FIFTH FORMERS of ST CLARE'S

St Clare's

Enid Blyton

St Clare's

1 The Twins at St Clare's
2 The O'Sullivan Twins
3 Summer Term at St Clare's
4 The Second Form at St Clare's
5 The Third Form at St Clare's (written by Pamela Cox)
6 Kitty at St Clare's (written by Pamela Cox)
7 Claudine at St Clare's
8 Fifth Formers at St Clare's
9 The Sixth Form at St Clare's (written by Pamela Cox)

Malory Towers

1 First Term at Malory Towers
2 Second Form at Malory Towers
3 Third Year at Malory Towers
4 Upper Fourth at Malory Towers
5 In the Fifth at Malory Towers
6 Last Term at Malory Towers

The Mysteries

1 The Mystery of the Burnt Cottage
2 The Mystery of the Disappearing Cat
3 The Mystery of the Secret Room
4 The Mystery of the Spiteful Letters
5 The Mystery of the Missing Necklace
6 The Mystery of the Hidden House
7 The Mystery of the Pantomime Cat
8 The Mystery of the Invisible Thief
9 The Mystery of the Vanished Prince
10 The Mystery of the Strange Bundle
11 The Mystery of Holly Lane
12 The Mystery of Tally-Ho Cottage
13 The Mystery of the Missing Man
14 The Mystery of the Strange Messages
15 The Mystery of Banshee Towers

Enid Blyton

FIFTH FORMERS of St CLARE'S

EGMONT

St Clare's

Enid Blyton

EGMONT

We bring stories to life

First published in Great Britain 1945 by Methuen & Co. Ltd
This edition published 2013
by Egmont UK Limited
The Yellow Building
1 Nicholas Road
London W11 4AN

978 0 6035 6939 5

A CIP catalogue record for this title is available from the British Library
Printed and bound in Great Britain by the CPI Group

56926/1

Contents

1

Back for the winter term

St Clare's had stood silent and empty during eight weeks of the summer holiday. Except for the sound of mops and brushes, and a tradesman ringing at the bell, the place had been very quiet. The school cat missed the girls and wandered about miserably for the first week or two.

But now everything was different. The school coaches were rolling up the hill, full of chattering, laughing children – St Clare's was beginning a new winter term!

'Who would think this was a winter term?' said Pat O'Sullivan, to her twin, Isabel. 'The sun is as hot as it was in the summer. We might be able to have a few games of tennis still.'

'I shall certainly have a swim in the pool,' said Bobby Ellis, whose face seemed even more freckled than usual. 'I hope there's fresh water in today – I might have a swim after tea.'

'Ah, you Bobbee! Always you must play tennis or swim or run or jump!' said Claudine, the little French girl. 'And your freckles! Never did I see so many on one face. I have been careful in the hot sun these holidays – not one freckle did I catch!'

The girls laughed. Claudine was always terrified of

getting freckles – but never did one appear on her pale face and white hands.

The girls poured into the school, running up the familiar steps, shouting to one another, dumping their lacrosse sticks everywhere.

'Hallo, Hilary! Hallo, Janet! Oh, there's Carlotta, looking more like a gypsy than ever. Hey, Carlotta, where did you go for your holidays? You look so tanned.'

'I have been to Spain,' said Carlotta. 'Some of my people live there, you know. I had a grand time.'

'There's Mirabel – golly, she's awfully tall now!' said Isabel. 'Gladys looks more like a mouse than ever beside her.'

'Hallo!' said the big, strapping Mirabel, coming up. 'How's everyone?'

'Hallo, Mirabel. Hallo, Gladys,' said the girls. 'You've been spending the hols together, haven't you? I bet you played tennis and swam all the time!'

Both Mirabel and Gladys were fond of games, and this term Mirabel was anxious to be sports captain at St Clare's. She had been in the fifth form for two terms, and Annie Thomas, the sports captain, had let Mirabel help her. Now Annie had left, and there was a chance that Mirabel might be captain, for there was no one in the sixth form really fitted to have that post.

'Let's go and look at our classroom,' said Bobby Ellis. 'It was going to be re-decorated in the hols, I know. Let's see what it's like.'

They all trooped upstairs to the big fifth-form room.

Certainly it looked very nice, painted a pale banana yellow. The light was clean and clear in the room, and the view from the windows a lovely one.

'We've only got this term here – and then we go up into the sixth form!' said Hilary. 'Fancy being at the top of the school! I remember when I first came to St Clare's, I thought the fifth and sixth formers were almost grown-up. I hardly dared to speak to them.'

'I expect the young ones think the same thing of us,' said Janet. 'I know most of them scuttle out of my way when I come along – like frightened rabbits!'

'I have a young sister in the second form this term,' said Claudine, the French girl. 'She came over with me from France. Look – there she is, the little Antoinette.'

The girls looked out of the window. They saw a girl of about fourteen, very like the pale-faced, dark-haired Claudine, standing watching the others. She looked very self possessed.

'Don't you want to go down and show Antoinette round a bit?' said Pat. 'I bet she feels lonely and new.'

'Ah, Antoinette would never feel so,' said Claudine. 'She can stand on her own toes, like me.'

'Stand on her own feet, you mean,' said Bobby, with a chuckle. 'You'll never get those English sayings right, Claudine. Ah – there's old Mam'zelle!'

The girls watched Mam'zelle going out into the garden, an anxious look on her face.

'She is looking for the little Antoinette,' said Claudine. 'She has not seen her for two years. Ah, Antoinette will now be swamped in love and affection! My aunt will think her little niece Antoinette is as wonderful as me, her niece Claudine!'

Mam'zelle was Claudine's aunt, and this fact was at times useful to Claudine, and at other times embarrassing. For Antoinette just then it was most embarrassing. The little French girl had been enjoying herself, watching the excited English girls catching hold of one another's arms, swinging each other round, chasing one another, and generally behaving in the usual schoolgirl way – a way, however, that the demure Antoinette had not been used to.

Then, quite suddenly, an avalanche descended upon her, two plump arms almost strangled her, and a loud and excited voice poured out French endearments in first one ear and then the other. Loud kisses were smacked on each cheek, and then another hug came which made Antoinette gasp for breath.

'Ah, *la petite Antoinette, mon petit chou,*' cried Mam'zelle at the top of her voice. All the girls stopped playing and stared at Antoinette and Mam'zelle. They giggled. It was plain that Antoinette was not at all pleased to be greeted in public in this way. She disentangled herself as best she could.

She caught sight of her elder sister, Claudine, leaning out of a high window, grinning in delight. She pointed up to her at once.

'Dear *tante* Mathilde, there is my sister Claudine who looks for you. Now that she has seen you greet me, she will wish you to greet her too.'

Mam'zelle glanced up and saw Claudine. Still holding Antoinette, she waved frantically and blew kisses. 'Ah, there is the little Claudine too! Claudine, I come to embrace you.'

Antoinette wriggled away and lost herself in the nearby crowd of girls. Mam'zelle turned her steps towards the door that led to the stairs. 'I come, I come!' she called to Claudine.

'And I go,' said Claudine, pushing away the giggling girls. 'Mam'zelle will be quite overcome this term with *two* nieces here.'

So, when poor Mam'zelle panted into the fifth-form classroom to embrace her second niece, Claudine was not to be found. 'I have missed her, but I will find her!' cried Mam'zelle, and she beamed round at the fifth formers there.

'Ah, Bobbee, you have come back – and you Angela – and Alison – all of you, the dear girls! And you are going to work hard for me this term, so hard – for is it not next term that you go up into the top form, the sixth form? That is indeed a solemn thought!'

The French teacher went out of the room, hunting for her dear Claudine. The girls laughed. 'Dear old Mam'zelle,' said Hilary, 'I shall never forget her, if I live to be a hundred! The tricks we've played on her – do you remember those awful stink balls you had, Janet, when we were in the fourth form? I laughed till I cried then, when I saw Mam'zelle's face as the smell reached her.'

'There's only one new girl this term,' said Janet, 'in our form, I mean. I saw her name on the list downstairs. She's called Anne-Marie Longden. And Felicity Ray has come up from the fourth form.'

'About time too,' said Mirabel. 'She's older than most of the fifth already. I think she's a bit batty.'

'No, she's not – it's only that she's a real musical genius,' said Gladys. 'You've said yourself heaps of times that she is, Mirabel. She doesn't seem to care about anything but music – other lessons just roll off her, like water off a duck's back. She's always bottom of everything except music.'

'Well, Miss Cornwallis won't be very thrilled if Felicity takes no notice of anything but music,' said Bobby, who had reason to know that the fifth-form mistress was what the girls called among themselves 'a real slave-driver'. 'I bet Felicity will know more geography, history and maths this term than she has ever known all the time she has been at school!'

'Any other girls?' said Mirabel.

'Well, it's funny, Alma Pudden's name was down on the list of fifth formers,' said Janet. 'But she's sixth form, isn't she? I mean, when she came last term, she was put into the sixth form – but now her name is down for our form. Perhaps she's been put back into the fifth for some reason.'

'Well, I wish she wasn't,' said Bobby. 'I can't say she thrills me. She's so like her name – puddeny! She's a bit like a suet pudding, fat and stodgy and dull.'

'She's got a beastly temper,' said Hilary. 'I guess she won't be too pleased at coming down into the fifth form!'

Matron appeared at the door of the classroom with a

tall, slender, dark-eyed girl, whose pale blonde hair made her eyes seem very black indeed.

'Hallo, fifth formers!' she said, her cheerful smile beaming at everyone. 'All back? Good girls. Now don't any of you dare to go down with mumps or measles, chickenpox or anything else! I've brought you the only new girl for your form – Anne-Marie Longden.'

Anne-Marie smiled nervously. She was not pretty, but her golden hair and dark eyes made her rather striking. 'Hallo,' she said, awkwardly, 'are you all fifth formers? What are your names?'

Hilary, who was head of the form, introduced everyone quickly.

'These are the O'Sullivan twins, Pat and Isabel. You'll probably know t'other from which in a few terms! This is Janet, and this is Roberta, commonly called Bobby. You'll always know her by her freckles! Look out for these two, for they know more tricks than anyone else.'

Anne-Marie smiled politely. Hilary went on, dragging first one girl forward and then another.

'This is Doris – she can mimic anyone under the sun. She'll be mimicking *you* before long, Anne-Marie!'

Anne-Marie did not look as if this thrilled her very much. She thought Doris looked a rather clumsy, stupid girl. She did not see the intelligent eyes and humorous mouth of the born actress that Doris was.

'Here's Carlotta, sun tanned as ever!' went on Hilary. Carlotta gave her usual cheeky grin.

'And please let me tell you, Anne-Marie, that I was

once a circus girl, and rode horses in a circus-ring,' said Carlotta. 'Angela is sure to tell you that sooner or later, so I may as well tell you now!'

The golden-haired beautiful girl called Angela flushed with annoyance. It was quite true that she looked down on Carlotta and always had – but she had hoped that Carlotta had not thought of it the last term or two. Carlotta had a very sharp tongue, and lashed out unmercifully at anyone she disliked.

Hilary hurried on, hoping to avert a quarrel between the hot-tempered Carlotta and the annoyed Angela. 'This is Angela,' she said. 'Our dream of beauty!'

'You've forgotten the Honourable,' said a malicious voice – Carlotta's. 'The *Honourable* Angela Favorleigh! Angela must have her label.'

'Shut up, Carlotta,' said Hilary. Angela scowled, making her lovely face quite ugly for a moment. Then she tossed her head and went out of the room. She had learnt by now that beauty and wealth were no match for a sharp wit like Carlotta's. Angela might be the most beautiful girl in the school and the richest, but Carlotta could always defeat her in a squabble.

'This is Pam, the brains of the form,' said Hilary, pulling a plain, undergrown girl forward, with great big glasses in front of her short-sighted eyes. 'She works much too hard, but nobody can stop her!'

Someone peeped in at the door. It was Claudine, come to see if her aunt was still there.

'It's all right. Mam'zelle is still looking for you, but not here,' said Carlotta. 'Anne-Marie, this is Claudine, the Bad Girl of the form – she only works at what she likes, she always gets what she wants – and she doesn't care how she does it. She has been here quite a long time already, trying to learn what she calls "the English sense of honour" – but she hasn't even smelt it yet!'

'Ah, you bad Carlotta,' said the good-humoured Claudine. 'Always you make fun of me. I am not so bad, and not so good.'

Mirabel and Gladys were pulled forward, and the plain, quiet Pauline, who had once been as big a boaster as Angela, but had learnt a bitter lesson, and was now a much nicer girl.

'There you are – that's the lot,' said Hilary, 'except Felicity, our musical genius, who is coming up from the fourth form, and hasn't arrived yet – and Alma Pudden who comes down from the sixth. I haven't seen her about yet, either.'

'I hope *you* don't do anything wonderful!' said Bobby, to Anne-Marie. 'What with Pam's brilliant brains, and Angela's film-star beauty, and Felicity's musical genius, the fifth form has got enough wonderful people in it! I hope you're a nice ordinary person, Anne-Marie.'

'Well – I'm not,' said Anne-Marie, flushing red. 'I'm – I'm a poet.'

There was a deep silence after this. A poet! What exactly did Anne-Marie mean by that?

'What do you mean – you write poetry, or something?' said Bobby. 'Oh, help!'

'You can't help being a poet, if you are one,' said Anne-Marie. 'You're born a poet. My grandfather was a famous poet, and my great-aunt was a great writer. It's in the family – and it's come out in me, I suppose. I'm always writing poetry. Mostly in the middle of the night.'

'Help!' said Bobby, again. 'We've had many odd things at St Clare's – but not a poet, as far as I remember. You and Felicity will make a pair! She gets up in the middle of the night to write a tune – you get up to write poems! Well – you'll be able to keep each other company!'

Another girl put her head in at the door and the twins yelled to her. 'Alison! Where have you been? Come and be introduced to our poet.'

A pretty, dainty girl came into the room, smiling. It was the twins' cousin, Alison.

'This is Alison,' said Pat. 'Our little feather-head. Thinks of nothing but her hair and her complexion and whether she has a shiny nose, and . . .'

Alison would have scowled, or burst into tears, a few terms before at this candid introduction, but she was thicker-skinned now. She merely lunged out at Pat, and nodded amiably at Anne-Marie.

'You'd better look out, Claudine,' she said, 'your aunt is coming along the passage.'

'You can't escape now,' said Hilary. 'You've got to go through with it – go on, it pleases old Mam'zelle. She really is fond of you, goodness knows why!'

Mam'zelle swept into the room, saw Claudine and flung herself on her. '*Ma petite Claudine*! How are you?

How are your dear father and mother, and all the family? I have seen the little Antoinette – ah, how lonely and shy the poor child looked. I have cakes and biscuits for you both in my room – you will come now, this very minute, and eat them with me!'

Claudine let herself be taken off. The others laughed. 'Funny to think of Claudine being a fifth former! Perhaps she will turn over a new leaf now she's so high up in the school.'

But that was the last thing Claudine meant to do. She went her own way, saying what she pleased, doing what she pleased, and always would. It was surprising that so many people liked her!

2

Studies of their own

It was the rule at St Clare's that as soon as any girl had been in the fifth form for two terms she should be allowed to have a small study of her own, which she shared with one other girl. These studies were tiny places, and the girls could, if they wished, furnish them themselves, though the school provided such things as a table, chairs and a carpet and shelves.

Most girls contented themselves with putting up a picture or two, bringing their own vases for flowers, a tablecloth or so, and a clock. A few were more ambitious and got a carpet from home, and maybe even an arm-chair.

The girls themselves chose the companion with whom they wanted to share a study. This was not usually difficult, because by the time they reached the top forms the girls had all more or less made their own friends, and, when they were in the fourth form, had planned with whom they were going to share the study.

It was fun arranging about the studies. The pairs had to go to Matron and tell her they were going to share a study, and then Matron would allot one to them.

'Fancy *you* having a study!' she would say. 'Dear me – it seems no time at all since you were in the first form and

I nearly gave you a scolding for not reporting your sore throats to me!'

Pat and Isabel O'Sullivan were to share a study, of course. Mirabel and Gladys wanted to as well. Angela had asked Alison to share with her – both girls had the same dainty tastes.

'I bet there will be nothing but mirrors all the way round the walls of your study!' said Bobby to Alison. It was a standing joke that Alison always looked into any mirror she passed, or even in the glass of pictures, to see if her hair was all right.

Bobby and Janet were to share a study. Both were tomboys, with a love for practical jokes. What tricks would be hatched out in their study!

One odd pair was Pam Boardman, the brainy one of the form, and Doris Edward, who was always near the bottom. For all her brilliance at mimicry and acting, Doris could not do ordinary lessons well, and admired Pam's brains deeply. Pam had tried to help the bigger girl at times, and a warm friendship had sprung up between them, which made Doris suggest sharing a study. Pam had left St Clare's once, but had missed it so much that her parents had sent her back again some time later.

The lonely little Pam, who had never had a real friend, at once welcomed the idea of sharing a study with Doris. Doris made her laugh, she teased her and put on her big glasses and mimicked her. She was good for Pam.

'Whom is Carlotta going with?' wondered Pat. 'Hilary, perhaps. They like one another very much.'

But no – Hilary, as head girl of the form, had the honour of a study all to herself. So Carlotta could not share with her. She chose Claudine!

Matron was openly doubtful about this.

'You'll have a mighty bad effect on each other,' she said. 'You're both as cheeky and don't-carish as can be. What you'll be like if you share a study, I can't think. But mind – any broken furniture or reports of rowdiness, and you'll go down to the common-room of the fourth formers.'

'Oh, Matron – how can you think that we should be rowdy?' said Claudine, putting on her most innocent look. 'I shall keep our study beautifully, so beautifully. Did I not in the holidays embroider two tablecloths, and three cushion-covers for our study?'

Anne-Marie and Felicity were to share a study, although Felicity had not been two terms in the fifth form, and Anne-Marie was new. Matron did not want them to be the only two without a study.

'Two geniuses together,' said Bobby, with a laugh. 'They ought to use up the midnight oil all right, writing poems and tunes!'

No one had asked Pauline to share a study with them, and she had no friend to ask. She was not a girl that anyone liked much, for she was envious, and had been very boastful till the others had found out that all her wonderful tales were made up. She had gone into her shell, and no one knew quite what the real Pauline was like.

'You had better share with Alma Pudden,' said Matron, ticking them off on the list. 'You're the only two left.'

'Oh,' said Pauline, dismally. She didn't like Alma very much. Nobody did. She was so fat and unwieldy and bad-tempered. But there was no one else to share with, so that was that.

'Well – that's the lot of you,' said Matron, shutting her book. 'You all know the study-rules, don't you? You can have your teas there by yourselves, if you don't want to go to the dining-room. You can get in someone from the first or second form to do any little job you want done. You can do your prep there in the evenings, and you can go up to bed when you want to, providing it is not after ten o'clock.'

The girls felt free and independent, having little rooms of their own. The studies were cosy corners, dens, bits of home – they could be arranged how the girls liked, and the tiny fire-places could burn cosy fires to sit by.

Angela, of course, furnished hers like a miniature palace. She bundled out every bit of the school furniture there, and got her mother to send down things from her own bedroom. She went down to the town with Alison, and the two had a wonderful time choosing curtain material, cushion-covers and rugs.

They cost a lot of money. Alison hadn't very much, but Angela had had magnificent tips from wealthy uncles and aunts in the holidays, and had saved them up for her study. She spent lavishly, and would let no one into their room till it was finished.

Then she and Alison gave a 'house-warming' as they called it. They had ordered in cakes and sandwiches from the local baker, and had bought lemonade and ginger beer.

The table was loaded with eatables, and a bright fire burnt in the grate, though the day was far too hot.

The girls crowded in curiously. They gasped at the polished furniture, beautiful mirrors and pictures, the two arm-chairs, and the lovely rugs. They fingered the silk curtains and looked at the brilliant chrysanthemums in the vases.

'*Well*!' said Bobby. 'Just wait till Matron sees all this! She'll tell Miss Theobald you have too much money to spend, Angela!'

'I don't see that it's anything to do with Matron,' said Angela, stiffly. 'Alison and I don't consider there is enough beauty or comfort at St Clare's – not as much as *we* are used to at home, anyway – and now that we have a study of our own, we don't see why we can't fill it with our own ideas. Don't you like it, Bobby?'

'Well – it's a bit too showy for me,' said Bobby. 'You know my simple tastes! But you certainly have made a marvellous job of it, Angela – and this tea is super!'

The other girls added what they wanted to their studies. Claudine put out her embroidered tablecloths and cushion-covers. Carlotta added a few things she had brought from Spain, one thing especially giving the little study colour and character – a deep red embroidered shawl from Seville.

The only study that was quite plain and without character was the one shared by Pauline and Alma. Neither of them had any taste or much money, and except for a blue vase contributed by Pauline and a tea-cosy as plump as Alma herself given by Alma, the little study was as bare as in the holidays.

Alma Pudden had a most unfortunate name. It would not have mattered a bit if she hadn't been so like a suet pudding to look at, but she was. Her school tunic always looked like a sack tied round in the middle. Her eyes were almost hidden in her round, pasty face.

It was the fifth formers who nicknamed her Pudding, and she hated it, which was not to be wondered at. If she had laughed, and said, 'Yes, I *am* rather puddingy – but I shall thin out soon!' the others would probably have liked her, and called her Pudding more in affection than in derision. But Alma flew into one of her bad rages when she was teased.

She had peculiar tempers – not hot ones, quickly flaring up and down, like Carlotta's or Janet's – but cold, spiteful rages. Try as they would, the others could not like anything about poor Alma.

Poor Pauline found sharing a study with Alma very dull indeed. Alma seldom had any intelligent remark to make, and though she pored over her prep she rarely got good marks. She was selfish too, and always took the more comfortable chair, and helped herself to more cakes than Pauline.

Felicity and Anne-Marie found it rather trying to live together in the same study. Felicity thought there was nothing in the world but music, and she was always singing or trying out tunes on her violin, when Anne-Marie wanted to work or to write.

'Felicity! *Must* you play that awful, gloomy tune again?' Anne-Marie would say. 'I'm trying to get the last verse of this poem right.'

'What poem? Is it the one you were doing last week?' Felicity would say. 'Well, it's a dreadful poem – all words and no meaning. You are no poet, Anne-Marie. Why should I stop my music in order that you should write third-rate poetry?'

Felicity did not mean to be rude or even hurtful. She was, as Bobby said, quite 'batty' about her music. She was working for a stiff exam, the L.R.A.M. and was very young indeed to take it. Miss Theobald, the head mistress, did not want her to work for it, and had already told Felicity's people that the girl must live an ordinary life, and take more interest in ordinary things.

'She is growing one-sided,' Miss Theobald explained to Felicity's parents, who came to see her one day. 'Sometimes I think she doesn't live in this world at all! That is bad for a young girl. She is already far too old for the fourth form, and yet is not fit to do the work of the fifth. But I think I had better put her up into the fifth, where the girls there of her own age will wake her up a bit. I wish you would say that Felicity must put off working for this difficult music exam for a year or two. She has plenty of time before her!'

But Felicity's people were too proud of their brilliant daughter to put off any exam. It would be wonderful to have a girl who was the youngest to pass such an exam!

'Put her up in the fifth form if you wish, Miss

Theobald,' said Felicity's father. 'But don't let her slacken in any way in her music studies. We have been told she is a genius, and a genius must be helped and encouraged in every way.'

'Of course,' said the head mistress, 'but we must be sure that our ways of encouragement are the *right* ones, surely. I don't like all this hard, musical work for so young a girl, when it means that other, quite necessary work has to be scamped.'

But it was no use talking like that to Felicity's parents. Their girl was brilliant, and she must go on being even more brilliant! And so it was that Felicity was put up into the fifth form, to be with girls of her own age even though her work was far below the form's standard – and yet had to work even harder at her music than before.

She did not like or dislike Anne-Marie. She was there and had to be put up with, but so long as she did not interfere too much with her music, Felicity did not really notice her study companion.

But Anne-Marie was jealous of Felicity and her undoubted genius. Anne-Marie was convinced that she too was a genius. Her people were sure she was, as well. They had her best poems framed, they recited them to visitors, who were too polite to say what they really thought, and they tried to get publishers to print them.

It was most annoying that the girls at St Clare's didn't seem to think anything of her loveliest poems. There was that one beginning:

Down the long lanes of the Future
My tear-bedimmed eyes are peering.

Only Angela and Alma had been impressed with it. Neither of them had enough brains to know a good poem from a bad one, and they could not see the would-be cleverness and insincerity of the long and ostentatious poem.

'What's it *mean*?' said Carlotta. 'I may be very stupid, but I don't understand a word of it. Why are your eyes tear-bedimmed, Anne-Marie? Are you so afraid of your future? Well, I'm not surprised, if that's the way you're going to earn your living! You won't get much money.'

'It's tosh,' said Bobby. 'You write something you really *feel*, Anne-Marie, and maybe you'll get something good out of your mind. This is all pretence – just trying to be awfully grown-up when you're not.'

So Anne-Marie was bitterly disappointed that *her* genius was not recognized, whilst everyone apparently agreed that Felicity really was gifted.

Still, on the whole, the study companions got on fairly well, some of them much better than others, of course. The twins rarely quarrelled, and had so much the same tastes and likings that sharing a study was, for them, a thing of delight. Bobby and Janet too were very happy together, and so were Mirabel and Gladys.

It was strange at first to get used to sending for the younger ones to do odd jobs. But on the whole that was quite a good idea too. Many of the first formers, for instance, had been head girls, or at least in the top forms of their prep schools, and it did them good to be at the bottom of another school, having, at times, to rush off to do the bidding of the older girls. The twins remembered how they had hated it at first.

'We thought it was beneath our dignity to light someone's fire, do you remember?' said Pat to Isabel, as she poked up the fire that a first former had just been in to light for her. 'It was jolly good for us. We were so stuck up – thought such a lot of ourselves too! We got our corners rubbed off all right.'

'We get to know the younger ones too,' said Isabel. 'They chatter away to us when they come to do their jobs. I'm getting to like some of the little first formers very much. One or two of them will be very good at games – they are awfully keen.'

'Angela sends for the young ones far too much, though,' said Pat, frowning. 'She and Alison make them do too many jobs. They've got a bit of power, and they are using it badly.'

'Better get Hilary to tick them off,' said Isabel, yawning. 'Golly, it's five to ten. Come on, we'd better pack up and go to bed. Isn't it fun to go when we like?'

'So long as it's not after ten o'clock!' said Pat, imitating Matron's crisp voice. 'Hurry – or it *will* be after ten!'

3

The new English teacher

That term there were a great many more girls at St Clare's in the younger forms, and Miss Theobald decided to engage an extra mistress, to take some of the work off the shoulders of the class-mistresses.

So, to the interest of all the girls, Miss Willcox appeared. She was present at Assembly the second day and looked round with vague, rather soulful eyes.

'Her name's Miss Willcox,' the girls whispered to one another. 'She's awfully clever. She's going to take English. She writes! She has had a book of poetry published.'

The girls all gazed at Miss Willcox with awe. They thought that anyone must indeed be clever to have written a book. Miss Willcox gazed back at the girls, her eyes dreamy and far away. What could she be thinking of? Another book, perhaps?

It was always exciting to have a new teacher. What would she be like in class? Strict? Humorous? Lenient? Dull? Would she be a good one to play a few tricks on?

'I think she looks most interesting,' said Alison. 'I do really. I think she looks as if all kinds of beautiful thoughts are passing through her mind.'

'She's probably wondering what there will be for

lunch,' said Bobby. 'I always suspect those people that look dreamily into the distance. Anne-Marie does it sometimes, and I know jolly well that half the time she's wondering if Felicity has remembered to get the cakes for tea, or something like that, and the other half she's thinking of nothing at all.'

Anne-Marie wished she could think of something smart to say back, but she never could. Well – poets were always misunderstood, she knew that. People laughed at them, and jeered at their work – but then, years after they were dead, people said how wonderful they were.

'Perhaps Miss Willcox will know that I am a real poet,' she thought. 'It would be nice to have someone on my side. I dare say if Miss Willcox reads my poems and likes them she will make the others change their minds. I'll work awfully hard in her classes, and get on her good side.'

Miss Willcox's lessons were certainly interesting. They were filled with plays and poetry, and the girls were allowed to debate anything they liked, so long as it had to do with literature.

There was no doubt that Miss Willcox 'knew her stuff' as Bobby put it. She was very widely read, had an excellent memory, and really did know how to pick out things that would interest the girls, and make them think.

She was a strange woman to look at, though – untidy, vague and given to 'bits and pieces' as Janet said. A scarf wound round her neck, a brilliant belt, a very striking handkerchief. She wore gold-headed pins in her black hair, and her dresses all had a drapy look about them. They did not really fit her.

She had an affected voice which rather spoilt her reading of poetry, for she pitched it deep and low, when really it should have been quite ordinary. She had graceful, dramatic gestures, which filled Alison's romantic soul with delight.

Alison copied one or two of the gestures. She flung out her hand dramatically when she was telling Pat and Isabel something, and hit Bobby with the back of her fingers.

'Hey!' said Bobby. 'Our feather-head is copying Miss Willcox! Alison, you're not going to lose your heart to *her*, are you?'

Alison went red. She always blushed very easily, which annoyed her. 'I don't know what you mean,' she said. 'I admire Miss Willcox, I must say. Her knowledge of English literature is marvellous.'

'Oh, Alison!' groaned Bobby. 'Don't say you're going to worship Miss Willcox. Haven't you got over that silly habit yet? You never choose the right people to worship, either!'

'Why isn't Miss Willcox the right person?' said Alison, trying to speak coldly, though she felt very hot and cross. 'She's clever – she's written a book of most marvellous poetry – she's got a lovely deep voice, and I think she's most picturesque-looking.'

'Untidy and messy, you mean,' said Bobby, in disgust. 'Picturesque-looking, indeed! What an idiot you are, Alison. I think Miss Willcox wants smartening up and making tidy. Gold-topped pins in her hair – gosh, it nearly made me sick to see them.'

Bobby was going to extremes and did not mean all she said. She was such a downright, boyish person, she so much hated nonsense and show, that people like Miss Willcox made her 'go off the deep end' and say more than she meant.

'Oh, Miss Willcox is not so bad as you make out, Bobby,' said Pat, seeing that Alison looked as if she was about to burst into tears. 'And she's not so wonderful as *you* make out, either, Alison. Anyway – for goodness' sake don't put on a worshipping act this term. You've been fairly sensible the last two terms or so.'

Alison turned away. 'Remember Miss Quentin,' said Bobby, warningly. 'Don't make the same mistake again!'

Miss Quentin had been worshipped by Alison when she was in a lower form, and Alison had been bitterly hurt by her, because she had found out that the mistress was laughing at her behind her back. She had learnt a hard lesson then and had been more careful about whom she gave her heart to. But now it looked as if she was going to start all over again!

'It's no good trying to stop her,' said Pat, watching her cousin as she left the room, her head high in the air, and her cheeks burning. 'You only make her worse, Bobby. She goes all loyal and intense.'

'Well, I've said my say,' said Bobby. 'It wouldn't matter a bit if only Alison would choose somebody decent, but she never does.'

'If Miss Willcox was sensible she'd nip Alison in the bud,' said Pat. 'Miss Cornwallis soon nips any silliness in the bud! So do the other mistresses. I can see that Miss Willcox is going to encourage that awful Anne-Marie too.'

'Well – let her!' said Bobby. 'If she wants the Alisons and Anne-Maries of the world sitting at her feet, she's welcome to them. Come on – let's go and see if the court is hard enough for tennis.'

They passed Alma Pudden on the way out. The girl looked rather dull and miserable. Pat felt sorry for her.

'Come and have a game!' she called. 'Make up a four.'

'I can't run,' said Alma, in her usual dull voice. 'I'm too fat.'

'Well, it will get your fat down a bit,' said Isabel. 'Come on!'

But no – Alma was almost as obstinate at refusing any exercise as Claudine was. Claudine got out of all games if she could, and even out of the nature-walks. At first she had arranged matters so that Matron piled mending on her, which had to be done in games time – but Matron had got wise to this little trick after a time, and Claudine suddenly found that she had not enough mending to make an excuse for missing out-door life.

But Claudine was not to be defeated in anything. If she did have to put on games clothes and shoes, and appear on the field or court, she would be taken with violent cramps, or would feel sick, and have to go off. It was simply amazing how she managed to slide out of the things she disliked.

She and Carlotta were a real pair in their study. Carlotta would not do things she disliked either, if she could get out of them, but she used open and direct methods, whereas Claudine really enjoyed getting her way secretly, putting on an innocent face all the time.

They both made war against Mirabel, who, to her intense delight, had been made sports captain for the school that term, as she had hoped. Gladys had been made vice-captain, and this pleased them both. Gladys was small, but very quick and deft on the playing-field or tennis-court, and a fine little swimmer. Also, she was very good at dealing with some of the shy, younger girls, who were a bit afraid of Mirabel's heartiness and drive.

Mirabel was a typical sports captain, loud-voiced, hearty in manner, strapping in figure, and not very sensitive to the feelings of others. She was always trying to make Alison, Claudine, Angela and Carlotta take more interest in games, and they were just as determined not to. It annoyed her intensely when they would not turn up at practices she had arranged, or got bored on the field and talked.

'This Mirabel, she is a pest,' complained Claudine to her aunt, Mam'zelle. 'Always she wants me to go to the field and make myself hot and dirty and untidy. Can you not tell her my heart is weak, *ma tante*?'

'Claudine! Have you a weak heart, my child? This you have never told me before!' cried Mam'zelle, in alarm. 'Have you a pain? You must go to Matron.'

This was the last thing that Claudine wanted to do. Matron was the one person who consistently disbelieved all that Claudine said.

'No, I have no pain,' said Claudine, demurely. 'Only

just a little flutter here – now and again when I run or go up the stairs.'

Mam'zelle looked at Claudine hard. She loved her dearly, but it did sometimes cross her mind that her niece might deceive her in order to gain her own ends. Claudine had pressed her hand over the place where she thought her heart was, to show where the flutter came – but unfortunately she wasn't indicating the right place.

'*Tiens*!' said Mam'zelle, half-alarmed still but a little angry. 'That is not your heart. That is your stomach. Maybe you need a dose of good medicine.'

Claudine disappeared at once. She was not going to have any of Matron's good medicine. She made up her mind to find out exactly where her heart was, so that another time she would not make a mistake.

After a few days the fifth form settled down into their usual familiar routine. They tackled their new work, grumbled and groused, laughed and talked, played games and went to bed tired out. It was a good life, an interesting, full and friendly one. Sometimes the fifth formers felt a little sad when they thought that they had only one more form to go into – and then St Clare's would be left behind for ever.

There was to be a stiff exam half-way through the term, which everyone was to take, even Doris and Alma and Felicity, who felt absolutely certain they would not be able to pass it.

'But it won't do you any harm to work for it,' said Miss Cornwallis, in her crisp voice. 'If you could just get a Pass

I should feel you had achieved something! I shall allow you to relax, all of you, after the exam is over, but I must insist that you do your very best for the first half of the term, and really study hard.'

So there was some very hard work done in the little studies that term. Carlotta groaned over her maths and Claudine puzzled over grammar. Felicity tried to learn her English literature and to write essays which usually ended abruptly because she had suddenly thought of a new tune. Anne-Marie rushed through all her prep except the English and then spent laborious hours over that, hoping to win approval from Miss Willcox.

Even Doris and Angela worked, though neither of them liked it. School was fun – but it *was* hard work too!

4

Angela loses her temper

The little first formers came and went at the bidding of the fifth. They ran errands, they made toast for tea and they chattered about their affairs to anyone who would listen.

Mirabel was always kindest to those who were good at games. She encouraged them to practise well at catching and running for lacrosse, she made up the teams for the school, and coached them well in her spare time. The younger girls thought she was wonderful.

'You know, that little Molly Williams is awfully good,' said Mirabel to Gladys, when she was making up the teams one day. 'I've a good mind to let her play in the third team, Gladys. And Jane Teal is good too, if she would practise running a bit more. She could be quite fast.'

'Little Antoinette is just as bad as Claudine,' said Gladys. 'I can't get her to practise at all, or to take any interest in games. Claudine doesn't back us up there, either. She is always telling Antoinette good excuses to make.'

'I'm tired of Claudine and her silly ways,' said Mirabel, impatiently. 'She's cunning. She'll get herself expelled one day!'

'Oh, no – she isn't as bad as that,' said Gladys, quite

shocked. 'She's just different from us, that's all. She's better than she was.'

'I should hope so, after all this time at St Clare's,' said Mirabel, writing the list of girls for the third team. 'Well – I've put Molly Williams down – she'll be thrilled.'

'It's a pity Angela and Alison order the young ones about so much,' said Gladys. 'They have always got one or other of them in their study, doing something for them. Angela even got Jane Teal in to do some mending for her, and that's not allowed.'

'I'll speak to Jane about it,' said Mirabel, in her direct way. 'I'll tell her she's not supposed to do Angela's mending, and she must use that time to get out on the practice field.'

'Well – wouldn't it be better to tell Angela that, not Jane?' said Gladys. 'It would come better from Angela, if she told Jane to stop doing her mending, than it would from you.'

'I'll deal with Jane myself,' said Mirabel, very much the sports captain, rather overbearing and arrogant that morning.

'Jane's fond of Angela,' said Gladys, as Mirabel went out of the roon. Mirabel snorted.

'She looks up to *me* no end,' she said. 'I'm pretty certain she'll do what *I* want, and not what Angela says. You really can leave these things to me, Gladys.'

Mirabel found Jane Teal and called to her. 'Hi, Jane! Come here a minute!'

The fourteen-year-old Jane, small, slight and quick,

went to Mirabel, her face flushing. She wondered if Mirabel was going to tell her she was to play in the third team with Molly. What a thrill that would be!

'Jane,' said Mirabel, in her direct way, 'I want you to do a bit more practising in the field the next few weeks. You'll be good if you really do practise. You ought to have been out this week. I hear you've been doing Angela's mending instead, and you know you don't need to do that.'

'I like to,' said Jane, flushing again. 'I'm good at sewing and Angela isn't. I like doing things for her.'

'Well, you give that up and pay more attention to games,' said Mirabel. 'I'm in charge of games and I want the good players doing their best.'

'I will do my best,' said Jane, proud to hear the great Mirabel say that she was one of the good players. 'But I did promise Angela to do all her mending this term – at least I offered to, Mirabel.'

'Well, you must tell her you can't,' said Mirabel, who quite failed to see that anything mattered except what she wanted herself.

'But – she'll be very cross and upset – and I do like doing things for her,' said Jane, half-frightened, but obstinate. 'I – I think she's beautiful, Mirabel. Don't you?'

'I don't see what that's got to do with it,' said Mirabel, impatiently. 'Anyway, I'm your sports captain and you've got to do as you're told. If you don't, I shan't let you play in even the fourth team, let alone the third.'

Mirabel's tone was sharp. She turned on her heel and went off. Jane looked after her, and tears smarted in her eyes. She admired Mirabel so much – and she did like Angela so much too. Angela had such a lovely smile and she said such nice things. The other girl she shared her study with was nice too – Alison.

Jane went to find her friend, Sally. She told her all that Mirabel had said and Sally listened.

'Well,' said Sally, 'you'll have to do what Mirabel tells you if you want to play in the third team and have some good matches. Why don't you go to Angela and tell her what Mirabel has said? You know quite well that if she is as sweet and kind as you say she is, she'll say at once that of course you mustn't do her mending any more.'

'Oh – that's a good idea,' said Jane, looking happier. 'I couldn't bear to upset Angela, Sally. I do really think she's wonderful. I should be miserable if she was angry with me.'

'Tell her when you go and make toast for her tea today,' said Sally. So that afternoon, rather tremblingly, Jane began to tell Angela what Mirabel had said.

'Angela,' she began, putting a piece of bread on to the toasting-fork, 'Angela, I've brought your mending back. I've done everything, even that stocking that had a ladder all the way down the back of the leg.'

'Thanks, Jane,' said Angela and gave Jane a smile that thrilled her.

'But – I don't believe I'll be able to do it much more,' went on Jane.

'Why ever not?' demanded Angela. 'You promised you would. I hate people who back out of things when they have promised to do them.'

'Well, you see – Mirabel spoke to me about it today,' said Jane, rather desperately. 'She said – she said – '

'Oh, I can guess what she said,' said Angela sneeringly. 'She said you were a wonderful player – and you must practise more – and you mustn't do odd jobs for that horrid Angela. And you meekly said you wouldn't. Little turncoat.'

'Oh, Angela, don't talk like that,' said poor Jane. 'It's not fair. Of course Mirabel didn't speak against you. But I have to do what she says, don't I? She's sports captain.'

'I don't see why *any*one has to do what dear, hearty, loud-voiced Mirabel says!' said Angela. 'I don't see why because *she's* mad on something she should expect everyone else to be mad on it too. This passion for games, games, games! I agree with Claudine that it's silly.'

'Oh, but Angela,' said Jane, shocked, 'games are lovely. And they make you get the team-spirit too, and play for your side instead of yourself – and – '

'Don't preach at *me,*' said Angela, angrily. 'You're only a half-baked first former. I don't care what you do, anyway. Go and practise running and catching morning, noon, and night if you want to. I shall certainly not allow you to do anything for me in future. I don't like turncoats. Leave that toast and go and find Violet Hill and send her to me. She can do my jobs instead of you.'

Jane was horrified at this outburst. She had given her heart to the beautiful, radiant Angela, and now it was treated as rubbish! Angela didn't want her any more. She would have that silly Violet Hill, who adored Angela from afar and would do anything for a smile from her.

Jane gave a sob and rushed out of the room. In a few minutes Violet Hill came in, thrilled to be sent for. Angela gave her orders in a lazy voice, amused to see how the little first former almost trembled with excitement as she tidied up the room, and hung on Angela's lightest word.

Alison came in after a while and looked surprised to see Violet there instead of Jane. 'Where's our devoted Jane?' she asked.

Angela told her in a few words what had happened. Violet Hill listened eagerly. She was glad that Jane was in disgrace. She would show Angela how much nicer she, Violet, was!

When Violet went out Alison spoke rather shortly to Angela. 'You shouldn't have said all that in front of Violet. You know how keen Jane was on you – she'll have a fit if she knows all this will be passed round her form.'

'Serves her right,' said Angela, viciously.

'Angela, you make these kids awfully silly,' said Alison, after a pause. 'I don't really think you treat them properly. You oughtn't to let them think you're so wonderful. I bet poor Jane is crying her eyes out. You know Miss Theobald dislikes that kind of thing.'

Angela went pale with rage. She always hated being found fault with. She glared at Alison and tried to think of something really cutting. She found what she wanted at last.

'Really, Alison,' she said, in her lightest, most jeering voice, 'really, Alison – who are *you* to talk of thinking people wonderful? You're a perfect ninny over that wonderful Miss Willcox of yours, aren't you? Why, you're even trying to copy that deep voice of hers. It just makes me laugh.'

Alison was deeply hurt. When she was fond of anyone she could not bear to hear a single word said against them.

'Miss Willcox is an absolutely sincere person,' she said, with dignity. 'That's why I like her. You've no interest in English literature, or anything at all really, except yourself, Angela – so you can't understand my admiring anyone with such an interesting character as Miss Willcox.'

'Tosh,' said Angela, rudely.

The two girls said no more to each other that evening. Angela fumed in silence and Alison wrote a long and, as she fondly hoped, intelligent essay for Miss Willcox. It was not a very happy evening.

Angela had her knife into Mirabel after that. She did not dare to go and tackle Mirabel openly about Jane, because she was afraid of Mirabel's rudeness. Mirabel was tasting power for the first time as sports captain, and she was rather arrogant and blunt in her speech. Also she was very thick-skinned and Angela despaired of being able to say anything that would hurt her.

So she had to content herself with looking at her sneeringly, and saying mocking things behind her back. But as sneering glances and words were typical of Angela when she was upset about something, no one took much notice, Mirabel least of all.

Angela made things up with Alison, not so much

because she wanted to, but because she simply had to have someone to talk to and air her views to. Also, Alison genuinely admired her looks and her clothes, and it was always pleasant to bask in admiration of that sort.

Alison was not foolish with Angela as she had been when she first came. She no longer spoilt her and praised her and agreed with everything. But she could not hide her real admiration of the lovely girl with her shining golden hair, and brilliant blue eyes.

She was glad to make up the quarrel with Angela, for she wanted to talk about Miss Willcox – how wonderful she was in class, what beautiful poetry she wrote, how well she recited in that soulful voice of hers.

So, in return for admiration, Angela listened, rather bored, to all that Alison wanted to say. They were friends again – but it would not take much to turn them into enemies once more!

5

Hard work – and a little fun

The fifth form were certainly working very hard. Miss Cornwallis kept their noses to the grindstone, as Pat said, and piled prep on to them. Miss Willcox expected a great deal of them too. Miss Theobald, the head, took the form for one or two lessons and although she did not give them a great deal of prep, the girls felt that what she did give them must be specially well done.

When Mam'zelle piled prep on them too, the girls grew indignant. 'Gracious! What with all that maths to do, and that map to draw, and those French poems to memorize, and that essay for Miss Willcox, we'll all have nervous breakdowns!' groaned Bobby.

Only Pam Boardman did not seem to mind. She had an amazing memory, and had only to look at a page once to know it by heart. Doris envied her this gift from the bottom of her heart.

'I've no memory at all for lessons,' she sighed. 'What I learn in the morning I've forgotten in the evening.'

'Well, if you're going to be an actress, you'll have parts to learn, won't you?' said Pam.

'The funny thing is, when I act a part and say the words out loud, I can remember them quite easily,' said

Doris. 'I never forget them then. It's sitting hunched up over a book, reading and re-reading the words that gets me down.'

'Well, Doris, stand up and recite the words out loud, and act them if you want to,' said Pam, a gleam of fun coming into her solemn eyes. 'Here – take this French poem – it's all about the so-beautiful country-side, as Mam'zelle would say. Recite it out loud, act the cows and the sheep, frisk when you come to the part where the little lambs play, and waddle like a duck when you get to them. You'll soon learn it.'

So, to the amazement of Pat and Isabel, who looked in at Pam's study to borrow a book, Doris threw herself heart, soul and body into the French pastoral poem.

She declaimed the poem loudly, with gestures of all kinds. She frisked like a lamb, she chewed cud like a cow, she waddled like a duck. It was perfect.

The girls shrieked with laughter. Doris had turned the solemn and rather heavy French poem into a real comedy.

'Now – do you know it?' said Pam, when Doris finished, and sat down panting in a chair.

Doris screwed up her nose and thought hard. 'Let me see,' she said, 'it begins like this . . .'

But until she got up and acted the poem as she had done before, she could not remember a word. It was evidently the acting that brought the words to her mind.

'Well – you do know the poem,' said Pam, pleased. 'You won't forget it now. Mam'zelle will be pleased with her *chère* Doris tomorrow!'

Doris, however, was not in Mam'zelle's good books the next day. Her French exercise was nothing but mistakes and was slashed right across with Mam'zelle's thick blue pencil. Mam'zelle never spared her blue pencil when she was annoyed, and a page disapproved of by her was always a terrible sight.

'Ah, you Doris!' began Mam'zelle, when she was going through the work with her class. 'You! Have I had you on my thumb . . .'

'*Under* my thumb,' said Bobby, with a grin. Mam'zelle glared at her and resumed.

'Have I had you on my thumb for all these terms and still you do not know that a table is she not he. Why are you not in the kindergarten? Why can you still not pronounce the French R? All the others can. You are a great big stupid girl.'

'Yes, Mam'zelle,' said poor Doris, meekly. When Mam'zelle flew into a rage, it was best to be meek. But for some reason Doris's meekness irritated Mam'zelle even more.

'Ah – you mock at me now! "Yes, Mam'zelle" you say, with your tongue in your mouth and butter melting in your cheek!' cried Mam'zelle, getting things mixed up as usual.

The girls giggled. 'You mean, with your tongue in your cheek, and butter that won't melt in your mouth,' suggested Bobby again.

'Do not tell me what I mean, Bobbee,' said Mam'zelle, exasperated. 'Always you interrupt. Doris, stand up.'

Doris stood up, her humorous mouth twitching. She would act this scene afterwards for the benefit of the girls. How they would laugh!

'Your written work is very bad. Now let me hear your oral work,' demanded Mam'zelle. 'You have learnt the French poem? Yes – then let me hear it. Begin!'

Doris couldn't think of a single word. She stared into the distance, racking her brains. She knew there were all kinds of animals in it – but how did the words go?

'She did learn it, Mam'zelle,' said Pam's voice, earnestly. 'I heard her say it all through without looking at the book once.'

'Then I too will hear it now,' said Mam'zelle. 'Begin, Doris.'

Pam sat just behind Doris. She whispered the first line to her. Doris began – and then she suddenly knew that if only she could act the poem, she could say every word – but not one line would come unless she acted it! Oh, dear – she couldn't possibly act it in front of Mam'zelle, who loved French poetry, and would think she was making fun of it.

'Well, Doris, I wait. I wait patiently,' said Mam'zelle, who was anything but patient at that moment. 'Can you or can you not say the poem to me?'

'Yes. I can,' said Doris. 'But – but only if I act it.'

'Then act it,' said Mam'zelle, losing the last of her patience. 'But if you are not telling me the truth, *ma chère* Doris, I complain to Miss Theobald. Act it – but say the poem through without mistake.'

So, in despair, Doris acted the French poem in her usual exaggerated, ridiculous manner, waggling herself, chewing the cud, waddling, frisking – and, of course, as soon as she acted the poem, she knew it all the way through without a single mistake. She certainly had a peculiar memory.

The girls were thrilled and amused at Doris's rendering of the solemn poem, but they felt certain that Mam'zelle would be exceedingly angry. It was Claudine who saved the situation.

She clapped her hands in delight. She threw back her head and laughed her infectious laugh. She held her sides and almost doubled herself up.

'Oh, *ma tante, ma tante*!' she cried to her aunt. 'The clever Doris, the marvellous Doris! Such a poem she makes of it – and not one single mistake. Ah, never never shall I forget this poem now!'

Mam'zelle pushed her glasses on to her nose more firmly. Her face changed. She let out a roar of delighted laughter, and the class breathed loudly in relief. So long as Mam'zelle saw the joke it was all right.

Mam'zelle took off her glasses and wiped her streaming eyes. 'It is clever, very clever, Doris,' she said. 'It is not the right way to recite such a poem, no. But it is very clever and very amusing. I will forgive you this time for your bad work. It is true that you know the poem, and you have made it very funny. Is it not so, Claudine?'

Claudine agreed. 'We too will say the poem like that,' she suggested, her eyes gleaming with fun. But Mam'zelle was not going so far as that.

'*Ah, non*!' she said. 'Doris has a gift that way. One girl is funny, but fourteen, fifteen girls would not be funny. *Tiens*! Look at the clock. We have wasted half the lesson on this bad, clever Doris. Get out your books, please.'

Doris found that she could learn anything if only she said it out loud and put ridiculous actions to the words. But so often she could not repeat what she had learnt unless she accompanied it with the absurd actions. Miss Willcox did not think this was funny. She called it 'playing the fool' and said it was very bad taste.

As for doing such a thing in Miss Cornwallis's class or Miss Theobald's, it was quite unthinkable. However much the girls begged Doris to recite the latest maths rules with appropriate – or inappropriate – actions she would not.

'I'm not going to get expelled just to make you laugh,' she said. 'I must go on plodding away, and get Pam's help as much as I can. I'll never be any good at lessons.'

'But you'll always be able to make people laugh!' said Isabel. 'I'd almost rather do that than anything, but I'm not much good at it.'

'I'd rather write a book or paint a beautiful picture,' said Alison.

'So would I,' said Anne-Marie. 'Much rather. To leave something of oneself behind, something one has made or created – now that's really worthwhile.'

'Deirdre fans!' said Carlotta, mockingly.

Alison had found out that Miss Willcox's first initial was D and had asked her what it stood for.

'Deirdre,' said Miss Willcox, and Alison had thought it

a most beautiful name, almost picturesque enough for her darling Miss Willcox. Deirdre Willcox – a lovely name for a poet!

She had told Angela and Angela had told everyone else. Both Anne-Marie and Alison were always round Miss Willcox, and the girls now called them 'Deirdre fans'. It annoyed them very much. Alison was sorry now that she had told anyone Miss Willcox's name – she would have liked to be the only one who knew it.

She and Anne-Marie both vied with each other for Miss Willcox's attentions. Alison was jealous of Anne-Marie because she could write poetry, and Miss Willcox encouraged her to bring her her poems. Anne-Marie was jealous of Alison because she felt sure that Miss Willcox liked Alison the better of the two, which was quite true. A little of Anne-Marie and her intenseness went a very long way.

'You're both silly,' said Bobby, who never could understand what she called 'sloppiness'. 'Can't you see that anyone who encourages a couple of idiots like you can't be worth sucking up to?'

But this kind of remark only made Alison and Anne-Marie more devoted. It even brought them together a little in their common indignation, which amused the girls very much. The 'Deirdre fans' were the cause of a lot of fun that half-term!

6

Angela and the younger girls

Little Jane Teal turned up on the lacrosse field and practised zealously, much to Mirabel's satisfaction.

'There you are,' she said to Gladys, triumphantly. 'You see, a little plain talking has done Jane Teal a lot of good. I shall make her a very good player in no time.'

Gladys had noticed that Jane had done exactly what Mirabel had told her, but she had also noticed too that Jane looked rather miserable.

'She doesn't seem very happy about it,' she said. 'And it doesn't seem to me that she puts much heart into all her practising. I bet Angela made things very unpleasant for her when she told her she couldn't do her mending any more.'

'Oh, well – it's a good thing if Jane gets that sort of nonsense knocked out of her,' said Mirabel. 'I can't bear these kids who go round worshipping people.'

'Well, a lot of them think no end of *you,*' said Gladys, 'and you like them to.'

'That's different,' said Mirabel at once. 'They look up to me because I'm sports captain, because I make them work hard, and because I don't stand any nonsense. I should tick them off if they got sloppy over me.'

'Well – all the same I think little Jane looks miserable,' said Gladys. 'Don't frown like that at me, Mirabel. After all, I'm your vice-captain, and I have a right to say what I think to you.'

Mirabel looked in surprise at Gladys, who was often called the Mouse, because she said so little and was so quiet. Mirabel was fond of Gladys – in fact she was the only girl in the school that she had any real affection for at all. All the same, she didn't think she could allow Gladys to find fault with her decisions – what was the sense of being captain if you didn't make your own decisions and stick to them? A little power had gone to Mirabel's head!

'You can say what you like to me, of course,' said Mirabel, stiffly, 'but that doesn't mean I shall pay attention to your suggestions, I'm afraid, Gladys. I shall *listen* to them, of course – but I am the one to decide everything.'

Gladys said no more. Mirabel was not going to be a very easy person to live with that term! Gladys wished she was bold like Carlotta, or forthright like Bobby, or a strong character like Hilary – they always seemed able to cope with others in the right way, but Gladys was afraid of hurting them, or of making them angry.

Angela made a fuss of Violet Hill, in order to punish poor Jane. She gave her one of her best hair-slides and a book, which sent the foolish Violet into transports of delight. Violet showed them to Jane and Sally.

'Look,' she said, 'isn't Angela a dear? She's so generous. I think she's wonderful. I do think you were silly to quarrel with her, Jane. I think Angela is worth three of Mirabel!'

Jane looked miserably at the book and the hair-slide. Angela had never given *her* a present. She wished she could dislike Angela, but she couldn't. Every time she saw the golden-haired girl, with her starry eyes set in her oval face, she thought how wonderful she was.

Sally was sorry for Jane. 'Cheer up,' she said. 'Angela isn't worth worrying about. I believe she's only making up to Violet just to make you jealous. I think she's being beastly.'

But Jane would not hear a word against Angela, however much she had been hurt by her. Violet too was cross at Sally's remarks.

'As if Angela would give me presents just to make Jane jealous!' she said, sharply. 'If you ask *me*, I think she gave me them because I mended her blue jumper so neatly. It took me hours.'

'Do you do her mending then?' said Jane, jealously.

'Of course,' said Violet. 'I don't care what Mirabel says to *me* – if I prefer to do things for Angela, I shall do them.'

Violet told Angela how upset Jane was, and Angela was glad. She could be very spiteful when anything upset her. She was especially sweet to Violet and to the other first former who came when Violet could not come. The two of them thought she was the nicest girl in the whole school.

Antoinette, Claudine's little sister, also at times had to do jobs for the fifth and sixth formers. She did not like Angela, and always found excuses not to go to her study, even when an urgent message was sent.

'That young sister of yours is a perfect nuisance,' Angela complained to Claudine. 'Can't you knock some sense into her, Claudine? When I sent for her yesterday, she sent back to say that she was doing her practising – and now I hear that she doesn't even *learn* music!'

'She might have been practising something else,' suggested Claudine, politely. 'Maybe lacrosse.'

Angela snorted. 'Don't be silly! Antoinette gets out of games just like you do – the very idea of thinking she might put in a bit of practice is absurd. I believe you encourage her in these bad ways – slipping out of anything she doesn't like.'

Claudine looked shocked. 'Ah, but surely the little Antoinette loves everything at this so-English school?'

'Don't pretend to me,' said Angela, exasperated. 'I should have thought that in all the time you have been here, Claudine, you would have got more English – you're just as French as ever you were!'

Claudine would not lose her temper at this ungracious speech. 'It is good to be French,' she said, in her light, amiable voice. 'If I were English I might have been *you*, Angela – and that I could not have borne. Better a hundred times to be a French Claudine than an English Angela!'

Angela could not think of any really good retort to this, and by the time she had found her tongue Claudine had gone over to speak to Mam'zelle. Angela knew she had gone to Mam'zelle on purpose – no one would dare to attack Claudine with Mam'zelle standing by! Mam'zelle was intensely loyal to her two nieces.

'All right,' thought Angela, spitefully. 'I'll just get that slippery sister of hers and make her do all kinds of things for me! I'll speak to Hilary about it, and she'll tell Antoinette she's jolly well got to come when I or Alison send for her.'

Hilary knew that Antoinette was being very naughty about coming when she was sent for – but she knew too that Angela used the younger girls far too much. She used her prettiness and charm to make them into little slaves. So she was not very helpful to Angela when the girl told her about Antoinette.

'I'll tell her she must obey the fifth and sixth formers,' she said. 'But Angela, don't go too far, please. Most of us know that you are using your power too much in that direction.'

'What about Mirabel?' said Angela, at once. 'Doesn't she throw *her* weight about too much? She's unbearable this term, just because she's sports captain!'

'There's no need to discuss Mirabel,' said Hilary. 'What we've all got to realize this term, the term before we go up into the sixth, is that this is the form where we first shoulder responsibilities, and first have a little power over others. You're not given power to play about with and get pleasure from, Angela, as *you* seem to think. You're given it to use in the right way.'

'Don't be so preachy,' said Angela. 'Really, are we never going to have any fun or good times again at St Clare's? Everyone looks so serious and solemn nowadays.

Bobby and Janet never play tricks in class. We never have a midnight feast. We never . . .'

'Remember that we are all working jolly hard,' said Hilary, walking off. 'You can't work hard and play the fool too. Wait till the exam is over and then maybe we can have a bit of fun.'

Hilary spoke to Antoinette and the small, dark-eyed French girl listened with the utmost politeness.

'Yes, Hilary, I will go to Angela when she sends for me,' said Antoinette. 'But always she sends for me at so – busy a time!'

'Well, make your excuses to me, not to Angela,' said Hilary, firmly. Antoinette looked at Hilary and sighed. She knew that Hilary would not believe in her excuses, and would insist, in that firm, polite way of hers, that Antoinette should do as she was told.

Angela saw Hilary speaking to Antoinette and was pleased. She decided to give Antoinette a bad time – she would teach her to 'toe the mark' properly.

'Violet, I shan't want you for a few days,' she told the adoring Violet. 'Send me Antoinette instead.'

'Oh, but Angela – don't I do your jobs well enough for you?' said Violet in dismay. 'Antoinette is such a mutt – she can't do a thing! Really she can't. Let *me* do everything.'

'Antoinette can sew and darn beautifully,' said Angela, taking pleasure in hurting Violet, who had been very silly that week. 'You made an awful darn in one of my tennis socks.'

Violet's eyes filled with tears and she went out of the

room. Alison looked up from her work.

'Angela, stop it,' she said. 'I think you're beastly – making the kids adore you and then being unkind to them. Anyway – you'll have a hard nut to crack in Antoinette! *She* won't adore you. She's got her head screwed on all right.'

'She would adore me if I wanted her to,' boasted Angela, who knew the power of her prettiness and smiles, and who could turn on charm like water out of a tap.

'She wouldn't,' said Alison. 'She's like Claudine – sees through everyone at once, and sizes them up and then goes her own way entirely, liking or disliking just as she pleases.'

'I bet I'll make Antoinette like me as much as any of those silly kids,' said Angela. 'You watch and see. You'll be surprised, Alison.'

'I'll watch – but I shan't be surprised,' said Alison. 'I know little Antoinette better than you do!'

7

Antoinette defeats Angela

The next time she was sent for, Antoinette arrived promptly, all smiles. She was just as neat and chic as Claudine, quick-witted and most innocent looking. Miss Jenks, the second-form mistress, had already learnt that Antoinette's innocent look was not to be trusted. The more innocent she looked, the more likely it was that she had misbehaved or was going to misbehave!

'You sent for me, Angela?' said Antoinette.

'Yes,' said Angela, putting on one of her flashing smiles. 'I did. Antoinette, will you clean those brown shoes over there, please? I'm sure you'll do it beautifully.'

Antoinette stared at Angela's beaming smile and smiled back. Angela felt sure she could see intense admiration in her eyes.

'The polish, please?' said Antoinette, politely.

'You'll find it in the cupboard, top shelf,' said Angela. 'How chic and smart you always look, Antoinette – just like Claudine.'

'Ah, Claudine, is she not wonderful?' said Antoinette. 'Angela, I have five sisters, and I like them all, but Claudine is my favourite. Ah, Claudine – I could tell you things about Claudine that would make you marvel, that would make you wish that you too had such a sister, and . . .'

But Angela was not in the least interested to hear what a wonderful sister Claudine was, and she was certain she would never wish she had one like her. Angela preferred being a spoilt only child. You had to share things with sisters!

'Er – the polish is in the cupboard, top shelf,' she said, her bright smile fading a little.

'The polish – ah, yes,' said Antoinette, taking a step towards the cupboard, but only a step. 'Now, Claudine is not the only wonderful sister I have – there is Louise. Ah, I wish I could tell you what Louise is like. Louise can do every embroidery stitch there is, and when she was nine, she won . . .'

'Better get on with my shoes, Antoinette,' said Angela, beginning to lose patience. A hurt look came into Antoinette's eyes, and Angela made haste to bestow her brilliant smile on her again. Antoinette at once cheered up and took another step towards the cupboard.

She opened her mouth, plainly to go on with her praise of Louise or some other sister, but Angela picked up a book and pretended to be absorbed in it.

'Don't talk for a bit,' she said to Antoinette. 'I've got to learn something.'

Antoinette went to the cupboard. She took a chair and stood on it to get the polish. Then she stepped down with a small pot in her hand, and a little secret smile on her mouth – the kind of smile that Claudine sometimes wore. Angela did not see it.

Antoinette found a brush and duster and set herself to her task. She squeezed cream on to the shoes and smeared it on well. Then she brushed it in and then rubbed hard with the soft duster. She held the pair of shoes away from her and looked at them with pride.

'Done?' said Angela, still not looking up in case Antoinette began talking again.

'They are finished,' said Antoinette. 'Shall I clean yet another pair, Angela? It is a pleasure to work for you.'

Angela was delighted to hear this. Aha – Alison would soon see that she could win the heart of Antoinette as easily as anyone else's.

'Yes, Antoinette – clean all the shoes you like,' she said, smiling sweetly. 'How beautiful that pair look!'

'Do they not?' said Antoinette. 'Such beautiful shoes they are too! Ah, no girl in the school wears such fine clothes as you, Angela – so beautifully made, so carefully finished. You have more chic than any English girl – you might be a Parisian!'

'I've been to Paris and bought clothes there two or three times,' said Angela, and was just about to describe all the clothes when Antoinette started off again.

'Ah, clothes – now you should see my sister Jeanne! Such marvellous clothes she has, like those in the shops at Paris – but all of them she makes herself with her clever fingers. Such style, such chic, such . . .'

'You seem to have got a whole lot of very clever sisters,' said Angela, sarcastically, but Antoinette did not seem to realize that Angela was being cutting.

'It is true,' she said. 'I have not yet told you about Marie. Now Marie . . .'

'Antoinette, finish the shoes and let me get on with my work,' said Angela, who felt that she could not bear to hear about another sister of Antoinette's. 'There's a good girl!'

She used her most charming tone, and Antoinette beamed. 'Yes, Angela, yes. I am too much of a chatter-tin, am I not?'

'Box, not tin,' said Angela. 'Now, do get on, Antoinette. It's lovely to hear your chatter, but I really have got work to do.'

Antoinette said no more but busied herself with three more pairs of shoes. She stood them in the corner and put the empty pot of cream into the waste-paper basket. 'I have finished, Angela,' she said. 'I go now. Tomorrow you will want me, is it not so?'

'Yes, come tomorrow at the same time,' said Angela, switching on a charming smile again and shaking back her gleaming hair. 'You've done my shoes beautifully. Thank you.'

Antoinette slipped out of the room like a mouse. She met Claudine at the end of the passage and her sister raised her eyebrows. 'Where have you been, Antoinette? You are not supposed to be in the fifth-form studies unless you have been sent for.'

'I have been cleaning all Angela's shoes,' said Antoinette, demurely. Then she glanced swiftly up and down the corridor to see that no one else was in sight, and shot out a few sentences in rapid French. Claudine laughed her infectious laugh, and pretended to box her sister's ears.

'*Tiens! Quelle méchante fille*! What will Angela say?'

Antoinette shrugged her shoulders, grinned and disappeared. Claudine went on her way, and paused outside Angela's study. She heard voices. Alison was there now too. Claudine opened the door.

'Hallo,' said Alison. 'Come for that book I promised you? Wait a minute – I've put it out for you somewhere.'

She caught sight of all Angela's shoes standing gleaming in a corner. 'I say! Did young Violet clean them like that for you? She doesn't usually get such a polish on!'

'No – Antoinette did them,' said Angela. 'She was telling me all about your sisters and hers, Claudine.'

'Ah, yes,' said Claudine, 'there is my sister Louise, and my sister Marie and my sister . . .'

'Oh, don't *you* start on them, for goodness' sake,' said Angela. 'What's the matter, Alison, what are you staring at?'

'Have you used up all that lovely face-cream al*ready*?' said Alison, in a surprised voice, and she picked an empty pot out of the waste-paper basket. 'Angela, how extravagant of you! Why, there was hardly any out of it yesterday – and now it's all gone. What *have* you done with it?'

'Nothing,' said Angela, startled. 'I hardly ever use that, it's so terribly expensive and difficult to get. I keep it for very special occasions. Whatever can have happened to it? It really is empty!'

The two girls stared at each other, puzzled. Claudine sat on the side of the table, swinging her foot, her face quite impassive. Then Angela slapped the table hard and exclaimed in anger.

'It's that fool of an Antoinette! She's cleaned my shoes with my best face-cream! Oh, the idiot! All that lovely cream gone – gone on my shoes too!'

'But your shoes, they look so beautiful!' remarked Claudine. 'Maybe the little Antoinette thought that ordinary shoe-polish was not good enough for such fine shoes.'

'She's an idiot,' said Angela. 'I won't have her do any jobs again.'

'Perhaps that's why she did this,' said Alison, dryly. 'It's the kind of thing our dear Claudine would do, for the same kind of reason, isn't it, Claudine?'

'Shall I tell Antoinette you will not need her again because you are very angry at her foolishness?' said Claudine. 'Ah, she will be so sad, the poor child!'

Angela debated. She felt sure that Antoinette had made a real mistake. She was certain the girl liked her too much to play such a trick on her. How thrilled Antoinette had seemed when she had smiled at her! No – the girl had made a genuine mistake. Angela would give her another chance.

'I'll try her again,' she said. 'I'll forgive her this time. We all make mistakes sometimes.'

'How true!' said Claudine. 'Now, my sister Marie, hardly ever does she make a mistake, but once . . .'

'Oh, get out,' said Angela, rudely. 'It's bad enough to

have you and Antoinette here without having to hear about your dozens of sisters!'

Claudine removed herself gracefully and went to find Antoinette to report the success of her trick. Antoinette grinned. '*C'est bien,*' she said. 'Very good! Another time I will again be foolish, oh, so foolish!'

Angela sent for her again the next day. Antoinette entered with drooping head and downcast eyes.

'Oh, Angela,' she said, in a low, meek voice, 'my sister Claudine has told me what a terrible mistake I made yesterday. How could I have been so foolish? I pray you to forgive me.'

'All right,' said Angela. 'Don't look so miserable, Antoinette. By the way, I think I'll call you Toni – it's so much friendlier than Antoinette, isn't it?'

Antoinette appeared to greet this idea with rapture. Angela beamed. How easy it was to get round these young ones! Well – she would get all the work she could out of this silly French girl, she would wind her round her little finger – and then she would send her packing and teach her a good sharp lesson!

'What would you have me do today?' Antoinette asked, in her meek voice. 'More shoes?'

'No,' said Angela. 'No more shoes. Make me some anchovy toast, Toni.'

'Please?' said Antoinette, not understanding.

'Oh, dear – don't you know what anchovy toast is?' sighed Angela. 'Well, you make ordinary buttered toast – and for goodness' sake toast the bread before you put the butter on – then you spread it with anchovy paste. You'll find it in the cupboard. Make enough for three people. Anne-Marie is coming to tea, to read us her new poem.'

'Ah, the wonderful Anne-Marie!' said Antoinette, getting out the bread. 'Now one of my sisters, the one called Louise, once she wrote a poem and . . .'

'Toni, I've got to go and see someone,' said Angela, getting up hurriedly. 'Get on with the toast, and do it really carefully, to make up for your silly mistake yesterday.'

'Angela, believe me, your little Toni will give you such toast as never you have had before!' said Antoinette with fervour. She held a piece of bread to the fire.

Angela went out, determined not to come back till Antoinette had made the toast and was safely out of the way. Talk about a chatterbox! She seemed to have a never-ending flow of conversation about her family. She might start on her brothers next – if she had any!

As soon as Angela had gone out of the room, Antoinette put aside her artless ways and concentrated on her job. She made six pieces of toast very rapidly and spread them with butter. Then she got a pot down from the cupboard shelf – but it was not anchovy. It was the pot of brown shoe polish that she should have used the day before!

It looked exactly like anchovy as she spread it on the toast. Carefully the little monkey spread the brown paste, piled the slices on a plate and set them beside the fire to keep warm. Then she slipped out of the room and made her way to the noisy common-room of her own form.

Soon Alison came in and sat down by the fire. Then

Angela popped her head round the door and saw to her relief that Antoinette was gone.

'I simply couldn't stay in the room with that awful chatterbox, drivelling on about her sisters,' said Angela. 'Ah, she's made a nice lot of toast, hasn't she? Hallo – here's Anne-Marie.'

Anne-Marie came in, her big eyes dark in her pale face. 'You look tired,' said Angela. 'Been burning the midnight oil? I wish *I* could write poems like you, Anne-Marie.'

'I worked on a poem till past twelve,' said Anne-Marie, in her intense voice. 'It's a good thing no one saw the light in my study. Ah – tea's ready, how lovely! Let's tuck in, and then I'll read my latest poem.'

8

Three disgusted girls

Angela lifted the toast on to the table. 'I got Antoinette to make anchovy toast for us,' she said. 'It looks good, doesn't it? Take a slice, Anne-Marie.'

Anne-Marie took the top slice. It seemed to have rather a peculiar smell. Anne-Marie looked rather doubtfully at it.

'It's all right,' said Alison, seeing her look. 'Anchovy always smells a bit funny, I think.'

She and Anne-Marie took a good bite out of their toast at the same second. The shoe-cream tasted abominable. Anne-Marie spat her mouthful out at once, all over the table. Alison, with better manners, spat hers into her handkerchief. Angela took a bite before she realized what the others were doing.

Then she too spat out at once, and clutched her mouth with her hands. 'Oh! Oh! What is it? I'm poisoned!'

She rushed to the nearest bathroom and the others followed, their tongues hanging out. Anne-Marie was promptly sick when she reached the bathroom. Tears poured from her eyes and she had to sit down.

'Angela! What filthy paste! How *could* you buy such stuff?' she said.

'Horrible!' said Alison, rinsing her mouth out over and

over again. 'All that toast wasted too. It's wicked. Angela, whatever possessed you to get paste like that? I've never tasted anchovy like that before, and I hope I never shall again. Ugh!'

Angela was feeling ill and very angry. What in the world had that idiot Antoinette done? They went back to the study and Angela opened the door of the little cupboard. She took down the pot of anchovy. It was untouched. So Antoinette couldn't have used it. Then what *had* she used? There was only jam besides the paste.

Alison picked up the pot of brown shoe-cream and opened that. It was practically empty. 'Look,' said Alison, angrily. 'She used the shoe-cream – plastered all the toast with it! She deserves a good scolding.'

Angela was white with anger. She put her head out of the door and saw a first former passing. 'Hey, Molly,' she called, 'go and find Antoinette and tell her to come here at once.'

'Yes, Angela,' said Molly, and went off. Very soon Antoinette appeared, her dark eyes wide with alarm, and her lips trembling as if with emotion.

'Antoinette! How *dare* you put shoe-cream on our toast?' almost screamed Angela. 'You might have poisoned us all. Can't you tell the difference between anchovy paste and shoe-polish, you absolute idiot? You've made us all ill. Matron will probably hear about it. You ought to be reported to Miss Jenks, you ought to . . .'

'Ah, ah, do not scold your little Toni so,' said Antoinette. 'You have been so kind to me, Angela, you have smiled, you have called me Toni! Do not scold me so! I will give up my tea-time, I will make you more toast, and this time I will spread it with the anchovy, there shall be no mistake this time.'

'If you think I'm ever going to trust you to do a single thing for me again, you're mistaken,' said Angela, still tasting the awful taste of shoe-cream in her mouth. 'I might have known a French girl would play the fool like this. I tell you, you've made us all ill. Anne-Marie was sick.'

'I am desolated,' wailed Antoinette. 'Ah, Angela, I pray you to let me come again tomorrow. Tomorrow I will be good, so good. Tomorrow you will call me Toni and smile at me again, tomorrow . . .'

'Tomorrow I'll get Violet Hill,' said Angela. 'Clear out, Antoinette, you're a perfect menace.'

Antoinette cleared out and there was peace. 'Well,' said Angela, 'she'll wish she'd been more sensible tomorrow. Serves her right! I was nice to her, and she thought the world of me – but I can't put up with idiots. She'll be jolly sorry when she sees I don't mean to give her another chance!'

'I don't feel like any tea now,' said Alison, looking at the remains of the toast with dislike. 'Do you, Anne-Marie?'

'No.' said Anne-Marie, and shuddered. 'I still feel sick. I don't even know if I can read my poem. It doesn't go very well with shoe-polish.'

'Oh, do read it, Anne-Marie,' begged Angela, who really did admire her poems. 'What's it about?'

'It's all about the sadness of spring,' said Anne-Marie, reaching for her poem. 'It's a very sad poem, really.'

'All your poems are sad,' said Alison. 'Why are they, Anne-Marie? I like poems that make me feel happy.'

'I am not a very happy person,' said Anne-Marie, very solemnly, and looked intense. 'Poets aren't, you know.'

'But some must have been,' objected Alison. 'I know lots of very cheerful poems.'

'Shut up, Alison,' said Angela. 'Read your poem, Anne-Marie.'

Anne-Marie began her poem. It was very doleful, full of impressive words, and rather dull. Neither Alison nor Angela liked it very much, but they couldn't help feeling impressed. However could Anne-Marie write like that? She must indeed be a genius!

'It must be nice for you, sharing a study with Felicity, who thinks as much of music as you do of poetry,' said Alison. 'You ought to get Felicity to set some of your poems to music. That would be wonderful.'

'I've asked her. She won't,' said Anne-Marie, shortly. The truth was that Felicity would not admit that Anne-Marie's poems were worth tuppence. It was very humiliating to Anne-Marie.

'Write something real, and I'll put a tune to it,' Felicity had said. 'I'm not going to waste my music on second-rate stuff.'

The door opened suddenly and Matron looked in. 'I hear you poor girls have had a nasty dose of shoe-polish,' she said. 'I hope it wasn't anything very serious.'

Angela thought she would take the chance of getting Antoinette into trouble, so she exaggerated at once.

'Oh, Matron, it was awful! We had our mouths absolutely full of the beastly stuff. Anne-Marie must have swallowed a lot, because she was sick. I shouldn't be surprised if we are ill, seriously ill, tonight,' said Angela.

'I'm sure I swallowed some,' said Anne-Marie, looking solemn. 'I expect we all did.'

'Then you must come and have a dose at once,' said Matron. 'That shoe-cream contains a poisonous ingredient which may irritate your insides for a week or more, unless I give you a dose to get rid of it. Come along with me straight away.'

The three girls stared at her in alarm. They simply could not bear Matron's medicines. They were really so very nasty! Angela wished fervently that she had not exaggerated so much.

She tried to take back what she had said. 'Oh, well, Matron,' she said, with a little laugh, 'it wasn't as bad as all that, you know. We spat out practically all of it – and we rinsed our mouths out at once. We're *per*fectly all right now.'

'I dare say,' said Matron. 'But I'd rather be on the safe side. I don't want you in bed for a week with a tummy upset of some sort. Come along. I've got something that will stop any trouble immediately.'

'But Matron,' began Alison.

It was no good. Nobody could reason with Matron once she had really decided to give anyone a dose. The three girls had to get up and follow her. They looked very blue, and felt most humiliated. As a rule Matron left the fifth and sixth formers to look after themselves, and seldom came after them, suggesting medicine. They felt like first or second formers, trooping after her for a dose.

Matron took them to her room, and measured out the medicine into tablespoons, one for each of them. It tasted almost as nasty as the shoe-polish toast!

'Pooh!' said Alison, trying to get the taste out of her mouth. 'Why don't you get some nice-tasting medicines, Matron? I've never tasted any so beastly as yours.'

'Well, I've got a much worse one here,' said Matron. 'Would you just like to try it?'

'Of course not!' said Alison. Then a thought struck her. 'Matron – how did you know we'd had shoe-polish on our toast today? We hadn't told a soul. Who told you?'

'Why, the poor little Antoinette told me,' said Matron, corking up the bottle. 'Poor child, she came to me in a terrible state, saying she had poisoned you all by mistake, and what was she to do if you died in the night, and couldn't I do something about it?'

The three girls listened to this with mixed feelings. So it was Antoinette who not only provided them with shoe-polish toast, but also with medicine from Matron! The little horror!

'You've no idea how upset she was,' went on Matron, briskly. 'Poor little soul, I felt really sorry for her. An English girl might have been amused at the mistake she had made, but Antoinette was so upset I had to comfort her and give her some chocolate. It's wonderful what chocolate will do to soothe the nerves of a first or second former! Nothing but babies, really.'

The thought of Antoinette eating Matron's chocolate was too much for Angela, Alison and Anne-Marie. They felt that they simply *must* get hold of Antoinette and tell her what they thought of her.

'Where is Antoinette, do you know, Matron?' asked Angela, wishing she could get the combined tastes of shoepolish and medicine out of her mouth.

'I sent her to her aunt, Mam'zelle,' said Matron. 'I'm sure she would cheer her up and make her think she hadn't done such a dreadful thing after all! Fancy thinking she really had poisoned you!'

The three fifth-formers went back to the study. It wouldn't be a bit of good going to fetch Antoinette now. She would probably be having a nice cosy tea with Mam'zelle, who would be fussing her up and telling her everything was all right, a mistake was a mistake, and not to worry, *pauvre petite* Antoinette!

'I'll send for her tomorrow and jolly well keep her nose to the grindstone,' said Angela, angrily. 'I told her she needn't do anything more for me – but I'll make her now. I'll make her sorry she ever played those tricks. Clever little beast – going off to Matron and play-acting like that. She's worse than Claudine!'

Alison was alarmed to hear that Angela was going to make Antoinette do some more jobs for them.

'For goodness' sake, don't be silly!' she said to

Angela. 'Antoinette is far too clever for us to get even with. She'll only do something even worse than she has already done. I told you she wouldn't be like the others, silly and worshipping. I told you she would size you up! I told you . . .'

'Shut up, Alison,' said Angela. 'I hate people who say "I told you, I told you!" I won't have Antoinette if you think she'll play worse tricks. She'd end in poisoning us, I should think. I wish I could pay her out, though.'

'It's partly your own fault, all this,' said Alison. 'If only you'd treat the younger ones like the others do, sensibly and properly, we shouldn't have all these upsets.'

Anne-Marie thought it was time to go. She always said that quarrels upset her poetic feelings. So she went, taking her mournful poem with her.

'We'd better not say a word about this to anyone,' said Angela. 'Else the whole school will be laughing at us. We won't let it go any further.'

But alas for their plans – Antoinette told the story to everyone, and soon the whole school was enjoying the joke. It made Angela furious, for she hated being laughed at. It humiliated Alison too, for even Miss Willcox got to hear of it and teased her and Anne-Marie.

'What about a little essay on "Anchovy Sauce"?' she said. 'Poor Alison, poor Anne-Marie, what a shame!'

9

Miss Willcox is in a bad temper

Miss Willcox was in a bad temper. She had just had back from her publishers her second book of poems, with a polite note to say that they were not as good as the first ones, and they regretted they did not see their way to put them into book form.

Miss Willcox had an excellent opinion of her own writings, just as Anne-Marie had of hers. Also she had boasted in advance of her second book of poems – and now it would not be published. She was disappointed, and, like many rather weak characters, her disappointment turned to resentment instead of to a determination to go on and do better.

So she went to her English class looking rather grim, and feeling that she could not stand any nonsense or bad work that morning.

As a whole, the class had been working really very well, for Miss Willcox's lessons were interesting. Alma Pudden had not been able to keep up with the class very well, and Doris could not learn by heart with any success unless she was allowed to act what she said. Felicity too was only really interested if the poems or plays aroused her sense of rhythm and music.

The girls were rather tired that morning. They had had a strenuous half-hour with the gym mistress, who, feeling rather brisk, had put them through a great many vigorous exercises. Then had come a very hard three-quarters of an hour over maths and then the English lesson. The girls were feeling that they wanted to relax a little – but here was Miss Willcox demanding intense concentration and attention.

Carlotta let out an enormous yawn which drew Miss Willcox's wrath upon her. Then Claudine said she felt sick and please could she go out of the room?

'It is astonishing how many times you manage to feel sick when you want to miss some part of a lesson,' said Miss Willcox, irritated. 'Go straight to Matron, please, and tell her.'

'I would rather not,' said Claudine, politely. 'I do not feel sick enough for that. I can be sick in here if you would rather I stayed for the lesson.'

It looked as if Miss Willcox was going to overwhelm Claudine with her wrath, when Felicity made them all jump. She began to tattoo on her desk, swaying to and fro in ecstasy.

'La-di-la-di-la!' she sang, 'oh, la-la-la-di-la!'

'Felicity! What in the world are you doing?' cried Miss Willcox, incensed with rage. Felicity took not the slightest notice. With eyes still closed, she continued her swaying, and her singing, at times thumping the desk to accent the rhythm.

'*Felicity*!' almost shouted Miss Willcox, one of her gold-topped pins falling out of her hair on to the desk. She didn't notice it. 'Do you hear what I say? What has come over this class this morning?'

Bobby gave Felicity a bang on the shoulder. Felicity opened her eyes with a start, and gazed round the room. She did not in the least seem to take in the fact that she was in class and that Miss Willcox was furious with her. She shut her eyes again and began swaying.

'She's music-mad,' said Bobby. 'She's in a kind of music-dream, Miss Willcox. I don't believe she can help it. Hi, Felicity!'

'She goes like this in our study at night, very often,' said Anne-Marie. 'I often think she does it on purpose. She always does it when I want to read one of my poems out loud.'

'Jolly sensible of her,' remarked Pat.

'La-di-la-di-la!' hummed Felicity. Miss Willcox stared at her very hard. She simply could not make out if the girl's actions were genuine or put on.

'Boom-di-boom, di-boom,' finished Felicity and banged the desk hard. 'Ah, I've got it at last!'

The girls laughed. Acting or not, it was very funny. Felicity beamed round. 'I have it!' she said. 'The melody I've had in my mind for the last two weeks. It goes like this – la-di-la-di-la . . .'

Now it was Miss Willcox's turn to bang on the desk. It was seldom that she really did lose her temper, for she considered that meant a loss of dignity, and Miss Willcox always liked to appear dignified and self-controlled.

But really, Felicity was too much for anyone!

'Leave the room,' commanded Miss Willcox, her voice trembling with anger. 'I won't have anyone in my class playing the fool like this. You shouldn't have come up into the fifth form – you should have gone down into the third!'

'Go out of the room?' said Felicity, puzzled. 'Why must I? I didn't mean to interrupt the lesson – I didn't do it on purpose. It came over me suddenly. Now I am quite all right.'

'Leave the room,' ordered Miss Willcox again. The girls were silent. It was almost unheard of for a fifth-form girl to be sent from the room. If Miss Theobald heard of it there would be serious trouble for Felicity.

Felicity got up and walked out of the room as if she was in a dream. She looked puzzled and shocked. She stood outside the door and leant against the wall. Her head ached. Then the new melody came back again into it and she began to sing it quietly. The sound came into the silent classroom.

'Anne-Marie, tell Felicity to go to her study, and to write out the whole of the act of the play she is now missing,' said Miss Willcox. 'I will not have this behaviour.'

'Felicity thinks she's a genius,' said Anne-Marie. 'She's always acting like this.'

'I didn't ask for any comment,' said Miss Willcox. She always forgot to put on her deep, rather drawling voice, when she was in a temper, and her voice now sounded rather harsh and unpleasant.

Almost everyone got into trouble that morning. Doris

was scolded for not knowing her part in the play they were reading. Alma was hauled up for eating sweets, 'like any silly little first former,' said Miss Willcox in disgust, taking the bag away from the unhappy Alma.

'Poor old Pudding!' whispered Pat to Isabel. 'I believe eating is her only pleasure in life!'

'Pat! What did you say?' demanded Miss Willcox. Pat went red.

'Well – I can't very well tell you,' she said, not wishing to repeat what she had said and hurt Alma.

Miss Willcox at once felt certain that Pat had been saying something rude about *her*. 'Miss games this afternoon and write out your part in the play instead,' she snapped. Pat looked upset, but did not dare to argue with Miss Willcox in her present mood.

The girls grew nervous. Pauline dropped her books on the floor and made Miss Willcox jump. She got a few sharp words that made her squirm and look at the mistress with resentment. Bobby debated whether or not to cheer things up by making Miss Willcox and the class laugh but decided that nothing on earth would get a smile out of the mistress that morning. Whatever could be wrong with her? She was not usually like this.

Only Alison and Anne-Marie gazed at her with admiration that morning. They both thought that their beloved Miss Willcox looked lovely with her dark soulful eyes flashing. A bit of Miss Willcox's hair came down and hung by her ear. Alison saw her feeling about for the pin that usually kept it up, and walked from her seat.

She picked up the pin that had dropped and put it on Miss Willcox's desk with one of her rather sweet smiles. Somehow the action and the smile soothed Miss Willcox.

'Thank you, Alison,' she said, using the deep voice that always thrilled Anne-Marie and Alison. 'You are always on hand to help!'

Anne-Marie felt jealous. She never liked it when Miss Willcox praised Alison in any way. She sat looking gloomy. The class was amused to see this little by-play.

After the reading of the play was finished, there were five minutes left. 'Has anyone found anything interesting to read?' asked Miss Willcox, who always encouraged the class to bring any poem they liked or to quote any prose lines they came across which pleased them.

Apparently no one had. 'We've been working too hard this week to read much,' said Hilary. 'We haven't time for anything till this awful exam is over.'

'Miss Willcox,' said Anne-Marie, nervously smiling. 'Could I read the class a poem of mine, please? I would so like to know if you like it.'

Miss Willcox was not really in the mood to hear poems by anyone, since her own had been sent back. But the class, thinking that they could sit back and have a little rest for five minutes, applauded Anne-Marie's suggestion loudly. Anne-Marie flushed with pleasure. She thought they were welcoming her poem. It didn't enter her silly little head that the girls wanted a rest, and wouldn't listen to a word of it.

'Well,' said Miss Willcox, rather ungraciously, 'you can read it if you like, Anne-Marie.'

Anne-Marie got a piece of paper out of her desk, covered with her sprawling hand-writing, which was always far too big. She cleared her throat, and began, putting on a deep voice that was supposed to be a flattering imitation of Miss Willcox's own style.

'THE LONELY MILL

Lost in the wreathing mists of time,
Silent as years that are lost,
Brooding . . .'

Nobody but Angela listened. The whole class was bored to tears by Anne-Marie's pretentious, solemn and insincere poetry. Anne-Marie let herself go, and her voice rang quite sonorously through the classroom.

But she was not allowed to finish it. Miss Willcox had listened in a state of irritation, and stopped her half-way through. The poem was plainly an imitation of one of her own poems, in the book she had had published, a copy of which the adoring Anne-Marie had bought.

Her poem was called 'The Deserted Farm', and the whole plan of it was much the same as Anne-Marie's, even to the ideas in the different verses. As an imitation it was very clever – but Anne-Marie had not meant it to be an imitation. She had thought she was writing a most original poem, and had not even realized that she had drawn on her memories of Miss Willcox's own poem.

'Stop,' said the mistress, and Anne-Marie stopped, puzzled. She glanced at Miss Willcox, who was frowning.

'When you write something *really* original, something out of your own mind, something which isn't copied from *my* work or anyone else's, I'll listen to it, Anne-Marie,' said Miss Willcox, putting on her deep, drawling voice again.

'But Miss Willcox – I didn't copy it from anywhere,' stammered Anne-Marie, horrified. 'I – I only tried to model it on your own style, which I admire very much. I – I –'

Even if Anne-Marie's poem had been as good as one by Shakespeare, Miss Willcox would not have admired it that morning, when she was still smarting from the sending back of her own precious collection of poems.

'Don't make excuses,' she said coldly. 'If I were you I should tear the poem up. Now – there's the bell. Put your books together and go out for break. Alison, you can stay and help me for a few moments. I want these papers put in order.'

In tears poor Anne-Marie went out of the room – and with smiles Alison helped Miss Willcox. The other girls hurried out thankfully – what a nerve-racking English lesson it had been!

10

About geniuses, sport, and mending

'You weren't sick after all, Claudine,' said Angela, rather maliciously, as they went out.

'It passed,' said Claudine, airily. 'Happily Felicity took Miss Willcox's attention, or I might have had to go to Matron.'

'We'd better go and get Felicity out of her study,' said Isabel to Pat. 'I wonder if she's written out the act of that play. It's an awfully long one.'

They went to Felicity's study. Anne-Marie was there, crying. She scowled at the others when they came in.

'Cheer up, silly,' said Pat. 'What does it matter what dear Deirdre says about your poem? I bet she's jealous, that's all!'

'You don't know anything about poetry,' sniffled Anne-Marie. 'I don't believe you heard a word of my poem, anyway.'

'Quite right, I didn't,' said Pat. 'I'd listen if I understood what you were trying to say in your poems, Anne-Marie, but it always seems to me as if you haven't got anything to *say*.'

'You're all unkind to me,' sobbed Anne-Marie,

thoroughly upset by two things – the fact that her precious poem had been scoffed at, and that her adored Miss Willcox had snubbed her.

'Oh, don't be such a baby,' said Pat, and turned to look at Felicity, who was writing feverishly in a corner, copying out the play in nervous, very small hand-writing.

'Bad luck, Felicity,' said Pat. 'Come on out now, though. Do you good to get a blow in the air this morning. You look awful.'

'I don't know what happened to me in class today,' said Felicity, raising her head for a minute. 'You see, I've been working so hard on my music, and the tune I've been groping for suddenly came to me – and my mind just went after it, and I forgot everything else.'

'It's because you're a genius,' said Pat, kindly, for she liked Felicity, who put on no airs at all, and was not in the least conceited. 'Geniuses always do funny unusual things, you know. They can't help it. They like working in the middle of the night, they go without food for days sometimes, they walk in their sleep, they are absent-minded – oh, they're not like ordinary people at all. So cheer up – you can't help being a genius. Personally, I think you're working too hard.'

Anne-Marie listened to this sympathetic speech with sniffles and a discontented look. She thought herself just as much a genius as Felicity – but nobody ever talked to *her* like that! Nobody ever called her a genius, except Angela – and Angela really didn't know the difference between a nursery rhyme and a great poem! Life seemed very hard to poor Anne-Marie just then.

'Perhaps,' thought Anne-Marie, suddenly, 'perhaps if I do some odd things, like Felicity does, the girls will realize I'm a genius too. It's worth trying, anyway – so long as I don't get myself into a row. It's no good doing anything in Miss Willcox's class – after Felicity's performance it would be silly.'

She cheered up a little and went out for break. Felicity would not go out. She was intent on finishing the writing out of the play, so that she could once more give her mind freely to the music that seemed always all around her. Felicity was finding things very hard that term. The work in the fifth form was more difficult than in the fourth, and there was the strain of the exam to face. She was also working even harder at her music, and very often could not sleep at night.

Mirabel also was working very hard at the sports standard of the whole school. She wanted to raise the standard of the lacrosse so that even the fourth and third teams would win all their matches. What a feather it would be in her cap, if she did!

Gladys did not approve of all this intense drive for high efficiency in games and gym and running practice. 'You're trying to do too much too quickly,' she said to Mirabel. 'You'll get much better results if you go more slowly, Mirabel. Look at this practice list of yours for the first form. You'll make them all fed up with games if you insist on so much time being given to them.'

'Do them good,' said Mirabel, intent on the second-form list. 'These kids ought to be very grateful for the interest I take in them. That Jane Teal, for instance – she is ten times better since she did what I told her and put in more practice. She's the best catcher in the first form.'

'Well, you can drive people like Jane Teal, who always want to do the best they can for anyone they like,' said Gladys, 'but you can't drive everyone. Some just get obstinate. I think you're not at all sensible with some of the fourth formers – and you really ought to know better than to go after people like Carlotta and Angela and Claudine.'

'I wish you wouldn't always find fault with me, Gladys,' said Mirabel, impatiently. 'You're quite different from what you used to be. You used to like being guided by me, you said I was the strong one, and you quite looked up to me.'

'I know,' said Gladys, 'and I do now. I only wish I had half your strength of will and purpose, Mirabel. But as I accepted the post of vice-captain, which does bring with it the responsibility of sharing with you most of your decisions, I can't sit back and not say things I ought to say. I don't *want* to say them – I know you won't like some of them – but I'd be a very poor thing if I *didn't* say them.'

Mirabel really was surprised at Gladys. Always she had been the leader of the two and Gladys had followed meekly and willingly. It was something new for Mirabel to find Gladys sticking up for her own ideas, and actually going against her sometimes! Mirabel should have admired her quiet friend for this, but instead, glorying in her position of sports captain, she only felt resentful.

'I mean to make St Clare's the best sports school in the country,' she said obstinately. 'I shan't listen to any excuses of overwork or tiredness from anyone. They'll just have to put as much into their games as they do into their school work.'

'Everyone is not as big and strong as you are,' said Gladys, looking at the huge, strapping girl. 'I don't wonder you are going to train as a games mistress. You're just cut out for it! You could take gym and games the whole day long and then go for a ten-mile walk in the evening! But do, do remember, Mirabel, old thing, that youngsters like Jane Teal really haven't the strength to do all *you* do!'

Jane Teal had most conscientiously done all that Mirabel had asked her, for she was a loyal and hard-working girl. She felt proud when Mirabel told her that she was now the best at ball-catching in lacrosse in the whole of her big form.

But she had never stopped worrying about Angela, and she longed to make up the quarrel with her, and do things for her again. She sat in prep and debated things in her mind. How could she become friends with Angela again? How could she do her jobs instead of Violet, who, after the upset with Antoinette, had been taken back into favour again. She could not for the life of her think how to get back into Angela's good books.

'You seem to be lost in dreams, Jane,' said Miss Roberts's voice. 'I can't think you are doing your maths, with that faraway expression on your face.'

'I – I was just thinking of something,' said Jane,

embarrassed, and bent her head to her work.

The next day Violet went down with a very bad cold, and was taken off to the sick-bay by Matron, sniffling and feeling very sorry for herself. She called to Jane as she went.

'Find that school story for me, and my new jigsaw puzzle and bring them in some time to me,' she said, and Jane promised she would. Accordingly she went to Violet's locker after morning school, and looked for the things she wanted.

She found them – and she also found two pairs of Angela's stockings, and two blouses, all wanting quite a lot of mending. She stared at them.

Violet would be away from school for three or four days. Should she, Jane, do the mending, and take it back to Angela, and ask if she might take Violet's place till she came back? It would be lovely to go to her study again, and tidy up the beautiful place, look at the pictures on the wall, fill the vases with water – do all the things she loved doing. Angela would smile at her again, and everything would be all right.

Jane mended everything beautifully, spending all her free time on the stockings and the blouses. Some of her free time should have been spent in learning a part in a play the first form were doing. How could she learn it, when she had to go to bed early, like all the other first formers?

'I'll take my torch to bed with me, and when the others are asleep, I'll switch it on under the bedclothes and learn my part then,' thought Jane. She was pleased at having thought of such a good way out. No one would know. She did not think of how tired she would feel the next day!

She took the things to Angela that afternoon when Angela sent for Violet. She went in timidly, her heart beating fast, for she was afraid of Angela's sneers and snubs.

Alison was there alone. She was surprised to see Jane. 'Hallo, kid,' she said. 'Where's Violet?'

'In the sick-bay with a cold,' said Jane. 'I mended Angela's things instead. Where is she, Alison?'

'Having a talk with Mirabel,' said Alison. Mirabel had been having serious talks with all the fifth form that day, asking them to help her in making the sports standard for St Clare's much higher. She would certainly not have much success with Angela, who detested getting hot and untidy!

'Oh,' said Jane, disappointed, and put the mended stockings and blouses down. Then her face brightened, for Angela came into the room and shut the door violently. She looked cross.

'That idiot of a Mirabel!' she said to Alison, not seeing Jane at first. 'She wants to turn us all into tomboys like herself, great strapping creatures, striding along instead of walking, shouting instead of speaking, playing . . .'

'Jane is here,' said Alison, warningly. Angela turned and saw her. She still looked cross, and Jane hastened to explain why she was there.

'Violet's ill, please Angela,' she said. 'So I have done your mending myself. I hope you don't mind. I – I – would like to do it for you again, if you'll let me.'

Angela stared at Jane unsmilingly. 'But what about dear

Mirabel, and her anxiety to make you into a wonderful little sportswoman?' she said in a mocking voice.

'I can do both,' said Jane, anxiously. 'I can make time for my work, and my games and for anything you'd like me to do too.'

Angela knew it would annoy Mirabel if she heard that she was making Jane spend her time on all kinds of jobs for her. So she nodded her head and gave the girl a slight smile, which was Heaven to Jane.

'All right,' she said. 'I'll have you again. I'm tired of that silly Violet anyway, with her big cow's eyes. You can come instead.'

Filled with delight Jane sped off. Everything was all right again! The wonderful Angela had smiled at her! She didn't mind if she had to work in bed every night so long as Angela went on being nice to her.

11

Mirabel makes herself a nuisance

Mirabel was really making herself a nuisance just then, especially with the fifth form, who were working very hard indeed for the exam. She was trying to get them interested in the younger ones, to make them go and take practice games with them. They objected to this very much.

'It's a silly idea,' said Pat. 'Those babies much prefer to practise on their own. They don't like being chivvied about by us big ones.'

'Besides, we've got to *work*,' said Hilary, exasperated. 'I can't imagine when you do any extra work for the exam, Mirabel – I'm sure you spend all your evenings in your study, preparing your sports lists and lists for matches, and goodness knows what.'

It was true that Mirabel was doing very little extra work. She was trusting to scrape through the exam, but she did not care whether she got good marks or not. Her whole soul was in the running of the school games, and she often annoyed the games mistress intensely. But Mirabel's thick skin made her quite invulnerable to cutting remarks or snubs.

'She just drives on like a tank,' said Bobby. 'Nobody can stop her. She'll have us all trailing after her helping her in her sports ideas just because we're so tired of arguing with her.'

'You can't argue with Mirabel,' said Doris. 'She never listens to a word anyone says. I doubt if she even listens to Gladys now. It's a pity Gladys isn't a stronger character. She might have some influence over our headstrong Mirabel!'

'Gladys *used* to have influence over her,' said Pat. 'Do you remember when Mirabel first came to St Clare's and was rude and defiant, and said she wouldn't stay longer than half-term, whatever happened?'

'Yes,' said Isabel, remembering. 'She was simply unbearable – quite unreasonable. And it was the little Mouse, Gladys, who got her round, and made her stay on, and become quite a decent member of St Clare's.'

'But Mirabel has got a swelled-head now she's sports captain,' said Bobby. 'Gladys can't do anything with her. I heard her arguing with Mirabel the other day, and all that happened was that Mirabel got angry and shut her up.'

'I have never liked this Mirabel of yours,' remarked Claudine, who had consistently got out of games and gym whenever she could, all the time she had been at St Clare's. 'She is always hunting me here, there and everywhere, calling upon me to do this and that.'

The girls smiled. Claudine usually found it quite easy to evade people who wanted her to do something she disliked, but few people were so persistent as Mirabel. No matter where Claudine hid herself, Mirabel would run her to earth, produce a list of games and try to pin Claudine down to a practice.

'Yesterday, in my great despair, I went to speak to Miss Theobald,' said Claudine, raising her eyebrows and her shoulders in an amusing way. 'There was Mirabel close behind me, waving a great list, and there was I, taking to my toes.'

'Heels,' said Bobby, laughing.

'I run fast,' said Claudine, 'and I find myself outside Miss Theobald's door. What shall I do to get away from this dreadful Mirabel? I knock at the door. I go in!'

The girls were amused and wondered what Claudine could have found so suddenly to say to Miss Theobald.

'What excuse did you make?' asked Janet.

'I held a long conversation with Miss Theobald,' said Claudine, solemnly. 'Ah, we talked, and we talked, whilst the poor Mirabel, she waited patiently outside the door!'

'What on earth did you talk about?' said Bobby, curiously.

Claudine looked mischievous. 'There was no Miss Theobald there!' she said. 'I talked to myself, and then I talked again as if I was answering. The door was shut. How could the good, patient Mirabel know that only I, Claudine, was in the room?'

'Was Mirabel outside the door when you went out?' said Bobby.

'Alas – Miss Theobald herself came to the door when Mirabel was still standing there,' said Claudine. 'The poor Mirabel! She must have been so surprised to see Miss

Theobald, as surprised as I was suddenly to hear her voice outside the door. Me, I did not stay in the room any longer. I jumped out of the window. The gardener was there, and he too jumped – how do you say it – he jumped out of his skin.'

The girls yelled at the thought of Claudine jumping out of Miss Theobald's window in order to avoid both Mirabel and Miss Theobald. None of the others, except perhaps Carlotta, would have thought of doing such a thing.

'You really are the limit,' said Bobby.

'What is this "limit" that you are always talking of?' inquired Claudine.

'Never mind. What happened next?' said Hilary, who always enjoyed Claudine's pranks.

'Ah, well – I went in at the side-door,' said Claudine, 'and I heard Miss Theobald and Mirabel being most surprised at each other. Miss Theobald said, "My dear Mirabel, how can Claudine be talking to me in the sitting-room if I am here, outside the door? Do not be foolish."'

The girls giggled. 'Didn't Miss Theobald open the door?' asked Janet.

'Yes,' said Claudine, 'and there was no one in the room. Ah, it was good to see poor Mirabel's face then! So surprised it was, so puzzled. And Miss Theobald, she was quite cross.'

'Did Mirabel ask you what had happened?' said Pat, grinning.

'Ah, yes – she asks me so many times,' said Claudine. And I say, 'I do not understand, Mirabel. Speak to me in

French. But the poor Mirabel, her French is so bad I do not understand that either!'

'Sh – here *is* Mirabel,' said Pauline, as the sports captain came into the room. You always knew when Mirabel was coming – she walked heavily, she flung doors open, and her voice was loud and confident. She came towards the girls.

'I say,' she said, 'I've just got Miss Theobald's permission to call a big sports meeting tomorrow night in the assembly hall. Seven o'clock. It's to discuss all the matches this term – and there are some jolly important ones. Seven o'clock, don't forget. And I shall expect every member of the fifth form to be there. The younger girls are all coming, of course, and it wouldn't do to let them see any of us slacking or not attending the meeting.'

'Yes, but Mirabel – it's Saturday night, and you know we were going to have a dance,' protested Angela. 'You *know* that. It was all arranged. The third and fourth form were coming too. It was to be real fun.'

'Well, I put the meeting tomorrow night because the dance isn't a bit important and the meeting *is*,' said Mirabel. 'We can have a dance any other Saturday. But I've got quite a lot of new ideas to put before the school. I've been working them all out.'

'You might ask *us* if we would agree to exchanging a dance for your silly meeting,' said Alison. 'You're so jolly high-handed! I shan't come to the meeting. I've got better things to do.'

Mirabel looked shocked. How could there be better

things to do than attend a sports meeting, and discuss the ins and outs of matches? She stared at Alison and frowned.

'You've got to come,' she said. 'Miss Theobald said I could arrange the meeting, and tell everyone to attend. It won't take long.'

'You always say that – but your meetings take hours,' said Carlotta. 'You stand up and talk and talk and talk. I shan't come.'

'I shall report anyone who doesn't,' said Mirabel, beginning to look angry.

'Mirabel – put the meeting another time,' said Hilary. 'You're only getting everyone's back up. You really are. We want a little fun tomorrow night. We've all worked hard this week.'

'I'm sorry,' said Mirabel, stiffly. 'The meeting will be held tomorrow night, and nothing will prevent it, not even *your* wish, my dear Hilary. You may be head of the form, but I am head of the whole school for sports.'

She went out and shut the door loudly. She knew the girls would say hard things about her, but she didn't care. She meant to have her way. The girls would thank her all right when every single match against other schools was won! She would put St Clare's at the top.

'She has a wasp in her hat, that girl,' said Claudine, disgusted.

'A bee in her bonnet, you mean,' said Pat. 'How you do get things mixed up, Claudine! Yes, old Mirabel certainly has got a bee in her bonnet – its sports, sports, sports with her all the time, and everyone else has got to be dragged into it too. I love games – but honestly, I find myself not wanting to turn out on the field now, simply because I know Mirabel will be there, ready to check all shirkers and late-comers!'

'Shall we *have* to go to this beastly boring meeting?' said Felicity. 'I wanted to work at my music.'

'And I wanted to finish my new poem,' said Anne-Marie at once.

'We'll have to go, if Miss Theobald has agreed to let Mirabel call the meeting,' said Hilary, reluctantly. 'I suppose she told Miss Theobald that we were all keen on the meeting. It's a nuisance – but we'll have to turn up.'

'Maybe the meeting will not be held after all,' said Claudine.

'Not a hope,' said Bobby. 'I know Mirabel. Once she makes up her mind about something, that something happens. She's a born dictator. She'll be appalling in the sixth form!'

'I think maybe the meeting will not happen after all,' said Claudine, looking dreamily into space.

'What do you mean?' said Bobby.

'I have a feeling here,' said Claudine, pressing a hand to her tummy. 'It tells me, this feeling, that something will stop the meeting tomorrow night. What can it be?'

Hilary looked suspiciously at Claudine, who was wearing one of her most innocent and angelic expressions. Claudine returned her look with candid wide-open eyes.

'Are you planning anything?' said Hilary. 'Because if so, don't. You can't meddle with things like school meetings once you're a fifth former.'

'How true!' said Claudine, with a sigh, and went off to her study with Carlotta.

That night, when everyone in Claudine's room was asleep, the little French girl slipped out of bed and went along the corridor. She went down the stairs and soon returned with something that shone brightly each time she passed under a dimmed light. She deposited it in an unused chest outside the dormitory door, covered it with an old rug, and then slipped along another corridor to the dormitory in which her sister Antoinette slept.

She awoke Antoinette by a light touch, and knelt by her sister's bed to whisper.

'*Oui, oui,*' whispered back Antoinette. 'Yes! Yes, Claudine, I will do as you say. Do not fear. It will be done!'

Claudine slipped back to bed like a little white ghost. She climbed between the sheets, grinning to herself. Dear Mirabel, it will be difficult for you to hold your meeting tomorrow, poor Mirabel, you will be disappointed, foolish Mirabel, you cannot get the better of the little French Claudine! With these pleasant thoughts Claudine fell fast asleep.

12

The meeting is spoilt

The third, fourth, and fifth forms were very much annoyed and upset by Mirabel's command to attend the sports meeting on Saturday night. They had looked forward to the dance so much – it was just like Mirabel to spoil everything!

'She walks about with those long strides of hers as if she owns the whole school,' said Belinda of the fourth form.

'I used to like games but now I'm getting fed up with them,' complained Rita of the third form. 'Mirabel ticks me off in public on the field as if I were one of the first form. I won't stand it!'

But she did stand it because Mirabel was a very strong personality determined to get her own way. She was using her power to the utmost and beyond.

The fifth formers all put away their various occupations that Saturday night as seven o'clock drew near. They grumbled as they shut their books, rolled up their knitting, put away their letters. But not one of them refused to go when the time came, for they knew that, as fifth formers, they must turn up even if only as a good example to the younger ones.

Mirabel was standing on the platform of the assembly

hall, running through the list of things she meant to say. She glanced up as the girls came filing in, her quick eyes watching to see that everyone turned up. Woe betide any unlucky first or second former who did not arrive! Mirabel would be after them the next day!

Antoinette came up to Mirabel. The sports captain glanced up impatiently. 'What is it, Antoinette?'

'Please, Mirabel, may the second form have a new ball to practise with?' said Antoinette. 'It seems that we have lost the one we had, and we are oh, so keen to practise hard for you.'

'Hm,' said Mirabel, rather disbelievingly, for Antoinette could not by any means have been called keen on games. 'Why didn't Violet come to me about it?'

'Violet is in the sick-bay,' said Antoinette.

'Well, come to me on Monday about the ball. I can't possibly deal with matters like that now,' said Mirabel. 'You ought to know better than to come just before an important meeting like this.'

'Yes, Mirabel,' said Antoinette, and sidled away. Mirabel thought of her with exasperation. She was a slacker, just like Claudine – but she would pin her down and make her play games properly if it took her three terms to do it!

The girls all filed in. Mirabel caught sight of Jane Teal in the first-form benches, looking rather pale. Jane was gazing at Angela, who was looking very beautiful that evening. She had had her hair washed, and it glistened like finest gold. Mirabel frowned. She wished that Jane and the other first formers would stop raving about that foolish Angela!

She ran her eyes over the fifth form. They all seemed to be there – but wait a minute, where was Felicity?

Mirabel spoke to Anne-Marie, who was passing by the platform at that moment. 'Where's Felicity?'

'She's coming, Mirabel,' said Anne-Marie, shortly, for she, like everyone else, resented giving up a jolly dance for a dull meeting. 'She had some music to finish copying out. She said she was just coming.'

'Well, I shall begin without her,' said Mirabel. 'She's always unpunctual. Such a bad example for the younger ones! It's a minute past seven already.'

Everyone was now in their seats. There was a great shuffling of feet, and an outbreak of coughing from the second form, who were a very lively lot this term.

Mirabel went to the front of the platform. She looked enormous there. She began very self-confidently, for she was seldom at a loss for words when her beloved games were the subject.

'Good evening, girls,' she began, in her loud, determined voice. 'I have called this important meeting here tonight for a very special reason. I want to make St Clare's the head of all the schools in the kingdom in their proficiency at games of all kinds. I want us to have hockey as well, I want us to . . .'

There came an interruption. A first-form girl stood up and stopped Mirabel.

'Jane isn't well. She says she won't leave the meeting,

but she must, mustn't she?'

It was Sally, Jane Teal's friend. Everyone turned to look at poor Jane, who, white in the face, felt quite faint with embarrassment.

'Take her out, Sally,' said Mirabel, rather impatiently. She did not like being interrupted in her opening speech. Sally helped Jane out. 'Are you going to be sick?' she asked in a loud whisper, which embarrassed poor Jane even more. She was terribly upset at holding up Mirabel's meeting, but she really did feel strange.

The two went out, and Mirabel resumed her speech, which went on for three or four minutes. 'I want us to win all our lacrosse matches, I want us to form a hockey team that is unbeatable, I want us to . . .'

But what else Mirabel wanted nobody ever knew. There came a sudden and unusual noise that made everyone jump violently. It was the loud clanging of the school fire-bell!

Clang! Clang! Clang! Clang!

Mirabel stopped and listened, startled. Fire! This was not just a practice alarm she was sure – Miss Theobald would never choose a time like this for an unexpected fire-practice; she knew there was an important meeting being held.

The first and second formers looked uneasily at one another, and then looked for a lead from the older ones. There were no mistresses present.

Hilary stood up, her face quite calm. 'Help me to get the first and seconds out quietly,' she said to the twins and to Janet and Bobby. 'We'll march them into the grounds, out by the side door.'

Mirabel also took quick command. Her strong voice rang out reassuringly.

'That's the school fire-bell. You all know what to do. Stand, please.'

The girls stood, glad to have a leader. Mirabel saw that Hilary, the twins, Bobby and Janet had moved across to the younger girls, and she saw that she could expect the utmost help from them. Some of the first formers looked rather scared.

'Right turn!' roared Mirabel. 'Follow Hilary Wentworth. *March!*'

In perfect order, without any panic at all, the first and second forms marched out, led by Hilary, who undid the garden door and went into the grounds. It was a dark night, but the girls knew the grounds well.

Pat and Isabel took out the second form. Bobby and Janet, and the head girl of the third form then marched off with that form. The fourth formers followed with the fifth, sniffing the air eagerly to see if they could smell smoke.

'Where's the fire?' cried Belinda. 'I can't see a sign anywhere!'

Mirabel went out of the hall last, pleased to find that she could handle an emergency so efficiently. Her loud confident voice had at once instilled trust into every girl. She wondered where the fire was.

The first of the mistresses to arrive on the scene was

Mam'zelle. Miss Theobald was out, and the French Mistress had been left in charge for that evening. The loud, distressed voice of Mam'zelle was heard long before she appeared in the doorway.

'Ah! Where are the girls? Yes, yes – in the assembly hall. To think that a fire should come when Miss Theobald is out! Girls, where are you? Claudine, Antoinette, show yourselves to me, I pray you! Are you safe?'

'Quite safe!' came Claudine's amused voice, and then Antoinette left the darkness of the grounds and went to where Mam'zelle stood in the doorway. 'I too am safe,' she said in her demure voice.

Mam'zelle threw her arms round Antoinette as if she had rescued her from flames. 'Ah, my little Antoinette! Do not be afraid. I am here, your strong Aunt Mathilde!'

'Where's the fire, Mam'zelle?' called a voice.

'Ah, the fire! Where is it?' repeated Mam'zelle, still feeling rather dazed.

Then Matron appeared on the scene, and took command at once. She had sped round the school immediately she had heard the fire-bell, to see where the fire could be. She had been to the place where the fire-bell was kept to see who was ringing it – but the fire-bell was standing in its place, and no one was near it!

She was puzzled, but as her nose, eyes and ears told her that certainly there was no fire raging anywhere near she felt sure that someone had been playing a joke. Matron had been long enough at St Clare's to smell a joke a mile away by now.

'Girls, come in at once!' she said, in her crisp, cool voice. 'There is no fire. But I must congratulate you on responding to the bell so quickly and quietly, and going out of doors in this sensible way.'

'Well, we were all at a meeting,' said Hilary, who was near the door. 'It was easy. We just marched out. But Matron – who rang the bell then?'

'We shall no doubt find that out later,' said Matron, drily. 'In the meantime, please march indoors again.'

The girls all marched in. Some of them were shivering, for it was a cold night. Matron saw this and hoped the sick-bay would not be inundated with people having colds the following week!

She looked at her watch and made up her mind quickly. 'You will all go to your common-rooms and your studies at once,' she said. 'Head girls, make up the fires in the common-rooms, please, and see that the rooms are warm. In ten minutes' time come to the kitchen, two girls from each form, and there will be jugs of hot cocoa ready, which I want you all to drink as soon as possible.'

This was pleasant news. The girls hurried in, glad to think of warm fires and hot cocoa. But Mirabel was annoyed. She spoke to Matron.

'Matron, I'm sorry, but I'm afraid the girls must go back to the hall. We were just beginning a most important meeting. Shall I tell them or will you?'

Matron looked hard at the self-confident Mirabel. 'We shall neither of us tell them,' she said. 'You heard what I said to them. They've had a spell out there in the cold and I don't want them to get chills. There will be no meeting tonight.'

'Hurrah!' said one or two low voices, as the girls hurrying in heard this welcome news. 'Good old Matron.'

Mirabel ought to have known that one person she could never flout was Matron. She began to argue. 'But, Matron – this is a most important meeting. I shall have to go to Miss Theobald, I'm afraid, and ask her for her authority to continue my meeting, if you won't give the girls permission.'

'Very well. Go and ask her,' said Matron, who knew quite well that Miss Theobald was out. So off went Mirabel, angry and determined, bitterly disappointed that her wonderful meeting was spoilt.

But Miss Theobald was not in her sitting-room. It was most annoying. Mirabel hardly dared to go back and take up the matter with Matron again. She had not at all liked the tone of Matron's voice. Her spirits sank and she felt rather miserable.

Then her face grew grim. 'Well, I shall find out who rang that bell and spoilt my meeting, anyway! And won't I give them a dressing-down – in front of the whole school, too!'

13

Who rang the fire-bell?

Mirabel went storming to her study. Gladys was there, warming herself in front of a cheerful little fire.

'Pity the meeting was spoilt,' she said, thinking that Mirabel would be in need of a little comfort about it. 'You were making a very good speech, Mirabel.'

'Gladys, who do you think rang that fire-bell?' said Mirabel, grimly. 'Is that cocoa in the jug? I'll have a cup. Not that I'm cold, but I do feel a bit upset at having the meeting completely spoilt by some silly idiot who thinks it clever to play a practical joke like that.'

Gladys said nothing. She had no idea at all who the culprit could be. Mirabel stirred her cocoa violently, and went on talking.

'Who wasn't there? Well, Felicity wasn't, of course! Gladys, could it have been Felicity?'

'Of course not,' said Gladys. 'I don't suppose Felicity even knows there is a fire-bell, let alone where it is!'

'Well – I shall certainly find out where she was all the time,' said Mirabel. 'This is really the sort of idiotic joke Claudine would play – but she was there all the time. I saw her myself – and Antoinette was there too, because she came up and spoke to me at the beginning of the meeting.'

'And she was out in the grounds with the others,' said Gladys, remembering. 'Didn't you see her go up to Mam'zelle and speak to her when Mam'zelle yelled out for Claudine and Antoinette?'

'Yes,' said Mirabel, frowning. 'Well, who else wasn't there? Violet is in the sick-bay. Everyone else was there as far as I can remember. I ticked people off as they came in, because I wasn't going to let anyone get out of the meeting if I could help it.'

Gladys offered no suggestion. Mirabel suddenly slapped the table hard and made Gladys jump. 'Don't, Mirabel,' she said. 'Don't be so violent.'

Mirabel took no notice. 'Of course – Jane Teal went out, didn't she – and Sally. Do you think either of them would have done it?'

'I shouldn't think so for a moment,' said Gladys. 'Why, Jane is very fond of you, and Sally is far too sensible to do a thing like that.'

'I shall find out,' said Mirabel, her face hard. Gladys looked rather distressed.

'Don't go about it too angrily,' she said. 'You'll only put people's backs up.'

'I don't care if I do,' said Mirabel, and she didn't. Gladys sighed. If only Mirabel did care a little more about other people's feelings, she would find them easier to tackle. She was always complaining that people would not co-operate with her or help her.

Mirabel gulped down her cocoa. 'I'm going off to Felicity's study first,' she said. 'See you later.'

She went out of the room. Gladys took up some knitting. She was making a jumper for her mother, and she had very little spare time for it, with all her exam work, sports work, and Mirabel's incessant demands to cope with. She couldn't help feeling rather glad that she had an unexpected hour to get on with her knitting!

Mirabel went into Felicity's study. Felicity was there, trying her violin softly, whilst Anne-Marie sat over the fire, a pencil and notebook on her knee, trying to compose a wonderful new poem. She kept frowning at Felicity's soft playing, but Felicity was quite unaware of Anne-Marie's frowns or even of Anne-Marie herself. She jumped violently when Mirabel came into the room.

Then, thinking she had come to see Anne-Marie, she went on with her soft playing. Mirabel spoke to her roughly.

'Felicity, why weren't you at the sports meeting this evening?'

Felicity looked startled. 'Oh, Mirabel – I'm so sorry. I really did mean to come, and I forgot all about it! I was playing my violin, and somehow forgot I had said I would go! How awful of me!'

'Where were you when the fire-bell went?' said Mirabel.

'Fire-bell?' said Felicity, looking astonished. 'What fire-bell?'

'She never hears anything but her music when she's really wrapped up in it,' said Anne-Marie. 'You know how she behaved in class the other day, Mirabel. I don't expect she heard the bell at all.'

'I didn't,' said Felicity, looking really bewildered now.

'Did it ring? Was there a fire? What happened?'

'Oh, you're hopeless,' said Mirabel, and went out of the study. Felicity stared at Anne-Marie, who made an impatient noise, stuffed her fingers in her ears, and tried to go on with her poem.

Mirabel went to find Jane Teal and Sally. They were in the first-form common-room, Jane still looking rather pale, but better. She flushed when Mirabel came in, quite thinking that the sports captain had come to see how she was.

But Mirabel hadn't. She came straight to the point. 'Jane and Sally – did either of you ring the fire-bell when you left the meeting?'

The girls stared at her in surprise. It would not have occurred to either of them to spoil such an important meeting! Jane felt very hurt to think that Mirabel should imagine her to be capable of such a thing.

'Well – haven't either of you tongues?' said Mirabel. The whole of the first form had now gathered round the three, and were listening with the greatest interest.

'Of *course* we didn't,' said Sally, indignantly. 'As if we'd do a thing like that! Anyway, poor Jane was feeling awfully ill. She had a terrible headache. She's always having headaches.'

'Shut up, Sally,' said Jane, who knew that Mirabel did not look very kindly on such things as headaches.

'Did you leave Jane alone at all?' said Mirabel to Sally. 'Yes – you came back to the meeting without her, didn't you? Then she could easily have slipped out of your common-room and rung the bell, couldn't she?'

'*Oh*!' said Sally, really indignant. 'As if Jane would do a mean thing like that! Yes, I did leave her here as she seemed a bit better and I went back to the meeting – and as soon as I sat down, the bell rang. But it wasn't Jane ringing it.'

Jane was terribly upset to think that Mirabel should even think she could spoil a meeting of hers. Her lips trembled, and she could not trust herself to speak.

'Now don't burst into tears like a baby,' said Mirabel to Jane. 'I'm not saying you *did* do it – I'm only saying that you had the *chance* to do it. It just puzzles me to know who could have done it, because everybody was at the meeting, except you and Felicity – and I'm pretty certain that Felicity didn't even know St Clare's possessed such a thing as a fire-bell!'

'Well, it looks as if I must have done the deed then,' said Jane, bitterly, trying to keep the tears out of her eyes. 'Think it was me, if you like. I don't care!'

'Now that's not the way to talk to your sports captain,' said Mirabel. 'I'm surprised at you, Jane. Well, I suppose I shall find out one day who rang that bell.'

She went out of the room and shut the door unnecessarily loudly. The first formers looked at one another.

'Beast,' said Sally. 'I shan't do one single minute's more lacrosse practice than I can help!'

'Nor shall I,' said Hilda, and the others all agreed, Jane mopped her eyes, and the others comforted her.

'Never mind, Jane. Don't you worry about it. We all know you didn't do it!'

'I wish I knew who *had* done it,' said Sally, her eyes sparkling. 'I'd go and pat her on the back and say, "Jolly good show!" '

The others laughed and agreed. It was strange how in a few short weeks Mirabel had changed from an object of great admiration into one of detestation.

Miss Theobald had to be told about the strange ringing of the fire-bell, apparently done by nobody at all. She was rather inclined to take a serious view of it and Mirabel was pleased.

'I am glad you too think it is a serious matter to have an important, pre-arranged meeting completely spoilt by somebody's stupid ragging,' said Mirabel.

'Oh, dear me, I was not thinking of your meeting,' was Miss Theobald's rather damping reply. 'I was thinking that I cannot have the fire-bell rung without proper cause. If it is, then the girls will not take warning when the bell is rung for a real fire. That is a very serious matter – not the interruption of your meeting.'

'Oh,' said Mirabel, rather crest-fallen. 'Well, could I have the meeting next Saturday night instead, Miss Theobald?'

'I'm afraid not,' said the head mistress. 'The heads of the third, fourth and fifth forms have already been to me to ask me if they may have the postponed dance then, Mirabel. I don't think we can possibly expect them to postpone it again. These forms are working very hard this term, and very well. I want them to relax when they can.'

Mirabel left Miss Theobald, angry and depressed.

She went into her study and sat down at the table to do some work. 'What's the matter?' said Gladys.

'Hilary and the head girls of the third and fourth have been to Miss Theobald behind my back and got her to say they could have their dance this coming Saturday,' said Mirabel, gloomily. 'It's absolutely the only chance I have of getting the whole school together on Saturday evenings, and they know it. Deceitful beasts!'

'Don't be silly,' said Gladys, feeling a wave of anger. 'They probably never even *imagined* you'd actually want them to give up *another* Saturday evening. Do be sensible, Mirabel. And look here – why have you left little Jane Teal out of next week's matches? She's very good and you know it. It will break her heart to be left out, when you've as good as told her she might play.'

'I'm not satisfied that she didn't have something to do with the ringing of that bell,' said Mirabel.

'*Well*!' said Gladys, exasperated. 'You might at least wait till you *are* sure, before you punish her like this. I think she's a very decent little kid, I must say, and I'm dead certain she wouldn't do a thing like that.'

'Look here, *I'm* captain, not you!' said Mirabel, losing her temper. 'I keep *on* having to remind you of that. I won't have you preaching at me and interfering.'

Gladys went rather white. She hated rows of any sort, and always found it difficult to stand up to Mirabel for any length of time. She took up a book and said no more. Mirabel took up a book too, and looked at it frowning. But she did not see a word that was printed there. She was turning over and over in her mind the same question – WHO rang that fire-bell?

She would have been interested in a little conversation between Claudine and Antoinette if she could have heard it.

'Very good, *ma petite,*' Claudine remarked to Antoinette. 'It was good to show yourself so well to Mirabel at the beginning of the meeting, and to appear out in the grounds when *tante* Mathilde called us. There is no one who thinks of you, no one at all.'

'Clang, clang, clang!' said Antoinette, her dark eyes gleaming with mischief. 'I felt like the old town crier at home. Clang, clang, clang, the meeting will not be held, clang, clang, clang! Ah, it is a good bell to ring!'

'Sh. Here come the others,' said Claudine. 'Slip away, Antoinette. Be sure *I* will help *you* if you want me to, since you have done this thing for me.'

Some of the fifth formers came up. 'What mischief are you thinking of?' said Bobby to Claudine. 'You look pleased.'

'I was remembering how I said, "I feel as if there will be no sports meeting,"' said Claudine. 'And I was right, was I not, Bobbee?'

14

The term goes on

The girls soon forgot about the strange ringing of the fire-bell – all except Mirabel, who felt sure Jane must have done it. In fact, she went even further in her thoughts and suspected Angela of having put Jane up to doing it! She took no notice at all of poor Jane, left her out of the matches, and altogether made her life miserable.

Angela tried to make things up to Jane, delighted at the chance of making a fuss of somebody neglected by Mirabel. Poor Jane was in a great state of mind, upset because Mirabel was unkind to her, thrilled because Angela was sweet to her, and overtired with all her learning in bed at night with the light of her torch.

She had headaches, felt terribly sleepy all the day, and could not see properly, for she was spoiling her eyesight by reading in bed by the dim light of the torch.

She was not the only one with headaches just then. Felicity, always more or less afflicted with them, was having them almost continuously. Also, to Anne-Marie's alarm, Felicity had begun to walk in her sleep at night!

This was something that Felicity had done as a child, when her mind was over-taxed, and now she had begun to do it again. Anne-Marie slept in the bed next to

Felicity's, and was awakened one night to see a dim white figure stealing out of the door. She sat up and switched on her torch. Felicity's bed was empty!

Has she gone to the study to do some more work? thought Anne-Marie. What an idiot she is! I'd better go and get her. She'll get into an awful row if Miss Cornwallis finds out.

Anne-Marie flung her dressing-gown round her shoulders and went after Felicity. To her surprise Felicity did not go in the direction of their study. Instead she went down the stairs and into the assembly room. She climbed up the platform steps, and stood in the middle of the platform.

'Felicity!' whispered Anne-Marie, astonished. 'What are you doing? Felicity!'

Felicity took absolutely no notice at all. She bowed gracefully, took a step backwards and then raised her arms as if she was playing a violin. It was strange to see her in the light of the moon that shone through a nearby window.

Up and down went Felicity's right arm, as the girl played an imaginary tune on an imaginary violin. Her eyes were wide open, fixed and staring. Anne-Marie shivered to see them.

She went up the steps and touched Felicity on the arm. The girl made no response. She went on with her tuneless playing, and then bowed as if she had finished. Anne-Marie took her by the arm. To her surprise Felicity came quite readily with her.

'Are you awake or asleep, Felicity?' said Anne-Marie, fearfully, as they went up the stairs. There was no reply. Felicity was fast asleep, though her eyes were wide open.

Anne-Marie took her safely to her bed and got her in. Felicity cuddled down, shut her eyes and breathed deeply. Anne-Marie got into bed too, but lay awake a long time puzzling over Felicity's sleep-walking.

'It must be because she's a genius,' thought the jealous Anne-Marie. 'She does odd things, as all geniuses seem to do. Sleep-walking must be a sign of genius, I suppose. I wish I did unusual things too. Then maybe everyone would think I was a genius – as I am! Suppose I start a little sleep-walking of my own? If only the girls would wake up and see it, it would be a good way of showing them I'm a genius too. But they all sleep so soundly!'

Still, it was an idea, and Anne-Marie pondered over it a good deal, making up her mind that when a suitable chance came she too would sleep-walk!

Felicity did not remember anything about her sleep-walking the next day and was half inclined to disbelieve Anne-Marie's account of it. She shrugged her shoulders, and went off to her music lesson. She could not find interest in anything but her beloved music these days.

Anne-Marie was still trying her best to win back Miss Willcox's smiles – but as the only way she knew was by pestering her to read her poems, she was not very successful. She so badly wanted praise and admiration for her talents that she did not see that Miss Willcox only had time for those who gave praise and admiration to *her*! Miss

Willcox was in many ways a grown-up Anne-Marie, posing and posturing, soaking up adulation and flattery from anyone who would give it to her. She had no time for people like Anne-Marie, who also demanded it.

For this reason Alison was very much her favourite. Alison had a real gift for making herself a willing slave to people of Miss Willcox's type. Like Jane for Angela, Alison was pleased to do all kinds of jobs at all kinds of hours, if she could please her idol. Miss Willcox took advantage of this, and kept the devoted Alison quite busy.

'It's a pity,' said her cousins. 'She's even beginning to dress like Miss Willcox – rather untidy and bitty!'

So she was. She would appear in class with a startling belt round her slim waist, or a scarf round her neck, and had even managed to get some pins rather like Miss Willcox wore in her hair – only Alison's were gilt-topped, not gold!

'Dear little Deirdre fan!' said Bobby, mockingly, when she saw the pins holding back Alison's pretty, curly hair. 'Golly, you and Anne-Marie really are a pair! Look at Anne-Marie, she's got on a brooch just like the big ones our Deirdre wears!'

It was really funny to see the way the two girls vied with each other to imitate Miss Willcox. But Miss Cornwallis was not pleased. She eyed the two girls each day, and said nothing at first, for the fifth formers were allowed more freedom with their clothes than the forms below.

But, when Alison appeared with two scarves of different colours twined round her neck, and Anne-Marie came with an out-size pewter brooch that had a brilliant orange stone in the middle, Miss Cornwallis could bear it no longer.

'Have you a sore throat, Alison?' she inquired politely. Alison looked surprised.

'No, Miss Cornwallis,' she said.

'Then why *two* scarves, Alison?' said Miss Cornwallis, still in a tone of great politeness, which rang a warning in the ears of the class. How well they knew that extra-polite tone! It always spelt Danger!

'I – I thought they looked nice,' stammered Alison, also hearing the warning in that cold, polite voice.

'Well, Alison, I had thought till this term that you had good taste,' said Miss Cornwallis. 'You always looked tidy and neat and dainty – well-turned out, in fact. But this term you look like a third-rate imitation of some little shop-girl who thinks the more colours and scarves and pins and brooches she wears, the better she looks.'

'Oh,' said poor Alison, scarlet in the face.

'And Anne-Marie seems to be going the same way,' said Miss Cornwallis, looking at the would-be poet in a way that made her squirm and long to take off the enormous brooch. '*What* is that dinner-plate you are wearing, Anne-Marie? Do you really think it becomes you?'

Anne-Marie removed the brooch with trembling fingers. She could not bear to have any faults pointed out in public.

'That's better,' said Miss Cornwallis. 'I don't know if you are imitating anyone, either of you – but let me tell you this – imitation is *not* always the sincerest form of flattery when you make yourselves look such silly little sights!'

'Poor little Deirdre fans!' whispered Bobby to Janet. 'That was a crack at dear Miss Willcox! I bet Corny knows all about what sillies they are over her!'

That was the end of Alison and Anne-Marie trying to dress like Miss Willcox – but they still went on trying to imitate her deep, drawling voice, her graceful gestures, and her rather round-shouldered walk. The girls got very tired of it, and tried to tease them out of it.

But Alison, thrilled because her dear Deirdre was making such a friend of her, was not in a state to listen to anything the others said, and Anne-Marie was too obstinate. If Alison could imitate Miss Willcox and please her by doing so, then Anne-Marie meant to as well!

Tempers began to be rather short as the exam drew near. Hard work and worrying about the exam made most of the fifth form feel harassed and worn. Only Bobby kept cheerful, and Claudine, of course, did not turn a hair. Even Carlotta worried a little, for she wanted to please her father, who had said he would be proud if she passed this rather stiff exam well.

Pauline worried a lot too. She was not brainless and could do quite well if she tried, but she did not like her study-companion, Alma.

'She's strange,' she told Alison. 'She doesn't seem to work at all, just sits and stares at her book and eats and eats, like a cow chewing cud. She's always grumbling too – says the food isn't enough here, and she wants more sweets and isn't allowed them. It's awful to swot over your work when a person like that sits opposite, glowering and grumbling and chewing!'

'Poor old Pudding!' said Alison, thinking of the fat, dull Alma, who was always at the bottom of the form. The mistresses did not seem to be unduly upset at Alma's position. In fact, they rather seemed to take it for granted, which was odd. Miss Cornwallis always had a few sharp words to say to any of the others who stayed too long at the bottom of the form! But she rarely spoke sarcastically to Alma about her work.

'It's awful to live with somebody like Alma all the time,' sighed poor Pauline. Carlotta heard her and made a suggestion.

'Come in and share our study with me and Claudine when you get too fed up,' she said, generously, for she did not really like Pauline very much. 'It's a bit bigger than most people's, so there'll be a corner for you if you like. But don't do it too often or you'll get Alma's back up.'

'Oh, thank you,' said Pauline, gratefully. 'It will make such a difference if I can sometimes pop in next door to your study, Carlotta. You will be cheerful company after Alma. She really *is* a pudding!'

Carlotta and Claudine got on very well together. The younger girls who came to do jobs for them liked them very much. Antoinette often came, and strangely enough, never made the kind of extraordinary mistakes she had made in Angela's study!

One day Antoinette found her sister alone and spoke to her with dancing eyes.

'Claudine! Our form is to have a midnight feast! Do you remember telling me of the fine feast you had when you were in the fourth form – you had a midnight picnic by the swimming-pool.'

'Yes, I remember,' said Claudine, and she sighed. 'It is a pity to be in the fifth form. We are so good now. We do not have midnight feasts, we do not play tricks. You will enjoy your feast, my little Antoinette.'

'Claudine, could you tell us a good place to keep our cakes and tins and ginger beer in?' asked Antoinette. 'We can't keep them in the common-room, and we daren't hide them in our dormitory. Tell me where we can keep them in safety.'

Claudine thought hard. 'There is a big cupboard just outside my study,' she said at last. 'It has a key. You shall put your things there, Antoinette, and I will take the key! Then everything will be safe and I can give you the key when you wish for it. You have only to put your head into my study and wink at me – and I will come out with the key!'

'Oh, thank you, a million times!' said Antoinette. 'The second form will be so pleased. What a fine sister you are!'

She disappeared, and in due time the cupboard was piled full of eatables and drinks. Claudine removed the key. 'Now no one will find them,' she said, and hung the key on a nail in her study.

But somebody did find them, which was very unfortunate!

15

Alma and the store cupboard

Alma did not at all like the way Pauline deserted the study they both shared in the evenings. Pauline would sit for a little while, trying to study, then, exasperated by Alma's continual chewing of chocolate, gum or toffee, she would gather up her books and disappear.

'Where are you going?' Alma would call after her. But Pauline did not bother to reply.

So Alma decided to see where Pauline went to. She popped her head out of her study door in time to see Pauline go into the next study, which was Claudine's and Carlotta's. She stood and frowned.

Pauline was not really friendly with either of them – so why, thought Alma, should she keep popping into their study? She sat and brooded over the matter. The next time that Pauline disappeared she made up her mind to follow her into the next study, after a while, and see exactly what she was doing there.

It so happened that Carlotta had had a big box of sugared candies sent to her by her grandmother, and, in her usual generous way, she opened it and laid it on the table in front of Claudine and Pauline.

'Help yourselves whilst you work,' she said. Claudine

looked longingly at the delicious candied sweets. There were bits of lemon and orange and nut, all candied round beautifully. Claudine, however, thought a great deal of her complexion, which was very good, and she took only one sweet, meaning to make it last all the evening. But Pauline helped herself liberally. She had very little pocket-money to buy herself luxuries, and sweets of this kind did not often come her way.

Just as she was choosing her fourth sweet, the door opened and Alma came in. 'Could you lend me a maths book?' she asked, rather self-consciously. 'Oh, *you're* here, Pauline! I say, what gorgeous sweets! You never told me you had a lovely box like that, Pauline.'

She thought it was Pauline's box because the girl was helping herself to them. Carlotta gave Pauline no time to reply, nor did Claudine. They both disliked Alma, and were afraid that, seeing Pauline there, she might sit down and stay for the whole evening. Then there would be no sweets left!

'Here's the maths book, Alma,' said Carlotta, and threw her one.

'Shut the door after you,' added Claudine.

Alma glared. She thought them very rude, as indeed they were. But who could bear to have Alma sitting there all the evening? Pauline looked uncomfortable as Alma went out and banged the door after her, almost shaking the pictures from the wall.

'She'll be simply beastly to me now,' she said. 'I suppose she spied after me and saw where I went. What's the matter with her? She's so terribly fat and pasty-looking.'

'Just over-eating, I should think,' said Carlotta, beginning to write an essay. 'Now shut up for a bit, both of you. I want to think.'

Alma was very angry that the three girls in the study had not asked her to have even one sweet. She did no work at all that evening. She sat and brooded over that enormous box of sweets. Alma had a craving for that kind of thing.

They're mean pigs, she thought. Really mean. I shall get even with them, though. I'll wait till Carlotta and Claudine are out, and I'll slip in and help myself to a few sweets. I suppose they're Pauline's, and she took them in there to share with the others, instead of sharing them with me.

So Alma kept a watch to see when Carlotta and Claudine went out. There was a little alcove some way up the passage, over which a curtain hung. If she stood there quite quietly she could see when the two girls left their study.

Two evenings later her patience was rewarded. Pauline had gone to a debate. Alma slipped into the alcove and waited to see if Carlotta and Claudine would go to it at half-time, as she had heard them say they would.

Sure enough, in a short while, the study door opened, and Carlotta and Claudine came out. They went down the corridor, talking. Alma waited till their footsteps had died away. She was just going to slip out of the alcove and into the study, when she heard footsteps returning. She peeped out to see who it was.

It was Claudine hurrying back. She had just met Antoinette, who had given her a tin of sugar biscuits to hide in the cupboard with the other things. Claudine ran into her study, took down the key of the cupboard, went outside and unlocked it, pushed in the tin, then locked the door again and hung the key on its nail. Alma watched in the greatest amazement.

Claudine hurried off to join the debate downstairs. Alma stepped out of the alcove, her little eyes gleaming. So that was where the fifth form kept their stores. They must be going to have a party of some kind, and they hadn't told her a word about it! Alma was trembling with rage.

How mean everyone was! It had been bad enough in the starchy sixth form the last term, but really, the fifth form were even worse, the way they left her out of things. Alma walked into her own study and sat down heavily. She looked across at the cupboard there. There was absolutely nothing to eat, nothing – and it was ages till supper-time – and even then there wouldn't be much to eat.

She wondered where Claudine kept the key of that store cupboard. It would be fun just to have a peep inside and see what was there – not to *eat* any of it, of course – oh, no, thought Alma, she wouldn't do that, mean though the others had been not to ask her to share. But she would dearly like to *look*.

There was no one about at all. She tiptoed to Claudine's study and pushed open the door. She looked round for the key. Could that be the one, hanging on the nail by the fire-place? She took it off and went to the cupboard in the passage outside.

With trembling fingers she slipped the key into the lock. It turned easily! It *was* the key. Alma opened the cupboard and looked inside.

The things that were there! It seemed as if every single thing she liked was there – sardines and tinned milk, strawberry jam and pineapple in tins, ginger beer and a box of sweets, biscuits and chocolate.

It was quite impossible for Alma to resist the temptation to pilfer the cupboard. Just one of those chocolates – just a biscuit to go with it – just a sweet or two! Guiltily the girl helped herself, then, hearing footsteps, hurriedly shut the door, turned the key, and slipped back into her own study.

She waited till the footsteps had gone by, then ran into Claudine's study next door, and returned the key to its nail.

For quite a long time Alma sat and brooded over her discovery. She felt certain that the fifth form were going to have a party. She hadn't heard a word about it – but then, nobody ever told her anything!

Alma badly wanted the things in the cupboard. Her continual craving for food made her find excuses for the wrong thing she wanted to do. 'It's only right I should share! Even if they don't ask me, I'm a fifth former and I ought to share in their treats. Well, I *shall* share – but in secret, instead of with them at the party! That will punish them for their meanness. It will give them a shock to find a lot of the things gone.'

It was a curious secret to have, but Alma found great pleasure in thinking about that store cupboard in bed at night, and in class the next day. She hugged the secret to herself, and gave Claudine many triumphant glances, which the French girl was quite at a loss to understand.

Alma began to go to the store cupboard whenever Claudine's study was empty. She was very artful, for she was careful not to take things whose absence would be very noticeable. She did not take much of the barley sugar in the bottle there, for instance, because she knew it might catch Claudine's eye. But she carefully took all the bottom row of the box of chocolates, which would not be noticed till the first row was eaten. She took a few biscuits from each row in the big tin, not one whole row. She drank half of each ginger beer bottle, but filled each one up with water so that it would seem as if the bottles had not been tampered with.

She enjoyed being cunning like this. Poor Alma – her whole interest seemed to lie in food, more food and yet more food. Fat, unwieldy and pasty-faced, with no friends, few brains, and a sly, suspicious nature, she was not a happy person.

She had a wonderful time pilfering the store cupboard. Claudine added a few more things to it, never suspecting that many had already gone. Alma was very clever at getting the key, and taking food when no one was about. If she had only used half as much brain in class as she did in stealing from the cupboard, she would not have been so far down at the bottom of the form.

Then one evening something happened. Pauline, Claudine, and Carlotta had gone down to the common-room of the fourth form to discuss something with the girls there, and Alma, alone in her study, planned to take some biscuits and some chocolate – perhaps she might even take a tin of sardines, as there were now five or six of them. She could open them when she was alone in her own study.

She stole out and got the key from the study next door. She had just put it into the lock of the cupboard and turned it, when she heard someone coming. In a panic she fled to her own study next door, only just disappearing in time. But the key fell out of the lock with a clang and lay on the floor.

It was Alison coming. She heard the key fall, and was surprised. She picked it up when she came to it, and put it into the cupboard lock. The door swung open – and to Alison's surprise she saw the stores there! She was still staring in amazement when Claudine came along, gave an exclamation and slammed the door shut.

She glared at Alison. 'Did you get the key from my study? Well, really, Alison, I did not think it of you! What business is it of yours?'

Alison was puzzled. 'From your study?' she said. 'Of course not! Someone must have been at the cupboard and opened it when I came along, because I heard footsteps scurrying away, and then heard the key fall out of the lock. I put it back, the door swung open – and I saw the things. I don't want to know anything at all about the food, Claudine, and I certainly shan't tell anyone – but it's obvious that somebody knows about the cupboard, isn't it?'

Claudine believed Alison at once. Alison might be weak and silly in many ways, but she was honest and truthful. Claudine swung the door open and looked into the cupboard very thoughtfully. So someone knew of the stores – someone knew where the key was kept – someone knew the secret!

It wasn't long before Claudine discovered that the someone had also taken various things from the stores. She shut the door and locked it, angry and puzzled.

'Someone's been at the things,' she said to Alison, 'but as far as I know only I and my little sister Antoinette knew the hiding-place. The second form are to have a midnight feast, and I have kept their food under lock and key for them. Who could have found out the hiding-place – and who could be dishonest enough to steal the things?'

'I can't imagine,' said Alison, amazed. 'It is such a mean, low-down thing to do. Whoever did it is absolutely despicable. It's unbelievable! Anyway, Claudine, if I were you I'd keep the key somewhere about your person. Then the thief, whoever it is, won't be able to get it!'

16

Alma – Alison – and Anne-Marie

Alma heard all this conversation quite clearly. She felt a wave of anger against Alison. Interfering little busybody! Now she, Alma, would not be able to feast herself on the hidden goodies any more. She sat perfectly still, hoping that neither of the girls would come into her study and see her there. She felt guilty, and was sure her guilt would show in her face.

But they did not come. It did not occur to either of them that the thief would be anywhere near. They felt sure she had run away. Maybe it was a second former – but how disgusting, whoever it was!

The next time Alma had a chance of tip-toeing into the study next to hers, the key was missing. She had feared it would be. She supposed that Claudine had it round her neck in safety. Now Alma would not be able to enjoy those delicious, deceitful little feasts any more!

The girl made a curiously big thing out of the whole happening, and for a few days thought of nothing else. She hated Alison for being the unwitting cause of depriving her of the food she craved for.

I'll pay her out, she thought. Spoiling things for me like this! I'll get even with her.

Alma was strangely clever in underhand ways. Stupid people can often be cunning, and Alma was no exception. She set her wits to work, and Alison began to go through an unpleasant and most annoying time.

Things kept disappearing out of her study. Never Angela's things, but always Alison's.

'*Where's* my hair-slide?' wailed Alison. 'It's gone, and I only *saw* it on the window-sill this morning. Have you borrowed it, Angela?'

'Of course not,' said Angela. 'You've dropped it somewhere.'

Then it was Alison's hair brush that disappeared from her dressing-table in the dormitory. She hunted all over for it, and then had to report the loss to Matron, who was not very pleased.

'How can you possibly mislay a *hair* brush?' she said to Alison. 'I suppose you've been using it in a bedroom battle or something, and it's flown out of the window!'

'We fifth formers don't have bedroom battles,' said Alison, with much dignity.

Then her geometry outfit went. It completely and utterly vanished, and no amount of hunting brought it to light. Bobby had two and lent her one.

'But for goodness' sake don't lose it,' she said. 'You seem to be losing everything this term!'

The same day Alison's knitting-needles disappeared out of the scarf she was knitting, and the stitches all pulled out loose when she took the work out of her bag.

'Now this is very strange,' said Alison, and she held it up

to show Angela. 'Look – the needles are gone – and all the stiches are dropped. Angela – what do you think of that?'

'Well,' said Angela, 'I think someone's doing beastly things to you, Alison. I do really. And I bet I know who it is, too!'

'Who?' said Alison, feeling shocked and hurt.

'Someone who is awfully jealous of you,' said Angela.

'You don't mean – Anne-Marie?' said Alison, still more shocked. 'Oh, *Angela* – surely she wouldn't do mean things like this! Do you think that she's been taking all those things of mine that disappeared too? Oh, *no* – she couldn't be as low down as that.'

'People say that when anyone is jealous they don't mind what they do,' said Angela. 'And you know Anne-Marie is awfully jealous because you are so well in with your dear Deirdre, and at the moment she isn't in Deirdre's good books. Why she can't see that her dear idol is bored stiff with her poems I really don't know!'

'She's a beast if she is really taking my things, and spoiling my knitting,' said Alison, almost in tears. The girl always loved to be liked by everyone, and it hurt her very much to think that one of her own form could be so unkind. 'I shan't listen to a single one of her silly poems now.'

So, much to Anne-Marie's surprise, neither Angela nor Alison evinced the slightest interest in a long new poem, called 'The Weary Heart', which she went along to their study to read out loud that evening.

'We're busy,' said Alison, shortly.

'And you ought to be, too,' said Angela, virtuously. 'The exam is coming jolly near.'

'It won't take long to read my poem to you,' said Anne-Marie, crestfallen. 'This is how it begins . . .'

'Do get out,' said Angela. 'I'm doing maths and they don't go with poetry, even if the poem *is* called "The Weary Heart", which is very descriptive of mine at the moment.'

'Why don't you write a poem called "The Missing Knitting-Needles"?' said Alison, unexpectedly. Anne-Marie stared at her, puzzled.

'Why knitting-needles?' she inquired at last.

'Well, you ought to know, oughtn't you?' said Alison. But Anne-Marie didn't. Thinking that Alison and Angela were rude and unkind, and a little mad, she went away, carrying her precious poem with her. She bumped into Miss Willcox on her way, and gave a gasp.

'Oh – Miss Willcox – please would you read this? I spent hours over it last night.'

Miss Willcox took the poem and glanced at it. It was the same kind as usual, pretentious, full of long words, solemn, sad and far too long. Miss Willcox felt impatient. She determined to be candid with Anne-Marie, now that she had her alone.

'Look here, Anne-Marie,' she said, in her deep voice. 'I want to give you a little advice – and I want you to listen to it carefully, and follow it.'

'Oh, *yes*, Miss Willcox,' said Anne-Marie, fervently. 'I will, indeed I will.'

'Well,' said Miss Willcox, 'you can't write poetry, and

you may as well know it. You can rhyme and get the metre right – but your ideas are rubbish. *Real* poetry has ideas in it, beautiful pictures, great feelings. Tear up all your poems, Anne-Marie, and set your mind on the coming exam. That is my advice to you. You think you're a genius. Well, you're not! You are just an ordinary little school girl who has got a swelled head, and thinks she can write. It is my opinion that unless your character changes considerably, you never *will* write a really good poem!'

Miss Willcox swept off, glad to have relieved her mind of the irritation that Anne-Marie and her never-ending poems always aroused in her. Anne-Marie, struck absolutely dumb, gazed after her, too hurt even for tears.

Her knees felt rather weak. She went to her study and sat down. Felicity was there, conning over some music theory, humming softly to herself. She did not even see Anne-Marie come in.

It took a little time for all that Miss Willcox had said to sink in. Poor Anne-Marie had had the greatest shock of her life. All her great ideas about herself began to totter and waver. *Wasn't* she a genius? *Couldn't* she write marvellously? She began to feel as if she wasn't Anne-Marie any more – she was nobody, nobody at all. She gave a sudden loud sob that entered even Felicity's ears.

'What's up?' said Felicity, looking round.

'Oh, *you* wouldn't understand!' said Anne-Marie, bitterly. 'You're a genius, you don't seem to live in this world, you don't notice anything that goes on at all. You don't even know I'm here half the time. Well, what does it matter? I'm nobody, not even Anne-Marie. I've had everything stripped away from me, everything I cared about.'

'Don't exaggerate so,' said Felicity, mildly surprised at this curious outburst. 'Can't you find the right rhyme for one of your poems? Is that what has upset you?'

'Oh, you're im*possible*!' said Anne-Marie, and threw a book at Felicity, which surprised her even more. Anne-Marie went out of the room. Felicity was at once absorbed in her work again, little creases between her eyes, her headache bothering her as usual.

Anne-Marie was hurt, shocked and resentful. She wondered if Miss Willcox could possibly be right. After all, she knew about poetry, so she ought to know if Anne-Marie's was good or bad. Anne-Marie thought a great deal about Miss Willcox that evening, and what she had said.

Her resentment made her begin to see the English mistress rather more clearly than usual. She remembered how the girls laughed at her posing and pretence, her vague ways and soulful looks. Almost in a flash her adoration turned to detestation. Poor Anne-Marie – all the things she cared for had indeed been reft from her suddenly. Her pride in herself and in her genius was gone, her hopes for the future, her confidence that Miss Willcox liked and admired her, even her poems now seemed worthless.

She half thought she would do as Miss Willcox had so coldly advised her, and tear them up. But a doubt still persisted in her mind about the teacher's ability to know, really *know*, whether her, Anne-Marie's, poems were good. Suppose she tore them up, and wrote no more – and suppose after all Miss Willcox was wrong, and her poems *were* good – what a loss to the world they might be!

If only I could find out whether or not Miss Willcox is as good a judge as she always sets out to be! thought Anne-Marie, quite obsessed by the subject. But how could I? I don't see *how* I could.

Then a way came to her, and she thought so deeply about it that she didn't even hear Alison speaking to her as she passed. I'll do it! thought Anne-Marie, exultantly. I'll do it! I'll find some little-known poem of one of the very great poets – Matthew Arnold perhaps, or Browning – and I'll write it out in my own hand-writing – and next time we have to write a poem for Miss Willcox, I'll send in not a poem of my own, but a classic!'

She got up to go to the school library to look through the books of poets there.

If Miss Willcox praises the poem, I shall know she genuinely appreciates good poetry – if she sneers at it, thinking it is mine, I shall know she doesn't! Ah, Miss Willcox, we shall see!

Anne-Marie was soon busy turning over the pages of Matthew Arnold, Tennyson and Browning. She felt as if her whole happiness, her whole future depended on this. She must be careful not to choose a poem at all well known, or certainly Miss Willcox would recognize it. She must choose one as like her own style as possible – something yearning and soulful and rather high-brow. Ah, Anne-Marie meant to test Miss Willcox, no matter whether she cheatcd or not in doing so!

Now that her liking for Miss Willcox had so suddenly vanished, Anne-Marie's jealously of Alison disappeared too. Silly little Alison, she thought, pityingly, as she shut one book of poems and opened another.

But Alison, not knowing anything about Miss Willcox's unkindness to Anne-Marie, and its result, still thought that the other girl was jealous of her, and put down the annoying disappearances of her things to spite on Anne-Marie's part.

Alma knew this and rejoiced. It made things much easier for her if Alison so clearly suspected someone else! She took a few more things, enjoying poor Alison's exasperation and annoyance. To Alma the loss of the hidden food in the cupboard was as great a blow as Miss Willcox's words had been to Anne-Marie!

17

Mirabel is very high-handed

The second formers decided to have their feast in their own dormitory, which was conveniently far from any mistresses' quarters. They asked the first form to join them and there was great rejoicing among the younger ones at this.

'Jolly decent of them,' said Sally. 'I vote we get in a spot of food ourselves. Don't you think so, Jane?'

Jane was not as thrilled as the others. She had been very quiet and subdued lately, hurt at Mirabel's neglect of her, and at her unjust suspicion regarding the ringing of the fire-bell, which mystery still had not been cleared up. She worked hard for Angela, finding comfort in the older girl's liking and praise, and still did a good deal of her work at night under the sheets.

'Cheer up, Jane!' Sally kept saying. 'You look like a hen caught in the rain. *Do* cheer up!'

Jane tried to smile. She had been very afraid of suddenly bursting into tears lately, a most unusual thing for her to do. 'It will be fun having a midnight feast,' she said, trying to think it *would* be fun. But somehow nothing seemed fun lately. It was so awful to be left out of matches, when she knew she was better than the others. What was the use of practising hard every spare minute she had, when Mirabel kept treating her like this? It wasn't fair, thought Jane, resentfully. It really wasn't.

Claudine had told Antoinette of the pilfering of the cupboard, and the second formers were annoyed and puzzled, for Antoinette had told no one of the hiding-place. Still there was plenty of food left, so never mind!

Antoinette went to Claudine. 'Claudine, we are to have our feast tomorrow night. Can I have the key of the cupboard please? I and one of the others will come up here very quietly just before midnight, and get the things.'

'Here is the key,' said Claudine, taking it off a thin string she wore round her neck. 'Now don't make a noise tomorrow night, whatever you do. Have a good time! I wish I was coming too!'

Antoinette grinned. She was enjoying this first term at St Clare's. Like Claudine, she had slipped out of things she did not like, had played many undetected pranks, and had enjoyed the fun and the jolly companionship. She took the key and went off. She hadn't gone far before she retraced her footsteps.

How many bottles of ginger beer were there? Would there be enough, now that the first form was coming? She slipped the key in the lock and turned it.

Alma, in her study, heard the click of the lock. How well she knew it! She peeped out of the door. Why, it was Antoinette at the cupboard, not Claudine. She went out of the door. Antoinette jumped violently and shut the door.

'What have you got in that cupboard?' said Alma, in a smooth voice. 'Let me see.'

Before Antoinette could object she grabbed the key from her and opened the cupboard. Then she pretended to be very surprised at the contents. 'Good gracious! What is all this? Does it belong to you, Antoinette?'

Antoinette hesitated. She disliked Alma and did not trust her. But what could she do? If she was rude, Alma might be most unpleasant.

'I see it is a secret,' said Alma, longing to take one of the tins of pineapple. 'Give me one of those tins, Antoinette, and I will not tell anyone of this at all. I suppose you are going to have a midnight feast?'

'Yes, tomorrow,' said Antoinette, disliking Alma even more. 'I'm sorry I can't give you a tin, Alma. I should have to ask the others first. It is not a nice thing for you to ask, anyway – I do not like a bargain of this sort!'

Antoinette shut the door firmly and locked it again, before Alma had made up her mind what to do. She took the key from the lock and stuffed it into her pocket, eyeing Alma defiantly. 'I will ask the others if you *may* have a tin of pineapple, if you wish me to, Alma,' she said. 'But – surely you do not wish me to?'

Alma scowled. Of course she could not have Antoinette telling the second form that she wanted a tin of pineapple. She tried to laugh it off.

'Don't be silly! I didn't really mean it. I don't like pineapple. Well – I hope you enjoy your feast!'

'You won't tell tales of us, will you?' said Antoinette, distrusting Alma more and more. 'You promise that, won't you? The second form would think you were terrible to tell such a tale, Alma. You have the English sense of honour, have you not, this honour that always you English girls are talking of?'

'Of course,' said Alma, walking off with what dignity she could muster. She went into her study. She thought of the food in that cupboard. She thought of Antoinette's half-veiled insolence. Probably she *would* tell the second formers about the tin of pineapple she had asked for – and they would nudge each other when she passed, and giggle.

Alma wished she *could* tell tales, and get the feast stopped! But who would listen to her? She would not dare to carry tales to Miss Theobald or Miss Cornwallis, nor was she certain that Hilary, the head girl of the form, would even listen to her!

Then a thought struck her. What about Mirabel? Mirabel was so keen on sports – and there was a match the day after next! She would not be at all pleased if she knew that the first and second form were going to have a midnight feast just before the match. Mirabel should be told about it, and maybe, in her blunt, overbearing way, she would stop it. That would punish Antoinette all right!

Alma did not dare to go to Mirabel direct. She printed a note, so that her handwriting would not be recognized, and did not sign her name at the end.

'DO NOT EXPECT THE THIRD TEAM TO WIN ITS MATCH ON FRIDAY,' said the note. 'THEY WILL ALL BE UP AT MIDNIGHT!'

Mirabel found the note on her table in the study that evening. She picked it up in curiosity and read it.

'Gladys,' she said, tossing the note over to her, 'what in the world does this mean?'

Gladys read it distastefully. 'It's a wretched anonymous letter,' she said, 'sent by someone who wants to tell tales and doesn't dare to do it openly. Beastly. Tear it up and put it in the waste-paper basket. Don't take any notice of it. That's the way to treat letters of that sort.'

'Yes, but Gladys – the third lacrosse team *won't* win their match if they are up at midnight,' argued Mirabel. 'And I do want them to. I've set my heart on it. I suppose they're going to have a midnight feast or something, silly kids. They'll be tired out next day.'

'Well, didn't *you* enjoy midnight feasts when you were in the lower forms?' said Gladys. 'Have you forgotten what fun they were?'

'We didn't have them just before an important match,' said Mirabel. 'We didn't, Gladys.'

'For goodness' sake don't think of stopping the feast, or whatever it is,' said Gladys, alarmed. 'You can't interfere like that, Mirabel, and be such a spoilsport.'

Mirabel thought for a few moments. 'I know what to do. I'll send a note to Katie, who's head of the second form, and inform her that I have heard there is to be something going on at midnight tomorrow, and I would like her to see that it is put off till after the match. They will respect my wishes I am sure – then they can play the match properly without being tired, and have their feast afterwards.'

'Well, I shouldn't even do that,' said Gladys. 'I don't think the feast will really make much difference to the match – and anyway, only about a quarter of the girls are playing in it – hardly that!'

'You never back me up in anything now,' said Mirabel, frowning. She said no more, but busied herself in writing a short note to the head girl of the second form.

Katie got it that day and read it in surprise. She showed it to Antoinette. 'However did Mirabel get wind of our plans?' she said. 'Have you told anyone, Antoinette?'

'Well – only Alma,' said the French girl, and she told Katie what had happened at the store cupboard.

'How awful!' said Katie, shocked at the tale and at Alma's behaviour. 'I say – I wonder if she was the one who pilfered our stores!'

'Perhaps,' said Antoinette. 'She is not a nice girl, that one.'

Katie called a meeting of the second formers in the common-room and read them Mirabel's note. It was, as might be expected, rather arrogant and peremptory. Evidently Mirabel expected to be obeyed, and that was that.

'I vote we have the feast tomorrow night as planned,' said Yolande. 'Mirabel has been throwing her weight about too much lately. I call that a most uncivil note. Anyway, what business is it of hers? She's always interfering now.'

Everyone followed Yolande's lead. It was curious how unpopular Mirabel had become. She had tried to drive everyone too fast, and now they were digging their toes in and refusing to budge!

'I'd better not answer this note of Mirabel's today, had I?' said Katie. 'I'll answer it *after* we've had the feast, then she can't stop it!'

Mirabel was surprised to have no answer from Katie, giving an undertaking to postpone the feast till after the match, but it did not occur to her at all that the first and second formers would dare to defy her. She felt puzzled and thought that Katie was not very mannerly – surely she knew that an answer should always be sent at once to any request from one of the top form girls?

The first and second form were getting excited. It was the first time they had had a feast at night, and to them it seemed a terribly exciting thing. Every single girl was going. Violet was back from the sick-bay now after a bout of flu, and was looking forward to it too.

Jane tried to look forward to it, but she was feeling very unhappy. Then a dreadful quarrel blew up between her and Violet, and Jane felt as if she couldn't bear things any more!

Violet had come back from the sick-bay expecting to do Angela's jobs as usual. She had been disappointed because Angela had not even sent a kindly message to her when she was ill. Never mind – Angela would be very glad to see her back, doing her cleaning and mending as before, thought Violet.

But Angela didn't want Violet mooning round again. She had got used to the quiet and efficient little Jane, who, so long as she got a smile and a word of praise now and again, seemed to be quite content. Violet was too talkative, and always liked to recount all her thoughts and doings, which was very boring to the self-centred Angela.

So, to Violet's enormous dismay, Angela did not greet

her warmly, and merely informed her that perhaps she would like to go and see to Pauline's jobs, as Jane was doing everything necessary. Violet did not dare to argue with Angela, but rushed off to Jane at once.

'You underhand thing!' she said, her eyes sparkling with anger. 'You go behind my back when I'm ill – and worm yourself into Angela's good graces again – and do all the things she was letting me do. Jane Teal, I shall never speak to you again, and neither will half the first form!'

Jane tried to defend herself, but Violet had a ready tongue, and could say some bitter, cutting things. Jane was tired out and unhappy, and she burst into tears.

'Just like you!' said Violet, scornfully. 'You think you'll get sympathy just because you cry. Well – you just burst into tears with Angela, and see what *she* says! She can't stand anything of *that* sort!'

Jane could not help feeling that perhaps she *had* done a mean trick to Violet. She hardly slept at all that night, and in the morning she awoke with a sore throat and a headache, which made her feel more miserable than ever. It's a good thing I'm not playing in the match tomorrow! she thought and wondered if Mirabel would ever put her name down for a match again.

Jane felt rather odd that day. She had a high temperature and didn't know it. She did badly on the lacrosse field and Mirabel ticked her off. She could not concentrate in class and Miss Roberts was not pleased. Violet avoided her and some of the other first formers, who were friends of Violet's, did not speak to her either.

'I wish I was at home,' thought Jane, longingly. 'If I could just tell Mother all about it I'd feel better. I can't write it in a letter. I wish I could go home.'

The idea grew and grew in her worried mind and at last Jane made a plan she would never have made if she had been quite well. Instead of going to the feast she would go home! Luckily for her, her home was actually in the next village, four miles away. Jane felt sure she could easily walk there in the middle of the night! Then she would see her mother, tell her everything, and things would be all right again.

She did not know she was beginning to have flu and had a temperature, she had no idea she was not normal just then. Sally could not get a word out of her and was worried. Poor Jane – she was not having an easy time just then. But never mind, she thought, I'll be home tonight!

18

A surprising night

That Friday night was to be a most astonishing one for Mam'zelle, though she did not know it. She never forgot it, and, whenever she took a holiday in her beloved France, she would often recount the happenings of that night, to show her enraptured listeners how odd were the English girls!

It was the night of the Feast, and the first and second formers were to have it at twelve o'clock sharp in one of their dormitories. Antoinette had already secreted some of the things on the top of a high cupboard in her dormitory, and meant to fetch the rest just before midnight.

Mirabel, unfortunately, had seen Antoinette hurrying along the corridor outside her study, carrying various suspicious parcels. She had called after Antoinette, but Antoinette had thought it advisable not to hear, and had scurried fast round the corner, almost knocking over Miss Willcox.

Mirabel stared after the disappearing Antoinette in exasperation. Really, these kids were getting too uncivil for words. She went back into her own study and frowned. *Could* those kids be going to have their feast that night after all – when she had asked them not to? Could they flout her request in that way – surely not!

All the same a doubt persisted in Mirabel's mind, and she could not get rid of it. She said nothing to Gladys, but she made up her mind to keep awake that night, and to go along to the first- or second-form dormitories about midnight, to see if anything was happening.

And if there is – won't I give them a talking to! thought Mirabel, grimly. I'll report them too. I'll make them see they can't disregard *my* orders!

Now Anne-Marie had planned to stage a sleep-walking act that night. She had thought of quite a lot of things to do which were extraordinary, and might make people say 'Ah, she does those because she's a genius,' as so often was said of the absent-minded Felicity. But she rather doubted her ability to carry them off in front of the sharp-eyed, quick-minded members of the fifth form.

It would never do to put on some sort of genius act, and have the others roar with laughter, disbelieve in it, and tell her it was all put on. It was getting to be quite imperative to Anne-Marie to be thought really clever. She had to do something to cancel out the damping effect of Miss Willcox's words.

Who would be taken in most easily? She thought for a while, and then decided on Mam'zelle. She had heard of the many tricks the girls had played on the French mistress through the years, and she felt sure she would take in Mam'zelle. Mam'zelle would exclaim, and waggle her hands, and tell everyone. She would say, 'Ah, *la petite* Anne-Marie, she walks in her sleep, she recites poetry as she walks, she is a genius! We must be careful of her, we must cherish this talented girl! One day she will be famous!'

Yes, certainly Mam'zelle would be the best one to impress. The middle of the night would be the best time. She would find some means of waking Mam'zelle, and bring her out in the passage, and then she would let her see her, apparently walking in her sleep, reciting lines and lines of poetry. Mam'zelle would be most impressed, and perhaps even Miss Theobald would think that Anne-Marie was a genius, and ask to see some of her poems.

Anne-Marie was really very pleased with her idea. She quite looked forward to putting it into practice that night. About half-past twelve or so, she thought. That would be the best time. Everyone will be asleep by then.

She had, of course, chosen a most unfortunate night for her sleep-walking, for quite a number of people were going to be wide awake! All the first and second formers would be revelling in their feast. Jane Teal would be stealing through the school, meaning to run off home. Mirabel would be on the prowl to find out if the younger girls were really having their feast. Alma would be snooping about to see if there was likely to be any food left in the cupboard. Antoinette and one or two others would be fetching the rest of the food.

And Felicity was to choose that night for sleep-walking too – but genuine sleep-walking, in her case. So there would be quite a number of people wandering about, though Anne-Marie hadn't the remotest idea of this.

All the girls went off to bed as usual at their ordinary times. The first and second formers went first, giggling with excitement, vowing that they wouldn't sleep a wink till midnight. Antoinette and Sally were to be responsible for rousing anyone who *did* go to sleep. It was thrilling to look forward to such an escapade.

The third and fourth formers went off to bed later.

The fifth and sixth could stay up till ten o'clock, and usually did. They all retired as usual, even Felicity, who often did not go till much later, lost as usual in her music. It was astonishing that no mistress had discovered her light burning so late in her study, but so far no one had.

Then the mistresses went to bed, yawning, having a last word together before they parted. Mam'zelle was the last to go. She had a pile of French essays from the sixth form to go through, and had left them rather late.

I will correct these, and then go, she thought, glancing at the clock. Half-past eleven already! How slow I have been tonight!

At just about five minutes to twelve Mam'zelle went into her bedroom. At twelve o'clock she was getting into bed, and the bed was about to creak under her rather heavy weight, when some sound caught her ears.

It sounded as if something hard had been dropped on the floor immediately above her head. Mam'zelle sat on the side of the bed and pondered over the various possible causes of the noise.

It was not the cat. It was not the unexpected groan or creak that furniture sometimes gave at night. It was not any mistress on the prowl, because all had gone to bed. Then what could it be? Mam'zelle thought hard. She knew that the fifth-form studies were above her bedroom, stretching in a long couple of rows down and around two corridors. Surely no one could possibly be up still? The fifth form must all be in bed!

Another small sound decided Mam'zelle. She had better go and investigate. It might be a burglar. Mam'zelle had a horror of burglars, but she felt it her duty to find out whether there was one in the school or not. Feeling extremely brave, and arming herself with a hair brush, she put on her dressing-gown and slippers, tied the belt tightly round her plump waist, and opened her bedroom door.

All the passages and corridors of St Clare's were lighted throughout the night, but with specially dimmed lights. It was possible to see a figure, but not to make out who it was. The corridors looked rather eerie to Mam'zelle as she set out on her journey of investigation.

The first thing that Mam'zelle did was to fall over the school's big black cat, much given to wandering around at night. Seeing Mam'zelle perfectly clearly, though she could not see him at all, he advanced upon her, and tried to rub against her ankles, delighted to see a fellow-wanderer in the night.

Mam'zelle gave a muffled shriek, and almost over-balanced. One of her big feet caught the cat on its side, and it gave one of its yowls. Mam'zelle recognized the cat's voice, and was relieved to find that it was not a burglar lying on the floor to catch her foot, but only the cat.

'Sssst!' she said, in a piercing, sibilant whisper, and the cat fled, grieved at Mam'zelle's lack of friendliness.

Mam'zelle went up the stairs to the next floor, where she had heard the noise. Antoinette was up there, on her third journey to collect the eatables with Sally. To her horror she suddenly heard Mam'zelle's piercing 'Ssssst!' noise from the floor below. She clutched Sally.

'Somebody's about! Did you hear that? Oh, how tiresome, Sally! What shall we do?'

'There's an alcove near here,' whispered Sally. 'Look – where that curtain is. We'll get behind there with our tins and bottles. Quick! Maybe whoever it is will pass by. Don't sneeze or anything!'

The two girls pressed themselves behind the curtain, their hearts beating fast. They heard Mam'zelle's footsteps coming along, making a soft swishing noise in her big bedroom slippers. They stood quite still.

Mam'zelle came to the alcove. She thought the curtain bulged suspiciously, and she put out a trembling hand. She distinctly felt some soft body behind it! She gave a gasp. Antoinette and Sally decided to make a bolt for it, and suddenly shot out from the alcove, dropping a ginger beer bottle on poor Mam'zelle's toes. She gave an anguished groan, lifted her foot, and did a few heavy hops over to the opposite wall, putting out a hand to steady herself when she got there.

She caught sight of two figures racing down the dim passage, and round the corner. She had no idea whether they were burglars or girls. As she felt her corns tenderly, wrath swept over her. How dared people drop things on her feet in the middle of the night, and then run away without apologizing? Mam'zelle determined to chase the scamps, whoever they were, and run them to earth.

She did not see the ginger beer bottle lying at her feet, and she fell over it as she went swiftly down the passage, stubbing her other foot this time. The bottle went rolling off and hit the wall. Mam'zelle stopped again and groaned.

She ran down the passage and came to the corner. There was no one to be seen there. The passage went completely round the third floor of the building, and came back again where it began, and Mam'zelle thought it would be a good idea to go the whole way and see if anyone was about on that floor. So off she set, determined to run to earth whoever was up so late at night.

Pad-pad-pad, went her feet, and every now and again Mam'zelle set her pince-nez firmly on her nose, for they had an irritating way of jumping off when she ran. Pad-pad-pad – the chase was on!

19

Mam'zelle on the war-path

Alma was the next one to be dimly seen by Mam'zelle. She had been certain that Antoinette would go to the store cupboard that night, and would probably make two or three visits. Probably in between she would leave the door open. Then, thought greedy Alma, she might be able to pop in and take something for herself. A tin of pineapple for instance. She seemed to crave a tin of pineapple!

So, making sure that the rest of her dormitory were asleep, Alma rose quietly from her bed, and went up the stairs to the third floor. She made her way to the cupboard just at the same moment as Mam'zelle, panting, came round the last of the four corners of the corridor, back again to where the alcove was. The store cupboard was quite near.

Mam'zelle saw a figure in the passage. Ah – there was *one* of the midnight wanderers, at least! Mam'zelle would teach them to drop things on her poor toes! She crept up behind the unsuspecting Alma, who was half in the cupboard, groping about for a tin of some kind.

Alma had the shock of her life when she felt a hand on her shoulder. She lunged out in fright and struck poor Mam'zelle square in the middle. Mam'zelle doubled up at once, and gave such a deep groan that Alma was horrified. She could not move an inch, but stood there, trembling.

Mam'zelle recovered rapidly. She felt certain that this must be a burglar rifling cupboards. He was dangerous! He had given her a terrible blow, the big coward! Mam'zelle was not going to come to grips with him. Giving Alma a sudden push, which landed her among the tins, bottles and old rugs, she shut the door firmly, locked it, and took the key.

'Ha!' said Mam'zelle, addressing the alarmed Alma in the cupboard. 'Now I have you under key and lock! I go for the police!'

With this terrifying threat she padded off to telephone to the police. She went downstairs, congratulating herself heartily on her smartness and bravery, and feeling her middle tenderly to see if she was bruised.

As soon as she got downstairs she saw Jane Teal, who had chosen that moment to creep away from the others, put on her hat and coat and go to find a side-door she could open quietly. But poor little Jane was now feeling very ill. The flu was sending her temperature high, and she felt as if she was in a dream. All she wanted was to get to her mother, and to do that she knew she must get out of St Clare's and walk and walk.

So, hardly knowing what she was doing, she felt with a feverish hand along the wall to find the side-door. She muttered to herself as she went. 'I must find the door. That's the first thing. I must find the door.'

Mam'zelle heard the muttering and stopped in

amazement and alarm. Could this be yet another burglar? Who was this person groping along the wall – with a hat on too! Mam'zelle could not see in the dim light what kind of a person it was, but having got the idea of burglars firmly in her mind, she felt certain this must be another – probably the second of the two she had first seen racing down the upstairs passage. She began to tiptoe cautiously after Jane.

Jane felt along the wall till she came to a door. 'Here is a door,' she muttered. 'I must open it and go out. I've found a door.'

But it was not the side-door, leading into the garden. It was the door of the second-form games cupboard, full of lacrosse sticks, old goal-nets, a few discarded raincoats and such things as this. Jane opened the door and went into the cupboard. Mam'zelle, triumphant, saw a chance of repeating her recent brilliance, and of locking this second burglar into a cupboard too.

She darted forward, shut the door and locked it, leaving poor Jane in the darkness among things that felt most extraordinary to her hot little fingers.

'I want to go home,' said Jane and suddenly sank down on to a pile of sticks and nets, for her legs felt as if they would no longer carry her. She lay there, feverish and half dreaming, not knowing or caring in the least where she was.

Mam'zelle could not help feeling very proud of herself. What other mistress at St Clare's could catch and imprison two burglars in one night like this? Mam'zelle began to think she was wasted as a French mistress. She should have been in the police force.

'Now I go to the telephone,' she said to herself, thinking with delight of the astonishment of the police when they heard her news. But she was not yet to broadcast her news, for, even as she went into the hall, she saw somebody else!

This time it was Felicity, walking in her sleep, trying to find the assembly room, so that she might once again mount the platform, and play her imaginary violin. She walked solemnly, her eyes wide open, humming a melody in a low, soft voice. She had on her white night-gown, and Mam'zelle was absolutely petrified to see this figure walking towards her, making a strange low humming.

'*Tiens*!' said Mam'zelle, and took a step backwards. For the first time she began to wonder whether the night's happenings were real or whether she might be dreaming. It seemed astonishing that so many people were about in the middle of the night.

This could not be a burglar. It looked like something unearthly – a spirit wandering about, lost and lone! Mam'zelle shivered. Burglars she had been able to deal with – but spirits were different. They faded away, they disappeared into thin air if they were touched, and Mam'zelle did not like things of that sort.

She decided not to go to the telephone just then, as she would have to meet this wandering spirit face to face. She would retire to her bedroom for a little while till the spirit had returned to wherever it had come from. So Mam'zelle turned tail and fled.

But for some reason Felicity, fast asleep as she was, seemed to perceive Mam'zelle as she disappeared towards the stairs. Into her dreaming mind came the idea that this person might take her to the platform, so that she might play her wonderful compositions, and she followed Mam'zelle up the stairs, her eyes glassy and wide open, her hands outstretched.

Mam'zelle glanced behind and was most alarmed to find the white spirit following her. She had not bargained for this at all. She almost ran to get to her bedroom on the second floor.

Felicity followed, seeming almost to float up the stairs, for she was tall and thin, and much too light for her age. Mam'zelle bolted into her bedroom and sat down on her bed, out of breath.

The door opened and Felicity came in, her eyes still wide open. As Mam'zelle had her light on, she saw at once that what she had thought was a frightening apparition was only Felicity.

'*Tiens*!' said Mam'zelle, putting her hand up to her forehead. '*Tiens*! What kind of a night is this, when burglars and children walk around? Felicity, my child, are you awake?'

There was something rather terrifying about Felicity's white, unawakened face. Mam'zelle saw that she was sound asleep, and was afraid to wake her. She was more than relieved when Felicity, feeling the bed, drew back the covers, got into it and shut her eyes. In a minute or two she was apparently sleeping quite peacefully.

Mam'zelle stared down at the pale face on her pillow. To have two burglars shut into two separate cupboards and a sleep-walking girl in her bed was rather bewildering. She could not make up her mind whether to telephone to the police or to go and call Miss Theobald and show her Felicity. Mam'zelle had had enough experience of girls to know that sleep-walking was not a good thing – something had happened to make Felicity act in this way, and that something must be investigated.

There was a noise upstairs again. Antoinette and Sally had returned to the cupboard for eatables, and had found the door locked, the key gone, and a prisoner in the cupboard! In amazement and fear they fled back to their dormitory to tell the others. Mam'zelle, disturbed by the noise they made, went out of her bedroom, and, as an afterthought, turned the key in the lock, in case Felicity should try a little more sleep-walking.

She was just in time to see Antoinette and Sally, two vague figures in the distance, running back to their dormitory.

'*Tiens*!' said Mam'zelle again, thunderstruck to find yet more people abroad that night. 'Do I sleep or wake? Everywhere I go I see people fleeing in the night!'

The next person Mam'zelle saw was Mirabel, who was creeping down the stairs to see if the second formers were holding their feast after all. Mam'zelle could not believe her eyes. Was the whole school wandering about that night – or was this yet another burglar?

Mirabel was a tall, strapping girl, and she wore

pyjamas. In the dim passage she looked as big as a man, and Mam'zelle felt certain this must be another of the gang of burglars that appeared to be infesting St Clare's that night. She followed her, trying to make no noise at all. It was becoming quite a common-place for Mam'zelle to lock people up that night, and she fondly imagined she could somehow imprison this burglar also.

Mirabel went towards the second-form dormitories. Mam'zelle, afraid that the burglar might scare the girls there, hurried her steps. The school cat reappeared at this moment, and tripped poor Mam'zelle up, so that she made a noise. Mirabel looked round, and slipped quickly into one of the bathrooms that ran opposite the dormitories. She did not want any of the second formers to know she was snooping round, in case by any chance they were *not* holding the feast after all.

Mam'zelle saw with great pleasure that once again she could lock somebody into somewhere. She began to think that burglar-catching was the easiest thing in the world – merely a matter of turning a key in a lock. She turned the key in the shut bathroom door – and there was yet another burglar accounted for!

Mam'zelle thought with delight of the surprise and admiration of the other mistresses when they heard of her exploits. She felt ready to imprison half a dozen more burglars into cupboards and bathrooms if necessary.

Mirabel was horrified at being locked in. She had no idea who had turned the key, but thought it was some silly trick of one of the younger girls. So she settled down to wait for the door to be undone. She felt sure no girl would keep her imprisoned all night long.

Mam'zelle decided that she would now go to Miss Theobald, as she felt that no policeman would be inclined to believe a telephone call from her about three locked-up burglars. So she padded along the passage to the stairs – but just as she was about to descend them, she caught sight of yet another night-wanderer.

This time it was Anne-Marie, who was now putting on her sleep-walking act in imitation of Felicity, and was on her way to wake up Mam'zelle. Mam'zelle could not believe her eyes when she saw yet another sleep-walker. No, really she must be going mad! There could not be so many people rushing about at night in the school passages!

Anne-Marie saw Mam'zelle standing under one of the dimmed lamps, and recognized her. At first she got a shock, for she had expected Mam'zelle to be in bed and not ambling about. But as soon as she was sure it really *was* Mam'zelle, she acted exactly as if she was walking in her sleep. She glided by Mam'zelle, her eyes set and staring just as Felicity's had been, muttering a poem.

Mam'zelle hesitated to grab her, for she had heard it was bad to awaken sleep-walkers suddenly. So she did not touch Anne-Marie, but followed her, whispering under her breath.

'The poor child! Here is another who walks in her sleep! I will follow her.'

Anne-Marie led Mam'zelle a fine dance, and finally ended up outside the second-form dormitories. The girl on guard there gave the alarm when she saw the two figures coming, and there was a terrific scramble as bottles and tins and plates were pushed under beds. The candles were blown out and girls got hurriedly into bed, those who didn't belong to that dormitory squeezing into wardrobes and under beds.

Anne-Marie, still acting, wandered into the second-form dormitory, meaning to walk to the end and back – but she fell over an empty bottle, and gave an exclamation. Mam'zelle followed her into the room and switched on the light.

Anne-Marie, dazed by the sudden light, blinked in confusion, watched in amazement by girls in bed. Then, remembering her sleep-walking act, she once again became glassy-eyed and glided between the beds.

The girls sat up, giggling. 'She's pretending!' called Antoinette.

'Ah, no, she walks in her sleep, the poor, poor child,' said Mam'zelle. 'What can we do for her?'

'I will cure her, *ma tante,*' said the irrepressible Antoinette, and leapt out of bed. She took a jug of cold water and threw it all over poor Anne-Marie, who, angry and wet, turned and gave Antoinette such a ticking off that all the girls knew at once that she certainly had not been sleep-walking before, but only play-acting. Mam'zelle realized it too, and tried to haul Anne-Marie out of the room, scolding her vigorously, and telling her to go and change her wet things at once. So engrossed was she that she entirely failed to see any signs of the midnight feast, nor did she notice any of the girls squashed into the wardrobes or under the beds.

'Golly!' said Sally, as soon as Mam'zelle had gone off with Anne-Marie. 'I don't believe she even *saw* the signs of our feast, not even that bottle that rolled out from under a bed!'

'Bit of luck for us,' said Violet. 'Come on, let's finish everything up quickly, and hide the things and get to bed before Mam'zelle thinks of coming back!'

The girls giggled. Mirabel, shut in the bathroom just opposite, heard them, and knew they were still enjoying their feast. She grew very angry indeed. She felt certain one of the second formers had locked her in, and she was determined to report the whole lot of them and have them well punished.

Mam'zelle took Anne-Marie to Matron's room, and woke Matron up, explaining volubly about Anne-Marie and why she was wet. Anne-Marie, her sleep-walking act quite ruined, wept copiously, fearing that she would be the laughing stock of the school next day.

'Now stop that silly crying,' said Matron briskly, giving Anne-Marie a vigorous rub-down with a very rough towel. She had long ago sized up Anne-Marie as a silly, swollen-headed girl, just the kind to act about like this.

'I must go,' said Mam'zelle, remembering the various people she had locked up that night. 'I have burglars to see to.'

Matron stared. 'What did you say?' she inquired.

'I said, I have burglars to see to,' said Mam'zelle, with

dignity. 'I have spent the night chasing people round the corridors, and locking them up. I go to Miss Theobald now, and she will telephone to the police. Ah, the people I have chased tonight. You would not believe it, Matron!'

Matron didn't. She thought Mam'zelle must be dreaming. 'Well, you go and get Miss Theobald and the police and whatever else you like,' she said, rubbing Anne-Marie so hard that she groaned. 'But don't bring me any more wet girls to dry in the middle of the night. I don't approve of them.'

Mam'zelle went off. She came to Miss Theobald's bedroom and knocked on the door. A surprised voice came from inside.

'Yes? Who is it?'

'It is I, Mam'zelle,' said Mam'zelle, and opened the door. 'Pardon me for coming at this time of the night, Miss Theobald – but I have burglars locked up in cupboards and a sleep-walker in my bedroom.'

20

A little unlocking

Miss Theobald listened to Mam'zelle's tale in the utmost astonishment. It seemed to her as if all the corridors of St Clare's must have been peopled with burglars, robbers, thieves, and others the whole of the night – but what was even more astonishing was the thought of Mam'zelle, who was terrified even of mice and beetles, valiantly chasing the burglars and, more remarkable still, locking them up wholesale!

She could hardly believe it. She looked closely at Mam'zelle, and wondered if the French mistress could possibly have dreamt it all. She got out of bed and put on her dressing-gown.

'I think, before I telephone the police, you had better show me where you locked these men up,' she said.

Mam'zelle trotted her off to the cupboard where she had locked in little Jane Teal. There was no sound from there at all. Miss Theobald was puzzled. She rapped on the door. Still no sound. Jane had fallen into a feverish doze. Miss Theobald suddenly heard the sound of overloud breathing, quick and hoarse.

She felt sure it was no burglar there. She unlocked the door, to Mam'zelle's dismay, and switched on the light inside the big cupboard – and there, before poor Mam'zelle's startled eyes, lay little Jane Teal, obviously ill, fully-dressed, even to her hat.

'This child's ill,' said the head mistress, feeling Jane's burning hot hand. 'Flu, I should think, and a very high temperature with it. What on earth is she doing dressed up like this, with hat and coat on? Was she going out?'

Mam'zelle was dumbfounded. She could not think of a word to say. Miss Theobald gently awoke Jane, and helped her to her feet. She could hardly stand. Between them the two mistresses took her to Matron's room, who, at one glance saw that Jane was seriously ill.

'I'll carry her to the sick-bay,' she said. 'I'll sleep there with her myself tonight.'

Matron's capable, strong arms lifted the half unconscious Jane easily, and bore her away to the quiet and comfortable sick-bay where all the ill girls were nursed. There was no one there at the moment. Matron soon had Jane undressed and in bed with a hot-water bottle.

'Well,' said Miss Theobald, thankful to have found poor Jane before worse befell her, 'what about your next burglar, Mam'zelle?'

Mam'zelle fervently hoped that the next prisoner *would* prove to be a burglar, even if he leapt out at them and escaped! She led the way to the bathroom opposite the second-form dormitory.

The second formers were still awake and heard the footsteps and voices in wonder. As the footsteps passed their door, they sat up and whispered, 'Who is it? What's up?'

Antoinette leapt out of bed and padded to the door. She peeped out cautiously. To her enormous astonishment she saw the head mistress standing by the bathroom door, with Mam'zelle, her aunt! Antoinette gaped as she saw Miss Theobald rap quietly on the door and say, 'Who's in here?'

A voice answered something, an angry voice. Miss Theobald heard that it was a girl's voice and not a man's, and she unlocked the door. Out shot Mirabel, expecting to see a group of grinning second formers – and stopped short in amazement when she saw Mam'zelle and the head mistress.

Mam'zelle's eyes almost dropped out of her head. She had shut her biggest burglar – or so she thought – into the bathroom – and now it was only Mirabel, that big, detestable, loud-voiced Mirabel, whose talk was all of games, games, and yet more games. Mam'zelle snorted in disgust.

'I want to complain,' said Mirabel, in a loud voice, surprised but unabashed by the sight of the head. 'I came to see if the second formers were having a midnight feast, which I had forbidden – and one of them locked me in this beastly cold bathroom. I want to report them, Miss Theobald. I know they held a feast, and there's a most important match tomorrow. And I demand that the girl who locked me in shall be punished.'

'It was Mam'zelle who locked you in,' said Miss Theobald. 'You had no right to be wandering about at night like this. Mam'zelle thought you were a burglar and locked you in.'

Antoinette stifled a giggle and rushed back into the dormitory. She related in whispers what she had heard. The girls were half amused and half angry – amused to think that Mirabel had been locked up, and angry to think she had been sneaking round, and had reported them.

Then Mam'zelle's loud voice penetrated into the listening dormitory. 'What is this untruthful thing you say, Mirabel? The second formers had *no* feast tonight! Did not I go there to chase Anne-Marie, after I had locked you in, and the good girls were all in bed and asleep! Not a thing to be seen, not a tin, not a bottle! You are a bad untruthful girl, trying to get others into trouble to protect yourself from blame!'

Mirabel was speechless. She glared at Mam'zelle, and Miss Theobald hastened to intervene.

'Well, if Mam'zelle was in the second-form dormitory, and the girls were in bed and asleep, it seems to me that you must be mistaken, Mirabel.'

'I'm not,' said Mirabel, rudely. 'Mam'zelle isn't speaking the truth. Go into the second-form dormitory and ask the girls if I or Mam'zelle is right, Miss Theobald. Then you will see.'

'I shall do nothing of the sort,' said the head mistress, coldly. 'Be more polite, Mirabel. You forget yourself.'

Mirabel, simmering with rage, dared say no more.

'Go back to bed,' said Miss Theobald. 'I will settle this tomorrow. I do not feel very pleased with you, Mirabel.'

Mirabel went back to bed with an angry heart. She knew she was right. Those second formers *had* had a feast, and Mam'zelle must be shielding them – because of Antoinette, she supposed. Well, she would get even with the little beasts. She would cancel the match next day! No one should play. She would show those youngsters she was sports captain, and make them toe the line!

'Well,' said Miss Theobald, looking at Mam'zelle, as Mirabel retreated, 'what about your next burglar, Mam'zelle?'

Mam'zelle took the head up to the corridor that ran round the fifth-form studies. She was feeling rather nervous now that her burglars were all turning into girls. It was really most extraordinary.

Miss Theobald rapped on the cupboard in which Alma was imprisoned. Alma's voice was heard.

'Let me out! It's awful in here!'

The head unlocked the door, and Alma staggered out, stiff and cold. Miss Theobald looked at her in surprise. 'Why were you wandering about at night?' she said, sharply.

'I – er – I heard a noise,' said Alma, stammering, for she was afraid of the head. 'And someone locked me in that cupboard.'

Miss Theobald switched her torch on and lit up the inside of the cupboard. She saw at a glance that it had been used as a storing-place for food.

'You went to take food from here, I suppose, Alma?' she said. 'Was it your own food?'

'I wasn't taking any,' said Alma. 'I was – well, I was just *looking*.'

'This girl is always eating,' said Mam'zelle in disgust.

'Always she chews something, always she eats.'

'Go back to bed, Alma,' said Miss Theobald. 'I will see you in the morning.'

Alma scuttled off thankfully. Miss Theobald turned rather coldly to Mam'zelle. 'Any more burglars?' she asked.

'Oh, Miss Theobald, truly I am sorry to have made so many mistakes!' said Mam'zelle, passing her hand through her hair in bewilderment. 'I pray you to forgive me, to . . .'

'Don't worry about it,' said Miss Theobald. 'It is perhaps a good thing that all this has happened: it seems that a great deal is going on this term at St Clare's that I must inquire into. Now – who is this girl you had in your bedroom – the one you found sleep-walking?'

'Felicity,' said Mam'zelle, fervently hoping that Felicity would still be there. She hurried down the stairs to her room, and unlocked the door.

Felicity was still there, lying asleep in bed. She looked very young and thin and, even in her sleep, her face wore a harassed, worried look. Miss Theobald looked at her for some time.

'This girl is obviously over-working,' she said, and sighed. 'Her music is too much for her, but her parents insisted on her taking her exams. I think, Mam'zelle, if you don't mind, we'll leave her in your bed. You had better sleep in the bed in Miss Harry's room – she is away for a few days. I suppose you have no more locked-up girls to show me tonight?'

'No,' said Mam'zelle, looking so crestfallen that the

head smiled. She patted Mam'zelle's plump arm.

'You meant well,' she said. 'If they had all been burglars, as you thought, you would have done a good night's work. Anyway, it is a good thing that so many things have come to light. Good night.'

Miss Theobald went back to bed, worrying about little Jane Teal, Alma, Mirabel and Felicity. It looked as if Jane had been trying to run away. She must find out about that.

Mam'zelle got into a strange bed, cold and puzzled. Why had so many girls been wandering about that night? Ah, that detestable Mirabel, how dare she say that she, Mam'zelle, was telling an untruth that night? And that dreadful Alma? Did she go snooping round every night to steal food from cupboards? There was something wrong with her, that girl!

Tomorrow I will talk with Claudine and Antoinette, thought Mam'zelle, screwing up her eyes, trying to go to sleep. They have good sense, they will tell me everything. It is a pity that English girls have not the good sense of French girls. It will be a pleasure to talk to my good little Claudine and Antoinette – *they* do not wander round at night for me to lock up. Alas, to think that I made so many prisoners, and now not one remains!

21
A few upsets

The next day the whole school knew the story of the night escapades, and how Mam'zelle had locked up so many girls. There was a great deal of giggling and chattering, and Anne-Marie had her leg pulled about her sleep-walking.

'How can I help sleep-walking?' she asked, trying to assume a dignity she did not feel. 'Felicity sleep-walks too, doesn't she? And you don't laugh at *her*.'

Miss Willcox heard about Anne-Marie's sleep-walking act and laughed too. She even teased her about it in class, which hurt Anne-Marie more than anything, and made her quite determined to get even with Miss Willcox if she could.

Felicity did not appear in class that day. It was reported that she had gone to the sick-bay for a rest and would not be taking the exam, which was the next week. Jane Teal was very ill indeed. Sally had been allowed to see her and had come back rather scared.

'Matron's worried about her and so is the doctor,' said Sally. 'Her mother is there in the sick-bay, too. I'm not allowed in any more. Matron shooed me out. I heard Matron say that Jane's worried about something and she can't get out of her what it is. But *I* know! It's all this business with Mirabel and Angela, and I know Jane reads in bed late at night with a torch. She learns her English and Latin that way. She told me so.'

'Well – hadn't you better go and tell Matron what you know?' said Katie. 'She might put things right for Jane then.'

'She can't, silly,' said Sally. 'You know what worries Jane more than anything – she's upset because Mirabel believes she rang that fire-bell to stop her meeting, and that's why Mirabel is so beastly to her. If only we could find out who did ring that bell, and make them own up, it would take a great load off poor Jane's mind!'

Violet Hill was feeling uncomfortable that morning, when she heard how ill Jane was. She remembered her quarrel with Jane, and the unkind things she had said. She wished she hadn't now.

'It will be a good thing to play in the match this afternoon,' said Sally. 'Take our minds off everything! We'll feel better out on the field, playing or watching.'

But Mirabel threw a bombshell that morning. She put a notice on the board, and soon everyone was round it, astonished and angry.

'The match today is cancelled, owing to the behaviour of the team members,' said the notice, and it was signed by Mirabel.

'*Well!*' said Sally. 'Would you believe it! How has she got the nerve to stick up a notice like that? And what right has she to cancel our match?'

'She's got the right because she's sports captain,' said Violet. 'Beast! I vote we send her to Coventry and don't speak a word to her, or smile at her, or turn up at any practices at all!'

Everyone agreed. It was an unheard of thing for the lower forms to treat an upper-form girl in this way, but they felt so indignant that not one member of the first or second form backed out of the agreement. Just because they had dared to have a feast in spite of Mirabel, she was treating them abominably, and putting up a notice in public to make them look small!

Gladys saw the notice and was shocked. She went straight to Mirabel.

'Mirabel! How *could* you put up that notice? Whatever were you thinking of? You *can't* cancel the match!'

'I can and I have,' said Mirabel grimly. 'I've sent a message to the school we were playing. They won't be coming. We shall have a practice match, instead. I have just written out another notice about that – the practice is to be at three o'clock, and every girl must attend from the two lowest forms.'

'Mirabel, you must be mad,' said Gladys, quite alarmed at her friend's grim face. 'You can't put all the girls against you like this, you really can't. You'll only get the worst out of them instead of the best.'

'I've told you before that I won't have you interfering with my decisions,' said Mirabel.

'Then what is the use of my being vice-captain?' said Gladys. 'Not a bit of use! I can't help you, because you won't let me!'

'Well, you're not much use, if you really want to

know,' said Mirabel, coldly, and went out of the room to pin the lacrosse practice notice on the board.

The girls held an informal meeting about the practice, and one and all determined not to turn up. It was Saturday, and, if they wished, they could go for nature-rambles. All the first and second forms decided to do this, even Antoinette, who detested walking.

So, to the astonishment of Miss Roberts and Miss Jenks, the whole of the two lowest forms went off in the sunshine together, taking with them nature notebooks and collecting tins and jars, chattering loudly as they passed by the windows of the mistresses' common-room.

'*Well!*' said Miss Roberts, looking after the laughing girls. 'What's come over them? Why this sudden, violent and wholesale interest in nature? I thought there was to be a match or lacrosse practice or something.'

Mirabel turned up on the playing-fields at five to three, grim-faced and determined. But nobody else arrived. Mirabel waited till ten past three, and then, rather white, went back to the school. One of the third formers, hardly able to hide her smiles, told her politely that the first and second formers had all gone out for a nature-walk.

Then Mirabel knew that she had lost. It had been her will against the wills of the first and second form, and they had won. They had ignored her orders. They had shown her what they thought of her and her authority. She sat down in her study, feeling dismayed.

She saw a note on the table addressed to her and opened it. It was a formal resignation from Gladys.

I wish to resign my post as vice-captain as I feel I cannot be of any use to you.
Gladys

Mirabel threw the note on to the floor. She felt unhappy and bitter. She had been so pleased to be sports captain. She had worked so hard for that position. She had had such high hopes of putting St Clare's at the very top of the lacrosse and tennis schools. Now the girls had defied her, and even her best friend had deserted her. It was a bitter hour for Mirabel.

The girls came back from their walk, rosy-cheeked and merry. They heard from the third form how Mirabel had gone out alone to the playing field, and had waited there in vain. They also heard that Gladys had resigned as vice-captain and they were pleased.

'Good old Gladys,' they said. 'We always thought it was funny she should back Mirabel up in her unpleasant ways!'

When Mirabel appeared in public at all that weekend the girls carefully turned away from her. Almost as if I was in quarantine for something beastly! thought Mirabel, bitterly. The girl was very worried and unhappy, but far too proud to appeal even to Gladys for comfort. Gladys was miserable too, and would have made things up with Mirabel at once if her friend had turned to her, or had admitted that she had been too high-handed with the younger ones. But Mirabel was cold and stand-offish, and gave Gladys no chance to be friendly.

The exam was to be held the next week, and most of the girls were feeling the strain. Only a few, like clever Pam, or the placid Hilary, did not seem to worry. Felicity was not to take the exam.

A specialist had come from London to see her. He spoke to Miss Theobald very seriously.

'This girl is on the verge of a nervous breakdown,' he said. 'Her mind seems full of music and nothing but music. See how she plays an imaginary violin, and strains to hear the tune. She must do no more work in music for a year.'

Miss Theobald nodded. How she wished Felicity's proud parents had not insisted on their gifted girl working for that difficult music exam! How much better it would have been for her to have dropped her music for a while, and to have entered into the ordinary, normal life of the other fifth formers, instead of losing herself night and day in her beloved music. Now her music might suffer because Felicity's brain had been worked too hard.

'Parents' fault, I suppose?' said the specialist, writing a few notes in his case-book. 'Why will parents of gifted children always push them so hard?'

'Just selfishness,' said Miss Theobald. 'Well – you think we must keep Felicity in bed for a time – then let her get up and wander round a bit, without any lessons – and then gradually join in with the others, without doing any music at all?'

'She can *play* at her music, but not work at it,' said the specialist. 'Let her enjoy it without worrying about it. She will probably do that anyhow when she knows she is not to work for the music exam for at least another two years.'

Felicity's parents came to see her, worried and dismayed. They remembered how Miss Theobald had pleaded with them not to push Felicity on so quickly. They were frightened when they saw her white face and enormous, dark-rimmed eyes.

'Don't worry too much,' said Miss Theobald. 'We have stopped her in time. Her sleep-walking gave us warning. Mam'zelle discovered that, and so we have been able to deal with Felicity quickly. Soon she will be a normal, happy girl again, and when she knows she need not work night and day for her music exam, a great weight will be off her mind, and she will laugh and chatter and be as cheerful as the others.'

It was a rather subdued father and mother that went home that day. 'Miss Theobald might have said, "I told you so," to us,' said Felicity's mother. 'But she didn't. Poor Felicity – I feel we are very much to blame for all this.'

The other sleep-walker, Anne-Marie, was not having a very good time. Whenever the first or second formers saw her coming, they immediately put on glassy stares, and with out-stretched hands began to glide here and there. Anne-Marie hated this teasing, and when it spread to the fifth form too, and glassy eyes appeared there also, Anne-Marie was very near tears.

'It's beastly of you,' she said to Alison and Angela, who laughed at her. 'I know I shan't pass the exam if you all jeer at me like this. It's mean of you.'

'Well, you're pretty mean yourself,' said Alison. 'You

keep on doing beastly things to *me,* don't you? Where have you put my geometry set you hid last week?'

Anne-Marie stared in surprise. She hadn't the least idea what Alison was talking about.

'Oh, don't put on that wide-eyed innocent look,' said Alison, impatiently. 'We all know you can act, but don't try to take *us* in by it! I know jolly well you're jealous of me because Miss Willcox likes me better than she likes you, and you're trying to get back at me by hiding my things and making silly bits of trouble for me!'

'I'm not,' said Anne-Marie, her voice trembling with indignation. 'I wouldn't dream of doing such a thing. I haven't *touched* your things! And as for being jealous of you, you needn't worry! I've no time for Miss Willcox now! I'm sure she's not as clever as you think. And what's more I'll show you she isn't.'

'Don't be silly,' said Alison. 'And don't talk about Miss Willcox like that. You're just plain jealous and you're taking my things and being beastly just to get even with me.'

'I tell you I'm not playing tricks on you, and I'm not jealous,' cried Anne-Marie. 'You can keep Miss Willcox all to yourself! I don't ever want to see her again! *Deirdre* Willcox indeed! Her name is Doris, just plain Doris – I saw it written in one of her books. I bet she calls herself Deirdre just because she thinks Doris is too ordinary. She's a – a – silly pretender!'

Anne-Marie flung herself out of the room, and Alison stared after her in rage. Angela laughed.

'You two amuse me,' she said. 'I'm glad I don't go off the deep end about anyone like you do! Silly, I call it!'

'Oh, *do* you!' said Alison, in a cutting voice. 'Well, let me tell you, you're just as bad in another way – you smile sweetly at the lower-form kids and get them all round you to wait on you – then when you're tired of them, you just tick them off – and they're as miserable as can be. I bet you're partly responsible for Jane Teal trying to run away!'

Angela opened her mouth to answer heatedly, but just then the door opened and Anne-Marie popped her head in again.

'I'll show Miss Doris Willcox up tomorrow, in front of the whole class!' she said. 'You see if I don't! Then you'll have to say I'm right, and you'll be jolly sick you didn't see through her. So there!'

The door banged and Anne-Marie disappeared. 'I'm tired of Anne-Marie and her silly ways,' said Alison, who still thought that it was she who was playing tricks on her, and had no idea it had been Alma. 'Let her do what she likes. I shall always like Miss Willcox!'

22

Anne-Marie traps Miss Willcox

Anne-Marie had prepared her little trap for Miss Willcox, and she had prepared it very carefully. Every week Miss Willcox set the girls some kind of composition to do, and they sent in their entries, which were carefully gone through by her and marked.

This week the subject set was a poem. It had to be only eight lines long, the first and third lines had to rhyme, and the second and fourth, the fifth and seventh and the sixth and eighth. The subject was to be 'Thoughts.'

The fifth form grumbled. They didn't like writing poetry, they *couldn't* write poetry, it was a silly waste of time for them in exam week. It was just like Miss Willcox to set a poem for them to do! So they grumbled and groaned, but all the same they managed to produce something that could be called a poem.

Anne-Marie had hunted through the poets for a lesser-known poem that would suit her purpose. If only she could find one that would just do! And by great good fortune she suddenly found exactly what she wanted. It was a little eight-line poem by Matthew Arnold, called 'Despondency', which seemed to Anne-Marie to be just what she wanted.

She copied it out in her big, rather sprawly handwriting. Really it seemed as if it was her own poem, it was just as sad as the ones she liked to write!

Anne-Marie sent the poem in with those of the others of her form. She signed her name at the bottom. Now, Miss Doris Willcox, we will see if you know good poetry when you see it!

The English lesson duly arrived, and Alison glanced curiously at Anne-Marie, who seemed excited. Was she really going to carry out her silly threat and do something to Miss Willcox? Alison felt a little disturbed. Ought she to warn Deirdre?

Miss Willcox arrived, carrying the sheaf of poems in her hand. She looked as soulful as ever, and wore a trailing crimson scarf round her swan-like neck.

The first part of the lesson was given to the reading of a play. Then came the time set apart for commenting on the girls' own work. Miss Willcox pulled the sheaf of poems towards her.

'Not a very good set,' she remarked, slipping the elastic band off the papers. 'I suppose the exam has had an effect on your creative powers. Pam's is the best – quite a praiseworthy little effort, simple and honest. Claudine, I can't pass yours. You may have meant it to be funny, but it isn't.'

Claudine made a face, which fortunately for her Miss Willcox did not see. Miss Willcox dealt with everyone's poems rapidly, quoting from one or two, praising here and there, and condemning the efforts of Doris, Angela and Carlotta.

Then she came to the last one, which was Anne-Marie's. She looked round the class, a rather spiteful look in her large eyes.

'And now at last we come to the poet of the class, Anne-Marie. A sad, heart-rending poem as usual. Listen to the wailings of our poet.

'THOUGHTS

The thoughts that rain their steady glow,
Like stars on life's cold sea,
Which others know, or say they know –
They never shone for me.

Thoughts light, like gleams, my spirit's sky,
But they will not remain.
They light me once, they hurry by,
And never come again.'

Miss Willcox read these lines out in a mock-heroic way, exaggerating the feeling in them, making fun of the whole poem. She put down the paper.

'Anne-Marie, why must you write like this? It is all so silly and insincere and quite meaningless. What for instance can you possibly mean by "Stars on life's cold sea?" What *is* life's cold sea? Just words that came into your head and you put them down because they sounded grand. Life's cold sea! Ridiculous!'

Anne-Marie stared at Miss Willcox steadily. She felt very triumphant. That wasn't *her* poem! It was written by a great poet, not by Anne-Marie at all! That just showed that Miss Willcox didn't know a thing and wasn't any judge of good poetry!

Miss Willcox didn't like the steady, oddly triumphant look on Anne-Marie's face. She felt a wave of anger against her.

'You have the scansion and the rhyming *quite* correct,' she said scornfully to Anne-Marie, 'but all the same I consider your poem the worst of the form.'

'Miss Willcox,' said Anne-Marie, suddenly, in a high, clear voice, 'I'm so sorry – I think I must have made a mistake in sending in that poem! I don't believe it is mine after all!'

The class turned to look at Anne-Marie. She sat tensely, still with that triumphant look on her face.

'What do you mean?' said Miss Willcox, impatiently. 'Not *your* poem? Then whose is it? I must say it *sounds* exactly like yours!'

'It's – it's very kind of you to say that,' said Anne-Marie, 'because you see – that poem is by Matthew Arnold, not by me at all. I'm glad you think his poetry is like mine. I feel honoured. Though I don't suppose, if he were alive, he would be at all pleased to hear the things you have just said about his little poem – it's strange to think you consider *his* poem the worst in the form!'

There was dead silence. Alison turned scarlet, seeing the trap Anne-Marie had set for Miss Willcox, and the prompt way in which she had fallen headlong into it. Anne-Marie pulled a volume of Matthew Arnold's poems from her desk and opened it at a certain page. 'Here's the poem,' she said, getting up from her desk. 'It's called "Despondency" not "Thoughts". I'll show it to you, Miss Willcox.'

Miss Willcox had gone white. She knew it had been a trap now – Anne-Marie's revenge for the cruel words she had spoken to her some days back. She had shown her up in front of the whole class. Oh, why, why had she said that the poem was the worst in the form? Why had she said such spiteful things? Only to hurt Anne-Marie, and because she thought she wanted taking down two or three pegs.

Alison was terribly distressed. She hated to see Miss Willcox trapped like that – and she also hated to think that the teacher had allowed herself to be trapped because of her own petty spite. She looked with dislike at the triumphant Anne-Marie.

'You have cheated, Anne-Marie,' said Miss Willcox, trying to regain her dignity. 'I shall have to report you to Miss Theobald for a grave act of deceit.'

'Yes, Miss Willcox,' said Anne-Marie maliciously, and the English mistress knew that it would be no good reporting Anne-Marie – for Anne-Marie would also report her own side of the matter, and Miss Theobald would not think very much of a teacher who condemned lines by a great poet just because she thought they were written by a schoolgirl she disliked.

The bell rang, and never did Miss Willcox feel so relieved to hear it. She gathered up her books and sailed out. The girls rounded on Anne-Marie.

'That was a beastly thing to do!' said Hilary.

'I thought it was funny,' said Claudine.

'You would!' said Pat. 'It was certainly clever, but it wasn't a decent thing to do.'

'I know it wasn't,' said Anne-Marie, defiantly. 'But I wanted to get my own back. And I did.'

'Well, I hope you're happy about it,' said Alison, bitterly. 'Trying to humiliate a good teacher in front of the whole class.'

'Did she feel sorry for poor little Doris-Deirdre then?' began Anne-Marie, but Hilary was not going to allow any spite of that sort.

'Shut up, both of you,' she said. 'Maybe you won't be such an ass over Miss Willcox now, Alison – and perhaps, now you've taken your revenge, Anne-Marie, you'll cool off and try to behave decently for the rest of the term. Alison has complained to me about your behaviour to her, and it's got to stop.'

'I don't know what you mean by my "behaviour to Alison",' said Anne-Marie, puzzled. 'She complains that I take her things, and play tricks on her, but I don't. Why should I? I'm not jealous of her or anything. She can keep Miss Willcox all to herself if she wants to! *I* don't mind!'

Most of the class, although they thought it was not a nice thing to humiliate a mistress publicly, had secretly enjoyed the excitement. Alma certainly had, for she had often been held up to ridicule by Miss Willcox for her complete inability to appreciate any fine literature at all. She was glad to see her defeated by Anne-Marie – and she was glad too when she heard Alison openly accusing Anne-Marie of the tricks she, Alma, had been playing on the unsuspecting Alison!

I'll play just one more and that shall be the last, she thought. I know she had a box of sweets sent to her today. I'll slip in and take those when she isn't there, and she'll blame Anne-Marie again!

But Alma tried her tricks once too often. When she slipped into Alison's study, it was empty, and she picked up the box of sweets quickly. She hurried to her own study and ran in.

To her dismay both Alison and Angela were there, waiting to ask Pauline something! Alison immediately saw the box of sweets in Alma's hand.

'Those are my sweets!' she said. 'You beast, you took them out of my study! Alma, you're a thief! I'm sure you were a thief before too – you pilfered the cupboard outside, when the second formers hid their stuff there. Angela, isn't she absolutely awful?

Alma stood there stubbornly, trying to think of some way out. 'I wasn't going to eat them,' she said at last. 'I was only playing a trick on you because I don't like you.'

'You were stealing,' said Alison, furiously. 'You know you meant to eat them! This will have to be told to Hilary. It's simply awful for a fifth former to be caught stealing.'

Alma sat down suddenly, feeling frightened. She had had a solemn and very serious talking to by Miss Theobald about being found in the cupboard the other night, and it had been impossible to convince the head mistress that she had not been doing anything wrong. If this got to her ears, matters would be even more serious.

'I didn't steal them, Alison,' she said, desperately. 'I tell you, I was just paying you out because you stopped me going to the cupboard where the second formers put their food – though you didn't know it. I took your knitting-needles – and your geometry set – and other things. Only to spite you, though, not to steal them. They're all here, look!'

She unlocked her desk in the corner and before Alison's astonished eyes lay all the things she had missed during the last week or two!

'Bring them into my study,' said Alison, completely at a loss to know what to do or say. 'I'll have to think about this. What a beast you are, Alma – especially as you knew I was blaming Anne-Marie all the time.'

Alma took everything back, weeping. Alison took one look at the puffy, pasty face and turned away in dislike. How could a girl who had been in the top form do things like this? Perhaps that was why she had been dropped back into the fifth – maybe because of some disgrace or other!

23

A few things are cleared up

'Wait till the exams are over before you make any fuss about Alma,' said Angela to Alison. 'Oh, dear – no wonder Anne-Marie didn't know what we were talking about when we kept accusing her of taking your things!'

'I shall have to apologize to her,' said Alison, gloomily. 'Blow Alma – what a first-class idiot she is, really! Isn't she odd? I don't understand her at all. Sometimes I think she's daft.'

The exams were now pressing on the girls, and they were working feverishly. Only Pam appeared to find them easy. Hilary worked through her papers methodically, and so did Pat and Isabel, Bobby and Janet, but Carlotta, Claudine and Angela got very hot and bothered. So, oddly enough, did Mirabel, which was unusual for her, but she had given so much of her time to the organizing of the school games that she had not worked as well at her exam tasks as the others had.

'These awful questions!' she said, as she read one after another. 'I can't seem to answer any of them!'

At last the exams were over and the whole form heaved a sigh of relief. What a week it had been! The girls wanted to yell and laugh and stamp and rush about. They became very boisterous, even the quiet Pam. But the teachers turned a blind eye and a deaf ear on the yelling girls, and did not even appear to see Carlotta doing cartwheels all round the gym.

'Thank goodness we haven't got to wait long for the results,' said Doris. 'I hate having to wait weeks. Miss Cornwallis says we shall know in a few days.'

'How's little Jane Teal?' said Pat, remembering the first former for the first time for a few days. 'Is she better?'

'She's over the flu,' said Isabel, 'but Matron says she's still worried in her mind. When she was so ill, she kept raving about the fire-bell, and Mirabel and Angela. I rather think there's going to be a few inquiries made about certain members of our form soon! Poor Jane – it's rotten to think no one ever owned up about that bell, but let Jane take the blame. It made Mirabel simply beastly to her. She is the only person who hasn't been to see Jane in the sick-bay. Did you know?'

'Just like her,' said Pat.

The exam results came out and were posted up on the board. Pam and Hilary were top with honours. The others came in turn down the list. Carlotta was glad to see she had passed. Doris just scraped through too, and so did Claudine and Alison.

Three girls failed. They were Angela, Alma – and, most surprisingly, Mirabel!

Alma had not expected to pass. Angela was amazed that *she* hadn't! As for Mirabel, she was humiliated beyond words. To think that she, sports captain of St Clare's, should have failed. She rushed off to her study, filled with shame and horror. How everyone would sneer!

Gladys, who had hardly spoken with Mirabel since she had resigned as vice-captain, stared in amazement at the exam results. Mirabel failed! She could hardly believe her eyes. With her heart full of sympathy and warmth she hurried off to find her one-time friend.

Mirabel was sitting by the window, her humiliation almost more than she could bear. Gladys went to her, and took her hand.

'Bad luck, old thing,' she said. 'I'm awfully sorry. You worked too hard at the matches and things, that's all. Don't worry too much about it. Two others have failed as well.'

Mirabel was touched by Gladys's warm sympathy. She had felt lonely and deserted. With tears in her eyes she gazed at Gladys, and tried to speak.

'I can't bear it,' she said at last. 'They'll all laugh at me. Me, the sports captain! They'll be glad to laugh too. They hate me. Everyone hates me. Where have I gone wrong? I meant to do so well.'

'Let's be friends again, Mirabel,' said Gladys. 'You need me, don't you? You wouldn't let me help you at all this term – but let me help you now. The girls don't really hate you – they admired you awfully at the beginning of the term, and there's no reason why they shouldn't again.'

Poor Mirabel – and poor Angela! Both liked to shine, and both had failed. What was the use of being sports captain, what was the use of being the most beautiful girl in the school, if your brains were so poor you couldn't even get as good marks as Doris or Alison!

Claudine had been rather quiet for a day or two. She had been to see Jane Teal and taken her a lovely little handkerchief she had embroidered for her. Then she sought out Antoinette and made a proposal to her that surprised that second former very much.

'What! Tell Miss Theobald that I rang the fire-bell!' said Antoinette, in surprise and disgust. 'Are you mad, Claudine?'

'Yes, perhaps,' said Claudine, thoughtfully. 'I am afraid I have caught a little of this English sense of honour, alas! I feel uncomfortable *here* when I think of Jane Teal worrying about the fire-bell, and of Mirabel thinking it is Jane. It is a great pity, but I fear I have caught this sense of honour, Antoinette.'

'Oh, is it catching?' said Antoinette, in alarm. 'I do not want to get it, it is an uncomfortable thing to have. See how it makes you behave, Claudine.'

'I will go to Miss Theobald and tell her it was all my fault,' said Claudine, at last. 'You do not need to come into it, Antoinette. After all, it was my idea, and you only carried it out. I will go and confess.'

She gave a huge sigh and went off. Miss Theobald was startled and amused to see Claudine arriving with a saintly and determined expression on her face.

'Miss Theobald, I have caught the sense of honour from somebody at St Clare's,' announced Claudine. 'I have come to make a confession. I told my little sister to ring the fire-bell when Mirabel was about to hold her stupid meeting. I did not mean to own up, but now I feel uncomfortable *here* about it.'

Claudine pressed her tummy, and Miss Theobald listened gravely. 'I am glad you have owned up, Claudine,' she said. 'It was a silly thing to do, but it became a serious thing when someone else was suspected of it. Please tell Hilary. I shall not punish Antoinette, but she too must own up to Jane Teal, and put her mind at rest.'

Claudine went out, knowing that her real punishment was to be owning up to the serious head girl of the form. Hilary did not favour misbehaviour of this kind now that they were top formers, and she had a way of talking that at times made Claudine feel very small. She made her feel small now.

'You don't realize that next term we shall all be in the top form,' she said to Claudine. 'From there we go out into the world. We can't behave like naughty children in the first form now. We have to set an example to the younger ones, we have to learn what responsibility means!'

'You should be a preacher, Hilary,' said Claudine, jokingly.

But Hilary was not in a mood to be joked with. She took her position as head girl very seriously, all the more so because she knew she would not be head girl of the sixth. She was only staying one term more, and the head girl must be someone staying for three terms. Everyone was wondering who would be chosen.

Claudine went off, abashed, and found Antoinette, who was highly indignant at being sent off to Jane Teal to confess. But when she saw Jane's face, she was not sorry she had gone.

'Oh,' said Jane, 'was it really you, Antoinette? Oh, I'm glad you told me. You know, I really began to feel it *might* have been me, I was so worried about it. Whatever will Mirabel say?'

Mirabel soon heard about it. Gladys told her. She flushed uncomfortably, thinking of the hard time she had given poor Jane because of her unjust suspicions. She thought for a while and then went straight off to the sick-bay, where Jane still was.

'Jane, I've heard who rang the fire-bell,' said Mirabel, hardly liking to meet Jane's eyes. 'It wasn't you, and I was sure it was. I was beastly to you – left you out of matches unfairly – and things like that. I'm – I'm sorry about it. I . . .'

'It's all right, Mirabel,' said Jane, eagerly. 'I don't mind now. Not a bit. All I want is to get up and practise hard for you again, and perhaps play in a match before the term ends.'

Jane's warm response and loyalty were very pleasant to Mirabel, who had been very miserable. She smiled at the first former, left her some barley sugar, and went back to her study, thinking how nice it was to have someone look at her with liking once again.

Mirabel's visit to Jane made a great impression on the lower forms. Jane soon spread it abroad, and spoke so glowingly of Mirabel's kind words to her, that the younger ones began to get over their dislike and defiance. They had deserted the practice field, and had shown little or no interest in games since Mirabel had cancelled their match – but now they gradually drifted back, and Mirabel found, to her delight, that they seemed as keen as ever.

Gladys took back her resignation, and Mirabel set to work humbly and happily to make out games lists again and to arrange matches – but she let Gladys do at least half of it, and was careful to listen to her and to take her advice when she gave it. The two were much happier than they had ever been before and Gladys was glad to see her friend learning from the bad mistakes she had made.

'Looks as if Mirabel will be a good captain after all,' said Bobby in surprise. 'Well, well – we're all turning over a new leaf! There's Felicity back again, not caring two hoots about her music for a bit, and being quite one of us – and there's Anne-Marie gone all friendly and jolly since Alison apologized to her for suspecting her wrongly – and there's Alison behaving sensibly too, now that she sees through dear Deirdre – and Angela isn't being such an idiot with the younger ones since she failed in her exam.'

'No – that was a shock that pulled her together a bit,' said Pat. 'She's working hard now. Did you know that Hilary gave her a most awful talking-to. She wept buckets of tears, and was furious with Hilary – but she certainly has been better since.'

'It's only Alma that's still a pain in the neck,' said Isabel. 'I hate speaking to her even. I know Hilary's gone to tell Miss Theobald about her taking those things of Alison's. I bet she'll be expelled or something if she isn't careful.'

But Alma was not expelled. Instead Hilary explained something to the girls that made them feel rather uncomfortable.

'I told Miss Theobald all about our trouble with Alma,' said Hilary, 'and she told me we must be patient with her and put up with her, because she can't help it just now. There's something wrong with her glands, that can't be put right for about six months. That's why she's so fat, and always hungry, and looks so pasty and funny. She was sent off from her last school in disgrace – but Miss Theobald wants to keep her here and help her, till she can have some sort of marvellous operation done that can put her right.'

'Poor old Pudding,' said Doris. 'She's her own enemy, I suppose – or her glands are, whatever they may be! Well – I suppose we must put up with our Alma, and grin and bear it when she chews and munches and eats.' Doris began to imitate Alma at a meal, and the girls screamed with laughter.

But there was no real unkindness in the laughter. One and all were ready to put up with Alma now and help her, even selfish little Angela, and wild Carlotta. They were growing up, they were fifth formers, they could behave decently. St Clare's put its mark on you by the time you were in the fifth form!

24

Who shall be head of the school?

After the exam the girls relaxed with pleasure and relief. The teachers gave them less prep to do, and the fifth formers spent pleasant evenings in their own studies or each other's, talking and laughing.

'Christmas will soon be upon us,' said Pat. 'The rest of this term will fly! I always like the Christmas term – it begins in summer-time, when the September sun is still hot, and it often ends in snow, with Christmas beckoning round the corner.'

'You sound quite poetic,' said Doris. 'Anne-Marie used to say things like that!'

Anne-Marie laughed. She had not written any poems for some time, for, after the success of her trick on Miss Willcox, she had felt rather ashamed of herself. After all, *she* had pretended too, just like Miss Willcox, *she* had tried to write poems that sounded very grand, but were quite worthless really. Now Anne-Marie was determined to wait till she had something to say, before she wrote poetry again.

She had had a talk with Miss Theobald, who had heard

of Anne-Marie's 'cheating' as Miss Willcox called it. The head mistress hadn't much time for the English teacher herself, sensing that she was insincere and rather conceited – but she could not allow any of the girls to flout authority, or be insolent, without reprimanding them severely.

So Anne-Marie had had a bad twenty minutes, and had come away a sadder and wiser fifth former, determined that she would write no more 'wonderful' poetry until, as Miss Theobald said, she had something real and honest and sincere in her heart to put into her writing and make it worthwhile.

Mirabel had got over the shock of failing in the exam, and was trying to make the lower forms forget her stupid arrogance and harshness. Her voice was still loud and clear, but not haughty or dictatorial, and she no longer walked as if the whole earth belonged to her. She was a wiser person altogether, and the girls respected her for being able to change herself so completely.

Jane Teal was once again working hard for Mirabel, exulting in her returned health and strength, a great weight off her mind. Angela no longer gave the younger ones so many jobs to do, and she and Alison did their mending together. Hilary had made a great impression on Angela when she had ticked her off, and had really frightened her.

'You're a poor, poor thing, Angela,' she had told her. 'You use your pretty face and smile to save yourself trouble, and you are getting a lazy mind and a lazy body, letting other people do the things *you* ought to do. No wonder you failed in the exam – and failed miserably too! If you're not careful you'll go on being a failure in all kinds of ways, and people will laugh at you instead of admiring and respecting you. What do you suppose Jane and Sally and Violet and the rest of your lower-form slaves think of their darling beautiful Angela now, when they see that she and Alma tied for bottom place in the exam? Pull yourself together a bit, for goodness' sake.'

Each term brought different things to learn, besides lessons. Those girls who faced their difficulties, saw and understood their faults, conquered their failings, and became strong characters and leaders would make the finest wives and mothers of the future. Miss Theobald watched the fifth formers carefully, and was proud of many of them.

She remembered them as silly little first formers, and a little less silly second formers. She remembered Pat and Isabel O'Sullivan, the 'stuck-up twins' as they had been called, when they first came. She remembered how Mirabel had vowed not to stay longer than half a term, and had misbehaved herself dreadfully in her first term. She remembered the wildness of Carlotta, who had come to St Clare's from circus-life, untamed and headstrong.

She remembered Bobby, whose brilliant brains were once only used in mad and clever tricks – and Claudine, untruthful, deceitful and unscrupulous, who was at last finding responsibility and a sense of honour. Here were all these girls now, dependable, honest-minded, hard-working, and responsible. Truly St Clare's was a school to be proud of.

Before the end of the term came the head mistress must choose the head girl for the whole school. All the sixth were leaving, and the fifth were to go up, with one or two new girls. Hilary was the only one of the fifth who was not staying on for one more whole year. She was only to stay one term more, and then she was to go to India to be with her parents there.

Otherwise Hilary would have been head of the sixth, and a good responsible head she would have made. But now someone else must be chosen. The girls wondered who it would be. It was a tremendous honour, for the head girl of the sixth would be the head girl of the whole school, a person of great influence.

'It won't be me, anyway,' said Doris, comfortably. 'I'm too stupid.'

'And it won't be me,' said Carlotta. 'I'm still too wild.'

'Nor me,' said Bobby, grinning. 'I'm still too much given to playing tricks. Didn't Mam'zelle jump when she drank her glass of milk this morning and found a black beetle at the bottom?'

The girls giggled. It was a silly trick, but had caused a lot of fun. Bobby had popped a little tin black beetle into Mam'zelle's glass of mid-morning milk, and her horror when she had drunk all the milk and then had suddenly seen the beetle at the bottom had been most amusing to watch.

'*Tiens*!' she had cried. 'What is this black animal I have

almost drunk? Oh là, là, that it should choose my glass and no one else's!'

The girls recalled all the tricks Bobby and Janet had played on poor Mam'zelle – the way they had made the plates dance – the dreadful stink balls – and many others. They had all been good fun, and Mam'zelle had always joined in the laughter afterwards.

'We break up in three days' time,' said Bobby. 'Then heyho for the holidays – and when we come back, we shall all be sixth formers, grave and serious and solemn! No tricks then – no giggles – no messing about!'

'Oh, rubbish!' said Carlotta. 'We shan't suddenly alter just because we're sixth formers. We shall be just the same. I do wonder who will be head girl. Perhaps one of the twins will.'

'I hope not,' said Pat, at once. 'I'd hate to be something Isabel wasn't, and she would hate it too. Otherwise we'd either of us love it. It's the thing I'd like best in the world at the moment. I love St Clare's, and I'm proud of belonging to it. If I could do something for it I would – but I don't want to do something that I can't share with Isabel.'

'I feel the same about that,' said Isabel. 'But if we *did* have the honour of being asked, either of us, to be head girl, we'd say no. Anyway, there are plenty of others who would make better head girls than we should.'

At that very moment the matter was being decided by Miss Theobald, Miss Cornwallis and Mam'zelle. They were sitting together in the head's sitting-room, discussing the very weighty and important question of who should be the next head girl. It was important because the head girl had a powerful influence on the whole school, and was, in fact, typical of the spirit of St Clare's.

They were going down the list of girls. 'Hilary can't be, of course,' said Miss Cornwallis. 'A pity, because she has had great experience of being head girl in three or four forms. Still, perhaps it is time someone else had a chance of showing leadership.'

'Janet?' said Miss Theobald.

The others shook their heads. Janet could still be hot-tempered and wilful at times. She had not yet learnt to guard her sharp tongue completely. A head girl had to have complete control of herself.

'Not Bobby, of course,' said Miss Cornwallis. 'Brilliant, trustable, but still a little unsteady. What about Gladys?'

'Too gentle – not enough of a leader,' said Miss Theobald, who knew the character of every girl in a most remarkable way. 'And Claudine I am afraid we must also cross out, Mam'zelle.'

Mam'zelle sighed. It had been a secret wish with her for two or three terms that Claudine, her little Claudine, might be head of St Clare's, the school in which Mam'zelle had taught for so many many years. But even Mam'zelle biased as she was, knew that Claudine was not fit to lead others.

'If she had been at St Clare's when she was thirteen now,' said Mam'zelle, 'ah, then my little Claudine might have had time to learn enough to become head girl!'

Both Miss Theobald and Miss Cornwallis had their

doubts about this. In fact, Miss Cornwallis thought that if Claudine had been at St Clare's ever since she was a baby, she would still not have been suitable for a head girl. But neither wanted to upset Mam'zelle, who adored her two nieces, so they said nothing.

'Alma, certainly not, poor girl,' said Miss Theobald. 'She is a most unfortunate child. Perhaps when she is in really good health, she will improve. Carlotta now – no, I think not. Still rather unaccountable and uncontrolled in her temper. I always feel she is still capable of scolding people if she doesn't approve of them.'

Mam'zelle remembered various scolding episodes in Carlotta's school-life and smiled. 'Ah, she would scold the first formers well if they did not behave!' she said. 'She would be an amusing head girl, but perhaps not a very good one.'

'Felicity, no,' said Miss Cornwallis. 'She will always be apt to forget everything when her music fills her mind. She will perhaps someday be one of the foremost musicians or composers, but only in her art will she be fit to lead others.'

'Angela and Alison – neither of them leaders in any way,' said Miss Theobald. 'How good it would be for both of them to be head girls, and feel the weight of leadership and responsibility on their shoulders – but how bad for the school! Alison is still such a feather-head, and Angela has a lot to learn yet. Three more terms to learn it in – well, maybe it will be enough.'

'Anne-Marie would be hopeless,' said Mam'zelle, 'so would Pauline.'

'That leaves Doris, Pam and the twins,' said Miss Theobald, looking at her list.

'Doris is too stupid,' said Mam'zelle. 'Still she cannot roll her Rs for me in the French way. Ah, she will be a great success on the stage, that girl, she is so clever a mimic. But she is stupid in all other ways, though a nice, nice girl.'

The others agreed. 'Pam would make an ideal head girl,' said Miss Theobald, 'but she is too young. Almost two years younger than the oldest in the fifth. She is staying on two years, so perhaps she will be head girl in the future. A nice, hard-working, quiet and dependable child.'

'That only leaves the O'Sullivan twins,' said Miss Cornwallis, 'and I am sure that we cannot choose one without the other. They are inseparable and always have been. The other twin would feel very much left out if we chose one of them.'

'Ah – I have it!' said Mam'zelle, suddenly, banging the table and making the other mistresses jump. 'I have it! Yes, we will have *two* head girls! Why not? Is not St Clare's bigger than ever it was? Has not the head girl more than enough to do? Then we will have *two* head girls, girls who will work together as one – so why not the O'Sullivan twins?'

Miss Theobald and Miss Cornwallis looked at each other. It was a good idea. Two head girls who were twins would certainly work very well together, and could share the responsibility well. Pat and Isabel had consistently done good work, and had grown into splendid, trustworthy and sensible girls.

'Yes,' said Miss Theobald, at last. 'It's a very good idea indeed. The twins will make fine head girls. It will do them a world of good, for they have never undertaken any kind of leadership here so far. They shall be joint head girls. I will make the announcement tomorrow.'

So, when the whole school was called together for the head to announce the changes in the coming term, the names of the two new head girls were given.

'We have carefully studied the question of who shall be head girl of the school for the coming year,' said Miss Theobald. 'And I think there is no doubt that our choice is wise and will be very popular. St Clare's is growing fast, and the head girl has a great deal to do; sometimes too much. So we have decided to have *two* head girls working together, and we have chosen a pair who have been with us from the first form, and have made their way up the school steadily and well, winning everyone's respect and admiration. Next term the O'Sullivan twins will be our head girls!'

There was a terrific outburst of cheering, clapping and stamping at these words. Everyone knew the like-as-pea twins, everyone liked them and trusted them. Now they were to be head girls together – splendid!

The twins were overwhelmed. They blushed scarlet, and when they heard the outburst of cheering, they felt sudden tears pricking their eyelids. It was a wonderful moment for them. To be chosen to head the school, to lead it, to hold the biggest honour St Clare's had to offer – that was something worthwhile.

'Thank you,' said Pat, standing up with Isabel, when the cheering had lessened. 'We'll – we'll do our very best!'

So they will – and their best will be very good indeed. And there we must leave them, about to have their dearest wish, head girls of St Clare's, the finest school they know.

CLAUDINE at ST CLARE'S

ST CLARE'S

Enid Blyton

St Clare's
The Twins at St Clare's
The O'Sullivan Twins
Summer Term at St Clare's
The Second Form at St Clare's
The Third Form at St Clare's (written by Pamela Cox)
Claudine at St Clare's
Fifth Formers of St Clare's
The Sixth Form at St Clare's (written by Pamela Cox)

Malory Towers
First Term at Malory Towers
Second Form at Malory Towers
Third Year at Malory Towers
Upper Fourth at Malory Towers
In the Fifth at Malory Towers
Last Term at Malory Towers

The Mysteries
The Mystery of the Burnt Cottage
The Mystery of the Disappearing Cat
The Mystery of the Secret Room
The Mystery of the Spiteful Letters
The Mystery of the Missing Necklace
The Mystery of the Hidden House
The Mystery of the Pantomime Cat
The Mystery of the Invisible Thief
The Mystery of the Vanished Prince
The Mystery of the Strange Bundle
The Mystery of Holly Lane
The Mystery of Tally-Ho Cottage
The Mystery of the Missing Man
The Mystery of the Strange Messages
The Mystery of Banshee Towers

Enid Blyton

Claudine at St Clare's

EGMONT

St Clare's

Enid Blyton

EGMONT

We bring stories to life

First published in Great Britain 1944 by Methuen & Co. Ltd
This edition published 2013
by Egmont UK Limited
The Yellow Building
1 Nicholas Road
London W11 4AN

978 0 6035 6938 8

A CIP catalogue record for this title is available from the British Library
Printed and bound in Great Britain by the CPI Group

56925/1

Contents

1
Back at school again

Pat and Isabel O'Sullivan walked into the fourth form-room at St Clare's, and looked round.

'Fourth form,' said Pat. 'Golly, we're getting on, aren't we, Isabel?'

'Yes – fourth form seems a long way from the first form,' said Isabel. 'I say – do you remember when we were in the first form – ages go? We were called the Stuck-Up Twins then, because we hated St Clare's, and didn't want to belong to it.'

The twins thought back to the days when they had been first formers. They remembered how they had settled down at St Clare's, their first dislike of it turning to pride and admiration, and now here they were, fourth formers at the beginning of the summer term!

'Don't the first formers seem babies now?' said Pat. 'We thought we were quite big when we first came, but when I see the first formers now they seem very young to me! I shall enjoy being in the fourth form, won't you, Isabel?'

'I shall,' said Isabel. 'I hope we shall stay on at St Clare's until we are in the top form – and I hope our friends do too.'

'Well, some of them have left already,' said Pat. 'Pam

isn't coming back, nor is Sheila. Lucy Oriell has gone too – to an art school. She was going to stay on here, but she's too brilliant at her art, and she's won a scholarship to the best art school in the country.'

'Good for Lucy!' said Isabel. 'We shall miss her though. I wonder if there are any new girls this term?'

'Sure to be,' said Pat. She looked round the big form-room. 'I say, this is a fine room, isn't it – the nicest classroom we've had so far. There's a wonderful view out of the window.'

So there was. The twins could see miles of beautiful country. It was country they knew well now, and loved very much. Down below, in the school grounds, were the tennis-courts, the games fields, and the big swimming-pool. The girls could see the school gardens too, and the big kitchen garden full of fresh vegetables.

'Bags I sit by the window,' said Pat. 'Hallo, there's Bobby, and Janet!'

Roberta and Janet walked into the classroom, grinning. Bobby's freckled face had a very boyish look, and she was very like a boy in her ways, full of fun and tricks.

'Hallo!' she said. 'Come to look at our new home? Nice room, isn't it?'

'What's our new form-mistress like?' said Pat. 'Miss Ellis – she's supposed to be quite nice, isn't she?'

'Oh, yes – very calm and unruffled and dignified,' said Bobby. 'She'll be all right.'

'Got any new tricks to play, Janet?' asked Isabel. Janet always had a stock of tricks each term, most of them from her schoolboy brother, who seemed to be a real scamp. Janet grinned.

'Wait and see,' she said. 'Anyway, I suppose I'd better go carefully now I'm a fourth former. Can't rag about so much when you get high up the school. And I'm going to work for my finals exam too, so I guess I won't have much time for tricks.'

'I guess you will, all the same,' said Pat. 'Any new girls, do you know?'

'Two or three,' said Bobby. 'Hallo, Hilary! Had good hols?'

Hilary Wentworth came into the room, dark and smiling. She had been at St Clare's even longer than the twins.

'Hallo!' she said. 'Yes, I had fine hols. I rode every day, and I played tennis on our hard court every day too. I say, who's the angel?'

'What do you mean?' asked the twins and Bobby.

'Oh, haven't you seen her?' said Hilary. 'She's just arrived, complete with posh new trunk, three tennis-rackets, and a handbag with gold initials on. What do you bet your Cousin Alison will think she's one of the world's seven wonders? She's got pale golden hair, bobbed like angels in pictures, and a pointed face like a pixie, and a voice like a princess.'

'Golly! Where is she?' said the others, with interest. 'Will she be in our form?'

'She's down in the hall,' said Hilary. 'She arrived in the biggest car I've ever seen, with a crest on the panels, and two chauffeurs.'

'Let's go and see her,' said Pat. So the five of them went

into the corridor, and hung over the stair banisters to see the newcomer.

She was still there – and it was quite true, she did look a bit like an angel, if an angel could be imagined dressed in school uniform, carrying three beautiful tennis-rackets!

'She's lovely, isn't she?' said Bobby, who, not being at all lovely herself, always admired beauty in others. 'Yes – I bet Alison will follow her round like a dog. Alison isn't happy unless she's thinking someone is just too wonderful for words!'

Alison came up at that moment. She was the twins' cousin, a pretty, feather-headed little thing, with not many brains. 'Hallo!' she said. 'Did I hear you talking about me?'

'Yes,' said Hilary. 'We were just saying that you'd be sure to like that schoolgirl angel down there. Did you ever see anything like her?'

Alison leant over the banisters – and, just as the others had guessed, she immediately lost her heart to thc new girl.

'She looks like a princess from a fairytale,' said Alison. 'I'll go down and ask her if she wants to be shown round a bit.'

Alison sped downstairs. The others grinned at one another. 'Alison has lost her heart already,' said Pat. 'Poor old Alison – the wonderful friends she's made and lost! Do you remember Sadie, the American girl, and how Alison was for ever saying, "Well, *Sadie* says so and so," and we made a song about it and sang it? Wasn't Alison cross?'

'Yes, and when she was in the second form she thought the drama mistress was simply wonderful, and when she was in the third form she lost her heart to the head girl and made herself a perfect nuisance to her,' said Janet. 'Really, the times Alison has lost her heart to people, and they never think anything of her for it.'

'Funny old feather-head,' said Pat. 'Look at her, taking the angel's arm and going off with her, all over her already!'

'There's another new girl down there too,' said Bobby. 'She looks rather forlorn. Well, I do think Alison might take her round as well. Hi, Alison!'

But Alison had disappeared with the golden-haired angel. The twins went down the stairs and spoke to the other new girl.

'Hallo! You're new, aren't you? You'd better come and see Matron. We'll take you.'

'What's your name?' said Pat, looking at the new girl, who was trying not to show that she felt new and lost.

'Pauline Bingham-Jones,' said the new girl in rather an affected voice. 'Yes, I'd be glad if you'd tell me what to do.'

'Well, Matron is usually here to see to all the new girls,' said Hilary, a little puzzled. 'I wonder where she is?'

'I haven't seen her at all,' said Pat. 'She wasn't here when we came, either.'

'Funny,' said Isabel. 'Let's go to her room and find her. We've got to see her, anyway.'

They went to Matron's room, taking Pauline with them. They banged on the door. They liked Matron, though they were very much in awe of her. She had been at St Clare's for years and years, and some of the girls' mothers, who had also been at St Clare's, had known her too.

A voice called out. 'Come in!'

'That's not Matron's voice,' said Pat, puzzled. She opened the door and went in, the others following. A woman in Matron's uniform sat sewing by the window. It wasn't the Matron they knew so well. The girls stared at her in surprise.

'Oh,' said Pat. 'We were looking for Matron.'

'I am Matron this term,' said the new Matron. 'Your old Matron fell ill during the holidays, so I have come to take her place. I am sure we shall all get on very well together.'

The girls stared at her. They didn't feel so sure about that. Their old Matron was fat and round and jolly, with a strong and comforting kind of face. This Matron was thin and sour-looking. She had very thin lips that met together in a straight line. She smiled at the girls, but her smile stayed at her mouth and did not reach her eyes.

'We came to find you,' said Bobby. 'Usually Matron meets the new girls. This is one of them. She has to give you her list of clothes and towels and things.'

'I know that, thank you,' said Matron, biting off the thread she was using. 'Send all the new girls to me, will you? How many have arrived?'

The girls didn't know. They thought it was Matron's business to find out, not theirs. They thought of their old

Matron, bustling about looking after the newcomers, making them welcome, taking them to their form-mistresses, or finding girls to take care of them.

'Well – this is Pauline Bingham-Jones,' said Pat, at last. 'There's another new girl somewhere. We saw her. Our Cousin Alison seems to be looking after her.'

The girls disappeared from the room, leaving Pauline to the new Matron. They looked at one another and screwed up their noses. 'Don't like her,' said Isabel. 'Looks like a bottle of vinegar!'

The others laughed. 'I hope our old Matron will come back,' said Bobby. 'St Clare's will seem funny without her. I wonder where Alison has gone with the angel.'

Alison appeared at that moment, looking flushed and radiant. It was quite plain that she had made a friend already. With her was the 'angel'.

'Oh,' said Alison, 'Pat, Isabel, Bobby, Hilary – this is the Honourable Angela Favorleigh.'

The Honourable Angela bent her head a little as if she was bowing to her subjects. Bobby grinned.

'I had a doll called Angela once,' she said. 'She was a bit like you! Well – I hope you'll like St Clare's. Alison, take her to Matron.'

'Where *is* Matron?' said Alison. 'I've been looking for her.'

'There's a new Matron this term,' said Bobby. 'You won't like her.'

The Honourable Angela Favorleigh didn't like Bobby. She gazed at her as if she was something that smelt rather nasty. She turned to Alison and spoke in a pretty, high little voice.

'Well – let's go to Matron. I want to take my things off.'

They went off together. Hilary laughed. 'Well, we shall all know where Alison will be most of this term,' she said. 'In the Honourable's pocket!'

2

In the fourth form

'Look,' said Bobby, 'there's another new girl. She's got her things off, too. She looks as if she'd be a fourth former, I should think.'

The new girl came up, walking quickly as if she had somewhere to go. 'Hallo,' said Bobby. 'You're new, aren't you? What form will you be in, do you know?'

'Fourth,' said the girl. 'My name's Eileen Paterson.'

'We're fourth form too,' said Pat, and she introduced herself and the others. 'Do you want to be shown round a bit? Usually Matron is here to welcome people, but there is a new one this term who doesn't know the ropes yet.'

The girl looked suddenly annoyed. 'I know my way about, thank you,' she said stiffly. 'I've been here a week already.'

Without saying any more she swung off. The others stared after her. 'What's bitten *her*?' said Bobby. 'No need to be rude like that. And what did she mean – that she's been here a week? Nobody comes back before the first day of term.'

Mirabel came up, with her friend Gladys. 'Hallo, Hallo!' said the others. 'Nice to see you again. I say, have you spoken to that girl who's just gone – new girl called Eileen

Paterson. Seems to think the whole school belongs to her!'

'No, I haven't spoken to her yet,' said Mirabel. 'But I know her mother is the Matron now – our old one is ill you know. Eileen is the new Matron's daughter, and she's going to be educated here. She came with her mother a week ago, when her mother came to take over the job and see to the linen and things.'

Bobby whistled. 'Oh! No wonder she was annoyed when we said the new Matron ought to be welcoming the new girls, and didn't know the ropes yet!' she said. 'And no wonder she knows her way about if she's already been here a week. I didn't like her much.'

'Give her a chance,' said Hilary. 'You know how you feel sort of on the defensive when you come to anywhere new, and meet girls who've been here ages. You feel a kind of outsider at first.'

There were new girls in the other, lower forms, but these did not interest the fourth formers much. They were glad to see one another again – the twins, Bobby, Hilary, Kathleen, Doris, Carlotta, and the rest. They had all come up together into the fourth form. There were a few old girls left in the fourth form, most of whom the twins liked. Susan Howes was head of the form, a pleasant, kindly girl with a good sense of responsibility and fairness.

The fourth form settled down under Miss Ellis. She was firm and calm, seldom raised her voice, expected good work and saw that she got it. She was interested in the girls and fond of them, and they, in return, liked her very much.

The Honourable Angela Favorleigh looked more like

an angel than ever in class, with her bobbed golden hair falling to her shoulders, the ends curling underneath most beautifully. All her school clothes, though cut to the same pattern as those of the others, were really beautiful.

'Do you know, she has every single pair of shoes especially made for her?' said Alison in a hushed voice to the twins. 'And she has a handbag to match every single frock she wears, all with gold initials on.'

'Shut up,' said Pat. 'Who cares about things like that? Your darling Angela is a snob.'

'Well, why shouldn't she be?' said Alison, ready to defend her new friend at once. 'Her family is one of the oldest in the country, she's got a third cousin who is a prince, and goodness knows how many titled relations!'

'You're a snob too, Alison,' said Isabel, in disgust. 'Why must you always suck up to people like that? Don't you know that it's what you *are* that matters, not what you have?'

'I'm not a snob,' said Alison. 'I'm pleased that Angela has chosen me for her friend, of course. I think she's lovely.'

'Pity she hasn't got more brains,' said Bobby. 'Honestly, I don't believe she really knows her twelve times table!'

Angela Favorleigh certainly was a snob. She was intensely proud of her family, of its wealth, its cars, and her own well-bred looks. She was very particular about making friends. She liked Alison because the girl was pretty and dainty, had beautiful manners and quite plainly adored the lovely Angela from the bottom of her foolish little heart.

Angela liked very few of her form. Bobby she detested because she had said she was like a doll. Carlotta she would have nothing to do with at all.

Carlotta didn't mind in the least. The dark-eyed, dark-haired girl had once been a little circus girl, and she was not at all ashamed of it. Her mother had been a circus-rider, but her father was a gentleman, and now Carlotta lived with her father and grandmother in the holidays, for her mother was dead. She had learnt to be lady-like, to have good manners, and was very popular indeed – but she had never forgotten the exciting days of the circus, and she often amused the others by turning cartwheels, or going completely mad in a Spanish way that the girls enjoyed very much.

Alison had told Angela the histories of all the girls, Carlotta included, and Angela had turned up her delicate little nose when she heard that Carlotta had actually ridden horses in a circus.

'How *can* they have her here, in a school like this?' she said. 'I am sure my people wouldn't have sent me here if they had known that.'

'Why did you come to St Clare's?' asked Alison, curiously. 'It's supposed to be a sensible, no-nonsense school, you know – not a swanky one.'

'I didn't want to come,' said Angela. 'My mother wanted to send me to a much nicer school, but my father has funny ideas. He said I wanted my corners rubbed off.'

'Oh, Angela! You haven't any corners!' said Alison. 'Honestly, I don't think you've any faults at all.'

This was the kind of thing that Angela loved hearing, and was one reason why she liked Alison for a friend. She looked at Alison out of innocent blue eyes, and smiled an angelic smile.

'You do say nice things, Alison,' she said. 'You are far and away the nicest girl in the form. I can't bear that common Eileen, nor that awful Carlotta, nor that dreadful Pauline Bingham-Jones.'

Pauline certainly wasn't much of a success. In her way she seemed as much of a snob as Angela, but she could not carry it off so well, because her clothes were not beautifully made, and she had no marvellous possessions such as Angela had. But she too turned up her nose at Carlotta, and disliked the ready-witted Bobby. As for Eileen, she would hardly speak to her at all.

'I don't see why Eileen should be allowed to join the school just because her mother is here as Matron,' said Pauline, in her rather affected voice. 'Good gracious me – we shall have the cook's daughter here next, and the gardener's too! It's bad enough to have Carlotta. She always looks so wild and don't-carish.'

Carlotta always did look a little wild at the beginning of term, partly because she was no longer under the rather strict eye of her grandmother. But nobody minded Carlotta's untidiness and wildness. It was all part of the vivacious, amusing girl. Carlotta knew that Angela and Pauline didn't like her, and she took a real pleasure in talking slang, making rude faces, and unexpectedly walking on her hands in front of them.

Miss Ellis, however, did not encourage things of this sort in the fourth form. Her form was a kind of half-way house, where girls had to learn to shed their irresponsible ways, and to become more serious, reliable members of the school. As soon as they moved up into the fifth and sixth, they had studies of their own, instead of common-rooms, and were expected to take a good deal of responsibility.

So Carlotta was often called to order by Miss Ellis, in her low, firm voice, and then Angela and Pauline looked down their noses at the one-time circus girl, and whispered mocking things to the girl next to them.

Pauline and Angela vied with each other in their boasting. The girls sometimes giggled to hear them.

'My third cousin – the one who is a prince,' Angela would say, 'he has an aeroplane of his own, and has promised to take me up in it.'

'Haven't you *been* up in an aeroplane yet?' Pauline would say, with affected surprise. 'Good gracious! I've been up three times already. That was when I was staying with the Lacy-Wrights. Fancy, they had sixteen bathrooms in their house – well, it was really a mansion, of course . . .'

'I bet you haven't more than one bathroom in your own home,' said Angela, spitefully. 'We've got seven.'

'We've got nine, if you count the two in the staff quarters,' said Pauline, at once. The other girls stared at her in surprise. They could well believe that Angela had scores of bathrooms, for wealth was written all over the little snob – but somehow Pauline didn't fit in with a number of bathrooms, a fleet of expensive cars and things like that.

'Well,' said Bobby, 'let me count *my* bathrooms. Three for myself – four for Mother – five for Daddy – two for visitors – er, how many's that?'

'Idiot!' said Pat, giggling. Angela and Pauline scowled.

'I can't remember whether we've got a bathroom at home or not,' said Hilary, entering into the fun. 'Let me think hard!'

But no amount of teasing would make either Angela or Pauline stop their vying with each other. If it wasn't bathrooms, it was cars; if it wasn't cars, it was their beautiful, expensively dressed mothers; if it wasn't mothers, it was clothes. The others really got very tired of it.

Eileen Paterson did not seem to mind very much being cold-shouldered by Angela and Pauline. She only spoke with eagerness of one thing – her elder brother. He was at work somewhere in the next big town, and it was quite plain that Eileen adored him.

'His name is Edgar,' she said. 'We call him Eddie.'

'You would,' said Angela, cattily. 'And if he was called Alfred, you'd call him Alf. And if he was called Herbert, you'd call him Herb – or Erb perhaps.'

Eileen flushed. 'You're a beast, Angela,' she said. 'You wait till you see Eddie – Edgar, I mean. He's marvellous! His hair's curly, and he's got the loveliest smile. He's the best brother in the world. He's working terribly hard at his job. You see, Mother lost a lot of money, so that's why she had to take a job as Matron, and why Eddie – Edgar – had to go to work.'

'Your family history doesn't interest me, Eileen,' said Angela, coldly, and went off with Alison. Eileen shrugged her shoulders.

'Little snob!' she said, loudly. 'She wants a good scolding.'

Carlotta agreed with her. 'Yes – sometimes I feel like throttling Angela,' she said. 'But now I'm a fourth former – what a pity! I shall quite forget how to scold anyone who needs it!'

'Oh no you won't,' said Bobby, laughing at the solemn Carlotta. 'When you fly into a temper, you'll forget all about being a fourth former – you'll just be the same wild Carlotta you've always been!'

3

The arrival of Claudine

Before a week had gone by, a fourth new girl arrived. Mam'zelle herself announced her coming.

'I have a surprise for you,' she beamed one morning, coming in to give a French lesson. 'We shall soon have another companion in the fourth form. She arrives today.'

'Why is she so late in coming?' asked Pat, in surprise.

'She has just recovered from the measle,' said Mam'zelle, who always spoke of this illness in the singular and not in the plural. 'The measle is a most tiresome disease. Claudine had a very bad measle, and she could not come back any sooner.'

'Claudine?' said Isabel. 'What a pretty name! I like it.'

'Ah, and you will like the little Claudine too!' said Mam'zelle. 'For she is French. She is my niece!'

This was news to the girls. They hadn't even known that Mam'zelle had a niece. One coming to St Clare's too!

'I hope she will be happy at St Clare's,' said Hilary, feeling that someone ought to say the right thing.

'Ah, she will be very happy,' said Mam'zelle. 'She would be happy anywhere, the little Claudine. There never was such a child for happiness. Always she smiles and laughs, and always she plays the trick and the joke.'

This sounded good. The girls began to look forward to Claudine's coming. They looked at Mam'zelle expectantly, hoping to hear more.

Then Mam'zelle's face grew solemn. She pinched her glasses more firmly on her nose and gazed at the listening girls with her short-sighted, much-magnified eyes.

'I have especially asked for Claudine to come here,' she said. 'Before, she has been to a Convent School, but it was too strict for her, and always they found fault with the poor little Claudine. They said she cared nothing for anyone, nor for any rules or customs. And I thought to myself, "Ah, the good, hard-working Bobby was once like that – and see what St Clare's has done for her! Now she works for her finals and she is as good as gold! Maybe the same thing will happen to my little Claudine." '

Bobby looked uncomfortable as Mam'zelle made this speech. She wasn't at all sure that she wanted to be referred to as 'good as gold'. But Mam'zelle was so much in earnest that Bobby made no protest. It wouldn't have been any good, anyway! Mam'zelle swept on with her speech.

'And so the little Claudine comes today, well-recovered from the measle, and you will all give her a grand welcome, will you not? For your old Mam'zelle's sake?'

'Of course we'll make her welcome,' said Susan Howes, and most of the others murmured the same, except Angela, Alison and Pauline, who all put on a bored look, as if a niece belonging to Mam'zelle wasn't worth giving a thought to.

'Ah, you are good kind girls,' said Mam'zelle. 'I will

introduce Claudine to you as soon as she comes. She will love you all. She is a good girl though she seems to care nothing for what is good and proper. But you will change all that, *n'est-ce pas*?'

The girls thought that Claudine sounded distinctly amusing. It would be fun to have a French girl in the class! They glanced at one another, thinking that of all the new girls, this latest one sounded the most promising.

About five minutes before the lesson finished the door was opened, and a strange girl appeared. She was small, dark and smart. She had a very cheeky look and she gave a quick sidelong glance at the girls before advancing to Mam'zelle.

Mam'zelle gave a shriek, and then flung herself on the new girl. She kissed her several times on both cheeks, she stroked her dark hair, and poured out such a torrent of French that no one could follow it.

The girl replied in smooth, polite French, and kissed Mam'zelle on each cheek. She did not seem to mind her aunt's outburst in the least.

'Ah, *ma petite* Claudine, here you are at last!' cried Mam'zelle. She swung the girl round to face the class. 'Now see, here is the little Claudine,' said Mam'zelle, her glasses falling off her nose in her violent delight. 'Greet your new friends, Claudine.'

'Hallo, buddies!' said Claudine, amiably. The girls stared in surprise and then giggled. It was funny to hear such an American expression from the little French girl.

'What did you say?' said Mam'zelle, who was not well

up on American slang. 'Did you say, "Hallo, bodies"? That is not correct, Claudine. You should say, "Hallo, everybody." '

The class roared. Claudine grinned. Mam'zelle beamed. She was plainly very proud of Claudine and very fond of her.

The bell rang for the end of class. Mam'zelle picked out Hilary. 'Hilary, you will take the little Claudine with you, please, and show her everything. She will feel strange and shy, poor little one.'

Mam'zelle was quite mistaken about that, however. Claudine didn't feel shy, and certainly didn't seem to feel strange. In fact she acted as if she had known the girls all her life! She spoke easily and naturally to them. Her English was good, though, like Mam'zelle, she sometimes put things in an unusual way.

She had been to school in France, and then had spent a term or two at a convent school in England. It seemed that Claudine did not want to remain at her last school and they did not want to keep her.

'You see – it was most unfortunate – the science mistress went up a ladder into a tree to collect some curious fungus that grew there,' explained Claudine, in her little French voice. 'And I came along and borrowed the ladder. So we did not have a science lesson that day.'

'Golly! Do you mean to say that you left the teacher stranded up the tree?' said Bobby. 'Well, you have got a nerve! No wonder Mam'zelle thinks St Clare's will be good for you. You can't do that sort of thing here.'

'No?' said Claudine. 'What a pity. Still, maybe you have good fun. I am sorry I did not come back to school on the first day. But I had caught a measle.'

The girls giggled. Everyone liked Claudine, except Angela. Even Pauline listened to the new girl, and Alison was much amused by her. But Angela as usual looked down her nose.

'What did I tell you?' she said to Alison. 'First we have to have Matron's daughter, and now we have to have Mam'zelle's niece! I can't see what you find to be amused at in Claudine, Alison. I'm surprised at you.'

'Well, I like her voice and her manners,' said Alison. 'I like the way she uses her hands when she talks – just like Mam'zelle does. She's really quite amusing, Angela.'

Angela did not like Alison to disagree with her about anything. She looked coldly at her friend and then turned away sulkily. That was always the way she punished anyone – by withdrawing from them and sulking. Alison couldn't bear it.

Alison tried to make it up. She went after Angela, and took her hand. She praised her and flattered her, and at last Angela condescended to smile again on her willing slave.

Then Alison was happy. 'You needn't think I shall bother about Claudine at all,' she said to Angela. 'She's a common little thing, really.'

'Not so common as Carlotta,' said Angela, spitefully. Alison looked uncomfortable. She sincerely liked Carlotta, who was absolutely honest, truthful and straight, besides being amusing company. Even her hot temper was likeable. Alison thought that Carlotta was more completely herself, more natural than any of the other girls. And to be natural was to be very likeable.

Claudine settled in at once. She took a desk at the back of the room, and bagged a locker in the common-room. She arranged her belongings in the locker, and put a photograph of her mother on top. She had brought a fine big cake with her and shared it generously all round, though Angela refused a slice. Alison did too, after hesitating. She was afraid that Angela might go into a sulk again if she saw her sharing the cake.

At first the girls were very much amused with Claudine, but they soon discovered that she had very un-English ways. For instance, she thought nothing of copying from someone else's book! She had a quick brain, but she was often lazy – and then she would simply copy the answers set down by the girl next to her. This was Mirabel, whose brains were not of the highest order. So, more often than not, Claudine copied down mistakes. But she did not seem to mind at all.

'Look here – we oughtn't to let Claudine cheat like this,' said Pat. 'She keeps *on* copying from Mirabel. Mirabel says Claudine didn't bother to do a single sum – she copied the answers of all hers!'

'The funny thing is, she does it so openly,' said Isabel. 'I mean – I really don't believe she thinks it's wrong!'

Claudine was very astonished when Susan Howes, the head girl of the form, spoke to her about the copying.

'It's cheating, Claudine! Surely you can see that!' said Susan, her honest face glowing scarlet, for she did not like accusing anyone of cheating.

'No, I do not see it at all,' said Claudine. 'You all see me do it. Cheating is a secret thing.'

'No, it isn't,' said Susan. 'Cheating is cheating whether you do it in front of anyone, or on the sly. Besides, it's so silly of you to copy from Mirabel. She gets so many answers wrong. Miss Ellis will find out and then you'll get into a row.'

'You think then it would be better to copy from Hilary?' asked Claudine, seriously. Susan sighed.

'Claudine, you mustn't copy from *anyone*. I know French people have different ideas from ours – Mam'zelle has, for instance – but you'll have to try and get into our ways if you're going to be happy here.'

'I am happy anywhere,' said Claudine at once. 'Well, Susan, I will perhaps not copy again – only if I have not done any of my prep at all.'

Another thing that the girls found irritating about Claudine was the way she borrowed things. She borrowed pencils, rubbers, rulers, books – anything she happened to want at the moment. And nine times out of ten she didn't give them back.

'I forget,' she explained. 'I borrow a pencil and I use it, and I am most grateful for it – and then I forget about it, and poor Hilary, she says, "Where is my pencil, I have lost my pencil" – and there it is on my desk all the time, not at all lost.'

'Well, you might *try* and remember to give back things you borrow,' said Hilary. 'After all, it was a silver pencil of mine you borrowed, one I like very much. And you might ask permission before you borrow things.'

'Oh, you English!' sighed Claudine. 'Well, I will be good, and always I will say, "Dear Hilary, please, please lend me your so-beautiful silver pencil." '

Hilary laughed. No one could help being amused by Claudine. She rolled her expressive black eyes round and used her hands in the same way that Mam'zelle did. After all, she hadn't been in England very long – she would learn English ways before the term was over!

4

Beware of Matron!

The first few weeks passed, and soon the fourth formers, those who had come up from the third form, felt as if they had always been in the fourth form! They looked down on the third formers, and as for the second- and first-form girls, well, they were very small fry indeed. No fourth former would have dreamt of taking any notice of them.

The summer term was always a nice one. There was tennis, and there was swimming. Angela proved to be an unexpectedly good swimmer, deft and swift. Alison, who disliked the water, did her best to shine in it in order to try to keep up with her beloved Angela.

Claudine frankly hated the water. She entirely refused to go in, much to the games mistress's annoyance.

'Claudine! What is the use of coming to an English school if you do not learn the good things in it?' she said.

'Swimming is not a good thing,' said Claudine. 'It is a horrible thing, wet and cold and shivery. And I do not like your habit of playing so many games. Tennis is also silly.'

As no one could undress Claudine by force, she did not go into the water. The others teased her by splashing her as much as they could. The games mistress saw that sooner or later Claudine would be pushed in, fully-dressed, and she sent her back to the school.

Claudine's tennis was even worse than Carlotta's. Carlotta had never managed to play properly. She was still very wild and uncontrolled in games, and the tennis ball was quite as likely to drop into the middle of the distant swimming-pool as over the tennis net! But Claudine did not even attempt to hit the ball!

'This is a so-silly game,' she would say, and put down her racket and go off by herself.

'But Claudine, it's your tennis-practice time. You *must* come,' Hilary would say.

'I must not,' was Claudine's reply, and that was that.

Angela played a neat and deft game. She always brought her three beautiful rackets out with her, in spite of everyone's teasing. Pauline was jealous of them. She tried to pay Angela out by being spiteful.

'I've two or three more rackets at home,' she said in a loud voice. 'But it isn't good manners to bring more than one to school. My mother says that would be showing off. No well-bred person shows off.'

Nobody liked Angela's conceit, but nobody liked Pauline's spite, either. In fact, few people liked Pauline for, rich and grand as she made out her people and her home to be, she was a plain and unattractive girl – unlike Angela, who was really lovely. Nobody could help looking at the angel-faced Angela without admiration and pleasure. Alison thought she was the prettiest girl she had ever seen.

Eileen was moderately good at both tennis and

swimming. She was moderately good at her lessons too. She took a liking to Alison, for some reason or other, and was very upset when Alison showed her far too plainly that she had no time for her.

'*Why* can't you sometimes walk with me when we go out in the afternoons?' Eileen said to Alison. 'You can't *always* walk with Angela. And *why* do you always refuse when I offer you sweets? They won't poison you!'

'I know,' said Alison, coldly. 'I just don't want them, that's all. And I don't particularly want to walk with you, either.'

'I suppose Angela told you not to!' said Eileen, angrily. 'You haven't got any mind of your own, have you? Whatever Angela thinks, *you* think! Whatever Angela does, *you* do! You're even trying to grow your hair the way she grows hers – down to your shoulders and curled under. Well, you look a perfect fright like that!'

Alison was very offended. She looked coldly at Eileen.

'Well, if you want to know, Angela doesn't approve of you, and as she is my friend, I respect her wishes. Anyway, I don't approve of you, either. You're a tell-tale!'

Eileen walked away, her face scarlet with rage. Alison's last hit had gone home. Eileen ran to her mother with tales, and there was nothing the fourth form did that the new Matron did not know about.

Worse than that, if Eileen told her mother that someone had been horrid to her, the Matron soon saw to it that that someone was called to her room, and shown a huge rent in one of her bed sheets to mend, or holes in her games stockings, or buttons off clothes.

'I believe she makes the holes on purpose and pulls the buttons off herself!' raged Angela, who had been given three stockings to darn in her spare-time. 'I've never darned a stocking in my life. What's a matron for if she doesn't keep our things mended?'

'Well, it is the rule at St Clare's that we do some of our own mending,' said Pat. 'But I must say, Angela, I can't think that you made all those enormous holes in your stockings! I've never seen you with a hole yet.'

'Oh, I *know* I didn't make them,' said Angela, trying in vain to thread a needle with wool. '*How* do you make the wool go through the needle's eye? I've been trying to thread this for ages.'

The girls laughed. Angela had no idea how to double over the end of the wool and thread the darning needle in the right way. Alison took the needle and stocking away from her.

'I'll do your darning, Angela,' she said. 'Don't worry. I bet it's that tell-tale Eileen that ran to her mother about something you said or did – and so Matron gave you this work to do out of spite.'

Alison darned the three stockings – not very well, it is true, because darning was not one of Alison's gifts. But Angela was grateful, and was so sweet to Alison that the girl was in the seventh Heaven of delight.

Pauline was the next to get into trouble with Matron. She, like Angela, turned up her nose at Eileen, and would have no more to do with her than she could help. When she told Bobby one morning that she had a sore throat, Eileen overheard. She went off out of the room, and in a short while Pauline was sent for.

'I hear you have a sore throat, Pauline,' said Matron, with a thin-lipped smile. 'You should report to me at once. Eileen felt worried about you, and told me. It was very kind of her. I have a gargle for you here, and some medicine.'

'Oh, my throat is much better now,' said Pauline in alarm. And it was – but Matron was not going to let her off. She made poor Pauline gargle for ten minutes with a horrible concoction, and then gave her some equally nasty medicine to drink.

Pauline went back to the others, angry and afraid. She glanced round the room to make sure that Eileen was not there.

'Eileen's been telling tales again,' she said. 'She told her mother I'd got a sore throat – and I've just been having an awful time. I feel quite sick. I know Eileen told Matron she didn't like me, and that's why Matron gave me such a beastly time.'

'We'll have to be careful what we say and do to Eileen,' said Alison, scared, for she hated medicine of any sort. 'Perhaps we'd better be friendlier.'

'I shall not be friendlier,' said Claudine. 'That is a girl I do not like.'

And, far from being friendlier, Claudine really seemed to go out of her way to be rude to Eileen! The result was that Matron came down heavily on Claudine, and gave her a whole basketful of mending to do!

'You have torn the hem of both your sheets,' she told Claudine. 'And you have holes in all your stockings, and you need a patch in one of your blouses. You are a very naughty, careless girl. You will do most of this mending yourself, as a punishment.'

Claudine said nothing. She took the basket of mending and put it on top of her locker. At first the girls thought she would simply forget all about it, and refuse to do it, as she refused to do other things. But, to their surprise, Claudine took down the mending and settled herself in a corner of the common-room to do it.

Bobby watched her needle flying in and out. 'I say – you do sew beautifully!' she said. 'You really do! And your darning is as good as embroidery. It's beautiful.'

'I like sewing and darning,' said Claudine. 'We are always taught that well in France. You English girls are clumsy with your needles. You can bang all kinds of silly balls about, but you cannot make a beautiful darn!'

'Claudine, put that mending away now, and come out and swim,' said Susan. 'It's such a nice sunny day.'

But nice sunny days did not appeal to Claudine at all. 'I can see the sun out of the window,' she said, sewing away hard. 'Leave me. I like sewing.'

Bobby stared hard at the bent head of the little French girl. Then she gave a chuckle.

'Claudine, you like sewing a whole lot better than you like swimming and games, don't you?' she said.

'Yes,' said Claudine. 'Sewing is very OK, I think.'

The others laughed. Claudine always sounded funny

when she brought American slang into her speech.

'I believe this is all a little trick of Claudine's,' said Bobby. 'She wants to have a real excuse for getting out of games! We all know we have to give up games time if we have mending to do – and Claudine has made Matron give her a punishment that will get her out of games, and give her something to do instead that she really likes!'

Miss Ellis came into the room. 'Hurry up and go out, girls,' she said. 'Don't waste a minute of this nice fine day. Claudine, put away your sewing.'

'I'm sorry, Miss Ellis, but Matron said I was to do my darning and mending before I could go to play with the others,' said Claudine, looking up with big innocent dark eyes. 'It is very sad – but I suppose I must do this, Miss Ellis?'

'Hmm,' said Miss Ellis, not at all taken in by the wide-open eyes. 'I'll have a word with Matron.'

But Matron was quite insistent that Claudine had been careless, and must mend her things, so Miss Ellis left the girl to her sewing. And Claudine had a very nice time, sewing away happily in a corner of the sunny room, hearing the shouts of the girls in the swimming-pool. She had no wish whatever to join them!

Horrible wet cold water! she thought to herself, and then looked up as she heard footsteps coming into the room. It was her aunt, Mam'zelle.

'Ah, *ma petite*!' said Mam'zelle, beaming. 'So you are here. Let me see your sewing. It is beautiful! Why cannot these English girls sew? Where are the others?'

'In the water,' said Claudine, in French. 'Always they are in the water, or hitting a ball, these English girls. Me, I prefer to sew, *ma tante*!'

'Quite right, little Claudine!' said Mam'zelle, who, for all her years in England had never been able to understand why English girls liked cold water, hitting balls, and running madly about. 'You are happy, my little one?'

'Yes, thank you, *ma tante*,' answered Claudine demurely. 'But I am a little dull. Does nothing ever happen in these English schools?'

'Nothing,' said Mam'zelle. But she was wrong. Things did happen – and they were just about to!

5

Angela gets a surprise

About the third week of the term, when everyone had settled down, and got into their work, Angela had a surprise.

She had been playing tennis, and one of the balls had been lost. 'Don't let's bother to look for it now,' said Bobby, who hated to stop in the middle of a game. 'It's sure to turn up. Tennis-balls always do. If it doesn't we'll look for it afterwards.'

The ball hadn't turned up, and Angela had offered to look for it. The others had music-lessons to go to, or elocution practice. Angela was the only one free.

'All right,' said Hilary. 'Thanks, Angela. You look for the ball, and pop it back into the box with the others if you find it.'

The other three girls ran back to the school, and Angela began to look for the lost ball. It was nowhere to be seen. The court they had been playing on backed on to a high wall, and Angela wondered if the ball could possibly have gone over it.

'I remember Bobby sending a pretty high ball once,' she thought to herself. 'Well, it doesn't seem to be *this* side of the wall – so I'll just slip out of the garden gate here and look in the lane.'

The girl opened the gate and went out into the narrow green lane. She looked about for the ball, and at last saw it. As she went to get it, she gave a start of surprise. A tall, rather thin young lad was behind the bush near the ball.

Angela picked up the ball and was about to go back into the school grounds, when the boy spoke to her.

'I say – do you belong to St Clare's?'

Angela looked at him and didn't like him. He had hair that was curly, and much too long. His eyes were small and puffy underneath, and he was very pale.

'What business is it of yours whether I belong to St Clare's or not?' said Angela, in her haughtiest voice.

'Now look here – don't go all stuffy and stupid,' said the boy, coming out from behind the bush. 'I just want a word with you.'

'Well, I don't want a word with *you*,' said Angela, and she opened the garden gate. The boy tried to stop her going through.

'Wait a bit,' he said, and his voice sounded so urgent that Angela turned round in surprise. 'I want you to take a message to one of the girls for me,' he said.

'Of course I shan't do that,' said Angela. 'Let me pass, please. You deserve to be reported for this.'

'Listen. You tell Eileen that Eddie wants to see her,' said the boy. 'Wait – I've got a note for her. Will you give it to her?'

'Oh – so you're Eileen's brother, are you?' said Angela. 'All right – I'll give her the note. But I can't think why you don't come right in and see your mother and Eileen too, if you want to. Your mother is Matron here, isn't she?'

'Yes,' said Eddie. 'But for goodness' sake don't go and tell my mother you've seen me. She doesn't know I'm here. I'd get into an awful row with her if she knew I was.'

'Your mother gets lots of people into rows besides you!' said Angela, taking the note.

The girl went through the gate and shut it. Then she stuffed the note into the pocket of her blazer, meaning to give it to Eileen when she saw her.

Eileen was not about when Angela went back to the cloakroom to change her shoes. The girl saw Alison there and began to tell her what had happened.

'I say, Alison!' she said. 'A funny thing happened just now. I went out into the lane to look for a tennis-ball, and there was a boy there, hiding.'

'Gracious!' said Alison, startled. 'What did you do?'

'He was an awful creature,' said Angela, beginning to exaggerate, as she usually did when she had a tale to tell. 'Honestly, he looked like the boy who brings the fish here every day – you know, that awful boy with the too-long hair and the piercing whistle! I half expected him to say, "I've brought the 'addock and 'ake and 'alibut, miss!" like the fish-boy said to Matron the other day, thinking she was the cook.'

Alison laughed. So did one or two other girls in the cloakroom. Angela loved an admiring audience. She went on with her tale, not seeing that Eileen had come in to put away gym shoes.

'Well, he asked me if I belonged to St Clare's, and I put

him properly in his place, you may be sure! And then he told me who he was. You'll never guess!'

The girls crowded round her in interest. 'Who?' said Alison. 'How should we know who it was?'

'Well, it was dear, darling wonderful Eddie, Eileen's big brother!' said Angela. 'As common as could be! I nearly asked him why he didn't get his hair cut!'

Someone elbowed her way roughly through the group round Angela. It was Eileen, her cheeks scarlet. She glared at Angela.

'You frightful fibber!' she said. 'My brother's nowhere near St Clare's! How dare you make up a story like that? I shall go and tell my mother at once – you hateful, horrid little snob!'

She burst into tears and went out of the door. The girls stared after her.

'I say,' said Alison, 'she really *will* go to Matron – and there's sure to be a row. You didn't make it up, did you, Angela?'

Angela raised her voice and shouted after Eileen. 'Well, go and tell if you like – but your darling Eddie begged and begged me *not* to let your mother know he was here. So you are just as likely to get *him* into a row, as me!'

Eileen turned round, looking scared. It was plain that she now believed what Angela said. It *had* been Eddie!

'What did he say to you?' she asked Angela, in a strangled voice. 'Did he want to see me?'

'Shan't tell you,' said Angela, in an irritating voice. 'I *was* going to do you a good turn and give you his message

– but if you behave like this I'm jolly well not going to be a go-between for you and dear, darling Eddie!'

Just at that very thrilling moment Miss Ellis put her head in at the door, looking most annoyed.

'Girls! Didn't you hear the bell? What in the world are you doing, chattering here in the cloakroom? You know that isn't allowed. Really, I do wish you fourth formers would realize that you are half-way up the school and not in the first form! I am most annoyed at having to come and fetch you.'

'Sorry, Miss Ellis,' said everyone, and hurried to go out of the cloakroom back to the classroom, where they had prep to do. Certainly they had heard the bell – but who could tear themselves away when a first-class quarrel was going on between the angelic Angela and the unpopular Eileen?

Angela felt delighted when she sat down at her desk. Now she had Eileen exactly where she wanted her – under her thumb! And if Eileen ever told tales of her again and got Matron to give her heaps of mending to do, she, Angela, would threaten to tell Matron about dear Eddie! Angela smiled a secret smile to herself, which made her look more like an angel than ever. It was extraordinary how Angela could look so innocently beautiful when she was thinking spiteful thoughts!

Eileen saw the secret smile. She pursed her lips together and ground her teeth. She hated Angela bitterly in that moment, with as deep a hatred as the love she had for Eddie. How dared Angela call Eddie common? How dared she say he was like that horrid little fishmonger's boy, with his long, greasy hair and shrill whistle?

To Eileen, her brother Edgar was the most wonderful being in the world. Their father had died when they were both very young, and their mother was a hard and stern woman. The little girl had turned to her big brother for love and companionship, and the boy had guarded and cherished his sister tenderly.

'As soon as I grow up, I'll get a fine job, and make heaps of money for you and Mother,' he told Eileen. 'Then Mother won't need to work so hard and be so tired and cross, and you shall have lots of nice presents. You'll see what wonderful things I'll do!'

And now Angela had poured scorn on darling, kind Eddie. Eileen felt as if she must burst with anger and tears. She was very anxious too. Why had Eddie left Woolaton, where he worked, and come to see her secretly? What had happened? Oh, if only that beast of an Angela would tell her!

Eileen thought of Eddie out there in the lane. She had not seen him for some weeks, and she was longing to talk to him and tell him everything. Perhaps he felt the same and had got some time off to slip along and see her. Perhaps he didn't want to come up to the school, because then he would have to see Mother too, and that would spoil the heart-to-heart talk they might have together.

Eileen looked at Angela. The girl was studying her French book, looking serene and lovely. Eileen gritted her teeth again, knowing that she would soon have to do something very difficult, something she would hate, yet which would have to be done gracefully.

I'll have to go and beg Angela's pardon and ask her to tell me what Eddie said, thought Eileen. Beast! I do hate her!

She gave a loud sigh. Miss Ellis looked up. She had already seen that Eileen was making no attempt at all to do her prep.

'Eileen, don't you feel well?' she inquired. 'As far as I can see you haven't done any work at all.'

'I'm all right, thank you, Miss Ellis,' said Eileen hurriedly. 'This – this French is a bit difficult today, that's all.'

'I should think it must be *very* difficult to learn your French out of your geography book,' said Miss Ellis in her calm voice. Eileen looked hurriedly down at her book – dash – it was her geography book she was holding! Trust the sharp eyes of Miss Ellis to spot that!

She said nothing, but got out her French book. Angela looked round and gave a scornful little smile. She knew quite well why it was that Eileen muddled her books just then – she was worried about dear darling Eddie. Well – let her worry!

Alison sat next to Eileen, and she couldn't help feeling a little sorry for her. Although she was such a little scatter-brain, Alison was sensitive to the feelings of others, and she knew that Eileen was desperately longing to know about Eddie. So, after prep was over she went to Angela and spoke to her.

'I say, Angela – hadn't you better tell Eileen her

brother's message? She's in an awful state. She sighed so hard in prep that she almost blew my papers off the desk!'

Angela was not amused at Alison's feeble little joke, neither did she like her giving her advice of any sort. She turned away, and Alison's heart sank. Now Angela was going to go all cold and sulky again. The beautiful little face was hard and haughty, and Alison knew it would be ages before she could get a smile out of her again.

She was just going after her when Eileen came up, a forced smile on her face. 'Angela! Can I speak to you for a minute? Alone, please?'

6

Angela and Eileen

'I'm busy,' said Angela, curtly.

'No, you're not,' said Eileen, trying to speak calmly and smilingly. 'It's important, Angela.'

'I hope you're going to apologize for your rudeness to me,' said Angela, haughtily. 'I certainly shan't speak to you unless you do. I'm not going to let people like you call me a hateful horrid snob.'

Eileen swallowed hard and forced herself to speak, though the words almost choked her.

'I beg your pardon, Angela. I – I just lost my temper!'

Carlotta overheard this conversation and unexpectedly came to Eileen's help. 'Well, if you ask *my* opinion I think Angela ought to apologize to *you*, Eileen, for some of *her* remarks!' said Carlotta, in her fresh, candid voice. 'I'm jolly certain I wouldn't apologize to *her* – little cat!'

Angela turned on Carlotta in a fury, her blue eyes gleaming with spite.

'You don't suppose we care what circus folk think, do you?' she said. But instead of being crushed, Carlotta gave one of her hearty laughs.

'If I wasn't in the fourth form I'd give you the biggest scolding you've ever had in your life, Angela,' she said, amiably. 'A good scolding would be the best thing you could have.'

'Nobody has ever raised their voice to me in my life,' said Angela, feeling an intense desire to smack Carlotta's vivid little face.

'I can tell that,' said Carlotta. 'You'd be a lot nicer if they had. Come on, Eileen, leave Angela to her haughty ways and come and play cards with me in the common-room.'

Eileen felt very grateful to Carlotta for her unexpected help, but she shook her head. She had simply *got* to find out about Eddie. How unfortunate it was that it should be Angela, of all people, that he had spoken to. Any of the others would have been decent about it – except Pauline perhaps.

Carlotta shrugged her shoulders and went off to find Bobby and the twins. She didn't like Eileen very much, because she thought, as the others did, that she was a tell-tale – but all the same Angela was behaving like a little cat to her, putting out those claws of hers and giving as deep a scratch as she could!

Angela turned to Eileen. 'Well,' she said, 'you've apologized and I accept your apology. What do you want to say to me?'

'Angela, *please* tell me what Eddie said,' begged Eileen. 'Did he give you a message for me?'

'Yes. He gave me a letter,' said Angela. Eileen went red with excitement and stared at Angela eagerly.

'Please give it to me,' she said.

'I don't see why I should,' said Angela. 'I don't think I

ought to take notes and deliver them, like this.'

Eileen knew that Angela was saying this to irritate her. She felt intensely angry, but she kept her temper.

'You'll never have to do it again,' she said. 'I'll tell Edgar he mustn't send in notes this way. He must post a letter. Please give me the note.'

'Now, listen,' said Angela, suddenly getting down to business, 'if I give you this note and don't tell your mother I saw her precious Eddie, you've got to promise *me* something.'

'What?' asked Eileen, in surprise. 'I'll promise you anything!'

'All right,' said Angela. 'You've jolly well got to promise me that you'll never run sneaking to your mother about *me*, see? I'm not going to have shoals of mending to do any more – I hate sewing and darning! I know you complained to Matron about me before, and that's why she presented me with stockings that had holes in *I* never made!'

'You're not to say things like that about my mother,' said Eileen.

'Well, I shall,' said Angela. 'We all know you sneak to her about us. Sneak about the others all you like – but don't you sneak about *me* any more. You'll be sorry if you do.'

There was nothing for it but to promise. So Eileen promised. 'I won't sneak about you,' she said in a trembling voice. 'I don't sneak. If Mother hands out sewing and mending, it's not my fault.'

'Hmm,' said Angela, disbelievingly, 'well, all I can say is – it's a funny thing that as soon as anyone dares to say anything about you, Matron heaps a beastly lot of mending on to them, so that they have to miss games and swimming. Anyway, Eileen, I warn you – you've got to tell your mother nice things about me, or I'll tell tales of *you*, and say I've seen Eddie and he didn't want his mother to know!'

Eileen bit her lip. It was very hard to keep her temper during this long speech. But she knew she had to, for Eddie's sake.

'I've apologized to you, Angela, and I've promised you what you want,' she said, in a low voice. 'Please give me the note now.'

Angela fished in her pocket for the note. She was a long time about it, pretending she had lost it, feeling in her blouse for it as well as in her pockets. Eileen hated her for this petty meanness, but she stood waiting patiently whilst Angela looked.

At last Angela produced the note. Eileen snatched it from her and without another word went off by herself to read it. It was very short.

Darling Sis, [said the note]
I must see you. Don't say a word to Mother. We simply must have a talk. Can you meet me outside the garden-door in the wall, any time this evening? I'll wait behind a bush till you come.
Your loving brother,
Eddie.

Eileen read the note three times and then tore it up. She was afraid her mother might find it, and then she would be angry with Eddie. Mother wasn't very sympathetic, somehow. She didn't seem to think much of Eddie, and was always telling him what a fine man his father had been and how curious it was that Eddie hadn't been much good at school, or won any scholarships, or made her really proud of him.

I'll slip down to the garden-door and see Eddie as soon as all the others are safely in the common-room, thought Eileen. Poor old Eddie – he must have been waiting a long time. He couldn't send a letter through the post, because Mother would have been sure to see it, and would have asked to read it.

The girl waited until she saw that all the fourth formers were in their common-room. She sat by the door and watched them. Doris and Carlotta were fooling about and the others were watching them, laughing. Claudine got up to join the two who were clowning, and Eileen saw that now was her chance. She slipped out.

But one person saw her go. That was Angela, who had been expecting Eileen to slip away down to the lane. It was forbidden for the girls to go out of the school grounds without permission after evening prep, and Angela smiled spitefully to herself.

If Eileen makes a habit of meeting dear brother Eddie out of hours, I shall be able to hold that over her, too, thought Angela. She went out of the room and walked into a little music-room that overlooked the school grounds. It was difficult to see anyone in the trees and bushes, but because she knew exactly where to look, Angela was able to catch a glimpse of Eileen now and again, hurrying through the trees to the little gate in the wall.

She went back to the common-room. Doris, Carlotta and Claudine were still fooling about, keeping everyone in fits of laughter. Doris was a wonderful mimic, Carlotta could do extraordinary tricks, and Claudine could imitate Mam'zelle, her aunt, to perfection.

Angela could not see anything to laugh at at all. Do they really think it's funny, to pull faces and make themselves ugly and stupid-looking? she thought to herself, as she watched Doris imitating an old charwoman, and Claudine playing up to her as a French maid. She patted her beautiful pale gold hair, comparing it with Carlotta's wild mop. A smug little smile came to her lovely face. She knew she was more beautiful than any other girl in the school! What did brains and gifts matter? Everyone stared at her in the street, everyone thought she must be a princess at least. And perhaps one day she would marry a prince and be a real princess! Angela dreamt away, not listening to the chatter around her at all.

Two people watched her, one with envy and the other with devoted admiration. The first was Pauline, who, plain and unattractive, envied Angela her beauty, and longed with all her heart to look like her. But her own perfectly straight hair, well-brushed as it was, would never shine like Angela's, nor would it curl under at the ends, as Angela's did, so prettily. Angela's eyes were a brilliant, startling blue – Pauline's were pale. Angela's cheeks were a beautiful rosy pink. Pauline's seldom had any colour. It was too bad that Angela had so much and she, Pauline, had so little in the way of looks!

The other person watching Angela, was, of course, her devoted slave, Alison. She wondered if Angela had forgiven her for offering advice about Eileen. She tried to catch Angela's eye, but Angela was lost in beautiful day-dreams.

'You do look so lovely, Angela,' whispered Alison, at last. Angela heard and smiled prettily. She had forgotten that she was offended with Alison. She spoke to her in a low voice, boasting of her conquest of Eileen.

'I ticked Eileen off properly for being a sneak,' she said to Alison. 'I forbade her ever to sneak again, and she promised she wouldn't.'

'Oh, Angela – did you really make her promise that?' said Alison. 'You're wonderful, you really are!' She looked round the common-room. 'I say – where *is* Eileen?'

'Would you like to know?' said Angela, looking at the expensive gold watch on her wrist, and seeing that there were only five minutes to go before bed-time. 'Well, come with me and I'll see if I can show you where our dear Eileen is!'

She took Alison into the little music-room. 'See the school wall, right down there?' she said. 'You know the little door let into it there, behind the tennis-courts? Well, I think Eileen has gone through there into the lane to talk to dear, darling Eddie!'

'Look – is that Eileen coming back?' said Alison. 'Golly, she'll get into a row if she's caught!'

'Yes – it's Eileen all right,' said Angela, as a figure came into view between the trees and then disappeared again. 'Let's wait outside the common-room door and catch her as she comes in!'

So the two waited there. Eileen came quickly up the passage to the room, and Angela spoke to her.

'Well – how's dear darling Eddie?'

Eileen stared at her, hardly seeming to see her. She looked pale and worried. She pushed at the shut door of the common-room, meaning to go and fetch her night-dress, which she had been mending. But Angela stopped her.

'You didn't answer my question,' she said, in a smooth little voice. 'How's dear darling Eddie?'

Eileen faced the spiteful girl. 'Eddie's all right,' she said, in a trembling voice. 'Eddie's fine. He had lots of good news to tell me. He's getting on well.'

She went into the common-room. Alison felt uncomfortable again. She didn't like this teasing, there was something spiteful in it – but how could she dare to find fault with the Honourable Angela?

7

Claudine gets her own way

'This is a jolly nice term,' said Pat to Isabel, as they dried themselves after swimming in the big swimming-pool. 'I simply adore all this open-air life – tennis and swimming and riding and gardening – and today we even had lessons out-of-doors, it was so hot!'

Isabel grinned. 'Poor old Claudine doesn't like the open air as much as we do!' she said. 'Wasn't she funny in maths?'

Claudine had indeed been funny. To begin with she had been quite horrified to hear that Miss Ellis proposed to take lessons out-of-doors under the trees. Apparently no school she had ever been to had ever thought of doing such a thing.

'Lessons out-of-doors!' said the little French girl. 'But why? What is the matter with indoors? I do not like this out-of-doors – the sun is too hot, it burns me.'

'Pity it doesn't burn you a bit more,' grinned Bobby, who was as brown as an acorn. 'Look at us, all brown and tanned – and you are like a lily, pale and white.'

Claudine looked down at her lily-white hands with great satisfaction. 'That is another thing I do not understand about you so-jolly English girls,' she said. 'It is not pretty to get burnt, it is ugly to grow freckles – and yet you try to grow as tanned as you can, all day long! Me, I like to be pale. It is more natural, more becoming. And now – what can Miss Ellis be thinking of to say lessons out-of-doors! I shall take a sunshade with me, for I will not grow one single freckle.'

But Miss Ellis did not approve of sunshades being brought out in a maths lesson. She looked at Claudine with disapproval. 'I don't know if you are merely being funny, Claudine, or if you seriously think that you need a sunshade under the trees, where there is no sun – but whatever your reason, the sunshade must go back to the school at once. I can't imagine where you got it!'

The sunshade had been used in a play, and was simply enormous. Claudine was quite lost under it. She looked at Miss Ellis pathetically.

'Please, *chère* Miss Ellis, I am not making a joke, it is because I do not wish to grow a freckle on my nose,' she said, beseechingly. 'A freckle is not for a French girl. Freckles are English, Miss Ellis, and I do not want to grow them.'

'Oh, freckles can be French as much as English!' said Miss Ellis. 'It will do your pale face good to have a few nice freckles here and there, Claudine. Take the sunshade back, please, and don't bring it out again.'

'Oh, please, Miss Ellis, couldn't Claudine and I share the sunshade?' said Angela, who also had a fear of freckles. Her face was tanned a rosy-brown, and she had no freckles at all – she was careful not to get too sunburnt, for she knew that would spoil her delicate beauty.

She gave Bobby's face a scornful glance. It was absolutely covered with little brown freckles, right to the tip of the up-turned nose. 'I couldn't bear to get freckled like poor Bobby,' went on Angela, no spite showing in her smooth little voice. 'This sun is so hot, Miss Ellis – just see how it has treated Bobby!'

'Don't you believe it,' said Bobby, not standing any nonsense of that sort. 'My face is freckled winter and summer alike. Nothing to do with the summer sun! I was born with freckles!'

The class giggled, and Bobby opened her mouth to continue. But Miss Ellis knew Bobby's speeches, and spoke first!

'That will do, Bobby. I don't want any more of the maths lesson wasted on freckles. Claudine, take the sun-shade back. Angela, don't look as if you are going to faint away – it would do both you and Claudine good to get a few freckles – Claudine because she sits too much indoors, and you because you think too much of your looks. It would be better if you thought a little more about your work. You may think it is amusing to be bottom each week, as you have been so far, but I must say I can't see the joke.'

Angela flushed. How horrid Miss Ellis could be! She caught a satisfied smile on Pauline's face. Pauline was cleverer than Angela – that was one way in which she was better than Angela, anyhow! Angela scowled and glanced at Alison for comfort. Alison gave it, smiling adoringly, and making a face at Miss Ellis.

Lessons out-of-doors were not a success at all, with Claudine in the class. She screamed whenever an insect flew near, and if a bird dared to fly suddenly out of a bush, she made everyone jump by her yells. Miss Ellis got very tired of her.

'*Now* what's the matter, Claudine?' she said, when a bee flew near the girl and hummed in her ear. Claudine had squealed, jumped up and run to the other end of the long table on which everyone was working.

'It is an animal that goes "Zzzz" and carries a sting, Miss Ellis,' said Claudine, looking genuinely frightened.

'A bee,' said Miss Ellis, in disgust. 'It won't sting you. Sit down. You are disturbing all the others.'

The next thing that upset Claudine was an ant. It crawled up her leg and she suddenly felt it. She gave such an agonized yell that everyone jumped violently.

'CLAUDINE! I shall send you indoors if you squeal again!' said Miss Ellis in exasperation. 'What's the matter now?'

Claudine was undoing her suspender with trembling hands, giving little squeals and French exclamations all the time. The ant had explored the inside of the top of her stocking. The girls went into fits of laughter, and Miss Ellis rapped angrily on her table.

'Claudine, what are you doing? Surely you are not taking off your stockings!'

Claudine was deaf to anything that Miss Ellis said. When she at last saw the ant, inside her stocking, she did not dare to touch it, and gazed round with such an agonized expression on her face that Bobby took pity on her, and flicked the ant deftly on to the grass.

'Ah!' said Claudine. '*Merci bien*, Bobbee! What a terrible thing to happen to me!'

'Much more terrible things will happen to you if I have any more disturbance,' said Miss Ellis, in such a grim tone that Claudine was much astonished. She sat down again, doing up her suspender.

'One more squeal from you and you go indoors,' said Miss Ellis. Claudine gazed at her thoughtfully. If there was one thing more than another that Claudine wanted at that moment it was to go indoors, where creatures that flew and crawled did not molest her.

She waited until Miss Ellis had bent her head to correct Hilary's book, and then she let out a piercing yell that made her neighbour, Pauline, jump so violently that she upset the ink over the table. Miss Ellis leapt to her feet, her usual calmness quite deserting her.

'Claudine! This behaviour is intolerable. Go indoors at once and find the mistress in the teachers' common-room who is free at the moment. Tell her I sent you in in disgrace and ask her to let you sit with her, whilst you do your maths. And if there is a single mistake in your paper I shall have a great deal to say about it. I am thoroughly displeased with you.'

With the greatest cheerfulness and alacrity Claudine obeyed Miss Ellis, scurrying indoors with her books before the mistress could change her mind. Doris exploded into one of her giggles. Miss Ellis glanced at her sharply, and Doris subsided. It then occurred to Miss Ellis that

Claudine, as usual, had got exactly what she wanted, in her usual unscrupulous way!

Miss Ellis wondered who the mistress was who would be in the teachers' common-room just then. She thought it would be Miss Rollins. That was good. Miss Rollins was very strict, and would make Claudine feel very small and humble before she had done with her.

But it was not Miss Rollins, much to Claudine's delight. When she knocked timidly on the mistresses' common-room door, she ran over in her mind what mistress was likely to be there. She hoped it would be the art mistress – she had a sense of fun and was very jolly.

She opened the door and went in – and she saw that it was Mam'zelle! Mam'zelle was having a cosy time by herself. She had taken off her big, flat-heeled shoes and had opened the collar of her high-necked blouse. It was such a hot day! She was half-asleep over her exercise books when the small neat figure of Claudine appeared. They stared at each other.

'Why are you here, Claudine?' asked Mam'zelle severely, in French. Claudine at once poured out a voluble and heart-rending explanation – how all the insects and winged beasts of that horrible English out-of-doors had molested her, yes, and bitten her and stung her, and altogether made life not worth living. And the sun had burnt her and she was sure she had dozens of those so-ugly freckles coming, and what would her dear mother say to that? Ah, life was very very hard at this so-sporting English school, with its love for the cold, cold water, and for striking at balls so many times a week, and for its detestable nature-walks, and . . .

Mam'zelle sympathized whole-heartedly. She too detested too much sun, and insects and reptiles of any kind filled her with fear and disgust. She forgot to inquire whether Claudine had come in of her own accord, or had been sent in in disgrace. Soon the two were talking nineteen to the dozen, going back in their thoughts to their beloved France, where girls were proper girls, and studied and did sewing and embroidery, and did not rush about in the mad way that all English girls did.

So, later on, when Miss Ellis asked Mam'zelle if she had scolded Claudine properly for being sent indoors in disgrace, Mam'zelle got a shock. She stared at Miss Ellis in dismay.

'Ah, the poor little Claudine!' she said at last. 'You must not be too hard on her, Miss Ellis. It is so difficult for a poor little French girl to learn your English ways.'

Miss Ellis snorted. 'I suppose that means that you and Claudine patted each other on the back, and that you believed everything the naughty little girl said – and I should think it is very likely that you helped her to do her maths too! She has never got all her sums right before.'

Mam'zelle felt extremely uncomfortable. She *had* helped Claudine with her work – and certainly she had believed every word she said. Would Claudine deceive her own good aunt? No, no – impossible!

But when Mam'zelle thought things over she knew that the clever little Claudine could and would deceive her if she felt inclined to. Mam'zelle loved Claudine very much, and thought the world of her – but all the same sometimes a doubt came into her mind – wasn't Claudine just a little *too* clever? Didn't she get her own way just a little *too* often? The trouble was – you never knew what Claudine wanted until she had got it, and then it was too late to do anything about it.

'My word,' said Bobby, when the maths lesson came to an end and the girls packed up their books. 'That little monkey of a Claudine can do anything she likes and get away with it! I bet she's had a perfectly lovely time indoors.'

So she had. She came beaming to meet Miss Ellis at the end of the morning, with a prettily worded apology.

'Ah, Miss Ellis! I am so, so ashamed of myself. You English, you are not frightened of anything, you keep the hairs on your head always, always you are calm – but me, I am a silly little French girl, so please excuse me and I will do better in future. My aunt was very, very angry with me, she caused me to cry bitterly, see how red my eyes are!'

Miss Ellis saw no signs of red eyes, and felt quite certain that Mam'zelle had not been angry at all. All the same, she found it difficult to hide a smile. Claudine was so very, very earnest and apologetic!

'I'll forgive you *this* time, Claudine,' she said. 'But you be careful *next* time!'

8

The term goes on

Although the girls knew quite well that Claudine told fibs when it suited her, borrowed without asking and still copied answers from other people's books if she wanted to, they couldn't help liking her. She was very funny, generous in her own way, and never took offence whatever was said to her.

She might easily have taken offence at things that Angela said, or Pauline. Angela looked down on her in the same way that she looked down on Eileen – because she was a pupil who was probably not paying the school fees.

'Charity girls, both of them!' she said to Alison, scornfully. 'I must say I didn't think we'd get them at schools like this.'

If Bobby, Hilary or the twins overheard things like this they ticked Angela off unmercifully.

'Look here,' Pat said once, 'we don't like Eileen any more than you do – but you've got to realize, Angela, that if Eileen's mother gets Eileen here for nothing, it's because of the work she does herself as Matron, and it doesn't matter tuppence if you pay for things in work or in money, it's good payment just the same, and Eileen isn't kept by "charity" as you call it. You're a disgusting little snob.'

Angela hated to be called a snob. She shut her book with a bang. 'Snob!' she said. 'That's a favourite word of yours for someone who happens to be out of the top drawer. Think of something more original to say.'

'Right,' said Bobby, at once. 'You think that Claudine is a charity girl too – well, instead of saying that to us, what about saying it to Mam'zelle – or even to Claudine herself? You're too cowardly to do that. You'll hit at Eileen because you've got some hold over her and she can't hit back – but you daren't hit at Claudine openly, because she's quite likely to fly at you and scratch your angelic face, or put Mam'zelle on the war-path after you!'

'Oh, you're impossible!' said Angela, angrily. 'I shall ask my mother to take me away at half-term. In fact, when she comes here and sees what kind of girls I have to live with, I'm certain she'll take me away with her, then and there!'

'Golly! If only your mother would be sensible enough to *do* that!' sighed Bobby. 'But she won't. I know mothers. She'll leave you here to be a pest to us for the rest of the term.'

Tears of anger came into Angela's eyes. In all her spoilt, petted life she had never been spoken to like this. She was angry, hurt, and miserable. She blinked back her tears, because a tear-stained face spoilt her beauty. She went to find Alison.

Alison could always put soothing ointment on Angela's wounds. In her usual feather-headed way she made herself quite blind to Angela's grave faults, and saw only the loveliness of Angela's face, and the beauty of her clothes and possessions. Poor Alison always seemed to attach herself to the wrong kind of people.

'She'll never learn!' said Hilary. 'I did think once, when she was in the second form, and was so keen on that awful drama mistress, Miss Quentin, that she had learnt a pretty sharp lesson – you remember how Miss Quentin let her down, don't you? She pretended to be awfully fond of Alison, and then laughed at her behind her back.'

The twins nodded. 'Yes,' said Pat. 'It's really a pity that Alison isn't happy unless she is worshipping someone. She's awfully bad for Angela. As soon as we get a bit of sense into Angela's head, Alison gets it out, by saying she's wonderful, too lovely for words, and all the rest of it.'

'I must say she's not a bit like you two,' said Bobby. 'You've got plenty of common sense. It's funny you should have a cousin like Alison!'

The weather went on being hot and sunny, with blue skies everyday. The girls swam and played games to their hearts' content. They all got very brown, except Claudine, who managed to remain pale as a lily in spite of everything. She worried very much one week because she felt sure she had a freckle coming on her nose. The girls teased her unmercifully.

'Golly! Isn't Claudine's freckle getting pronounced?' said Hilary, staring at Claudine's dainty little nose.

'Yes. It's going to be a real beauty,' said Pat.

'Big as a penny piece,' said Isabel.

Claudine gave a squeal of horror and fished out the

little mirror she always carried with her. She and Angela and Alison always carried small mirrors about with them, and were for ever examining their faces for something or other.

'I have no freckle,' she announced indignantly. 'You talk under your hats!'

The girls laughed. 'Claudine, you talk *through* your hat, not under it,' said Bobby. 'But if you want to keep a secret you keep it *under* your hat! See?'

Claudine sighed. 'Ah, your English sayings are so difficult. I will remember – to talk *through* your hat means to be silly – to keep something *under* your hat means to keep a secret. Ah – there goes one who keeps something under her hat!'

The girls turned to see who Claudine meant. It was Eileen Paterson.

'Yes – Eileen does seem to be all bottled up, somehow,' said Hilary, rather worried. 'As if she's got a secret and is afraid someone will get to know it. She's been looking rather miserable sometimes.'

'Well, she's got her mother here to tell anything to,' said Pat. The others made scornful noises.

'Pooh!' said Bobby. 'Would *you* tell Matron anything if she were *your* mother? I know I wouldn't. She's as hard as nails! I hope to goodness I'm never ill whilst she's here as Matron. I shouldn't fancy being looked after by her!'

The girls were all rather careful in the way they treated Eileen now, because they felt certain that any slight, intended or otherwise, that they showed Eileen was reported to Matron, and then Matron landed them with all kinds of unexpected mending to do. All except Angela. Angela could say and do what she liked to Eileen. Matron always seemed to look on Angela with a favourable eye. Eileen did not dare to tell tales of her.

'I think Eileen misses that dear brother of hers,' said Bobby. 'You know what Angela told us – how he came to see her, but didn't want to see his mother. I bet he's in some kind of trouble, and Eileen's worried about it.'

'Poor Eileen!' said Hilary. 'I'll just pump her a bit and see.'

So Hilary kindly and tactfully 'pumped' Eileen, but she learnt very little.

'How old is your brother, Eileen?' she said. 'Is he like you at all?'

Eileen fetched a snapshot and showed it to Hilary. She seemed glad of the chance of talking about Eddie.

'Eddie's eighteen,' she said. 'Two years older than I am. He's fine, Hilary. But he's never had much chance. You see, my father died when we were so little. Eddie ought to be at college now, but he's got to earn his living.'

Hilary looked at the snap of the rather weak-looking boy in the picture. He looked kind but that was about all one could say.

'What work is he doing?' she asked.

'He's in engineering works,' Eileen said. 'He's doing awfully well. He'll make a lot of money one day.'

'You're not worried about him, are you?' said Hilary, kindly, looking at the flushed face of the girl beside her.

Eileen answered at once. 'Worried about him? Of course not! Why should I be? I wish I saw him more often, that's all. You see, until this term, when Mother took this job, we all lived together. Now he's in lodgings and I do miss him a lot.'

Hilary said no more. She still thought that Eileen looked worried, and certainly she did not pay as much attention to her lessons as Miss Ellis expected – but after all, thought Hilary, it was enough to make anyone look worried if they had to listen to Matron's grumbles in their spare-time!

Eileen had to help her mother with the school linen every week, and sometimes when the girls passed Matron's room they could hear her grumbling away at Eileen. True, Eileen answered back sometimes, but usually she listened in silence. Some of the girls felt sorry for Eileen, others were glad, because they knew she was a tale-teller when it suited her to pass on things she had heard in the fourth form.

Another week or two went by, and half-term began to come near. Three or four fourth-form birthdays came along too, and there was a good deal of present-buying.

Angela had unlimited pocket-money and bought most extravagant presents. Pauline tried to vie with her and to buy marvellous gifts too. But it was impossible to spend as much as Angela did! She thought nothing of spending two pounds on a bottle of bath salts or a lace-edged handkerchief.

Eileen gave no presents at all. 'Sorry,' she said to

Hilary, whose birthday it was. 'I'd like to give you something – but I've no money at the moment. Many happy returns of the day, anyway!'

'Thanks,' said Hilary, thinking that Eileen could be very straightforward and honest, and liking her at that moment for being courageous enough to own up to having no money at all.

Angela presented Hilary with a magnificent blotter, made of real leather, and decorated very beautifully at the corners. Hilary liked it very much. Then Pauline presented her with a purse on which were Hilary's initials, H.W.W.

'Oh, Pauline – how beautiful!' said Hilary. 'But I wish you wouldn't spend so much money on me! I'm sure you can't afford it!'

This was an unfortunate remark to make to Pauline, who was very touchy about money, and was always trying to compete with Angela. She flushed and answered stiffly.

'You know that my family, the Bingham-Joneses, are wealthy,' she said, putting on the affected voice that Hilary detested. 'I have as much money as I wish. It's true I don't splash it about in the vulgar way that Angela does – I hope I am better bred than that. But I have all I ask for, Hilary, so please accept this purse with my best wishes, and don't think it cost any more than I could afford!'

'What with the Bingham-Joneses and the Honourable Favorleighs we're just overwhelmed with high-and-mightiness!' said Pat to Isabel, with a giggle. 'Well – I think I prefer Pauline of the two – Angela is really too spiteful for words, sometimes – and she says the cattiest things with the most angelic smile on her face!'

'I can't say I think a great deal of any of the four new girls, considering everything,' said Isabel, wrinkling her forehead and thinking. 'Angela's a spiteful snob. Pauline is an envious snob. Claudine is amusing but quite unscrupulous – hasn't any sense of honour at all, as far as I can see – and Eileen is a sneak and a bit of a bore!'

'Golly – you sound pretty catty yourself, Isabel!' said Pat.

'No, I'm not,' said Isabel, earnestly. 'I'm only just sizing them all up. I'm not like Alison, unable to see beyond a pretty face. And though I don't think much of any of those four, you know jolly well I'd help every one of them if they were in trouble. And if you're really catty, you don't feel like that, do you?'

'No, you don't,' said Pat. 'You're quite right, old thing – it doesn't matter seeing people for what they are, and even disliking them – so long as you're willing to help if necessary!'

9

Preparing for half-term

Half-term came along very shortly, and the girls were excited because their parents were coming to see them. There were to be tennis matches and swimming for the parents to watch. Hilary, Bobby, the twins and one or two others were excited about these, because they hoped to be in the teams.

'I'd like my mother to see me swim under water for the whole length of the pool,' said Bobby. 'She was a very good swimmer herself when she was young. Hope I'm chosen for the swimming competitions.'

The twins hoped to be in one of the tennis matches. They were both good at tennis, and it would be lovely for their mother to see them play together and win a match. Both girls were intensely proud of St Clare's, and badly wanted to show off their school, and their own prowess to the best advantage.

Hilary was to play in a singles match with one of the fifth formers. She had been chosen for her very graceful style, and it was to be an exhibition match more than a battle. Both girls had a beautiful natural style and the games mistress was proud of them.

Mirabel was hoping to win the one-length race in the

swimming. She was very fast and very strong. Her smaller friend, the mouse-like Gladys, was also in the swimming competitions for, although she was small, she was a beautiful little swimmer. She was longing for her mother to see her. She had no father and no brother or sister, so her mother was everything to her.

'Half-term will be fun,' said Hilary. 'Is your mother coming, Angela?'

'Of course,' said Angela. 'And Daddy too. I'm longing to see their new car. It's a Rolls Royce, black with a green line, and . . .'

'I bet you're looking forward to seeing the new car more than to seeing your people!' said Bobby, with a chuckle. 'You never talk of your parents except in terms of the wealth they own, Angela. Did you know that?'

Angela looked sulky. 'I don't know what you mean,' she said. 'I guess you'd talk about cars and things if your parents had the same as mine. And you just see my mother when she comes! She will stand out above everyone else. She's absolutely beautiful – golden hair like mine – and the bluest eyes – and she wears the most marvellous clothes . . .'

'And even the safety-pins she uses are made of pure gold set with diamonds,' finished Pat.

'That's not funny,' said Angela, as the others shouted with laughter. 'I tell you, you just wait and see my mother! She's the most beautiful person you'll ever see.'

'*What* a pity you don't take after her, Angela!' said Bobby, sorrowfully. 'Isn't your mother sorry to have a daughter like you? You must be a terrible disappointment.'

Angela flushed with anger. She could never bear this kind of teasing. 'All right,' she said, in a bitter voice. 'All right. But just wait till you see my mother – and then tell me if she isn't the most wonderful person you ever saw in your lives. I hope she wears her double-string of pearls. They are worth five thousands pounds.'

'Well,' said the soft voice of Gladys, who rarely butted in on any conversation of this sort, 'well, I don't care if *my* mother wears her very oldest clothes, I don't care if she's got a ladder in her stockings, I don't care if she hasn't even powdered her nose – so long as my mother comes to see me and I can be with her for a few hours, she can be the untidiest, ugliest, poorest-dressed there – but I shall still be proud of her, and think she's the best of all!'

This was a long speech for the timid Gladys to make. Everyone was silent when she stopped. Pat found that she suddenly had tears in her eyes. There was such love in Gladys's voice – and what she said was fine. That was the way to love someone – not to care how they looked or what they did – but just to welcome them all the same!

Even Angela was taken aback. She stared at Gladys in surprise. She was about to make a sneering remark but Bobby stopped her.

'Now you shut up,' said Bobby, in a warning voice. 'Gladys has said the last word about mothers, and she's right. Good for you, Gladys.'

After that Angela said no more, but privately she rejoiced when she thought of her own beautifully dressed mother, and how the girls would have to admire her and her clothes when she came.

'Are *your* parents coming?' said Hilary to Pauline.

'Oh, yes,' said Pauline, in a bright voice, and she began to talk eagerly of them. 'My father is such a good-looking man, and Mother is sweet. I do hope she wears the dress she bought in the holidays – it's really beautiful. It makes her look so young and pretty.'

Pauline chattered away about her parents, in her way as much of a snob as Angela, though, far more than Angela, she talked of them as real people, generous, kind, amusing, instead of people cluttered up with great possessions.

'Pauline's people sound rather nice,' said Pat. 'I shall take a good look at Angela's family – I sort of feel that her father will wear diamond buttons on his coat and her mother will wear the crown jewels!'

Isabel giggled. 'Well, I'm rather glad that our mother is just ordinary,' she said, 'pretty and kind and sensible, just an ordinary nice mother!'

The girls all practised hard for half-term, swimming and playing tennis as much as they could, so that their parents might be proud of them. There was to be an exhibition of pictures too, done by the girls themselves, and a show of needlework. Here Claudine expected to shine. She had done a really beautiful cushion-cover, on which was embroidered a peacock spreading its lovely tail.

Mam'zelle was intensely proud of this. She bored everyone by talking about it. 'It is exquisite!' she said. 'Ah, the clever little Claudine! Miss Ellis, do you not think that

Claudine has done the tail most perfectly?'

'I do,' said Miss Ellis. 'Much better than she does her maths or her history, or her geography or her literature, or her . . .'

'Come, come!' said Mam'zelle, hurt. 'It is not given to us to have great gifts at everything. Now, the little Claudine, she . . .'

'I don't expect Claudine to have great gifts at anything but needlework,' said Miss Ellis. 'All I ask is a *little* attention in class, and a *little* thought in prep time! You spoil Claudine, Mam'zelle.'

'I! I spoil Claudine!' cried Mam'zelle, her glasses falling off her nose in rage. 'I have never spoilt any girl, never. Always I am strict, always I am fair, always I am . . .'

'All right, Mam'zelle,' said Miss Ellis, hastily, seeing that Mam'zelle was going to make one of her long and impassioned speeches, 'all right. I must go. You can tell it all to me when you see me next.'

Mam'zelle sought out Claudine. She fell upon her and hugged her, much to Claudine's surprise. But it had suddenly occurred to Mam'zelle that 'the poor little Claudine' would not have parents visiting her at half-term, for they were in France. So, immediately on thinking this, she had gone to comfort Claudine, who, however, was not in any need of comfort at all. She liked her parents, but as she was one of a very large family, and had only got a small share of their love and attention, she had not missed them very much.

'Ah, my little Claudine!' said Mam'zelle, flinging her

arms round the astonished Claudine. 'Do not be sad, do not be discouraged! Do not fret yourself – you shall not be alone at half-term.'

Claudine wondered if her aunt had gone mad. 'I am not sad, *ma tante,*' she said. 'What is the matter? Has anything happened?'

'No, no,' said Mam'zelle, still full of tender thoughts for her little Claudine, 'nothing has happened. It is only that I feel for you because your parents will not be with you at half-term. When everyone else has their handsome fathers and their so-beautiful mothers, you will have no one – no one but your loving Aunt Mathilde!'

'Well, that's OK,' said Claudine in English. Mam'zelle wrinkled up her nose and her glasses fell off.

'Do not use these expression!' she said. 'They are vulgar. Ah, my little Claudine, you will not have any parents to admire your so-fine cushion-case with its magnificent peacock – but I will be there, my little one, I will stand by your cushion-cover all the time, not one minute will I go away, and I will say to everyone: "See! See the beautiful cover made by the clever Claudine! Ah, it needs a French girl to do such work as this! Regard the tail, regard each feather so finely done in silk, regard the priceless cushion-cover, the most beautiful thing in this school today!'

'Oh, Aunt Mathilde, I wish you wouldn't think of saying anything like that,' said Claudine in alarm. 'The girls would laugh like anything. They would tease me terribly. Please don't. I shan't be lonely. I shan't mind not having anyone there.'

'Ah, the brave little one!' sighed Mam'zelle, wiping away a tear from her eye. 'I see your courage. You will not show others that you suffer.'

'I *shan't* suffer,' said Claudine, getting impatient. 'I shan't really, Aunt Mathilde. Please don't make a fuss like this. It would be dreadful if you stood by my cushion-cover all the afternoon and made remarks like that.'

The idea of Mam'zelle standing like a bull-dog on guard, telling surprised parents of her poor lonely little Claudine, and praising to the skies the little cushion-cover filled Claudine with horror. She began to wish that half-term was safely over.

But it hadn't even come! Four days away – three days – two days – the night before. Ah, now it really *was* near! The girls went to bed very excited that night and talked in whispers long after lights were out. Susan Howes, the head girl of the form, pretended to be asleep. She could not bear to be a spoil-sport on the night before half-term, strict as she was on all other nights.

Angela was thinking of the wonderful impression her mother would make, and how she would bask in her reflected glory. She hoped her mother would wear her famous pearls.

Eileen was thinking about her own mother. She would be there as Matron, not all dressed up and pretty as other people's mothers would be. She wished that Eddie could be there – not because she was going to do anything in the swimming or tennis matches, or had anything in the art or needlework exhibition – but because it would have been lovely to have seen him looking for her – her own darling big brother!

Alison was looking forward to seeing her own pretty mother, and also to seeing Angela's mother too. She hoped the two would be friends. It would be lovely if they liked one another, and what fun if Angela's mother asked her, Alison, to stay with them in the holidays. That *would* be fine!

Pauline was thinking of her parents too. So was Bobby. It seemed a long time since the last holidays. School was fun – but your own home and people were something very solid and real and lovely. It would be nice to get a bit of them tomorrow.

One by one the girls fell asleep. Bobby was the first to wake up. She sat up and spoke loudly. 'Wake up, you sleepy-heads! It's half-term!'

10

Half-term at last

Half-term Saturday was a perfectly beautiful day. The sun shone down from a blue sky that hadn't a single cloud in it.

'Gorgeous, isn't it, Claudine?' said Doris happily to the little French girl. 'Couldn't be better.'

Claudine groaned. 'To think we shall all have to be out-of-doors in this terrible sun!' she said. 'I know I shall get a freckle. I wish it had rained.'

'You spoil-sport!' said Bobby, grinning. 'You would like to huddle indoors even on a day like this. Come on, cheer up and smile – it's really a heavenly day.'

The art exhibition was all ready for the parents to admire. There were some really good pictures there. Miss Walker, the art mistress, was proud of them. She had a water-colour class which went out regularly to paint country scenes with her, and some of them were very good.

'Good enough to sell!' said Claudine. 'Do we sell our work? How much would you get for this so-beautiful picture, Hilary?'

Hilary laughed. 'You have got funny ideas, Claudine,' she said. 'Of course we don't sell our work. As if our proud parents would let us! No, they will take our pictures home, and our pottery, and place them in conspicuous places on the walls, or mantelpiece, so that all their friends can admire them, and say, "How clever your daughter must be, Mrs So-and-So!" '

'I bet your mother will be pleased if you send her that lovely cushion-cover of yours for her birthday,' said Pat. Claudine laughed.

'I have three sisters who do much more beautiful work than I do,' she said. 'My mother would look at my cover and say, "Ah! The little Claudine is improving! This is not bad for a beginning." '

'Mam'zelle thinks it's wonderful, anyhow,' said Bobby, grinning. 'There's one thing about you, Claudine – you're not in the least conceited. With all the fuss that everyone has made of your embroidery, you might quite well have begun to swank about it. But you don't.'

'Ah, I know that it is good compared with the sewing of you English girls,' said Claudine, seriously, 'but, you see, I know that it would be quite ordinary in France. I have a different standard to compare that so-beautiful cover with, and I cannot think it is as wonderful as you do.'

Claudine was a very funny mixture of honesty, sincerity and deceitfulness. Even her deceitfulness was odd, because she did not attempt to hide it. She often tried to deceive Miss Ellis, for instance, and if Miss Ellis saw through it, Claudine would at once admit to her attempted deceit without any shame. It was almost as if she were playing a game with the teachers, trying to get the better of them, but not trying to hide the fact that she *was* trying to get the better of them. The girls could not quite make her out.

Pat and Isabel were playing together in a school match, and they were delighted. They looked out their white skirts and blouses, their red socks and white shoes, and took the clothes to Matron for the laundry staff to iron. Everyone had to look their best when parents came!

Pauline looked a little miserable at breakfast-time, and the girls wondered why. Hilary spoke to her in her usual kindly way.

'What's up, Pauline? You're looking glum. You're not upset because you haven't been chosen to play in the school matches, are you?'

'Oh, no,' said Pauline. 'I've had a great disappointment, that's all.'

'What?' asked Hilary, and the other girls came round to hear.

'Well, you see,' said Pauline, 'it's most unfortunate – Mother is ill, and my father doesn't like to leave her – so they won't be coming today! And I was *so* looking forward to them being here and seeing everything.'

'Bad luck, Pauline!' said the twins, sympathetically. A disappointment of that kind was awful at the last minute. Everyone was very sorry.

'I hope your mother isn't really ill,' said Susan Howes.

'No, not seriously,' said Pauline. 'But she can't possibly come. Oh, dear – and I did so badly want you all to see my good-looking father and my pretty mother. I even wrote to ask her if she would wear the pretty new frock I liked so much, and she said she would.'

'Well, never mind,' said Isabel, feeling very sorry indeed. 'You can come out with us and our people, if you like, Pauline. Then you won't feel so lonely.'

'Oh, thank you,' said Pauline, and after that she seemed to cheer up a good deal, and entered into everything with enthusiasm.

Mam'zelle had displayed Claudine's beautiful cushion-cover in a very prominent place. She still seemed inclined to fall on Claudine's neck, and tell her she must not feel lonely, and the little French girl kept out of her way as much as possible, slipping deftly round the corner whenever she saw her aunt approaching.

'Sort of hide-and-seek you're playing, Claudine!' said Bobby. 'You'll have to have a word with Mam'zelle soon, or she'll burst. She's longing to show you how beautifully she has arranged your so-marvellous cushion-cover!'

Lunch was a very scrappy affair that day because the cooks were concerned with the strawberry tea that the parents were to have in the afternoon, and scores of pounds of strawberries were being prepared in big glass dishes. The cooks had made the most lovely cakes and biscuits, and there were sandwiches of every kind. The girls kept peeping into the big dining-room, where the dishes were all set out.

Claudine slipped in and sampled some of the strawberries. She was the only one who dared to do this.

'You'll get into a row if anyone catches you,' said Bobby.

'You go and taste them,' said Claudine, running her

little pink tongue round her crimson lips. 'They are so sweet and juicy!'

'No,' said Bobby. 'We've been put on our honour not to sample this afternoon's tea, and I wouldn't dream of breaking my honour.'

'This honour of yours, it is a funny thing,' said Claudine. 'It is a most uncomfortable thing. It stops you from doing what you want to do. I have no honour to worry me. I will never have this honour of yours. I do not like it.'

'You're awful, Claudine,' said Angela, screwing up her nose. 'You do exactly as you like. I'm glad I'm not as dishonourable as you are.'

The tone was very unpleasant, but Claudine only laughed. She hardly ever took offence. 'Ah, Angela,' she said, 'you think it is worse to take a few strawberries than to tell untruths about another girl behind her back? Me, I think it is really dishonourable to speak lies against another girl as you do. To me you are dishonourable, a worth-nothing girl, not because of a few strawberries but because of your evil tongue!'

The listening girls laughed at this. It was said in a pleasant voice, but there was such truth in it, and the tables had been turned so cleverly on Angela that the girls couldn't help being amused. Only Angela was angry. But there was little time to quarrel on half-term day. There were so many jobs to do, and everyone had her own allotted task.

Some had to do the flowers all over the school, and this

took a long time. The vases had to be washed, old flowers thrown away, new ones picked, and then arranged to the best advantage in all kinds of bowls, jars and vases. The twins were especially good at this, and were very busy all the morning.

After lunch everyone changed into either sports clothes or school uniform. The summer uniform was a brightly coloured tunic. The girls could choose any colour they liked, so every girl was able to wear the one that suited her best. Dark girls, like Carlotta, chose reds and oranges, fair girls like Angela chose pale colours, blues and pinks. They looked like flowers, moving about against the green lawns of the school grounds, on that hot summer day.

'The parents are arriving!' squealed Alison, as she heard the sound of wheels coming up the drive. 'The first lot are here. Who are they?'

The fourth formers looked out of their windows, but nobody knew the people in the car. 'They must belong to some of the lower school,' said Bobby. 'Here come some more!'

'They're mine!' cried Janet. 'Oh, goody-goody! I hoped they'd come early. I say, doesn't my mother look nice and tanned. I'm going to greet them.'

She sped off happily. More and more cars drove up the drive, and soon the lawns were crowded with fathers and mothers and aunts, and with younger or older brothers and sisters. How Eileen wished that Eddie could be there!

Eileen's mother was very trim and starched in her

Matron's uniform and white apron. Some of the parents went to talk to her about the health of their children. Eileen was glad that her mother was sought out by so many parents – but she could not help wishing that she had on a pretty frock and looked as sweet and attractive as many of the other girls' mothers.

Mother ought to smile more, thought Eileen. She looks so strict and hard. Look at the twins' mother over there – she's really sweet. And I do like the way she's got her arm round both Pat and Isabel. Mother never puts her arm round me or Eddie.

An enormous car rolled up the drive, with a smartly uniformed chauffeur in front. It was a beautiful new Rolls Royce, black with a small green line. It came to a stop and the chauffeur got out. Angela gave a loud squeal.

'That's our new car! Look, everyone, isn't it a beauty! And do you like the chauffeur's uniform, black with green piping to match the car? The cushions are black too, with green edges and green monograms.'

'I should have thought you would have been so excited to see your parents that you wouldn't even have noticed the car!' said Janet's cool voice. But Angela took no notice. She was very pleased indeed that so many of the fourth formers were near when her grand new car drove up!

The chauffeur opened the car door. Angela's mother stepped out. Certainly she was a vision of beauty! She looked very young, was extraordinarily like Angela, and she was dressed in a most exquisite fashion.

The girls stared at her. She looked round with brilliant

blue eyes, also very like Angela's. After her came her husband, a tall, military-looking man, with rather a serious face. Angela gave another squeal.

She ran to her parents and flung her arms round her mother as she had seen the others do, purposely exaggerating everything because she knew they were watching.

'Angela dear! Be careful of my dress!' said her mother. 'Let me see how you are looking.'

Her father gave Angela a good hug, and then pushed her a little way away so that he could have a good look at her.

'She looks very well indeed,' said her father.

'But this awful school uniform spoils her,' said her mother. 'I do think it is most unbecoming. And I can't bear those terrible school shoes, with their flat heels.'

'Well, all the girls wear the same,' said Angela's father, reasonably. 'I think Angela looks very nice.'

'If only the school had a prettier uniform!' said Angela's mother, in a complaining voice. 'That was one reason why I didn't want to send her here – the dress was *so* ugly!'

11

Angela's 'wonderful' mother

The complaining voice of Angela's mother could be heard very often indeed that afternoon. Beautiful as she was, attractive and exquisite in her dress and looks, the lovely face was spoilt by an expression of discontent and boredom.

She complained of so many things, and her voice was unfortunately harsh and too loud! She complained of the hard bench that she had to sit on to watch the tennis matches. She found fault with the cup of tea that Angela brought her. 'What terrible tea! They might at least provide China tea. You know I can't drink Indian tea, Angela.'

She complained of the cake she took. 'Awfully dry,' she said. 'I can hardly eat it.'

'Leave it then,' said Angela's father. And to Angela's horror her mother dropped the cake on the ground, where it could be trodden underfoot. The sharp eyes of the other girls noted all these things, and Angela began to feel rather uncomfortable.

'Isn't my mother lovely?' she whispered to Alison. 'Don't you think those pearls are marvellous? Hasn't she got beautiful hair?'

Alison agreed. Privately she thought that Angela's mother acted like a spoilt child, complaining and grumbling all the time. She did not praise the pictures in the art exhibition, neither did she show any enthusiasm for the pottery work. She was forced to express a good opinion on Claudine's cushion-cover, because Mam'zelle stood there like a dragon, looking so fierce that everyone felt they must praise her niece's handiwork.

'Ah! So this is your mother, Angela?' said Mam'zelle, in a most amiable voice. 'We will show her the work of the little Claudine! Is it not beautiful? See the exquisite stitches! Regard the fine tail, spreading so well over the cover!'

Angela's mother looked as if she was going to pass the cover by without saying anything, but Mam'zelle was certainly not going to let that happen. She took hold of the visitor's arm and almost forced her to bend over Claudine's cushion-cover. 'You have not seen it! It is a work of art! It is the finest thing in the exhibition!' said Mam'zelle, getting excited.

'Very nice,' said Angela's mother, in a tone that seemed to say 'Very nasty!' She took her arm away from Mam'zelle's hand, brushed her sleeve as if it had some dust left on it, and turned away impatiently.

'Who is that awful old woman?' she asked Angela, in much too loud a voice. 'Surely *she* doesn't teach you, my dear? Did you ever see anyone look so dowdy?'

The girls were very fond of Mam'zelle, and they were angry to hear this remark. Bobby felt certain that Mam'zelle herself had caught some of it. The French-woman was standing looking after Angela and her parents with a puzzled and hurt expression in her eyes.

'Well – I always thought Angela was pretty beastly,' said Bobby to Pat, in a low tone, 'and now I see where she gets her cattiness from! How ashamed I'd be of *my* mother if she walked round like that, criticizing things and people at the top of her voice. Poor old Mam'zelle! It's a shame to hurt her.'

Claudine had overheard the remarks made by Angela's mother, and she too was hurt and angry. She was fond of her Aunt Mathilde, and though she was cross with her for standing by her cushion-cover and behaving in such an exaggerated way about it, she saw that it was the intense love and pride she had for Claudine herself that made her do it.

She looked at Angela's beautiful mother. She noted her discontented face, and the petulant droop of the mouth that at times quite spoilt its loveliness. She thought of all the hurts and insults that that beautiful mouth must have uttered through the years. And Claudine longed to punish Angela's mother in some dramatic way for the cruel words she had spoken about her Aunt Mathilde!

Angela took her parents to the swimming-pool. St Clare's was proud of this, for it was one of the finest and biggest swimming-pools owned by any school in the kingdom. The water lapped against the sides, a beautiful blue-green colour.

But even here Angela's mother had fault to find. 'I suppose they change the water every day, Angela?' she said.

'No, Mother, twice a week, sometimes three times,' said Angela. Her mother gave a little disgusted squeal.

'Good gracious! To think they can't even change the water every day! What a school! I really must make a complaint about it. Angela, you are not to bathe in the pool unless the water has just been changed. I forbid it.'

'But, Mother,' began Angela, uncomfortably, 'I have to do what the others do – and really, the water *is* quite clean, even when it's two days old, or three.'

'I shall complain,' said Angela's mother. 'I never did like the idea of sending you here. It's a second-rate school, I think. I wanted to send you to High Towers School. *Such* a nice school! I can't think why your father wanted to send you here. Perhaps now he has seen it he will think again.'

'Pamela, don't talk so loudly,' said Angela's father. 'People here don't like to listen to what you are saying. You are in a minority – it is plain that all the other parents here think as *I* do – that St Clare's is splendid in every way!'

'Oh, *you*,' said Angela's mother, as if what her husband thought was of simply no account at all. She shut up her scarlet lips, and looked just as sulky as Angela always did when anybody ticked her off.

No – Angela's mother was certainly not a success! Beautiful she might be, expensive she certainly was – but she had none of the graciousness of the twins' mother, or the common sense of Bobby's jolly-looking mother, or the affection of Gladys's plainly dressed but sweet-faced mother.

'I'm jolly glad I haven't got a mother like Angela's!' said Janet to Alison. 'Isn't she perfectly awful?'

Loyal though Alison wanted to be to Angela, she

couldn't help nodding her head. She had overheard many of Angela's mother's rude remarks, and she had not liked them, because even feather-headed Alison felt a deep sense of loyalty to St Clare's and all it stood for. She was not at all eager to be introduced to Angela's mother now – but the time came when she had to be, for Angela sought her out and took her off.

'Mother, this is Alison, the friend I told you about in my letters,' said Angela. Her mother looked at the pretty, dainty girl with approval. Alison was like Angela, and could wear the school uniform well.

'Oh, so this is Alison,' said Angela's mother. 'How do you do? I must say you look a little more attractive than some of the girls here. One or two that Angela has introduced me to have been perfect frights!'

Bobby had been introduced to Angela's mother and was presumably one of the 'frights'. Her frank freckled face was not at all attractive to anyone as exquisite as Angela's mother.

'Where is your mother?' asked Angela. 'We must introduce her to mine. Mother wants to ask if you can spend some of the summer hols with me.'

But, rather to Alison's relief, when the introduction had been made, and the two mothers had greeted one another, the invitation was quite firmly declined by Alison's own mother!

'Thank you,' she said, 'but I am afraid I have other plans for Alison.'

She did not explain what these were. She did not say

that she had watched Angela's mother, and had heard some of her insolent remarks and detested them. She did not say that Angela's mother was the sort of person she would hate Alison to spend even a day with! But Alison knew what her mother was thinking, and silly girl as she was, she knew that her mother was right.

Angela's mother sensed that the other mother was snubbing her, and she was surprised and annoyed. She was about to say something more, when a bell rang loudly.

'Oh! Must they ring bells like that!' said Angela's mother, putting her hands to her ears. 'How crude!'

'But sensible, don't you think so?' said Alison's mother drily, and left her.

'That's the bell to tell us to go and watch the swimming,' said Alison, slipping her hand into her mother's arm. 'Come on, Mummy. You'll see Bobby swimming there – you know, the freckled girl you liked. And Mirabel too – she's awfully fast.'

The hot sun blazed down as the company took its place round the swimming-pool. The parents sat at the edge of the baths, but the girls were in the big gallery above, watching eagerly.

Many of them were not taking part in the swimming, but they were all keen to see the performers diving, somersaulting and swimming. It was fun to hear the continual splashes, and to see the rippling of the blue water.

'Isn't it a gorgeous afternoon?' said Janet, happily. 'I *am* enjoying myself! I feel so glad that it's a fine day so that we can show off St Clare's at its very best.'

'All our parents seem to think it's a great success,' said Bobby. 'Well – except *one* parent!'

She meant Angela's mother. Angela heard this remark and flushed. She had been so pleased to show off her beautiful mother – but somehow everything had been spoilt now. She couldn't help wishing that her mother had made nice remarks like the others had made. But then, Mother wasn't usually very pleased with things, no matter what they were.

Claudine, Alison, Angela and many others not in the swimming got front places in the big gallery above the water. Claudine leant over rather far, not so much to look at the swimmers, in their navy-blue swim-suits, but to see the rows of parents.

'Look out, Claudine, you'll fall in!' said Alison, in alarm, trying to pull her back.

'I shall not fall,' said Claudine. 'I am just looking at that so-discontented person below, with the voice that makes loud and rude remarks!'

'Sh,' said Alison. 'Angela will hear you.'

'I do not care,' said Claudine. 'Why should Angela expect us to praise a mother who is beautiful only in appearance, and whose character is ugly?'

'Do be quiet,' said Alison, afraid that Angela would hear. 'I'm sorry Angela's mother said that about your aunt, Claudine. I heard it, and I'm sure poor Mam'zelle was hurt.'

The swimming began. Angela's mother looked disgusted when a drop of water splashed on to her beautiful dress. She shook it daintily and tried to move backwards a little – but other people were behind her and she couldn't.

It was an exciting hour, for the swimmers were fast and good, and the divers graceful and plucky. But the most exciting bit of the whole afternoon was not the swimming or the diving, or the backward somersaulting done so cleverly by Bobby.

It was an unexpected and highly dramatic performance, quite unrehearsed, given by Claudine!

She was leaning well over the gallery balcony. She suddenly gave a piercing shriek that made everyone jump in alarm – and then to the horror of all the lookers-on, the little French girl fell headlong from the gallery into the water below!

12

A happy time

She made a most terrific splash. The water rose up and fell all over Angela's mother, soaking her from head to foot!

'Good gracious!' said Miss Theobald, the head mistress, startled out of her usual calm dignity. 'Who has fallen into the water? Get her out, quickly!'

Claudine could not swim. She sank under the water, and then rose to the surface, gasping. Bobby and Mirabel, who were in the water, too, at once swam over to her. They got hold of her and helped her to the steps.

'Claudine! Whatever happened?' said Bobby. 'You *are* an idiot!'

Claudine was gasping and spluttering. She cast an eye towards Angela's mother, and saw, to her delight, that she was drenched. Miss Theobald was by her, apologizing, and saying that she must come at once to the school, and allow her, Miss Theobald, to lend her some clothes whilst hers were drying.

Angrily Angela's mother followed the head mistress from the swimming-pool. She looked a dreadful sight, with her dress soaked and clinging tightly to her, and her beautiful hat dripping with water. Angela looked very distressed.

'You too, Claudine, you must go with Matron and get into dry clothes,' said Miss Ellis to the soaking wet fourth former. 'Get into another tunic, quickly, or you'll catch cold. Hurry, now.'

Claudine, out of the tail of her eye, saw Mam'zelle bearing down upon her, alarm and anxiety written all over her. The little French girl at once fled off up to the school. She felt she could not bear to be enwrapped in Mam'zelle's overwhelming affection just then.

'Wait, wait, Claudine,' called Matron, who was annoyed that Claudine had caused her to leave the company and go back to the school. But Claudine did not wait. Better to face Matron's annoyance than Mam'zelle's loud exclamations of dismay and sympathy!

'How exactly like Claudine to cause such a disturbance!' said Pat to Isabel. 'Oh, Isabel – I can't help feeling delighted that the person who got soaked was Angela's tiresome mother!'

'I suppose Claudine couldn't possibly have done it on purpose, could she?' said Isabel, doubtfully. 'You know, she doesn't care in the least what she does, if she wants to get a result she has set her heart on. I bet she wanted to punish Angela's mother for her rudeness to Mam'zelle!'

'But Claudine simply hates and detests the water!' said Pat. 'Nothing will make her undress and have a swim. And to let herself fall from the gallery into the water would be a very brave thing to do, considering she can't swim.'

Claudine soon returned, in dry clothes, looking

demure and innocent. She could look just as innocent as Angela when she liked – and now that the girls knew her better, they were certain that the more innocent Claudine looked, the worse mischief she had done or was about to do!

Angela's mother also returned, after a while – dressed in Miss Theobald's clothes! Miss Theobald was about the same size as Angela's mother, but a little taller, and although she always looked nice, her clothes were very simple, plain and dignified.

They did not suit Angela's mother at all. In fact she looked very extraordinary in them and she knew it. She was angry and she showed it. It was bad enough to be drenched like that by some silly, careless girl, but much worse to be made to wear clothes too long for her, and so dowdy and frumpish after her own!

But somehow Angela's mother could not be rude to Miss Theobald. The head mistress was extremely kind and apologetic, but she was also calm and dignified, and she acted as if she expected Angela's mother to be calm and dignified also. And, much to her surprise, the spoilt woman found herself guarding her tongue and behaving quite well, whilst she changed into Miss Theobald's clothes.

The rest of the time went quickly. The matches and competitions were all over. Parents went off with their children, taking them out to dinner in the various hotels round about, for a treat.

Pauline went with Mrs O'Sullivan, the twins' mother. The twins had told their mother about the girl's great disappointment, and she had at once said that Pauline must come with them.

Alison's mother spoke to Alison. 'Is there anyone you would like to bring with you this evening? I hope you don't want to go with Angela and her people, because your father and I would rather be on our own with you.'

Alison understood that her mother had no wish to become at all friendly with Angela's mother. If she could choose someone to go with her, it would be easy to refuse Angela, if she asked for the two families to have dinner together. Alison wondered whom she could ask.

She took a look round at the girls. Most of them were clustered around their parents, chattering gaily, waiting for the various cars to come along. Eileen stood alone, watching. Her mother had disappeared – gone to see to some of the younger children, probably. The girl had such a forlorn look on her face that Alison was touched.

'I'll ask Eileen, Mother,' she said. 'I don't like her much – or her mother, who is Matron – but she would so enjoy coming! And oh, Mother – could I ask someone else too?'

'Who?' said her mother, in surprise.

'Could I ask Claudine, the little French girl who fell into the water?' said Alison. 'Her parents are in France. She's only got her aunt here, Mam'zelle. I know she would simply love to come! She adores going out.'

'All right, dear. Ask them both,' said her mother, pleased. Anything rather than having that spoilt little Angela and her equally spoilt mother with them!

Alison tore off to Eileen. 'Eileen. Go and ask your

mother if you can come out to dinner with my people. Hurry up.'

'Oh!' said Eileen, her eyes suddenly shining like stars. 'Oh, Alison – do you really mean it? You *are* decent!'

She rushed off to find her mother. Alison went up to Claudine. 'Claudine, will you come out with me and my people? Mother said I could ask you. Eileen is coming too.'

'Thank you,' said Claudine, all her pretty manners coming into play. 'It is indeed very kind of you, Alison, and of your mother too. I will go to ask my aunt.'

Mam'zelle was delighted. She liked Alison, although she despaired over her French. 'Yes, you go, my little Claudine,' she beamed. 'You need a treat after your so-terrible shock this afternoon. Poor little one – to fall into the water like that, to be nearly drowned, to . . .'

'Well, I wasn't nearly drowned really, you know,' said Claudine, a twinkle coming into her eye. 'I knew I *shouldn't* be drowned, Aunt Mathilde, because Bobby and Mirabel were both in the water – and oh, wasn't it grand when I splashed that hateful woman from head to foot? I never guessed I would drench her like that!'

Mam'zelle's mouth fell open, and she stared at Claudine as if she could not believe what she heard.

'Claudine! Claudine! What is this that you are saying? Surely, no it is not possible – you could not have fallen on purpose! You would not be such a bad girl!' Poor Mam'zelle could hardly get the words out.

Claudine answered demurely. 'On purpose, Aunt Mathilde! Why, how could you think of such a thing? Do you suppose that your niece could do a so-shocking thing as that? But how wonderful that it should happen just by Angela's mother! Ah, truly, that was a miracle!'

With a wicked twinkle in her eye, the unscrupulous Claudine walked off to get herself ready for going out. Mam'zelle stared after her. Ah, this Claudine – she was a bad, bad girl – and yet what a good, good girl she was too, to throw herself into the water in order to splash and punish an unkind woman, someone who had hurt and puzzled her aunt! Mam'zelle sat down on a hall-seat, feeling quite breathless. Which *was* Claudine – a bad girl or a good one? For the life of her Mam'zelle could not decide.

Meanwhile all the girls and their parents had gone off in their different cars. Angela had rolled away in her magnificent car – but a very quiet and subdued Angela. Somehow things had not turned out quite as she had planned. She hadn't shone in the reflected glory of her beautiful mother. She had only felt the scorn of the other girls because her mother had criticized their school in loud and complaining tones.

Angela looked out of the car window and saw the happy faces of the twins, and saw Pauline walking with Mr and Mrs O'Sullivan. They were all going off together, chattering gaily.

'You all did *mar*vellously!' she heard Mrs O'Sullivan say, in clear, happy tones.

Then she saw her friend Alison – and to Angela's enormous surprise, Eileen and Claudine were with her, all getting into a car together! Oh! How mean of Alison! Why hadn't she asked Angela to join up with her and her people? Fancy asking that common little sneak, Eileen, and that awful outspoken niece of Mam'zelle's, Claudine! How *could* Alison do such a thing!

Angela did not think of what the real reason might be – a real feeling of kindness on Alison's part. She was angry and annoyed. She would show Alison exactly what she thought of her when she saw her next! If Alison wanted to make friends with charity girls, let her – but she wouldn't have Angela Favorleigh, the Honourable Angela Favorleigh, for her friend too!

There were two or three fairly big towns within easy reach of the school by car, and the different families chose their own town and hotel, and drove off. To Eileen's intense joy, Alison's mother chose to go to the town where Eddie lived!

'Oh,' she said, as the car slid into the town. 'This is where my brother lives. I wonder if I shall see him.'

'Would you like to ask him to come and have dinner with us?' said Alison's mother.

Eileen shook her head. 'Oh, no, thank you. It's kind enough of you to ask *me* without asking *him* as well! But – if you wouldn't mind – I would love to slip along and see him after we've had dinner. His lodgings aren't very far from the hotel. He'd love to see me.'

'Just as you like, dear,' said Alison's mother. So they had their dinner, and a very good one it was, and then Eileen slipped off to see Edgar.

Claudine proved a great success with Alison's people.

The French girl had naturally good manners, she was vivacious and amusing, and she was extremely pleased to have such a treat. Alison's parents really enjoyed the girl's company.

'Alison, I wish that French girl was your friend, and not Angela,' said her mother. 'She really is nice. Don't you like her?'

'Yes, Mother, I do,' said Alison. 'She's quite different from us English girls, though – I mean, she hasn't our sense of honour – and honestly, she simply doesn't care *what* she does. But she's fun, quite sincere, and awfully kind.'

'Here comes Eileen back again,' said Alison's mother. 'She must be very fond of her brother. She really looks happy now!'

Eileen did. Eddie had been delighted to see her. She beamed at Alison and Claudine in an unusually friendly manner. What a lovely day it had been!

13

Janet and the 'stink balls'

After the excitements of half-term the girls felt flat and dull. There didn't seem anything to look forward to now. Lessons were boring. The weather was too hot. It seemed a long time till the summer holidays.

'Janet! Bobby! Can't you think up some trick or other?' said Pat, with a yawn. 'I wish you would. I shall die of boredom this week if something doesn't happen.'

Janet grinned. 'I've got rather an awful trick from my brother,' she said. 'I don't really know if we ought to play it, now we're fourth formers.'

'Oh, don't be an idiot!' said Doris. 'Why can't we have a few jokes, even if we *are* fourth formers! What's the trick?'

'Well – it's a perfectly frightful smell,' said Janet. 'Wait a bit – I'll get the things.'

She went up to her dormitory, rummaged about in one of her drawers and then came down again with a small box.

The others crowded round her. The box was full of what looked like tiny round glass balls, full of some sort of clear liquid.

'What are they?' said Pat, puzzled. 'I've never seen them before.'

'They are smell balls,' said Janet. 'Stink balls my brother calls them. When you break one and let out the liquid, it dries up at once – but leaves the most frightful smell behind.'

'What sort of smell?' asked Doris, with great interest. 'Like drains or something?'

'Well – like very bad eggs,' said Janet. 'My brother – he's simply awful, you know – he broke one of these balls at a very solemn meeting once, in our sitting-room at home – and in less than a minute the room was empty! You simply can't imagine what it was like!'

Bobby chuckled. 'Let's break one in French class tomorrow,' she said. 'It's going to be terribly dull – translating pages and pages of that book Mam'zelle is so keen on – that French play. This trick is absolutely *sent* for things like that. Will you break one of these balls tomorrow, Janet, or shall I?'

'Well, you take one and I'll take one,' said Janet. 'Then if mine doesn't work – my brother says they are sometimes disappointing – you can use yours. See?'

The whole class were thrilled about the 'stink balls'. Everyone but Eileen knew about them. The girls were afraid of telling Eileen in case she sneaked to Matron, and the secret was found out. So Eileen was not told a word. She was astonished to find that so many of the girls hurriedly stopped talking when she came up, and then began chattering very loudly about quite silly things. She was sure they had been talking about her, and she felt hurt.

If they're going to be beastly to me, I shall tell Mother, and they'll all get dozens of stockings to mend! thought Eileen, spitefully.

Janet and Bobby went into the French class the next day with the little 'stink balls' in their pockets. The lesson was just before break.

'We'd better not choose any lesson except one just before break,' Janet had said, 'because if the smell goes on too long, it might still be there in Miss Ellis's class, and I bet she'd smell a rat.'

'She'd smell much worse than a rat once she sniffs one of your "stink balls",' said Bobby, with a grin.

'You see, we can open all the windows and doors and let the smell out well during break,' said Pat. 'There won't be anything of it left by the time maths lesson comes afterwards with Miss Ellis.'

The class were standing politely and silently when Mam'zelle came in. She beamed at the girls.

'Sit! Now today we will go on with this play of ours. I will allot the parts. You, Janet, can take the part of the old servant; you, Alison . . .'

The girls opened their books, hiding their grins as best they could. A trick performed by Janet or Bobby was always fun, great fun! The girls remembered the many other tricks the two had played, and chuckled. This would liven up a dull French lesson very considerably.

'Janet, will you please begin?' said Mam'zelle, aimiably. She liked this fourth form. They were good, hard-working girls – and her dear little Claudine was there too, her face buried in her book – the good, good little girl!

Janet began reading in French. Her hand stole to her pocket. The girls behind her saw it, and tried to choke back their giggles. That was the worst of playing a trick – you always wanted to begin giggling far too soon, and it was terribly difficult to stop real giggles. Doris gave one of her sudden snorts, and Mam'zelle looked up in surprise.

Doris turned it into a long cough, which set Mirabel off into giggles too. Mam'zelle glared at Mirabel.

'Is it so funny that the poor Doris has a bad cough?' she enquired.

This seemed funnier still to Mirabel and she went off into more helpless giggles which began to infect the others. Janet turned round and frowned. She didn't want Mam'zelle to suspect too soon that she was playing a trick. The others caught her warning look, and became as serious as they could again.

The lesson went on. Janet slid the little glass ball out of her pocket. Her hand was behind her, and the girls saw her press firmly on the tiny glass ball. The thin glass covering broke, and the liquid ran out, drying almost as soon as the air touched it. The liquid disappeared, and the tiny fragments of thin glass dropped unheeded to the floor.

After a few moments a curious smell drifted all round. Doris coughed. Alison sniffed loudly and said 'Pooh!'

It was a horrid smell, there was no doubt about that. It smelt of bad eggs, drains, dead rats, old cats' meat . . . all that was horrid!

Mam'zelle did not smell the smell at first. She was

astonished at the sudden outburst of sniffing and coughing. She looked up. She saw expressions of disgust on everyone's face, mixed with the desire to giggle.

'What is the matter?' demanded Mam'zelle, suspiciously. 'Why do you pull these faces? Alison, stop saying, "Pooh!" Janet, why do you look so disgusted?'

'Oh, Mam'zelle – can't you smell it?' said Janet, an agonized expression on her face.

'Smell *what*?' said Mam'zelle, exasperated. The smell had not drifted her way as yet.

'Oh, Mam'zelle – the *smell*!' chorused half a dozen voices.

Mam'zelle looked puzzled and angry. She took a few enormous sniffs of the air, which made Doris explode into laughter.

'I smell no smell,' said Mam'zelle. 'This is a silly trick, yes. Stop sniffing, Janet. If you say "Pooh" again, Alison, I will send you out of the room. Claudine, do not look like a duck that is dying.'

'But, Aunt Mathilde, the smell, the smell! *C'est abominable*!' cried Claudine, who detested bad smells, and looked as if she was about to faint.

'Claudine! You too!' rapped out Mam'zelle, who, safely away at the end of the room, had not even got so much as a sniff of the evil smell yet. 'Now listen, *mes enfants* – one more mention of a smell, and I fetch Miss Theobald herself here to smell it! It is all pretence. You are bad children.'

This was a truly terrible threat! Miss Theobald would certainly be able to smell the smell as soon as she got into the room, and then there would be a big row. The girls looked at one another in dismay. They put their handkerchiefs to their noses and tried not to sniff up the ghastly odour.

Mam'zelle began to read out loud from the French play. After a few lines, she stopped. Strange! She felt as if she too now could smell something. She took a cautious sniff. Was it a smell, or was it not? Nonsense! Strange and horrible smells do not invade classrooms all of a sudden. Mam'zelle took another breath and went on reading.

The smell stole round her. Mam'zelle could smell it quite distinctly now. She stopped reading again and sniffed wildly. Yes, there was no doubt about it, a perfectly horrible smell was in the room! The poor, poor girls – they had smelt it first – and she had not believed them.

Mam'zelle gave a gulp and a choke as the smell really took hold of her. She fished about for her handkerchief. The girls, divided between disgust at the smell and an intense desire to giggle at Mam'zelle's horrified face, stuffed their hankies into their mouths, making all kinds of most peculiar noises.

'Girls,' said Mam'zelle, in a choking kind of voice, 'girls, you are right. There is a terrible smell in here. What can it be?'

'A dead rat under the floorboards?' said Doris, obligingly, removing her hanky from her mouth for a moment.

Mam'zelle gave a small shriek. Rats, dead or alive, gave her shivers all down her back.

'Perhaps a drain has burst outside the window,' said Pat, speaking in a muffled voice. 'I'll look.'

She went to the open window and leant out, taking in deep breaths of the pure air there. One or two others joined her, thinking it was a very good idea.

'Perhaps it will go away,' said Mam'zelle, hopefully.

'Open the door, Janet, and maybe it will help to clear the room of this evil odour.'

Janet thankfully opened the door. This was an amusing trick to play – but it had its drawbacks!

The draught of air took a good strong dose of the smell over to Mam'zelle's desk. She gave a loud exclamation. '*Tiens*! This is terrible! We shall all be ill. Pick up your books quickly and we will finish our lesson in the garden. I will tell Miss Theobald and maybe she will have the boards up to seek for a rat that is quite dead.'

All but Claudine were delighted to go out into the garden. Claudine did not know which was worse – the smell in the classroom, or the insects out-of-doors. She thought there was very little to choose between them!

Soon the girls were sitting in a nice shady part of the garden, giggling whenever they thought of the awful smell drifting round their classroom. The lesson was no longer boring or dull! The smell had made it a great success.

Mam'zelle kept her word and reported the smell to Miss Theobald. 'Ah, Miss Theobald,' she said, 'it is a smell truly unbelievable! Of dead rats and mice, of eggs that are bad, of drains that are broken! It came into our classroom whilst the girls were reciting their French lesson, and it spoilt the whole hour. We had to leave the room and go into the garden.'

Miss Theobald was surprised to hear of such a very strong and disgusting smell. In all her experience of schools, she had never yet come across a smell that had driven a class from the room.

'I will go and smell it,' she said to Mam'zelle. 'If it is a dead rat, or bad drains, then, of course, we must have the smell seen to at once, this very afternoon. The smell will remain there, if those are the causes.'

But, to Mam'zelle's great astonishment and to Miss Theobald's mild astonishment, not a trace of the smell remained. The two of them sniffed all round the room, but it smelt fresh and clean.

'Extraordinary,' said Miss Theobald, gazing at Mam'zelle. 'You are quite sure, Mam'zelle, that it *was* a strong smell, a really bad one?'

Mam'zelle was most indignant. What, the head mistress was doubting her word? Mam'zelle at once began to describe the smell all over again, this time making it a smell ten times worse than before. Miss Theobald smiled to herself. She knew Mam'zelle's indignant exaggerations by this time.

'Well,' she said, 'I won't have the floorboards up, or the drains inspected today – maybe the smell will not return. If it does, Mam'zelle, kindly report it to me at once, please, so that I may smell it myself before it goes away.'

'Yes, Miss Theobald,' said Mam'zelle, and went to the mistresses' common-room, full of the smell and of its power in sending her class into the garden. Everyone listened in astonishment. It didn't occur to anyone but the first-form mistress, Miss Roberts, that it might be a trick. But Miss Roberts had had much experience of Janet's jokes, and it did cross her mind to wonder if this could be one of them.

'Let me see, Mam'zelle,' she said, thoughtfully, 'Janet is in the fourth form, isn't she?'

'Yes,' said Mam'zelle, 'but what has that got to do with my smell?'

'Oh – nothing I expect,' said Miss Roberts. 'But – if I were you, Mam'zelle, if that smell appears again, you trot down to Miss Theobald *at once*. I think she may be able to find the cause of it without taking up any floorboards and examining any drains!'

'Of course I shall report to the head at once,' said Mam'zelle, with dignity.

And the time came when she did!

14

Miss Ellis plays a trick too

The girls had been really delighted with the success of Janet's 'stink ball'. Whenever Eileen had not been in the room, they had chattered and laughed about Mam'zelle's disgust and astonishment.

'All the same, we'd better not do it again,' said Janet. 'I have a sort of feeling that once would be a success, but that twice would be a failure! You can pull Mam'zelle's leg beautifully once in a while, but not all the time.'

'If you do the smell again, I shall be sick and go out of the room,' said Claudine. 'It is the worst smell I have ever sniffed.'

'We won't do the smell again,' promised Bobby. 'But I tell you what we *will* do – we'll pre*tend* there is a smell, shall we – and get old Mam'zelle all hot and bothered expecting one – she'll sniff and snuff, and we shall die of laughing!'

'Oh, yes – that's a good idea,' said Janet. 'Doris, you can start off about the smell again in tomorrow's French grammar class.'

Doris grinned. She could act that kind of thing very well. So the next day, when Mam'zelle was ensconced safely at her desk at the end of the room, Doris began her act.

There was a very nice smell in the room, for Alison, the

girl doing the flowers for the classroom that week, had filled a big vase with white pinks, and they scented the room beautifully. The girls could smell them as they worked.

Doris began to sniff. At first she gave very little sniffs. Then she gave two or three bigger ones.

'Doris! Have you a cold?' said Mam'zelle, impatiently. 'Are you a first former, come to class without a handkerchief?'

'I've got a hanky, thank you, Mam'zelle,' said Doris, humbly, and took it out.

Then Janet began to sniff. She screwed up her nose, sniffed, and looked all round. Bobby gave a chuckle and turned it into a long cough. Mam'zelle frowned. She did not like behaviour of this sort! It made her angry.

Then Pat began to sniff, and pulled out her hanky too. Soon the whole class, all except Eileen, who was not in the joke, were sniffing as if they had bad colds.

Mam'zelle gazed at the sniffing girls, exasperated. 'What is all this noise? Sniff-sniff-sniff! I cannot bear it.'

Doris put on an expression of disgust. Mam'zelle saw it, and an alarming thought came into her head. Could it be that terrible smell again?

'Doris,' she said, urgently, 'what is the matter?'

'I can smell something,' murmured Doris. 'Distinctly. It's very strong just here. Can't you smell anything, Mam'zelle?'

Mam'zelle couldn't, which was not at all surprising. But she remembered that before she could not smell the smell until after the girls. She looked anxiously at the class. They all seemed to be smelling it.

'I will report it at once,' said Mam'zelle, and she left the room in a hurry.

'Crumbs!' said Bobby. 'I don't know that we wanted her to go to the head about it! I say – she shot off so quickly we couldn't stop her!'

Unluckily for Mam'zelle the head was out. Mam'zelle was annoyed and upset. Here was the smell again, and no Miss Theobald to smell it, and to know that she, Mam'zelle, had not exaggerated last time!

Mam'zelle popped her head in at the mistresses' common-room as she hurried back to the classroom. Miss Ellis was there, correcting exercise books belonging to the fourth form.

'Miss Ellis – I regret to say that that terrible smell is back again,' said Mam'zelle. 'It is abominable! I do not think you will be able to take the fourth form in your room next lesson.'

She withdrew her head and hurried back to the fourth form. She went in, expecting to be greeted by a wave of the terrible smell. But there seemed to be no smell at all. Very strange!

'Miss Theobald is out,' said Mam'zelle. 'Alas, she cannot smell our smell. Neither do I smell it yet!'

It was good news that Miss Theobald was out! The girls felt cheerful about that. Doris spoke up at once.

'Don't worry, Mam'zelle. We know what the smell was this time – quite different from last time. It was only these pinks!'

Doris picked up the big bowl of pinks, walked jauntily to Mam'zelle and thrust them under her big nose. Mam'zelle took a sniff and the strong and delicious scent went up her nose.

'So!' she said to Doris. 'It was the pinks you smelt. Well, it is a good thing Miss Theobald was not in. She would have come to smell for nothing!'

There were a few giggles – and then, as the door opened, the girls fell silent, and looked to see if it was Miss Theobald coming in after all.

But it wasn't. It was Miss Ellis, who, curious to smell this extraordinary smell that Mam'zelle seemed continually to get excited about, had come to smell it herself. She stood at the door, sniffing.

'I can't smell anything, Mam'zelle,' she said, surprised. Mam'zelle hastened to explain.

'I smelt nothing, either, Miss Ellis. It was the pinks the girls smelt. Doris has just told me.'

Miss Ellis was surprised and most disbelieving. 'I don't see how the girls could mistake a smell of pinks for the kind of awful smell you described to me last time,' she said. 'I am not at all sure I believe in that smell at all.'

She gave her form a glare, and went out.

Mam'zelle was indignant. Had she not smelt the smell herself last time? For the rest of the lesson the class had a very peaceful time, discussing smells, past and present, with their indignant French mistress.

After break came geography, taught by Miss Ellis. She came into the room looking rather stern.

'I just want to say,' she said, 'that I shall regard any mention of smells, bad or good, as a sign that you want a little extra work given to you.'

The class knew what that meant. 'A little extra work' from Miss Ellis meant a good two hours extra prep. So everyone immediately made up their minds not to mention the word smell at all.

But a terrible thing happened in ten minutes' time. Bobby had quite forgotten that she still had her 'stink ball' in her pocket, left over from the day before. And, in sitting down rather violently, after going with her book to Miss Ellis, she broke the thin glass surrounding the liquid. Then, in a trice, the perfectly awful smell came creeping round the classroom once more!

Doris smelt it. Janet smelt it. Bobby smelt it and put her hand at once into her pocket, desperately feeling about to see if she had accidentally broken the little 'stink ball'. When she found she had, she gazed round, winking and nodding at the others, to tell them of the awful accident. Miss Ellis's sharp eyes caught Bobby's signs. So she was not really very surprised when she smelt the smell coming towards her. What a terrible smell it was!

Miss Ellis thought things out quietly. Evidently yesterday's smell had been this same horrible one – and the one Mam'zelle had reported today, and which Doris had said was pinks after all, was nothing to do with the real smell – just a silly joke played on Mam'zelle.

But this awful smell is the real thing again, thought Miss Ellis. And, judging by Bobby's signs to the others, was a mistake. I don't think the girls would dare to play a trick like this on me. Well – I will just play a little trick on *them*!

Quietly Miss Ellis wrote a few directions on the board. Then she turned and left the room, closing the door after her. The girls stared at the board.

'Page 72. Write down the answers.

'Page 73. Read the first two paragraphs and then rewrite them in your own words.

'Page 74. Copy the map there.'

'I say!' exploded Doris. 'She's gone – and we've got to stay here in this awful smell and do that work. Bobby, you absolute idiot, why did you break that stink ball?'

'It was an accident,' said Bobby, most apologetically. 'I sat on it. I quite forgot it was there. Isn't this frightful? Miss Ellis has smelt it, of course, guesses it's a trick, and for punishment we've got to sit through the smell and work at our geography – and we simply daren't complain!'

'I am not going to sit in the smell,' announced Claudine, emphatically. She got up. 'I feel sick. I go to be sick.'

She went off, and she made such wonderful sick-noises as she passed Miss Ellis in the passage outside, that Miss Ellis said nothing, but let her go to the bathroom. Trust Claudine to do what she wanted! Not one of the others dared to leave the room.

They sat there, choking into their handkerchiefs, moaning over their fate, but not daring to scamp their work. At the end of the hour, when the smell had somewhat lessened, Miss Ellis opened the door.

She left it open. 'You may go for a short run round the

garden and back,' she said. 'Bobby, remain behind, please.'

With a wry face Bobby remained behind whilst the others fled out gladly into the fresh air.

'I was the one who caused that terrible smell this time,' said Bobby, at once. It was never any good beating round the bush with Miss Ellis – not that Bobby was given to that, anyway. She was a straightforward and truthful girl. 'But it was an accident, Miss Ellis, really it was. Please believe me.'

'I do,' said Miss Ellis. 'But it is an accident that is on no account to happen again. You have all had your punishment, so I shall say no more about it. But I want you to warn the fourth formers that any future smells will result in quite a lot of punishment!'

15

A birthday – and a grand idea!

'Isn't it gorgeous weather?' said Isabel to Pat. 'Day after day we get nothing but sun and blue sky. I wish we could have lessons sitting in the swimming-pool!'

'The coolest part of the day is the night!' said Doris. 'I should like to sleep all day and work all night in the cool night breeze.'

'Last night I woke up and saw the moon shining in at the window,' said Hilary. 'I got up and looked out – I simply can't tell you how beautiful the country looked, all lit up by moonlight. I wished I could go for a walk – have a moonlight picnic all by myself!'

'I *say*!' said Bobby, at once. 'A moonlight picnic! What an absolutely marvellous idea! Let's!'

'Oooh,' said the others, staring at Bobby, really impressed by the unusual idea. 'Golly – what fun!'

'Yes, it would be,' said Hilary, 'but – now that we're fourth formers, do you think we *ought* to?'

'Oh, Hilary – don't be so pious!' said Janet.

'I'm *not*,' said Hilary, indignantly. 'That's a thing I've never been. Well – perhaps it wouldn't matter. We could picnic in the school grounds. Oh, I *say* – let's picnic by the swimming-pool, and have a moonlight swim!'

'Better and better!' said Bobby, giving a whoop of delight. 'Golly – that would be super! Look here – let's wait till full-moon night – that's two nights from now – and have it then. The pool would be brilliantly lit and we could have a gorgeous time.'

'It's my birthday then,' said Mirabel. 'That very day. Oh, let's make it then, and I'd feel it was a birthday treat too!'

'Right,' said Janet. 'Now we'd better make plans quickly, because we haven't much time to get anything.' She turned to the quiet and responsible head girl of the form, Susan Howes. 'Susan, you'll come, won't you?'

Susan nodded. She was a good and trustworthy girl, but she loved a bit of fun, and she could not see that there was any harm in a moonlight picnic.

'I'll go down to the town today with Hilary, and buy a few things,' she said. 'I'll leave word at the grocer's and the baker's that you will all go in at different times and fetch one or two things. Then no one will suspect anything – we shall just quietly return to school with small parcels!'

'Shall we tell Eileen or not?' said Janet.

'No, of course not,' said Bobby. 'I bet she'd split on us and tell her mother – and then we'd all get caught and everything would be spoilt.'

'Well – it's a pity to leave Eileen out of everything like this really,' said Pat, 'but we can't risk being found out. And these midnight affairs *are* such fun!'

Mirabel was thrilled that it was her birthday that day!

It would make it all the nicer. She and Gladys, her quiet little friend, talked and talked about it.

'I'll take my birthday cake, of course,' said Mirabel. 'I'll save it up till then. Mother said she would send sixteen candles separately, and we'll stick them on the cake in their holders, and light them in the moonlight!'

Eileen was by now used to the others planning things without her. She knew that the tricks they whispered about together were not told her beforehand because she was known as a sneak. So she did not prick up her ears at all when she saw the girls talking together in low tones.

What do I care for their silly tricks? she thought. If they want to act like that, let them!

So she did not try to overhear or find out their fresh secret. She went her own way, looking rather pale and unhappy. She rarely smiled now, kept herself quite to herself, and did not try to make friends with anyone. She had been nice to Alison after the half-term treat, and Alison had benefited from her kindness by having no mending of her own at all to do ever since! But she still struggled with Angela's darning, though Angela was never very grateful.

Mirabel's birthday came. As usual her form gave presents. Some were small presents, if the girls had little money left, some were extravagant, like Angela's.

Angela gave Mirabel a book of very expensive music that she wanted. It cost five pounds and Mirabel was really quite overcome. 'You shouldn't spend so much money on a birthday!'

'Why not?' said Angela. 'My grandfather sent me ten pounds last week. What's the good of having money if you don't spend it?'

Pauline, not to be outdone, gave Mirabel a music-case of fine leather. Mirabel was amazed. It was not usual to have such beautiful presents for a school birthday. She had not even known that Pauline had noticed that her own old music-case had a broken strap and was almost worn out.

'Oh, Pauline – this is beautiful!' said Mirabel, red with surprise and delight. 'But you shouldn't do it. It's bad enough for Angela to do it – and for you to give me something so extravagant too, well really, I feel quite overwhelmed!'

'If Angela can do it, I can as well,' said Pauline, a little stiffly. That took the pleasure out of the gift somehow, thought Mirabel. If Pauline only gave her something fine just because she didn't want to be outdone by Angela, well, there wasn't much kindness or affection behind the gift!

Claudine surprisingly gave Mirabel a very pretty bag. Claudine was one of the girls who had very little money, and said so – so Mirabel was really touched to have such a nice gift from her.

'Oh, thank you, Claudine,' she said. 'It is really lovely. But it's too extravagant of you! I know you don't have much pocket-money.'

But Claudine seemed to have plenty that week! She bought eight pounds of cherries as her share of the picnic's goodies, and they came to three pounds. Everyone thought it was decent of her.

'Ah, when I have a little money, I like to spend it,' said Claudine. 'It is nice to spend. I wish I could spend always. That would be fine, to be like Angela and to say, "I will have this, I will have that!"'

'Yes – but it does mean you don't have many treats, real *treats,*' said Gladys. 'I mean – if Mother and I save up for ages to go on a good holiday together, it means much more to us and is a greater treat than any holiday could possibly be to Angela – who can have expensive holidays whenever she likes. To have a lot of money doesn't mean that you get more enjoyment than those who haven't much.'

'Quite right as usual,' said Isabel, giving the quiet Gladys a little pat. 'Well, I wish I and Pat could buy more for this picnic, but it was our granny's birthday last week and we spent most of our money on that mauve silk scarf we sent her. So we're cleaned out for a bit. I hope you won't turn up your nose at our birthday offering, Mirabel – it's only two drawing pencils with your name on!'

'That's very decent of you,' said Mirabel, who really did not mind whether gifts cost ten pounds or ten pence. 'I think you're all decent to me, everyone of you. Everybody has given me a present.'

Even Eileen had, though with many apologies for the poorness of her gift. 'It's only a little hanky,' she said to Mirabel. 'And I'm afraid it's not even new. It's one of my own, but please take it, Mirabel, with my birthday wishes. I don't want to be the only one not giving you anything!

You know I have hardly any pocket-money, and it's Eddie's birthday soon and I'm saving every penny for that.'

Everyone knew that Eileen had less money than any girl in the school. Her mother was mean over pocket-money. Certainly she had to work hard for her own money, but she seemed to think that the sixteen-year-old Eileen could manage on a penny or two a week, just as she had managed when she was a small six-year-old.

'I wish we could ask Eileen to go with us tonight,' said Mirabel. She was usually a thick-skinned girl, who had little feeling for anyone else, except for her friend Gladys – but she had been touched by Eileen's little gift, and her honest confession of having no money.

'Well, we can't,' said Bobby, decidedly. 'I know she told her mother that Janet said that there seemed to be more torn sheets in the fourth-form dormitories than in the whole of the rest of the school put together – and poor Janet has done oceans of mending this week. But who can help thinking our sheets are torn on purpose? On purpose to give us work to do! They were never torn like this before. Why, I could go a whole term without having to mend a pillow-case or sheet at all when our old Matron was here!'

'All right. We won't ask Eileen,' said Mirabel. 'I don't really care. She *is* a dreadful sneak, I suppose.'

Everything was prepared in readiness for the moonlight picnic and swim. The sky was clear when the girls went to bed that night. They went to bed in the daylight, for the evenings were very long just then.

'There won't be any darkness at all, I should think,' said Bobby, looking out of the window. 'When daylight begins to go, the full moon will come swimming up the sky, and then everything will be almost as bright as day again. Golly, isn't it hot? I shall adore being in the water at midnight!'

Luckily for the girls, Eileen was a very sound sleeper. Once she was asleep, nothing ever seemed to wake her, and even when the fire-practice alarm had gone once in the middle of the night, she had not awakened. So the girls felt sure she would know nothing.

It was too hot to sleep! Some of the girls dozed off, and Eileen and Mirabel slept soundly. But the others tossed and turned, half-asleep and half-awake. So, when the big clock in one of the towers struck half-past eleven, there was only Mirabel to wake!

Eileen slept in a bed by the door of one of the fourth-form dormitories, and the girls had to tip-toe past her. But she did not stir. She had looked rather pale and tired lately, and now she slept very deeply. The girls had on swimming-costumes under their dressing-gowns, and rubber shoes on their feet. They made no sound as they stole down the corridors, went down the stairs, and came to the big cupboard where they had hidden their food and drink.

With giggles and whispers they loaded themselves with the goodies, and then undid the garden door as quietly as they could. They left it a little open so that they could get in easily when they returned. There was no wind to bang it shut.

Keeping in the cover of the trees, the line of excited girls made their way towards the swimming-pool. How gorgeous the still water looked, lying calm and deep in the brilliant moonlight. The moon was now up, and was flooding the grounds with cold, silver light. Everything could be plainly seen. Only the warm colours of daylight were missing.

'We mustn't make too much noise,' said Janet. 'Our voices would carry a good way on a still night like this. I only hope no one will hear the splashing of the water when we go in! Let's go in first, before we eat. I'm so hot.'

Off came the dressing-gowns. Bare long legs gleamed in the moonlight. One after another the girls dived in or jumped in – all but Claudine, who had steadfastly refused to come in a swimming-costume, but had on her night-gown under her dressing-gown. The little French girl liked the excitement of the midnight picnic but, hot though it was, nothing would persuade her to go in the water! She would throw herself in to punish a spiteful-tongued woman – but she certainly would not go in for pleasure!

She stood and watched the girls, laughing. She glanced away from the pool – and suddenly saw a figure slipping silently between the trees. Whoever could it be?

16

Claudine deals with Matron

Claudine ran quietly in her rubber shoes to see who was out in the grounds that night, besides the fourth formers. It was Eileen! Eileen, whom the girls had left sound asleep in bed.

'The sneak!' said Claudine to herself. 'She comes to peep and pry at us, and then she goes back to her so-severe mother to tell a tale! I will follow her back.'

But somehow she missed Eileen, and could not see where she had gone. Claudine rushed back to the pool and almost fell into the water in her excitement at telling the others what she had seen.

'Oh, blow!' said Bobby, climbing out, the moonlight shining on the silvery drops running down her legs. 'I suppose that sneak of an Eileen will go straight off to Matron – and before we can have anything to eat, she'll be here scolding us and rowing us and sending us back in disgrace.'

'I will go back to the school, and keep watch,' said Claudine, eagerly. 'I know where Matron sleeps. I will go outside her door and stand there till I know for certain that either she is coming here, or that Eileen has not told tales after all.'

'Right,' said Bobby. 'Hurry! And be sure to race back and warn us if you hear Matron dressing or wandering about. We simply mustn't be caught. But oh, what a shame if we can't have the moonlight picnic. And I bet Matron will confiscate Mirabel's lovely cake!'

Claudine sped off in her rubber shoes. She did not see Eileen at all. She went in at the open garden door and ran quietly up the stairs to the corridor at the end of which Matron slept.

She stood outside Matron's door and listened. There was not a single sound from inside. She could not hear either Eileen's voice or Matron's. On the other hand, she could not hear slight snores or heavy breathing. Claudine stood there, wondering what to do. *Had* Eileen seen the picnickers? *Did* she mean to tell tales? Where had she gone?

Then Claudine's quick ears caught a sound from inside Matron's room. The bed was creaking! Plainly Matron was awake. The bed creaked a little more, and then there came the sound of someone shuffling into slippers.

'Now she puts on a dressing-gown,' thought Claudine. 'Now she ties the belt. But why is she getting up just now, if Eileen has not been to tell her?'

The little French girl squeezed herself into a dark corner as Matron's door suddenly opened. The thin narrow-shouldered figure appeared framed in the doorway, full in the moonlight. Matron looked rather grim.

She set off silently down the passage and turned off in the direction of the dormitory belonging to the fourth formers. Claudine followed her like a moving black shadow, keeping cleverly in the dark corners. Matron went into the dormitory where Eileen always slept.

'Eileen!' said Matron, in a whisper. But there was no answer. Then Matron evidently patted the bed and found no one there. There came an exclamation, and Matron switched on the light. In a moment she saw the empty beds!

She went into the next dormitory, where the fourth formers also slept, and again switched on the light. No girls there!

'Where are they?' said Matron, angrily. 'I will not have this sort of thing! Why didn't Eileen warn me of this? She ought to know better than to join in tricks of this sort!'

Claudine heard these muttered words, and was surprised. So Eileen *hadn't* warned her mother! She had followed the others out, and must be hiding somewhere in the grounds, watching the fun.

And now Matron was going to spoil everything. Why should she? Claudine felt a sudden and intense dislike for the severe and spiteful Matron. There was no harm in a moonlight swim and picnic! Quite likely if the girls had asked Miss Theobald's permission, she would have laughed and granted it, just for once! And now Matron was going to interfere.

Matron went down the stairs. She came to the cupboard where the girls had stored their picnic food and drink. They had left the door open. Matron gave an angry exclamation and went to shut it.

And it was then that the Great Idea came to Claudine!

It was an idea that might have occurred to any angry girl, but only Claudine would have carried it out.

Matron suddenly got the shock of her life! Someone gave her a violent push so that she landed inside the cupboard, among old lacrosse sticks and tennis-rackets. Then the door was shut – and locked!

Matron was a prisoner! Claudine took the key out of the cupboard and put it into her dressing-gown pocket. Choking with laughter she ran out of the garden door and made her way to the swimming-pool. She could hear Matron hammering on the door. But the little back-hall beyond the garden-door, near the cupboard, was seldom used, and far from any sleeping-quarters. It was quite likely that no one would hear Matron at all.

Now we are safe! thought Claudine, triumphantly. What a fine joke! But will these English girls think it is a joke?

For the first time a doubt came into her mind. She, Claudine, knew it to be a grand, grand joke to lock that so-detestable Matron up in a dark cupboard, to stop her from spoiling the fun – but would the others think like Claudine? Might not this curious 'honour' they were always talking about prevent them from thinking it a joke? Might not Susan Howes, fourth-form head girl, think it her duty to go and rescue Matron? One could never tell what the English would think right or wrong!

Then I shall not tell them what I have done! thought Claudine, as she sped along to the pool. If they do not know, they cannot worry. Now I will only tell them that it is all right, Eileen has not told tales, and that Matron is quite, quite safe.

The girls climbed out of the pool and surrounded Claudine when she came running back.

'It's all right,' said Claudine. 'Very much OK. Eileen has not told tales. She is not back at the school. And Matron is quite, quite safe!'

'Oh, *good*!' said all the girls, and shook the water from themselves. 'What about some eats now?'

'Where's Eileen then, if she isn't in bed and didn't go back to school?' said Bobby, puzzled.

But nobody knew and nobody cared. Let Eileen wander where she liked so long as she didn't spoil their fun. And how good that Matron was safe too!

The girls were very hungry after their swim. They sat down to enjoy the food. There was bread, butter, potted meat, tins of sardines, marmalade, apricot jam, cherries, biscuits and Mirabel's big birthday cake. The candles did not show up very well in the bright moonlight, but still, it was fun to light them.

The girls had their picnic by the edge of the water, dangling their legs in the pool. The water was lukewarm, for the sun had warmed it thoroughly. It was simply lovely. There had never been such midnight fun as this!

'This cake is gorgeous,' said Bobby, eating an enormous slice. 'My word – I don't ever remember feeling so hungry. Are those sardine sandwiches? Pass them along, Susan.'

Claudine enjoyed her meal more than anyone. True, she was not so hungry as the others, for she had not been in for a swim – but she could not help thinking of Matron shut up in the dark cupboard, quite unable to spoil the fun of the fourth formers! And that gave a very keen edge to her enjoyment of the picnic. She felt no anxiety as to what would happen when Matron was let out. Claudine never let things like that worry her at all!

The meal was over at last. Every scrap was finished. Even Angela said she had enjoyed it. Alison had not enjoyed it quite so much as the others because she had fallen into the water in her dressing-gown, and was worried as to how to dry it before Matron saw it. Mirabel said she had never enjoyed a birthday so much in all her life.

'It's been a great success,' said Janet, pleased. 'Now we'd better go back. Hark – there's one o'clock striking – Dong! Golly, I'm tired now.'

Everyone was tired. The swim had been rather strenuous, for there had been a lot of good-humoured racing and teasing. The girls cleared up crumbs, cartons and paper-bags, and put empty ginger-beer bottles into a locker up in the gallery, meaning to collect them when it was safe.

'That's all, I think,' said Susan, looking round. 'Isn't the water lovely, gleaming in the moonlight. I just hate to leave it!'

But they had to leave the gleaming pool. They made their way back through the trees, whispering together. They came to the garden door, which was still open.

And then they heard a most peculiar noise. Bang, bang, bang, knock, knock, knock!

'Crumbs! What's that?' said Susan, startled.

'Let me out, let me out!' cried a muffled voice, and somebody kicked against a wooden door.

Alison and Angela were terrified. 'It's a burglar!' said Alison, and tore up the stairs as fast as ever she could. Angela followed her, trembling.

Claudine pushed the others towards the stairs quickly. 'Don't stop,' she whispered. 'Get back to the dormitories as quickly as you can. Don't stop. I will explain everything.'

In the greatest astonishment the girls went upstairs to their dormitories. They crowded into the one in which Claudine slept, and demanded to know what the explanation of the curious noises was.

'It's Matron,' said Claudine. 'She's locked in that cupboard.'

There was an amazed silence.

'*Who* locked her in?' said Bobby at last.

'I did,' said Claudine. 'She came into our dormitories and saw we weren't there. I did not want her to spoil your fun – so I pushed her into the cupboard and locked her in. Was I not quick and clever?'

17

An infuriated Matron

For a minute or two no one said anything at all. The girls found it simply unbelievable that Claudine should have done such a thing. Locked Matron into a games cupboard! Left her there, shouting and hammering! Really, the French girl must be completely mad.

'No, I am not mad,' said Claudine, reading their thoughts. 'It was the only thing to do, wasn't it? She would have spoilt your fun, and I could stop her. So I stopped her.'

'But Claudine – you'll get into the most fearful row!' said Janet at last.

'That matters nothing,' replied Claudine, and certainly she acted as if she did not mind what happened! She was not in the least excited or upset. The girls went on staring at her, hardly able to take in the fact that Matron had been, and still was, a prisoner downstairs.

Then an awful thought came to Bobby. 'Who's going to let her out?'

Nobody said anything. Not even Claudine wanted to set free a woman who would be sure to be violently and spitefully angry. But certainly she could not be left in the cupboard till the morning.

'Where's the key?' said Janet. Claudine produced it

from her dressing-gown pocket. It was a large key. Claudine put her finger in the hole at the top of it and swung it thoughtfully to and fro.

'As I was the one who locked her in, I will also be the one to let her out,' she said at last. 'But I shall unlock the door very, very quietly, then open it a tiny way, and then I shall fly up the stairs, taking my heels with me.'

The girls couldn't help smiling. 'You mean, you will take to your heels and fly upstairs!' said Bobby. 'You do say ridiculous things, Claudine. Honestly, I can't imagine how you dared to do such a thing – locking Matron into a cupboard – golly, it's unheard of! Why didn't you tell us what you had done, when you came back to the pool and joined the picnic?'

'I thought you would say, "Ah, it is not honourable to do such a thing,"' explained Claudine. 'I thought maybe Susan would feel she ought to go and set Matron free. So I said nothing.'

'I never met anyone quite like you before,' said Pat. 'You do the most awful things for perfectly good reasons! I mean – you throw yourself into the pool when you *hate* the water, just to punish someone who's been unkind to your aunt – and you go and lock Matron up in a cupboard just so that we shan't have our picnic spoilt! I must say you do the most dramatic things – we never know what you're going to do next!'

'Well – what are we going to do about Matron?' demanded Susan, who was getting worried. 'Shall we let Claudine let her out?'

'I go,' said Claudine, and got up with much dignity. She loved moments like this, when she took the stage and everyone looked at her. She was not at all conceited, but there was to her a very satisfying feeling in doing something unusual and dramatic.

She went. The girls scrambled into bed, feeling that very shortly Matron would come bursting into the dormitories like an angry bull!

Claudine crept downstairs to the little back-hall by the garden-door. Matron was still shouting and hammering. Claudine slipped along to the door and put the key quietly into the key-hole – but just as she was about to turn it and unlock the door, she heard the sound of quiet footsteps on the gravel path outside!

She darted up the stairs at once, without turning the key. Let whoever it was coming by unlock the door! They would be sure to hear Matron, and set her free. Then she, Claudine, could get away in safety!

The footsteps came to the garden-door, and then someone slipped inside. It was Eileen! She stood still in the greatest astonishment as she heard the muffled cries and the banging on the door of the games cupboard.

'Why – it's Mother's voice!' said Eileen out loud, in the very greatest amazement. 'Where is she? She can't be in that cupboard!'

But she was, as Eileen very soon realized. The girl turned the key at once and opened the door. Matron stumbled out, almost beside herself with rage. She caught hold of Eileen in a fierce grip, not seeing which girl it was. Eileen cried out in pain.

'Mother! Don't! It's me, Eileen. However did you get into that cupboard?'

'*You*!' cried Matron, and let go Eileen's arm. 'What are *you* doing here? Where have you been? How dare you go out at night like this? Tell me what you have been doing, at once!'

Eileen said nothing at all. Her mother gave her a shake. 'You've been out somewhere with the fourth form. They are all out of their beds! What have you been doing? I shall report you all to Miss Theobald. Why didn't you tell me what was happening?'

'I can't say anything, Mother,' said Eileen, in a frightened voice. It was news to her that the fourth form had been out that night. She had not noticed any empty beds when she had slipped out herself. She had not heard any noise from the swimming-pool either. She had been out to meet her brother Eddie in the lane, and she was not going to tell her mother this. She no longer dared to meet him in the daytime, for she felt that anyone might see her, and report her. So she had been meeting him once a week in the middle of the night, when all her dormitory was sound asleep.

Nobody knew this. And certainly she must not let her mother know, or Eddie would get into trouble too. What had the fourth formers been doing? How mean of them to go off on a spree at night and leave her out! Somehow or other she must make her mother think she had been with them.

'You won't say anything?' said her mother in a threatening voice. 'Well, tell me this – who locked me in here? I can't imagine that *you* would dare to!'

'Of course I didn't,' said Eileen. 'And I don't know who did, either. Carlotta might have. It's the kind of thing she would do. I really don't know, Mother. Please let me go back to bed!'

But Matron was far too angry and humiliated to let the matter drop. She swept up the stairs to the fourth-form dormitories, and switched on the lights. The girls all pretended to be asleep. Matron walked into the dormitory where Eileen slept, and spoke in a loud and angry voice.

'It's no good your pretending to be asleep. I know you're not. I've come to find out who locked me into that cupboard! I insist on knowing, here and now. That girl will be expelled from St Clare's!'

Susan Howes sat up and looked at the angry Matron. 'We all take the blame for that,' she said, quietly. 'We are very sorry, Matron, and we hope you will accept our apologies.'

Matron made a fierce explosive noise. 'Accept your apologies! Of course I don't! You won't get out of this as easily as that! I insist on knowing who locked me in. Otherwise I shall go straight to Miss Theobald, here and now, in the middle of the night.'

Claudine sat up in bed, ready to speak. She did not in the least mind owning up. But Bobby laid a warning hand on her shoulder, and pulled her over towards her, to whisper into her ear.

'Don't own up to Matron! She will go to your aunt too, and make a fearful fuss, and there's no reason why Mam'zelle should be brought into this. You can tell Miss Theobald yourself tomorrow if you want to.'

'*Bien*!' said Claudine, snuggling down into bed again. 'Very good! I do as you say, Bobbee.'

Matron stood glaring round the room. Then she stamped heavily with her foot and almost shouted. 'All right! I shall go to Miss Theobald. You will all have to explain what you were doing in the middle of the night, leaving your beds like that – and I warn you, I shall show no mercy to the person who has not owned up to locking me in. Eileen, get into bed. I am absolutely ashamed to think that a daughter of mine should have joined in midnight wrong-doing, and should refuse to tell me anything about it!'

She went off down the corridor, walking angrily. The girls sat up.

'Whew!' said Bobby. 'What a volcano! I say, Eileen, where were you? Does your mother really think you were with us?'

'Yes,' said Eileen, in a low voice. 'Please don't give me away. I was only meeting Eddie, my brother. I was afraid to tell my mother that, so I let her think I was with you. I didn't know what you had been doing, so I couldn't possibly tell her, of course, and that has made her very wild with me. We're all going to get into a most fearful row.'

'I bet Miss Theobald won't be too pleased at being

wakened up at this time of night,' said Janet, looking at her watch. 'It's half-past one! We'd better try and get some sleep – though I expect the next thing will be Miss Theobald coming in and demanding explanations too!'

The girls tried to settle down and go to sleep. Mirabel fell asleep first, and then one by one the others did . . . all except Eileen, who lay awake, staring into the dark, worried and unhappy. Everything was going wrong! Everything was getting worse! Oh dear, she did hope the girls wouldn't give her away and say she had not been with them that night. They might quite well sneak about her. She had done plenty of sneaking that term, and it would not be at all surprising if they got a bit of their own back!

Matron walked down the corridor and made her way to the separate wing in which the head mistress, Miss Theobald, had her set of rooms. She knocked loudly on the bedroom door.

'Come in!' said a startled voice, and there was the sound of a light being switched on. Matron opened the door. Miss Theobald was sitting up in bed, eyes heavy with sleep.

'What is the matter?' she said anxiously. 'Is someone ill, Matron?'

'No,' said Matron, her thin face still purple with rage. 'Something much worse than that!'

'Good gracious, what?' asked Miss Theobald, hurriedly getting out of bed and reaching for her dressing-gown. 'Quick, tell me!'

'It's the fourth form,' said Matron, in a grim voice. 'All out of their beds, every one. Even my Eileen. Goodness knows what they were doing!'

Miss Theobald sat down on her bed in relief. 'Oh,' she said, 'a midnight feast, I suppose? I thought you had come to report something really serious! Couldn't this have waited till the morning, Matron?'

'Indeed it couldn't,' said Matron, 'and for a very good reason, too. Somebody locked me for hours into the games cupboard in the back-hall by the garden-door!'

Miss Theobald stared at Matron as if she really could not believe her ears. 'Locked you into the cupboard?' she said at last. 'Are you quite sure? I mean – I really cannot imagine any of the fourth formers doing that.'

'You don't know half that goes on in the school,' answered Matron in a grim and righteous tone. 'Not half! My Eileen tells me most things, and you'd be surprised if I told you some of them.'

'I don't think I want to hear,' said Miss Theobald, 'and I can't help thinking it is a mistake, Matron, to encourage Eileen to tell tales to you. Also I think you need not worry whether I know all that goes on or not. That is my concern.'

Matron sensed the rebuke in Miss Theobald's words, and she began to feel angry that the head had not expressed more anger and concern over her imprisonment in the cupboard. She looked grimmer than ever.

'Eileen set me free,' she said. 'Otherwise I might have been in the cupboard till the morning. A fine thing to happen to the Matron of a school like this! I went up to the fourth-form dormitories at once, and there were all the girls pretending to be asleep. Little hypocrites!'

'Oh, Matron, don't be quite so vindictive!' said Miss Theobald, feeling rather shocked at the Matron's tone. 'You have never been Matron in a girls' school before, and you are not yet used to the mischievous ways of the various forms. But as a rule there is little harm in them. Who locked you in?'

'The girls won't say,' said Matron, angrily. 'But I demand that whoever locked me in should be expelled, Miss Theobald. A girl that does a thing like that is a very bad influence on the others!'

'Well, I expect they were all in it,' said Miss Theobald. 'I should never expel a girl without a much stronger reason than mere mischief, Matron. I am certain that the whole form shared in the fun, and you would not expect me to expel the whole lot, would you? Do try and see things in a reasonable light. You are angry and annoyed now – you will not be so inclined to want girls expelled in the morning.'

'Aren't you coming back to the dormitories with me to demand who it was that locked me in?' demanded Matron, furiously, as she saw Miss Theobald taking off her dressing-gown and slippers.

'The girls will, I hope, be asleep by now,' said the head, getting into bed. 'I see no reason for waking them all up again. This can easily wait till the morning.'

Matron was infuriated. She had planned a most

dramatic return to the dormitories with Miss Theobald, and had gone so far as to hope that the head would demand to know the culprit and announce her expulsion there and then. She bit her thin lips and glared at Miss Theobald so angrily that the headmistress began to feel annoyed.

'Please go now, Matron,' she said. 'We will continue this rather complicated conversation in the morning.'

Matron took a step forward, and her face took on a malicious look. 'Well,' she said, 'I wasn't going to tell you till I'd found out the thief – but there's somebody in the fourth form who's been stealing, Miss Theobald! I've missed money – yes, and stamps too – and all kinds of things like notepaper and envelopes. You've got a nasty little thief in the fourth form, and I shall want *that* matter cleared up too! Otherwise, I am afraid – I shall go to the police!'

18

Claudine scores again

Miss Theobald disliked Matron intensely at that moment. It was quite plain that she took a real pleasure in saying these poisonous things.

'I think all these things must wait till the morning, Matron,' said the head. 'I will go into them thoroughly then. We can do nothing satisfactory tonight. Good night.'

Matron walked out of the room without answering. She hoped she had given Miss Theobald a shock. She had not meant to talk about her missing money, for she was taking a great pleasure in trying to track down the thief herself – and then she had meant to take her by the shoulder and lead her triumphantly to Miss Theobald. Matron hoped that the thief and the one who had locked her into the cupboard were one and the same. She felt certain they were. Surely only a very bad character could lock her into a cupboard!

'We shall perhaps get to the bottom of things tomorrow!' she thought, as she got into bed. 'I'll make Eileen tell me all that the fourth form did. I shan't say anything about my missing money to her, though, in case she warns the fourth form and the thief isn't caught.'

The fourth-form girls woke up tired and sleepy and

rather fearful the next morning. Had Matron been to Miss Theobald? What was going to happen?

Matron appeared at breakfast, grim and stern. Eileen had tear-stained eyes. Her mother had scolded her and demanded to know what the fourth form had been doing the night before. But Eileen had not told.

Bobby had spoken seriously to her. 'Look here, Eileen – we didn't ask you to our picnic last night because we were afraid you'd sneak to your mother, as you often do. But we'll make a bargain with you. We will say nothing at all about your not being with us – Matron can go on thinking you *were* with us – but you in your turn aren't to give us away any more at all. See? And if you do, the bargain is automatically broken, and we shall tell on you. It's the only way to teach you that sneaking doesn't pay.'

Eileen, looking pale and unhappy, had nodded. 'Thank you,' she said. 'I couldn't bear Mother to know I go and meet Eddie. She would be so angry with him. I won't split on any of you any more. I've sneaked, I know – but it's so difficult not to answer Mother's questions sometimes.'

Bobby guessed it was. Eileen had her own problems – but they wouldn't be solved by being weak and telling-tales! She had to find that out sooner or later.

But this morning Eileen had been determined and strong, for once, and had not answered Matron's insistent questions. Her mother had been very angry, and had scolded her severely. Matron had a fierce temper when she let herself go, and poor Eileen had had to bear the brunt of it.

'Claudine,' said Susan, in a low voice at breakfast-time, 'if you want to own up to Miss Theobald about locking Matron up, you'd better go immediately after breakfast. But if you don't want to own up, you needn't. We'll all stick by you, and ask Miss Theobald to hand out a punishment to the whole form. After all, we had a good time, because of you, and we none of us want you to be punished for something we would all dearly like to have done ourselves.'

'Thank you, Susan,' said Claudine, thinking that these English girls could be very nice and fair and generous. 'But I shall go to Miss Theobald. I am not ashamed of what I did. She is a nasty woman, the Matron, and I shall tell Miss Theobald that it filled me with pleasure to punish her for some of the unkind things she has done this term.'

'Well – do and say what you like,' said Susan, thinking that Claudine would, all her life, quite probably do and say exactly what she liked! 'And good luck to you!'

So Claudine went to the head, knocked firmly at the door and went in.

She began without any beating about the bush. 'Please, Miss Theobald, I have come to say that it was I who locked Matron in last night. I suppose it is not a thing that any English girl would have done, with their so-fine sense of honour, but I am French, and I did not like Matron, and I wanted the fourth form to have a good time. We went for a moonlight picnic, Miss Theobald, and swam in the pool. At least, I did not swim, but the others did, and they said it was magnificent.'

Miss Theobald found it difficult not to smile at the frank confession. Claudine always had such a very disarming and innocent air, even when she was doing or owning up to the most extraordinary things. The head looked keenly at the intelligent French girl.

'Why do you dislike Matron?'

'You wish me to say the truth to you?' asked Claudine. 'Well, then, I will say this. Matron can find out, through Eileen, all the little stupidities and mischiefs of the fourth formers, and then, see what happens! Miraculously our sheets get torn and we spend hours mending them. Suddenly stockings are full of holes, blouses are without buttons. Alas, Miss Theobald, we do not all like Eileen, and if we show it, then these unhappy things happen, and we sit indoors mending, whilst others play games.'

'I see,' said Miss Theobald. She had suspected this. 'Claudine, you cannot go about locking people into cupboards. I am certain that even French school girls do not do this!'

'Ah, Miss Theobald, I do not go about always locking people up!' said Claudine, beginning to launch herself on one of her long and involved speeches. 'No, no – only those people who deserve it should be imprisoned into cupboards. Me, I would never . . .'

Miss Theobald thought that Claudine had many of Mam'zelle's own ways. She smiled to herself and stopped the voluble explanation.

'That will do, Claudine. You will please apologize to Matron this morning, and you will accept what punishment she gives you. There is one thing more . . .'

She stopped and looked keenly at Claudine. The little French girl listened intently, for she had a great liking and respect for the wise and kindly head mistress.

'That one thing more is about the English sense of honour,' said Miss Theobald. 'You speak lightly of it, even mockingly – but I think, Claudine, in your heart of hearts you see it for the good and fine thing it really is. When you go back to France, Claudine, take one thing with you – the English sense of honour.'

Claudine looked solemn. She was very much moved.

'Miss Theobald,' she said, 'believe me when I say that I do not really mock at it. First I did not understand it. Then I thought it was tiresome in others and even more tiresome to have oneself. But now I begin to learn it, and it is good, very good.'

There came a knock at the door and Matron came in, looking grimmer than ever. She meant to have things out with Miss Theobald at once. Claudine was simply delighted to see her. 'Now,' thought the clever girl, 'now I will apologize to Matron in front of Miss Theobald, and she will not dare to be too spiteful to me nor to give me too great a punishment!'

So Claudine went meekly up to Matron, cast her eyes down to the ground, and spoke in a very timid voice.

'Matron, it was I who locked you in last night. I apologize to you and beg your forgiveness. I will gladly bear what punishment you give me!'

Miss Theobald looked on with much amusement. She

knew that Claudine was acting a part, and had cleverly taken advantage of Matron's coming, to apologize at once, in front of the headmistress herself.

Matron went purple in the face. She glared at Claudine and scolded her severely.

'You're a very naughty girl! You deserve to be expelled! And what is more, I *would* have you expelled if it was not that your aunt is the French mistress here, and it would break her heart to have a thing like that happen.'

Actually Matron was afraid of Mam'zelle, who was apt to fly off into even more violent tempers than Matron herself. Matron even felt that Mam'zelle might come and scratch her face and pull her hair out if she dared to try and get Claudine expelled.

'It is good of you to consider my kind aunt,' replied Claudine, still in a very meek voice. 'What is my punishment to be?'

'You will spend every hour of your spare-time this week helping me to mend the school linen,' said Matron. She did not see the flash of joy in Claudine's downcast eyes. Ah, now she would be able to get out of games and walks for a whole week! 'Very well, Matron,' she said, putting on a most miserable voice, that did not deceive the listening Miss Theobald in the least. She turned to the head.

'I will return now to my class,' she said, and gave Miss Theobald a brilliant and grateful smile. She went out of the room, shutting the door quietly. Miss Theobald thought that no one could help liking the naughty little girl, clever as she was at always getting her own way!

'Well, Miss Theobald,' said Matron, in a war-like tone, 'can we get down to this business of stealing? I can't have it happening any longer. It's got beyond me. Day after day it happens. And what's more, some more of my money has gone since last night! Only two pounds, it is true – but stealing two pounds is as bad as stealing ten pounds. It's thieving, right down bad thieving. And I think the girl who does it ought to be expelled. You wouldn't agree to expelling the girl who locked me in last night – but maybe you'll have to, Miss Theobald! Yes, maybe you'll have to!'

'What do you mean?' asked Miss Theobald in surprise.

'I mean this,' said Matron, 'I think it's that little French girl who's taking things! She's always in and out of my room with mending – and I hear she's been throwing a lot of money about lately – and *I* know she hasn't much, because Mam'zelle herself told me. So maybe, Miss Theobald, you will find that it's best to get rid of a girl of that sort, and will agree with me that it would be a good thing to expel her!'

19

Pauline's mother

Before Miss Theobald could make up her mind that day what would be the best way to tackle the Matron and her accusations, a nasty accident happened in the gym.

It happened to Pauline. She was climbing one of the ropes, and somehow slipped and fell to the ground. She fell with one leg doubled up under her, and there was a sickening crack.

Pauline crumpled up on the floor, went very white, and then quietly fainted. The games mistress hurried to her in alarm, and Matron was at once called and the doctor telephoned for.

'Broken her leg,' he said. 'Clean break. Nothing to worry about.'

He set it, and Pauline was put to bed, still white from the shock. Miss Theobald went to see her, and Pauline looked beseechingly up at her.

'Don't tell my mother,' she said. 'I don't want to worry her. Please don't tell her.'

'My dear child, I have already telephoned her,' said Miss Theobald in surprise. 'Why shouldn't she be told?'

'I don't want to worry her,' said Pauline, faintly. 'Please ring her up again, Miss Theobald, and say she is not to worry, and of course she is not to bother to come and see me. Say I will write to her today.'

'You can't write today,' said Miss Theobald gently. 'You must keep absolutely quiet today. I will ring your mother up again this evening, and tell her not to bother to come and see you if she cannot do so.'

'Tell her *not* to,' said Pauline. 'She – she hasn't been well, you see. I don't want her to be worried.'

Everyone was sorry about Pauline. The girls were not allowed to go and see her that day, but they sent her in little gifts of flowers and fruit and books.

'Everything seems to be happening at once,' said Bobby. 'I say – wasn't that a perfectly awful talk that Miss Theobald had with us this morning?'

It had been a very serious and solemn talk indeed, and had happened just before dinner that morning. All the fourth formers, except Pauline, who was in the sickbay, under Matron's care, had been called to Miss Theobald's sitting-room.

The head had lightly touched on the night before, telling them that Claudine had confessed, and had apologized to Matron and received a punishment for her extraordinary behaviour. She said that she would have given permission herself for a moonlight picnic and swim if she had been asked, but she realized that girls as young as the fourth still thought it was more fun to do things with*out* permission, than with.

This made the more responsible ones squirm a bit. They did not like being considered young and silly. Then

Miss Theobald passed on to Matron's other complaint. This was very much more serious, of course, and the fourth form listened in great discomfort as the head told them that a thief was in their midst, and must be found out, or must come and confess.

'You must realize that what would be a small thing, comparatively speaking, in the lower school, among the younger children, is a much more serious thing among you older girls,' said the head, 'and Matron is quite rightly concerned about the matter. Whoever is taking things from her room is doing it deliberately and continually – it is not something done in a moment of urgency and perhaps regretted bitterly afterwards – it is, apparently, quite cold-blooded, frequent and deliberate.'

The girls talked about it all afterwards, the affair of Matron being locked up in the cupboard taking second place to this much more serious accusation. Who in the wide world could it be?

'Matron is certain it's someone in the fourth form because our common-room is the only one near to her room,' said Bobby. 'It would be easy for someone to slip out now and then, see if the coast was clear, and then pop into Matron's room and sneak something.'

'Such peculiar things have been stolen besides money,' said Janet, puzzled. 'Stamps – and notepaper and envelopes. Why those? Matron says that biscuits and sweets have been taken too. It almost looks as if somebody has been taking anything they could, just out of spite.'

'Well, we none of us loves Matron!' said Bobby,

grinning. 'If it was just a question of paying her out for her meannesses, any one of us might be the culprit!'

'I am glad such things happen to her,' said Claudine. 'She deserves to have unhappiness, because she gives so much sadness to others. The poor Eileen has red eyes all day long today!'

'Yes, I can't help feeling sorry for her,' said Doris. 'It's bad enough to have Matron as Matron, but to have her as mother as well must be pretty awful!'

Pat, Isabel, Janet, Bobby and Hilary discussed the matter between themselves on the tennis-court that day.

'Who *could* it be?' said Bobby.

'Has anyone suddenly been having more money than usual?' wondered Pat. The same thought at once came into everyone's mind.

'Yes – Claudine has! She's been splashing it about like anything!'

'And she has plenty of chance of going into Matron's room because she is always taking mending there!'

'But it *can't* be Claudine! It's true she hasn't our sense of honour – but she wouldn't do a thing like that!'

'You know she doesn't care *what* she does when she dislikes somebody or wants to get even with them. She wouldn't think it was wrong, even.'

The five looked at one another, suddenly feeling extremely uncomfortable. They knew Claudine had very little money indeed – and yet she had given Angela that lovely bag – and had spent three whole pounds on cherries for the picnic. It did really seem as if it might be Claudine.

The bell rang for tea-time and the girls sped into the school. After tea Angela and Alison went off together down to the town to get something they wanted. On the way back they overtook an elderly woman, dressed in sober black clothes, sensible flat-heeled shoes, and a plain hat. She wore glasses, and her face was thin and worn, but kindly.

'I bet that's a cook come after the job at St Clare's,' said Angela to Alison. The girls passed her and she turned and spoke to them.

'Could you tell me if I am on the right road for St Clare's? You are St Clare girls, aren't you?'

'Yes,' said Alison. 'Keep straight on.'

The girls made as if to go on, but the woman stopped them with a question that astonished them very much.

'How is my girl Pauline now? The head mistress telephoned me to say she had broken her leg this morning, and I caught the first train I could. I'm Mrs Jones.'

Angela and Alison stopped dead in the road and stared open-mouthed at the little elderly woman. They remembered Pauline's wonderful stories of Mrs Bingham-Jones, her beautiful and wealthy mother. They simply could not understand this plain, tired-looking woman, almost old, being Pauline's supposedly wonderful mother.

Scorn welled up at once in Angela's heart. So Pauline, who was always trying to out-do and out-boast Angela herself, had, for a mother, a woman who looked like a worn-out cook. She tried to pull Alison up the road quickly.

But something in Mrs Jones's tired face had touched

Alison. Alison had many faults, but she was sensitive to other people's feelings, and she could sense Mrs Jones's worry and anxiety. She shook her arm away from Angela's.

'Pauline is all right,' she said, kindly. 'We couldn't see her today but we've all sent her something – you know, flowers and books and things – just to cheer her up. Are you better now? Pauline was *so* disappointed that you and her father couldn't come and see her at half-term, because you were ill.'

Mrs Jones looked extremely surprised. 'I haven't been ill,' she said. 'I wanted to come at half-term, but Pauline wrote to say there was a case of scarlet fever at the school, and the half-term matches had been put off, so would I not come.'

Alison was horrified. In a flash she saw that Pauline, afraid that her mother would not shine among the other mothers, knowing that she had told all kinds of lies that would be found out when the girls saw her elderly, tired mother, had actually made up the lie about scarlet fever to stop her people from coming at half-term – and had pretended to be bitterly disappointed because they weren't coming!

Angela, of course, heard what was said, and an expression of scorn and contempt came over her face.

'*Well*!' she said. 'There was no case of . . .' But Alison was not going to let Angela interfere in the matter. She gave her friend a sharp nudge that made her squeal in surprise. Then she gave her such a fierce look that Angela said no more, but thought in surprise that Alison must be mad to treat her, Angela, like that.

'I hope Pauline is happy at St Clare's?' said Mrs Jones. 'She has always wanted to go there, ever since she heard about it. I didn't see that I could afford to send her, but I managed to scrape enough together. Her poor father is an invalid, you know – has been for years – but I expect she's told you all that. We haven't a lot of money, but I did want Pauline to have a good time at a nice school. I said to her, "Well, my dear, you won't have as much pocket-money as the others, and you won't have as many treats, but there you are, if you like to go under those conditions, I won't stop you."'

Mrs Jones talked to Alison, not to Angela. She liked Alison's pretty, kindly little face, and was glad to have someone to talk to. Angela gave a snort of contempt, and went quickly on, up the hill towards St Clare's.

'It's quite a way, isn't it?' said Mrs Jones, beginning to pant. 'I didn't take a taxi, because taxis are expensive and I thought I could easily walk. Poor little Pauline – it is terribly bad luck to have broken her leg like this. I thought she would be so pleased to see me, if I can hurry along at once.'

Alison didn't feel so certain. She thought that if Pauline had kept her mother away by lies at half-term she would certainly not want her at St Clare's now, with all her lies exposed for what they were.

'Pauline is disgusting,' thought Alison. 'She really is. She takes everything from this poor little mother of hers, who probably goes without a lot of things she wants in order to pay for Pauline here – and then keeps her away from the school because she is ashamed of her! Beast!'

Alison took Mrs Jones to the school door and left her there in charge of a teacher. She went to take off her hat and blazer and joined the rest of her form in the common-room.

'I hope Angela doesn't go and hold forth about Pauline's poor old mother,' thought Alison uncomfortably. 'I feel sorry for the old thing. She looked so tired and worn.'

She heard Angela's voice as she opened the common-room door.

'And, my dear, *I* know who it was that took Matron's beastly money and everything! There's not a doubt of it. It was Pauline!'

'Pauline! What do you mean? Why do you say that?' came Janet's voice at once.

'I'll tell you why,' said Angela, and paused dramatically. 'I and Alison walked up the road with Pauline's mother today – and from what she said to us it's pretty certain that our dear Pauline is a frightful story-teller and quite likely a horrid little thief!'

20

Angela – and Claudine

'You'll have to tell us why you say all this,' said Bobby. The whole of the fourth form crowded round to hear. Only Claudine was not there, and neither, of course, was Pauline.

'Well, listen,' said Angela, spitefully, 'I and Alison were walking up the road and we saw an ugly little elderly woman, awfully plain, dressed in black, in front of us. I thought she must be a cook coming to try for the job going here. And it turned out to be Mrs Jones, Pauline's mother – not Mrs *Bingham*-Jones, if you please, but just plain Mrs Jones.'

'She's a nice little woman,' said Alison, not liking the contempt in Angela's voice.

'*Nice* little woman!' said Angela, rounding on Alison scornfully. 'Common as dirt, you mean! And when I think of Pauline's airs and graces – trying to make out her mother was as good as mine – trying to pretend that her family were as grand as mine really are – swanking about her cars and things – and they're as poor as church mice, and can only just afford to send Pauline here! Golly, won't I tell Pauline what I think of her when I see her! *I'll* tell her what I think of dear Mrs Jones, dressed up like a cook, moaning about her poor little Pauline.'

Before anyone else could speak, Alison stood up. She was rather white, and there was a strange look on her face.

'You won't tell Pauline anything of the sort,' she said. 'You won't tell Pauline *any*thing that's going to make her ashamed of that poor old mother of hers. Don't you realize how you'll make her hate her mother, if she knows you saw her and are saying this kind of thing about her? I think Pauline has behaved disgustingly about things, but I'm not going to have you making matters worse for Mrs Jones by saying horrible things about her to Pauline.'

Angela was amazed. Could this be her friend Alison talking to her like this? She stared at her, unable to say a word. Then she found her tongue.

'Well, if you stick up for people like Pauline's awful mother, I'm jolly glad you're not coming to stay with me for the holidays,' she said, spitefully. 'I'm going! I shan't stay here to be insulted by somebody I thought was my best friend.'

Poor Alison was now trembling, for she hated rows. Angela moved towards the door. But to her intense surprise and annoyance, two girls caught firmly hold of her arms and sat her down violently, almost jerking the breath out of her body.

'You may not want to listen to Alison, but you're jolly well going to listen to *us*!' said Carlotta, her eyes flashing fire. 'Now *we* will say a few things!'

'Let me go, you beasts,' said Angela, between her teeth.

'You seem to be talking a lot about mothers,' said Carlotta, bending over the angry Angela, and talking in such a fierce tone that Angela drew back, afraid. 'Well, we *will* talk about mothers – *your* mother! We would not talk about her if it was not necessary – but it is very necessary now, in order to get some sense into your thick head!'

'I'll scream if you don't let me go,' said Angela, in a rage.

'Every time you scream I shall pinch you hard, like that,' said Carlotta, and gave Angela such a pinch on her plump shoulder that she squealed in pain.

'Shut up, Carlotta,' said Bobby. 'You can't act like that.'

'Yes, I can,' said Carlotta, coolly. And Angela knew she could, so she made no further sound.

'Pauline's mother may be tired and old and plain and poor,' said Carlotta, 'but that's no reason to despise her. Now there *is* reason to despise *your* mother, Angela! She is a spoilt, rude, discontented, horrible little snob – just like you are! And will you please tell her on no account to come here again, turning up her nose at everything, because we don't want to see her, we dislike her and despise her, and we want her to take you away as soon as ever she will!'

'Hear hear!' said Bobby, Janet and the twins. Angela went very pale. These were terrible things to hear, but she had brought them on herself. She, too, had been ashamed of her spoilt mother when she had come at half-term – but she had not guessed how bitterly the girls had resented her contemptuous attitude towards the school and all it stood for.

'That's enough, Carlotta,' said Susan Howes, uncomfortably. And it was enough. Angela looked as if she was about to faint. She wanted to sink through the floor. She, who had boasted and bragged of herself and her family, who had set herself up as better than any of them, was being spoken to as if she were dirt. She gave an enormous sob, and fled from the room.

'Well, thank goodness she's gone,' said Pat. 'Cheer up, Alison. I was proud of you when you spoke up like that. Perhaps now you will see Angela as clearly as *we* see her.'

'Yes – I do,' said poor Alison, really distressed. 'I think she's awful. I did feel so sorry for that poor Mrs Jones – and Angela had nothing but scorn for her. There's no kindness in her!'

'None at all,' said Janet. 'Well – she's got to learn that kindness breeds kindness, and spite breeds spite. She'll have an awful time if she doesn't.'

'Do you think it's right, what Angela said, that Pauline might be the thief?' said Doris. 'She *has* splashed money about very much lately – and if she's really poor – where did it come from?'

'We half thought it might be Claudine,' said Isabel. 'You know, she's poor too – hardly ever has a penny – and then, quite suddenly, she had lots of money. And you know how unscrupulous Claudine is! I like her – but she simply has no sense of honour at all! We did wonder if it could be her.'

'Sh! Sh!' said someone. But too late – for Claudine, who had come in unnoticed, had heard what Isabel had said!

The little French girl at once pushed her way to the front of the crowd of girls. Isabel saw her coming, and was horrified. Not for the world would she have had Claudine hear what she had said!

'Claudine!' she said. 'I'm sorry you heard. Don't be angry. We only thought it because you seem so different from us in your ideas of honour. And it did seem to us that if you disliked Matron, you might pay her out in that way.'

Claudine looked round the little group, intense anger in her small face. She saw Isabel's earnest face, Pat's scared one, Bobby's watchful one – and then, to the enormous astonishment of the listening girls, the anger in her face melted away – and Claudine threw back her head and laughed!

The girls stared at her in surprise. Honestly, thought Doris, you simply never know what Claudine will do!

Bobby thought how like Mam'zelle she was, in her swift changes from anger to laughter. But what a blessing that Claudine could see some humour in Isabel's words!

'I am not angry,' said Claudine, at last, wiping away the tears of laughter. 'No, I am not angry. You English girls, you are so serious and solemn and so very, very honourable. I too have my own honour, and although it is not quite like yours yet, perhaps, one day it will be. The good Miss Theobald, she said to me this morning that one thing I must take back to France with me, one only – the English sense of honour.'

'Just like Miss Theobald to say a thing like that,' said Janet. 'But why did you laugh just now, Claudine?'

'I laugh because I was thinking so suddenly of the

reason why I have so much money now to spend,' said Claudine, smiling her infectious smile. 'But first, if I tell you, you must promise, on your English honour, that never, never will you tell my Aunt Mathilde what I have done!'

'Oh, Claudine – *what* have you done?' said Pat, imagining the most awful things.

'You remember my so-beautiful cushion-cover that my aunt loved so much?' said Claudine. 'Well, I sold it to one of your mothers for quite a lot of money! You see, I needed money – there were birthdays coming, and I do not like to have so little. And one of your mothers, she was so nice to me, and she bought my so-beautiful cover, and I sent it to her by post. I explained to her that it was my own, and I lacked for money, and she was so, so kind to me.'

'Was that *my* mother?' asked Alison, suspiciously. 'I saw you talking nineteen to the dozen to her at half-term. Mother *would* do a nice thing like that, and never say a word about it. I hope she puts the cushion-cover in my bedroom, that's all!'

'Well,' said Claudine, grinning all over her little monkey-face, 'it *might* have been your so-nice mother, Alison. My sense of honour forbids me to say. And now I appeal to *your* sense of honour also, not to tell my aunt what has happened to my cushion-cover. I told her I had sent it to my mother.'

'You *are* an awful story-teller, Claudine,' said Gladys, shocked. 'You deceive people right and left! I just can't understand you. Why couldn't you tell Mam'zelle you had sold the cover, instead of telling lies and keeping it a secret?'

'Ah, me, I adore secrets!' said Claudine, her eyes dancing. 'And Aunt Mathilde would have written to the so-kind mother and got the cover back and repaid the money, and I should have been so, so sad, for it is nice to earn money, do you not think so?'

'I think you're a puzzle,' said Janet. 'I'll never make you out, Claudine. You go and tell lies in order to sell your cushion-cover and get money for somebody's birthday – you shut Matron up to give us a good time – you . . .'

'Ah, say no more of my badness,' said Claudine, earnestly. 'One day I may become good. Yes, certainly I shall become good if I stay at this so-fine school for another term!'

'Well, you're jolly decent not to have taken offence at what I said,' said Isabel, warmly. 'I'm glad you told us where you got the money from. I'm afraid now it means that Pauline must have taken it. She's had such a lot of money lately. Blow! I wish beastly things like this wouldn't happen! What do you think we ought to do about it?'

'Hilary and I will go to Miss Theobald and tell her everything,' said Susan. 'We can't tackle Pauline now, she won't be fit enough. But Miss Theobald ought to know what we think and why. Come on, Hilary. Let's get it over!'

21

Alison is a good friend

Hilary and Susan went to Miss Theobald's room and knocked on the door. She called out to them to come in. Fortunately she was alone. She looked up with a pleasant smile as the two girls came in.

'Well,' she said, 'what do you fourth formers want? You haven't been getting into any more trouble I hope?'

'No, Miss Theobald,' said Susan. 'But we are rather worried about this stealing business – and we have an idea who it is.'

'Why doesn't the girl herself come to me, then?' said Miss Theobald, looking very serious.

'Well – she can't,' said Susan. 'You see – we think it's Pauline – and you know she's in the sickbay with a broken leg.'

'*Pauline*!' said Miss Theobald, astonishment showing in her face. 'I can't think it is Pauline. She isn't the type. No – surely it cannot be Pauline.'

'We thought it might be Claudine at first,' said Hilary. 'But it isn't.'

'Ah, I am glad of that,' said Miss Theobald. 'I still cannot think it is Pauline. She is not altogether sensible in some ways – but she did not seem to be at all a dishonest girl.'

'Well, Miss Theobald, we have something else to tell you about Pauline, which will show you that she is really peculiar in some ways, and not at all truthful,' said Susan, gravely. 'We are not, of course, telling tales to you – but we know we can't deal with this ourselves, so we have come to you.'

'Quite rightly,' said Miss Theobald, also very gravely. 'Well – what is there to say about Pauline? Her mother is with her now, and possibly I might be able to have a talk with her about Pauline before she goes.'

Hilary and Susan together told Miss Theobald of Pauline's ridiculous boasting and lying – of how she had put off her mother coming at half-term by telling an absurd story about a scarlet-fever case – how she had pretended to be bitterly disappointed – how she had always seemed to have plenty of money, and yet her mother had told Alison she was afraid that Pauline would always be short of pocket-money.

'So, you see,' said Hilary, 'putting everything together, and knowing what an awful fibber Pauline was, we felt it was probably she who stole from Matron.'

'I see,' said Miss Theobald. 'Curiously enough, people who tell lies for the reason that Pauline tells them, are rarely dishonest in other ways. You see, Pauline lies because she longs to be thought better than she is – that is the *only* reason she lies. Now, if she stole, she would know herself to be despicable, and that others would despise her too. So she would not steal. But from all you tell me I am afraid that she does steal. Having so much money when it is clear that her mother cannot supply her with much is very curious.'

'Yes, it is,' said Susan. 'Well, Miss Theobald, we have told you all we know and think. We would all like this stealing business to be cleared up – the fourth form hate it, as you can imagine – and we are glad to leave it in your hands to settle.'

There came a knock at the door. Miss Theobald called, 'Come in.' Before anyone entered she nodded to the two fourth formers to dismiss them.

'I will see to everything,' she said. 'I will talk to Pauline – possibly tomorrow or the day after – as soon as she has recovered from the shock of her broken leg. The doctor is to put it in plaster, and then she will return to school to do lessons, whilst it is healing. It is essential that I should have this matter cleared up before she returns to the fourth form.'

A staff member had entered the room and waited until Miss Theobald had finished speaking. 'Mrs Jones would like a word with you before she goes.'

'Tell her to come in,' said Miss Theobald. Mrs Jones came in. Hilary and Susan glanced at her curiously as they went out. So this poor, tired, worried-looking little woman, so plainly dressed, was Pauline's marvellous, pretty, beautifully dressed, wealthy mother! What an idiot Pauline was!

Mrs Jones plunged into her worries as soon as the door shut. 'Oh, Miss Theobald, I'm really bothered about Pauline. She didn't seem at all pleased to see me. She cried her heart out when I told her I'd met some of her school-fellows on the way up, and had talked to them. I just can't understand her. I thought she'd be so pleased to see me. She even blamed me for coming – said I was making a fuss – and after all she's my only child, and very precious to me.'

Miss Theobald looked at the distressed woman and was very sorry for her. She wondered whether or not to say anything about Pauline's stupid boasting, and to explain that Pauline's unkindness was because she was ashamed of having her lies exposed for what they were – she was ashamed of her mother, ashamed of not having enough money, ashamed of everything, so that she had forced herself to make up a whole new family and home of her own.

Then she decided not to say anything. It would only hurt and worry the poor little woman even more. She must have a serious talk with Pauline first, and perhaps she could persuade Pauline herself to put matters right.

So she listened, and tried to comfort Mrs Jones as best she could. 'Don't worry,' she said. 'Pauline has had a shock, through falling like that. Don't take any notice of what she says.'

Mrs Jones went at last, only half comforted, feeling puzzled and hurt. Miss Theobald sighed. There suddenly seemed to be quite a lot of difficult problems to solve. How upset poor Mrs Jones would be if she had to be told that her only child was a thief, as well as a stupid boaster!

'I will have a talk to Pauline tomorrow or the next day,'

thought Miss Theobald. 'I only hope Matron does not make any more fuss – really, she is a most unpleasant woman.'

Matron did make plenty more fuss! She went storming into Miss Theobald's room the next morning, with another complaint.

'Five pounds gone this time! A five-pound note! Out of my purse too. And I had hidden it for safety in my mending-basket. But it's gone all the same. Miss Theobald, that girl has got to be found and expelled!'

Miss Theobald listened in astonishment. How could *Pauline* be the thief if she was in the sickbay with a broken leg? But, as Matron went on complaining, it appeared that her mending-basket had been in the sickbay. She had taken it there to do her mending, as she had to sit with Pauline.

So Pauline *might* have been able to take the note from the purse. Other girls had popped in and out too, as Pauline was allowed to see her form that day. It was all very tiresome. Miss Theobald got rid of Matron as soon as she could, thinking that a lot of trouble was coming out of the fourth form that term!

The fourth formers had been very cool towards Angela since the row. Angela looked pinched and unhappy but nobody felt sorry for her, not even Alison. At half-past twelve Alison saw Angela putting on her hat to go out.

'Where are you going?' she asked. 'You know we mustn't go down to the town alone – do you want me to come with you?'

'No,' said Angela, sulkily. 'If you want to know what I'm going to do, I'll tell you. I'm going down to the nearest telephone box to telephone my mother and tell her all the beastly things you've said about her, and ask her to come today and take me away!'

'No, don't do that,' said Alison, distressed. 'We only said those things because you were so horrid about poor old Mrs Jones, Angela.'

But Angela's mind was made up and off she went. Alison waited about miserably, not liking to tell the others. She pictured Angela's mother sweeping down in her Rolls Royce, spiteful and malicious, ready to say all kinds of horrible things about St Clare's and its girls. It was not a pleasant thought.

Presently, about five minutes before the dinner-bell, she saw Angela coming back. But what a miserable, tear-stained Angela! Alison went to meet her, unexpectedly liking this humble, unhappy Angela far more than she had liked the bright and boastful one.

'What's the matter?' she said. Angela turned to Alison, and began to weep bitterly.

'Oh, Alison! Mother's away – and I got on to Daddy instead. But instead of listening to me and comforting me, he was very angry. And oh, he said Mother hadn't any right to talk as she did at half-term – and he was going to see *I* didn't grow up thinking I could say hurtful things to people – and he's coming today to see Miss Theobald about me!'

'Oh, Angela!' said Alison, in dismay. 'How simply

awful! He *must* have been angry. Miss Theobald won't be at all pleased when she hears you've been telephoning to your people and complaining. You'll get into a row from everyone!'

'Oh, I know, I know,' wept Angela. 'I don't know what to do. Oh, Alison, I know I've been beastly. But please don't desert me now. I was awful yesterday about Pauline's mother. I'm ashamed of it now. Do, do be my friend again.'

'Angela,' said Alison, looking very serious all of a sudden, 'I've been a very bad sort of friend to you. I've praised you and flattered you and thought the world of you, when all the time it would have been better to have laughed at you and teased you, like the others do. Bobby would have made you a much better friend, or the twins. They would have been sensible with you. I've spoilt you and been silly.'

'Well, never mind, go on being my friend,' begged Angela, who, now that things were looking black, felt that she simply *must* have someone who liked her. 'Please do, Alison. I'll try and be nicer, I really will. But oh, what shall I say to Daddy when he comes this afternoon? I'm so afraid of him when he gets really angry.'

'Listen,' said Alison, 'immediately after lunch we'll go down to the telephone box again. You get on to your father, and then say that you've been thinking things over, and you've come to the conclusion you've been an idiot but you'd like another chance. Then let me have a word with him, and maybe between us we can stop him coming.'

'Oh, Alison, you're a brick!' said Angela, drying her

eyes, and sniffing. 'Daddy liked you. He'll listen to you. Oh, thank you for your help.'

The dinner-bell had long since gone. The two girls were late. Miss Ellis, taking a look at Angela's swollen eyes, contented herself with a few sharp words and then said no more.

Immediately after dinner the girls went off to the telephone box. Angela got through to her annoyed father, and made her little speech. 'I've been an idiot. I see it now. Don't come down, Daddy. I'm going to try and do better. Here's my friend Alison to talk to you.'

The telephone receiver was passed to Alison who, rather nervous, spoke the little speech she herself had prepared.

'Good afternoon! This is Alison speaking, Angela's friend. Angela is all right now. She was upset before, and rather silly. But I am sure she is going to settle down now and be a sport. So I don't think you need to leave your work and come to St Clare's.'

'Oh,' said Angela's father, in a grim voice. 'Well, as I'm very busy, I won't today. But any more nonsense from Angela and I shall come down and make a Big Row. I put Angela into St Clare's because it's the finest school I know. And there she is going to stay until she, too, thinks it's the finest school *she* knows. If you really are her friend, you'll help her to realize this. You've been there some time, I know.'

'Yes, I have,' said Alison, earnestly. 'And it is the very finest school in the kingdom! I'll teach Angela that, really I will, and so will the others.'

'Well, don't spoil her,' said the far-off voice, not sounding quite so grim. 'Shake her up a bit! She may look like a golden princess, or an angel, but she's not a bit like one inside. And I'd like her to be. Tell her to speak to me again.'

Angela took the receiver. What she heard comforted her. 'Thank you, Daddy,' she said. 'I'll try. I really will. Goodbye.'

She put the receiver back, looking much happier. 'Daddy said that although he is often angry with me, he will always love me,' she said to Alison. 'And he said if I loved him, I'd try to be a bit more like he wants me to be. So I shall try now. Thanks, Alison, for your advice!'

She squeezed her friend's arm. Alison took Angela's arm in hers and they walked back to the school. Alison was talking sternly to herself as they went.

'Now, no more telling Angela she is lovely! No more flattering her! No more praising her up to the skies because she looks like an angel! It's no good looking like one if you're just the opposite inside. Tease her and laugh at her and scold her and point out her faults – that's what I've got to do if I'm to be a real friend to Angela.'

And, to the astonishment of all the fourth form, things between the two friends appeared now to be quite changed! Angela was now the docile one, accepting teasing criticism, and Alison was the leader!

'Good for both of them!' said Bobby, with a grin. 'This will make Angela a nicer person altogether, and will end in giving Alison quite a lot of common sense!'

22

Matron has a shock

'I wonder whether Miss Theobald has tackled Pauline about taking Matron's money and other things yet,' said Hilary to Susan, after tea that day.

Eileen looked up, startled. She had not been there the day before when the matter had been discussed and Hilary and Susan had gone off to see Miss Theobald. She had been cross-examined continually by her mother, who had tried to find out exactly what the fourth formers had done on Mirabel's birthday night – but Eileen had kept her word, and had not told her anything.

'Pauline – taking Mother's money?' said Eileen, amazed. 'What's all this? I haven't heard a word about it.'

'*Haven't* you?' said Janet, surprised. 'Oh, no – you were with Matron when we discussed it yesterday – and today we haven't had a minute to say anything about it. Not that there's anything much to say, really, except that we all think it's Pauline who has taken the things belonging to your mother. You see, we know now that her people can hardly afford to send her here and that she hasn't much pocket-money – so, as she has been splashing money about lately, we felt sure she was the thief. She's such a fibber, she could quite well go a bit further and be a thief as well!'

'And Miss Theobald is going to tackle her about it,' said Susan. 'Hilary and I went and told her everything yesterday. I'm sorry Pauline broke her leg – but really, if she's a thief as well as a story-teller, I think it's a good punishment for her.'

Eileen sat and stared at the chattering girls. Bobby thought she looked rather strange.

'Do you feel all right?' she asked. 'You look a bit funny.'

'Of course I'm all right,' said Eileen. She got up and went out. To the girls' astonishment they saw her, a minute later, flying down the drive at top speed.

'What's up with Eileen?' said Hilary, in amazement. 'Has she forgotten we've got prep to do tonight?'

She apparently had. She did not turn up for prep at all, and Miss Ellis sent to ask Matron if she had kept Eileen with her for any reason. Matron appeared at the classroom door, looking annoyed.

'I can't imagine where Eileen is,' she said. 'I hope you will punish her, Miss Ellis. She has been such an obstinate, stubborn girl lately.'

Eileen did not even return for supper, and it was only when the fourth formers were getting undressed that they saw her again. Doris looked out of her dormitory window and saw Eileen coming up one of the school-paths. With her was somebody else.

'It's Eddie!' said Alison. 'Gracious, won't Eileen get into a row! She must have shot off to see Eddie, and now he's come back with her.'

Eileen looked strung-up and tearful. Eddie looked

much the same. They disappeared into the school. Instead of going up to their mother's room, they went straight to Miss Theobald's room.

'Cheer up!' whispered Eddie. 'I'm here! I'll take care of you, Eileen.'

The two went into Miss Theobald's room. The head mistress looked surprised to see Eileen with a boy. Eileen told her who Eddie was.

'This is my brother Edgar,' she said, and then she broke down, and began to sob bitterly and piteously. Miss Theobald was distressed. Eddie put his arm protectively round his sister.

'Don't cry,' he said. 'I'll tell about everything.' Then he turned to Miss Theobald.

'Miss Theobald,' he said, 'today Eileen heard that another girl, Pauline, was going to be accused of stealing from Matron, our mother. Well – it was Eileen that took all the money and other things, not Pauline or anyone else!'

'*Well*!' said Miss Theobald, thinking that surprises were coming thick and fast in the last few days. 'But, why? What made her do such an extraordinary thing?'

'It was because of me,' said Eddie. 'You see, I got a job in an engineering works at the beginning of this term, and Mother was very pleased. Well, I hadn't been there long before I had an accident with a car, and they sacked me. I – I didn't dare to tell my mother, Miss Theobald.'

Miss Theobald looked at the weak, thin face of the lad in front of her, and was not surprised that he feared his bad-tempered, spiteful-tongued mother. How she would tear him and rend him with her tongue if she knew he had failed in his job!

'Well,' went on Eddie, swallowing hard, and still holding his arm round Eileen, 'well, I thought maybe I'd be able to get another job fairly soon, and then Mother need only be told that I'd changed jobs. But, you see, I'd no money, and I had my lodgings and food to pay for – so I managed to hitch-hike over here one day and see Eileen without Mother knowing. And I asked her to give me what money she had.'

'I see,' said Miss Theobald, very grave. 'And Eileen stole from her mother to give to you.'

'I didn't know she was taking Mother's money,' said Eddie. 'I thought it was her own – out of her money-box or out of the post office savings. I knew she'd got a little. And she brought me biscuits too, and some notepaper and stamps to apply for other jobs. She's – she's been such a brick to me, Miss Theobald.'

'Oh, Eddie, I'd do anything for you, you know that,' sobbed poor Eileen. 'But Miss Theobald, when I knew Pauline was going to be accused of something *I'd* done – then I rushed out and went to Eddie, and told him everything. And he came back with me to tell you. Oh, Miss Theobald, we don't dare to tell Mother!'

'What a mix-up!' said Miss Theobald, looking at the two scared, unhappy young faces before her. She could not help in her heart blaming Matron very much for all this. If she had been a kindly, loving mother, helping her children instead of expecting far too much of them, this would never have happened. They would have gone running to her for comfort and help, instead of hiding things from her, and stealing from her, too frightened to do anything else.

'You see,' said Eileen, drying her eyes, 'as Eddie is Mother's son, I didn't really think it was wrong to take her money and other things to help him.'

'I see,' said Miss Theobald. 'But it *was* wrong all the same. Eileen, I am glad to think that you had the courage to realize that you could not let another girl bear the blame for your own wrong-doing. That is a great point in your favour.'

There was a pause. Then Eddie spoke, rather nervously. 'Miss Theobald – do you think you could see Mother for us? Please do. She might not be so terribly angry if you spoke to her first.'

Miss Theobald felt a little grim. 'Yes,' she said, 'I *will* see her. You two can wait in the next room until I have spoken to her.'

Eddie and Eileen retired to the next room, looking forlorn and frightened. Miss Theobald sent a message asking Matron to come and speak to her.

Matron soon appeared, crackling in starched apron and uniform.

'Sit down, Matron,' said Miss Theobald. 'I have found out who has taken your money and I wanted to tell you about it.'

'I hope you will expel the girl,' said Matron, in a severe voice. 'After all, Miss Theobald, I've got a girl here myself, in the fourth form. It's not a very good influence for her, is it, to have a thief living side by side with her?'

'Well, Matron,' said Miss Theobald, 'I have made up my mind that I myself will not decide whether to expel this poor little thief or not. You shall decide, and you alone.'

Matron's eyes sparkled. 'Thank you,' she said. 'You may consider that my decision is taken. The girl will go – and go tomorrow!'

'Very well,' said Miss Theobald. 'Now listen to my story, please. This girl did not steal for herself, but for someone she loved, who was in trouble.'

'Stealing is always stealing,' said Matron, in a righteous voice.

'She was afraid to go to her mother for help, afraid to go to her for advice,' continued Miss Theobald.

'Then the mother is as much to blame as the girl,' said Matron. 'Mothers who have children so scared of them that they will steal have done a very bad job as mothers.'

'I thoroughly agree with you,' said Miss Theobald. 'Nevertheless, this girl had the courage to come and tell me, and she asked me to tell you.'

'Where *is* the little thief?' said Matron, fiercely. '*I* shall have a few words to say to her, I promise you! Out she goes tomorrow!'

Miss Theobald stood up and opened the door connecting her sitting-room with her study. 'You will find the little thief in here,' she said. 'With her brother.'

Matron walked firmly into the study, ready to lash out at the thief. She saw there her two children, Eileen and Eddie. They stared at her nervously.

'What's this?' said Matron, in a faint voice. 'Why is Eileen here – and Eddie?'

'Eileen is the thief, Matron – and Eddie is the one she stole for – and you are the hard mother they were too scared to come to for advice and help,' said Miss Theobald, in a grave and serious voice. 'And I think, knowing you as I do – that Eileen is not the one who should leave St Clare's – but you!'

Matron's face suddenly crumpled up and her mouth began to tremble. She stared unbelievingly at Eileen and Eddie. Eileen was crying again.

'You are a hard and spiteful woman,' went on Miss Theobald's solemn voice. 'This boy and girl need help and comfort, but they would never get it from you!'

'I've got another job, got it today, Mother!' said Eddie. 'I shall pay back every penny Eileen took. You're not to scold her. She did it for me because she loved me. Soon I shall earn enough money to let her live with me and keep house for me. Then you won't be bothered by either of us. We've always disappointed you. We weren't clever or gifted, though we did our best. But I'll look after Eileen now.'

'Don't, Eddie, don't,' said his mother, in a choking voice. 'Don't talk like that. What have I done? Oh, what have I done to have this punishment on my shoulders?'

Miss Theobald shut the door. They must sort things out for themselves. Matron had made her own bed and must lie on it. Those two children would probably be all right because they loved each other and would always stick together. They were weak-willed and not very attractive characters – but their love for each other would give them strength and courage.

Miss Theobald took up the telephone receiver. She got through to the old Matron, who was now almost recovered from her illness.

'Matron?' said Miss Theobald. 'Can you come back tomorrow? You can have as easy a time as you want to – but we can't do without you any longer! Yes – I have a feeling that the present Matron will be gone by tomorrow! Good – we *shall* be pleased to see you back!'

23

Things settle down at last

And now still one more thing remained to be done. Pauline must be seen, and her affairs put right too. So accordingly next day Pauline was astonished to see Miss Theobald coming into the sickbay looking much more serious than usual.

It was the second surprise Pauline had had that day. The first was when quite a new Matron had appeared, plump and jolly and twinkling. Pauline had stared at her in astonishment, delighted not to see the other Matron.

'Hallo!' said this new Matron. 'So you've broken your leg! Very careless of you. Don't make a habit of it, will you?'

'Where's the other Matron?' asked Pauline.

'She's had to leave in a hurry,' said Matron, putting Pauline's bedclothes straight. 'So I've come back. And let me warn you I'm a Real Old Bear! I've been here for years and years, I'm probably a hundred years old, and I've scolded most of the girls' mothers as well as the girls themselves!'

'Oh, you're the old Matron the girls have told me about,' said Pauline, pleased. 'That's good! Why did Matron leave in such a hurry? Has Eileen gone too?'

'Yes,' said Matron. 'They both had to leave in a hurry.

Not our business why, is it? Now then – what about those pillows?'

Pauline had hardly got over her astonishment at seeing a different Matron, when Miss Theobald came in. As usual the head went straight to the point, and soon the horrified Pauline was realizing that Miss Theobald, and the girls too, all knew what a stupid, untruthful boaster she had been.

She lay back in bed, feeling ashamed and miserable. Miss Theobald went relentlessly on, and finished by telling her how unhappy and puzzled she had made her mother.

'She came rushing to see you,' said Miss Theobald. 'She panted up from the station because she could not afford a taxi – and you know what sort of a welcome you gave her!'

Pauline turned her face to the wall and a tear trickled down her cheek.

'And there is yet another thing,' said Miss Theobald, remembering. 'Someone has stolen money – and because you seemed to have plenty, though the girls heard this week you were supposed to have very little pocket-money, *you* were suspected of being the thief! So you see, Pauline, to what big and terrible suspicions bragging and story-telling can lead us!'

'Oh! I've never stolen a thing in my life!' cried Pauline. 'I had some money in the savings bank – and without Mother knowing I took my savings book here with me – and when I wanted money I took some out. That's how I had plenty of pocket-money, Miss Theobald. Please believe me!'

'I do believe you,' said Miss Theobald. 'But you must hand over your book to me and not withdraw any more money without your mother's permission. And, if you stay here at St Clare's, you will have to do what some of the other girls do who have very little money – say so quite honestly! Nobody minds. We should never judge people by the amount of money or possessions they have, but by what they *are*. You must learn that, Pauline, or you will never know what real happiness is.'

'I feel very miserable,' muttered Pauline, anxious for a kind word. 'I – I don't know how I shall face all the girls after this!'

'Tell Susan or Hilary or the twins that you have been foolish,' said Miss Theobald, getting up. 'They are all sorry you have broken your leg, and I think they will see that you are treated kindly – but you will have to *earn* their kindness and friendship now, Pauline – not try to buy it with tales of wealth and great possessions! Earn their friendship by being sincere and natural and kindly. As for feeling very miserable – well, that is part of the punishment you have brought on yourself, isn't it, and you will have to bear it as bravely as you can!'

Miss Theobald turned to go. She smiled down at Pauline, her smile kinder than her words, and the girl felt a little comforted.

She did as Miss Theobald had advised and confided in Hilary when she came to see her. Hilary was outspoken but helpful.

'You're a frightful idiot, really frightful. And I shall only help you, and make the others decent to you, on one condition, Pauline.'

'What?' asked Pauline.

'That you write to your mother, and say you are sorry for being such a beast to her when she came to see you, and tell her you'll give her a great welcome next time she comes,' said Hilary. 'I'm not going round putting everything right for you, my girl, unless you first do a little putting-right yourself! And don't you dare to brag about a single thing more this term, or we'll all sit on you good and hard!'

And with that piece of advice, Hilary went off to tell the others that Pauline had come to her senses at last, and, as she had broken her leg, and was feeling pretty miserable, what about giving her a chance when she came back to class?

'Well, what with Eileen gone, and Angela reforming herself fast, and Pauline getting a little sense knocked into her, and Matron disappeared for good, we seem to be getting on nicely!' said Bobby, with one of her grins.

'It only remains for Claudine to get the English sense of honour,' put in Pat. 'Then we shall indeed be a form of saints!'

Alison had a letter from Eileen the following week. She read it to the others.

Dear Alison,

I don't know whether you were ever told, but I was the thief. You see, Eddie was out of a job (he's got a good one now) and hadn't any money, so he asked me to help him and I did. But I hadn't much money myself, so I took Mother's, and some other things too.

Well, it was a most frightful shock to Mother, and she said she couldn't bear to stay at St Clare's another day. So we packed and went. Miss Theobald was frightfully decent to Eddie and me. I simply can't tell you how decent. She even offered to keep me on at St Clare's when Mother went. But I couldn't face you all, and anyway I don't fit in there. I know I don't.

So I am going to study shorthand and typing, and then I am going to get a job in the office where Eddie works, and we shall be together. Mother is quite different now. I think it was an awful shock to her to find out how bad I was – but it was for Eddie, and I couldn't help it. Mother has been kinder and gentler. Really, you would hardly know her. Eddie and I think that when we are both earning money Mother won't need to work, and then she can take a rest and perhaps feel happier.

I thought I had better let you know what happened to me, because I left so suddenly. I left my silver thimble behind, in the school work-box – the one in the fourth-form cupboard. Will you please have it yourself in gratitude for taking me out at half-term, as I can never repay that?

I hope Pauline's leg is better. Please, Alison, don't always think unkindly of me, will you? I know I was a sneak, but you can't imagine how difficult things were for me sometimes.

Yours with gratitude,

Eileen Paterson.

The girls were all rather touched by this letter. Alison at once found the thimble and said she would wear it and not think too badly of Eileen.

'It was mostly her mother's fault she was such a little sneak and beast,' said Bobby. 'Golly, we're lucky to have decent mothers, aren't we?'

Angela went red at this remark but said nothing. She had been so much nicer lately – and she had determined that when she went home for the holidays, she was going to praise St Clare's night and day, and not allow her mother to say a single word against it! Mothers could make bad or good children – but, thought Angela, maybe children could alter mothers sometimes too. She was going to have a good try to make her mother change her mind about quite a lot of things. Miss Theobald would have been very delighted if she had known some of the thoughts that went through Angela's golden head those days.

'Hols will soon be here now,' said Pat to Isabel.

'It's been an exciting term, hasn't it – and aren't you glad our old Matron is back? Hi, Bobby – what about a really good trick to round off the term? Can't you and Janet think of one?'

'I dare say we can,' grinned Bobby, her good-natured face looking tanned and even more freckled than usual.

'We could put a frog in Claudine's desk, or fill her pencil-box with earwigs,' suggested Janet with a wicked look at the horrified Claudine.

'If you do such a thing I take the train and the boat to France at once,' declared the French girl.

'She would too,' said Janet. 'Well – perhaps we'd better not try out anything of that sort on Claudine. It would be a pity if she went back to France before she had had time to get that "sense of honour" she is always talking about!'

Claudine threw a cushion at Janet's head. It knocked over Doris's work-basket. Doris leapt up and threw a heap of mending at Claudine. It scattered itself over Mirabel who was just coming into the room. The girls shrieked with laughter to see Mirabel standing in surprise with somebody's blouse over her head.

In no time, there was a fine fight going on, with squeals and yells. Arms, legs, and heads stuck out in all directions.

The door opened again and Miss Theobald looked in with a visitor.

'And this,' she said, 'is the fourth-form common-room. Girls, girls, what *are* you doing? What *will* you be like as six formers, if you behave like kindergarten children now?'

What will they be like? Not very different I expect! We'll wait and see.

FIFTH FORMERS of ST CLARE'S

'Felicity! Must you play that awful, gloomy tune again?' said Anne-Marie. 'I'm trying to get the last verse of this poem right.'

The fifth form are sharing studies this year. And tempers are fraying. It's going to be a very tense term!

THERE'S MORE TROUBLE at ST CLARE'S!

Second Form at St Clare's

St Clare's

Enid Blyton

St Clare's
The Twins at St Clare's
The O'Sullivan Twins
Summer Term at St Clare's
The Second Form at St Clare's
The Third Form at St Clare's (written by Pamela Cox)
Claudine at St Clare's
Fifth Formers of St Clare's
The Sixth Form at St Clare's (written by Pamela Cox)

Malory Towers
First Term at Malory Towers
Second Form at Malory Towers
Third Year at Malory Towers
Upper Fourth at Malory Towers
In the Fifth at Malory Towers
Last Term at Malory Towers

The Mysteries
The Mystery of the Burnt Cottage
The Mystery of the Disappearing Cat
The Mystery of the Secret Room
The Mystery of the Spiteful Letters
The Mystery of the Missing Necklace
The Mystery of the Hidden House
The Mystery of the Pantomime Cat
The Mystery of the Invisible Thief
The Mystery of the Vanished Prince
The Mystery of the Strange Bundle
The Mystery of Holly Lane
The Mystery of Tally-Ho Cottage
The Mystery of the Missing Man
The Mystery of the Strange Messages
The Mystery of Banshee Towers

Enid Blyton®

Second Form at St Clare's

EGMONT

St Clare's

Enid Blyton

EGMONT

We bring stories to life

First published in Great Britain 1944 by Methuen & Co. Ltd
This edition published 2013
by Egmont UK Limited
The Yellow Building
1 Nicholas Road
London W11 4AN

978 0 6035 6937 1

A CIP catalogue record for this title is available from the British Library
Printed and bound in Great Britain by the CPI Group

56924/1

EGMONT LUCKY COIN

Our story began over a century ago, when seventeen-year-old Egmont Harald Petersen found a coin in the street.

He was on his way to buy a flyswatter, a small hand-operated printing machine that he then set up in his tiny apartment.

The coin brought him such good luck that today Egmont has offices in over 30 countries around the world. And that lucky coin is still kept at the company's head offices in Denmark.

Contents

1.

Off to school again

The last week of the summer holidays flew by, and the twins, Pat and Isabel O'Sullivan, seemed to be in a rush of buying clothes, fitting them on, looking out lacrosse sticks, finding lacrosse boots, and hunting for all kinds of things that seemed to have completely disappeared.

'Where *is* my knitting-bag?' said Pat, turning a whole drawerful of things upside down. 'I know I brought it home at the end of last term.'

'I can only find *one* of my lacrosse boots,' wailed Isabel. 'Mummy, have you seen the other?'

'Yes, it came back from the bootmaker's yesterday,' said Mrs O'Sullivan. 'Where did you put it?'

'Packing to go to school is always much more muddling than packing to come back home,' said Pat. 'I say, Isabel – won't it be fun to be in the second form this term?'

'Who is your form teacher there?' asked their mother, unpacking half Pat's things and packing them all over again.

'Miss Jenks,' said Pat. 'I'll be sorry to leave Miss Roberts and the first form, in some ways. We did have fun there.'

'I bet we'll have some fun in Miss Jenks's class too,' said Isabel. 'I don't think she's quite so strict as Miss Roberts.'

'Don't you believe it!' said Isabel, trying to cram a tin

of toffees into a corner. 'She may not have Miss Roberts's sarcastic tongue – but she's all there! Don't you remember how she used to deal with Tessie when Tessie used to try on her pretend-sneezes?'

'Yes – sent her to Matron for a large dose of awful medicine, supposed to stop a cold!' giggled Pat. 'All the same, I bet we'll get away with quite a lot of things in Miss Jenks's form.'

'I hope you mean to work,' said Mrs O'Sullivan, putting in the top tray of Isabel's trunk. 'I was quite pleased with last term's report. Don't let me have a bad one as soon as you go up into another form, will you?'

'We'll work all right, Mummy,' said Pat. 'I can tell you, the teachers at St Clare's aren't easy-going where work is concerned. They keep our noses to the grindstone! Mam'zelle's the worst. She really seems to think we ought to learn to talk French better than we speak English!'

'No wonder your French accent is so much improved, then,' said Mrs O'Sullivan, with a laugh. 'Now Pat – let me see if I can possibly shut your trunk. You'd better sit on it whilst I try to shut the clasps.'

The trunk wouldn't shut. Mrs O'Sullivan opened it again and looked inside. 'You can't take all those books,' she said, firmly.

'Mummy, I *must,*' said Pat. 'And I simply must take those games too – we love jigsaws in the winter term.'

'Well, Pat, all I can say is, you'd better take books, games, toffees, biscuits and knitting things, and leave behind your clothes,' said the twins' mother. 'Now – be sensible – take out three books and we can shut the trunk.'

Pat took out three books, and, when Mrs O'Sullivan was not looking, put them hurriedly into Isabel's trunk. Her own trunk now shut down fairly easily, and was locked. Then Mrs O'Sullivan went to Isabel's.

'This won't shut, either,' she said. 'Gracious, the things you girls take back with you to boarding school nowadays! When *I* . . .'

'When *you* were a girl you only took a small case, and that held everything!' chanted the twins, who had heard these remarks before. 'Mummy, we'll *both* sit on Isabel's trunk, shall we?'

Mrs O'Sullivan opened the trunk and firmly removed three books from the top layer. She looked at them in surprise. 'I seem to have seen these before!' she said. The twins giggled. They sat on the trunk and it shut with a groan.

'And now to pack your hand-bag with night-things in,' said Mrs O'Sullivan, looking at the school-list to make sure nothing had been forgotten. 'That won't take long.'

Nightgowns, tooth-brushes, face-flannels and sponges went into small bags. Then the twins were ready. They were both dressed neatly in their school winter uniforms of grey, with blue blouses and scarlet ties. They put on grey coats and grey felt hats with the school ribbon round, and looked at each other.

'Two good little St Clare girls,' said Pat, looking demure.

'Not so very good,' said her mother, with a smile. 'Now – there is the car at the door, ready to take us to the station. Have we really got everything? You must write and tell me if you want anything else.'

'Oh, we're sure to want lots of things!' said Pat. 'You're a darling, the way you send us things. It's fun to be going back to St Clare's. I'm awfully glad you sent us there, Mummy.'

'And how you hated going at first!' said Mrs O'Sullivan, remembering the fuss the twins had made, because they had wanted to go to another, much more expensive school.

'Yes – we made up our minds to be so awful that the school wouldn't keep us,' said Pat. 'And we *were* awful too – but we couldn't keep it up. St Clare's was too much for us – we just *had* to be decent in the end!'

'Do come on,' said Isabel. 'We shall miss the train! I'm longing to meet all the girls in London, and see them again, aren't you, Pat? I do like the journey down to St Clare's.'

They were off at last. They had to travel to London, and go to the station where the St Clare train started. The whole train was reserved for the St Clare girls, for it was a big school.

There was a terrific noise on the platform, where scores of girls were waiting for the train. Their mothers were there to bid them goodbye, and teachers moved about, trying to collect the girls together. Porters shoved luggage into the van, and everyone was excited.

'Bobby! Oh, there's Bobby!' yelled Pat, as soon as they arrived on the crowded platform. 'And Janet too. Hi, Bobby, hi, Janet!'

'Hallo, twins!' cried Bobby. Her merry eyes crinkled up as she smiled.

'It's good to see your turn-up nose again,' said Pat, slipping her arm through Bobby's. 'Hallo, Janet! Got anymore tricks from that brother of yours?'

'Wait and see,' grinned Janet. A mistress came up at that moment and overheard the remarks.

'Ah – did I hear the word *tricks*, Janet?' she said. 'Well, just remember you're in *my* form this term, and there are really Terrible Punishments for tricks like yours!'

'Yes, Miss Jenks,' grinned Janet. 'I'll remember. Are all the others here yet?'

'All but Doris,' said Miss Jenks. 'Ah, there she is. Now we must get into the train. The guard is looking rather worried, I see.'

'Carlotta! Get into our carriage!' yelled Bobby, seeing the dark-eyed, dark-haired girl running down the platform. 'What sort of hols did you have? Did you go back to the circus?'

Carlotta was a source of great attraction and admiration to the girls, for she had once been a circus girl, and her understanding and handling of horses was marvellous. Now she had to settle down at St Clare's, and learn many things she had never heard of. She had found her first term very difficult, but at the end of it she was firm friends with most of her form, and the mistresses were pleased with her. She ran up to the twins and Bobby, her vivid little face glowing with pleasure.

'Hallo!' she said. 'I'll get into your carriage. Oh, look –

there's your cousin Alison. She looks rather miserable.'

'I *feel* miserable,' said Alison O'Sullivan, coming up, looking very woe-begone. 'I shall miss my friend Sadie dreadfully this term.'

Sadie had been an American girl with no ideas in her head at all beyond clothes and the cinema. She had had a very bad influence on Alison, but, as she was not coming back that term, it was to be hoped that the feather-headed Alison would pull herself together a little, and try to do better. She was a pretty little thing who easily burst into tears. Her cousins welcomed her warmly.

'Hallo, Alison! Don't fret about Sadie. You'll soon find other friends.'

They all got into the carriage. Doris arrived, panting. Hilary Wentworth, who had been head of the first form, flung herself down in a corner seat. She was very much wondering if she would be head of the second form. She was a trustworthy and responsible girl who liked being head.

'Hallo, everybody,' she said. 'Nice to see you all again. Well, Carlotta – been riding in the ring, I suppose! Lucky kid!'

'You know I don't belong to a circus any more,' said Carlotta. 'I went to spend my holidays with my father and my grandmother. My father seems to like me quite a lot – but my grandmother found a lot of fault with my manners. She says I must pay more attention to them this term even than to my lessons! You must all help me!'

'Oh, no!' said Pat, with a laugh. 'We don't want you

any different from what you are, my dear, hot-tempered, entirely natural, perfectly honest little Carlotta! We get more fun out of you than out of anyone. We don't want you changed one little bit! Any more than we want Bobby changed. We shall expect some marvellous tricks from you this term, Bobby.'

'Right,' said Bobby. 'But I tell you here and now, I'm going to work too!'

'Miss Jenks will see to that,' said Hilary. 'Remember we shall no longer be in the bottom form. We've got to work for exams and pass them!'

'We're off!' said Pat, leaning out of the window. 'Goodbye, Mummy! We'll write on Sunday!'

The train steamed slowly out of the station. The girls drew in their heads. All the carriages were full of chatterers, talking about the wonderful hols they had had, the places they had been to, and what sort of term it would be.

'Any new girls?' said Isabel. 'I haven't seen one.'

'I think there's only one,' said Bobby. 'We saw a miserable-looking creature standing a little way up the platform – I don't know whether she'll be second form or first form. Not second, I hope – she looked such a misery!'

'Alison's doing her hair again already,' said Pat. 'Alison! Put your comb away. Girls, I think we'll have to make it a rule that Alison doesn't do her hair more than fifty times a day!'

Everyone laughed. It was good to be back, good to be all together once more. The winter term was going to be fun!

2. In the second form

It was very strange at first to be in the second form, instead of the first. The twins felt very important, and looked down on the first formers, feeling that they were very young and unimportant. But the third formers also looked down on the second form, so things soon shook themselves out, and everyone settled down.

'It's funny to go to the second-form classroom instead of to Miss Roberts's room,' said Pat. 'I keep on going to the first-form room, as I always used to do.'

'So do I,' said Janet. 'Miss Roberts is beginning to think we're doing it on purpose. We'd better be careful.'

'There's a whole lot of new girls in the first form, after all,' said Pat. 'Miss Roberts must have collected them altogether on the train. That's why we didn't see them. There's about twelve!'

'I shall never know all their names,' said Isabel. 'Anyway – they're only little kids – some of them not yet fourteen!'

'All the first formers have been moved up,' said Bobby. 'Except young Pam – and she's only just fourteen. I bet she'll be head of the first form!'

Pam Boardman had been new the term before, and

was a very hard-working child. As Bobby said, she was made head of the first form, and was extremely proud of the honour. She had many new girls under her, and was eager to help them all.

Only two girls had been left down in the second form – Elsie Fanshawe and Anna Johnson. The girls who had just come up were sorry to see them there, for they were not much liked. Elsie Fanshawe was spiteful, and Anna Johnson was lazy.

'I suppose one of them will be head girl,' said Hilary, with a grimace. 'Well – I don't fancy either of them, do you, Bobby?'

'They both think themselves very superior to us,' said Bobby. 'Just because they've been second formers for a year.'

'*I* should be ashamed,' said Carlotta. 'I would not like to spend more than a year in any form. But Anna is so lazy she will never get up into the third form, I'm sure!'

'I believe Miss Jenks didn't send them up because she hoped they'd buck up a bit if they were heads,' said Pat. 'I rather think she's going to make them joint head girls. We shall have to look out if Elsie's head – she's really catty.'

'We've got that Misery-girl in our form after all,' said Bobby, looking at the new girl, who was standing mournfully not far off, looking at nothing. 'She never says a word, but looks as if she'll burst into tears at any moment!'

The Misery-girl, as the others called her, was named Gladys Hillman. The girls tried to make her talk and Bobbie did her best to make her laugh, but Gladys took no notice of anyone. She walked by herself, seemed to dream all the time, and hardly spoke a word.

'Better leave her alone,' said Hilary. 'Perhaps she's homesick.'

Not many of the St Clare girls felt homesick when they returned to school, because it was all so jolly and friendly, and there was so much to do that there seemed no time to miss home and parents. The beginning of term was always fun – new books given out, new girls to size up, new desks to sit in, and sometimes new forms to go to.

'There's a new mistress,' said Bobby, in excitement. 'She's to take elocution and drama! Look – there she is – isn't she dark?'

Miss Quentin certainly was dark, and extremely good looking. She had black piercing eyes, and a beautiful voice. Alison thought she was wonderful.

'You *would*!' said Bobby. 'You'll be doing your hair like Miss Quentin next, swept over your brow and round your ears. There'll always be someone for you to copy, my dear Alison! Do you remember last term how you copied everything your dear friend Sadie did?'

Alison flushed. She was always being teased and she never seemed to get used to it. She turned away with a toss of her pretty head. The others laughed at her. There was nothing bad in Alison – but on the other hand there was nothing very good either. She was, as Pat so often said, 'just a pretty little feather-head!'

The second form soon settled down with Miss Jenks. At first it seemed strange to them not to have Miss Roberts teaching them for most of the morning. They missed her dry remarks and crisp words of praise. Miss Jenks was not so shrewd as Miss Roberts, nor was she so cool when angry. She could not bear the slightest hint of rudeness, and she had no sympathy at all for 'frills and fancies' as she put it. No girl dared to fuss her hair out too much, or to wear anything but a plain gold bar for a brooch in Miss Jenks's class.

'Alison is in for a bad time!' grinned Bobby one morning, when Alison had been sent to remove a bow from her hair and a brooch from her collar.

'So is Carlotta!' said Pat. 'Miss Jenks doesn't like frills and fancies – but she doesn't like untidiness either! Just *look* at your hair, Carlotta. It's wild enough in the ordinary way – but it looks like a bird's nest at the moment.'

'Does it really?' said Carlotta, who never cared in the least what she looked like. 'Well, those sums we had to do were so hard I just had to clutch my hair all the time!'

'Old Mam'zelle's still the same,' said Isabel. 'Funny, old, hot-tempered, flat-footed thing – but I like her all the same. She always gives us *some* excitement – and I bet she will this term, too. Do you remember how she and Carlotta nearly came to blows last term?'

Yes – the summer term had been a very exciting one. The girls looked at Mam'zelle and remembered all the jokes they had played on her. Dear old Mam'zelle, she always fell for everything. She was very terrifying when she lost her temper, but she had a great sense of humour, and when her short-sighted eyes twinkled behind their glasses, the girls felt a real fondness for her.

'Ah,' said Mam'zelle, looking round the second form. 'Ah! You are now the second form – very important, very responsible, and very hard working, *n'est-ce pas*? The first formers, they are babies, they know nothing – but as soon as you arrive in the second form, you are big girls, you know a great deal. Your French will be quite per-r-r-rfect! And Doris – ah, even Doris will be able to roll her 'r's in the proper French way!'

Everyone laughed. Poor Doris, always bottom at oral French, could never roll her 'r's. Doris grinned. She was a dunce, but nobody minded. She was a wonderful mimic and could keep the whole form in roars of laughter when she liked.

'R-r-r-r-r-r-r!' said Carlotta, unexpectedly. She sounded like an aeroplane taking off, and Mam'zelle frowned.

'You are now in the second form, Carlotta,' she said, coldly. 'We do not do those things here.'

'No, Mam'zelle,' said Carlotta, meekly. 'Of course not.'

'Tricks and jokes are not performed in any form higher than the first,' warned Mam'zelle. 'Whilst you are first-form babies, one does not expect much from you – but as soon as you leave the bottom form behind, it is different. We expect you to behave with dignity. One day the head girl may be one of you here, and it is not too soon to prepare for such an honour.'

Winifred James, the much-admired head girl, had left, and Belinda Towers, the sports captain, had taken her place. This was a very popular choice, for Belinda was well known by the whole school, and very much liked. As sports captain she knew practically all the girls, and this would be a great help to her as head girl. She was not so gentle and quiet as Winifred, and many girls were afraid of her out-spokenness, but there was no doubt she would make an excellent head girl.

Belinda visited every common-room in turn and made the same short speech to the girls there.

'You all know I'm head girl now – and I'm still sports captain too. You can come to me if you're in a spot of trouble at any time and I'll help if I can. You'll all have to toe the mark where games are concerned, because I want to put St Clare's right on the map this winter, with lacrosse. We must win every match we play! We've got some fine players for a school team, but I want every form to supply players for the second and third match-teams too. So buck up, all of you, and practise hard.'

Alison groaned as Belinda went out of the second-form common-room. 'Why *do* we have to play games?' she said. 'They just make us hot and untidy and tired.'

'You forget they do other things as well,' said Janet. 'We have to learn to work together as a team – each one for his side, helping the others, not each one for himself. That sort of thing is especially good for *you*, my dear Alison – you'd sit in a corner and look at yourself in the mirror all day long if you could – and a fat lot of good that would do you or anybody else.'

'Oh, be quiet,' said Alison. 'You're always getting at me!'

It *was* fun to be back again, and to hear all the familiar

school chatter, to groan over prep, to eat enormous teas, to talk about lacrosse, to laugh at somebody's joke, and to look forward to the class you liked the best – painting, maybe, or music, or elocution – or even maths!

There was a surprise for the second form at the end of the first week. Another new girl appeared! She arrived at tea-time, with red eyes and a sulky mouth. She looked defiantly at everyone as she took her place at the second-form table.

'This is Mirabel Unwin,' said Miss Jenks. 'She has arrived rather late for beginning of term – but still, better late than never, Mirabel.'

'I didn't want to come at all,' said Mirabel, in a loud voice. 'They tried to make me come on the right day but I wouldn't. I only came now because my father promised I could leave at half-term if I'd come now. I suppose he thought once he got me here I'd stay. But I shan't.'

'That will do, Mirabel,' said Miss Jenks, soothingly. 'You are tired and over-wrought. Don't say any more. You will soon settle down and be happy.'

'No, I shan't,' said the surprising Mirabel. 'I shan't settle down and I shan't be happy. I shan't try at anything, because what's the use if I'm leaving at half-term?'

'Well, we'll see,' said Miss Jenks. 'Be sensible now and eat some tea. You must be hungry.'

The girls stared at Mirabel. They were not used to people who shouted their private affairs out in public. They thought Mirabel was rather shocking – but rather exciting too.

'I thought she was another Misery-girl at first, but I believe she's just spoilt and peevish,' said Pat. 'I say – the second form is going to be quite an exciting place this term!'

3.

Two head girls and two new girls

Miss Jenks made both the old second formers into joint head girls of the form. She and Miss Theobald, the head mistress, had had a talk about them, and had decided that perhaps it would be the making of them.

'Elsie is a spiteful type,' said Miss Jenks. 'She has never been popular, though she would have liked to be – so she gets back at the others by being spiteful and saying nasty things. And Anna is bone-lazy – won't do a thing if she can help it!'

'Well, a little responsibility may be good for them,' said Miss Theobald, thoughtfully. 'It will give Elsie a sense of importance, and bring out any good in her – and Anna will have to bestir herself if she wants to keep her position. Let them both try.'

'I don't know how they will work together,' said Miss Jenks, doubtfully. 'They don't like each other very much.'

'Let them try,' said Miss Theobald. 'Elsie is quick, and she may stir Anna up a bit – and Anna is too lazy to be spiteful, so perhaps she will be good for Elsie in that way. But I too have my doubts!'

Elsie Fanshawe was delighted to be a joint head girl – though, of course, she would very much rather have been the only one. Still, after being thoroughly disliked and kept down by the whole of the second form, it was quite a change to be top-dog!

Now I can jolly well keep the others down and make them look up to *me*, thought Elsie, pleased. I can get some of my own back. These silly little first formers, who have just come up, have got to learn to knuckle under a bit. I can make Anna agree with all I do – lazy thing! I'll have every single one of the rules kept, and I'll make a few of my own, if I want to – and I'll report anyone who gets out of hand. It's worthwhile not going up into the third form, to be top of the second!

The others guessed a little what Elsie was thinking. Although they had not known the girl very well when they were first formers, they had heard the others talking about her. They knew Elsie would try to 'get her own back'.

'Just what a head girl shouldn't do,' said Janet. 'She should try and set some sort of example to the others, or what's the use of being a leader? Look at old Hilary, when she was head of the first form! She was a good sport and joined in everything – but she always knew where to draw the line without getting our backs up.'

'I can't bear Elsie,' said Carlotta. 'I would like to slap her hard.'

'Oh, Carlotta! Have you still got that habit?' said Bobby, pretending to be shocked. 'Really, a second former, too! What *would* Elsie say?'

Elsie overheard the last remark. 'What would I say to what?' she asked, coming up.

'Oh, nothing – Carlotta was simply saying she'd like to slap someone,' said Bobby, with a grin.

'Please understand, Carlotta, that you are in the second form now,' said Elsie, in a cold voice. 'We don't even *talk* of slapping people!'

'Yes, we do,' said Carlotta. 'Wouldn't you like to know whom I want to slap, dear Elsie?'

Elsie heard the danger-note in Carlotta's high voice, and put her nose in the air.

'I'm not interested in your slapping habits,' she said, and walked off.

'Shut up now, Carlotta,' said Bobby. 'Don't go and get all wild and Spanish again. You were bad enough with Prudence last term!'

'Well, thank goodness old Sour-Milk Prudence was expelled!' said Carlotta. 'I wouldn't have stayed if she had come back!'

It was the hour when all the second form were in their common-room, playing, working or chattering. They loved being together like that. The radio blared at one end of the room, and Doris and Bobby danced a ridiculous dance to the music. Gladys Hillman sat in a corner, looking as miserable as usual. Nobody could make anything of her. Isabel looked at her and felt sorry. She went over to her.

'Come and dance,' she said. Gladys shook her head.

'What's the matter?' asked Isabel. 'Are you homesick? You'll soon get over it.'

'Don't bother me,' said Gladys. 'I don't bother you.'

'Yes, you do,' said Isabel. 'You bother me a lot. I can't bear to see you sitting here all alone, looking so miserable. Haven't you been to boarding school before?'

'No,' said Gladys. Her eyes filled with tears. Isabel felt a little impatient with her. Hadn't she any courage at all?

'You don't seem to enjoy a single thing,' said Isabel. 'Don't you like any lesson specially – or games – or something?'

'I like acting,' said Gladys, unexpectedly. 'And I like lacrosse. That's all. But I don't like them here. I don't like anything here.'

She wouldn't say any more, and Isabel gave her up. She went across to Pat. 'Hopeless!' she said. 'Just a mass of self-pity and tears! She'll fade away and we'll never notice she's gone if she doesn't buck up! I'd almost rather have that rude Mirabel than Gladys.'

Mirabel had been the source of much annoyance and amusement to the second form. She was rude to the point of being unbearable, and reminded everyone every day that she wasn't going to stay a day beyond half-term.

'Don't tell me that any more,' begged Bobby. 'You can't imagine how glad I am you're going at half-term. It's the only bright spot I can see. But I warn you – don't be too rude to Mam'zelle, or sparks will fly – and don't get on the high horse too much with our dear head girl, Elsie Fanshawe, or you'll get the worst of it. Elsie is pretty clever you know, and you're rather stupid.'

'No, I'm not!' flashed Mirabel, angrily. 'I only seem

stupid because I don't want to try – but you should hear me play the piano and the violin! *Then* you'd see!'

'Why, you don't even *learn* music!' said Bobby. 'And I've never seen you open your mouth in the singing class. We all came to the conclusion that you couldn't sing a note.'

'That's all *you* know!' said Mirabel, rudely. 'Golly, what a school this is! I always knew boarding school would be awful – but it's worse than I expected. I hate living with a lot of rude girls who think they're the cat's whiskers just because they've been here a year or two!'

'Oh, you make me tired,' said Bobby, and walked off. 'Really, what with you and the Misery-girl, and spiteful old Elsie, we're badly off this term!'

Miss Jenks kept a very firm hand on Mirabel. 'You may not intend to work,' she said, 'but you are not going to stop the others from working! You will do one of three things, my dear Mirabel – you will stay in the classroom and work – or you will stay in the classroom and do nothing at all, not even say a word – or you will go and stand *out*side the classroom till the lesson is finished!'

At first Mirabel thought it was marvellous to defy Miss Jenks and be sent outside. But she soon found it wearisome to stand there so long, waiting for the others to come out. Also, she was always a little afraid that the head mistress, Miss Theobald, would come along. Loudly as Mirabel declared that she cared for nobody, nobody at all at silly St Clare's, she *was* in awe of the quiet head mistress.

'Did you tell Miss Theobald that you didn't mean to

stay here longer than half-term?' asked Pat. Every girl had to go to see the head mistress when she arrived on the first day.

'Of course I did!' said Mirabel, tossing her head. 'I told her *I* didn't care for anyone, not even the head!'

This was untrue. Mirabel had meant to say quite a lot – but Miss Theobald had somehow said it first. She had looked gravely at the red-eyed girl when she had come in, and had told her to sit down. Mirabel opened her mouth to speak, but Miss Theobald silenced her.

'I must finish this letter,' she said. 'Then we will talk.'

She kept Mirabel waiting for ten minutes. The girl studied the head's calm face, and felt a little awed. It would be difficult to be rude to someone like this. The longer she waited, the more difficult it would be to say what she had meant to say.

Miss Theobald raised her head at last. 'Well, Mirabel,' she said, 'I know you feel upset, angry and defiant. Your father insisted you should come away to school because you are spoilt and make his home unbearable. You also domineer over your smaller brother and sister. He chose St Clare's because he thought we might be able to do something for you. No – don't interrupt me. Believe me, I know all you want to say – but you don't know what I have to say.'

There was a pause. Even defiant Mirabel did not dare to say a word.

'We have had many difficult girls here,' said Miss Theobald. 'We rather pride ourselves on getting the best out of them. You see, Mirabel, difficult children often have fine things hidden in their characters – things that perhaps more ordinary children don't possess . . .'

'What things?' asked Mirabel, interested in spite of herself.

'Well – sometimes difficult children have a great talent for something – a gift for art or drama, a talent for music – or maybe they have some great quality – outstanding courage, perhaps. Well, I don't know if this is the case with you, or whether you are just a spoilt and unruly girl – we shall see. All I want to say now is – give yourself a chance and let me see if there *is* anything worthwhile in you this half-term. If there is not, we don't want you to stay. We shall be glad for you to go.'

This was so unexpected that Mirabel again had nothing to say. She had meant to say that nothing on earth would make her stay at St Clare's beyond the half-term – but here was Miss Theobald saying that she didn't want to keep her longer than that – unless – unless she was worthwhile! Worthwhile!

I don't care if I'm worthwhile or not! thought Mirabel to herself, indignantly. And how dare Daddy write and tell Miss Theobald those things about me? Why couldn't he keep our affairs to himself?

Mirabel voiced this thought aloud. 'I think it was horrid of my father to tell you things about me,' she said, in a trembling voice.

'They were said in confidence to someone who understood,' said Miss Theobald. 'Have you kept your own tongue quiet about *your* private affairs this afternoon, Mirabel? No – I rather think you gave yourself away to the whole school at tea-time when you arrived!'

Mirabel flushed. Yes – she had said far too much. She always did. She could not keep control over her tongue.

'You may go,' said Miss Theobald, picking up her pen again. 'And remember – it is not *St Clare's* which is on trial – it is *you*! I hope I shall not say goodbye to you and rejoice to see the last of you at half-term. But – I shall not be surprised if I do!'

Mirabel went out of the room, her ears tingling, her face still red. She had been used to getting all her own way, to letting her rough tongue say what it pleased, and to ruling her parents and brother and sister as she pleased. When her father had at last declared in anger that she must go away, there had been a royal battle between them. The spoilt girl had imagined she could rule the roost at St Clare's too. But she certainly could not rule Miss Theobald!

Never mind – I'll lead everyone else a dance! she thought. I'll show Daddy and the others that I mean what I say! I won't be sent away from home if I don't want to go.

And so Mirabel set herself to be as annoying as possible, to spoil things for the others, and to try and domineer in the classroom, as she had always done at home. But she had not bargained for the treatment she got at last from an exasperated class.

4.

Mirabel is a nuisance

The second form did not so much mind when Mirabel was annoying in classes they disliked, such as the maths class, which they found difficult that term – or even in Mam'zelle's class when she took irregular French verbs, hated by every girl. But they did dislike it when she spoilt, or tried to spoil, the English class, or the art class.

'It spoils our reading of *The Tempest* when you make idiotic remarks, or flop about in your seat and make Miss Jenks keep on saying, "Sit up!" ' said Hilary, angrily. 'Either behave badly enough to get sent out of the room at once, idiot, or else keep quiet.'

'And if you dare to upset your paint-water all over somebody again, and make us lose ten minutes of the art class whilst we all get ticked off by Miss Walker, I'll throttle you,' said Carlotta, all in one breath. 'We wouldn't mind so much if you did something really funny, like Bobby or Janet did last term – what you do *isn't* funny – just idiotic, spoiling things for the whole class.'

'I shall do what I like,' said Mirabel.

'You will not,' said Elsie, spitefully. 'I'm head girl of this form – with Anna – and we say you are to behave yourself, or we'll know the reason why.'

'You do know the reason why,' said Mirabel, pertly.

'Anyone would think you were six years old, the way you behave,' said Bobby, in disgust. 'Well – I warn you – you'll be sorry if you keep on like this. We're all getting tired of you.'

The explosion came during the drama class. This was taken by the new teacher, Miss Quentin, and was really rather an exciting class. The girls were to write and act their own play. Dark-eyed Miss Quentin was full of good suggestions, and the play was almost written.

The new teacher was not much good at discipline. She relied on her good looks and rather charming manner, and on the interest of her lessons, to help her to discipline her classes. Alison adored her, and, as the girls had already foreseen, was copying her in everything, from her little tricks of speech, to the way she did her hair.

Most of the girls liked Miss Quentin, though they did not very much respect the way she coaxed them to behave when they became a little unruly. They really preferred the downright methods of Miss Roberts or Miss Jenks. Mirabel, of course, soon found that Miss Quentin was quite unable to keep her in order.

'Your turn now, Mirabel dear,' Miss Quentin would say, smiling brightly at her. Mirabel would pretend not to hear, and Miss Quentin would raise her voice slightly.

'Mirabel! Your turn now, dear!'

The class disliked Miss Quentin's 'dears' and 'lambs' and other names – except Alison. She loved them. They all looked at Mirabel impatiently. She was always losing time like this, when they wanted to get on.

Mirabel would pretend to come back to earth with a start, fumble for the place, be gently helped by Miss Quentin, and at last say something, usually incorrect. When there was any acting to be done she came in at the wrong moment, said the wrong lines, and altogether behaved in a most annoying manner. Miss Quentin was at a loss to know how to deal with her.

'Mirabel! I have never yet sent a girl out of my class,' she would say, in such a sorrowful voice that it quite wrung Alison's heart. 'Now come – pull yourself together and try again.'

One morning Alison was waiting to act a part she loved. She had rehearsed it over and over again to herself, acting it, as she thought, to perfection. She was longing for her turn to come, so that she might gloat over the sugared words of praise she felt sure would drop from Miss Quentin's lips.

There were ten more minutes to go – just about time for Alison's turn to come. And then Mirabel chose to be stupid again, saying her lines incorrectly, doing the wrong things so that Miss Quentin had to make her speak and act two or three times. The teacher, following her usual rule of being patient and encouraging, wasted nearly all the precious ten minutes on Mirabel.

Alison cast her eye on the clock, and bit her lip. All her rehearsing would be wasted now. How she hated that stupid Mirabel, holding up every class in order to be annoying.

'Now, Mirabel *dear,*' said Miss Quentin, in her

charming, patient voice, 'say it like this . . .'

It was too much for Alison. She stamped her foot. 'Mirabel! Stop fooling! It's hateful the way you take Miss Quentin in – and she's so patient too. You've wasted half the time – and now I shan't have my turn.'

'Poor little Alison!' said Mirabel, mockingly. 'She so badly wanted to show off to her precious Miss Quentin, and hear her say, "Well done, *darling*!" '

There was a dead silence. Then Alison burst into a flood of tears, and Carlotta trod on Mirabel's toe very neatly and smartly. Miss Quentin stared in horror.

'Girls! Girls! What are you thinking of? Carlotta! You amaze me. I cannot have this behaviour, I really cannot. Carlotta, apologize at once to Mirabel.'

'Certainly not,' said Carlotta. 'I don't mean to be rude to *you*, Miss Quentin – but you must see for yourself that Mirabel deserved it. I knew no one else but me would dare to do it – and it's been coming to Mirabel for quite a long time.'

The bell rang for the next class. Miss Quentin was most relieved. She had no idea how to tackle things of this sort. She gathered up her books quickly.

'There is no time to say any more, girls,' she said. 'I must go to my next class. Carlotta, I still insist that you put things right with Mirabel by apologizing.'

She went out of the room in a flurry. Carlotta grinned round at the others. 'Well,' she said, 'don't stand staring at me like that as if I'd done something awful. You know quite well you've all wanted to chastise Mirabel yourselves. We're as tired of her as we can be. It's a pity half-term isn't here and we can see the back of her.'

'Carlotta, you shouldn't do things like that,' said Janet. 'Alison, for pity's sake, stop howling. Mirabel, you deserved it, and now perhaps you'll shut up and behave properly.'

Mirabel had gone rather white. She had not attempted to hit back at Carlotta. 'If you think that will stop me doing what I like to spoil things for anybody you're mistaken,' she said, at last, in a tight kind of voice. 'It'll make me worse.'

'I suppose it will,' said Hilary. 'Well – I'll give you a warning. If you don't stop being an idiot, we shall make things uncomfortable for *you*. I don't mean we shall thump you. We shan't. But there are other ways.'

Mirabel said no more – but as she made no attempt that day or the following to behave sensibly, the girls made up their minds that they must carry out their threat.

They met in one of the music-rooms. Elsie Fanshawe was pleased. This excited her – it gladdened her spiteful nature, and added to her sense of importance, for, as she was one of the head girls, she could direct everyone in what they had to do.

'We've met together to decide how to get back at Mirabel,' she began.

Hilary interrupted her. 'Well – not exactly "get back", Elsie,' she said. 'It's more to prevent her from going on disgracing herself and our class.'

'Call it what you like,' said Elsie, impatiently. 'Now – what I propose is this: we'll take her books from her desk and hide them. We'll make her an apple-pie bed each night. We'll stitch up the pockets and sleeves of her out-door coat. We'll put stones into her Wellingtons. We'll . . .'

'It all sounds rather spiteful,' said Hilary, doubtfully. 'Need we do quite so many things? I know Mirabel is perfectly sickening and needs a good lesson – but don't let's make ourselves as bad as she is!'

'Well – do as you like,' said Elsie, rather sneeringly. 'If you're too goody-goody to follow the lead of your head girls, well, there will be plenty of us who'll do what I say.'

'I bet Anna didn't think of any of those things,' said Bobby, looking at the plump, placid Anna, sitting beside Elsie.

The meeting discussed the matter a little more, and then, at the sound of a school bell, broke up. Only Gladys had said nothing. She had sat, as usual, in a kind of dream, paying hardly any attention to what was said. The girls were becoming so used to the Misery-girl, as they called her, that they really hardly noticed whether she was there or not.

'Well,' said Hilary, as the girls ran off to change for games, 'I suppose we must do something to teach Mirabel that two can play at being annoying – but somehow a lot of spitefulness seems to have got mixed up in it.'

'It's bound to, with Elsie Fanshawe to lead us!' said Bobby. 'I wish she wasn't our head girl. She's not the right sort. As for Anna, she's no use at all – just a lazy lump!'

'Mirabel's going to have a few shocks from now on,' said Alison, who was more pleased than anyone to think of the tricks that were to be played on Mirabel. 'I for one will do everything with the greatest pleasure!'

'I hope your darling Miss Quentin will be pleased with you!' said Bobby, with a grin, and scampered off to the field before Alison could think of any reply.

5.

Mirabel and the Misery-girl

It was not pleasant to be thought a tiresome nuisance by girls and teachers alike. Mirabel was getting tired of her defiant pose. Nobody had ever thought it was funny, as she had hoped. Nobody had ever laughed. They had just got impatient. The girl began to feel sorry she had ever started her irritating behaviour.

A great feeling of misery overtook her the evening of the day Carlotta had turned against her. She felt that no one liked her, and certainly no one loved her. Hadn't her own father sent her away? And her mother had agreed to it! How could she put up with that? There was no way to answer things like that except by being defiant.

Mirabel felt that she did not want to be with the others that evening in the noisy common-room. She stole away by herself to one of the music-rooms. She had spoken truly when she had told Bobby that she could play the piano and the violin. She loved music, and was a really good performer on the piano, and a beautiful player of the violin. But because of her defiant obstinacy, she had refused to learn either of the instruments at St Clare's, when her father had spoken to her about them.

'You can learn well there,' he had told her. 'There are excellent teachers of both.'

'What's the use?' Mirabel had flashed back at him. 'I'm only going to be there for half a term – and you don't want to have to pay full fees for two lots of music lessons, do you, as well as full fees for the ordinary lessons?'

'Very well. Have it your own way,' said her father. So nothing had been said about learning music, and the girl had missed her weekly lessons very much. Music had always helped her strong, domineering nature – and now, without it, she felt lost. She was depressed and unhappy tonight – her mind longed for something to fasten on, something to love. She thought of her violin at home, and wished with all her heart that she had brought it with her.

It was dark in the music-room. Mirabel did not turn on the light, for she was afraid somebody passing might see her, and she did not want any company just then. She leant her arms on a little table and thought.

Her hands touched something – a violin case. Something in the feel of it stirred her, and suddenly, with hands that trembled a little, she undid the strap and took out the violin inside. She put it lovingly under her chin, and groped for the bow.

And then the little dark music-room was full of music, as Mirabel played to herself. She played to comfort herself, to forget herself, and the notes filled the little room, and made it beautiful.

'That's better,' said Mirabel at last. 'That's much better! I didn't know how much I'd missed my music. I wonder whereabouts the piano is. I'll play that too. Why didn't I think of this before?'

She groped her way to the piano, and began to finger the notes gently in the darkness. She played from memory, and chose melodies that were sad and yearning, to match her own mood.

She thought she was alone, and she put her whole heart into her playing. Then suddenly she heard a sound in the room beside her, and she stopped at once, her heart thumping. She heard a stifled sob.

'Who's there?' said Mirabel, in a low voice. There was no answer. Someone began softly to grope her way to the door. Mirabel felt a stir of anger. Who was it spying on her? Who had come into the room like that? She jumped up and grabbed wildly at the someone near the door. She caught a blouse sleeve and held on.

'Who is it?' she said.

'Me – Gladys,' said a voice. 'I was in here alone – when you came in. I didn't know you were going to play. But you played such beautiful music I had to stay – and then it got sad, and I cried.'

'You're always crying,' said Mirabel, impatiently. 'What's the matter?'

'I shan't tell you,' said Gladys. 'You'll only tell the others, and they'd laugh. They call me Misery-girl, I know. It's hateful. They'd be Misery-girls too if they were like me.'

'Like *you* – why, what's the matter with you?' asked Mirabel, her curiosity aroused. 'Look here – tell me. I shan't jeer at you or anything.'

'Well, don't turn on the light then,' said Gladys. 'You'll think I'm very feeble, so I'd rather tell you in the dark.'

'You *are* an odd fish,' said Mirabel. 'Come on – what's the matter?'

'It's my mother,' said Gladys. 'She's awfully ill – in hospital – and I don't know if she'll get better. I simply can't tell you how much I love her, and how much I miss her. I haven't a father, or brothers or sisters – only my mother. I've never been away from her even for a night till now. I know it sounds silly to you – you'll call me babyish and mother's girl – and so I am, I suppose. But you see, Mother and I haven't had anyone but each other – and I'm so terribly, terribly homesick, and want to be with Mother so much . . .'

Gladys burst into sobs again, and cried so miserably that Mirabel forgot her own troubles for the moment and put her arm awkwardly round the girl. She saw how little courage Gladys had got – she saw how little she tried to face what had come to her – and she felt a little scornful. But no one could help feeling sorry for the miserable girl. Mirabel had no idea what to do for the best.

'Well,' she said, saying the first thing that came into her head, 'well, how would you like to be *me*? Sent away from home by your mother and father because they didn't want you, and said you upset your brother and sister and made everyone unhappy! That's what *I've* got to put up with! I'm not so lucky as you, I think!'

Gladys raised her head, and for the first time forgot her unhappiness in her scorn of Mirabel.

'*You* unlucky! Don't be silly – you don't know how lucky you are! To have a father *and* a mother, a brother *and* a sister, all to love and to love you. And I only have my mother and even she is taken away from me! Mirabel, you deserve to be sent away from home if you can't understand that families should love one another! I can tell you, if I had all those people to love *I* wouldn't behave so badly to them that they'd send me away. You ought to be ashamed of yourself.'

Coming from the silent Gladys, this was most astonishing. Mirabel stared into the darkness, not knowing what to say. Gladys got up and went to the door.

'I'm sorry,' she said, in a muffled voice. 'You're unhappy – and I'm unhappy – and I should be sorry for you, and comfort you. But you made your own unhappiness – and I didn't make mine. That's the difference between us.'

The door banged and Mirabel was alone. She sat still in surprise. Who would have thought that Gladys could say all that? Mirabel thought back to her own home. She saw the golden head of her little sister, the dark one of her brother, bent over homework. She saw the gentle, patient face of her mother, who always gave in to everyone. She remembered the good-humoured face of her father, changed to a sad and angry countenance because of her own continual insistence on her own way.

It was Mother's fault for giving in to me, she thought. And Harry and Joan should have stood up to me. But it's difficult for younger ones to stand up for themselves – and after all, I *am* difficult. I wish I was home now. I'm lonely here, and I've behaved like an idiot. I know Mother would always love me – and yet I've been beastly to her – and turned Daddy against me too. Harry and Joan will be glad I've gone. Nobody in the world wants me or loves me.

Self-pity brings tears more quickly to the eyes than anything else. Mirabel put her head on the table and wept. She forgot Gladys and her trouble. She only felt sorry for herself. She dried her eyes after a while, and sat up.

I shall stop behaving badly, she thought. I shall leave at half-term and go back home and try to do better. I'm tired of being silly. I'll turn over a new leaf tomorrow, and perhaps the girls will feel more friendly.

She got up and switched on the light. Her watch showed five minutes to nine – almost bed-time. She sat down at the piano and played to herself for a while, and then, when the nine-o'clock bell sounded, made her way upstairs to bed, full of good resolutions. She began to make pictures of how nice the girls would be to her when they found she was turning over a new leaf. Perhaps the twins would find she was somebody worth knowing after all.

Poor Mirabel! When she got into bed that night, she found that she could only get her legs half-way down it! The girls had made a beautiful apple-pie bed, and, not content with that, Elsie had put a spray of holly across the bend of the sheet. Mirabel gave a shout of dismay as the holly pricked her toes.

'Oh! Who's put this beastly thing into my bed? It's scratched my foot horribly!'

Mirabel had never had an apple-pie bed made for her before. She could not imagine what had happened. She tried to force her legs down to the bottom of the bed, but only succeeded in tearing the sheet.

The girls were in fits of laughter. They soon saw that Mirabel had not experienced an apple-pie bed before, and had no idea that the top sheet had been tucked under the bolster, and then folded in half, half-way down the bed, and brought back to fold over the blanket. Doris rolled on her bed in glee, and even placid Anna squealed with joy.

'Golly! You'll have to report that tear to Matron in the morning,' said Elsie, when she heard the sheet torn in half. 'You idiot! You might have guessed that would happen. You'll spend the next sewing-class mending a long rent.'

Mirabel threw the holly at Elsie. She had now discovered what had happened, and was angry and hurt. She got into bed and drew the covers round her. The others chuckled a little and then one by one fell asleep.

In the morning Mirabel awoke early. She lay and thought over what she had decided the night before. It wasn't going to be easy to make a complete changeover, but she didn't see anything else to do. She simply could *not* go on being idiotic. Once you were ashamed of yourself, you had to stop. If you didn't, then you really were an idiot.

So, full of good resolutions still, Mirabel went to her classes. She would work well. She would give Mam'zelle a great surprise. She would please Miss Jenks. She would make up for her rudeness to Miss Quentin. She would even be decent to that wild little Carlotta, and forgive her for treading on her toe. The girls would see she wasn't so bad as they thought she was, and they would turn over a new leaf too, and be friendly to her. Everything would be lovely again – and at the half-term she would leave, and people would be sorry to see her go!

It was with these pleasant thoughts that poor Mirabel entered on a day of horrid shocks and unpleasant surprises!

6.

A day of shocks and surprises

Alison and Elsie were the two who enjoyed punishing Mirabel more than any of the others – Elsie because she was naturally spiteful, and Alison because she had been so annoyed at losing her turn in Miss Quentin's class.

'I'll sew up the sleeves of Mirabel's coat,' said Alison to Elsie. 'I'll do them awfully tightly. She'll be furious!'

'I'll take out some of her books and hide them,' said Elsie. 'Anna, go and find Mirabel's Wellington boots and put small pebbles inside – right in the toes.'

'Oh, can't someone else do that?' said Anna. 'I shall have to go down to the games-room to get the boots. Bobbie, you go.'

Elsie went to the classroom before morning school and removed various books and exercise papers. There was no one else in the room. The girl spitefully dropped ink on to a maths paper that Mirabel had done. 'This will teach her to behave better!' said Elsie to herself. 'Now – where shall I put the books?'

She decided to put them at the back of the handwork cupboard, and cover them with the loose raffia there. So into the cupboard went the books, and then Elsie, having a few minutes to spare, looked round for something else to do.

She saw the list of classroom duties hung up on the wall and went to read them. It was Mirabel's turn that week to keep the vases well-filled with water. Elsie pursed up her lips spitefully.

I'll empty out the water – and then, when the flowers begin to droop, Miss Jenks will notice and Mirabel will get ticked off for forgetting the water, thought Elsie. So out of the window went the water from the four big vases. The flowers were hurriedly replaced just as the first bell went for lessons.

The second form trooped in to take their places. Alison went to hold the door for Miss Jenks. Mirabel took a look round at the girls, hoping to get a smile from someone. She was longing to say that she meant to turn over a new leaf. But nobody looked at her except Elsie, who nudged Anna and then turned away.

'She's coming!' hissed Alison. The class stopped lounging over their desks and talking. They stood up and waited in silence. Miss Jenks was very strict about politeness and good manners in her class.

'Good morning, girls,' said the mistress, putting her books on her desk. 'Sit, please. We will . . . good gracious, Alison, what is that you are wearing on your left wrist?'

'A bracelet,' said Alison, sulkily. The girls looked at it and giggled. It was very like one that Miss Quentin wore. Alison loved to wear anything that even remotely resembled her beloved Miss Quentin's belongings.

'Alison, I am getting tired of asking you to remove bows and brooches and bracelets and goodness knows what,' said Miss Jenks. 'What with putting up with Mirabel's stupidities, and your vanities, I'm going really grey!'

Miss Jenks had flaming red hair, with not a scrap of grey in it. The girls smiled, but were not certain enough of Miss Jenks's temper that day to laugh out loud.

'Bring me that bracelet, Alison,' said Miss Jenks, in a tired voice. 'You can have it back in a week's time providing that during that time I haven't had to remove any other frills and fancies from you.'

Alison sulkily gave up the bracelet. She knew it was the rule that no jewellery should be worn with school uniform, but the little feather-head was always trimming herself up with something or other.

'And now please get out your maths books and the exercise you did for prep and we will go on to the next page of sums,' said Miss Jenks. 'It's much the same as the one we did yesterday. Work them out, please, and if there is any difficulty, let me know. Come up one by one as I call you, with your maths exercise paper, and I will correct it at my desk with you.'

The class got busy. Desks were opened and books got out. Pencils were taken from boxes. Exercise books were opened, and there was a general air of getting down to hard work.

Mirabel hunted all through her desk for her maths book. How curious! It didn't seem to be there. 'Have you borrowed my maths book?' she asked Janet in a whisper.

'No whispering,' said Miss Jenks, who had ears like a

lynx. 'What is it, Mirabel? One of your usual interruptions, I suppose.'

'No, Miss Jenks,' said Mirabel, meekly. 'I can't find my maths book, that's all.'

'Mirabel, you're always pretending you can't find this and that,' said Miss Jenks. 'Get your book at once and begin.'

'But, Miss Jenks, it really isn't here,' said Mirabel, hunting frantically through her desk again. The girls nudged one another and grinned. They all knew where it was – at the back of the handwork cupboard. Mirabel might look through her desk all day but she wouldn't find her book.

'Share Janet's book, then,' said Miss Jenks, shortly, only half-believing Mirabel. Mirabel heaved a sigh of relief, and opened her arithmetic book to copy down the sums from Janet's textbook. She put ready her maths paper, which she had done in prep the night before, to show to Miss Jenks. But as she turned it over the right way, she stared at it in horror. It was covered with ink-spots!

Just as I've made up my mind to turn over a new leaf, all these things happen! thought Mirabel in dismay. I can't imagine how I got that ink on my paper. Miss Jenks will never believe I didn't know it was there.

Mirabel was right – Miss Jenks didn't believe it! She looked in disgust at the untidy paper. She would not even correct it.

'Another of your nice little ways, I suppose,' she said. 'Do it again, please.'

'Miss Jenks, I really didn't make all those ink-spots,'

said Mirabel. But she had given in too many badly done papers before, on purpose, for Miss Jenks suddenly to believe her now.

'I don't want to discuss the matter,' said Miss Jenks. 'Do it all again, and let me have it this evening, without any mess on it at all.'

Mirabel went back to her desk. She caught Elsie's spiteful smile, but she did not guess yet that there was a campaign against her. She sat down, angry and puzzled.

The French class came next, and Mirabel discovered, to her dismay, that not only her French books, but also the French paper she had written out the day before as homework, had disappeared. She hunted through her desk again and again, and Mam'zelle grew sarcastic.

'Mirabel, is it possible for you to come out of your desk before the lesson is ended? Soon I shall forget what your face is like.'

'Mam'zelle, I'm sorry, but I can't seem to find the French paper I did yesterday,' said Mirabel, emerging from her desk flushed and worried.

If there was one thing that Mam'zelle could not stand, it was the non-appearance of any work she had set the class to do. She frowned, and her glasses slid down her big nose. The girls watched gleefully. The knew the signs of gathering wrath. Mam'zelle replaced her glasses on the bridge of her nose.

'Ah, Mirabel! You cannot seem to find the work you did, you say? How many times have I heard that excuse since I have been here at St Clare's? A thousand times, ten thousand times! You have not done the work. Do not deny it, I know. You are a tiresome girl – you have been tiresome ever since the first day you came. You will always be tiresome. You will give me that work before the end of the morning or you will not play lacrosse this afternoon.'

'But, Mam'zelle, I really *did* do it!' protested Mirabel, almost in tears. 'I can't find my ordinary French books, either. They're gone.'

'Always this Mirabel holds up my class!' cried Mam'zelle, raising her hands to the ceiling and wagging them in a way that made Doris long to imitate her at once. 'She loses things – she looks for them – she makes excuses – I cannot bear this girl.'

'Nor can anybody,' said Alison, delighted at the success of the trick. Mirabel flashed an angry glance at her. She was beginning to wonder if the girls had had anything to do with the mysterious disappearance of her things.

It's too bad all this happening now, she thought. Mam'zelle might believe me. I really am speaking the truth.

But Mirabel had so often been silly and untruthful that she had only herself to blame now if no one believed her when she did actually tell the truth. She tried once more with Mam'zelle.

'Please do believe me, Mam'zelle,' she begged. 'Elsie saw me doing the paper last night. Didn't you, Elsie?'

'Indeed I didn't,' said Elsie, maliciously.

'Ah, this untruthful Mirabel!' cried Mam'zelle. 'You will do me the paper once because you have not done it

– and again you will do it for me because you have told an untruth.'

Mirabel saw her time at break going. She would have to do the two papers then. She looked round the class for sympathy. Usually, comforting glances were sent from one girl to another when somebody got into trouble. But there were no comforting glances for Mirabel. Everyone was glad that the Nuisance was in trouble.

Poor Mirabel! Her troubles were never-ending that morning. Miss Jenks noticed all the drooping flowers in the waterless vases during the next lesson, and spoke sharply about it.

'Who is Room Monitor this week?'

'I am,' said Mirabel.

'Well, look at the flowers,' said Miss Jenks. 'It doesn't seem as if they can have a drop of water in the vases, by the look of them.'

'Why, I filled them all up yesterday,' said Mirabel, indignantly. 'I did really.'

Miss Jenks went to the nearest vase and tipped it up. 'Not a drop of water,' she said. 'I suppose you will suggest next that somebody has emptied all the vases, Mirabel?'

It flashed across the girl's mind that someone might actually have done that, to pay her back for all the annoying things she had done. But it seemed such a mean trick – to make flowers die in order to get somebody into trouble! She flushed and said nothing.

'I suppose you thought I would let you miss part of the lesson whilst you filled up the flowers,' said Miss Jenks, in disgust. 'Hilary, have you finished answering the questions on the blackboard? Good – then just go and get some water for the vases, will you?'

Mirabel spent the whole of break doing the French paper twice over. She guessed now, by the grins and nudges among the girls, that most of her troubles were due to them, and she was angry and hurt. Just as I had made up my mind to be decent! she thought, as she wrote out the French papers quickly. It's beastly of everyone.

She was late for games because she could not put on her coat in time to go to the field with the others. Alison had sewn up the sleeves well and truly – so tightly that it was impossible to break the stitches. Mirabel had to go and hunt for a pair of scissors to cut the sewn-up sleeves. She was almost in tears.

And then, when she put on her Wellingtons to go across the muddy field-path, she squealed in pain. Nasty little pebbles made her hobble along – and at last she had to stop, take off the boots, and empty the pebbles into the hedge.

Miss Wilton, the sports mistress, had already started the lacrosse game going. 'You're late, Mirabel,' she called. 'Stand aside until half-time. If you can't bother to be in time, you can miss part of the game.'

It was cold standing and watching. Mirabel felt miserable. Everybody and everything was against her. What was the use of trying to be different?

Miss Wilton took her to task at half-time. 'Why were you so late? You know the time perfectly well. You were almost fifteen minutes after the others!'

She waited to hear Mirabel's excuse. The other girls listened. They had not bargained for Miss Wilton enquiring into the matter. Alison felt uncomfortable. She didn't want to get into trouble for sewing up Mirabel's coat-sleeves. She did not want another bad report. Last term's had been very poor, and her father had had a good many things to say that were not pleasant to hear.

Mirabel opened her mouth to pour out her woes – how her coat-sleeves had been sewn up – stones put into her Wellingtons – and goodness knows what else done to her! Then she shut her mouth again. How often had she scolded her young brother and sister for telling tales of her when she had made things unpleasant for them? She had always said that a tale-bearer was someone quite impossible.

The girls deserve to have tales told about them, thought Mirabel, but I shan't make myself into something I hate just to get back at them.

So she said nothing at all.

'Well,' said Miss Wilton, impatiently, 'as you have no excuse, it seems, take off your coat and join in the second half of the game. But next time, if you are late, you will not play in the game at all – you can just go back to school and ask Miss Jenks to give you something to do.'

The game went on. One or two of the girls began to feel uncomfortable. It was decent of Mirabel not to give them away. You couldn't attack people if they behaved well. It's time we stopped going for Mirabel, thought Hilary. I'll tell Elsie so tonight!

7.

A meeting in the common-room

Another meeting, this time called by Hilary, was held that night. It was held in the common-room. Everyone was there but Mirabel, who was doing her maths paper all over again in the classroom.

'What's the meeting for?' asked Elsie, half-indignant that anyone but herself should call a meeting.

'It's about Mirabel,' said Hilary. 'You know, she didn't split on us when she had the chance to – so I vote we stop playing tricks on her now. Anyway, we pretty well put her through it today!'

'We're certainly not going to stop,' said Elsie, at once. 'What, stop when she's only just begun to learn her lesson! She'll be as bad as ever if we don't go on showing her we can make things just as tiresome for her as she has made them for us!'

'No, we've done enough,' said Hilary. 'It makes me feel rather mean. I rather wish we hadn't done *quite* so many things – and anyway, I don't know who spilt ink over her maths paper, and took the water out of the flowers. We didn't arrange that. Who did it?'

There was a silence. Elsie went red. She did not dare to say she had done anything more than had already been arranged – the others might think her spiteful, or mean.

'I believe it was Elsie!' said Carlotta, suddenly. 'Look how red she's gone!'

Everyone looked. Elsie scowled. 'Of course I didn't do anything,' she said. 'I don't think we did nearly enough. I think a girl who openly says she's jolly well going to make herself too beastly to stay more than half a term ought to be well shown up!'

'Well, she *has* been shown up – by her own self!' said Janet. 'No one would have known anything about her or her private affairs if she hadn't gone round yelling them out! I think Hilary is right – we won't do anything more.'

'You talk as if Hilary is head girl,' said Elsie, spitefully.

'Well – so she was in the first form,' said Bobby, losing her temper. 'And let me tell you she was a much better one than you, Elsie.'

'Don't forget that Anna is head girl too,' said Pat. Anna smiled sleepily. Bobby turned on her at once.

'As if anyone can remember that Anna is head girl, or anything! What's the good of a head girl who is always too lazy to do a single thing? We've got two head girls in this form – and one is spiteful and catty and overbearing – and the other is fat and lazy!'

'Shut up, Bobby,' said Hilary, uncomfortably. 'It's no good losing your temper like that. Let's get back to the point – and that is, we're not going to persecute Mirabel any more. Let's give her a chance and see if today's lessons have taught her anything. She knows well enough we have all been working against her – and that must be a very horrid experience.'

'Hilary Wentworth – if you don't stop talking as if you were head of this form, you'll be sorry,' said Elsie, angered by Bobby's candid speech. 'Anna – for Heaven's sake sit up and back me up.'

'But I don't think you're right,' said Anna, in her gentle voice. 'I don't want to persecute Mirabel, either. I don't feel spiteful towards her now.'

'You're too lazy to feel anything,' said Elsie, surprised and furious at Anna's unexpected refusal to back her up. 'You know perfectly well that as head girls we must work together – and it's an unwritten rule that the form go by what we say.'

'Well, I can't work with you in this,' said Anna. 'I may be fat and lazy and all the other things you probably think about me, and don't say – but I am not catty. So I say, as head girl of the form – we will not continue with our tricks against Mirabel.'

'Well,' said Pat, 'this is going to be difficult – two head girls, each saying different! I suppose we'd better put it to the vote, which girl we follow. Now – hands up for Anna and doing what she says!'

Every single hand went up at once. Anna grinned and for once sat up really straight. Elsie went white.

'Now – hands up those who wish to follow Elsie,' said Pat. Not a single hand went up, of course. Elsie stood up angrily.

'This is what comes of having to stay down with a lot

'How do you know?' asked Janet. 'She's never played any instrument here – and she doesn't even open her mouth in the singing-class.'

'I know because I've heard her,' said Gladys. 'She was in the music-room last night – you know, the one next to the boot-cupboard – and first she played a violin – oh, most beautifully – and then she played the piano. And it was all in the dark too.'

'In the *dark*!' said Carlotta, in surprise. 'Whatever were you two doing there in the dark? How odd! Do you usually go and sit in the music-rooms in the dark?'

Gladys didn't know what to say. She couldn't confess that she often went to the lonely little music-rooms by herself when she felt extra-homesick – the girls would laugh at her, and she couldn't bear that. She stared at Carlotta and said nothing.

'Well, can't you answer?' said Carlotta, impatiently. 'Do you often go and listen to Mirabel playing in the dark?'

'No – of course not,' said Gladys. 'I – I just happened to be there – when Mirabel came in – and she didn't see me. So I heard her playing, you see.'

The girls looked at one another. So Gladys disappeared into the dark little music-rooms at night – all alone. What a strange girl she was! They looked at her thin white little face, and two or three of them felt a pang of sympathy for the Misery-girl and her lonely thoughts, whatever they might be. Nobody laughed or teased her about being in the dark in the music-room. Even downright Carlotta made no remark about it.

'You know,' said Janet, looking round at the little company of girls, 'Mirabel reminds me in some ways of the O'Sullivan twins!'

'What do you mean?' said Pat, indignantly.

'Well – don't you remember how awfully difficult you were a year ago, when you first came to St Clare's?' said Janet. 'You just made up your minds to be awkward, and you were! You ought to understand Mirabel's point of view, and be able to tell us how to tackle her. What made you two change your ideas and want to stay here?'

'Oh – as soon as we realized we were acting stupidly – and you were friendly to us – we just sort of settled down and loved everything,' said Pat, trying to remember that first exciting term.

'Right,' said Anna, taking charge of the meeting again. 'That's just what *we*'ll do! We think Mirabel was decent for not splitting on us today – so we'll be friendly towards her now instead of beastly – and perhaps if we get her to play to us, and praise her up a bit – she'll settle down too. What about it?'

'Yes, Anna!' said everyone, Gladys too. Hilary gazed in surprise at Anna. She would never have thought that sleepy Anna could have come to the fore like this – why, she really seemed to be taking a keen interest in everything! And taking the lead too. Perhaps it would be a good thing that the class had broken away from Elsie's leadership. Anna seemed as if she was going to take the chance offered to her by the unexpected quarrel.

'Sh! Here comes Mirabel!' said Pat, as the door opened.

At once the girls began to chatter and gabble about anything that came into their heads. Mirabel looked at them suspiciously. She felt sure they had been discussing her! Horrid things. Well – if they had been planning fresh tricks to play on her, she would go back to her old ways and upset every single class she could!

8.

Mirabel gives the form a surprise

The twins talked together that night when they were in bed. Their beds were next to one another and they could whisper without anyone else hearing what they said.

'We ought to have a few excitements now!' whispered Pat. 'I bet Elsie won't sit down under this! She'll find some way of getting back at Anna – and all of us as well!'

'I hope Mirabel will be sensible now,' said Isabel. 'She looked most suspiciously at all of us, I thought – and she hardly answered Janet at all when she spoke to her.'

'Well, I'm not surprised, really,' said Pat, with a yawn. 'After all – we did do an awful lot of things to her today. It was funny at first – but I didn't like it much afterwards – even though I must say I think Mirabel deserved a little rough-handling. I say – didn't you think it was funny, Gladys speaking up like that – and admitting she was in the music-room all alone? Funny kid, isn't she?'

'Pat, what Janet said was quite true,' said Isabel, speaking rather loudly.

'Sh! Don't speak so loud,' whispered Pat. 'What do you mean?'

'Well, you know – we did behave a little bit like Mirabel – and we did hate it when everyone disliked us – it was a miserable feeling,' said Isabel. 'So let's make a bee-line for Mirabel tomorrow, and buck her up a bit. St Clare's has done a lot for us – let's do a bit for Mirabel.'

'Pat! Isabel! If you don't stop talking at once, I'll report you to Miss Jenks tomorrow!' suddenly came Elsie's sharp voice through the darkness.

'You can't. You're not head girl,' came Carlotta's cheeky voice, before the twins could answer.

'I'll report you too, for untidy drawers and cupboard,' said Elsie, furiously.

'Well – it will only be the fiftieth time, I should think,' said Carlotta, lazily. 'Go ahead, Miss Catty Elsie!'

There was a delighted squeal of laughter from the dormitory at this. Elsie sat up in bed, furious.

'Carlotta! If you dare to talk like a low-down circus girl to me . . .' she began. But at that everyone sat up in bed, indignant.

'Listen,' began Bobby, 'anyone who calls Carlotta low-down deserves a good scolding! We're all proud of Carlotta – remember how she saved Sadie from being kidnapped last term! It's *you* who are low-down, Elsie! Now – just you remember what I said about that scolding!'

Elsie was furious. She began to tell Bobby exactly what she thought of her. She forgot to keep her voice low, and when Miss Jenks came along to see that all was quiet in the dormitory, she was amazed to hear a voice going on and on in the darkness – an angry voice, a spiteful voice!

She switched on the light and stood in silence by the door. Every girl was sitting up in bed. Elsie's voice died away in horror. She stared wide-eyed at Miss Jenks.

'Who was that talking just now?' enquired Miss Jenks, in her cool voice.

Nobody answered. Elsie simply could not bear to own up. She swallowed hard, hoping that Miss Jenks would deliver a general lecture and go. Miss Jenks didn't. She just stood and waited.

'Who is in charge of this dormitory?' she asked. 'Oh you, I suppose, Elsie – as you are one of the head girls for this form. Well – as the culprit does not seem to have enough courage to own up, perhaps you, as head girl, will see to it that the girl is punished by going to bed one hour earlier tomorrow. Will you?'

'Yes, Miss Jenks,' answered Elsie, in a very subdued tone. There was a smothered giggle from Carlotta's bed, hurriedly turned into a loud cough.

'You seem to have a cold, Carlotta,' said Miss Jenks, pretending to be quite concerned. 'Perhaps you had better go to Matron tomorrow morning and get a dose of medicine for it.'

'Oh, I shall be quite all right tomorrow morning, Miss Jenks, thank you,' Carlotta hurriedly assured her.

'Good night, girls,' said Miss Jenks, and switched off the light. As soon as her footsteps had died away, the girls began to giggle and whisper.

'Elsie! See you put yourself to bed an hour earlier tomorrow!' whispered Carlotta.

Elsie lay in bed, her cheeks burning. Why hadn't she owned up? Then she wouldn't have been so humiliated! She jolly well wouldn't go to bed early the next night, anyway. She shut her ears with her fingers, so as not to hear what the girls were whispering. She did not dare to tell them to stop – and as for threatening to report them – well, that would make them laugh all the more!

Everyone felt scornful of Elsie – but they also thought the whole thing was funny. The girls were quite determined that Elsie *should* go to bed early the next night. They were not going to let her off the punishment she had meekly promised to wreak on the culprit!

The next day the twins gave Mirabel a cheerful grin at the breakfast-table. She smiled back, surprised and warmed. She had been expecting a few more tricks, and the unexpected smile surprised her very much.

After breakfast Pat and Isabel spoke to Mirabel. 'Did you hear about the row in our dormitory last night?' asked Pat.

'I knew there was something up,' said Mirabel. 'I heard the others talking about it. What was it?'

The twins told Mirabel about Elsie and Miss Jenks, and the girl smiled. 'Thanks for telling me,' she said, 'it was funny. I say – is the form going to do beastly things to me today? You know, I'd just decided to turn over a new leaf – when you did all those things.'

'Had you really decided to change?' said Pat, in surprise. 'Well – don't worry – we're not going to get back at you anymore. But for goodness' sake do your bit too.

It's pretty sickening having class after class upset, you know. You may feel in a temper about your home-affairs – but that really isn't any reason for venting your temper on the class!'

'No – I see that now,' said Mirabel. 'I'm an idiot – always have been. Well – I bet you'll be glad to see the back of me at half-term.'

'Wait and see,' said Isabel. 'I say – our form is giving a concert next week, in aid of the Red Cross. Everyone is to do something. Could you play the violin for us, do you think? And perhaps the piano too?'

'How do you know I play?' asked Mirabel, in surprise. But at that moment Miss Jenks bustled the whole class off for a nature-walk, and Mirabel found herself walking with the timid Gladys, who, remembering the night in the dark music-room, felt afraid to say a word. Mirabel felt awkward too, so the two hardly exchanged a single word.

The twins, when the chance came, hurriedly told the rest of the form that they had asked Mirabel to play at the concert planned for the following week. Every form had been asked to get up something in aid of the Red Cross, and this was to be the second form's contribution.

'Did she say she would?' asked Bobby.

'No – but we'll put her name down on the programme,' said Pat. 'I bet she will! She was quite nice this morning.'

Mirabel found her books back in her desk that day. Anna had taken them from their hiding-place and put them back. Elsie had scowled, but had said nothing. She didn't know whom she hated most – Anna – or that saucy Carlotta!

When the programme for the Red Cross concert was drawn up that evening, Isabel called across to Mirabel.

'Hi, Mirabel! I've put you down for a violin solo, and a piano solo. What will you play? Can you tell us the names of the pieces?'

'I haven't my violin here,' said Mirabel hesitatingly.

'Pooh – you can easily send a message home for it,' said Pat. 'And Anna will lend you hers to practise on this week – won't you, Anna?'

'Of course,' said Anna. 'I'll go and get it now and you can see if you like the feel of it. It's a good one.'

Anna went to fetch her violin. She took it out of its case and put it into Mirabel's hands. As she had said, it was a good one. Mirabel drew the bow across it lovingly.

'Play something,' said Isabel. And then, as in the dark music-room, Mirabel played some of the melodies she loved. She forgot the girls in the common-room, she forgot St Clare's, she forgot herself. She was a real little musician, and she put all her heart into the music she loved.

The girls listened spell-bound. Two or three girls in the school played the violin very well – but Mirabel made it speak. The notes rang out pure and true, and Anna was amazed that her violin could produce such music.

When Mirabel stopped, everyone clapped frantically. 'I say! You *are* marvellous!' said Pat, her eyes shining. 'Golly – you'll make everyone sit up at the concert next week, I can tell you. Now go and play something on the piano. Go on. You simply must!'

Mirabel looked round at the admiring audience, with flushed cheeks and bright eyes. Only Elsie Fanshawe did not applaud. She sat at a table, reading a book, taking no notice at all.

'Go on, Mirabel – play us something on the piano!' insisted Pat.

Mirabel went across to the old piano in the common-room. It was there for the girls to strum on, if they wanted to. Usually dance music or popular songs were hammered out on it – but tonight something quite different was played!

Mirabel's long, sensitive fingers ran over the notes, and one of Chopin's nocturnes filled the quiet common-room. Most of the girls loved good music, and they listened in delight. Gladys shut her eyes. Music always stirred her very much, though she learnt no instrument, and knew little about it.

The notes died away. The girls sat up, pleased. 'Look here – play that at the concert next week,' said Hilary. 'It's heavenly. I heard it on the radio in the hols – but you play it much better!'

'I don't,' said Mirabel, red with embarrassment and pleasure. 'All right – I'll play it. And if you really want me to play something on the violin too, I'll send a message tomorrow asking for my own violin to be sent. Anna's *is* a lovely one – but I'm more at home with my own.'

'Good,' said Isabel. 'I say – aren't you a dark horse –

never saying a word about your music – keeping it up your sleeve like that! You've got a real gift. I wish *I* had a gift. You're lucky!'

Mirabel went to help Isabel to draw up the programme. Her words echoed in her mind. 'You've got a real gift!' She remembered Miss Theobald's words too. 'Difficult children often have some hidden quality – some gift – something to make them worthwhile!'

Nobody at home thought her worthwhile – or surely they wouldn't have sent her away! But she *was* worthwhile! See how the girls loved hearing her play. It was a pity she hadn't accepted her father's offer to learn music at St Clare's. She had no other gift but music, and she had refused to develop that, out of obstinacy.

'I bet you could pass any music exam you went in for,' said Isabel, handing Mirabel a few programmes to print. 'Nobody in our form is specially good at music. It's a pity you don't learn. You would be a credit to us – you'd make some of the top formers sit up, I bet! And I guess you'd win the music-prize.'

'Well – I'll certainly send that message tomorrow,' said Mirabel, printing the programmes neatly. She felt happy for the first time that term. It was nice to be working in friendliness with someone like Isabel. It was lovely to be praised for something. Nobody thought a great deal of her music at home, because none of them were musical – except her brother – and dear me, how she snubbed him! Mirabel felt annoyed with herself when she remembered that. She ought to have encouraged him.

I really must have been tiresome, she thought. Well – going away from home does make you see things clearly. When I go back at half-term I'll show them I'm not as bad as they think!

That night, at eight o'clock, all the second form winked at one another. If Elsie was going to bed an hour earlier, it was time she went. But she showed no sign. She had come back from supper and had settled down to read again, saying nothing to anybody.

'Bedtime for little girls!' said Carlotta. Elsie took no notice.

'Naughty girls must go to bed early,' said Bobby, loudly. Elsie did not move.

The girls looked at one another. It was quite clear that Elsie was not going to get up and go. She had not only been afraid to own up to Miss Jenks the night before – but she was now going to evade the punishment!

To everyone's surprise Anna spoke. 'Elsie!' she said. 'You know perfectly well what you have to do. Don't make us all ashamed of you.'

'You can't talk to *me* like that!' said Elsie, turning over a page.

'I can,' said Anna, calmly. 'I am head girl of the form. I have the right to tell you what to do.'

'You haven't,' said Elsie, furiously. 'I'm head girl too.'

'You're not, you're not!' cried a dozen voices. 'We only recognize Anna as head girl now. We don't want *you*!'

'Only Miss Jenks can decide a thing like that,' said Elsie, looking round at the girls.

'Perhaps you are right,' said Anna, in her slow voice. 'Come with me and we will let Miss Jenks decide.'

Hilary looked at Anna in admiration. She knew that this was the one thing that would defeat Elsie. On no account would Elsie go to Miss Jenks at the moment! It would be far too humiliating.

Elsie hesitated. The girls waited. They knew Elsie would not consent to go with Anna. Anna stood up as if she was going.

'I'm not going to Miss Jenks,' said Elsie, in a low voice.

'I thought not,' said Anna, and sat down again. 'Well – either Miss Jenks decides this matter or the girls do. I don't mind.'

'*We*'ll decide – we've already decided!' said Janet. 'Anna is our head girl, and we don't want Elsie. And that being so, Elsie – you'll just do as Anna says, and go off to bed. It's your own silly fault.'

That was too much for Elsie. Her obstinacy rose up and she pursed her thin lips. 'I'm not going,' she said. 'I'm not obeying Anna. She may be your head girl – but I won't admit she's mine!'

'Right,' said Carlotta, cheerfully, getting up. 'Come on, Bobby – Janet – twins. Get hold of Elsie, and we'll bump her all the way upstairs to bed! We can't have her disobeying Miss Jenks's orders like this! My word – won't the third form stare when we go by with poor Elsie!'

'No – don't!' cried Elsie, in dismay, jumping to her feet. She knew the wild little Carlotta would stop at nothing. 'I'll go. I'll go. But I hate you all!'

She burst into tears, and with loud sobs went to the door. Carlotta sat down. When Elsie had gone, she looked round.

'I didn't really mean us to bump her up the stairs to bed,' she said, 'but I guessed she'd go of her own accord if I suggested it.'

'She'll be awful tomorrow,' said Bobby. Anna shook her big head.

'No,' she said. 'I know Elsie. She will begin to feel a martyr, and terribly sorry for herself. She will try to get our sympathy by being subdued and meek.'

'Yes – I think you're right,' said Janet. 'Well – the best thing is not to take any notice of her at all. We don't want to get spiteful – just let's leave her alone and take no notice at all.'

'That's the best thing,' said Anna. She took up her knitting again. 'Oh, dear – being the only head girl is very wearing. There seem so many things to decide!'

9.

Anna sees the head mistress

The next morning Mirabel wanted to send for her violin. Anna told her what to do.

'You'll have to go and get permission from Miss Theobald.'

Mirabel went to ask permission. She knocked at Miss Theobald's door and was told to come in. The head mistress looked up. She did not smile.

'What is it, Mirabel?' she asked.

'Please, Miss Theobald, may I send a message home?' asked Mirabel.

Still Miss Theobald did not smile or unbend in any way. She looked really stern. Mirabel began to feel very uncomfortable.

'What is the message about?' she asked. 'You know that you cannot leave before half-term.'

'It's nothing to do with my leaving,' said Mirabel. 'It's – it's – well, Miss Theobald, I just want to ask my mother if she'll send my violin, that's all.'

The head looked surprised. 'Your violin?' she said. 'Why? You don't learn music, do you?'

'No,' said Mirabel. 'I wish I did now. But I wouldn't when Daddy gave me the chance. You see – the second form are giving a concert for the Red Cross next week – and I said I would play for them. I'd like my own violin to play on. It's a beauty.'

Miss Theobald looked at Mirabel. 'So you *have* a gift, Mirabel!' she said. 'You remember what I said to you? I wonder if there is anything worthwhile in you after all!'

Mirabel went red. She stood on first one foot and then on the other. She felt certain that Miss Theobald had had bad reports of her from every mistress.

'I'm not sure that I shall let you ask for your violin,' said Miss Theobald at last. 'I hear that you misbehave at practically every class. You try to spoil everything, it seems. How do I know that you will behave at the concert?'

'I will,' said Mirabel, earnestly. 'You won't believe me, perhaps – but I've turned over a new leaf now. I've got tired of being silly.'

'I see,' said Miss Theobald. 'You've stopped misbehaving just because you're tired of it – not because you're ashamed of it, or want to do better, or want us to think well of you. Only just because you're tired of it. You disgust me, Mirabel. Go, please. I'm disappointed in you. I had hoped that possibly you might turn over a new leaf for some better motive. I thought I saw some courage in you, some real intelligence that might help you to realize your foolishness and selfishness in behaving as you did. Now I see that you have none – you only stop because you yourself are tired of misbehaviour and, possibly, are tired also of having the others unfriendly towards you. Please go.'

Mirabel was struck with horror at the cold, stern words. She had felt so pleased with herself to think she was turning over a new leaf. She *had* been ashamed of herself. She hadn't only got tired of being silly. She opened her mouth to defend herself, but the sight of Miss Theobald's stern face frightened her. She went out of the room without a word.

Miss Theobald sat and thought for a few minutes. Then she sent a message to ask Miss Jenks to come to her for a few minutes.

Miss Jenks soon appeared. 'Sit down for a moment,' said Miss Theobald. 'I want to talk to you about Mirabel Unwin. I have had continual bad reports from you about her. Is there any improvement at all?'

'Yes,' said Miss Jenks at once. 'She seems suddenly to be settling down. I don't quite know why. Has anything happened? I saw her just now, and she looked as if she had been crying.'

'Probably she had,' said Miss Theobald, and told Miss Jenks what had just passed between her and Mirabel.

'I should like to know if the girl has suddenly changed for the right reasons, or the wrong ones,' she said. 'Perhaps the head girls could tell me. Send them, will you?'

'There seems to be some sort of upset between the two head girls of my form,' said Miss Jenks. 'I don't think Elsie Fanshawe has gone down very well with the first formers who came up into my form. But Anna seems unexpectedly to be showing some signs of responsibility and leadership. I'll go and send the two girls to you.

Perhaps they can tell you more about Mirabel. Personally I think we might give her a chance now, and let her have her violin.'

She left the room and went to find Anna and Elsie. They were in the common-room with the others. As the door opened and Miss Jenks appeared all the girls rose to their feet and stopped chattering. Janet turned off the radio.

'Miss Theobald wants the two head girls to go to her for a few minutes,' said Miss Jenks in her cool voice. 'Will you go at once, please?'

She left the room. There was a silence. Anna stood up to go. So did Elsie. But quick as thought Carlotta pulled her down again to her chair.

'You're not head girl, Elsie. You know you're not. We won't have you – and if we won't have you, then Anna is the only head girl. You are not going to Miss Theobald!'

'Don't be an idiot!' snapped Elsie, scrambling up again. 'You know I've got to go. I can't tell Miss Theobald I'm no longer head girl.'

'Well, Anna can,' said Hilary. 'It's unfortunate, Elsie – but we all happen to think the same about this. You were a bad head girl – and we won't accept you. You wouldn't let Miss Jenks decide it – you accepted *our* decision – and you've got to abide by it. Anna must go alone.'

'She's not to, she's not to,' said Elsie, half-crying. 'It's shameful. What will Miss Theobald think?'

'You should have thought of these things before,' said Hilary. 'Anna, go. Say as little as you can about Elsie, of course – but please let it be understood that you are the only head girl of the second form now.'

Anna went. Elsie saw that the whole of the second form would stop her by force if she tried to follow. So she lay back in her chair, looking as forlorn and miserable as she could, letting the tears trickle down her cheeks. She hoped that the girls would feel uncomfortable, and very sorry. But nobody did. In fact, they took no notice of her at all, and went on cheerfully chattering among themselves. It was Saturday morning, and except for an hour's lessons, they were free to do as they chose.

Mirabel was not there. She had had a shock, and it had upset her very much. She did not want anyone to see that she had been crying, so she had gone to the cloakroom to bathe her eyes. She came out of the room just as Anna passed it on her way to the head. Anna spoke to her.

'Hallo! Did you get permission from the head to send for your violin?'

'I didn't get permission,' said Mirabel, miserably. 'Anna, Miss Theobald was awful to me. She thinks I've only turned over a new leaf because I was tired of being an idiot. But I haven't. I'm awfully ashamed of myself now. It was dreadful having you all doing beastly things to me the very day I'd made up my mind to do better – and now even Miss Theobald is against me. What's the use of trying? It's just no good at all. I shan't play at the concert. I shan't do anything.'

Anna stared at Mirabel, surprised. 'Look here, I can't wait now,' she said. 'I've been sent for by the head. But I'll have a talk with you afterwards, see? I'm awfully sorry, Mirabel. Really I am. Cheer up.'

She ran down the passage to Miss Theobald's sitting-room and knocked.

'Come in!' said the head's pleasant voice. Anna entered, half-scared. Miss Theobald was kind and just – but her wisdom and dignity awed every girl, and it was quite an ordeal to go for any kind of interview.

'Good morning, Anna,' said Miss Theobald. 'Where is Elsie Fanshawe?'

'Elsie isn't head girl now, Miss Theobald,' said Anna, feeling awkward. Miss Theobald looked most surprised.

'I hadn't heard this,' she said. 'Why isn't she?'

'We all decided that she wasn't quite fit to be at present,' said Anna, finding it difficult to explain without giving Elsie away too much.

'Miss Jenks knows nothing of this,' said the head. 'Why didn't you ask her advice?'

'Elsie didn't want us to,' said Anna. 'She said she would rather accept our decision, without us taking matters any further. It's – it's rather difficult to explain, Miss Theobald, without telling tales.'

'Did Hilary Wentworth and the O'Sullivan twins agree to this?' asked the head. She had great faith in the fairness and common sense of these three girls.

'Oh, yes,' said Anna. 'I wouldn't have done it myself – I'm too lazy, I'm afraid. But once the girls wanted me to accept responsibility and carry on without Elsie, I had to take it.'

'Of course,' said Miss Theobald, sensing in Anna something better and stronger than she had known before in the lazy slow-moving girl. 'Well – I won't ask any more questions, Anna. I think probably the second form are right – all I hope is that some good will come out of this for Elsie. I can see an improvement in *you* already!'

Anna blushed. Responsibility was a nuisance – but it did bring definite rewards, not the least of which was an added self-respect.

'Anna, I sent for you because I want to ask you about Mirabel Unwin,' said Miss Theobald. 'I always take the head girls of any form into my confidence, as you know. Will you tell me what your opinion is of Mirabel – whether it is bad or good – anything that can help me in dealing with her. You know all the details as to why she was sent here because she has told the whole school!'

Anna seldom wasted words. She said shortly what Miss Theobald wanted to know. 'Mirabel has been awfully tiresome, and the second form punished her for it. She's ashamed of herself now – and she wants to show us she's some good. Could you let her send for her violin?'

'Very well,' said Miss Theobald, smiling at Anna's directness. 'I refused her permission a little while ago. Will you, as head girl, tell her I have changed my mind, and she can send for her violin. Tell her, too, that I shall like to hear her play at the second-form concert.'

'Yes, Miss Theobald,' said Anna. 'Thank you.' The girl left the room, pleased. For the first time in her lazy life she felt that she had some importance. The head had sent for her and actually listened to her. It was worth making an effort if people like Miss Theobald appreciated it.

She went to look for Mirabel. She found her in the common-room, reading rather soberly, her eyes still red.

'Mirabel! Miss Theobald says you may send for your violin. And she says she looks forward to hearing you play at the concert next week.'

Mirabel looked up, astonished and delighted. This was a lovely surprise after having her hopes dashed and her good resolutions misunderstood. She stood up, glowing.

'Anna! It's because of you Miss Theobald said I could send for it. Thanks awfully. You're a brick.'

'It wasn't altogether me,' said Anna. 'Hurry up and get that message sent off.'

The message caused much surprise in Mirabel's home!

'She wants her violin!' said her mother, in astonishment. 'Why, she must be settling down a bit. I *am* glad!'

So the violin was packed up, registered and sent off at once. It arrived on the Monday of the week following, and Mirabel unpacked it joyfully. Her own violin! Now she would be able to play beautifully. She would show the second form what real music was!

And I'll astonish Miss Theobald a bit too, thought Mirabel. She'll see I have a real gift – even if I haven't anything else! I'd like her to think I was worthwhile – I really would.

10.

Gladys is surprising

The second form were very busy preparing for their concert. They were going to charge fifty pence for the tickets, and all the first form, most of the third form, and even a few of the higher-form girls had promised to come. All the mistresses had promised too. It was to be quite a big affair.

The girls were to manage everything themselves. They prepared the programmes and the tickets. Isabel drew a fine big poster and coloured it. She put it up in the big assembly room where everyone could see it.

The concert was to be held in the gym, where there was a fine platform. The second form grew quite excited about it. Too excited for Mam'zelle's liking. She could not bear to feel that the class were thinking about something else in her lessons.

'Isabel! Pat! Did you not sleep last night, that you dream so this morning? What was the question I have just asked the class?'

The twins stared at Mam'zelle in alarm. Neither of them had heard the question. Carlotta whispered softly.

'She said, "Has anyone here seen my glasses?"' whispered Carlotta, grinning. This was quite untrue, as everyone knew! But the twins fell into the trap at once. They stared innocently at Mam'zelle, seeing her glasses perched as usual on her big nose.

'Well?' said Mam'zelle, sharply. 'What did I ask the class?'

'You asked if we had seen your glasses anywhere,' said Pat, 'but they are on your nose, Mam'zelle.'

There was a squeal of laughter from the class. Mam'zelle banged on her desk angrily. '*Ah, que vous êtes abominable*!' she cried. '*Insupportable*!'

The twins glared at Carlotta, who was holding her sides. She shook her head at them, tears of laughter in her eyes. 'Wait till break, you wretch!' said Pat.

'*Taisez-vous*!' said Mam'zelle. 'Pat! Isabel! Of what were you thinking just now when I addressed the class? Be truthful!'

'Well, Mam'zelle – I was thinking of the concert our form is holding on Saturday,' said Pat. 'I'm sorry. My thoughts just wandered away.'

'So did mine,' said Isabel.

'If they wander away again I shall not come to the concert,' threatened Mam'zelle. There was a loud and universal groan.

'We shan't hold the concert unless you come!'

'You *must* come, Mam'zelle! You laugh louder than anyone!'

'I will come if you write me a nice composition,' said Mam'zelle, suddenly beaming again. 'You shall write me a beautiful essay and tell me all that is to happen at this wonderful concert. With no mistakes at all. That will please me greatly. That shall be your prep for tomorrow.'

The girls groaned again. French essays were awful to do – and this one would be difficult. Anyway, the idea had put Mam'zelle into a better temper, so that was something!

Two girls were doing nothing in the concert at all. Elsie had refused to do anything, and had announced her intention of not even coming. And nobody had asked the little Misery-girl to do anything. Everyone felt certain that Gladys would not and could not do a thing. They thought it would be kinder to leave her out altogether.

Gladys was hurt because she was not asked, yet glad that she was not pressed to do anything. She shut more and more up into herself, only spoke when she was spoken to, and was so quiet in every lesson that the teachers hardly knew she was there. Only in Miss Quentin's class did she show any real animation. Not that Miss Quentin ever asked her to act a part, because, like everyone else, Miss Quentin always passed over Gladys, thinking that such a little mouse could never do anything!

But Gladys watched the others acting, and for once in a way forgot to brood over her troubles when she saw Bobby strutting across the room as a king or duke, and Carlotta playing the part of a jester.

Alison adored Miss Quentin's classes. She really did work hard in those – harder than she worked in anyone else's. For one thing she was pretty and graceful, and parts such as princesses or fairies were given naturally to her, and for another thing, she lived for Miss Quentin's words of praise. She thought Miss Quentin was 'just wonderful'!

The preparations for the concert went on well. Doris was to give some of her clever imitations. She meant to mimic Mam'zelle, who had all kinds of mannerisms which were a joy to the class. She meant to imitate Clara, the cook, a jolly, rough-and-ready person much liked by the girls. And she meant to dress up as Matron, and imitate her doling out advice and medicine to various girls.

'Doris, you really are a scream,' said Bobby, enjoying the girl's clever performance in rehearsal. 'You ought to be on the stage.'

'I'm going to be a doctor,' said Doris.

'Oh – well, you'll be a jolly good one because you'll make all your patients scream with laughter!' said Bobby.

Everyone was doing something – either reciting, playing the piano or violin, singing or dancing – everyone, that is, except Elsie and Gladys. Carlotta was going to give a display of acrobatics. She was marvellous at such circus tricks as turning cartwheels, walking on her hands and so on.

'You and Doris, Carlotta, will be the hits of the evening,' said Pat. She and Isabel were going to give a dialogue, supposed to be funny, but they both felt it was not nearly so good as anyone else's contribution. Bobby was to do conjuring tricks! She was very good at these, and had a lot of idiotic patter that fell from her lips in a never-ending torrent.

'I bet Mirabel will be a hit too,' said Janet, after the girl had played her concert piece to them, during rehearsal. 'Good thing we found out she could play!'

'By the way – how *did* you find out?' asked Mirabel, putting her violin into its case. 'I kept meaning to ask you. I didn't think anybody knew.'

'Yes – somebody did,' said Janet, looking round to see if Gladys was in the room; but she was not. 'It was Gladys who told us.'

'*Gladys*!' said Mirabel, suddenly remembering the night in the dark music-room. 'Yes – of course – she heard me that night.'

'She said you were in the dark,' said Pat. 'So that means she was too. Funny kid, isn't she, sitting about in dark rooms all by herself. She really is a little misery. I can't think what's the matter with her. She never tells anyone. If she did, we might help her a bit – get a smile out of her occasionally, or something.'

'Oh – she told me what's the matter,' said Mirabel, remembering everything Gladys had said.

'*Did* she?' said Bobby, in surprise. 'Well, what *is* the matter with her?'

'It's her mother,' said Mirabel. 'She's in hospital – awfully ill – perhaps she's going to die. Gladys said she's only got her mother – no father or brothers or sisters – and they were sort of all-in-all to one another. She'd never been away from her mother even for a night till she was sent here when her mother went to hospital. She said she was awfully homesick, and missed her mother terribly. I suppose she thinks every day she may hear bad news or something.'

The girls heard all this in silence. They felt sorry and uncomfortable. The little Misery-girl really did have something to worry about. Everyone there but Carlotta had mothers they loved – and fathers – and most of them had brothers and sisters. Even slow-minded Anna, who had little imagination, knew for one short moment the sort of heartache that Gladys carried with her day and night.

'Why didn't you tell us this?' asked Bobby.

'I didn't remember it till now,' said Mirabel.

'Well, I think you should have told us at once,' said Hilary. 'We might have been decenter to Gladys. She's a poor little thing, without any courage or spunk – but we haven't exactly made things any easier for her. You really are to blame for not having told us, Mirabel.'

Mirabel was really conscience-stricken. She couldn't think how she could have forgotten Gladys's troubles. She had been so wrapped up in her own, and then, when the girls had become friendly and helped her, she had been so happy that she had not given a thought to the little Misery-girl. She stared unhappily at Hilary.

'I'm sorry,' she said. 'I *should* have told you. All the same, I don't think Gladys would like it if she knew that everyone knew about her troubles. So don't tell her you know. Just be nice to her and notice her a bit.'

The second form received this advice in silence. Mirabel sensed that they did not think very much of her for forgetting another person's troubles. She said no more, but went off to put her violin away.

I wonder where Gladys is, she thought. I've a good mind to hunt for her and ask her if she's heard any news of her mother lately. After all, it might help a bit if someone shares the news with her.

Mirabel went to look for Gladys. She could not seem to find the girl anywhere. It was puzzling.

'Well, she simply *must* be somewhere!' said Mirabel to herself. 'I wonder if she's up in the box-rooms. I saw her coming down from there the other day and wondered whatever had taken her there.'

She went up the stairs to the top of the school. Trunks and bags were kept in the attics, but little else. There was a light showing under the door of one of the attics – and from the room came a voice.

It didn't sound like Gladys's voice. It was deep and strong. Mirabel listened in surprise. The voice was declaiming one of the speeches in *The Tempest,* which the second form were taking that term with Miss Jenks.

That's not Gladys, thought Mirabel. I wonder who it is. Ah – now there's a different voice. There must be two or three people there. But who can they be? Only the second form are doing *The Tempest* this term – and all but Gladys were at rehearsal this evening.

A third voice spoke, gentle and feminine. Mirabel could bear it no longer. She really must see who the speakers were. They were declaiming Shakespeare's words beautifully.

She opened the door. The voice stopped at once. Mirabel stared into the room, expecting to see three or four people there, rehearsing the play. But there was only one person there – Gladys!

'Golly! It's only you!' said Mirabel, in astonishment. 'I thought there must be lots here. I heard all kinds of different voices. Was it *you*?'

'Yes,' said Gladys. 'Go away. Can't I even do this in peace?'

'What are you doing?' asked Mirabel, going into the room and shutting the door. 'Do tell me. It sounded fine. Do you know it all by heart?'

'Yes, I do,' said Gladys. 'I love acting. I always have. But Miss Quentin never gives me a chance in the drama class. I could act the parts well. I know I could. You see me act Bobby's part in that play we're doing with Miss Quentin!'

And before Mirabel's astonished eyes, the girl began to act the part that had been given to Bobby. But she acted it superbly. She was the part! The little Misery-girl faded, and another character came into the attic, someone with a resonant voice, a strong character, and a fierce face. It was extraordinary.

Mirabel stood and gaped. Her astonishment and admiration were so plain that Gladys was impelled to show her another part in the play – Carlotta's part. Here again she was twice as good as the fiery Carlotta, and her voice, wild and strong, quite different from Gladys's usual meek, milk-and-water voice, rang through the attic.

'Gladys! You're simply marvellous!' said Mirabel.

'You're to come and show the girls. Come on. Come on downstairs at once. I never saw anything like it in my life. *You* to act like that! Who would have thought it? You're such a mouse, and your voice is so quiet – and yet, when you act, you're Somebody, and you quite frighten me. You simply *must* come down and show the girls what you can do.'

'No,' said Gladys, becoming herself again and looking half the size she had seemed two minutes before.

'Oh, Gladys,' said Mirabel, suddenly remembering why she had been looking for the girl. 'Gladys – how's your mother? I do hope you've got good news.'

'Thank you – it's just about the same,' said Gladys. 'Mother can't even write to me, she's so ill. If I could just get a letter from her, it would be something!'

'Does she get *your* letters?' asked Mirabel.

'Of course,' said Gladys. 'I keep telling her how much I miss her, and how lonely and unhappy I am without her.'

'But, Gladys – how silly!' said Mirabel.

'What do you mean?' asked Gladys, half-indignantly. 'Mother wants to know that.'

'I should have thought she would have been much gladder to think you were trying to settle down and be happy,' said Mirabel. 'It must make her very miserable indeed to feel you are so lonely and sad. I should think it would make her worse.'

'It won't,' said Gladys, her eyes filling with tears. 'If she thought I was happy here, and getting other interests, she would think I was forgetting her.'

'I do think you're silly, Gladys,' said Mirabel, wishing she was Hilary or Anna, so that she might know the best way of tackling someone like Gladys. 'Don't you want your mother to be proud of you? She'll think you are an awful coward – no spunk at all – just giving in like this, and weeping and wailing.'

'Oh, you *are* hateful!' cried Gladys. 'As if my mother would ever think things like that of me, ever! Go away. I won't come down with you. And don't you dare to tell anyone what you saw me doing. It's my secret. You'd no right to come spying like that. Go away.'

Mirabel looked at Gladys's angry little face, and wondered what to do or say. She hadn't done any good, that was certain. I suppose I haven't got the character to help people properly, like Hilary or Anna, thought Mirabel, going soberly downstairs. I've got a lot to learn. When I go home at half-term next week, I'll really try and do better.

She went down to the library to get a book. But, as she hunted through the shelves, she kept thinking of Gladys. She couldn't just do nothing. If she, Mirabel, couldn't help Gladys, maybe somebody else could. Hilary could. She was always so sensible. So was Bobby – and the twins, too. She would go and tell them what had happened, and leave it to them to do what they could. Mirabel was beginning to have a very low opinion of herself and her powers.

She left the library and went to find Hilary. She was lucky enough to see her in a music-room with

Bobby, Janet and the twins, practising something for the concert. Good! This was just the chance to tell them what had happened!

11.

A disappointment for the second form

'I say!' said Mirabel, opening the door. 'Can I interrupt a moment?'

'I suppose so,' said Bobby. 'What's up?'

'It's about Gladys,' said Mirabel, and she told them how she had found the girl acting all by herself in the box-room. Then she went on to tell them what she had said to Gladys, and how she had failed to help her – only made her angry.

'Well,' said Hilary, listening intently. 'I think, Mirabel, you gave Gladys some very sound advice. Really I do. Of course Gladys ought to stop moaning to her mother. She must find a little pluck somewhere, or she'll go to pieces. You did right to say that it would help her mother if she knew Gladys was settling down, and trying to do well.'

'Oh – I'm glad you think that,' said Mirabel. 'I'm not so good as you are at knowing what to do for the best for people. By the way – Gladys said she didn't want me to tell everybody.'

'Well, you haven't,' said Hilary. 'You've only told us five – and we understand perfectly. But, Mirabel, as it seems that Gladys has taken *you* into her confidence and nobody else, I think you'd better go on tackling the matter!'

'Yes!' said all the others.

'Oh, *no*,' said Mirabel, horrified. 'I came to ask *you* to help. I'm no good at this sort of thing.'

'Well, it's time you were,' said Hilary, firmly. 'Now come on, Mirabel – we all tried to help you when you needed it – you've got to do the same to Gladys. Be friends with her, and buck her up – and if you can persuade her to show us how she can act, we'll all listen and applaud – and she must be in the concert!'

'She can't be. It's the day after tomorrow, and all the programmes are written out,' objected Isabel. 'We really can't write them all out again.'

'She wouldn't want to be in the concert, anyhow,' said Mirabel. 'All right, Hilary – I'll do what I can. But I really am very bad at this sort of thing.'

It was distasteful to Mirabel to mention the matter to Gladys again. She always felt awkward at anything involving tact or understanding another's troubles. She would very much rather have left it to the others. Still, once she said she would do a thing, she did it.

Gladys was surprised, and not too pleased to find Mirabel always at her elbow the next day. 'Gladys, I didn't mean to make you angry,' Mirabel said, when they were alone for a few minutes. 'I'm clumsy in what I say. I know I am. But I really and truly am sympathetic. I don't expect I can help at all – but I'd like to.'

'Well,' said Gladys, looking at Mirabel's earnest face,

'I *was* angry yesterday. Nobody likes being told they're cowardly. But I thought it all over and in some ways I think you're right. I shouldn't keep writing to my mother and telling her how miserable and lonely I am. I know it would worry her – and that might keep her from getting well.'

'Yes, it might,' said Mirabel, pleased that what she had said had, after all, had some effect on Gladys. 'I say – look here – wouldn't she be *thrilled* if she knew you were in the concert – acting like that – being clapped by everybody! I do wish you'd let the girls see you act.'

Gladys hesitated. She did know, quite certainly, that her mother would be pleased to hear of any success she made – but she was such a mouse, so afraid of everything – it would be a real ordeal to show off in front of the girls. And, of course, she couldn't possibly be in the concert! She would be scared out of her life!

Mirabel saw her hesitate, and she went on pressing her. 'Gladys! Come on – be a sport. Look – if you'll show what you can do, and get the girls to put you into the concert, *I'll* write to your mother myself and tell her how well you did. See? Because I know you'll do well. And then think how pleased she'll be!'

The thought of Mirabel actually writing to her mother for her touched Gladys more than anything else could have done. She stared at Mirabel's earnest face, and tried to blink back the tears that came far too easily.

'You are a good sort,' she said, rather chokily. 'You really are. I thought at first you were such a selfish, cold-hearted sort of girl – but you're not. Be friends with me, Mirabel. You haven't any friend here and neither have I. I'll do anything you ask me, if you'll be friends.'

'Well,' said Mirabel, remembering that it was the half-term the following week, 'I'm leaving soon, you know – at half-term. I never meant to stay longer than that. So it's not much use your being friends with me really – because I'll soon be gone.'

'Oh,' said Gladys, turning away. 'That's just my luck. People I like always go away.'

'Now don't start that sort of thing again,' said Mirabel, half-impatiently. 'All right. I'll be your friend till I go – but mind, you've got to be sensible and do what I say. And the first thing I say is – you've got to show the girls how you can act!'

It was quite pleasant to have someone taking such an interest in her! Gladys felt warmed, and looked gratefully at Mirabel. She was a weak, timid character – Mirabel was strong and decided, even though she was often wrong.

'Yes – I will show the girls if you want me to,' Gladys said.

'Well, after tea, in the common-room this evening, you show them,' said Mirabel. 'I'll clap like anything at the end, so you needn't be afraid. Perhaps the girls will put you in the concert after all, when they see how good you are. Isabel said something about not being able to alter the programmes – but I'm sure it could be done. I could help.'

Mirabel felt rather proud of having got her own way with Gladys. She told Hilary and the others, and they looked forward with interest to seeing what Gladys could do that evening.

It certainly was a surprise to everyone! Gladys looked terribly nervous at first, and her voice shook. But in a minute or two, as she forgot herself, and threw herself heart and soul into the part she was acting, it seemed as if the little Misery-girl was no longer there – but someone quite different, that nobody had seen before!

Gladys acted many parts from different Shakespeare plays – Lady Macbeth – Miranda – Malvolio – Hamlet. She knew them all by heart. Her mother had been very fond of Shakespeare's works, and the two of them had studied them together evening after evening. Gladys's dead father had been a fine actor, and Gladys had inherited the gift.

Gladys stopped at last, changing from Bottom the Weaver to her own timid self. The girls roared with delight at her, and clapped loudly.

'You monkey! Fancy not telling us you could do all that!' said Pat. 'You'll bring the house down at the concert! I say – we simply MUST put her in! Can't we possibly?'

'Please, please don't,' begged Gladys in alarm. 'I couldn't possibly do it in front of most of the school. Well, I might, if I'd more time to rehearse with you. But the concert's tomorrow. I should die if you made me be in it! Please don't!'

'Well – if you feel so strongly about it, I suppose we'll have to leave you out,' said Janet. 'Is there, by any chance, anything else you've kept us in the dark about?

Can you paint marvellous pictures – or work wonderful sums in your head?'

Gladys laughed – the first laugh since she had been at St Clare's. 'There's only one other thing I'm good at,' she said. 'That's lacrosse.'

'Well, you don't seem to have shone there to any great extent,' said Bobby, in surprise.

'I know. I didn't bother,' said Gladys. 'I just didn't care whether I ran fast or not, or scored a goal, or anything. That's why Miss Wilton kept making me goalkeeper, I expect. She thought I was only good for stopping goals, not for anything else. But I *can* play well, if I try. I was in the top team at my day school.'

'Good,' said Mirabel. 'We'll make you shoot dozens of goals and then you can write that to your mother, too.'

'Sorry about your mother, Gladys,' said Hilary. 'Tell us any news you get. We're all interested.'

Gladys went to bed really happy that night. She had a friend. She had been clapped and applauded. She had thrown off her reserve, and let the other girls speak to her of her mother. Things didn't seem so bad now. For the first time she fell asleep without laying and worrying.

In the middle of the night, five of the girls lay and tossed restlessly. Pat and Isabel, Doris, Bobby and Carlotta could not sleep. Their throats hurt them. They coughed and sneezed. It was most annoying – because the concert was to be the next evening!

I shan't be able to speak a word, thought Doris, as she tried to ease her throat. This really is bad luck. I can't possibly be in the concert. Blow! I was so looking forward to it.

In the morning all five went along to Matron, feeling very miserable and sorry for themselves. She took their temperatures.

'You've got the horrid cold that has been running round the school,' she said, briskly. 'You've all got temperatures except Carlotta – and it would take a lot to give *her* one! But she can go to bed just the same. To the sickbay, all of you.'

'But, Matron – it's the concert tonight!' said Bobby, hoarsely. 'We can't possibly go to bed.'

'Put your coats on and your hats and scarves,' said Matron, taking no notice of Bobby at all. 'And go across to the sickbay, immediately. You've all got the same feverish cold, that's plain – caught the chill watching lacrosse in that cold wind the other day, I suppose – so the germ found you easy prey. Bobby, are you deaf? Go and get your coat and hat at once and don't stand arguing.'

It never was any good trying to argue with Matron. She had dealt with girls for many, many years, and bed and warmth and the right medicine in her opinion cured most things very quickly. So, concert or no concert, the five girls were bundled into bed in the sickbay, and there they lay, moaning about the concert and wondering what was going to happen.

It didn't take the rest of the form long to decide what was to happen.

'We can't *possibly* hold the concert without those five!' said Hilary.

'Doris was one of the stars,' said Janet.

'*And* Bobby,' said Hilary. 'And Carlotta too. It would be a very weak affair without those three. We'll have to postpone it. We'll have it just before half-term.'

'We can't,' said Anna. 'The third form are having theirs.'

'Well, the week after then,' said Hilary. 'That will give the invalids time to get over their colds. I hope nobody else feels like sneezing or coughing! If they do, for goodness' sake go to the sickbay, and get it over, so that we can have the concert all right in a fortnight's time!'

'Gladys can be in it this time!' said Kathleen. 'That makes another good performer.'

'Oh, good!' said Anna, looking at Gladys. 'That will be fine. You'll have loads of time to practise and rehearse now, Gladys.'

Gladys couldn't help feeling thrilled. She did love acting – and it would be fun to rehearse with the others. It hadn't been nice to be left out. Now she would be able to join in, and would be clapped just as the others were. There would be a lot to tell her mother when she wrote. She felt a wave of gratitude welling up for Mirabel. It was Mirabel who had made all this possible for her.

She went up to Mirabel and slipped her arm through hers. 'It's a pity about the others, isn't it?' she said. 'But they'll be better in a fortnight – and I *shall* like being in the concert now. I shall clap like anything when your turn comes, Mirabel. I think you'll be the best of us all.'

Mirabel did not smile. She looked rather cold and blank. Gladys wondered what the matter was.

'How many pieces are you going to play?' she asked. 'Do you want me to turn over the pages for you at the piano?'

'I shan't *be* in the concert,' said Mirabel, in a funny, even voice. 'You know I'm going home at half-term – and by the time the concert comes, I'll be gone. I feel disappointed, of course – so don't keep on rubbing it in!'

She took her arm from Gladys's and walked off. How sickening everything was!

12.

Gladys tackles Mirabel

The second form seemed to have dwindled considerably now that five of them were away. Hilary and Alison went down with the cold the next day, so there were many empty desks. The concert was put off for two weeks, and the second-form girls felt very flat and gloomy.

Elsie was the only one who was at all pleased. She had consistently refused to take any interest at all in the concert, and she felt glad that this disappointment had come upon the others. As Anna had predicted, Elsie had adopted a martyr-like attitude, looking left-out and miserable all day long. But no one took the slightest notice of her.

The girl's pride was hurt. She had not liked to ask Anna what she had said to Miss Theobald on the day when both of them had been sent for. But it was clear to her now that not only did the girls no longer regard her as one of their heads, but Miss Jenks also appeared to think that only Anna was head girl. It was most exasperating. Elsie sometimes wished she was like Carlotta and could scold people when she felt like it! She would scold everyone in the form!

The seven girls in the sickbay had a bad time for

the first day or two, and then, when their temperatures went down, they sat up and recovered their spirits. It was fun for so many to be together. They could play games and talk.

'It's half-term next week,' said Isabel. 'Our mother's coming over to take us out.'

'So's mine,' said Doris. 'Carlotta, is your father coming to take you out?'

'Yes – and my grandmother too,' said Carlotta, gloomily. 'I get on with my father all right now – but I just seem to go all common and bad-mannered with my grandmother. I remember all my circus ways, and she just hates them. Oh, dear – I meant to try and get terribly good-mannered this term, and not scold anyone or lose my temper or anything.'

'Mirabel is supposed to be going at half-term, isn't she?' said Bobby, suddenly. 'She won't be in the concert then – and she won't know if she's been chosen to play in any of the lacrosse matches, either – and she'll miss the birthday feast that Carlotta's going to give.'

'She's an idiot,' said Doris. 'She can't think straight. That's what's the matter with her.'

'She wouldn't be a bad sort if she made up her mind to shake down and be sensible,' said Pat. 'I quite like her now. And I must say she's good to that timid little Gladys. When Kathleen came in to see us yesterday, she said that Mirabel really does look after her and walk with her – and Gladys is like a little dog with her – trots after her and does everything she's told.'

'Well, who would have thought that those two would pair up?' said Isabel. 'And there's another astonishing thing too – who would have thought that lazy old Anna would pull herself together as she has done?'

Before long the seven invalids were very much better. They could not possibly have attended the concert, if theirs had been postponed only a week, so it was just as well that it had been put off for two weeks. They would be well enough to go to the third form's concert, which was on the Thursday before half-term.

Mirabel was looking very glum. Half-term seemed to be coming quickly. The postponing of the concert had been a bitter disappointment. It was dull without half the class at lessons.

The only bright spot was her new friendship with Gladys. The girl was showing unsuspected sides of her character to Mirabel. She could make excellent jokes, and had a fine sense of humour. She was fun to walk with because she could keep up a merry chatter. She seemed to have quite thrown off her preoccupation with her own troubles. She really was very fond of Mirabel, and the girl, although embarrassed by any show of affection in the ordinary way, liked to feel Gladys slipping her arm through hers.

'Mirabel! You won't really go home at half-term, will you?' Gladys said that week. 'There are only a few days more. It's lovely being friends with you. Don't go, will you?'

'Of course I'm going,' said Mirabel, impatiently. 'I told

you I'd made up my mind to go at half-term, even before I arrived here! And I'm not going back on that. I never go back on what I've said.'

'No. I know you don't,' said Gladys, with a sigh. 'It's only people like me who change their minds and alter what they meant to do. But I do wish you weren't going, Mirabel.'

Gladys said the same thing to Hilary that day, when she went to see her in the sickbay. 'I do so wish Mirabel wasn't going,' she said. 'I feel a different person since she was nice to me, and all of you clapped me that time I acted for you.'

'What's she got to go for?' said Hilary. 'She has settled down all right. She's happy. She's one of us now, and she enjoys life here. Whatever does she want to go home at half-term for, now she's all right?'

'Well, you see,' said Gladys, earnestly, 'she can't go back on what she said. She *said* she was going home at half-term – she made up her mind about that – so she can't *possibly* change her mind, can she? She's such a strong character, you see.'

'Well, it's strong characters who ought to be able to change their minds at times,' said Hilary. '*I* call it weak to stick to something when you know it's silly. And it is silly for Mirabel to go back home now. We want her for the concert. She knows that. She's just being weak, not strong!'

Gladys was astonished to hear this. It seemed to make things quite different. Weak little Gladys had thought that strong characters must be able to make right decisions and carry them out – but now she saw that a strong character could do something wrong or stupid because it was too proud to unmake a decision! It was something quite new to her. She stared at Hilary.

'I wish you'd say that to Mirabel,' she said.

'Say it yourself,' said Hilary. 'You're her friend, aren't you? Well, *you* tell her!'

'She wouldn't listen to *me*,' said Gladys.

'What you mean is – you're afraid to tackle her!' said Hilary, with a laugh. 'Go on, Mouse – take the bull by the horns – and if you really do care for Mirabel and want her for your friend, don't be afraid of telling her what you think. Get a little spunk!'

Poor Gladys! Everyone always seemed to be telling her to get a little 'spunk'. It was something she was sure she would never possess. She had been such a mother's girl that now it was difficult for her to stand on her own feet.

All the same – it's no good having a friend unless you'll do something for them, thought Gladys, trying to screw up her courage. I shall lose Mirabel if I don't tackle her – and if I lose her because she's angry with me for tackling her, well, I shan't be any worse off. So I'll do it.

It wasn't easy. It never is easy for a timid person to tackle a strong one, especially if it is to point out that the strong one is wrong. Gladys went to Mirabel and slipped her arm through hers.

'Mirabel,' she said, 'I've been thinking over what you said about going home – and not changing your mind and all that – and I really do think you're wrong.'

'That's my own business,' said Mirabel, rather roughly.

'No, it isn't. It's mine too,' said Gladys, hoping her voice would not begin to tremble. 'You're my friend, and I don't want you to go.'

'I've told you I can't change my mind. I never do,' said Mirabel. 'Don't bother me.'

'If you were really as strong a character as you make out, you *would* change your mind,' said Gladys, boldly. 'You know you could stay here happily now – but you're too proud to own you've been silly – and you call it being strong enough not to change your mind!'

'Gladys! How *dare* you talk to me like this?' cried Mirabel, astonished and angry. 'Anybody would think you are Miss Theobald – picking me to pieces – telling me I'm no good – not worthwhile!'

'I'm not telling you that,' said Gladys, getting distressed. 'I'm only saying – don't let your pride stand in the way of your happiness. That's all.'

Mirabel wrenched her arm out of Gladys's and walked off, red in the face. How dare Gladys say things like that to her? She put on her hat and coat and went out into the school grounds, fuming.

Gladys stared after her, miserable. I knew it wouldn't be any good, she thought. Of course Mirabel wouldn't let me say things like that. Now she won't even be friends with me for the last two or three days before she goes!

Mirabel walked round the grounds, hot and angry. But, as her anger died, her mind began to work more calmly. There was a great deal in what Gladys had said. 'Though how that timid little thing ever thought that all out beats me!' said Mirabel to herself. 'There must be more in her than I thought. And the way she stood up to me too! She *has* come on. She must like me a lot to make up her mind to go for me like that, in order to try and make me change my mind, so that she can still have me for a friend.'

The wind cooled her hot cheeks. She sat on the wall and looked down over the valley. It was very pleasant there. It would be marvellous in the summer. St Clare's was fun – there was no doubt about that.

'Now, let's think things out calmly,' said Mirabel to herself. 'I was angry because my family sent me away because I didn't fit in at home – and I vowed to get back as soon as I could just to show them they couldn't send me away! Now I like being here – and I see that I *am* better away from home, and shall go back really thrilled to see everyone. I dare say I'll learn lots of things here I ought to have learnt before – thinking of other people, not always having my own way and things like that. Well, then – what is stopping me from staying here?'

She gazed down on the valley, and did not like to think out the answer. But she had to.

'All that is stopping me is, as Gladys pointed out, my pride. I'm too proud to tell Daddy that I'll stay. I was so angry at being sent away that I wanted to pay them out by coming back as soon as possible and being beastly. And I think I'm a strong character! Golly, all this makes me sound as hateful as catty Elsie!'

She stayed for a few minutes longer and then she

sprang down from the wall. She went into the school building and took off her outdoor things. She went straight to Miss Theobald's room and knocked at the door.

'Come in!' said Miss Theobald. She was talking to Miss Jenks and Mam'zelle. Mirabel was a little taken aback when she saw all three teachers there – but what she had come to say had to be said, no matter how many people were in the room.

'Miss Theobald,' she said, rather loudly. 'May I stay on, please, and not go home at the half-term? Would you let me? I like being here, and I'm sorry I was so silly at first.'

Miss Theobald looked at the girl, and smiled her nicest smile, warm and friendly.

'Yes – we shall be very glad to have you,' she said. 'Isn't that so, Miss Jenks – Mam'zelle?'

'It is,' said Miss Jenks and nodded kindly at Mirabel.

'Ha!' said Mam'zelle. '*C'est bien, ça*! I too am pleased.'

'I will telephone your parents,' said Miss Theobald. 'I am glad, Mirabel, that you have something "worth-while" in you – no, I don't mean your music! Something better than that. Well done!'

Praise like this was very sweet. Mirabel walked out of the room, warm and happy. She knew she had a great deal to learn – things would go wrong, and she would make mistakes – but nothing could take that moment from her.

She went to find Gladys. She found her curled up in a corner of the common-room, looking rather small and woe-begone. She went over to her and gave her an unexpected hug.

'Well, old thing! I'm staying on! I've just been to tell Miss Theobald. And all because you ticked me off like that, and set me thinking!'

Half in tears Gladys returned the hug. It was marvellous. She, a weak person, had summoned up enough strength to tackle a strong one – and had actually got what she wanted. It was too good to be true.

'You'll be in the concert!' she said. 'And you'll come to Carlotta's feast. What fun we'll have! Oh, Mirabel I'm so proud of you!'

'I'm rather proud of you too,' said Mirabel, awkwardly. 'You gave me a surprise, telling me home-truths like that. You're a good sort of friend to have.'

'What a lot I shall have to write and tell my mother!' said Gladys. 'And I say – won't everyone be pleased you've changed your mind and are staying on!'

The girls *were* pleased. They had begun to like Mirabel now, and they admired her for being able to alter her mind and own that she had been wrong. Soon they would forget Mirabel's extraordinary behaviour the first few weeks of the term.

Only one girl was displeased. That was Elsie. Why should such a fuss be made of that ridiculous Mirabel, who had behaved so badly, and who had been partly the cause of Elsie's disgrace? Elsie brooded over this and cast many spiteful glances at Mirabel, wondering what she could do to pay her out for being popular, when she,

Elsie, was never taken any notice of at all!

But Mirabel was thick-skinned. She neither saw nor felt Elsie's hostility, but looked forward happily to the remainder of the term at St Clare's.

13.

Half-term holiday

Half-term came and went. It was a pleasant break for everyone. Most parents came to take out the girls for some kind of treat, and those that lived near enough went home for a day or two. Alison's parents were away so she went out with the twins and their mother.

'Well, how are you all getting on this term?' asked Mrs O'Sullivan. 'Working hard, I hope?'

But nobody said anything about work. The twins poured out their news about the concert, and about lacrosse, and how Carlotta was going to have a feast on her birthday. Alison talked of nothing but her beloved Miss Quentin.

'She's awfully clever,' said Alison. 'It's lovely learning drama under her. She says I have the making of a good little actress.'

'Oh, do shut up talking about Miss Quentin,' groaned Pat. 'Mummy, last term Alison was all over Sadie Greene, that American girl – who, by the way, has never even *written* to you, Alison! And this term it's Miss Quentin! Isn't there any medicine or pill we can give Alison to stop her raving about people?'

Alison had been very hurt that her 'best' friend, Sadie,

had not taken the trouble to write to her at all. She thought it was mean of Pat to remind her of it.

'Well, Miss Quentin wouldn't be like that,' she said. 'I've made her promise to write to me every week in the holidays. She's loyal, I know. I think she's marvellous.'

'She's beautiful, she's wonderful, she's marvellous, she's magnificent,' said Isabel, with a grin. 'But the thing is – what does she think of *you*, Alison? Not much, I bet! You're always going about thinking somebody is wonderful – you never seem to imagine they might be bored with you.'

The idea of her beloved Miss Quentin being bored with her made Alison hot and angry. She glared at the twins. Mrs O'Sullivan saw the look.

'Now, now,' she said, 'don't let's waste our precious time in quarrelling, please. I've no doubt Miss Quentin is a very admirable person and I'm sure Alison works hard in *her* class, at least, if she doesn't in anyone else's.'

Mirabel's father and mother came over to see her at half-term, and took her out to lunch, a theatre, and tea afterwards. Mirabel was intensely excited at the thought of seeing them. She forgot all about the temper in which she had been when she had parted from them. She forgot the horrid things she had said, and the threats she had made. She stood at the front door, eagerly waiting for them.

When they arrived, they were startled by someone who hurled herself at them, flung her arms round them, and exclaimed in a choky voice, 'Mummy! Daddy! It's lovely to see you again!'

Her mother and father looked at the excited girl, whose eyes shone with welcome. This was a different Mirabel altogether! They hugged the girl, and looked with interest at the school. Neither of them had seen it. It had been a very sudden decision on Mirabel's father's part to send Mirabel away, and he had chosen a school recommended to him very highly by a friend. It had all been done in such a hurry that the parents had not had time to see the school itself.

'What a lovely place!' said Mrs Unwin. 'Is there time to look round?'

'Mummy, you simply *must* see everything,' cried Mirabel, and she dragged her parents all over the school, from top to bottom, even showing them the bathroom where she had her nightly bath. There was great pride in the girl's voice. Her parents exchanged happy glances with each other. It was quite plain to them that Mirabel was extremely proud of St Clare's already, and felt it to be her own splendid school.

'Daddy, I'm so pleased you chose St Clare's,' said Mirabel, when they came back to the front door at last. 'It's marvellous. It really is.' She looked at her parents and hesitated a little. She had something to say that was difficult. Mirabel hated saying she was sorry about anything.

'You know – I really am sorry I was so awful at home,' said the girl, rushing her words out. 'I can see you all better now, because I'm far away from you – and I think I was awful to everyone.'

'We've forgotten it all,' said her father. 'We shall never

remember it again. All that matters to us is that you are happy – and will be happy when you come home again. We felt so proud when Miss Theobald let us know that you wanted to stay on. She said one or two nice things about you.'

'Did she really?' asked Mirabel, pleased. 'I hated her at first – she said some awful things to me – but now I think she's fine. Oh, Mummy – I do wish you'd brought Joan and Harry with you! I did want to see them.'

'They wanted to see you too,' said her mother. 'But it was too far to bring them. Now – what about going? We shall never get any lunch if we don't start soon.'

'Mummy – would you do something for me?' asked Mirabel, suddenly. 'I've got a friend here – and her mother's ill in hospital, so there's no one to take her out for a half-term treat. Could she possibly come with us, do you think?'

'Of course,' said Mrs Unwin, surprised and pleased to think that her difficult daughter had actually made a friend. She wondered what the friend would be like. She had never liked Mirabel's chosen friends before – they had always been noisy, impolite and out-of-hand – a little like Mirabel herself.

'I'll go and get her,' said Mirabel. She ran off to find Gladys. She was getting ready for the school lunch, feeling a little lonely, for nearly all the other girls had left for the half-term holiday.

Mirabel rushed at her. 'Gladys! You're to come with me! Go and ask Miss Jenks if you can come, quickly!

Mummy and Daddy say you can come.'

A shock of joy ran through Gladys. She felt nervous of meeting Mirabel's parents – but to think that Mirabel wanted her to come was marvellous. Her depression fell away from her at once, and she stared in joy at her friend. She had had few treats in her life, and it did seem to her that going out to lunch and a theatre was too good to be true.

'Gladys, don't stand staring there!' cried Mirabel, impatiently. 'Hurry up. Go and find Miss Jenks. I'll get your outdoor things.'

In three minutes Gladys was at the front door with Mirabel, red with shyness, hardly able to say a word. Mr and Mrs Unwin took a look at the nervous girl, and were astonished. So this was Mirabel's friend – well, what a change from the tiresome girls she had chosen before! They took a liking to Gladys immediately, and Mrs Unwin smiled a motherly smile at her.

In some ways Mrs Unwin resembled Gladys's own mother. Both were the gentle, kindly type, and Gladys warmed to Mrs Unwin at once. In no time at all she was telling Mrs Unwin all about her own mother, revelling in the understanding and kindness of Mirabel's mother.

'I say! I do think you've got a nice mother!' she whispered to Mirabel, when they went to wash their hands at the hotel, before lunch. 'Next to mine, she's the nicest I've ever met. And isn't your father jolly? I feel a bit afraid of him but I do like him. Aren't you lucky?'

Mirabel was pleased. She was seeing her mother and

father with different eyes, now that she had been away from them for some weeks. It was pleasant to hear someone liking them so much. She squeezed her friend's arm.

'It's fun having you,' she said. 'I'm glad my people like you.'

A real surprise was in store for Gladys. When Mrs Unwin asked her what hospital her mother was in, she heard Gladys's answer with astonishment.

'Why – that's quite near where my sister lives. I often go over to see my sister – and perhaps I could go to the hospital and find out how your mother is. I might even see her, if she is allowed visitors.'

Gladys stared at Mrs Unwin, red with delight. It would bring her mother much closer somehow, if she knew someone was going to the very hospital where her mother was. And just suppose she was allowed to see her! Mrs Unwin could write and tell her about it.

'Oh, thank you,' said the girl. 'If you only could! It would be marvellous!'

The half-term went all too quickly. All the girls enjoyed it. It was a very pleasant break indeed, and they went back to school full of chatter about what they had done.

'Hallo!' said the twins, meeting Carlotta when they arrived back. 'How did *you* get on? Was your grandmother very stand-offish?'

'No – she seemed quite pleased with me,' said Carlotta, grinning. 'I didn't walk on my hands or do anything she disapproves of – and I made my hair so tidy you wouldn't know me. I was most frightfully polite to her, and my father was awfully pleased with me. He gave me a five-pound note for my birthday!'

'Gracious!' said Pat. 'What luck!'

'And my grandmother told me I could order anything I liked for my birthday party, at the shop in the town,' said Carlotta, her eyes lighting up with delighted expectancy. 'I say – won't we order lots of things! She gave me some things out of her store cupboard too. I've got a big box in the cupboard in our dormitory. I don't know what's in it yet, but I bet my grandmother has given me plenty.'

'How gorgeous!' said the twins. 'You sound as if you've got enough to feed the whole school.'

'No – just our form,' said Carlotta. 'And I'm not sure yet if we'll have it properly, in the afternoon at tea-time – or whether we'll make it really exciting, and go in for a midnight feast again. I think we ought to have a midnight feast every term, you know! School doesn't seem really complete without that!'

It looked as if the latter half of the term was going to be exciting. There was the concert to look forward to that week – several lacrosse matches – and now Carlotta's feast! All the girls glowed. What fun they had!

Bobby had a secret, and so had Janet. They had gone out together with Bobby's parents, and with Janet's brother, whose half-term holiday was the same weekend. He was as much of a monkey as Janet, always up to tricks. He had given Janet and Bobby an old trick to play on Mam'zelle. It was a curious-looking thing, consisting of a long stretch of narrow rubber tubing, with a little bladder on one end, and an india-rubber bulb on the other, which, when pressed, sent air down the tube into the little bladder, which at once expanded and became big.

'But what's it for?' asked the twins, in curiosity.

'You put the bladder under someone's plate at mealtime,' giggled Bobby, 'and run the tubing under the table-cloth. Then, when you press the bulb, the bladder fills and up tips the plate. Imagine Mam'zelle's astonishment when her plate starts dancing about! We shall all be in fits of laughter!'

This was really something to look forward to as well. Mam'zelle was a marvellous person to play tricks on. She was always taken in, and had caused more enjoyment than all the mistresses in the school put together.

'Oh, Bobby! Let's do it soon,' begged Doris. 'Do let's. We haven't played any tricks this term, at all.'

'Well, after all, we *are* the second form,' said Janet, teasingly.

'Bobby will be playing tricks when she's head girl!' said Isabel. 'I'm surprised she has gone as far as half-term without thinking of any.'

'Oh, I've *thought* of plenty,' said Bobby. 'But Miss Jenks isn't an easy person to play about with. She doesn't keep her temper like Miss Roberts did. She flares up suddenly, and I don't particularly want to be sent to Miss Theobald now I'm in the second form. It may have escaped your notice that I'm working hard this term! Don't forget I'm not Don't-Care Bobby as I was last term. I'm using my brains for other things besides tricks and jokes.'

'Let's have a rehearsal for the concert,' said Pat. 'We've only got a few days now. Bring your violin, Mirabel – and Gladys, make up your mind what you're going to act, out of all the hundreds of parts you seem able to play. Come on, everybody – let's enjoy ourselves!'

14.

A marvellous show

The days flew by, and the night of the concert came. Miss Jenks had to be lenient with the second form, because she could see that they really did mean their show to be a great success. Mam'zelle was the only teacher who would not make allowances, so the class groaned and worked for her as best they could.

'It is bad to have concerts in the middle of the term,' Mam'zelle grumbled to Miss Jenks. 'These girls, they think of anything but their work. Now, when I was a schoolgirl . . .'

'You worked all day, and you worked all night, you had no games, you prepared no concerts . . .' chanted Miss Jenks, with her wide smile. The teachers had heard a thousand times of Mam'zelle's hard-worked youth.

'There are other things as important as lessons,' said Miss Roberts. 'We are not out to cram facts and knowledge into the girls' heads all day long, but to help them to form strong and kindly characters too. This concert now, that you grumble at – it is making the second form work together in a wonderful way, it is bringing out all kinds of unexpected talent – look at Mirabel and Gladys, for instance – and it will help a great cause. It makes the girls resourceful and ingenious too – you should see the costume Doris has made for herself as Matron and as Cook.'

Mam'zelle did not know that Doris was going to imitate her as well. The other mistresses guessed it and they were looking forward to it. They all liked Mam'zelle, and admired her sense of humour. She could take a joke against herself very well.

'The third-form concert was quite good,' said Miss Lewis, the history teacher. 'But I think the second form will be more entertaining. The third form were rather high-brow, and didn't provide a single laugh for anyone. I fancy we shall find plenty to laugh at this Saturday!'

The second form were getting very excited. Only Elsie was apart from all the thrills and enjoyment. The girl still obstinately refused to take part in anything, and would not even be prompter.

'But Elsie, everyone will think it very funny that you are the only second former out of things,' said Pat, impatiently. 'We keep on offering you things to do, and you keep turning them down. I think it's very decent of us to be so patient with you.'

'I'll take part on one condition,' said Elsie, sullenly.

'What?' asked Bobby, coming up.

'That you let me be head girl again with Anna,' said Elsie. 'You've punished me for weeks now, by taking away my authority as head girl. Isn't it about time you let me have it back again?'

'Well – we'll ask the rest of the form,' said Pat. So that

night in the common-room, before a rehearsal was held, Anna put the question to the meeting.

'Elsie says she will take part in the concert if we let her be joint head girl again. What does everyone think about it?'

'Why should she bargain with us?' cried Carlotta. 'It is we who should bargain with her! We should say, "You can be head girl again if you show that you are worthy of it!"'

'Quite right,' called Doris.

'Look how she has behaved all these weeks,' said Janet. 'Has she tried to give us a better opinion of her? Has she shown us she could be trusted to lead us again? No – all she has done is to look spiteful, be catty when she has a chance, pose as a martyr and hope she'll get our sympathy. Well, she hasn't. We've just taken no notice at all, and she hasn't liked it.'

'I don't see why we should bother with her,' said Isabel. 'I really don't.'

'Will you show in the usual way whether you would like her again or not?' asked Anna. 'Hands up those who will give Elsie another chance as head girl.'

Not a single hand went up. Anna grinned. 'Well,' she said, 'that's that. Elsie will have to put up with it. She hasn't come at all well out of this, I must say. I would have been willing to work with her again, if you'd said so – but I'm glad I haven't got to.'

Elsie was not there, and nobody bothered to fetch her to tell her what had happened. They began their rehearsal and were soon busy criticizing and applauding as one after another performed. Gladys was by now used to an audience and she acted as naturally as everyone else. She and Doris were both natural actresses, though in a different way. Doris could imitate anyone she had seen, but not act a part – and Gladys, quite unable to imitate anyone around her, was excellent at interpreting any part in a play. The two admired each other and Gladys was fast making another friend.

'Well – I really think we've got everything all right now,' said Bobby at last. 'It *will* be fun! Doris, you'll bring the house down with your imitation of Mam'zelle. I only hope Mam'zelle won't mind. But I don't think she will.'

The door opened and Elsie came in. 'You held the rehearsal without me,' she said. 'What do you want me to do at the concert?'

'Well, Elsie – you said you would only be in it if we recognized you as head girl again,' said Anna, rather awkwardly. 'We put the question to the second form, and I'm afraid they decided not to give you the chance. So we didn't think you'd want to help with the concert, in that case.'

'Couldn't you have told me you wouldn't have me as head girl, and still let me be in the concert?' said Elsie.

The others stared at her. 'Don't be silly,' said Bobby, at last. 'That's not the point. The point is, you always refused, and then wanted to make a bargain with us – and we wouldn't make it. I suppose you're beginning to feel very awkward about being left out of the concert in front of the whole school, so you're climbing down a bit, and want to help even if we won't accept you as head girl again. Well – help if you like – but don't expect us to fall on your neck and give you a warm welcome, because we shan't.'

This was a long speech and Elsie listened to it in growing anger. All that Bobby said was true. Elsie was now beginning to feel horrified at being left out. Everyone in the school would notice it. They would whisper about her. They would nudge one another as she passed. Elsie couldn't bear it. But neither had she the strength to overrule her rage and accept Bobby's luke-warm offer to let her help. She made a curious explosive noise of rage and walked out of the room.

Doris immediately imitated the explosive noise, and the whole form burst into laughter. Elsie heard the squeals, and stopped. She felt inclined to go back and hit out at everyone. Then a wave of self-pity overcame her and she burst into tears.

The concert was an enormous success. Half the school was there and all the mistresses. The curtain was drawn at exactly eight o'clock, and everything went like clockwork. The third form had been late in starting, and there had been long intervals between the various turns, which had bored the audience. But the second form were most efficient.

Turn after turn was put on and loudly applauded. Mirabel's playing was encored twice. The girl was so thrilled at her success that she could hardly speak for joy. Her piano-playing was really excellent, and as for her violin solo, it amazed everyone, even the four music teachers, who were by now used to gifted children springing up in their classes at times.

Carlotta's acrobatics were hailed with delight by the whole school. Everyone knew that Carlotta had once been a circus girl, and they clapped till their hands smarted when she did some of her graceful circus-tricks. The first formers gaped in admiration and secretly determined to try out all the acrobatics themselves.

Gladys got an encore too. When the nervous, white-faced girl stepped on to the stage, the audience waited, rather critical, expecting to be bored. But before their eyes the girl changed into the characters she acted, and held the whole school spell-bound. She was really gifted, there was no doubt about it.

The most surprised person in the whole of the audience was Miss Quentin. She took the drama class herself, and prided herself on knowing the capacities of everyone in the second form. Privately she had thought that Doris and Carlotta were the only ones worth teaching – and now here was the quiet little mouse, Gladys, bringing down the house with her polished and beautiful interpretations of many of the most difficult parts in Shakespeare's plays!

Miss Theobald leant across to Miss Quentin. 'I must congratulate you on one of your pupil's performances!' she said, in her quiet voice. 'I can see that you must have helped the child a great deal. She could never have done all this by herself. It is amazing.'

Miss Quentin was not honest enough to say that she was as astonished as Miss Theobald. She loved praise as much as Alison did, and she nodded her head, pretending that she had taught Gladys all that she knew. Secretly she made up her mind to cultivate Gladys Hillman and give her the most important part in the play the second form were doing with her. She knew Alison had hoped for it – but she couldn't help that. Gladys must certainly have it. Then Miss Quentin could take all the credit herself for the excellent performance she was sure Gladys would give!

The concert went on. The twins were applauded and so was Janet. The first formers loved Bobby's conjuring tricks, and her ceaseless, ridiculous patter, and gave her an encore! But it was Doris who was the real star of the evening!

When she stepped on to the stage, dressed up as the jolly, fat old cook, there was a roar of delighted laughter. Doris pretended to make a pudding, keeping up a monologue in the cook's Irish accent, bringing in all the phrases that the girls knew so well. They squealed with laughter.

Then she altered her cook's uniform deftly – and lo and behold, there was Matron! Bobby ran on with some big bottles of medicine and a thermometer, and Doris proceeded to imitate Matron interviewing various girls sent to her for treatment or inspection.

Matron was in the audience, shaking with laughter. The girls roared with delight, missing many of Doris's jokes because they could not stop laughing. She was extremely clever and extremely funny.

'She should be on the stage,' said Matron, wiping her streaming eyes. 'Oh, am I really as funny as that? It's time I retired if I'm such a joke. This girl will be the death of me! Wait till she comes for medicine! I'll get my own back then!'

Doris went off the stage, grinning. The audience looked at the next item she was to do – another impersonation. Who?

They knew as soon as she appeared again. She had made herself plump with padding. She had scraped back her hair into a bun, put on enormous flat-heeled shoes, secretly borrowed from Mam'zelle's room, and wore glasses crookedly on her nose.

'Mam'zelle!' shrieked the girls, in delight. 'Marvellous!'

Doris approached the edge of the stage and addressed the girls in Mam'zelle's identical voice, taking off her English accent to perfection. The audience roared with laughter as Doris scolded them for misbehaviour.

'*C'est abominable*!' she finished. Then she turned away, re-arranged some things on a desk behind, and proceeded to take a lesson in the way that Mam'zelle took it, with hands wagging towards the ceiling, and her glasses slipping down over her nose.

Everyone looked at Mam'zelle herself to see how she was taking it. Mam'zelle was lying back in her chair, helpless with laughter, tears pouring down her cheeks. The girls felt a warm wave of liking for her – how nice she was to laugh at someone taking off her little foibles and mannerisms! The girls had to laugh at Mam'zelle's squeals as much as at Doris's acting.

It was a marvellous show and a great success. Everyone had loved it, and crowded round at the end to clap the performers on the back, and congratulate them. It was pleasant for both Mirabel and Gladys to feel these pats and hear the generous words of praise.

'Mother will hardly believe it all,' said Gladys to herself, her face shining with delight. 'I must tell her every single thing. And wasn't Mirabel's playing good? I clapped till my hands were sore.'

'We've made ten-pounds-fifty by selling tickets, programmes and getting in extra subscriptions,' announced Anna. 'Isn't that good? I bet no form will do as well as that.'

The second form enjoyed coffee and biscuits for a treat after the show, generously provided by Matron and Mam'zelle. 'Though why we should do this for a form whose chief success is putting up Mam'zelle and myself to be laughed at, I really don't know!' said Matron, beaming round. 'By the way – where's Elsie? She wasn't in the concert, and I don't see her now.'

The second form were so elated by their success that they wanted Elsie to join in the coffee and biscuits. But she was nowhere to be found.

She was in bed, alone – but not asleep; the only girl who had not shared in or applauded her form's success! Poor Elsie – her thoughts were very bitter that night, as she heard the echoes of laughter from the concert-room!

15.

Elsie is foolish

The next big event was Carlotta's birthday. She was fifteen, and planned a really good feast. She had opened the box of goodies given to her by her grandmother, and it had proved to be even better than the second form had hoped.

'Sardines!' said Bobby, taking out three or four of the oblong tins. 'And what's this – an *enormous* tin of pine-apple chunks. It's ages since I've tasted pineapple. And what a fine big tin!'

'Bars of chocolate-cream!' said Janet. 'Enough to feed the whole school, I should think!'

'Tins of prawns!' cried Hilary. 'I say – I do like prawns. Golly – prawns and pineapple – what a heavenly mixture that would be!'

'Here's a gingerbread cake,' said Alison. 'Isn't it big? Carlotta, I must say you own a first-class grandmother! Mine's good for a cake and a bottle of boiled sweets, but that's about all. Yours is super!'

'Well, she's only just begun to be super,' said Carlotta, with a grin. 'When she didn't approve of me, she handed me out ten pence and a new comb. See what happens when she *does* approve of me!'

'Let's teach Carlotta some really marvellous manners,' said Janet, 'so that she will make a wonderful impression on her grandmother in the Christmas hols. She'll come back with half a grocer's shop then, I should think!'

'Oh, I say – what's this?' said Bobby, pulling out what looked like a large medicine bottle full of a yellow liquid. She read the label on it, then laughed.

'Do listen. "One table-spoonful of this to be taken by each girl after the birthday feast!" Oh, Carlotta, your grandmother is a scream.'

'Did you say you could go down to the shop in the town and order anything else you liked for your birthday?' asked Hilary, looking at the fine selection of things spread out on the floor. 'I shouldn't think you want anything else, do you?'

'I'd like a good big birthday cake with fifteen candles on,' said Carlotta. 'I know candles are childish when you're fifteen, but I can't help it. I think a cake looks so pretty when they are all lit. And, if we have the party at night, we can let the cake-candles light us!'

'Are we *really* going to have the feast at night?' asked Mirabel, thrilled. 'I've often read of midnight feasts in school-stories, but I didn't really think they happened.'

'Of course they happen!' said Bobby. 'You wait and see what we'll do.'

'I must order heaps and heaps of ginger beer,' said Carlotta. 'I always feel I can drink a lot at night. And I'll get lemonade too. And buns we can butter and put jam on. I like those. It's a pity we can't cook kippers too. I do like kippers.'

Everyone laughed. Carlotta loved kippers and pineapple, two things she had had a good deal of in her circus days. She had often described to the girls how lovely frying kippers smelt, being cooked on a stove in the open-air, in the dark of the night after a show.

'No, Carlotta – we must draw the line at kippers,' said Anna. 'The smell would wake the whole school. You know how we smell kippers frying even when Cook has the kitchen and the scullery door shut.'

Elsie heard all the talk about Carlotta's birthday. She knew there was to be a feast or a party of some sort. She saw the amount of goodies taken out of Carlotta's box, and she wondered if she was going to be asked or not.

The others debated the point when Elsie was not in the room.

'Are we going to ask Catty Elsie, or not?' said Pat.

'Not,' said almost everyone.

'Oh, yes, let's,' said easy-going Anna. 'She likes good things as much as anyone.'

'I dare say – but we don't want her spiteful face glowering at us all the time,' said Isabel.

At this moment Elsie came to the door of the common-room. She stood outside, listening. She was always wondering if the others were discussing her. This time they were!

'Well, as it's my birthday I can choose my own guests,' said Carlotta. 'It's for me to say whether I'll ask Catty Elsie or not.'

'Yes – all right – *you* say, Carlotta!' cried half a dozen voices at once.

'Well – I say this – I'll ask her, but at the same time I'll tell her she's got to drop this awful pose of being a miserable martyr and act sensibly,' said Carlotta. 'She goes about looking like a wet dishcloth. I'm sure everyone in the school must laugh at her. She's a disgrace to our form. Anyway, I'll ask her to the feast, and see if she's properly grateful, and will behave herself.'

'Yes, do that,' said Anna, who was as tired as anyone else of seeing Elsie walking about looking as if she was going to weep at any moment. 'Maybe she learnt her lesson when she was left out of the concert. Perhaps she will jump at the chance of being friends again.'

'Poor Catty Elsie,' said Doris, and she began to imitate Elsie's rather high, silly voice, tearful and excited. Everyone roared with laughter.

They had no idea at all that Elsie was outside the door, listening. They would have been very scornful of her if they had known that, for eavesdropping was not looked on favourably by any member of the second form. They had very strict ideas of honour and liked to keep to them.

Elsie forgot that those who listen behind doors seldom hear any good of themselves. She stood there, trembling with anger and self-pity, hating all the girls who tossed her name about so scornfully, and laughed at her so unkindly.

A movement towards the door made her hurry away quickly. She turned a corner and went into a cloak-room, pretending to fetch a pair of shoes. The second formers, pouring out of their common-room to go to a Nature meeting, did not guess that she had overheard nearly all they had said.

There was no time then to ask Elsie to the party, for the girls were already late for the meeting. Elsie joined them, and sat sulkily silent whilst the second and third formers decided various matters concerning the Nature Club. She didn't hear a word that was said. She remembered instead what she had just overheard, and looked with rage at Carlotta and the others. How she wished she could punish them in some way!

That night Carlotta went up to where Elsie was sewing in the common-room. 'Elsie! I expect you know I'm having a birthday soon, don't you?'

'I should think the whole school knows,' said Elsie, spitefully.

'Well – I'm having a party or a feast of some kind,' said Carlotta. 'And everyone is coming. The thing is – I'd like you to come too – but only if you'll pull yourself together and act sensibly. We're all tired of the way you're behaving. Come on, Elsie, now – can't you have a bit of common sense and be one of us? We don't like you a bit as you are now, but we are quite willing to change our ideas of you, if you'll be sensible.'

'Very kind of you, *very* kind of you indeed,' said Elsie, in a trembling, sarcastic voice. 'The great Carlotta is *most* bountiful and condescending! And I know I should be very grateful and bow before her, thanking her for her great kindness!'

'Don't be an idiot,' said Carlotta, uncomfortably.

'I'm not,' said Elsie, changing her tone of voice and almost snarling at the surprised Carlotta. 'I'm just saying – "No, thanks! *I'm* not coming to your beastly feast." Ho – be a good little girl and you can come to the party! That's what you've said to me – me, who ought to be your head girl! I would *hate* to come! And what is more, if you're going to hold it at night, Anna had better look out. You're second formers now, not first formers, and if you're caught, Anna will soon find *she* isn't head girl any more, either.'

'You're impossible, Elsie,' said Carlotta, in disgust at Elsie's tone of voice. 'Well, if you don't want to come, don't. I for one am pleased.'

'So are we all!' cried Pat, Isabel and a few others, who had listened in indignation to Elsie's stinging speech. 'Keep away, Elsie. The party will be better without you!'

Elsie went on with her sewing, pursing up her thin lips scornfully. She badly wanted to go to the party, for she loved good things as much as anyone else. But her spitefulness and obstinacy made it impossible for her to climb down and accept. She sat sewing, thinking that if she could possibly prevent the party from being held, she would.

If I could find out when and where Carlotta is going to hold it, I could drop a hint to Miss Jenks, she thought. Miss Jenks doesn't look kindly on things like that. I've only got to say a word – or write an anonymous note – and the feast would be stopped before it had begun. That would be fine!

But the others did not mean to let Elsie know when the feast was to be held! They felt certain she would try to spoil it in some way. They had decided to hold it on the night of Carlotta's birthday, in the common-room itself. If they drew the blinds, and shut the door, they were reasonably safe. The common-room was a good way away from any mistresses' room, and yet fairly near their own dormitories.

They talked about it with excitement whenever Elsie was not in the room. As soon as she appeared they dropped the subject at once. Not one girl, not even silly little Alison, mentioned the subject when Elsie was there, much as they sometimes wanted to.

Carlotta had been down to the shop in the town and ordered what she wanted. The cake was to be a magnificent affair, with fifteen coloured candles. It was to have pink icing, with roses round the edge, and silver balls and sugared violets for decoration. The candles were to be fixed in roses made of sugar. Everyone was very excited about it.

'The ginger beer has come,' announced Carlotta, gleefully. 'I got the boy who brought it to put it at the back of the bicycle shed. I was afraid Miss Jenks would have a fit if she saw all those bottles of ginger beer and lemonade arriving for me. We'll each have to bring in a bottle or two when it's safe.'

'It will be fun,' said Mirabel. She looked at Gladys, who was beaming too. 'I'm glad I stayed on. Fancy missing Carlotta's feast! I would have been an idiot.'

'You would,' said Gladys. The mouse-like girl was no longer the Misery-girl. She laughed and smiled with the rest, and followed Mirabel about like a shadow. The bigger girl was very fond of her, and the two were quite inseparable. St Clare's had already done a good deal for both of them!

'We'd better not cook anything at all,' said Pat. 'I remember when we fried sausages once in the middle of the night, they made a terrific smell. We'd better just be content with cold things. We'll borrow some plates from the dining-room cupboard. There are heaps of old ones on the top shelves that won't be missed for a day or two.'

It was fun to plan everything – fun to smuggle glasses and mugs, plates and dishes and spoons and forks into the common-room. Carlotta's birthday was coming nearer and nearer. The birthday cake was made and the girls went down to the shop to inspect it. It was marvellous.

'I wish your birthday night would come, Carlotta!' said Pat. 'What sport we'll have! And *what* a feast!'

16.

Carlotta's birthday party

The girls were gathered in their common-room, the day before Carlotta's birthday. Alison took a quick look round the room. Elsie was not there.

'What time's the feast tomorrow night?' she asked. 'Exactly at midnight? Let's make it *exactly*! It's much more thrilling. Miss Quentin calls it the "witching midnight hour", and somehow . . .'

'I suppose you'd like to ask your beloved Miss Quentin?' said Isabel, pulling Alison's curly hair. 'Can you see her sitting here in our common-room, her hair done up in curlers, her face shining with grease, eating pine-apple chunks and sardines? I can't.'

'She *doesn't* do her hair in curlers,' said Alison, indignantly. 'She's got beautiful, naturally wavy hair. Why are you always so unkind about her? I wish she *could* come to the feast. I'm sure she'd love it.'

'Well, *we* shouldn't,' said Pat, who had no great liking for the rather affected teacher of drama. 'You make me sick the way you go mooning round after Miss Quentin. She's not so marvellous as you think she is. I think it was pretty mean of her to take the credit herself for Gladys's acting at our concert the other night.'

'Whatever do you mean?' cried Alison, indignantly.

'Well, Alison, you know when Gladys put up that grand performance of Shakespeare's characters the other night,' said Pat, who thought it was about time that Alison was cured of her senseless admiration for Miss Quentin.

'Yes,' said Alison.

'Well, at the end of it, Miss Theobald leant across to Miss Quentin and congratulated her on Gladys's performance and said she was sure she herself had coached her for it,' said Pat, mercilessly. 'And your wonderful Miss Quentin just nodded and smiled and looked pleased – and didn't say that she knew nothing about Gladys Hillman's acting powers at all! We all think that was pretty mean.'

'I don't believe it!' cried Alison, quick to defend the mistress she so much admired.

'Well, Pam Boardman was sitting near, and she heard it all,' said Pat. 'She told us. So now just stop thinking Miss Quentin is the world's greatest wonder.'

Alison changed the subject quickly. It really hurt her to hear such things of Miss Quentin. She was always one to shut her ears to possibly unpleasant things.

'To come back to what I was saying,' she said, 'what time's the feast tomorrow night?'

'Well, as you so badly want it at exactly midnight, we'll have it then,' said Carlotta. 'I've got a dear little alarm clock I'll set for the time – and one of you in the other dormitory can stick it under your pillow so that it'll wake you without rousing everyone in the building. I daren't put it under *my* pillow because Miss Catty Elsie sleeps near me and would wake too. We want to be sure she doesn't know the time.'

'All right then – midnight exactly, tomorrow night,' said Doris, in her clear voice.

At that moment the door opened, and Hilary came in. She had been to the school library to choose a book. She looked round at the others.

'I hope you haven't been talking about anything that matters,' she said, 'because dear sweet-natured, honest-souled Elsie was outside the door, listening for all she was worth!'

The others stared at her in dismay.

'Blow!' said Carlotta. 'We *have* been talking – about the feast – and we said a good many times it was to be midnight tomorrow. Blow, blow, blow!'

'Well, Elsie will certainly do her best to spoil it for us tomorrow night,' said Pat. 'She's sure to split on us somehow – absolutely sure to.'

'I'm not *going* to have our feast spoilt,' said Carlotta, in a determined voice. 'Pat, go to the door and see if Elsie's anywhere about now. Stay by the door and warn us if she comes.'

Pat looked outside the door. There was no one there. Elsie had got the information she wanted, and was content!

'Now listen,' said Carlotta, 'the feast is off for tomorrow night – but it's *on* for tonight instead!'

'Goody, goody!' said everyone, pleased.

'We must make sure Elsie doesn't hear us creeping out of the room,' said Bobby.

'She sleeps very soundly,' said Carlotta. 'I think we can manage it all right. Now, not a word, anyone! We'll hold the feast tonight – and Elsie will get a frightful shock tomorrow when she finds it's all over, and she hasn't been able to spoil it!'

Elsie had no idea that the time of the feast was altered. She hugged her secret all day long, pondering how she could spoil the feast without anyone guessing it was she who had done so.

Should she tell Miss Jenks? That would certainly stop the feast, but Miss Jenks did not like tale-bearers. Should she write a note to Miss Jenks, informing her of the feast, but not sign her name? This seemed quite a good idea – but then Miss Jenks might throw the note into the fire and take no notice of it. Elsie had once heard her say that no one should ever take notice of anonymous letters – they were too despicable even to read.

It's no good writing a note that Miss Jenks won't read or take notice of, thought the girl. I wish I knew the best way to spoil the feast.

She thought about it earnestly – so earnestly that Mam'zelle nearly 'went up in smoke', as Bobby put it, because Elsie paid so little attention in the French class.

'Elsie! This is the third time I have asked you to come out and write on the blackboard,' said Mam'zelle, exasperated. 'Ah, I have the patience of a donkey or I would not put up with you.'

'You mean, the "patience of an *ox*", Mam'zelle,' chuckled Bobby.

'A donkey is patient too,' said Mam'zelle. 'I need the patience of cows, donkeys, sheep and oxen too, when I deal with such a person as this Elsie. You will either depart from this room, Elsie, or pay attention to what I say. I will not have inattention in my class.'

Elsie had to give her thoughts to the French lesson after that – but during prep time that evening she suddenly made up her mind what she would do.

I'll wait till they're all out of the room tomorrow night – then I'll slip along to Miss Jenks's room and say I'm very worried because all the others have vanished, thought Elsie. She'll come back to see – and will then go and hunt around, and find everyone feasting in the common-room. I can say I am afraid they've been kidnapped or something. After all, that American girl, Sadie, was nearly kidnapped last term – so I can pretend to be afraid it's happened again!

This seemed to Elsie a good idea. If she really pretended to be frightened that the others had been kidnapped, Miss Jenks would not think she was telling tales – and the others would not know she had given them away, because it would be Miss Jenks who suddenly came along and found them!

Elsie had no idea that the feast was for that night not the next. The second formers kept their secret well. In fact, Carlotta and Bobby went a bit further, and whispered loudly together, in Elsie's hearing, about all that was to happen the night following! Elsie took it all in, and grinned to herself. Just wait, you second formers, and see what happens to your wonderful feast tomorrow night!

That night Carlotta wound up and set her tiny alarm clock. She gave it to Kathleen, who slept in the next room with the others. 'Put it under your pillow,' she said. 'When it goes off, wake the others quietly. Then come and wake me in the next dormitory. I'll wake our lot and we'll all go to the common-room as quiet as mice.'

Kathleen put the clock under her pillow. She felt sure she would not need it, because she was too excited to sleep. But sleep overtook one tired girl after another, and soon both dormitories were peacefully dreaming.

Elsie was fast asleep too. She was a heavy sleeper, and sometimes snored. Tonight she was huddled up beneath her blankets, because it was cold. She meant to sleep well that night so that she would be well-rested, and able to keep awake the following night.

Everyone was asleep at midnight. The alarm clock under Kathleen's pillow suddenly went off with a tiny ringing noise. Kathleen woke with a jump. She put her hand under the pillow and stopped the alarm from ringing. No one else had woken up. Kathleen sat up in bed, hugging herself in joy. The midnight feast was about to begin!

She sprang out of bed and put on her slippers and dressing-gown. Then she went softly from one bed to another, shaking the sleepers, and whispering the magic words into their ears: 'Midnight feast! Midnight feast!'

Everyone sat up at once. Dressing-gowns and slippers were groped for in the dark. Excited whispering rose.

'I can't find my slippers!'

'Blow this dressing-gown! The belt's all tied in a knot!'

'Sh!' warned Kathleen. 'We've got to be careful not to wake dear Elsie, you know.'

She slipped into the next dormitory and made her way quietly to Carlotta's bed. Carlotta was under sheets and blankets, curled up like a little animal. Kathleen shook her gently. Carlotta shot upright in bed and Kathleen pressed her shoulder warningly.

'Midnight,' she whispered in Carlotta's ear. Carlotta's heart jumped for joy. Her birthday feast, of course! She padded round the dormitory as quietly as a cat, waking everyone but Elsie.

There was no whispering in that room, and not a single giggle! Each girl took slippers and dressing-gown and crept quietly to the door. Elsie snored a little, much to everyone's relief. Carlotta shut the door quietly – and locked it! She took out the key, and put it into her dressing-gown pocket. Now, if Elsie *did* wake up, she couldn't get out and spoil the feast!

Everyone went to the common-room. Not until the door was fast-shut and cushions put along the bottom to hide the crack of light, was the light switched on. Then what a whispering and giggling there was!

'Elsie snored as we went out!' giggled Carlotta. 'Such a nice, gentle little snore! Now – come on – set out the plates and things!'

Everything was taken from the hiding-places – from the bottom of cupboards, and the back of shelves, from tuck-boxes and tins, and from behind books in bookcases. Soon the common-room tables were set with the empty plates and dishes. The largest plate of all was put in the middle. That was for the lovely birthday cake.

'Now for a real, proper feast!' said Carlotta, happily. She and the others set out the goodies they had – the cakes and the buns, the biscuits and the sweets. They opened the tins and emptied the contents on to dishes – sardines, fruit salad, pineapple, prawns – the most wonderful selection of things imaginable!

Carlotta opened a dozen ginger beer bottles. At each pop there was a giggle.

'Here's to our dear, sleeping-beauty, Elsie!' said Bobby, with a laugh, and drank the fizzy ginger beer. 'Come on, everyone – let's really enjoy ourselves!'

17.

The second form play a trick

The second formers certainly *did* enjoy themselves. After a bit they forgot to whisper, and began to speak in their normal voices. It didn't matter, really. They were too far from any sleeping mistress to be heard. They giggled at everything, and laughed till the tears came at Doris and her idiotic antics with empty ginger beer bottles.

They ate everything. Carlotta even ate sardines and pineapple together. Alison tried prawns dipped in ginger beer, which Pat and Isabel said were 'simply super', but they made her feel sick taken that way. However, the others didn't mind, and mixed all the food together with surprising results.

'Nobody would dream that sardines pressed into gingerbread cake would taste so nice,' said Janet. 'My brother told me that and I didn't believe him. But it's true.'

The birthday cake was marvellous. It melted in the mouth! The candles were lit very soon and the light turned off. All the girls sat munching happily, watching the fifteen candles flicker and glow. It was lovely.

'A happy year to you, Carlotta!' said Pat, holding up her mug of ginger beer. 'It's your birthday now, because it's past midnight. Many happy returns of the day!'

'Thanks,' said Carlotta, her vivid little face radiant. Her dark eyes sparkled as she looked round at her friends. It was lovely to give people pleasure. She would tell her grandmother all about it.

'Happy returns!' said one voice after another. 'Happy birthday! Good old Carlotta!'

Carlotta cut second slices of her big birthday cake for everyone. There was a fairly big piece left, enough for two extra slices.

'Two more bits,' said Carlotta, slicing the piece in half. 'Who shall we give them to?'

'One to Miss Jenks!' said Pat. 'You needn't say we had the cake at midnight!'

'And one to Miss Quentin,' said Alison eagerly.

'Don't be silly,' said Carlotta. 'Do you think I'm going to waste my birthday cake on Miss Quentin! I'd rather give a slice to Elsie!'

'Well, let's,' said Anna, unexpectedly. 'It's supposed to be good for people to heap coals of fire on their head – you know, return good for evil – and anyway, what a shock for Elsie when we give her a bit – and she realizes we've had the party!'

'We'll give it to her after the next night then,' said Carlotta, grinning. 'Let her try and spoil the feast this coming night – and then the next day we'll present her with a bit of cake. That really would be funny.'

Everyone agreed to that – not that they wanted to make Elsie a present at all – they just wanted to see her face when she saw the piece of cake, and realized that the feast had been held in peace without her, and hadn't been spoilt.

'Well, one bit for Miss Jenks, and the other for darling Elsie,' said Carlotta, and put them away in a tin. 'Now, girls, is there anything else left to eat?'

There wasn't – and very little to drink either. 'It's a good thing,' said Anna. 'I simply couldn't eat another crumb!'

'Fancy *you* saying that, Anna!' said Pat, with a laugh, looking at the plump, round-faced girl. 'I should have thought you could have gone on eating till breakfast-time!'

'Don't be rude to your head girl,' said Anna, lazily. Nothing ever ruffled her good temper. 'Carlotta, we'd better clear up and get back. We've been here ages!'

'What a pity!' said Alison, with a sigh. She never liked clearing up. The girls set to work and stacked the dishes and plates neatly at the back of a cupboard, hoping they would be able to wash them and put them back into their proper places in the morning.

They swept up the crumbs and threw them out of the window. They put the ginger beer and lemonade bottles into a cupboard outside in the passage. Then they looked round the common-room. There was not a single sign of the lovely feast they had had.

'Good girls,' said Anna. 'Now come along – as quietly as you can, so as not to wake Elsie.'

The second formers crept quietly back to their rooms. Carlotta unlocked her dormitory door. The first sound that greeted her was the light snoring of the sleeping Elsie! She had not even stirred.

Good, thought Carlotta, cuddling into bed. Everything went off marvellously. Oh, I wish we could have it all over again tomorrow night!

The second formers were very sleepy the next morning. They found it difficult to get up. Alison said she felt sick, and so did Kathleen.

'Well, never mind, it was worth it, wasn't it?' said Pat. 'Do you want to go to Matron?'

'No,' said Alison and Kathleen together. Matron would only give them a large dose of nasty-tasting medicine. She had an unfailing way of knowing when a midnight feast had been held, and kept special medicine for girls who complained of feeling sick the next day!

Elsie did not for one moment suspect that the feast had been held. Nobody said a word about it in front of her. The common-room had been so well cleared up that there was not a crumb left to give the secret away.

Elsie looked at the second formers as they worked in Miss Jenks's geography class. You may think you are going to have a lovely time tonight, she thought, but you won't! Miss Jenks will come and spoil it all – and that will serve you right for being so mean to me!

Neither Alison nor Kathleen were sick after all, but because they would eat no breakfast and no dinner, Miss Jenks sent them to Matron. Matron took their temperatures, and found they had none.

'H'mmmm!' she said, thoughtfully. 'Anyone had a birthday in the second form?'

'It's Carlotta's today,' said Kathleen.

'I thought so,' said Matron. 'You are both suffering from Too-Much-To-Eat. A dose of medicine will soon put you right!'

That night the second form went to bed with giggles and nudges. They felt quite certain Elsie was going to give them away – or was hoping to. They had made a lovely plan.

'We'll all wake up at midnight and creep out of the room,' planned Bobby. 'Then, as soon as we're gone, I bet Elsie will go off to tell Miss Jenks, or even Miss Theobald! You never know! When we see her go, we'll all creep back into bed and be there, pretending to be sound asleep, when Miss Jenks comes. What a sell for dear Elsie!'

Everyone approved of this plan. Elsie saw them whispering and giggling, and felt certain it was about the feast that night! She made up her mind to keep awake, whatever happened.

Carlotta set her alarm clock for midnight once more – this time under her own pillow, as she wanted to make sure of waking Elsie up that night! It went off at twelve o'clock, and Carlotta sat up. She grinned to herself in the darkness.

She went from bed to bed, waking everyone up, making rather a noise. Elsie woke up too, for she had fallen asleep after all. She pretended to lie fast asleep, and did not stir until all the girls had crept out of the dormitory. Then she sat up and pulled on her own dressing-gown.

The beasts! Enjoying themselves without me! she

thought maliciously, forgetting that she could have joined in the party if she had said she would behave sensibly. Well, now I'll go and wake Miss Jenks – and pretend I'm frightened because the others have all disappeared!

She slipped out of the dormitory. Carlotta, who was hiding round a corner, saw her going down the passage in the opposite direction, on her way to Miss Jenks's room.

'Come along,' she whispered to the second formers, who were giggling nearby. 'She's gone! I bet Miss Jenks will be along in half a minute! What will she say to Elsie when she sees us all safe and sound in our warm beds!'

The girls took off dressing-gowns and slippers, and hurried back into their beds, which were still nice and warm. They cuddled down and waited, giggling every now and again when someone made a silly remark.

Meanwhile Elsie was knocking on Miss Jenks's door. There was no answer. She knocked more loudly. There was a creak from the bed and then Miss Jenks's voice. 'Who's there? What's the matter?'

Elsie opened the door. Miss Jenks switched on the light beside her bed. She saw Elsie, who had put on a very frightened expression indeed.

'Is somebody ill?' asked Miss Jenks, springing out of bed and dragging her dressing-gown on. 'Quick, tell me!'

'Oh, Miss Jenks – I'm so frightened,' stammered Elsie, filling Miss Jenks with foreboding, she looked so scared. 'All the girls out of my dormitory have disappeared – every one of them. Oh, Miss Jenks – do you think they can have been kidnapped? I feel so scared.'

Miss Jenks snorted. She had a wonderful snort which was often faithfully copied by Doris.

'My dear Elsie, don't be a ninny! As if seven or eight girls could be kidnapped in your room and you hear nothing! Use your common sense, for pity's sake!'

'Miss Jenks, they really aren't there,' said Elsie, looking more wide-eyed than ever. 'Not one of them. Where can they be?'

'It's Carlotta's birthday, isn't it?' said Miss Jenks, crossly. 'I suppose it's a feast. Just like you to try and spoil it!'

'Oh, Miss Jenks, I never thought of that!' cried Elsie, pretending to be astonished and hurt. 'Oh, so long as they aren't kidnapped!'

'You really make me cross, Elsie,' said Miss Jenks who, having had Elsie for more than a year in her form, knew her very well indeed. 'Well, come along – I suppose I'll have to look into this – but you'll just come along with me too, my girl – and the second form can see who's spoilt things for them!'

This was not what Elsie had planned at all! But it was no use, she could not draw back now. She had to go with Miss Jenks.

They went along to the dormitory where Elsie slept. The girls heard them coming and cuddled closer into bed, shutting their eyes tightly, hoping they would not giggle g7and give everything away. Doris gave one or two beautiful little snores, so real that Carlotta wondered if she could possibly have gone to sleep! Miss Jenks heard the snores. She switched on the dormitory light.

She stared in silence at the beds, all except Elsie's occupied by apparently sleeping girls. Doris gave another marvellous little snore, and then, with a realistic grunt, turned over in bed and settled down again. Miss Jenks watched her. She felt certain Doris was awake.

Elsie stared in the utmost astonishment and horror at the occupied beds. She simply could not understand it. She had not been more than three minutes away, surely – and yet here were all the girls asleep in bed. Could she have dreamt it all? Had the girls not stirred from their beds at all? What had happened?

'Well, Elsie,' said Miss Jenks, not troubling to lower her voice, for she felt certain every girl was awake, 'you appear to have brought me out on a wild-goose chase. We shall have to have a talk about this tomorrow, I think. I don't feel at all pleased to be woken up with a story of wholesale kidnappings, and then to find that the only girl out of bed is yourself. Not a very creditable performance on your part, I feel.'

Elsie got into bed without a word. Miss Jenks snapped off the light and went back to bed, shutting her ears to the giggling and whispering that immediately broke out. No one said a word to the cowering Elsie. Let her try to puzzle out what had happened! After ten minutes giggling the room went to sleep again – all but Elsie, who lay awake worrying about what was to happen to her the next day!

The first thing that happened had its funny side. Carlotta solemnly approached her and offered her a piece of the birthday cake. 'You weren't there, so we saved it for you,' she said, a very goody-goody expression on her glowing little face.

Elsie was startled out of her silence. She stared at the cake and said, 'So you *did* have the feast after all? When did you?'

'We had it when we were kidnapped,' said Carlotta, solemnly. 'Oooh, Elsie – it was thrilling! Somebody came in the middle of the night – and kidnapped us all – and took us away – but we offered them a bit of the birthday cake and they were so pleased with it that they set us free!'

'Don't tell such untruths!' said Elsie, angrily. There were squeals of laughter at this.

'Untruths! Why, who was it went and told Miss Jenks we had been kidnapped? *You* can't talk about untruths!'

Elsie turned away. She would not take the cake. She was sick at heart, and longed for a friendly look or a friendly word. Now she had to go and face Miss Jenks. That would be awful too. She had to go just before morning school, at ten minutes to nine in the classroom.

She went. Miss Jenks was there, busy as usual correcting piles of exercise books. On the desk in front of her was a most surprising sight – a large piece of birthday cake! It had been offered to her by Carlotta with a merry twinkle – and had been accepted with a merry twinkle also! Elsie stared at it and bit her lip. To think that Miss Jenks had accepted the cake! Why, she must have guessed about the feast – and here she was accepting a bit of the cake! It was too bad.

'Elsie, there is something seriously wrong with you this term,' began Miss Jenks. 'You had a great chance as head girl, and both Miss Theobald and I hoped you would take it. Apparently you haven't. None of the girls will accept you. Instead of standing up to things and realizing you had to do better and change your attitude, you chose to do stupid things like coming to me last night with a cock-and-bull tale, in order to spite the others. They were too smart for you, I am pleased to see. Now what is to be done? Are you going to go on like this for the rest of the term? Your report will not make pleasant reading if so. Or are you going to show that you really have a little courage and common sense in you, and try to make up for your silly behaviour before it is too late?'

Plain speaking was Miss Jenks's strong point. Elsie listened in silence. She looked at the calm eyes of her form mistress. There was absolutely nothing else to be done now but admit herself to be in the wrong, and say she had courage to do better. That was hard – but the alternative was harder – getting a thoroughly bad report, and having to bear the sneers of the girls for the rest of the term.

'I'll try to make up for being silly,' said Elsie, in a half-sulky tone.

'You've been more than silly,' said Miss Jenks. 'Pull yourself together. You know that St Clare's only keeps the girls it can do something with. The second formers are decent. If they see you showing a little courage and common sense, they will help you.'

'All right,' said Elsie, ungraciously. 'But, Miss Jenks –

don't make me tell them I'm sorry or anything. I can't do that. I really can't.'

'My dear Elsie, I haven't had you in my form for over a year without knowing that I can't expect you to have either the good feeling or the courage to say you're sorry,' said Miss Jenks, impatiently. 'Now here come the others. Go and get my books for me out of the mistresses' common-room, and put on a little brighter face. I simply cannot bear to see you looking like a hen left out in the rain any longer!'

Elsie went to fetch Miss Jenks's books as the second formers crowded into the room. They sat down at once, surprised to see their form mistress there before them.

'I want to say a word to you this morning,' said Miss Jenks. 'About Elsie. She has agreed to try and have a little courage and do better from now on – rather unwillingly, I must admit. She tells me she cannot possibly say she is sorry to you for her stupid conduct – and in any case, I don't think she *is* sorry – but try to act towards her in a way to help her efforts, not hinder them, will you? After all – you played a wonderful trick on her last night, didn't you?'

This unexpected ending made all the girls smile delightedly. So Miss Jenks guessed everything – and there was the birthday cake, sitting waiting to be eaten! Good old Miss Jenks! The girls were ready to do anything she asked them.

'All right, Miss Jenks – we'll put up with Elsie as graciously as we can,' said Hilary, smiling. 'We got our own back last night – so we can afford to be generous!'

Elsie came back into the room. She had tried to make her face pleasanter. She placed the books on the desk. 'Thank you, Elsie,' said Miss Jenks, in a pleasant tone, and gave her a smile. The girls saw it and approved. What Miss Jenks could do, they could do also. Things would be easier for Elsie than she deserved!

18.

An exciting match

The term went on its way, happy and busy with lessons, games and fun. Lacrosse matches were played, and the whole school turned out to watch and cheer at the home matches.

The second form were very proud of Gladys. Anna had told Miss Wilton, the games mistress, that she thought Gladys would be worth trying in some other position than goal-keeper, and Miss Wilton rather doubtfully agreed to try her.

'She has never shown any aptitude for running, catching or tackling,' she said. 'However – we will see.'

So Gladys, to her delight, was put in a position where running and catching would count, and after once or twice the girl proved herself to be very good. She was small, but very wiry and agile, and she was amazingly good at dodging the enemy and passing the ball quickly to someone else.

'Good, Gladys, good!' Miss Wilton said, time after time, one Monday afternoon. 'You *are* coming on!'

Gladys flushed with pleasure. She looked very happy these days. Miss Quentin was taking a good deal of notice of her in the drama class, and now Miss Wilton was praising her at lacrosse – the two things she liked most. She was writing very happy letters to her mother now, and although she still had no reply, she had had a letter from Mirabel's mother that had delighted her.

Dear Gladys [the letter had said],
I thought you might like to know that I was able to go today to the hospital your mother is in. The nurse actually allowed me to see her for two minutes, as it was one of her good days. I told her about you, and how you and my Mirabel were friends. She could not say much, but she did say how delighted she was to hear what a success you were at the concert. Perhaps you will be able to see her in the holidays. It is early days to say yet whether she is really making progress, but I think you may be hopeful. I will go to see her again if I can.

Give my love to Mirabel, and say I hope she is treating you properly! You are such a little mouse and Mirabel is just the opposite!

Love from
Elise Unwin

This letter Gladys treasured greatly. She thought with intense gratitude of Mrs Unwin. She began to hope that her mother really might get better. She knew that when she was well enough she had to have a serious operation, and this thought worried her greatly – but now that she was happier things did not seem so bad.

Meantime there was lacrosse, and the excitement of the next match, which was to be a home one, against St

Christopher's. Belinda Towers had let it be known that she would like to choose one girl from the second form for the team. No one in the first form was good enough as yet – but the second form were on the whole not at all bad at the game.

'*You* might be chosen, Gladys!' said Mirabel, half-teasingly. She did not seriously think that the shy girl would be picked out, for although she certainly was very good at the game now, she was not half the size of some of the other girls in the form.

'I wish I could!' said Gladys. 'But I know who will be – Hilary! She's terribly good, I think.'

Hilary certainly was very good – very sure and very swift. Her catching was graceful to watch, and it seemed certain she would be chosen for the match.

But two days before the match Hilary went down with a cold again. Matron popped her into bed, in spite of her wails about lacrosse.

'Belinda said I could play in the match!' she said. 'Can't I get up tomorrow for certain?'

'Nothing is certain with bad colds,' said Matron. 'So don't count on anything.'

Thus it came about that Hilary, although chosen by Belinda, could not play – and Belinda, running her pencil down the list of names in the second form, suddenly came to a stop by Gladys Hillman's name. She sat and thought.

That kid's good, thought the head girl. I watched her yesterday. She's fast – and jolly good at tackling although she is small. I've a good mind to try her.

So, when the list of names was put up on the big noticeboard, showing the girls chosen for the next match, Gladys Hillman's appeared at the bottom – the only one chosen from the second form! Mirabel saw it and went hurriedly in search of Gladys.

'Gladys! What do you think? You're down for the match!'

'Really?' said Gladys, her face flushing brightly. 'Oh – how marvellous! Golly, I *shall* be nervous, though!'

'No, you won't. You'll just remember that your mother is longing to hear that you've shot twelve goals for St Clare's, and that you've won the match for the school!' said Mirabel, laughing. 'Oh, I say – I *am* pleased. Good for you!'

Gladys was happy to see Mirabel's real pleasure. That was the best of friends – they shared your troubles with you, and they doubled your joys. It was good to have a friend.

The school turned out as usual to watch the match. The St Christopher girls came in a big coach, their lacrosse sticks beside them. The St Clare's girls gave them a cheer.

The game began. Belinda was referee, and blew her whistle sharply. There was the click of lacrosse sticks as the two girls in the centre of the field began the game. Then the ball was flicked quickly away, and Margery Fenworthy, of the third form, picked it up in her lacrosse net and flew down the field with it. She passed to Lucy Oriell, her friend, and then when Lucy was tackled, cleverly caught the ball once more and passed to Gladys, who was hopping about in excitement, ready for any chance.

Click! Gladys caught the ball, dodged a tackling enemy, and threw to Lucy. From one to another went the ball, and Lucy tried to throw a goal, which was deftly stopped by the St Christopher's goal-keeper.

The game was very even. The St Clare girls were better runners and catchers, but the St Christopher goal-keeper was marvellous. She had a quick eye, a firm wrist, and a real talent for stopping the ball every time the St Clare girls threw at the goal.

St Christopher's threw a goal first, and the St Clare girls clapped, though their faces were rather anxious. This was going to be a stiffer match than they thought. Thank goodness both Margery Fenworthy and Lucy Oriell were playing today – they were always first-class. Some of the St Clare girls looked doubtfully at Gladys Hillman. She seemed very small in comparison with the others. Margery Fenworthy, for instance, was a big strapping girl who over-topped Gladys by a head and a half!

'Play up, Gladys!' yelled Mirabel, every time her friend came near her. 'Go on – play up!'

And the whole second form would yell in chorus, 'Play *up*, Gladys! What about a goal from you?'

Half-time – and no goals for the St Clare girls! One-love! The St Clare girls who were watching crowded round their team, trying to buck them up and spur them on.

'You are doing well, Margery and Lucy,' said Belinda Towers, approvingly. Her eye caught the flushed face of Gladys Hillman, and she gave her one of her sudden wide smiles. 'You're not doing too badly either, kid! But keep a bit closer to Margery, will you? You might be able to score a goal off one of her passes to you.'

'Yes, Belinda,' said Gladys, happily. 'I'll try.' She kept her word. She hovered closer to Margery, and caught the ball slickly each time. Twice she was tackled and had to pass before she could shoot at the goal – but the third time she threw the ball with all her might at the net in the distance.

'Goal, goal!' yelled the St Clare girls. But no, the St Christopher goal-keeper deftly flicked the ball away. No goal – but a jolly good try!

'Go it, Gladys, go it!' yelled the second form, dancing about in excitement. 'Try again!'

Gladys did her best. She was everywhere, in and out, running, tackling, passing. Time slipped on, and still no goals were scored by St Clare's. On the other hand no more were scored by St Christopher's, either. It was the closest match the schools had ever played.

'Oh, golly, it's almost time!' groaned Mirabel, glancing at her watch. 'Gladys! Play up. There's only four minutes more!'

Gladys heard, and ran to tackle an enormous St Christopher girl. The girl dodged, and Gladys tripped. She wrenched her ankle, and gave a groan. It was going to be painful to run now. But she couldn't possibly give up!

The ball rolled near her. She nipped it up into her lacrosse net, and ran, limping, down the field. She passed to Margery, who at once passed back again when she was tackled. Gladys didn't catch the ball. It was neatly caught by a much taller girl, who leapt into the air. The ball fell into her net, and she turned to run down the field. But quick as thought Gladys hit her lacrosse stick upwards, and the ball flew into the air. Gladys caught it, and ran again. She shot for the goal.

It was not such a good shot as before – but the ball bounced over a tuft as it rolled towards the goal, and avoided the waiting lacrosse net of the goal-keeper. In the greatest dismay she saw it roll into the goal!

The St Clare girls nearly went mad with joy. The second form thumped each other on the back and yelled 'Good old Gladys' at the tops of their voices. It was all very thrilling.

The match was a draw – one all. The St Christopher girls went back to tea with St Clare's, and discussed the match at the tops of their voices. The second form treated Gladys to a special cake for making the score even.

'Good for you, kid!' said Belinda, as she passed. That was Gladys's biggest reward! Words of praise from the great head girl were words of praise indeed!

19.

Alison and Miss Quentin

The term hurried on its way. The girls began to talk about Christmas holidays and what they were going to do – pantomimes, parties and theatres were discussed. Gladys looked a little bleak when the girls began to talk excitedly about the coming holidays.

'Will your mother be well enough to leave the hospital and have you home with her?' asked Mirabel.

'No. I'm staying at school for the hols,' said Gladys. 'Matron will still be here, you know, and two girls from the third and fourth form, whose parents are in India. But I shall be very lonely without you, Mirabel.'

'Poor Gladys!' said Mirabel in dismay. 'I should hate to stay at school for the hols I must say. After all, most of the fun of being at boarding school is being with crowds of others, day and night – it won't be any fun for you being with one or two! Won't your mother really be better?'

'She's going to have a serious operation soon,' said Gladys. 'So I know quite well she won't be able to leave the hospital, Mirabel. But the operation may make her well again, so I'm just hoping for the best – and I'm quite willing to stay on at school for the hols if only I hear that Mother is getting better after the operation.'

Mrs Unwin had written to Mirabel about Gladys's mother. She had told Mirabel not to show the letter to Gladys.

'I feel rather worried about Gladys's mother,' she wrote. 'She is to have the operation soon – and I can't help wondering if she really will get over it, because she is very weak. If there is bad news, you must comfort Gladys all you can. She will be very glad to have a friend if sadness comes to her. I will let her know at once if the news is good.'

Mirabel said nothing to her friend about the letter – but she was extra warm and friendly towards Gladys. It was unusual for the rather selfish, thick-skinned Mirabel to think of someone else unselfishly and tenderly. It softened her domineering nature and made her a much nicer girl.

Gladys was pleased to be able to tell her mother about the match. She wished she had shot a winning goal – but it was something to shoot the goal that made a draw!

'*I* shall write and tell your mother too,' said Mirabel, who could not do enough for her friend just then.

'Oh, Mirabel – you are good!' said Gladys, delighted. 'You wrote to Mother after the concert, and I guess she was pleased to hear all you said. My word – what a silly I was at the beginning of the term, all mopey and miserable, couldn't take an interest in anything. I should think you hated me.'

'Well, I didn't like you very much,' said Mirabel, honestly. 'But I guess you didn't like *me* much, either!'

Gladys was shining not only at lacrosse but in the

drama class as well! Miss Quentin, who had been really amazed at Gladys's performance on the night of the concert, was making a great fuss of her and her talent. Alison didn't like it at all. She was jealous, and there were some days when she could hardly speak to Gladys.

The play was to be performed at the end of the term. Miss Quentin had tried out Alison, Doris, Carlotta and now Gladys in the principal feminine part. There was no doubt that Alison looked the prettiest and the most graceful, and that she was quite word-perfect and had rehearsed continually. But Gladys was by far the best actress.

Miss Quentin had given Alison to understand that she would have the chief part. She had not actually said so in so many words, but the class as a whole took it for granted that Alison would take the part. They found it quite natural too, for they knew how hard the girl had worked at learning the words, a task always difficult for her.

Alison was really silly about Miss Quentin. She waited round corners for her, hoping for a smile. She hung on every word the teacher said. She was worse than she had been with Sadie Greene the term before – for one thing Sadie had had a little common sense and often laughed at Alison, but Miss Quentin had no common sense at all! So Alison became worse instead of better, and the second formers became quite exasperated with her.

Then Alison heard some news that gave her a great blow – Miss Quentin was not coming back the next term!

'Are you sure?' asked Alison, looking with wide eyes at Hilary, who had come in with the news.

'Well, I heard Mam'zelle say to Miss Quentin, "Well, well – so you will be on the stage next term, whilst we are all struggling with our tiresome girls!" Apparently Miss Quentin had only just heard the news herself – she had a letter in her hand. I think she must only have been engaged for a term – it's the first time we've had a proper drama class. Perhaps Miss Theobald was trying out the idea.' Hilary looked at Alison, who had tears in her eyes. 'Cheer up, Alison – the world won't come to an end because your beloved Miss Quentin isn't here next term! You'll find someone else to moon round, don't fret!'

It was a great shock to Alison. She had dreamt of term after term in Miss Quentin's drama classes, with herself taking all the chief parts in every play, hearing honeyed words of praise dropping daily from the teacher's lips. She went away by herself and cried very bitterly. The silly girl gave her heart far too easily to anyone who attracted her, or made a fuss of her.

'What's come over Alison?' asked Pat, in surprise, when her cousin appeared with swollen eyes. 'Been in a row, Alison?'

'She's only sorrowing because her beloved Miss Quentin won't be here next term to pat her on the back and tell her she is very very good!' said Janet.

'Alison, don't be an idiot!' said Isabel. 'You know perfectly well Miss Quentin won't be much loss. We all think she's too soft for words! And think how mean she was in taking the credit for Gladys's performance at the concert.'

'I have never believed that,' said Alison, tears coming

into her eyes again. 'You don't know Miss Quentin as I do – she's the truest, honestest, most loyal person! I've never met anyone like her.'

'Nor have I!' said Pat. 'And thank goodness I haven't. Alison, why must you go and choose the wrong people to moon round? Sadie Greene was amusing but she hadn't anything in her at all – and neither has Miss Quentin. Now, take Miss Jenks for instance . . .'

'Miss Jenks!' said Alison, with an angry sniff. 'Who would want to moon round Miss Jenks, with her snappy tongue and cold eyes?'

'Well, I think she's pretty decent,' said Pat. 'Not that I should want to moon round her or anyone, for that matter. I'm only just saying you will keep on choosing the wrong people to lavish your affections on! Sadie has never even written to you – and I bet Miss Quentin won't, either!'

'She will! She's very fond of me,' said Alison.

The others gave it up. Alison would never learn sense! 'It's a pity she can't find out how silly her Miss Quentin really is – how undependable,' said Hilary. 'Your feather-headed cousin, Pat, wants to learn common sense – it's a pity she can't find out that all her ideas about Miss Quentin are only dreams – the real Miss Quentin isn't a bit as Alison pictures her!'

'Well, we can't teach her,' said Pat. 'She'll make herself miserable for the rest of the term now, and for all the hols too, I expect!'

Alison was really unhappy to hear that her favourite teacher was leaving. She thought she would hang about near the common-room of the junior mistresses, and watch for Miss Quentin to come out. Then she would tell her how upset she was.

So she went to a little lobby near the common-room, and pretended to be hunting for something there. She could hear Miss Quentin's voice talking to Mam'zelle, behind the closed door of the common-room, but she could not hear anything that was said.

Then someone opened the door and came out. It was Miss Lewis, the history teacher. 'Leave the door open,' cried Mam'zelle, 'it is stuffy in here!'

So Miss Lewis left the door open, and went off towards the school library. Alison stood in the little lobby, her heart beating fast, waiting for Miss Quentin to come out. Surely she would come soon!

The mistresses went on talking. Some of them had clear, distinct voices, and some spoke too low for Alison to hear anything. She did not mean to listen, she was only waiting for Miss Quentin – but suddenly she heard her own name, spoken by Miss Quentin herself. Alison stiffened, and her heart thumped. Was Miss Quentin going to praise her to the others? It would be just like her to say something nice!

'Alison O'Sullivan is going to get a shock,' said Miss Quentin, in the low, clear voice that Alison thought so beautiful. 'The silly girl thinks she's good enough to play the lead in the second-form play! She's been wearing herself out rehearsing – it will do her good to find she's not going to have the part!'

'Who's going to have it, then?' asked Miss Jenks.

'Gladys Hillman,' answered Miss Quentin, promptly. 'I've had my eye on that child ever since the beginning of the term. She's three times as good as anyone else. She will be marvellous as the Countess Jeannette.'

'I wish Alison worked as hard in my classes as she does in yours,' remarked Mam'zelle, in her rather harsh, loud voice. 'Ah, her French exercises! But I think, Miss Quentin, she really does work at drama.'

'Oh, well, she simply adores me,' said Miss Quentin, easily. 'I can always make her type work. She'll do anything for a smile or a kind word from me – like a dear little pet dog. But give me somebody like that wild Carlotta – somebody with something in them! Alison bores me to tears with her breathless, "Yes, Miss Quentin! No, Miss Quentin! Oh, *can* I, Miss Quentin?" It will be good for her to have a shock and find she has to take back place to Gladys Hillman.'

'I'm not so sure,' said Miss Jenks, in her cool voice. 'Shocks are not always good for rather weak characters, Miss Quentin. I hope you will break your news kindly to poor Alison – otherwise she will weep all day, and as exams are coming on tomorrow, I don't want bad work from her because of you!'

'Oh, don't worry! I'll just pat her curly head and say a few kind words,' said Miss Quentin. 'She'll eat out of my hand. She always does.'

Miss Lewis came back and shut the door. Not a word more could be heard. Alison sat on a bench in the lobby, sick at heart, shocked and hurt beyond measure. Her mind was in a whirl. She had not been able to help hearing – and once she had grasped that her idol, Miss Quentin, was poking fun at her, she had not even been able to get up and go. She had had to sit there, hearing every cruel word.

She was not to have the leading part in the play. Miss Quentin wasn't fond of her – only amused with her, thinking her a little pet dog, someone to pat and laugh at! Miss Quentin had told a lie – she had not noticed Gladys Hillman at all until the night of the concert! Miss Quentin was bored with her!

Alison was too shocked even to cry. She sat in the lobby quietly, looking straight in front of her. What was it that Miss Jenks had said? 'Shocks are not always good for weak characters!' Was she, Alison, such a weak character then? The girl rubbed her hand across her forehead, which was wet and clammy.

I have to think all this out, said Alison to herself. I can't tell anyone. I'm too ashamed. But I must think things out. Oh, Miss Quentin, how could you say all that?

Poor Alison! This was the greatest shock she had ever had in her easy-going life! All her admiration and love for Miss Quentin vanished at once – passed like a dream in the night. There was nothing of it left, except an ache. She saw the drama teacher as the others saw her – someone pleasant and amiable, but undependable, disloyal, shallow.

Alison was a silly girl, as changeable as a weather-vane, swinging now this way and now that, easily upset and easily pleased. As the others often said, 'she hadn't much in her'! But in this hour of horror – for it *was* horror to her – she found something in herself that she hardly knew she possessed. And that something was a sense of dignity!

She wasn't going to go under because of someone like Miss Quentin! She wasn't going to be a pet dog, eating out of her hand! She had too much dignity for that. She would show Miss Quentin that she was wrong. Hurt and shocked though she was, Alison had a glimmering of common sense all at once, and she held up her head, blinked away the tears, and made up her mind what she was going to do.

So it came about that when Miss Quentin broke the news to the drama class that Gladys was to have the leading part, and not Alison, the girl gave no sign at all of being disappointed. Her face was pale, for she had slept badly that night, but it had a calmness and dignity that astonished the watching girls.

'So Gladys is to have the part, you see,' finished Miss Quentin. She lightly touched Alison's curly head. 'I'm afraid my Alison will be disappointed!'

'Of course not, Miss Quentin,' said Alison, moving away from the teacher's hand. 'I think Gladys *should* have the part! She is the best of us all – and I am very glad.'

The girls stared at Alison in the greatest amazement. They had expected tears – even sulks – but not this cool acceptance of an unpleasant fact.

'Who would have thought Alison would take it like that?' said Janet. 'Well – good for her! All the same, I think it's a shame. Miss Quentin made us all think Alison would have the part.'

Alison would not meet Miss Quentin's eye. She played the part she was given very well, but seemed quite unmoved when Miss Quentin praised her. Miss Quentin was puzzled and a little hurt.

'Girls, I have something to tell you,' she said at the end of the lesson. 'I shall not be here next term. I shall miss you all very much – especially one or two of you who have worked extremely hard!'

She looked hard at Alison, expecting to see tears, and to hear cries of 'Oh, Miss Quentin! We *shall* miss you!'

But Alison did not look at the teacher. She gazed out of the window as if she had not heard. Hilary cleared her throat and spoke politely. 'I am sure we are all sorry to hear that, Miss Quentin. We hope you will be happy wherever you go.'

Miss Quentin was hurt and disappointed. She spoke directly to Alison.

'Alison, I know you worked specially hard for me,' she said.

'I worked hard because I like drama,' said Alison, in a cool voice, looking Miss Quentin in the eyes for the first time. This was a direct snub and the girls gasped in surprise. Whatever made Alison behave like that? They gazed at her in admiration. So Alison had seen through her beloved Miss Quentin at last – and instead of moaning and wailing, had put on a cloak of dignity and coolness. One up to Alison!

Miss Quentin retired gracefully to her next class, very much puzzled. The girls crowded round Alison.

'Alison! What's happened? Has your beloved Miss Quentin offended you?'

'Shut up,' said Alison, pushing her way between the girls. 'I can't tell you anything. I don't want to discuss it. Let me alone.'

They let her go, puzzled, but respecting her request. 'Something's happened,' said Hilary, watching the white-faced girl going out of the room. 'But whatever it is, it's for the best. Alison seems suddenly more grown-up.'

'Time she was,' said Pat. 'Anyway – if she stops mooning round somebody different each term – or at any rate chooses somebody worthwhile – it will be a blessing!'

Nobody ever knew what had made Alison 'grow up' so suddenly. Only Alison herself knew, and out of her hurt came something worthwhile, which was to help her in many years to come.

20.

An exciting end of term

Exams were being held, and girls were groaning daily over them. Mam'zelle was in a state of trepidation in case any of the girls fell short of pass-marks. The girls were in a far greater state, feeling quite certain that nobody at all would pass in French! Mam'zelle always threatened to give them such difficult papers – but when the time came, they were not so bad after all!

Gladys found the exams difficult because her mother was to have her operation that week. She was very anxious indeed. Mirabel did all she could to help her to prepare each evening. It was good to see the patience and kindliness of the bigger girl. The others warmed greatly to Mirabel because of it.

Even Elsie felt sorry for the anxious girl. 'I hope you'll hear good news soon,' she said. Gladys looked at her in surprised gratitude. Fancy Elsie saying anything kind! The others heard the low words, and looked at one another with raised eyebrows. They had kept their promise to Miss Jenks, and had not hindered Elsie in any way in her efforts to behave more reasonably.

But, on the other hand, no girl had been able to show any liking for Elsie. It was impossible. The girl had been too spiteful, too exasperating altogether to be liked now. She would be tolerated, but nothing else. Miss Jenks watched everyone's behaviour, and came to the conclusion that it was hopeless to expect any happiness or real help for Elsie from the second formers. On the other hand, the lazy Anna had been a great success as head girl of the form. She had thrown aside her laziness, and had come to the fore, taking responsibility and making decisions capably and quickly. Miss Jenks was pleased with her. She was now ready to go up into the third form, and take her part with the older girls there. Hilary Wentworth could be head girl next term.

Miss Jenks spoke to Miss Theobald about it and the head agreed. 'But what are we to do with Elsie?' she said. 'I will have a talk with her.'

So Elsie was sent for, and sat rather sullenly in Miss Theobald's sitting-room, expecting to be scolded, or something even worse – she might be told that St Clare's didn't want her any more!

'Elsie,' said Miss Theobald, 'I know you have found things difficult this term – mostly your own fault, as I think you will admit.'

Elsie looked at Miss Theobald's solemn face. 'Yes,' she said at last. 'I suppose things were mostly my own fault. The second form don't like me at all. They will never have me as head girl. They just tolerate me, that's all. It makes things hard for me. I feel I can never do anything to alter their opinion, and so I can't very well take any pleasure in being there.'

'You see, Elsie, one of the hardest things in the world to forget and forgive is spitefulness,' said Miss Theobald. 'Malice and spite rouse such bitter feelings in others. Other faults, such as greed, irresponsibility, silliness – these arouse disgust, but are forgotten and forgiven. Spite always rankles, and is never forgotten. I can see you will never do any good either to yourself or to others in the second form.'

Elsie waited, her heart sinking. This meant that she was to be asked to leave. She didn't want to do that. She did like St Clare's. She stared at Miss Theobald miserably. The head guessed what the girl was thinking.

'I'm not going to say you must leave St Clare's,' she said quickly. 'I think the school can do a lot for you, Elsie, and you may be able to do something for St Clare's too. No – you shan't leave! I think you must go up into the third form instead – leave behind the second formers who have seen such a bad side of your character – and go into the third form, which, next term, will have five or six new girls. You will have a chance then to show a different side of your character! You are not really ready to go up, either in your work, or in your behaviour – but I will send you up if you will tell me that you will take this chance, and work hard and, more important still, try to get the "cattiness" out of your nature that every schoolgirl detests!'

Elsie's heart lifted in relief. Go up into the third form – and leave behind the girls who would always dislike her! Wouldn't she work hard! Wouldn't she be kind and friendly and helpful to the new girls who didn't know anything about her! She smiled gladly.

'What about Anna?' she asked. 'Is she going up too?'

'Yes – but you can trust Anna not to give you away at all,' said Miss Theobald. 'She's a good girl – she really has turned out well as head girl. Now, Elsie – take this chance and make good!'

'I will,' said Elsie. 'Thank you, Miss Theobald. I never thought of going up into the third form! It makes all the difference in the world!'

The girl went out, pleased and hopeful. She saw Gladys Hillman in the passage and went up to her with a warm gesture of friendliness.

'Any news of your mother, old thing?' she asked.

'Not yet,' said Gladys, wondering whatever could have made Elsie look so friendly and glad. Elsie went on her way and met Bobby.

'I say,' she said, 'I saw poor old Gladys just now. Can't we do something to take her out of herself a bit? She's moping again.'

'Good idea!' said Bobby at once. 'I'll play that trick on Mam'zelle – you know, the trick that makes plates jump about! Mam'zelle is taking lunch today at our table, because Miss Jenks is going out. It will be sport!'

So the second formers were told that a trick was about to be played, and they all cheered up, forgot about exams, and looked at Bobby with bright eyes. The first trick that term! It was time one was played!

Mam'zelle was in a good temper. The first form had

done unexpectedly well in their French exam. She beamed at everybody. The second formers beamed back, and Doris gave a deep chuckle, exactly like Mam'zelle's.

'Ah, this bad Doris!' said Mam'zelle, clapping Doris on the shoulder. 'She can imitate me per-r-r-rfectly – but she cannot roll her 'r's yet in the true French way! Now – let us go to the dining-room. The bell for luncheon has gone. Today I take you for the meal, because the good Miss Jenks is out!'

The second form seated themselves at their table. Mam'zelle was at the head. Bobby was three places away from her. The others looked at her, grinning. They hoped she had been able to slip into the dining-room and lay her plans!

Bobby had prepared everything carefully. There was a pile of plates at Mam'zelle's place, ready for her to serve the stew for each girl. Bobby had removed the plates, and had deftly placed the long rubber tubing under the table-cloth, so that it ran from where the plates were to Bobby's own seat, and hung down under the cloth. The bladder-end was where the plates were, and the bulb to press was by Bobby's place. Bobby replaced the pile of plates over the bladder-end. The plates were too heavy to move when the bulb was pressed – but when all the girls were served and only Mam'zelle's plate was there, it would tip up beautifully as soon as Bobby pressed the bulb which filled the bladder-end with air!

Mam'zelle served out the stew rapidly. The girls began their meal hungrily, one eye on Mam'zelle's plate. It was the only one left now. Mam'zelle filled it with stew and gravy. She was very fond of gravy.

'At first,' said Mam'zelle conversationally, taking up her knife and fork, 'at first when I came to England I did not like this stew of yours! But now – ah, it is wonderful!'

Bobby pressed the rubber bulb she was holding under the cloth. The bladder-end under Mam'zelle's plate filled with air and became fat and big. Mam'zelle's plate tilted up on one side, gave a little wobble and subsided again as Bobby let go the bulb she was pressing.

Mam'zelle was overcome with astonishment. She felt her nose to see if her glasses were there. Yes, they were. But could she have seen right? Her plate had moved!

She took a quick look round at the girls. They seemed to have noticed nothing – though actually all the girls had seen the plate lift and wobble, and were fighting hard to keep from giggling.

Mam'zelle dismissed the matter from her mind. She had imagined it! She began to make conversation again.

'Tomorrow you second formers will have your French tests,' she said, smiling round. Then she tried to cut a piece of meat with her knife – whilst Bobby at the same moment pressed the rubber bulb. Air ran through to the bladder, and Mam'zelle's plate lifted itself up very suddenly, and spilt some gravy over one side.

Mam'zelle looked at her plate in alarm. It had done it again. It was alive! It had spilt its gravy on the cloth.

'*Tiens*!' said Mam'zelle, very much startled. 'What is this?'

'What is what, Mam'zelle?' asked Janet, with a solemn face.

'Nothing, nothing!' said Mam'zelle, hastily, not liking to say that she feared her plate was alive. But something certainly was the matter with it. She looked down at it, hardly daring to eat her meal.

Bobby gave the plate a rest. Mam'zelle looked at it warily for a little while, and then plucked up her courage to eat her meal once more. The plate seemed to be behaving itself. Then it suddenly went mad again!

It tipped up and down slowly and solemnly three times, then jerked from side to side spilling some more gravy. Mam'zelle grew really alarmed. She glanced at the girls. How strange that they did not seem to see what was happening! She must be going mad!

'Don't you like your stew, Mam'zelle?' asked Pat, solemnly. 'I thought you said it was wonderful.'

Mam'zelle looked suspiciously at her plate which was now quiet. Doris made a silly joke in order to let the girls laugh loudly, for two or three of them were almost hysterical by now, and would certainly have given the game away if they had not been able to laugh loudly.

The rest of the school looked in amazement at the bellowing girls. Miss Theobald, who sat at the head of the sixth-form table, was displeased.

'Quiet, please,' she called to the second formers. They choked and became quiet. Doris was purple in the face with trying not to laugh again. Mam'zelle looked round with a frown.

'Such a noise!' she said, reprovingly. But her attention was soon drawn to her plate again when it solemnly rose up and down twice, and then became quite still.

Mam'zelle frowned. This could not really be happening! Plates could not behave like that. It was nonsense. She would eat her dinner and not think about it.

'Don't do it again till the pudding comes,' whispered Carlotta to Bobby. 'We can't help squealing with laughter now. We shall get into a row. Give us a rest!'

So for the rest of the first course the plate behaved itself, and Mam'zelle was much relieved. But when the pudding arrived, and she had served it out, leaving only her own plate in its place, the fun began again. The pudding-plate leapt quite wildly, and Mam'zelle pushed her chair back with a scream. The girls choked and the tears ran down their cheeks.

'Ah! This plate!' cried Mam'zelle. 'It is as bad as the other one. See how it jumps!'

Bobby kept the plate quite still. Doris exploded into laughter and two or three joined her helplessly. Miss Theobald began to look really vexed. The rest of the school craned their necks to see whatever could be happening at the second-form table.

The plate moved again, and Mam'zelle backed away still farther. Miss Theobald, amazed and puzzled, left her place and walked over to the second-form table. Every girl was rocking in helpless laughter. Not even the presence of the head mistress could stop them. This was the funniest thing they had ever seen.

'Mam'zelle! What *is* the matter?' asked Miss Theobald, really annoyed. Mam'zelle turned to her wildly.

'My plate!' she said. 'My plate!'

'Well, what is wrong with it?' asked Miss Theobald, impatiently, thinking that Mam'zelle must really have gone mad. 'It seems all right to me.'

'Miss Theobald, it jumps, it dances, it leaps around the table,' said Mam'zelle, earnestly, exaggerating in the hope that Miss Theobald would be impressed. 'It is a mad plate. I cannot bear it.'

The head mistress looked at the plate of pudding. It lay quite still on the table, perfectly ordinary. She glanced round at the giggling girls. She supposed they were laughing at Mam'zelle's behaviour. Well, it certainly was extraordinary.

'You had better go and lie down, Mam'zelle,' she said at last. 'I think you can't be well.'

'*I* am well,' said poor Mam'zelle. 'It is the plate that is mad. You should see it jump, Miss Theobald.'

Miss Theobald looked doubtfully at the plate – and Bobby had a tremendous urge to make it jump again. She pressed the bulb hard, and the plate jumped up at once, wobbled and fell back again. Miss Theobald looked astonished and Mam'zelle gave another squeal. The girls screamed with laughter.

Miss Theobald lifted up the plate, and pushed back the table-cloth. There, underneath, was the little rubber bladder attached to the tubing that led to Bobby's place. Mam'zelle's eyes nearly fell out of her head when she saw it.

'I think, Mam'zelle, one of the girls is playing a trick on you,' said Miss Theobald. 'I will leave you to deal with it. I dare say Roberta can explain how it was done.'

The girls stopped laughing. They stared at Miss Theobald walking back to her seat. They looked at Mam'zelle, who glared at poor Bobby.

'What is this horrible trick?' she inquired in a loud voice.

Bobby explained, and Mam'zelle listened carefully. She removed the whole thing and looked at it. Then she put back the table-cloth and her plate and began to eat her pudding, looking straight in front of her with her sloe-black eyes.

The girls felt uncomfortable. Was Mam'zelle really offended, really angry? The trick was quite a harmless one. They finished their pudding and sat still.

Suddenly there came a snort from Mam'zelle and all the second formers looked up in surprise. Mam'zelle threw back her head. She roared, she bellowed! She laughed so much that the relieved second formers couldn't help laughing again too.

'It was a good trick,' said Mam'zelle at last, wiping her eyes. 'Yes, a good trick. I shall make my sister laugh till she cries when I tell her. When I think of that plate jumping at me like that – ah, *magnifique*!'

'I'll lend you the whole trick, if you like,' said Janet. 'It belongs to my brother. You can play the trick on your sister.'

Mam'zelle stared at her in delight. 'What a good idea!' she exclaimed, beaming. 'This will cheer my good sister immensely. You shall show me how it works.'

Miss Theobald smiled as she left the room. It really had been funny. What a good thing Mam'zelle had seen the funny side – but she could generally be trusted to. Poor Mam'zelle – the hundreds of tricks that had been played on her during her years at St Clare's! She would never learn to be suspicious of the girls!

'Marvellous!' said Janet, when the second formers were in their common-room again, discussing the affair. 'Simply super. Bobby, you did it awfully well. I thought I should have died, trying to keep in my laughter. Oh, dear – when I think of that plate jumping about – and Mam'zelle's horrified face – I want to scream all over again!'

Everyone was amused, and Gladys, who had seen few tricks played in her life, laughed as much as anyone. She forgot her worry for a while, and Mirabel was glad to see her smiling face as she listened to the talk.

The next day Mam'zelle gave out the French papers. They were much easier than the class expected and everyone gave a sigh of relief. Even Doris hoped she might get enough marks for a pass!

In the middle of the exam when everything was perfectly quiet, the door opened and a junior girl looked in. Mirabel glanced up. She looked across at Gladys. Gladys had gone white. She wondered if there was any news for her. 'Please could Gladys Hillman go to Miss Theobald,' she said. Gladys stood up, her knees shaking. She was sure that her mother was dead. She went out of the room as if she was walking in a dream. Mirabel stared after her, miserable. She feared the worst too.

But in two minutes Gladys was back! The door was flung open, and she burst into the room, her face beaming, and her eyes shining. She rushed to Mirabel.

'Mirabel! Mother's had the operation, and she's come through it wonderfully! She's going to get better! I'm to see her soon, just for an hour! Perhaps next week, Mirabel! Isn't it marvellous!'

Mirabel was as glad as if it had been her own mother. She forgot about the class, and put her arm round the happy girl.

'Oh, Gladys!' she said. 'It's marvellous! I *am* glad!'

'Hurrah!' yelled Bobby, as delighted as anyone. 'Good old Gladys!'

'I too am glad,' beamed Mam'zelle, forgetting all about the French exam, for a wonder. 'Such a surprise for you! Now you will be able to smile again!'

Gladys glanced round the room, suddenly remembering where she was. She had forgotten everything for the moment except that she must tell Mirabel, her friend, the great news. She went back to her seat, so happy that she felt she might cry with gladness at any moment.

'And now, we must look at our exam papers again,' said Mam'zelle, in a kindly voice. 'Gladys, you should do a wonderful paper, with such good news to help you!'

Everyone was glad. The term had only two more days to go, and the girls were pleased to think that Gladys had something to look forward to. They were as nice to her as they could be, even Elsie!

The last day came, and packing was begun. Gladys couldn't help feeling a little sad as she saw everyone preparing to go away for the holidays. She would have to stay at school – but, never mind, she would be able to see her mother soon. What a pity she was so far away – it would be difficult to see her more than once.

Just as the second form were in a complete muddle over their packing, Miss Theobald came into the room with a letter in her hand. She had just received it. The girls stood up and listened.

'Oh, Mirabel,' said Miss Theobald in her clear voice, 'I have just received a letter from your mother. She says you can take Gladys home with you for the holidays if I will give my permission, as then she can go to see her mother twice a week quite easily from your home, which is not very far from the hospital.'

Mirabel gave a shriek of delight. Gladys turned as red as a beetroot.

'Miss Theobald! How marvellous! Isn't mother a brick? Can Gladys come with me?'

'Of course,' said the head mistress, smiling at the bewildered, radiant Gladys. 'But she will have to pack very quickly. Hurry up, Gladys, and see if you can be ready by the time the school-coaches arrive!'

Ready! Of course she could be ready! Helped by willing hands Gladys flew here and there, cramming everything in, her heart singing with joy. To go home with Mirabel – see her friend's brother and sister – visit her own mother twice a week! What wonderful luck!

And if I hadn't tackled Mirabel that time, and got her to change her mind and stay on, nothing like this would have happened! thought the girl, packing her jerseys. It just shows you've got to have courage and go straight for things. Oh, it's too good to be true!

But it was true, and Gladys went off in the school-coach with Mirabel beside her, singing heartily with the others as they rolled down to the station. Alison clapped her on the back. 'Happy holidays, Gladys!' she said.

'Same to you,' said Gladys. Alison was changed. Not so silly, thought Gladys. I like her better now. I like lots of people better – but most of all Mirabel!

'Goodbye, everybody!' yelled the twins. 'Merry Christmas and Happy New Year when they come!'

'Goodbye! Don't eat too much Christmas-pudding, Anna!'

'Goodbye, Elsie! Happy hols!'

'Goodbye, Bobby! Think out a few more tricks. I say, *do* you remember Mam'zelle's face when the plate jumped?'

'Goodbye, Hilary. See you next term. Nice to think you'll be our head girl again!'

'Goodbye, everybody! Goodbye!'

The Third Form at St Clare's

written by Pamela Cox

'Girls!' cried Janet. 'We just have to make sure that the play goes ahead somehow!'

There's lots of drama this term! The third form have written a school play and jealous Fern plots to ruin it. Then there is a terrible accident . . .

THERE'S MORE TROUBLE ST CLARE'S!

CLAUDINE at St CLARE'S

Mam'zelle beamed.

'You will like the little Claudine!

For she is French.

She is my niece!'

But Mam'zelle is in for a SHOCK!

Out to break every school rule,

New girl Claudine is no teacher's pet . . .

THERE'S MORE TROUBLE AT St CLARE'S!

EGMONT PRESS: ETHICAL PUBLISHING

Egmont Press is about turning writers into successful authors and children into passionate readers – producing books that enrich and entertain. As a responsible children's publisher, we go even further, considering the world in which our consumers are growing up.

Safety First
Naturally, all of our books meet legal safety requirements. But we go further than this; every book with play value is tested to the highest standards – if it fails, it's back to the drawing-board.

Made Fairly
We are working to ensure that the workers involved in our supply chain – the people that make our books – are treated with fairness and respect.

Responsible Forestry
We are committed to ensuring all our papers come from environmentally and socially responsible forest sources.

For more information, please visit our website at www.egmont.co.uk/ethical

MIX
Paper
FSC FSC® C018306

Egmont is passionate about helping to preserve the world's remaining ancient forests. We only use paper from legal and sustainable forest sources, so we know where every single tree comes from that goes into every paper that makes up every book.

This book is made from paper certified by the Forestry Stewardship Council (FSC®), an organisation dedicated to promoting responsible management of forest resources. For more information on the FSC, please visit **www.fsc.org**. To learn more about Egmont's sustainable paper policy, please visit **www.egmont.co.uk/ethical**.

EGMONT PRESS: ETHICAL PUBLISHING

Egmont Press is about turning writers into successful authors and children into passionate readers – producing books that enrich and entertain. As a responsible children's publisher, we go even further, considering the world in which our consumers are growing up.

Safety First
Naturally, all of our books meet legal safety requirements. But we go further than this; every book with play value is tested to the highest standards – if it fails, it's back to the drawing-board.

Made Fairly
We are working to ensure that the workers involved in our supply chain – the people that make our books – are treated with fairness and respect.

Responsible Forestry
We are committed to ensuring all our papers come from environmentally and socially responsible forest sources.

For more information, please visit our website at www.egmont.co.uk/ethical

MIX
Paper
FSC FSC® C018306

Egmont is passionate about helping to preserve the world's remaining ancient forests. We only use paper from legal and sustainable forest sources, so we know where every single tree comes from that goes into every paper that makes up every book.

This book is made from paper certified by the Forestry Stewardship Council (FSC), an organisation dedicated to promoting responsible management of forest resources. For more information on the FSC, please visit **www.fsc.org**. To learn more about Egmont's sustainable paper policy, please visit **www.egmont.co.uk/ethical**.

ST CLARE'S

Enid Blyton

St Clare's
The Twins at St Clare's
The O'Sullivan Twins
Summer Term at St Clare's
The Second Form at St Clare's
The Third Form at St Clare's (written by Pamela Cox)
Claudine at St Clare's
Fifth Formers of St Clare's
The Sixth Form at St Clare's (written by Pamela Cox)

Malory Towers
First Term at Malory Towers
Second Form at Malory Towers
Third Year at Malory Towers
Upper Fourth at Malory Towers
In the Fifth at Malory Towers
Last Term at Malory Towers

The Mysteries
The Mystery of the Burnt Cottage
The Mystery of the Disappearing Cat
The Mystery of the Secret Room
The Mystery of the Spiteful Letters
The Mystery of the Missing Necklace
The Mystery of the Hidden House
The Mystery of the Pantomime Cat
The Mystery of the Invisible Thief
The Mystery of the Vanished Prince
The Mystery of the Strange Bundle
The Mystery of Holly Lane
The Mystery of Tally-Ho Cottage
The Mystery of the Missing Man
The Mystery of the Strange Messages
The Mystery of Banshee Towers

Enid Blyton®

Summer Term at St Clare's

EGMONT

St Clare's

Enid Blyton

EGMONT

We bring stories to life

First published in Great Britain 1943 by Methuen & Co. Ltd
This edition published 2013
by Egmont UK Limited
The Yellow Building
1 Nicholas Road
London W11 4AN

978 0 6035 6936 4

A CIP catalogue record for this title is available from the British Library
Printed and bound in Great Britain by the CPI Group

56923/1

EGMONT LUCKY COIN

Our story began over a century ago, when seventeen-year-old Egmont Harald Petersen found a coin in the street.

He was on his way to buy a flyswatter, a small hand-operated printing machine that he then set up in his tiny apartment.

The coin brought him such good luck that today Egmont has offices in over 30 countries around the world. And that lucky coin is still kept at the company's head offices in Denmark.

Contents

1.

Going back to school

'Four weeks' holiday!' said Pat O'Sullivan, as she sat up in bed the first morning of the Easter holidays. 'How lovely! Hope it's good weather!'

Her twin yawned and turned over. 'How nice not to have to get up as soon as the school bell goes,' she said, sleepily. 'I'm going to have another snooze.'

'Well, I'm not,' said Pat, hopping out of bed. 'Oh, Isabel – it's a simply perfect day! Do get up and let's go round the garden.'

But Isabel was asleep again. Pat dressed and ran downstairs. She felt happy and excited. The first day of the holidays was always grand. Everything at home looked so new and exciting and welcoming. Even the staid brown hens in the yard seemed to cluck a welcome!

School is lovely – but holidays are grand too, thought Pat. Oh, there's the first daffodil coming out – and look at those scillas – exactly the colour of the April sky!

Both the twins enjoyed the first day of the holidays in their own way. Isabel lazed around, peaceful and happy. Pat rushed here, there and everywhere, seeing everybody and everything. Their mother laughed to see the different ways in which they enjoyed themselves.

'You're as like as two peas to look at,' she said, 'but you often act in quite the opposite way. I hope this lovely weather goes on – you'll be quite nice and brown! Well – make the most of it, my dears, because your four weeks will soon go!'

'Oh, Mother – four weeks is a lovely long time – simply ages!' said Pat.

But although it seemed ages at first, it began to slip by very quickly after the first few days! The twins were astonished to find that a week had gone by – and then ten days – and then a fortnight!

'Cousin Alison is coming to spend the last two weeks with us, isn't she, Mother?' said Pat. 'When is she coming? This week?'

'On Thursday,' said Mrs O'Sullivan. 'By the way, her mother said to me on the telephone yesterday that she is much better for being a term at St Clare's – not nearly so vain and silly.'

'That's quite right,' said Isabel, thinking of the teasing and scolding her feather-headed cousin had had at St Clare's the last term. 'She learnt quite a lot of lessons – well, so did we the first term too. I'm glad you sent us there, Mother. It's a fine school. I'm already beginning to look forward to going back. Summer term ought to be grand!'

'Two more weeks,' said Pat. 'I say – won't it be fun to play tennis again? I wonder if we'll play any matches? Isabel and I were tennis captains at Redroofs, our old school. But I expect St Clare's tennis is a pretty high standard.'

'Let's mark out the court and play a few games,' said Isabel, eagerly. But Mrs O'Sullivan shook her head.

'Not in April,' she said. 'You would spoil the lawn. Ring up Katie Johnston and see if you can fix up a four on her hard court.'

It was all because of poor Isabel's eagerness to have a few practice games at tennis that the rest of the holidays were spoilt! They went over to Katie Johnston's, and played a tennis four there, with another girl, Winnie Ellis. Winnie played a very poor game, and quite spoilt it for the others.

Katie apologized for Winnie when she had the twins alone for a minute. 'Can't think what has happened to her today,' she said. 'She usually plays such a good game. She's sending everything into the net. She says her head aches, so maybe she isn't very well.'

Poor Winnie was certainly not well. She went down with mumps that evening, and her mother rang up Katie's parents at once.

'I'm so very sorry,' she said, 'but Winnie has mumps! I hope Katie has had it. Otherwise she will be in quarantine, I'm afraid.'

'Yes, Katie's had it, thank goodness,' said Mrs Johnston. 'But I don't know about the other two girls who were here playing tennis today – the O'Sullivan twins. I must ring up their mother and tell them.'

The telephone rang that evening as the twins were having supper with their parents. Mrs O'Sullivan went to answer it. She soon came back, looking a little worried.

'What's the matter?' asked Mr O'Sullivan.

'That was Mrs Johnston,' said the twins' mother. 'Pat and Isabel went over to Katie's to play tennis today – and the fourth girl was Winnie Ellis. She has just developed mumps this evening – and the twins haven't had it!'

'Well, Mother, we didn't breathe her breath or anything,' said Pat. 'We shall be all right.'

'I hope you will, dear,' said her mother. 'But the thing is – you'll both be in quarantine now – and the quarantine for mumps is rather long. You won't be able to go back to school at the beginning of the term, I'm afraid.'

The twins stared at her in dismay. 'Oh, Mother! Don't let's miss the beginning of term! It's one of the nicest parts. Can't we possibly go back in time?'

'Well, you certainly can't, of course, if you get the mumps,' said Mother. 'I'll see the doctor and find out exactly how long you will have to be away.'

Alas for the twins! The doctor said firmly that they could not go back to school for just over a week after the beginning of term. Pat and Isabel could have cried with disappointment.

'Well, well – anyone would think you liked school, the way you are looking,' said their father, laughing at their gloomy faces. 'I should have thought you would have been pleased at the chance of an extra week's holiday.'

'Not when everyone else is back at school bagging the best desks and hearing all the holiday news and seeing if there are any new girls,' said Pat. 'The first week is lovely, settling in together. Oh, blow Winnie Ellis! What did she want to go and have mumps for, and spoil things for us?'

'Well, these things do happen,' said Mother. 'Never mind. Try to enjoy your extra week. Keep out in the open air as much as you can, and let's hope you don't develop the mumps, either of you!'

During their quarantine time the twins could not go out to tea, and could have no one in to play with them, so they felt rather dull. They were glad to have each other, especially when the day came for all the girls to return to St Clare's for the summer term.

'I wonder if they'll miss us?' said Pat.

'Of course they will,' said Isabel. 'Our Cousin Alison will tell them what's happened to us. Lucky for Alison she didn't come and stay with us before we were in quarantine, or she'd have been caught like this too! Oh blow, blow, blow! What's the time? They'll all be catching the train now, and gabbling like anything in the carriages.'

'Wonder if there are any new girls?' said Pat. 'Or any new teachers? Oh dear – do you remember the tricks that Janet played on poor old Mam'zelle last term? I nearly died of laughter!'

'We shan't be able to share the tuck-boxes,' said Isabel, gloomily. 'All the cakes and things will be eaten before we get back. Oh, how I wish we were back today. Old Janet will be there – and Hilary – and Doris – and Kathleen – and Lucy and Margery – though *they* may have gone up into the second or third form, I suppose – and Sheila will be back, and Tessie.'

'Let's not think about it,' said Pat. 'Do you feel as if

you are getting the mumps, Isabel? Have you got a headache or a pain in the jaw or neck or anything?'

'Not a thing,' said Isabel. 'I say, wouldn't it be perfectly awful if we got mumps on the very last day of our quarantine and couldn't go back even then!'

'Anyone would think you disliked your home thoroughly!' said Mrs O'Sullivan, coming into the room. 'Well, it's nice to think you look forward to school so much. But do be sensible girls and make the most of this last week. I don't think you will get the mumps, so just be happy and look forward to going back next week.'

They tried to take their mother's advice. It was lovely weather, and they were out in the garden all day long, helping the gardener, or lazing in the hammock. But the time went very slowly, and each night the twins looked anxiously at each other to see if they had any sign of the mumps.

At last the final day of their quarantine came and in the evening the doctor arrived to make quite sure they could go back to school. He smiled cheerfully at them as he examined them, and then made their hearts sink with his next words.

'Well, my dears – I'm afraid – I'm very much afraid – that you'll have to go back to school tomorrow!'

The twins had looked full of dismay at his first words – but as he finished the sentence they beamed, and yelled with delight.

'Hurrah! We can go to school tomorrow. Hurrah! Mother, can we go and pack?'

'It's all done,' said Mrs O'Sullivan, smiling. 'I thought you were quite all right – so I packed today for you. Yes – even your tuck-boxes!'

So the next day up to London went the twins with their mother, and were put into the train for St Clare's. They were happy and excited. They would soon see all their friends again, and be lost in the excitements of school-life. They would sit in class under Mam'zelle's stern eye, they would giggle at Janet's tricks, and they would hear all the latest news. What fun!

The train sped away from the platform. It seemed to take ages to get to the station that served St Clare's. At last it drew up, and out got the two girls, shouting to the porter to get their luggage. Usually the mistresses saw to the luggage and looked after everything, tickets included – but as they were by themselves, the twins had to do all this. They quite enjoyed it.

They got a taxi, had their luggage put in, and set off to the big white building in the distance, whose tall twin towers overlooked the beautiful valley.

'Good old St Clare's,' said Pat, as she saw the building coming nearer and nearer. 'It's nice to see you again. I wonder what all the girls are doing, Isabel?'

They were at tea when the twins arrived. It was strange to arrive alone, and to have the great front door opened to them by Jane, looking very smart indeed.

'Hallo, Jane!' cried the twins. 'Where's everyone?'

'Having tea,' answered Jane. 'You'd better go along in before everything's eaten up!'

The twins ran to the big dining-hall and opened the door. A great babel of sound came to their ears – the girls all talking together happily. No one saw them at first. Then Janet happened to glance up and saw the twins standing at the door, still in their coats and hats.

'Pat! Isabel!' she yelled. 'Look, Hilary, look Kathleen, they're back! Hurrah!'

She jumped up and rushed to greet them. With a look at the astonished Miss Roberts, the mistress who was at the head of the first-form table, Kathleen and Hilary did the same. They dragged the twins to their table, and made room for them. Miss Roberts nodded at them and smiled.

'Glad you're back!' she said. 'You can take off your hats and coats and hang them over your chairs for now. I don't know if these greedy first formers have left much for you to eat, but I've no doubt we can get more from the kitchen if not!'

How good it was to be back among the girls once more! What fun to have questions hurled at them, and to call back answers! How friendly everyone was, clapping them on the back, and smiling with welcoming eyes! The twins felt very happy indeed.

'How are the mumps?'

'So you've turned up at last!'

'Your Cousin Alison told us the news. Bad luck you couldn't come back the first day!'

'Mam'zelle has missed you terribly – haven't you, Mam'zelle?'

'Ah, *ma chère* Pat, the French class is no longer the

same without you and Isabel. There is now no one to shout at and say, "*C'est abominable*!"' said Mam'zelle, in her deep voice.

'It's good to be back!' said Isabel, helping herself to bread and butter and jam. 'I say – we've got our tuck-boxes with us. We must open them tomorrow.'

'We've finished all that was in ours,' said Hilary. 'Never mind – two or three of us have birthdays this term and you can have a double share of birthday cake to make up for missing our tuck-boxes!'

Only four or five girls around the big table said nothing. They were all new girls, and they did not know the twins. They stared at them in silence, thinking that the two must be very popular to get such a welcome. Pat and Isabel took a quick look at the strange girls, but had no time to size them up for they were so busy exchanging news and eating.

Plenty of time to know the new girls afterwards, thought Pat. My, it's good to be back at St Clare's again!

2.

Settling down again

It really was lovely to be back at school again, and to hear the familiar chattering and laughing, to see the piles of books everywhere, and to hear the familiar groans of 'Who's taken my pen?' or 'Gracious, I'll never get all this prep done!'

It was good to see the smiling mistresses, and to catch a glimpse of Winifred James, the dignified head girl. It was fun to have a word with Belinda Towers, the sports captain. The twins greeted her with beaming smiles, for they liked her immensely. She was one of the top formers, but because she arranged all the matches for the whole school, she was much better known to the lower forms than the other big girls.

'Hallo, twins!' she said, stopping to greet them after tea. 'What about tennis this term? I hope you're good. We want to play St Christopher's and Oakdene, and beat them hollow. Have you played any in the hols?'

'Only once,' said Pat. 'We used to be good at our old school, but I don't expect we shall shine much at St Clare's.'

'My word, haven't you changed since you first came two terms ago!' said Janet, with a sly smile. 'The stuck-up twins would at once have said that they were champions at tennis!'

'Shut up, Janet,' said Pat, uncomfortably. She never liked being reminded of the way she and Isabel had behaved the first term they had arrived at St Clare's. They had been called the stuck-up twins then, and had had a very difficult time.

'Don't mind Janet's teasing,' said Lucy Oriell, slipping her arm through Pat's. 'You know her bark is worse than her bite. Pat, I shan't see as much of you this term as I'd like, because I've been moved up into the second form.'

'I thought you would be,' said Pat, sadly. She and Isabel were very fond of Lucy. Lucy's father had had an accident the term before, which meant he could no longer do his usual work, and for a while everyone had thought that the popular, merry-eyed Lucy would have to leave. But there was a chance that she could win a scholarship and stay on at St Clare's, for she was very clever and quick. So she had been moved up and would now work with the scholarship girls.

'Margery's been moved up too,' said Lucy. Margery came up at that moment, a tall, older-looking girl. She gave the twins a slap on the back.

'Hallo!' she said. 'Did Lucy tell you the sad news? I'm in the second form too, and I feel very superior indeed to you tiddlers! And gosh – I'm working hard! Aren't I, Lucy?'

'You are,' said Lucy. Margery was her friend, and the two had been glad to be moved up together.

'Who else has been moved up?' asked Isabel, as they all went to the common-room together.

'Vera Johns, but that's all,' said Janet. 'Otherwise our form is the same – except for the new girls, of course. By the way, your Cousin Alison has palled up with one of them – an American girl, stiff-rich, called Sadie Greene. There she is, over there.'

The twins looked for Sadie. There was no mistaking her. Although she wore the school uniform it was plain that her mother had got the very best material possible and had had it made by the very best dressmaker! It was plain too that her hair was permed, and her nails were polished so highly that each small finger-tip shone like a little mirror.

'Golly!' said Pat, staring. 'What a fashion victim. What's she been sent to St Clare's for?'

'Can't imagine,' said Janet. 'She thinks of nothing but her appearance, and nearly drives poor Mam'zelle mad. She has the most atrocious French accent you ever heard, and her American drawl is worst Hollywood. You should hear her say "Twenty-four!" The best she can manage is "Twenny-fourr-r-r-r-r!" no matter how many times Miss Roberts makes her repeat it. Honestly we've had some fun in English classes, I can tell you. Sadie's not a bad sort though – awfully good tempered and generous really. But she's jolly bad for that silly cousin of yours. They walk together whenever we go out and talk of nothing but clothes and haircuts and film stars!'

'We'll have to take Alison in hand,' said Pat, firmly. 'I

thought she looked a bit more feather-brained than usual when I saw her just now. I say – who's that? What a wild-looking creature!'

'That's our Carlotta,' said Hilary with a grin. 'She's half-Spanish, and has a fiercer temper than Mam'zelle's, and that's saying something! She speaks very badly, and has the most awful ideas – but she's pretty good fun. I can see a first-class row boiling up between her and Mam'zelle some day!'

'Oh, it *is* good to be back,' said Pat, thoroughly enjoying hearing all this exciting news. 'The new girls sound thrilling. I did hope there would be some. But I'm sorry the other three have gone up into the second form – I shall miss Lucy and Margery especially.'

Pat and Isabel had no prep to do that night but they had to unpack and put away their things instead. They left the noisy common-room and went upstairs to their dormitory.

Hilary called after them. 'You're in Number Six, twins. I'm there, and Janet, and Prudence Arnold, a new girl, and Carlotta Brown. And Kathleen and Sheila are there too. You'll see which are your cubicles.'

The twins went up the broad stairway and made their way to the big dormitory. It was divided into eight cubicles, which had white curtains hung round them that could be pulled back or drawn round, just as the girls wished. Pat found their cubicles at once. They were side by side.

'Come on, let's be quick,' said Pat. 'I want to get down and have a talk again. There are still three new girls to hear about. I rather liked one of them – the one with the turned-up nose and crinkly eyes.'

'Yes, I liked her too,' said Isabel. 'She looked a monkey. I noticed she and Janet ragged each other a lot. I bet she's good at tricks too. I say – it looks as if we'll have some fun this term, Pat!'

They unpacked happily, and stowed their things away in the drawers of their chests. They hung up their dresses and coats in the cupboard, and set out the few things they had for their dressing-table. They put out the pictures of their father and mother, and their brushes and mirrors.

'I expect we'd better go and see Matron and Miss Theobald,' said Pat, when they had finished. So down they went and made their way to Matron's room. She was there, sorting out piles of laundry. 'Come in!' she called in her cheerful voice. She looked up and beamed at the twins.

'Two bad eggs back again!' she said. 'Dear, dear – and I've had such a peaceful time without you for a whole week of term. Why couldn't you get the mumps and give me a little longer spell? Well – all I say is – don't you dare to go down with the mumps now, and start an epidemic of it!'

The twins grinned. Everyone liked Matron. She was full of common sense and fun – but woe betide anyone who lost too many hankies, tore their sheets, or didn't darn their stockings at once! Matron descended on them immediately, and many a time the twins had had to go to Matron's room and try in vain to explain away missing articles.

'We're glad to be back,' said Pat. 'We're looking forward to tennis and swimming, Matron.'

'Well, remember that your swimming-costumes have to be brought to me after swimming,' said Matron. 'No screwing them up and stuffing away into drawers with dry things! Now run away, both of you – unless you want a dose out of a nice new bottle of medicine!'

The twins laughed. Matron had the largest bottles of medicine they had ever seen anywhere. There was a big new one on the mantelpiece. Matron picked it up and shook it. 'Try it!' she said.

But the twins fled. Downstairs they went to see Miss Theobald, the wise and kindly head mistress. They knocked at the sitting-room door.

'Come in!' said a voice, and in they went. Miss Theobald was sitting at her desk, writing. She took off her glasses and smiled at the blushing twins. They liked the head mistress very much, but they always felt nervous in front of her.

'Well, twins?' she said. 'I still don't know which is which! Are *you* Patricia?' She looked at Isabel as she said this and Isabel shook her head.

'No, I'm Isabel,' she said, with a laugh. 'I've got a few more freckles on my nose than Pat has. That's about the only way to tell us at present.'

Miss Theobald laughed. 'Well, that's an easy way to tell one from the other when you are both in front of me,' she said, 'but it wouldn't be very helpful when there was only one of you. Now listen, twins – I want you to work hard this term, because Miss Roberts thinks you should go up into the second form next term. So just see what you can do! I should like you to try for top places this term. You both have good brains and should be able to do it.'

The twins felt proud. Of course they would try! What fun it would be to go up into the next form – and how pleased their parents would be.

They went out of the room determined to work hard – and to play tennis hard and swim well. 'Thank goodness we didn't get the mumps,' said Pat, happily, as they went back to the common-room. 'Wouldn't it have been awful to have missed more weeks of the summer term?'

It was supper-time when they reached the common-room and the girls were pouring out to go to the dining-hall, chattering loudly. Janet was arm-in-arm with the new girl, the one with the turned-up nose and crinkly eyes.

'Hallo, Pat, hallo, Isabel,' she said. 'Come and be introduced to the Bad Girl of the Form – Bobby Ellis!'

Bobby grinned, and her eyes became more crinkled than ever. She certainly looked naughty – and there was a sort of don't-care air about her that the twins liked at once.

'Is your name really Bobby?' asked Pat. 'It's a boy's name.'

'I know,' said Bobby. 'But my name is Roberta and the short name for Robert is Bobby, you know – so I'm always called Bobby too. I've heard a lot about you two twins.'

'Good things I hope, not bad,' said Isabel, laughing.

'Wouldn't you like to know!' said Bobby, with a twinkle, and went off with Janet.

It was fun to sit down at supper-time again and hear the familiar chatter going on, fun to take big thick slices of bread and spread it with potted meat or jam. Fun to drink the milky cocoa and yell for the sugar. Everything was so friendly and jolly, and the twins loved it all. Afterwards the girls returned to the common-room and put on the radio or the record player. Some of the girls did their knitting, some read, and some merely lazed.

By the time that bedtime came the twins felt as if they had been back at school for weeks! It seemed quite impossible to think they had only been there a few hours.

They went upstairs yawning. 'What's the work like this term?' asked Pat, poking her head into Janet's cubicle as they undressed.

'Fierce,' said Janet. 'It always is in the summer term, don't you think so? I suppose it seems extra difficult because we all so badly want to be out in the sunshine – but honestly Miss Roberts is driving us like slaves this term. Some of us will have to go up into the second form next term, and I suppose she doesn't want us to be backward in anything. My goodness, the maths we've had the last week! You just wait and see.'

But not even the thought of Miss Roberts being fierce

with maths could make the twins feel unhappy that first night! They cuddled down into their narrow beds and fell asleep at once, looking forward to the next day with enjoyment.

3.

Back in Miss Roberts's class

The twins awoke before the bell went the next morning. They lay whispering to each other whilst the May sunshine shone warmly in at the window. Then the bell went and the eight girls got out of bed, some with a leap, like Carlotta and the twins, some with a groan like Sheila, who always hated turning out of her warm bed, winter or summer.

They met their Cousin Alison coming out of her dormitory arm-in-arm with the American girl, Sadie Greene. They stared at Alison, because she had done her hair in quite a different way.

'Alison! What have you done to your hair?' said Pat. 'It looks awful. Do you think you are a film star or something?'

'Sadie says I look grand like this,' said Alison, setting her little mouth in an obstinate line. 'Sadie says . . .'

'That's all Alison can say nowadays,' remarked Janet. 'She's like a record always set to say, "Sadie says . . . Sadie says . . . Sadie says . . ." '

Everyone laughed. 'It's sure a wunnerful way of fixing the hair,' said Doris, with a very good imitation of Sadie's American accent. Sadie laughed. She was very good tempered.

'I don't know what Miss Roberts will say though,' went on Doris. 'She isn't very keen on fancy hair styles, Alison.'

'Well, but Sadie says . . .' began Alison, in an injured sort of voice – and at once all the girls took up the refrain.

'Sadie says . . . Sadie says . . . Sadie says!' they chanted in a sort of chorus, whilst Doris jumped up on to a nearby chair and beat time for the chanting. Alison's eyes filled with the easy tears she always knew how to shed.

'You can see your cousin can turn on the water tap just as easily as last term,' said Janet, in her clear voice. Alison turned away to hide her face. She knew that the girls had no patience with her tears. Sadie slipped her arm through hers.

'Aw, come on, sugar-baby,' she said. 'You're a cute little thing, and I won't let them tease you!'

'I can't think how your cousin can make friends with that vulgar American girl,' said a soft voice at Pat's side. 'It's good thing you've come. Sadie has a very bad influence on the class.'

Pat turned and saw the girl called Prudence Arnold. She didn't know whether she liked the look of her or not. Prudence was pretty, but her mouth was hard, and her eyes, set too close together, were a pale blue.

The breakfast bell went and saved Pat the bother of answering. She ran down the stairs with the others and whispered to Janet. 'Is that Prudence? She looks awfully goody-goody.'

'Yes, you'd better mind your Ps and Qs with her!' said Janet. 'She's so good she'll burst with it one day –

and as for playing a trick on anyone, well the thought of it would send her into a fit. You should have seen her face one day last week when I flipped a rubber at Hilary in class. It was enough to turn the milk sour. Oh and by the way – according to her she's related to half the lords and ladies in the kingdom. Get her on to the subject – she's funny!'

'No talking now please,' said Miss Roberts as the girls stood for grace to be said. Pat took a quick look at Prudence. The girl was standing with her head bent and her eyes shut, the very picture of goodness.

Now Lucy Oriell is *really* good, thought Pat, glancing at Lucy, and I like her awfully, and did from the first – and yet I don't take to Prudence at all, and *she* sounds good too. Perhaps it is because she hasn't any sense of fun, and Lucy has. I wonder if she's as clever as Lucy at lessons. Well, we shall soon see.

That morning Miss Roberts read out the class marks for the week, and the last new girl, Pamela Boardman, was top with ninety-three marks out of a hundred. Prudence Arnold was only halfway down the list. Sadie, Alison, Carlotta and Doris vied for places at the bottom.

'Pamela, you have done very well for the first week,' said Miss Roberts. 'I can see you set yourself a high standard, and you work steadily in each subject. Considering that you are the youngest in the form – not yet fourteen – this is very good.'

All the girls stared at Pamela, who was sitting upright at her desk, red with pleasure. The twins looked at her curiously. They were nearly fifteen, and it seemed marvellous to them that a thirteen-year-old should be top of their form.

'She's very small even for thirteen,' thought Pat. 'And she's pale now that she's not red any more. She looks as if she worked too hard!'

Pamela was not very attractive looking. She wore big glasses, and her straight hair was tightly plaited down her back. She had a very earnest face, and paid the greatest attention to everything Miss Roberts said.

Miss Roberts had some more to say. She flipped at the marks list with her first finger and then looked firmly at Alison, Sadie, Doris and Carlotta.

'You are all bottom,' she said. 'Well, we know *someone* has to be bottom – but nobody needs to be quite so very low down as all of you are. Sit up, Sadie! Carlotta, there is no need to grin round the class like that. It isn't funny to get so few marks in any and every subject!'

Carlotta stopped grinning round and scowled. Not even her school uniform could make her look ordinary. She glared at Miss Roberts.

Miss Roberts took no notice of the scowl or the glare, but went calmly on. 'Doris, you have been in my form for four terms now, and I'm really tired of seeing you at the bottom still. You will have extra coaching this term, because you really mustn't stay in my form much longer.'

'Yes, Miss Roberts,' murmured poor Doris. The girls glanced at her, trying to cheer her up. Doris was a real dunce and knew it – and yet of all the girls in the school she could be the very funniest, sending the class into squeals of laughter by her imitations of mistresses and other girls. Everyone liked her, even the mistresses who laboured so hard trying to teach her.

'Now you, Alison,' began Miss Roberts again, looking at the twins' cousin with the intention of telling her that she also could do better, 'now you, Alison . . .' Then she stopped and looked at the girl carefully.

'Alison,' she said, 'there is something very strange about you this morning. It seems to me that you have forgotten to do your hair.'

'Oh no, Miss Roberts,' began Alison, eagerly. 'Sadie showed me a new way. She said I had the kind of face that . . .'

'Alison, you don't really mean to tell me that your hair is done like that on *pur*pose!' said Miss Roberts, in pretended horror. Alison subsided at once, and the girls giggled. Alison really did look a little silly with her hair done in a fancy way. Miss Roberts never could stand what she called 'frippery' in dress or hair style.

'Much as I hate you to lose any part of my lesson, Alison,' she said, 'I must ask you to go and do something to your hair that will make you look a little less amazing.'

'I thought she'd be sent out to do her hair properly.' whispered Janet to Pat. Miss Roberts's sharp ears caught the whisper.

'No talking,' she said. 'We'll now get on with the lesson. Open your maths books at page sixteen. Pat and Isabel, bring your books up to my desk, please, and I will try and explain to you what the class did last week when you were away. The rest of you get on with what you began yesterday.'

In a little while all was silence as the class applied itself to its work. Alison slipped back into the room quietly, her cheeks flaming. Her hair was now taken down and brushed back properly, and she looked what she was, a fourteen-year-old schoolgirl. Sadie sent her a look of sympathy.

Prudence and Pamela bent their heads almost to their desks, so concentrated were they on their task. They sat next to each other. Prudence took a quick look at Pamela's book to see if her own sums showed the same answers. Janet nudged Hilary.

'Our pious little Prudence isn't above having a peep at Pam's work!' she whispered, opening her desk to hide the fact that she was speaking. Hilary nodded. She was about to open her own desk and make a remark, but Miss Roberts's eye caught hers and she decided not to. Miss Roberts didn't seem to be standing any nonsense that term! She meant her class to do well, and to make a good showing when most of it went up into Miss Jenks's form the next term!

Pat and Isabel stood beside Miss Roberts struggling to understand what she was explaining. Their five weeks' holiday had made them rusty, and it was difficult to get back the habit of concentration again. But at last they understood and went back to their places to work.

Miss Roberts got up to go round the class.

A suppressed giggle made her look round. Bobby Ellis had balanced a sheet of blotting-paper on the bent head of the unsuspecting Prudence. It sat there, moving slightly whenever Prudence turned her head a little to refer to her textbook. Then it floated gently to the ground, much to Prudence's surprise.

'I imagine that, as you find time to play about with blotting-paper, Roberta, you have also found time to do every one of the sums set,' said Miss Roberts in a cold sort of voice. Bobby said nothing. She hadn't done even half the sums.

'Well, if you haven't done all the sums, and got them right too, by the time I get round to you, you will stay in at break and do them then,' said Miss Roberts. 'Prudence, pick up the blotting-paper and put it on my desk.'

'Miss Roberts, I didn't know anything about what Bobby was doing,' said Prudence, anxiously. 'I was quite lost in my work. I . . .'

'Quite so, Prudence,' said Miss Roberts. 'Now pick up the blotting-paper please and get lost again.'

Poor Bobby lost her time at break. There was no doubt about it – Miss Roberts was on the war-path that term!

'What did I tell you?' said Janet, when the morning ended at last, and the girls trooped out to wash for lunch. 'What a morning! Alison sent out to do her hair again – most of us scolded – Bobby kept in for break – Janet ticked off for talking twice – Doris pulled up for dreaming in geography – Carlotta sent out of the room for answering back – and double the amount of prep we usually have! Golly, this *is* going to be a term!'

4.

The five new girls

In a day or two the twins had settled down so well again that no one even remembered they had been late in coming back. They felt that it was a little unfair that the teachers so soon forgot this, for once or twice they were scolded for not knowing things that the rest of the class had been taught during the first week.

But the twins had good brains and soon caught up with the others. They had always loved the summer term at their old school, and they found that it was just as nice at St Clare's. There was no lacrosse that term, of course, but instead there were tennis and swimming – and they were grand!

There were eight courts at St Clare's, and Belinda Towers, who had charge of them, drew up a careful timetable so that every girl could have her turn at tennis practice. Miss Wilton, the sports mistress, was an excellent coach, and soon picked out the girls who would do well.

Margery Fenworthy, one of the old first formers who had gone up into the second form, was brilliant at tennis, as she was at all sports. Miss Wilton was delighted with her.

'She's so strong,' she told Belinda, 'and she has a lovely

style. Watch her serve, Belinda. See how she throws the ball up high, and gives it just the right smack when it comes down – and skims it over the top of the net. You know, I shouldn't be surprised if she wins the school championship this term, and beats all you top formers!'

'I don't mind if she does,' said Belinda, 'so long as she wins the matches against the other schools we play! Oakdene and St Christopher's are both running singles championships, you know, this term. Perhaps we can put Margery in for our player. She's better than I am.'

'Well, there's not much to choose between you,' said the sports mistress, 'except that Margery is immensely strong.'

The twins were quite good at tennis, and Miss Wilton was pleased with their style. 'Practise well and you may be in the tennis team for the first form,' she said. 'We shall be playing plenty of matches this term, so you'll have some fun if you get into the team.'

The twins flushed with pleasure, and made up their minds to practise every minute they could. They loved their school and were very anxious to do everything they could to bring it fame among other schools.

But Miss Wilton was not so pleased with their cousin Alison. Alison did not like games. 'They make me get hot and messy,' she always complained. 'I hate running about, especially in the hot weather. My hair gets all wet at the back of my neck.'

'Alison, you make me feel sick,' said Bobby Ellis, who always said straight out what she was thinking. She was a bit like Janet that way, without Janet's hot temper. 'You're nothing but a little peacock, always hoping someone's going to admire you!'

'Alison got much better last term,' said Pat, trying to stick up for her cousin. 'She really did try to get on with lacrosse.'

'Well, Sadie says . . .' began Alison, quite forgetting what the girls thought about this refrain of hers. At once the girls nearby took up the chorus.

'Sadie says . . . Sadie says . . . Sadie says . . . What does Sadie say?' they chanted.

Alison turned away in a temper. She was usually quite a good-tempered girl, but she hated being teased, and she certainly was getting a lot of it that term. She flew off to find her precious Sadie. Sadie didn't care about games either. It was difficult to find out what she did care about, with the exception of clothes, hair, nails, complexion – and the cinema!

Sadie frankly didn't try at tennis or swimming. She hated the water. So did Alison. Alison couldn't bear going in. 'It's so icy cold!' she complained, as she stood at the top of the steps leading down into the deliciously green water. She would stand there, shivering, until one of the girls gave her an exasperated push and sent her in with a gasp and a flop. Then she would come up, spluttering in fury, and glare round for the girl who had pushed her in. But Bobby or Janet or whoever it was would be well away at the top of the swimming-pool!

Only one of the new girls really took to tennis and

swimming. That was Bobby Ellis. She was a good sport, and so daring that she even pushed Miss Wilton unexpectedly into the pool, a thing that no other girl would have dared to do. Nobody ever knew what Don't-Care-Bobby would do next. She really seemed to care for nothing and nobody, and went her own sweet way regardless of rules or punishments. She was good at tennis and a fast swimmer – but not one of the other new girls was any good at sports.

Prudence was no sport. She thought games were a waste of time, but only because she was no good at them. She fancied herself clever at conversation, and was always trying to get the other girls to argue about politics.

'Oh, shut up!' Janet would say. 'Keep that sort of thing for the debating hour, for goodness' sake! If you took a bit more interest in the jolly things of life, and *did* something instead of always talking and prating and airing your wonderful opinions, you'd get on better. I consider you're a silly little empty-head, for all your talk. Golly, you can't even play a simple game of cards!'

'My father says cards lead to gambling,' said Prudence. Her father was a clergyman, and the girl had been brought up very strictly. 'My aunt, who married Sir Humphrey Bartlett . . .'

There was a groan at this. The girls were getting heartily sick of Prudence's grand relations, who were brought into the conversation whenever possible.

'Let me see,' said Bobby, pretending to be interested, 'was that the aunt who always had blue silk sheets on the beds? Or was it the one who threw a fit because the home help dared to give her a hot-water bottle with a cover that didn't match the eiderdown? Or was it the one who kept table napkins embroidered with every letter in the alphabet so that no matter what the names of her guests were, there was always a napkin with the right initial?'

Prudence flushed. She had once boasted about an aunt who had blue silk sheets for her beds, but she hadn't said anything about hot-water bottles or table napkins. Those were clever make-ups on Bobby's part. She said nothing.

'Well, go on, tell us!' said Bobby. 'We're all eager to hear the latest Society News!'

But Prudence had sense enough not to be drawn into an argument with Bobby. Clever as she was at debating things, she was no match for the quick-witted Bobby, who got all the laughs whenever she argued with any one.

Pamela Boardman was very earnest over her tennis and swimming, but she was no good at them at all. 'You see, I always had a governess before I came here,' she explained to the girls, 'and my governess didn't play games. Anyway, I was never interested in them. I loved working at lessons.'

'All work and no play makes Jack a dull boy,' said Pat. 'You're much too clever for thirteen! I think it would do you good to be bottom of the form for once, and really enjoy yourself out in the open air! You're always stewing over a book.'

Carlotta had never played tennis before, and she was quite wild at it. Miss Wilton said that she really thought Carlotta imagined the tennis net to be about two miles high, the way she hit the ball into the air, sky-high!

'Carlotta, when I was small, I played a game with my brothers called "Chimney-pot tennis",' she said solemnly to the fiery little girl. 'We sent the ball up to the roof and tried to get it down a chimney. Well, it seems to me you would be very good indeed at that game! But as you are not playing with chimney-pots, I really would be very glad if you could have a look at the net over there, and see if you can get the ball anywhere near it when you serve. Now – throw it into the air – and hit it straight towards the net!'

There would be a shriek of laughter from the watching girls as Carlotta hit wildly at the ball and, as likely as not, sent it over the wall into the kitchen-garden!

Her swimming was much the same, though she liked the water and was quite at home in it. But, as Belinda complained, she swam just like a dog, splashing out with legs and arms just anyhow.

'You swim like my dog Binks,' said Kathleen. 'He sort of scrabbles along in the water, and so do you, Carlotta!'

Sadie couldn't swim at all, and though she didn't mind the cold, as Alison did, she hated having to put her carefully done hair under a tight swimming-hat, and complained that the water ruined her complexion. So, with the exception of Bobby Ellis, the first formers voted the new girls a complete failure at sports.

'It's a pity our form have lost Margery Fenworthy,' said Isabel, as she watched the straight-limbed girl swimming the whole length of the pool under water. 'She would win the championship for the school, and wouldn't we first formers be proud!'

May was a glorious month that year, warm and sunny. Swimming was in full swing, and daily tennis made the grass become worn at the service lines. A good many of the girls had school gardens, and these patches were soon full of growing seedlings of all kinds. Gardening was the one outdoor thing that Pamela really seemed to like. She took a big patch and sowed many packets of seeds there. She bought little plants too, double-daisies, velvet pansies and pretty polyanthus to make the borders of her patch bright.

There were nature-walks over the hills and through the woods. Sadie and Carlotta knew nothing about nature, it seemed, and made some curious mistakes. When Pat exclaimed at the amount of frogs in the pond, Sadie looked at them with interest.

'I got some early frog-spawn in the spring,' said Pat, 'and I got heaps of tadpoles from it. Most of them have turned into tiny little frogs now. They're sweet.'

'Do tadpoles turn into frogs, then?' said Sadie in the greatest surprise. The girls laughed at her. They couldn't imagine how it was that Sadie knew so little about the most ordinary things.

'Didn't you ever go to school before?' said Pat.

'Well, I lived mostly in hotels in America with my mother,' said Sadie. 'I had a sort of governess but she didn't know much! You see, most of the time my mother was fighting a law case.'

'What's that?' asked Isabel.

'Well, when my father died he left a funny sort of will,' said Sadie. 'And it seemed as if all his money would go to his sisters. So Mother had to go to law about it, and it took years to settle. She won in the end – and I'm to have the money when I'm twenty-one. It's a proper fortune.'

'So you're an heiress?' said Prudence, admiringly. 'No wonder you have such nice clothes and things.'

It was the first time that Prudence had heard of Sadie's fortune. After that everyone noticed that the girl hung around Sadie continually.

'See dear Prudence sucking up to the rich heiress?' said Janet, scornfully. 'She's made friends with Pamela so that she can pick her brains – and now she's making friends with Sadie because one day she'll be rich. Nasty little humbug!'

'That's a bit unkind,' said Pat. 'After all, Sadie's kind and generous, and we all like to be friends with her because of those things, not because she's well off. And Pam's a nice little thing, though she's such a swot. I'm not friends with her because I want to pick her brains but because there's something rather nice about her, in spite of her head always being inside a book.'

'Well, stick up for Prudence if you like,' said Janet. 'I think she's a humbug. I can't stick her goody-goody ways. Can you, Bobby?'

Bobby agreed. There was no humbug about Bobby. You always knew where you were with her. She was warm, friendly and sincere for all her don't-care attitude to everyone and everything.

'We're a mixed bunch this term,' said Pat to Isabel, as she gazed round her form one morning. 'A very mixed bunch. There'll be a few busts-up before we all shake down together!'

5.

Bobby plays a trick

After two or three weeks the first form began to work quite well. The girls saw that Miss Roberts meant to have her way about the work, and they soon found that it was quicker to prepare work thoroughly, than to have it all to do again after the lesson because it was carelessly prepared beforehand.

Janet badly wanted to go up with the others the next term, so she worked hard. But Bobby Ellis, who had become her firm friend, could not work hard for more than a few days at a time. After that she became bored, and then the class had some fun. For when Bobby was bored with work, she found relief in tricks and jokes. Janet had always been marvellous at these, but Bobby was ten times more ingenious!

Bobby always found the maths lesson far too long. She hated maths and could never see the use of them. 'I wish I could make the lessons ten minutes shorter,' she sighed, as she dressed one morning. 'Miss Roberts said she was going to give us an oral test at the end of maths today, and I know I shall be bottom. I can't even think what seven times eight are!'

'Well, can't you think of some way of making the

lesson short?' said Janet. 'I don't like oral maths tests any more than you do. If only we could put the clock on when Miss Roberts isn't looking!'

'She's got eyes at the back of her head,' said Bobby. 'No good doing it when she's there. If only she'd go out of the room for a minute. But she never does.'

'Can't you make her?' said Pat. 'You're always full of ideas. Go on – I dare you to make her!'

Bobby always took on any 'dare'. She looked at Pat, and grinned. 'Right!' she said. 'I'll bet you a stick of toffee to a peppermint drop that Miss Roberts disappears from our classroom during the maths lesson.'

All the girls began to feel excited. Bobby was such fun. They knew she would do something unusual!

She did. She sat lost in thought at breakfast-time, and forgot to have any marmalade with her toast. Between breakfast and the first class, which was geography, Bobby disappeared.

She went to the common-room, which was empty, for the girls were now tidying their cubicles and making their beds. She got down her writing-pad and pen, and in neat, mature writing, penned two lines.

'Kindly attend at the mistresses' common-room in the lesson after break.'

She added a squiggle at the bottom that looked like anybody's initials, popped the note into an envelope and printed Miss Roberts's name on it. Then she placed the note inside her writing-pad in readiness for when she meant to use it.

'Thought of a plan yet?' asked Janet, when Bobby rejoined the girls upstairs. 'I've made your bed for you. What have you been doing?'

'Wait and see,' said Bobby, with a grin.

Maths was the first lesson after break. The girls waited impatiently for it, wondering what was going to happen. At break they begged Bobby to tell them what she was going to do, but she wouldn't.

She slipped off to the common-room whilst the others were out in the garden. She took the note she had written, and went into Miss Jenks's classroom, next to Miss Roberts. She laid the note on Miss Jenks's desk, and then, making sure that no one had seen her, she slipped out again and went into the garden.

'Miss Jenks will see the note and think it has been left in the wrong classroom by mistake.' Bobby grinned to herself. 'She'll send one of her girls in with it to Miss Roberts – and then maybe we'll see our Miss Roberts trotting off to the mistresses' common-room. And if I don't move the hands of the clock on whilst she's gone, my name isn't Roberta Henrietta Ellis!'

All the girls trooped back when the school bell rang. They went to their classroom and waited for the mistresses to come and take the next lesson. Hilary stood at the door watching for Miss Roberts.

'Sssst! Here she is!' warned Hilary. The girls stood up at once, and became silent. Miss Roberts came in and went to her desk.

'Sit,' she said, and the girls sat down with clatters

and scrapes of their chairs.

'Now today,' said Miss Roberts, briskly, 'we will try to do a *little* better than yesterday, when Pamela was the only one who got even *one* sum right. At the end of the lesson there will be a ten minutes' oral test – and I warn you, no one is to get less than half-marks, or there will be trouble. Alison, please sit up. I don't like to see you draped over your desk like that. You are here to do maths not to act like the Sleeping Beauty and go to sleep for a hundred years!'

'Oh, Miss Roberts, *must* we have an oral test on a hot day like this?' said Alison, whose brains worked slowly in the hot weather. 'This hot sun does make me feel so sleepy at the end of the morning.'

'Well, I shall wake you up thoroughly if you seem sleepy in your oral test,' said Miss Roberts, grimly. 'Now – page twenty-seven, please. Bobby, why do you keep looking at the door?'

Bobby had had no idea that her eyes were continually on the door, waiting for it to open and a second former to appear. She jumped.

'Er – was I looking at the door?' she said, at a loss what to say, for once.

'You were,' said Miss Roberts. 'Now for a change, look at your book. Begin work, everyone!'

Bobby looked at page twenty-seven, but she didn't see the sums there. She was wondering if Miss Jenks had seen the note. What a pity if she hadn't! The whole joke would be spoilt.

But Miss Jenks had. She had not noticed it at first,

because she had put her books down on it. Then she had written something on the blackboard for the class to do, and had gone round the form to make sure they all understood what she had written. It was not until she sent Tessie to her desk to fetch a book that the note was discovered.

Tessie lifted up the books – and the note was there underneath. Tessie glanced at it and saw that Miss Roberts's name was printed on it.

'There's a note here on your desk for Miss Roberts, Miss Jenks,' she said. 'Do you suppose it was left here by mistake?'

'Bring it to me,' said Miss Jenks. Tessie took it to her. 'Yes – someone thought this was the first form, I suppose,' said Miss Jenks. 'Take it straight in to Miss Roberts, Tessie – and come straight back.'

Tessie took the note and left the room. She knocked at the door of Miss Roberts's classroom. All was complete silence inside.

Bobby's heart jumped when she heard the knock. She looked up eagerly. 'Come in!' said Miss Roberts, impatiently. She always hated interruptions to her classwork. Tessie opened the door and came in.

'Excuse me, Miss Roberts,' she said, politely, 'but Miss Jenks told me to come and give you this.'

This was better than Bobby had hoped! Now it sounded as if Miss Jenks herself had sent the note. Miss Roberts wouldn't suspect a thing. Miss Roberts took the note, nodded to Tessie, and opened the envelope.

She read what was inside and frowned. It was a nuisance to have to leave her class in the middle of a difficult maths lesson. Well, she would slip along straightaway whilst the form was hard at work, and see why she was wanted.

She put the note back on her desk and stood up. 'Go on with your work, please,' she said. 'I shall be away a minute or two. No talking, of course. Finish what you are doing, and work hard.'

All the girls looked up, astonished, for they guessed that Bobby somehow had been the cause of Miss Roberts's disappearance – but how could she have made Miss Jenks send in a note to get her away? They gaped round at Bobby, who grinned back in delight.

'How did you do it, Bobby?' said Janet in a whisper, as soon as the door was shut.

'Bobby! You didn't write that note, did you?' said Pat, amazed. Bobby nodded and leapt to her feet. She ran quietly to the mantelpiece and opened the glass covering of the big schoolroom clock. In a moment she had put the hands on more than ten minutes. She shut the glass with a click and returned to her place.

'You really are a monkey!' said Hilary, thrilled. Even Pamela was amused. Only Prudence looked disapproving.

'It seems rather a deceitful thing to do,' she murmured. Sadie gave her a push.

'Aw, don't be a ninny!' she said, in her American drawl. 'Can't you ever see a joke?'

'I wonder what poor Miss Roberts is doing,' said Janet.

'What did you say in the note, Bobby? How clever of you to leave it in the wrong classroom so that Tessie had to bring it in!'

'Miss Roberts is probably waiting all alone in the mistresses' common-room,' said Bobby, with her wide grin. 'I don't know how long she'll wait!'

Miss Roberts was feeling very puzzled. She had hurried to the common-room belonging to the Junior mistresses, and had found no one there. Thinking the others would come in a minute or two, she went to the window and waited. But still nobody came.

Miss Roberts tapped her foot impatiently on the floor. She hated leaving her class at any time. There were too many mischief-makers in it that term! They couldn't safely be left for two minutes. What they would be up to now she couldn't think.

'I'll go and see if Miss Jenks knows what it's all about,' she thought. So she went to the second form, and was soon questioning a surprised Miss Jenks about the supposed meeting.

'I don't know anything about it,' said Miss Jenks. 'I just sent the note in by Tessie because it was left on my desk for you by mistake. How funny, Miss Roberts!'

Miss Roberts, very much puzzled, went back to her class. She took a quick look round, but every head was bent and it seemed as if every girl was hard at work.

Too good to be true! thought Miss Roberts disbelievingly. Half the little monkeys have been playing about, and the other half talking. It's impossible to realize that when they are top formers they will all be thoroughly trustworthy, more dignified than the mistresses even, and so responsible that we could probably trust the whole running of the school to them. Who would have thought that Winifred James, our worthy head girl, was sent out of my class three times in one morning for playing up with her best friend?

Miss Roberts was, for once, too engrossed in her thoughts to look at the clock. She began to go round the class to see what work had been done. When she came to the last girl she stood up and gave an order.

'Time for the oral test. Shut your books please.'

Then she took a glance at the clock, and stared in surprise. Why, it was the end of the lesson already! How quickly the time had gone – but of course she had had to waste some of it waiting about for nothing in the common-room.

'Good gracious, look at the time!' she said. 'We can't have the oral test after all. Put away your books quickly please. Mam'zelle will be here in a moment.'

With grins of delight, and secret nudges, the girls put away their books quickly. Miss Roberts went out of the room to the fourth form, where she was due to give a maths lesson also. They were filled with surprise to see her arrive so early!

'Oh, Bobby, good for you! You've let us off that awful oral test!' said Alison. 'I do think you're a marvel!'

'Yes, you really are!' said Pat. 'It acted like clock-work. Wonderful!'

'Oh, it was nothing,' said Bobby, modestly, but secretly very thrilled at the admiration she was getting. Other girls loved to be praised for their work or their games – but Bobby revelled in admiration for her jokes and tricks!

Only Prudence again disapproved. 'Somehow it doesn't seem quite honest,' she said.

'Well, go and sneak about it to Miss Roberts then,' said Bobby at once. 'Little Miss Goody-Goody, aren't you? Where's your sense of fun?'

'What Prudence wants is a few jokes played on her,' said Janet. 'She's just too good to be true. Let's see if your wings are growing yet, Prudence!'

She pretended to feel down Prudence's thin back and the girl squirmed away angrily, for Janet's fingers were sharp. 'The budding angel,' said Janet. 'Tell me when you feel your wings sprouting, won't you?'

Miss Roberts was very much puzzled about the note and the fact that she was unexpectedly early for her next class. But this time she did not suspect a trick of any sort. She simply thought that some mistake had been made and dismissed it from her mind. She would never have thought of it again if Bobby and Janet, made bold by the success of the first trick, hadn't tried another of the same kind – far too soon!

6.

Janet in trouble

The girls were allowed to go down to the town together, either out to tea in a tea-shop, to the shops or to the cinema. No girl was allowed to go alone unless she was a top former. The younger ones loved to slip off together. They went to buy sweets, records, or cakes, and if there was anything good on at the cinema, it was fun to go.

That week there was a fine film being shown about Clive of India, and as the first form were then doing the same period with Miss Lewis in the history lesson, they all made up their minds to see it.

Miss Lewis encouraged them. 'You should certainly go,' she said. 'It will make your history lesson come alive for you. I will give a special prize to the best criticism written of the film by any first or second former.'

It was more difficult for the first form to go that week than for the second form. The first form had every afternoon full, and four of its evenings were taken up by meetings of some sort or other.

'I shan't be able to go until Friday,' sighed Janet. 'I've got to clean out the art cupboard for Miss Walker tonight, when most of you others are going. Oh, why did I offer to do it? The kindness of my heart runs away with me!'

'Well, it's not likely to run very far,' said Bobby. 'So cheer up!'

Janet threw a rubber at Bobby. They were in the common-room with the others, and there was a terrific noise going on. The radio was on at one end of the room, someone had set the record player going at the other, and Sheila and Kathleen were arguing at the tops of their voices about something.

'NEED we have both the radio AND the record player on together when nobody is listening to either?' pleaded Pamela's voice. 'I'm trying so hard to read and remember what I'm reading, and I simply can't.'

'Well, Pam, you shouldn't be working now,' said Pat, looking up from her knitting. 'You should slack off, like the rest of us. Why, you were saying history dates in your sleep last night, Sadie said!'

'Bobby, book me a seat for Friday night,' said Janet, looking everywhere for her rubber. 'I shall have an awful rush, I know, unless I can get Miss Roberts to let me off prep that night.'

'She let *me* off,' said Hilary. 'I went last night, and Miss Roberts was an awful brick – let me off half an hour early so that I could see the film.'

'Well, I'll ask her if she'll be a sport and let me off too,' said Janet. 'Oh blow, where *is* my rubber? Why did I throw it at Bobby? What a waste of a rubber!'

The next day was Thursday, and that evening the rest of the first form went to the cinema, except Janet, who kept her promise and turned out the untidy art cupboard for Miss Walker.

'I'll ask Miss Roberts to let me off early tomorrow,' thought Janet, as she threw all sorts of peculiar things out of the cupboard on to the floor. 'Golly, what a collection of things the art classes get! I don't believe this cupboard has been turned out for years!'

The next day Janet was unlucky. She had to do the flowers for the classroom that week, and Miss Roberts discovered that there was very little water in the vases. She looked disapprovingly at Janet.

'No wonder our flowers look sorry for themselves this week, Janet,' she said, poking a finger into the nearest vase. 'This bowl is almost empty. I do think you should attend to your responsibilities better, even the little ones.'

Janet flushed. Usually she was good at remembering small things as well as big, but the flowers had just slipped her memory that day. She muttered an apology and went to get a jug of water.

She came into the classroom with it, and was just about to pour water into a vase on the windowsill when the school cat jumped in at the window.

Janet was startled. She jumped violently and jerked the jug of water. A stream flew into the air – and landed very neatly on the back of Prudence's head! It dripped down her neck at once and the girl gave a loud squeal. Miss Roberts looked up, annoyed.

'What's the matter, Prudence? Janet, what have you done?'

'Oh, Miss Roberts! Janet has soaked me!' complained Prudence. 'She deliberately poured the water down my neck!'

'I didn't!' cried Janet. 'The cat sprang in through the window and made me jump, that's all.'

Miss Roberts eyed Janet coldly. She had seen too much of Janet's mischief to believe that it was entirely an accident.

'Prudence, go and dry yourself in the cloakroom,' she said. 'Janet, Prudence was engaged in writing out that list of geography facts for future reference. As she will not be able to finish it now, I would be glad if you would take her book and write the facts out for her during prep this evening.'

Janet stared in dismay, remembering that she had meant to ask for early leave. 'Miss Roberts, it really and truly was an accident,' she said. 'I'll write out what Prudence was doing, but may I do it in break, not in prep?'

'You will do it in prep,' said Miss Roberts. 'Now will you kindly finish playing about with that water and do a little work?'

Janet pursed up her lips and took the water out of the room. It looked as if she wouldn't be able to see the film now. As she went to the cloakroom to put away the jug, she met Prudence, who had dried herself quickly, for she was not really very wet.

'Prudence! You know jolly well it was a complete accident,' said Janet, stopping her. 'I want to leave prep early tonight, to see *Clive of India*. I shan't be able to unless you're decent and go and tell Miss Roberts you know it was an accident and ask her to let me off.'

'I shan't do anything of the sort,' said Prudence. 'You and Bobby are always playing silly tricks. I'm not going to get you out of trouble!'

She marched back to the classroom. Janet stared after her, angry and hurt. She stuck the jug back into the cupboard and slammed the door shut. Janet had a hot temper, and would willingly have poured a dozen jugs of icy-cold water all over Prudence at that moment!

When break came she told Bobby what had happened, and Bobby snorted in disgust. 'Prudence makes out she's so goody-goody,' she said, 'and yet she won't do a little thing like that. Now – let's see – is there any way of getting you off early to go to the film, Janet, in spite of everything?'

'No,' said Janet, dolefully. 'Miss Roberts is taking the first and second form together for prep tonight. If Miss Jenks was taking it I'd take a chance and slip out, hoping she wouldn't notice. But Miss Roberts will have her eye on me tonight.'

'I wonder – I just wonder – if I can't get Miss Roberts out of the room again,' said Bobby, her eyes beginning to gleam.

'Don't be an ass, Bobby,' said Janet, 'she can't be taken in twice that way – so soon after, too.'

'Well – what about doing it a bit differently?' said Bobby. 'Getting *you* called out, for instance?'

'Oooh,' said Janet, and her eyes danced. 'That *is* an idea! Yes – we might work it that way. But what about that beastly stuff I've got to write out for Prudence?'

'I'll do that for you,' said Bobby. 'I can make my writing like yours, in case Miss Roberts wants to see it.'

'All right,' said Janet. 'Well, now – how are we going to work it?'

'I'll ask Miss Roberts if I can go and fetch a book from the library,' said Bobby. 'And when I come back I'll say, "Please, Miss Roberts, Mam'zelle says can Janet go to her for some extra coaching?" And I bet Miss Roberts will let you go like a lamb – and you can slip off in time to see the whole of the picture.'

'It's a bit dangerous,' said Janet, 'but it's worth a try. Hope I shan't be caught.'

Don't-Care-Bobby grinned. 'Nothing venture, nothing have!' she said. 'Well, I'll do my best for you.'

So when the first and second form were all sitting quietly doing their prep that evening, Bobby put up her hand. 'Please, Miss Roberts, may I just slip along and get a book from the library?'

'Be quick, then,' said Miss Roberts, who was busy correcting books, and hardly looked up. Bobby grinned at Janet and slipped out of the room. She arrived back with a book under her arm and went to Miss Roberts's desk.

'Please, Miss Roberts, may Janet go to Mam'zelle now for a little extra coaching?' she said. Janet went red with excitement.

'Well,' said Miss Roberts, rather astonished, 'Mam'zelle didn't say anything to me about it when I saw her in the common-room. I suppose she forgot. Yes, Janet – you had better go – and you can write out those geography facts later on this evening, when you are in the first form common-room.'

'Thank you, Miss Roberts,' murmured Janet and scuttled out of the room like a rabbit. She rushed to the cloakroom, got her hat, flew out of the garden-door, went to the bicycle shed and was soon cycling down to the town as fast as she could go! How she hoped she would not meet any mistress or top former who would see that she was alone!

She slipped into the cinema unseen and was soon lost in the film, whilst the first form went on silently doing their prep for the next day. Only Prudence was suspicious, for she had seen the looks that passed between Janet and Bobby.

She was even more suspicious when she could not see Janet in the common-room that night, after prep. 'Janet is having a very long lesson with Mam'zelle,' she said to Bobby.

'Really?' said Bobby. 'How nice for them both!'

Bobby had copied out the geography for Prudence, trying to make her writing as like Janet's as possible. She laid the book down on Prudence's desk when the girl was out of the common-room for a minute. Prudence found it there when she came back. At first she thought Janet had written out the pages and she looked round for her. But Janet was still not there. How strange!

Prudence looked closely at her book. She saw that the writing was not really Janet's, and she stared at Bobby, who was lying in a chair, unconcernedly reading, her feet swung over the arm.

'This isn't Janet's writing,' said Prudence to Bobby. Bobby took no notice but went on reading. 'BOBBY! I said this isn't Janet's writing,' said Prudence, annoyed.

'Did you really say so?' said Bobby. 'Well, say it again if you like. I don't know if anyone is interested. I'm not.'

'I believe you and Janet made up a plot between you,' said Prudence, suddenly. 'I don't believe Mam'zelle wanted Janet at all – and I believe *you* wrote out these pages.'

'Shut up, I'm reading,' said Bobby. Prudence felt angry and spiteful. So Janet had managed to slip off to the cinema after all! Well, she would see that Miss Roberts knew it, anyway!

So the next morning, when Miss Roberts asked to see her geography book, to make sure that Janet had written out what she had been told, Prudence gave the game away. She went up to Miss Roberts's desk with her book and held it out. Miss Roberts gave a quick glance at it and nodded.

'All right!' she said, not noticing anything wrong with the writing.

'Bobby has written it out very nicely, hasn't she?' said Prudence, in a low, soft voice. Miss Roberts glanced sharply at the book and then at Prudence. She knew at once what the girl meant to tell her.

'You can go to your place,' she said to the girl, for she disliked sneaking. Prudence went, pleased that Miss Roberts had guessed what she meant.

Miss Roberts spoke to Mam'zelle when next she saw her. 'Did you by any chance give Janet Robins any extra coaching last night?' she asked. Mam'zelle lifted her eyebrows in astonishment.

'I was at the cinema,' she said. 'And so was Janet. I saw her! Why do you ask me such a question? I do not give coaching in the evenings.'

'Thank you,' said Miss Roberts, and beckoned to a passing girl.

'Go and find Janet Robins and ask her to come to me,' she said, grimly. The girl sped off and found Janet on the tennis-court.

'Wow!' said Janet when she got the message. 'Now I'm for it. The cat's out of the bag – but who let her out? Bobby, say goodbye to me for ever – I've got to face Miss Roberts in a rage – and I shan't come out alive!'

Bobby grinned. 'Poor old Janet!' she said. 'Good luck to you. I'll wait for you here, old thing.'

7.

Janet, Bobby – and Prudence

Janet went quickly to find Miss Roberts. When there was trouble brewing Janet faced up to it at once. She didn't run away from it, or make excuses. She wasn't looking forward to the interview with Miss Roberts, but she thought the sooner it was over the better.

Miss Roberts was in the first-form classroom correcting books. She looked up as Janet came in. Her face was very cold and stern.

'Come over here, Janet,' she said. Janet went to her desk. Miss Roberts finished correcting the book she had before her and then put down her pencil.

'So you didn't go to Mam'zelle for extra coaching last night?' she said.

'No, Miss Roberts, I didn't,' said Janet. 'I went to see *Clive of India* at the pictures. Bobby had booked me a seat the night before.'

'And who wrote out Prudence's geography lists then?' asked Miss Roberts.

'Well, Miss Roberts, I didn't,' said Janet after a pause. 'I – I can't tell tales.'

'I don't want you to tell tales,' said Miss Roberts. 'There is nothing that I detest more. I merely wanted to make sure you hadn't done the lists yourself.'

'I suppose Prudence split on me?' said Janet, her good-tempered face suddenly flushing.

'Well, I'm not telling tales either,' said Miss Roberts, 'but it won't be difficult for your own common sense to tell you how I found out about your gross disobedience. Janet, I'm not going to have you behaving like this. You have plenty of character, you are plucky, just and kind, though you have too quick a temper and too rough a tongue sometimes – but you and Roberta have got to pull yourselves together and realize that I am not here to play tricks on, but to make you work and really learn something. Especially this term, which should be your last one with me. I really feel ashamed of you.'

Janet went red again. She hated being scolded, but she knew it was just that she should be. She looked Miss Roberts straight in the face.

'I'm sorry,' she said. 'I didn't feel it was fair having to miss going to the cinema when I really didn't mean to spill that water on Prudence. It was a pure accident. If I'd done it deliberately, then I wouldn't have minded being punished.'

'You will leave it to me to judge whether or not a punishment is just,' said Miss Roberts, coldly. 'Now, as you used a bit of trickery to go down to the town last night, I feel you are not to be trusted for some time. You will not go down again unless you come to me, say why you want to go, and get my permission. Even so, I shall not grant any for a week or two. You will also do what I told you to do yesterday and write out the geography facts yourself – in Prudence's book as I said.'

'Oh, need I do it in her book?' said Janet in dismay. 'After all, the geography is already written out there once. Prudence will grin like anything if I go and ask her for her book.'

'You've brought it on yourself,' said Miss Roberts. 'And just remember this, my dear Janet – that much as I admire many things in your character, there is still plenty of improvement to be made – especially in your classwork. I feel very much inclined to go into the matter of that note I had the other day, which resulted in my leaving the maths class – it seems to me that that episode and this have a certain likeness that makes me feel very suspicious. Any more of that kind of thing from either you or Roberta will be instantly punished. Please tell Roberta this from me.'

'Yes, Miss Roberts,' said Janet, seeing from Miss Roberts's face that the teacher was in no mood to be generous or soft hearted. Miss Roberts hated being tricked, and usually prided herself on the fact that her first formers never *did* get the best of her. She was annoyed to think that her class might be laughing up their sleeves at her.

'You can go,' she said to Janet, and reached out for another book to correct. Janet hesitated. She badly wanted to get back into Miss Roberts's good books again, but somehow she felt this was no time to try and make amends. She must find a chance some other time, and bear her punishment as gracefully as she could.

She left the room and went gloomily back to the tennis-court, where Bobby was anxiously awaiting her. Bobby slipped her arm in Janet's.

'Was it very bad?' she asked, sympathetically.

'Beastly,' said Janet. 'I feel as small as that beetle on the grass down there. I can't go down to the town for a week or two, and after that I've got to go to Miss Roberts and beg for permission whenever I want to go. It's so humiliating. And oh, Bobby – I've got to write out those hateful geography lists again – in Prudence's book!'

'That's too bad,' said Bobby, feeling at once that Prudence would crow over Janet in delight. 'How did old Roberts find out about you?'

'There's only one way she could have,' said Janet, fiercely. 'That rotten Prudence must have split on me! I'll jolly well tell her what I think of her, that's all!'

The twins came up at that moment and heard with sympathy all that had happened to Janet. 'I heard that sneak of a Prudence say, "Bobby has written it out very nicely, hasn't she?" when she showed Miss Roberts one of her books this morning,' said Pat. 'I didn't know what she meant, of course. I just thought she was being nice about Bobby's writing. I didn't realize it was her horrid way of splitting on poor old Janet.'

'The beast!' said Bobby, her eyes flashing and her cheeks flaming. She was very fond of Janet. 'I'll pay her out all right! I'll make her squirm. The nasty little tell-tale. She always pretends to be so goody-goody too. I think she's a hypocrite. I'll go and get her beastly book for you,

Jan. You shan't have to go and do that, anyway – and if she dares to say a single word to me in that soft sneering way she has, I'll pay her back.'

'No, Bobby, don't do that,' said Janet. 'It's never any good to do things like that. Leave that to our Carlotta!'

Everyone grinned. Carlotta was a really fierce little creature when she was in a temper, and had berated Alison fiercely the day before, because Alison had pointed out that Carlotta's uniform was not tidy. Carlotta had listened with a wild expression on her face, and had then screamed at Alison, which had made Alison dissolve into tears.

'You find fault with me again, and you'll regret it!' threatened Carlotta.

'Carlotta, we don't behave like that here,' Hilary had said. 'Maybe you do in Spain – but you can't do it here; it just isn't right.'

Carlotta made a rude explosive sort of noise. 'Pah! If I want to shout, I shout! What right has this silly little peacock to talk about my uniform? See how she cries, the baby! She does not even argue back!'

Alison was not even thinking of such a thing. She was very hurt and upset, especially when Sadie Greene gave a laugh.

'My, Alison, you're just cat's-meat to that little savage! Cheer up. Don't you see she wanted to make you howl?'

The twins, Janet, and Bobby remembered this episode as they stood on the tennis-court listening to Bobby's suggestion that she should treat Prudence in the same way that Carlotta had treated Alison. They all knew that such things as screaming and threatening were out of the question! But nevertheless each one of them would dearly have loved to give Prudence a good scolding!

'It's what she wants,' said Pat, with a sigh. 'However – we'll see she's made to feel what a little beast she is, somehow. She won't get away with this.'

'I'll go and get the geography book from her,' said Bobby, and marched off. She went to the common-room, thinking that Prudence might be there. She was like Pam, always to be found indoors!

She was sitting doing a jigsaw puzzle. Bobby went up to her. 'Where's your geography book?' she said. 'I want it.'

'Oh, have you got to write something else in it?' said Prudence, in her clear, soft voice. 'Poor Bobby! Are you going to do it again for Janet? What will Miss Roberts say?'

'Look at me, you nasty little sneak!' said Bobby, in such a peculiar, threatening voice that Prudence was alarmed. She raised her eyes and looked at Bobby. Bobby was white with rage, and her eyes glinted angrily.

'You're going to be sorry for this,' said Bobby, still in the same peculiar voice, as if she was talking with her teeth clenched. 'I hate sneaks worse than anything. If you dare to tell tales again, I'll make you very sorry.'

Prudence was frightened. Without a word she got up, went to her shelf and fetched her geography book. She gave it to Bobby with a trembling hand. Bobby snatched it from her and went out of the room.

'I say!' said a small voice from the corner of the room. 'I say! Wasn't Bobby in a rage, Prudence? Whatever have you done?'

It was from Pam Boardman, curled up with a book as usual. She looked through her big glasses, her eyes very large.

'I've done nothing,' said Prudence. 'Nothing at all. I haven't sneaked or told any tales. But Bobby has got her knife into me because I think her tricks are a silly waste of time. Don't *you* think they are, Pam?'

'Well, I'm not very fond of games or jokes or tricks,' said Pamela. 'I've always liked my work better. But some of Bobby's jokes and Janet's do make me laugh. Still, I agree with Miss Roberts – if most of the first form have got to go up next term, tricks and things are a silly waste of time.'

'You're such a sensible girl, Pam,' said Prudence, going over to her. 'And so brainy, I wish you'd be my friend. I like you and Sadie better than anyone else in the form.'

Pam flushed with pleasure. She was a shy girl who found it very difficult to make friends, because she could not play games well, and found it impossible to think of funny things to say or do, as the others did. She did not see that Prudence wanted to make use of her.

'Of course I'll be friends,' she said, shyly.

'You've got such brains,' said Prudence, admiringly. 'I'd be so glad if you'd help me sometimes. I wish that Sadie would be friends with you too – it would do her good to think of something besides her hair and skin and nails. I like Sadie, don't you?'

'Well, I'm a bit afraid of her,' said Pam, honestly. 'She's got such grand clothes, and she does look so lovely sometimes, and she seems so very grown-up to me. I always feel small and dowdy when she comes along. I don't know whether I like her or not.'

Prudence tried to forget Bobby's unpleasant words to her, but it was difficult. She wondered what had happened. Had Miss Roberts made Janet write out those geography things all over again? What punishment would she give the girl?

When her book was returned to her, Prudence looked with curiosity inside the pages. Yes – there were the geography lists neatly written for the second time – this time in Janet's rather sprawly writing – and Miss Roberts had ticked it.

So she had to do it after all, thought Prudence. Good! Serves her jolly well right. Now perhaps she and Bobby will leave me alone for a bit, in case Miss Roberts gets after them again!

8.

Carlotta is surprising

The five new girls 'shook down' at St Clare's each in their different ways. Sadie Greene sailed through the days, taking no notice of anything except the things she was really interested in. Miss Roberts's cold remarks passed right over her head. Mam'zelle made no impression on her at all. She thought her own thoughts, looked after her appearance very carefully and took an interest in Alison because the girl was really very pretty and dainty.

Prudence and Pam settled down too, though Prudence was careful not to come up against Bobby and Janet more than she could help. Bobby settled in so well that to the old first formers it seemed as if she had belonged to St Clare's for years. Carlotta too settled down in some sort of fashion, though she was a bit of a mystery to the girls.

'She seems such a common little thing in most ways,' said Pat, overhearing Carlotta talking to Pam in her curious half-cockney, half-foreign voice. 'And she's so untidy and hasn't any manners at all. Yet she's so natural and truthful and outspoken that I can't help liking her. I'm sure she'll come to blows with Mam'zelle some day! They just can't bear each other!'

Mam'zelle was not having an easy time with the first

form that term. The girls who were to go up into the second form were not up to the standard she wanted them to be, and she was making them work very hard indeed, which they didn't like at all. Pam was excellent at French, though her accent was not too good. Sadie Greene was hopeless. She didn't care and she wasn't going to try! Prudence seemed to try her hardest but didn't do very well. Bobby was another one who didn't care – and as for Carlotta, she frankly detested poor Mam'zelle and was as nearly rude to her as she dared to be.

So Mam'zelle had a bad time. 'Do you wonder we called her "Mam'zelle Abominable" the first term we were here?' said Pat to Bobby. 'She has called you and your work "abominable" and "insupportable" about twenty times this morning, Bobby! And as for Carlotta, she has used up all the awful French names she knows on her! But I must say Carlotta deserves them! When she puts on that fierce scowl, and lets her curls drip all over her face, and screws up her mouth till her lips are white, she looks like a regular little tornado.'

Carlotta was really rather a surprising person. Sometimes she gave the impression that she was really doing her best to be good and to try hard – and then at other times it seemed as if she wasn't in the classroom at all! She was away somewhere else, dreaming of some other days, some other life. That would make Mam'zelle furious.

'Carlotta! What is there so interesting out of the window today?' Mam'zelle would inquire sarcastically. 'Ah – I see a cow in the distance? Is she so enthralling to you? Do you wait to hear her moo?'

'No,' Carlotta said, in a careless voice. 'I'm waiting to hear her bark, Mam'zelle.'

Then the class would chuckle and wait breathlessly for Mam'zelle's fury to descend on Carlotta's head.

It was in gym that Carlotta was really surprising. Since Margery Fenworthy had gone up into the second form, there had been nobody really good at gym left in the first form. Carlotta had done the climbing and jumping and running more or less as the others had done, though with less effort and with a curious suppleness – until one day in the third week of the term.

The girl had been restless all the morning. The sun had shone in at the classroom window, and a steady wind had been blowing up the hill. Carlotta could not seem to keep still, and paid no attention at all to the lessons. Miss Roberts had really thought the girl must be ill, and seriously wondered if she should send her to Matron to have her temperature taken. Carlotta's eyes were bright, and her cheeks were flushed.

'Carlotta! What *is* the matter with you this morning?' said Miss Roberts. 'You haven't finished a single sum. What are you dreaming about?'

'Horses,' said Carlotta at once. 'My own horse, Terry. It's a day for galloping far away.'

'Well, I think differently,' said Miss Roberts. 'I think it's a day for turning your attention to some of the work you leave undone, Carlotta! Pay attention to what I say!'

Fortunately for Carlotta the bell went for break at that

moment and the class was free to dismiss. After break it was gym. Carlotta worked off some of her restlessness in the playgrounds, but still had plenty left by the time the bell went for classes again.

Miss Wilton, the sports mistress, was gym mistress also. She had to call Carlotta to order several times because the girl would climb and jump out of turn, or do more than she was told to do. Carlotta sulked, her eyes glowing angrily.

'It is such silly baby stuff we do!' she said.

'Don't be stupid,' said Miss Wilton. 'You do most advanced things considering you are the lowest form. I suppose you think you could do all kinds of amazing things that nobody else could possibly do, Carlotta.'

'Yes, of course I could,' said Carlotta. And to the astonishment of the entire class the dark-eyed girl suddenly threw herself over and over, and performed a series of the most graceful cart-wheels that could be imagined! Round and round the gym she went, throwing herself over and over, first on her hands, then on her feet, as easily as any clown in a circus! The girls gasped to see her.

Miss Wilton was most astonished. 'That will do, Carlotta,' she said. 'You are certainly extremely good at cart-wheels – better than any girl I have known.'

'Watch me climb the ropes as they should be climbed!' said Carlotta, rather beside herself now that she saw the plain admiration and amazement in the eyes of everyone around. And before Miss Wilton could say yes or no, the little monkey had swung herself up a rope to the very top.

Then she turned herself completely upside-down there, and hung downwards by her knees, to Miss Wilton's complete horror.

'Carlotta! Come down at once. What you are doing is extremely dangerous!' ordered Miss Wilton, terrified that the girl would fall and break her neck. 'You are just showing off. Come down at once!'

Carlotta slid down like lightning, turned a double somersault, went round the gym on hands and feet again and then leapt lightly upright. Her eyes shone and her cheeks were blazing. It was plain that she had enjoyed it all thoroughly.

The girls gazed open-mouthed. They thought Carlotta was marvellous, and every one of them wished that she could do as Carlotta had done. Miss Wilton was just as surprised as the girls. She stared at Carlotta and hardly knew what to say.

'Shall I show you something else?' said Carlotta, breathlessly. 'Shall I show you how I can walk upside-down? Watch me!'

'That's enough, Carlotta,' said Miss Wilton in a firm voice. 'It's time the others did something! You certainly are very supple and very clever – but I think on the whole it would be best if you did the same as the others, and didn't break out into these odd performances.'

The gym class went on its usual way, but the girls could hardly keep their eyes off Carlotta, hoping she would do something else extraordinary. But the girl seemed to sink into her dreams again, and scarcely looked at anyone else.

After the class was over the girls pressed round her.

'Carlotta! Show us what you can do! Walk on your hands, upside-down.'

But Carlotta wasn't in the mood for anything more. She pushed her way through the admiring girls, and suddenly looked rather depressed.

'I said I wouldn't – and I have,' she muttered to herself, and disappeared into the passage. The girls looked at one another.

'Did you hear what she said?' said Pat. 'I wonder what she meant. Wasn't she marvellous?'

It seemed to have done Carlotta good. She was much better in her next classes after her curious performance in the gym, quieter and happier. She lost her scowl and was not at all rude to Mam'zelle in French conversation.

The girls begged her to perform again when the gym was empty, but she wouldn't. 'No,' she said. 'No. Don't ask me to.'

'Carlotta, wherever did you learn all that?' asked Isabel, curiously. 'You did all those things just as well as any clown or acrobat in a circus! The way you shinned up that rope! We always thought Margery Fenworthy was marvellous – but you're far better!'

'Perhaps Carlotta has relations who belong to a circus,' said Prudence, maliciously. She didn't like the admiration and attention suddenly given to the girl, and she was jealous. She thought Carlotta was common and she wanted to hurt her.

'Shut up, Prudence,' said Bobby. 'Sometimes you make

me think how lovely it would be to teach you a lesson.'

Prudence flushed angrily. The other girls grinned. They liked seeing Prudence taken down a peg or two.

'Come on to the tennis-court,' said Pat to Bobby, seeing that a quarrel was about to begin. 'We've got to practise our serving, Miss Wilton said. Let me serve twenty balls to you, and you serve back to me. Next month there are going to be matches against St Christopher's and Oakdene, and I jolly well want to be in the team from the first form.'

'Well, I'll come and let you practise on *me*,' said Bobby, with a last glare at Prudence, 'but it's not a bit of good me hoping to be in any tennis team. Come on. Let's leave old Sour Milk behind.'

How Prudence hated that name! But whenever she made one of her unkind remarks, someone was sure to whisper 'Sour Milk'. Prudence would look round quickly, but everyone would look most innocent, as if they hadn't said a single word.

Prudence hated Bobby because she had begun the nickname, but she was afraid of her. She would dearly have loved to give Bobby a clever, unkind name too – but she couldn't think of one. And in any case Bobby was 'Bobby' to the whole school. Even the mistresses presently ceased calling her Roberta, and gave her her nickname. Much to Prudence's anger, Bobby was one of the most popular girls in the form!

9.

Prudence makes a discovery

Two or three quite exciting things happened during the next week or two, and all of them had to do with Carlotta. The first happened at the swimming-pool. Carlotta was no swimmer, but she adored diving and jumping. She was excellent on the spring-board too, which jutted out over the water.

Most of the girls could run lightly along the board and dive off the end of it – but Carlotta could do far more than that! She could run along it, leap high into the air, turn two or three somersaults and land in the water with her body curled up into a ball – splash! She could stand at the end of the board, bounce herself up and down till the board almost touched the water, and then with one last enormous bounce send herself like a stone from a catapult into the air, turning over and diving in beautifully as she came down.

She jumped or dived from the topmost diving platform, and she came down the water-chute in every possible position, even standing, which was a quite impossible feat for any other girl. Her swimming was always peculiar, but for acrobatic feats in the water no one could possibly beat Carlotta.

She didn't show off. She did all these things perfectly naturally, and with the utmost enjoyment. Prudence, who was a bad swimmer and disliked the water, never joined in the general praise and admiration that the other girls gave to Carlotta.

'She's just showing off,' Prudence said in a loud scornful voice, as Carlotta did a beautiful somersault into the water near her. Prudence herself was shivering at the top of the steps, not yet having gone in. The water was cold that morning, and courage was not Prudence's strong point. Alison was beside her, also shivering.

'She's not showing off,' said Janet, who overheard what Prudence said. 'It's just natural to her to do all those things. You're jealous, my dear Prue! What about going down another step and getting your knees wet? You've been shivering there for the last five minutes.'

Prudence took no notice of Janet. Carlotta climbed up to the topmost diving platform and did a graceful swallow dive that made even Miss Wilton clap in admiration.

'There she goes, showing off again,' said Prudence, talking to Alison. 'Why people encourage her I can't imagine. She's conceited enough as it is.'

'That's just the one thing Carlotta isn't,' said Bobby. 'Hold that horrid tongue of yours, Prudence. It's difficult to believe you were brought up in a vicarage when we hear you talk like that.'

'Well, it's quite plain our dear Carlotta was not brought up in any vicarage,' said Prudence, spitefully. Carlotta overheard this and grinned. She never seemed to mind remarks of this sort, though it made the others angry for her when Prudence said them. Bobby pursed up her mouth and looked at Prudence's white shivering back with distaste.

'What about a dip, dear Prue?' she said suddenly, and gave the girl a violent push. Into the pool went the surprised Prue with a loud squeal. She came up angry and spluttering. She looked round for Bobby, but Bobby had dived in immediately behind her and was now under the water groping for Prudence's legs!

In half a second Prudence felt somebody getting tight hold of the calf of her left leg and pulling her under the water! Down she went with another agonized squeal and disappeared below the surface, gasping and spluttering. She came up again, almost bursting for breath – but no sooner had she got her wind again than once more Bobby caught hold of her leg and pulled her under.

Prudence struggled away and made for the side of the pool at once, calling to Miss Wilton.

'Miss Wilton, oh, Miss Wilton, Bobby is almost drowning me! Miss Wilton, call Bobby out!'

Miss Wilton looked round in surprise at the yells from Prudence. Bobby by this time had got to the other end of the pool and was almost dying of laughter.

'What do you mean, saying that Bobby is drowning you?' said Miss Wilton, impatiently. 'Bobby's right at the other end of the pool. Don't be an idiot, Prudence. Pull yourself together and try to do a little swimming. You seem to spend most of your time standing on the steps like a scared three-year-old.'

There were a few titters from the girls nearby. Prudence was so angry that she fell back into the water and swallowed about two pints all at once.

'I'll pay you out for that!' she called to Bobby, but Bobby merely waved her hand and grinned.

'Perhaps you'll keep your tongue off Carlotta a bit if you think you're going to have Bobby after you for it!' remarked Janet, who was nearby, enjoying the fun.

Prudence unburdened her mind to Pamela Boardman as they walked back to the school building that afternoon. 'It's so bad for that common little Carlotta to have us all staring at her open-mouthed, and thinking she's wonderful,' said Prudence. 'I don't see why people like Carlotta should be allowed to come to a good school like this, do you, Pam? I mean, it's not fair on girls like us, is it, who come of good families and have been well brought up? Why, Carlotta might have a very bad influence on us indeed.'

'Perhaps her parents think that we might have a good influence on Carlotta?' suggested Pam, in her soft voice. 'She *is* odd, I agree – but she's quite fun, Prudence.'

'I don't think the things she does are really clever,' said Prudence, spitefully. 'I don't think she's fun, either. I think there's a decided mystery about our Carlotta – and I'd dearly like to know what it is!'

Pam was younger than Prudence, and although she was a clever girl at her work, she was very easily influenced by Prudence. Soon she was agreeing to all that the older girl said, and even when Prudence said things that were plainly untrue and unkind about others, Pam listened to her respectfully and nodded her head.

It was Pam and Prudence who discovered Carlotta doing something extraordinary, not long after the episode at the swimming-pool. The two of them were going for a nature-walk together, taking with them their notebooks and their nature specimen cases. They set off over the hill and went across the fields that lay behind the school. The country swept upwards again after a little, and big fields lay behind high hedges. It was a beautiful day for a walk, and Pam, who seldom went out, was quite enjoying herself.

Prudence would not have gone out at all for a walk if she hadn't seen Carlotta making off by herself. The girls were not allowed to go out alone, unless they were top formers, and two or three times Prudence had suspected that Carlotta was disobeying the rules.

Today she had seen Carlotta slipping off through the school grounds to the little gate that was set in the garden wall a good way behind the school. Prudence had been in the dormitory, and her sharp eyes picked out the girl at once. 'I wonder what she does when she goes off alone,' thought Prudence, spitefully. 'Where does she go? I bet she's got some common town friends that nobody knows anything about. I'd like to follow her and find out.'

Prudence was cunning. She knew it would be no good to go to Pam Boardman and suggest spying on Carlotta because Pam, though having a great respect for Prudence, shied away from anything underhand. So Prudence ran downstairs and found Pam curled up as usual, reading.

'Hallo, Pam!' she cried. 'Let's go out for a nature-walk! The fields look lovely behind the school this afternoon. Do come with me. It will do you good.'

Pam was good natured. She shut up her book and went to get her hat and notebook. The two girls set off. Down through the grounds they went, out of the gate and then across the field paths. Prudence kept a sharp look-out for Carlotta, and soon caught sight of the figure in the school blazer, a good way off, going up the hill opposite.

'I wonder who that is,' she said carelessly to Pam. 'We'll keep her in sight and perhaps join up with her on our way home.'

'We can't do that,' said Pam. 'She's alone so it must be one of the top formers. She wouldn't want to walk home with *us*!'

'Oh, I forgot that,' said Prudence. 'Well, we may as well go the same way as she does. She probably knows the right paths.'

So the two girls kept Carlotta in sight. The girl made her way over the top of the hill and then down into the next valley. Here there was a big camp, for a circus had come to the next town. In a vast field many caravans and cages were arranged, and in the centre an enormous tent towered up.

'There must be a circus at Trenton,' said Prudence. 'But Carlotta can't be going to it, because the show won't be on now.'

'How do you know it's Carlotta?' said Pam, in surprise.

'It can't be! She's not allowed out by herself. However *can* you tell who it is so far away?'

Prudence was annoyed with herself. She hadn't meant to let Pam know she knew it was Carlotta. 'Oh, I've got wonderful eyesight,' she said. 'You have to wear glasses, so probably your eyes don't see as far as mine. But I'm pretty sure it's Carlotta. Isn't that just like her – slipping out and breaking the rules?'

'Yes, it is rather like her,' said Pam who, however, could not help rather admiring the fiery little girl for her complete disregard of rules and regulations when she wanted to do something very badly. Carlotta always went straight for a thing, riding over objections and obstacles as if they were not there.

They followed Carlotta to the big field. They saw her speak to an untidy-haired, rough-looking groom. He smiled at Carlotta and nodded. The girl left him and went into the next field where there were some beautiful circus horses. In half a minute the girl had caught one, leapt on to its back and was galloping round the field, riding beautifully, although it was bareback.

Pam and Prudence stared in the utmost surprise. Whatever Prudence had imagined Carlotta might be going to do she certainly hadn't thought of this! She could hardly believe her eyes. The two girls watched Carlotta on the beautiful horse, which first galloped swiftly round the field, and then fell to a canter. The man she had spoken to came to watch her. He called out something to her and pointed to another horse. This was more the cart-horse type, broad backed and staid.

Carlotta called something back to the man. She leapt off her horse and ran to the one he had pointed out to her. In a trice she was up on its back, calling to it. It began to run round the field.

And then Carlotta did something that made the two hidden girls gape even more! She stood up on the horse's back and, keeping her balance perfectly, made the horse trot round and round as if it were in a circus ring! Prudence's mouth shut in a straight line.

'I always thought there was something strange about Carlotta,' she said to Pam. 'Now we know what it is. I'm sure she's nothing but a jumped-up circus-girl. How *could* Miss Theobald have her here? It's wicked! Whatever will the others say?'

'Don't let's sneak, Prudence,' begged Pam, timidly. 'Please don't. This is Carlotta's secret, not ours. We'd better say nothing.'

'Well, we'll bide our time,' said Prudence, in a spiteful voice. 'We'll just bide our time. Come on – we'd better get back before she sees us watching.'

So the two girls made their way back to the school, mostly in silence. Prudence was gloating because she had discovered something so peculiar about Carlotta – and Pam was puzzled and worried, fearful that Prudence would give away Carlotta's secret, and drag her, Pam, into the unpleasantness too. They arrived back at school just in time for tea.

Pat and Isabel saw them going indoors and called to

them in surprise. 'I say! You don't mean to say you two have actually been for a nature-walk! I thought neither of you could be dragged out of doors!'

'We had a *lovely* walk,' said Prudence, 'and we saw some very interesting things.'

'What have you brought back, Pam?' asked Hilary, seeing that Pam had her nature-specimen case slung over her shoulder.

Pam flushed. She had nothing, and neither had Prudence. It seemed as if the whole walk had been nothing but following Carlotta, spying on her, and then thinking about her all the way back. Prudence certainly hadn't spoken a word about nature, and Pam hadn't liked to ask her to stop when she saw anything that she herself was interested in.

Prudence saw that Pam was uncomfortable because they had brought nothing back for the nature-class. So she lied glibly.

'We've heaps of things,' she said. 'We'll keep them till after tea. We're hungry now – and there's the tea bell.'

Prudence knew that no one would be interested enough to ask to see any nature specimens after tea. She pushed Pam in the direction of the cloakroom, so that they might wash their hands.

Pam was silent as she washed. She was a truthful person herself, and it puzzled her when Prudence told fibs, for the girl was always condemning others who did wrong – and yet here she was lying quite cheerfully!

'Perhaps it was because she didn't want to say we'd seen

Carlotta,' said Pam to herself. 'She was just shielding her.'

Carlotta arrived late for tea. She muttered an apology to Miss Roberts and sat down. She was red with running, and although she had brushed her unruly dark curls, she looked untidy and hot.

'Wherever have you been, Carlotta?' said Pat. 'I looked all over the place for you this afternoon. It was your turn to play tennis. Didn't you know?'

'I forgot,' said Carlotta, taking a piece of bread and butter. 'I went out for a walk.'

'Who with?' said Janet.

'By myself,' said Carlotta, honestly, lowering her voice so that Miss Roberts could not hear. 'I know it's breaking the rules – but I couldn't help it. I wanted to be by myself.'

'You'll get caught one of these days, you monkey,' said Bobby. 'I break a good few of the rules myself at times – but you seem to act as if there weren't any at all. You be careful, Carlotta!'

But Carlotta only grinned. She had a secret which she meant to keep to herself. She didn't know that somebody else found it out!

10.

An uproar in Mam'zelle's class!

The next thing that happened was an uproar in Mam'zelle's French class. The term was getting on, and many of the first formers seemed to have made no progress in French at all. The weather was very hot just then, and most of the girls felt it and were disinclined to work hard. Girls like Pam Boardman and Hilary Wentworth, both of whom had brains, a steady outlook on their work, and a determination to get on, worked just as well as ever – but the twins slacked, and as for Sadie and Bobby, they were the despair of all the teachers.

But it was Carlotta who roused Mam'zelle's anger the most. When Carlotta disliked anyone she did not hide it. Neither did she hide her *liking* for any girl or teacher – she would do anything for a person she liked. The twins, and Janet and Bobby, found her generous and kind, willing to do anything to help them. But she thoroughly disliked Alison, Sadie, Prudence, and one or two others.

Carlotta's idea of showing her dislike for anyone was childish. She would make faces, turn her back, even slap. She would stamp her foot, call rude names, and often lapse into some foreign language, letting it flow out in an angry stream from her crimson lips. The girls rather enjoyed all this, though Hilary, as head of the form, often took the girl to task.

'Carlotta, you let yourself down when you act like this,' she said, after a scene in which Carlotta had called Alison and Sadie a string of extraordinary names. 'You let your parents down too. We are all more or less what our parents have made us, you know, and we want them to be proud of us. Don't let your people down.'

Carlotta turned away with a toss of her head. 'I don't let my parents down!' she said. 'They've let *me* down. I wouldn't stay here if I hadn't made a promise to someone. Do you suppose I would ever choose to be in a place where I had to see people like Alison and Sadie and Prudence every day? Pah!'

The girl almost spat in her rage. She was trembling, and Hilary hardly knew what else to say.

'We can't like everyone,' she said at last. 'You *do* like some of us, Carlotta, and we like you. But can't you see that you only make things worse for yourself when you act like this? When you live in a community together, you have to behave as the others do. I'm head of the form, and I just can't let you go around behaving like a four-year-old. After all, you are fifteen.'

Carlotta's rage vanished as suddenly as it had appeared. She genuinely liked the steady responsible Hilary. She put out her hand to her.

'I know you're right, Hilary,' she said. 'But I haven't been brought up in the same way as you have – I haven't learnt the same things. Don't dislike me because I'm different.'

'Idiot!' said Hilary, giving her a clap on the shoulder. 'We like you because you *are* so different. You're a most exciting person to have in the form. But don't play into the hands of people like Prudence, who will run to Miss Roberts if you bring out some of your rude names. If you really want to let off steam, let it off on people like me or Bobby, who won't mind!'

'That's just it,' said Carlotta. 'I *can't* go for you – you're too decent to me. Hilary, I'll try to be calmer. I really will. I'm getting on a bit better with Miss Roberts now – but Mam'zelle always drives me into a rage. I'll have to be extra careful in her class.'

It was Bobby who really began the great uproar in Mam'zelle's class one morning. Bobby was bored. She hated French verbs, which had an irritating way of having different endings in their past tenses. Just as if it was done on purpose to muddle us, thought Bobby, with irritation. And I never can remember when to use this stupid subjunctive. Ugh!

Nearby Bobby was a vivarium, kept by the first formers. It was a big cage-like structure, with a glass front that could be slipped up and down. In it lived a couple of large frogs and a clumsy toad. With them lived six large snails. The first formers regarded these creatures with varying ideas.

Kathleen, who loved animals, was really attached to the frogs and toad, and vowed she could tell the difference between the six snails, which she had named after some of the dwarfs in the story of Snow White. The rest of the form could only recognize Dopey, who never seemed to move, and who had a white mark on the spiral of his shell.

The twins liked the frogs and toad, and Isabel often tickled the frog down his back with a straw because she liked to see him put his front foot round, with its funny little fingers, and scratch himself. Some of the class were merely interested in the creatures, the rest loathed them.

Sadie and Alison couldn't bear them, and Prudence shuddered every time she saw the frogs or toad move. Doris disliked them intensely too. Bobby neither liked nor disliked them, but she had no fear of the harmless creatures as Prudence and the others seemed to have, and she handled them fearlessly when their vivarium needed to be cleaned or rearranged.

On this morning Bobby was bored. The French class seemed to have been going on for hours, and seemed likely to continue for hours too, though actually it was only a lesson lasting three-quarters of an hour. A movement in the vivarium caught the girl's eye.

One of the frogs had flicked out its tongue at a fly that had ventured in through the perforated zinc window at the back. Bobby took a quick look at Mam'zelle. She was writing French sentences on the blackboard, quite engrossed in her task. The girls were supposed to be reading a page of French, ready to translate it when she was ready.

Bobby nudged Janet. Janet looked up. 'Watch me!' whispered Bobby with a grin. Bobby slid the glass front of the vivarium to the back and put in her hand. She took one of the surprised frogs out and then shut the glass lid.

'Let's set him hopping off to Prudence!' whispered Bobby. 'It'll give her an awful fright!'

No one else had noticed Bobby's performance. Mam'zelle was irritable that morning, and the class were feverishly reading over their page of French, anxious not to annoy her more than they could help. Bobby reached over to set the frog on Prudence's desk.

But the poor creature leapt violently out of her hands on to the floor near Carlotta. The girl caught the movement and turned. She saw the frog on the floor, and Bobby nodding and pointing to show her that it was meant for the unsuspecting Prudence.

Carlotta grinned. She had been just as bored as Bobby in the French class, and the page of French had meant nothing to her at all. She hardly understood one word of it.

She picked up the frog and deposited it neatly on the edge of Prudence's desk. The girl sat next to her, so it was easy. Prudence looked up, saw the frog and gave such a scream that the whole class jumped in fright.

Mam'zelle dropped her chalk and the book she was holding, and turned round with an angry glare.

'PRUDENCE! What is this noise?'

The frog liked Prudence's desk. It hopped over her book and sat in the middle of it, staring with unwinking brown eyes at the horrified girl. She screamed loudly again and seemed quite unable to move. She was really terrified.

The frog took a leap into the air, and landed on Prudence's shoulder. It slipped down to her lap, and she leapt up in horror, shaking it off.

'Mam'zelle! It's the frog! Ugh, I can't bear it, I can't bear it! Oh, you beast, Carlotta! You took it out of the vivarium on purpose to give me a fright! How I hate you!' cried Prudence, quite beside herself with rage and fright.

Most of the class were laughing by now, for Prudence's horror was funny to watch. Mam'zelle began to lose her temper. The frog leapt once more and Prudence screamed again.

'*Taisez-vous,* Prudence!' cried Mam'zelle. 'Be silent. This class is a garden of bears and monkeys. I will not have it. It is *abominable*!'

More giggles greeted this outburst. Prudence turned on Carlotta again and spoke to her with great malice in her voice.

'You hateful creature! Nothing but a nasty little circus girl with circus-girl ideas! Oh, you think I don't know things about you, but I do! I saw you take the frog out of the vivarium to make him leap on me. I saw you!'

'*TAISEZ-VOUS,* Prudence,' almost shouted Mam'zelle, rapping on her desk. 'Carlotta, leave the room. You will go straight to Miss Theobald and report what you have done. That such things should happen in my class! It is not to be believed!'

Carlotta did not hear a word Mam'zelle said. She had sprung up from her seat and was glaring at Prudence. Her eyes were flashing, and she looked very wild and very beautiful. Like a beautiful warrior, Isabel thought.

She began to speak – but not one of the girls could understand a word, for Carlotta spoke in Spanish. The words came pouring out like a torrent, and Carlotta stamped her foot and shook her fist in Prudence's face. Prudence shrank back, afraid. Mam'zelle, furious at being entirely disregarded by Carlotta, advanced on her with a heavy tread.

The whole class watched the scene, breathless. There had been one or two Big Rows, as they were called, in the first form at times, but nothing to equal this. Mam'zelle took Carlotta firmly by the arm.

'*Vous êtes in-sup-por-table*!' she said, separating the syllables of the word to make it even more emphatic. Carlotta shook off Mam'zelle's hand in a fury. She could not bear to be touched when she was in a rage. She turned on the astonished French mistress, and addressed her in a flow of violent Spanish, some of which Mam'zelle unfortunately understood. The mistress went pale with anger, and with difficulty prevented herself from giving Carlotta a box on the ears.

In the middle of this the door opened and Miss Roberts came in. It was time for the lesson to end, but everyone had been far too engrossed in the scene to think of the time. Miss Roberts had been surprised to find the classroom door shut, as usually it was held open for her coming by one of the class. She was even more astonished to walk in and see Mam'zelle and Carlotta apparently about to have a free fight!

Mam'zelle recovered herself a little when she saw Miss Roberts. 'Ah, Miss Roberts!' she said, her voice quite weak with all the emotion she had felt during the last few minutes. 'You come in good time! This class of yours is shocking – yes, most shocking and wicked. That girl Carlotta, she has defied me, she has called me names, she has – oh la, la, there is the frog again!'

Everyone had forgotten the frog – but it now made a most unexpected appearance again and leapt on to Mam'zelle's large foot. Mam'zelle had no liking for frogs. All insects and small creatures filled her with horror. She gave a squeal and stumbled backwards, falling heavily on to a chair.

Miss Roberts had taken everything in at a glance. Her face was extremely stern. She looked at Mam'zelle. She knew Mam'zelle's hot temper, and she felt that the best thing to do was to get the angry French mistress out of the class before making any inquiries herself.

'Mam'zelle, your next class is waiting for you,' she said in her clear cool tones. 'I will look into this matter for you and report to you at dinner-time. You had better go now and leave me to deal with everything.'

Mam'zelle could never bear to be late for any class. She got up at once and left the room, giving Carlotta one look of fury before she went. Miss Roberts nodded to Hilary to shut the door and then went to her own desk. There was a dead silence in the room, for there was not a girl there who did not dread Miss Roberts when she was in this kind of mood.

Carlotta was still standing, her hair rumpled over her forehead, her fists clenched. Miss Roberts glanced at her. She knew Carlotta's fiery nature by now, and felt that it was of no use at all to attack her in that mood. She spoke to her firmly and coldly.

'Carlotta, please go and do your hair. Wash your inky hands too.'

The girl stared at her teacher, half mutinous, but the direct order calmed her and she obeyed it. She left the room and there was a sigh of relief. Carlotta was exciting – but this time she had been a little *too* exciting.

'Now please understand that I am not encouraging any tale-bearing,' said Miss Roberts, looking round her class with cold blue eyes, 'but I am going to insist on finding out what this extraordinary scene is about. Perhaps you, Hilary, as head of the class, can tell me.'

'Miss Roberts, let *me* tell you!' began Prudence, eager to get her word in before anyone else. 'Carlotta opened the vivarium and took out the frog, and . . .'

'I don't want any information from you until I ask for it, Prudence,' said Miss Roberts, in such a cutting tone that the girl sank back into her seat, flushing. 'Now, Hilary – tell me as shortly as you can.'

'Well, apparently someone took a frog out of the vivarium and put it on Prudence's desk,' said Hilary reluctantly. Bobby got up, red in the face.

'Excuse me interrupting, Miss Roberts,' she said. '*I* took the frog out.'

'It was that beast Carlotta who played the trick on me!' exclaimed Prudence. 'You're shielding her.'

'Prudence, you'll leave the room if you speak again,' said Miss Roberts. 'Go on, Bobby.'

'I was bored,' said Bobby, honestly. 'I took out the frog to make it jump on to Prudence for a bit of fun, because she's scared of frogs. But it leapt out of my hand on to the floor – and so I nodded to Carlotta to pick it up and put it on the desk – and she did. But I was the one to blame.'

Bobby sat down. 'Now you go on with this extraordinary tale, Hilary,' said Miss Roberts, wondering if her class could really be in its right senses that morning.

'Well, Miss Roberts, there isn't much else to tell except that Prudence got an awful fright and screamed and Mam'zelle was angry, and Prudence blamed it all on to Carlotta and said some pretty horrid things to her, and Carlotta flared up as she does – and when Mam'zelle ordered her from the room she wouldn't go – I really think she didn't even *hear* Mam'zelle! Then Mam'zelle was furious because Carlotta didn't obey her and went over to her – and Carlotta turned on her and said something in Spanish that made Mam'zelle even more furious. And then you came in,' finished Hilary.

'And spoilt your fun, I suppose,' said Miss Roberts in the sarcastic voice that the class hated. 'A very entertaining French lesson, I must say. You appear to have begun it all, Bobby – Carlotta certainly had a hand in it –

and the rest of the tale appears to be composed of bad tempers on the part of several people. I imagine that everyone was simply delighted, and watched with bated breath. I'm disgusted and ashamed. Bobby, come to me at the end of the morning.'

'Yes, Miss Roberts,' said Bobby, dismally. Prudence looked round at Bobby with a pleased expression, delighted that the girl had a punishment coming to her. Miss Roberts caught sight of the look. She could not bear Prudence's meanness, nor her habit of tale-bearing and gloating over others' misfortunes. She snapped at her so suddenly that Prudence jumped.

'Prudence! You are not without blame, either! If you *can* make trouble for others, you invariably do. If you had not made such a stupid fuss none of this would have happened.'

Prudence was deeply hurt. 'Oh, Miss Roberts,' she said, in an injured tone, 'that's not fair. Really I . . .'

'Since when have I allowed you to tell me what is fair and what is not?' inquired Miss Roberts. 'Hold your tongue and sit down. And while I think of it – your last essay was so bad that I cannot pass it. You will do it again this evening.'

Prudence flushed. She knew that Miss Roberts definitely meant to be unkind at that moment, and she felt that all the girls, except perhaps Pam, silently approved of Miss Roberts's sharp tongue, and were pleased at her ticking-off. Her thoughts turned to Carlotta, and she brooded with bitterness over the fiery girl and what she had said. Miss Roberts had said nothing about punishing that beast Carlotta! Surely she wasn't going to let her go scot-free! Think of the things she had said to Mam'zelle! Carlotta was strange and bad – see how she broke the rules of the school and went off riding other people's horses!

The class was in a subdued mood for the rest of that morning. Bobby went to Miss Roberts and received such a scolding that she almost burst into tears – a thing that Bobby had not done for years! She also received a punishment that kept her busy for a whole week – a punishment consisting of writing out and learning all the things that Miss Roberts unaccountably appeared to think that Bobby didn't know. It is safe to say that at the end of that week Bobby knew a good deal more than at the beginning!

Carlotta appeared to receive no punishment at all, which caused Prudence much anger and annoyance. Actually, as Pat and Isabel knew, Carlotta had been sent to the head, Miss Theobald, and had come out of that dread sitting-room in tears, looking very subdued and unlike herself. She told no one what had passed there, and nobody dared to inquire.

Mam'zelle received a written apology from Bobby and from Carlotta – and, much to Prudence's anger, one from Prudence herself too! Miss Roberts had demanded it, and would not listen to any objections on Prudence's part. So the girl had not dared to disobey but had written out her apology too.

I'll pay Carlotta out for this! she thought. I'll go and

find that man she was talking to – and ask him all about that horrid beast of a Carlotta! I'm sure there's something funny about her.

11.

Carlotta's secret

The first chance that Prudence had of going for a walk over to the circus camp was two days later. She sought out Pam and asked her to go with her.

'Oh, Prudence! I did so badly want to finish reading this book,' said Pam, who was in the middle of a historical novel dealing with the class's period of history. It was quite a joke with the first form that Pam never read any book unless it had to do with some of the classwork.

'Pam, do come,' begged Prudence, slipping her hand under Pam's arm. Pam had had very little affection shown to her in her life and she was always easily moved by any gesture on Prudence's part. She got up at once, her short-sighted eyes beaming behind their big glasses. She put away her book and got her hat. The two girls set off, going the same way as before.

In half an hour's time they reached the camp. 'Why, we've come the same way that we came last week!' said Pam.

'Yes,' said Prudence, pretending to be astonished too. 'And look – the circus camp is still there – and those lovely horses are still in the field. Let's go down to the camp and see if we can see any elephants or exciting things like that.'

Pam wasn't at all sure that she wanted to find

elephants, for she was nervous of animals, but she obediently followed Prudence. They went into the field where the caravans and cages were arranged. No one took any notice of them.

After a while Prudence's sharp eyes found the untidy-haired man that she had seen Carlotta talking to. She went up to him.

'Does it matter us looking round the camp a bit?' she asked, with her sweetest smile.

'No, you go where you like, missy,' said the man.

'Are those the circus horses in that field over there?' asked Prudence, pointing to the field where she had seen Carlotta riding.

'They are,' said the man, and he went on polishing the harness that lay across his knees.

'I wish we could ride them like Carlotta,' said Prudence, gazing at the horses with an innocent expression. The man looked at her sharply.

'Ay, she's a fine rider,' he said. 'Fine girl altogether, I say.'

'Have you known her long then?' said Prudence, still looking very innocent indeed.

'Since she was a baby,' said the man.

'She's had an awfully interesting life, hasn't she?' said Prudence, pretending that she knew far more than she did. 'I love to hear all her stories.'

Pam stared at Prudence open-mouthed. This was news to her! She wondered uncomfortably if Prudence was telling one of her fibs - but why should she do that?

'Oh, she's told you about her life, has she?' said the

man, looking rather surprised. 'I thought she wasn't . . .'

He stopped short. Prudence felt excited. She really was discovering something now. She looked at the untidy man, her eyes wide open with a most honest expression in them. No one could beat Prudence at looking innocent when she wasn't!

'Yes, I'm her best friend,' said Prudence. 'She told me to come over here and look round the camp. She said you wouldn't mind.'

Pam was now quite certain that Prudence was telling dreadful untruths. In great discomfort the girl went off to look at a nearby caravan. She felt that she could not listen any more. She could not imagine what Prudence was acting like this for. She had so little spite in her own nature that it did not occur to her to think that Prudence was trying to find out something that might damage Carlotta.

Prudence was pleased to see Pam go off. Now she could get on more quickly! She felt certain somehow that Carlotta really had been connected with circus life in some way, so she took the plunge and asked the man the question.

'I expect Carlotta loved circus life, didn't she?'

The man apparently saw nothing odd about the question. He plainly thought that Carlotta had told Prudence a great deal about herself. He nodded his head.

'She oughtn't to have left it,' he said. 'My brother, who was in the same show as Carlotta was, said it would break her heart. That girl knew how to handle horses better than a man. I was glad to let her have a gallop when she came over here the other day. We move tomorrow – so you tell her when you get back that if she wants another gallop, she'll have to come along pretty early tomorrow morning, like she did two weeks ago.'

Prudence was almost trembling with excitement. She had found out all she wanted to know. That nasty little Carlotta was a circus girl – a horrid, common, low-down little circus girl! How dare Miss Theobald accept a girl like that for her school! Did she really expect girls like Prudence, daughter of a good family, to mix with circus girls?

She called Pam and the two set off to go back to the school. Both were silent. Pam was still feeling very uncomfortable about Prudence's untruths to the man in the camp – and Prudence was thinking how clever she had been. She did not realize that it was not real cleverness – only shameful cunning.

She wondered how she could get the news round among the girls. Should she drop a hint here and there? If she could get hold of that foolish Alison, she would soon bleat it out everywhere! She went to find Alison that evening in the common-room. The girl was sitting doing a complicated jigsaw. She loved jigsaws, although she was very bad at them, and usually ended in losing half the pieces on the floor.

It was an interesting jigsaw. Four or five girls came to see how Alison was getting on. Bobby picked up a piece.

'Doesn't that go there?' she said, and tried it. Then

Hilary picked up another piece, and in trying to make it fit, pushed the half-finished picture crooked.

'Oh!' cried Alison, exasperated. 'If there's one thing I hate more than anything else it's having people help me with a jigsaw puzzle. First it's Bobby, then it's Hilary, then it's somebody else. I could finish it much more quickly if only people didn't help me!'

'I've never seen you finish a jigsaw puzzle yet, Alison,' said Pat, teasingly.

'Why don't you do it properly?' said Doris who, however poor she was at lessons, was astonishingly quick at jigsaws. 'You always begin by putting little bits together here and there. What you should do is begin with the outside pieces. You see, they've got a straight edge, and . . .'

'I know all that,' said Alison, impatiently, 'but Sadie says . . .'

Immediately the chorus was taken up with the greatest delight by the girls around.

'Sadie says – oh, Sadie says – Sadie, Sadie, Sadie SAYS!'

The girls at the back of the room took up the chorus too, and Sadie good-naturedly lifted her pretty head. 'Don't you mind them, Alison,' she said. But Alison did. She never could take teasing well. She muddled up her half-made jigsaw in peevishness, piled it into its box, dropped two or three pieces on the floor and went out of the room.

Prudence followed her, thinking she might drop a few words into Alison's ear. 'Alison!' she called. 'What a shame to tease you like that! Come out into the garden with me. It's a lovely evening.'

'No, thanks,' said Alison, half rudely, for she did not like Prudence. 'I'm not in the mood to hear nasty things about half the girls in the form!'

Prudence flushed. It was true that she lost no chance of telling tales about the girls, trying to spread mischief among them – but she had not realized that the girls themselves knew it. It was plainly no use trying to get Alison to listen to tales about Carlotta.

'I'll have to think of some other way,' said Prudence to herself. But she did not have to think – for the whole thing came out that same evening far more quickly than Prudence had ever expected.

She went back into the common-room. Carlotta was there, laughing as she told some joke in her half-foreign voice, which was rather fascinating to listen to. The girls were grouped around her, and Prudence felt a sharp twinge of jealousy as she saw them.

Her face was so sour as she looked at Carlotta that Bobby laughed loudly. 'Here comes old Sour Milk!' she said, and everyone giggled.

'Sour Milk!' said Carlotta. 'That is a very good name. Why have you gone sour, Prudence?'

Prudence was suddenly full of spite. 'It's enough to make anyone go sour when they have to live with a low-down circus girl like you!' she said, her tone so full of hate that the girls glanced at her in astonishment. Carlotta laughed.

'I'd like to see *you* in a circus!' she said cheerfully. 'The tigers would like you for their dinner. And I don't believe anyone would miss you.'

'Be careful, Carlotta,' said Prudence. 'I know all about you. All – about – you!'

'How interesting!' said Carlotta, though her eyes began to gleam dangerously.

'Yes – very interesting,' said Prudence. 'The girls would soon despise you if they knew what I know. You wouldn't have any friends then. No one would want to know – a common little circus girl!'

'Shut up, Prudence,' said Bobby, afraid that Carlotta might lose her temper. 'Don't tell silly lies.'

'It's not silly lies,' said Prudence. 'It's the truth, the whole truth. There's a circus camp over near Trenton, and I talked to a man there – and he told me Carlotta was a circus girl, and knew how to handle horses, and was nothing but a common little girl from a circus belonging to his brother. And *we* have to put up with living with a girl like her!'

There was a complete silence when Prudence had finished. Carlotta looked all round the girls with flashing eyes. They stared at her. Then Pat spoke.

'Carlotta – did you *really* live in a circus?'

Prudence watched everyone, pleased with her bombshell. Now Carlotta would see what decent, well-brought-up girls would say to her. She, Prudence, would have a fine revenge. She waited impatiently for the downfall of the fiery little Carlotta.

At Pat's question Carlotta looked towards the twins.

She nodded her head. 'Yes,' she said. 'I *was* a circus girl. And I loved it.'

The girls looked in amazement and delight at Carlotta. Her eyes were glowing and her cheeks were red. They could all imagine her quite well riding in a circus ring. They pressed round her eagerly.

'Carlotta! How marvellous!'

'I say, Carlotta! How simply wonderful!'

'Carlotta, you simply *must* tell us all about it!'

'I always knew there was something unusual about you.'

'Oh, Carlotta, to think you never told us! Why didn't you, you wretch?'

'Well – I promised Miss Theobald I wouldn't,' said Carlotta. 'You see – it's a funny story really – my father married a circus girl – and she ran away from him, taking me with her, when I was a baby. She died soon after, and I was brought up by the circus folk. They were grand to me.'

She stopped, remembering many things. 'Go on,' said Kathleen, impatiently. 'Do go on!'

'Well – I loved horses, just as my mother did,' said Carlotta, 'so I naturally rode in the ring. Well, not long ago, my father, who'd been trying to find me and my mother for years, suddenly discovered that mother was dead and I was in a circus. Father is a rich man – and he made me leave the circus, and when he found how little education I'd had he thought he would send me to school to learn.'

'Oh, Carlotta – how awfully romantic!' said Alison. 'Just like a book. I always thought you looked unusual,

Carlotta. But why are you so foreign?'

'My mother was Spanish,' said Carlotta, 'and some of the folk in the circus were Spanish too, though many of them came from other parts of Europe! They were grand people. I wish I could go back to them. I don't fit in here. I don't belong. I don't think like you do. Our ideas are all different – and I'll never never learn.'

She looked so woe-begone that the girls wanted to comfort her.

'Don't you worry, Carlotta! You'll soon fit in – better than ever now we know all about you. Why didn't Miss Theobald want us to know you'd been a circus girl?'

'Well, I suppose she thought maybe you might look down on me a bit,' said Carlotta. The girls snorted.

'Look down on you! We're thrilled! Carlotta, show us some of the things you can do!'

'I promised Miss Theobald I wouldn't do any of my tricks,' said Carlotta, 'in case I gave the show away. I broke my promise the other day in the gym – but somehow I simply couldn't help it. I'd been thinking and dreaming of all the old circus days – and of my darling beautiful horse, Terry – and I just went mad and did all those things in the gym. I can do much more than I showed you then!'

'Carlotta! Walk on your hands upside-down!' begged Bobby. 'Golly! What fun you're going to be! You're a fierce creature with your fly-away tempers and ready tongue – but you're natural and kind and we shall all like you even better now we understand the kind of life you've lived before. It's a wonder you've fitted in as well as you did.

What a mercy you were honest about it – we wouldn't have admired you nearly so much if you'd been afraid to own up.'

'Afraid to own up – why, I'm proud of it!' said Carlotta, with sparkling eyes. 'Why should I be ashamed of knowing how to handle horses? Why should I be ashamed of living with simple people who have the kindest hearts in the world?'

The girl threw herself lightly over and stood on her hands. Her skirt fell over her shoulders as she began to walk solemnly round the room on her strong, supple little hands. The girls crowded round her, laughing and admiring.

'My word – the second form will be jealous when they hear about Carlotta!' said Bobby.

'They certainly will!' said Sadie, who was just as full of astonishment and admiration as anyone else. It all seemed most surprising and unreal.

Everyone was pleased and thrilled – save for one girl. That girl, of course, was Prudence. She could not understand the attitude of the girls. It was completely opposite to what she had expected. It was hard to believe.

Prudence stood in silence, listening to the squeals of delight and admiration. Her heart was very bitter within her. The bombshell she had thrown had certainly exploded – but the only person it had harmed had been the thrower! Instead of making the girls despise Carlotta and avoid her, she had only succeeded in making them admire her and crowd round her in delight. Now Carlotta would show off even more – she would get more friends than ever. How could everyone like a nasty common little girl like that?

No one took any notice of Prudence. For one thing they were so excited about Carlotta – and for another thing they despised her for her mean attempt to injure another girl for something she couldn't help. Bobby elbowed her a little roughly, and Prudence almost burst into tears of rage and defeat.

She slipped out of the room. It was more than she could bear to see Carlotta walking on her hands, cheered on by the rest of the first formers. The last words she heard were, 'Let's get the second formers in! Where are they? In the gym? Do let's go and tell them to come and see Carlotta! She's marvellous!'

I meant my news to hurt her – and it's only brought her good luck and friendship, thought Prudence bitterly. Whatever shall I do about it?

12.

Bobby gets a shock

Carlotta was a very popular person after this upheaval. Her complete honesty and frankness had disarmed everyone, and to most of the girls she suddenly appeared as a most surprising and romantic person. Even the second formers were thrilled, though as a rule they professed rather to turn up their noses at anything that happened in the first form. But Tessie, Queenie and the rest of the second form were just as persistent as the lower form in begging Carlotta to show off her circus tricks and accomplishments.

'It must have been a bit of a shock to that sneak of a Prudence to find that instead of looking down on our Carlotta we looked up to her and admired her instead!' said Pat. 'I bet dear darling Prudence thought we'd be shocked to the back teeth to hear she was a circus girl. I vote we punish her by not taking a scrap of notice of her, and not listening to anything she says!'

'I think we ought to do the same to Pam then,' said Bobby. 'Pam's Prudence's friend, you know, and she was with her when they spied on Carlotta. She's a silly little creature and thinks the world of Prudence. It will do her good to feel that we don't approve of Prudence's ways, and don't particularly want to be pleasant to Prudence's friends.'

'Well, I'm rather sorry for Pam,' said Isabel. 'She's a nervous little thing and awfully hard working. Don't let's be too hard on her.'

Prudence didn't at all like the treatment meted out to her by the first formers. The girl was very fond of the sound of her own voice, and it was most annoying to her to find that whenever she began to air her views about anything, all the girls around either suddenly disappeared, or else began to talk nonsense to one another at the tops of their voices.

Prudence would perhaps address herself to Hilary and say, 'Hilary, what side are you taking in tonight's debate on "Should Women rule the World?" I'm taking the side that they certainly should. After all, don't we . . .'

Then Hilary would suddenly address Janet in a very loud voice and say something perfectly ridiculous, such as, 'I say, Janet, old thing, how many legs has a kitten?'

And Janet, perfectly solemn, would answer in a loud voice, 'Well, usually four. But you'd better count and see.'

Prudence would stare in astonishment, and then begin again. 'What I say is, if women ruled the world . . .'

Then Kathleen would chime in, cutting right across Prudence's rather affected little voice. 'Hilary, Janet! Do you suppose a worm really grows into two worms when it's cut in half?'

Then Bobby would cut in, rather cruelly. 'What about cutting dear Prudence in two, then we'll see!'

And so it went on, nobody ever paying any attention to Prudence at all. Prudence was hurt and angry and went to Pam for comfort. She squeezed out a few tears and Pam tried to comfort her.

'Pam, you know quite well I wasn't spying on Carlotta,' wept Prudence. 'Can't you tell the girls I wasn't? Do stick up for me. What's the good of being my friend if you don't?'

And then poor Pam, trying her hardest to be loyal, would stick up for Prudence, although in her heart of hearts she no longer really trusted or liked her. But the thirteen-year-old girl was easily swayed, and anyone in tears moved her heart.

So it came about that very soon the first formers began to ignore poor Pam too, and laughed at her efforts to stick up for Prudence. Pam retired into her shell and felt very unhappy. She worried about the whole thing and turned to her work more than ever to help her to forget the many unpleasantnesses that seemed to be cropping up in those weeks.

Now that her secret was out, Carlotta was very happy. Hers was an honest nature, and she had not liked keeping everything to herself. Now the whole school knew what she was and eyed her with wonder, half expecting her to do something extraordinary at any time. The twins took her under their wing, and they and Carlotta, Bobby and Janet were continually about together.

Carlotta had gone to Miss Theobald and had told her that everyone now knew she had once been a circus girl.

'But they don't seem to mind,' said Carlotta, looking straight at the head mistress with her fearless eyes. 'You thought they would, didn't you?'

'No, Carlotta, I didn't think that most of them would mind at all,' said Miss Theobald. 'But I thought it might be easier for you to settle down if the girls did not regard you as anything out of the ordinary. Also your father begged me to keep your "secret" as he called it. Well – it's out now – and you must just show me that it doesn't matter. You are all your father has, you know – so try and get used to the kind of life you will have to lead with him later on.'

Carlotta sighed. She didn't want to lead any other kind of life except the one she had always known – the life of the circus camp, always on the move, always visiting new places, always making new friends. She left Miss Theobald's sitting-room looking rather subdued.

After a while the excitement caused by the row in Mam'zelle's class, and by Carlotta's secret, died down a little. This was partly because matches were looming ahead – tennis and swimming – and the school was putting in a good deal of practice, hoping to win all the matches against other schools.

The twins were practising hard, and Bobby was helping them. Don't-Care Bobby would not do anything much to help herself on, but never minded how much time she gave to help anyone else to become better at anything. Janet and Hilary were both practising too, but were not so good as the twins.

'You're getting a grand style at tennis, both of you,'

said Belinda Towers, approvingly, as she watched the twins one afternoon. 'If you go on like this you'll be chosen for the first-form team against St Christopher's! Bobby, you're getting better too. Why don't you try a bit harder and see if you can't be the reserve girl?'

Two out of each form were chosen to play against two girls from each form of the opposing school, and for each two there was a reserve girl, in case one of the two fell ill or could not play for any other reason. Bobby shook her head when she heard Belinda say this.

'No, thanks!' she said. 'It makes tennis too much like hard work if I have to practise up for reserve girl!'

Belinda was not amused by this answer. She gave Bobby a look that rather surprised her, because it held a certain amount of scorn in it.

'Oh, well,' said Belinda, 'of course we can't expect Don't-Care Bobby to care enough for the school, or to have enough pride in her form to do anything that might seem like hard work. Foolish of me to suggest it!'

She walked away and the three stared after her. 'What's bitten *her* this afternoon?' said Bobby, surprised. The twins looked at her uncomfortably.

'Well, Bobby, I suppose it must seem to the top girls that you do just what you like and don't bother about working or playing as hard as you might,' said Pat, at last. 'Mind you, I'm not blaming you, not one bit – I think you're grand as you are – but the top formers have other ideas about things. You know how good and proper they get as they go up the school. Maybe one day *you'll* be good and proper too – though I jolly well hope you won't!'

'Don't worry, I shan't,' said Bobby, shortly. She hadn't at all liked what Belinda had said. She wondered if she ought to put in a bit of hard practice at tennis herself, just to please Belinda. But she was obstinate and didn't, though she went on helping the twins all she could, standing at the other end of the court for a long time whilst they served ball after ball across the net, trying to improve their style.

Sadie, Alison, Pam, Prudence, and Carlotta made no pretence at all of trying to better their tennis. They either played because they had to, or because there wasn't anything better to do at the moment. Not one of the five, with the exception of Carlotta, visited the swimming-pool except on the days when it was compulsory to do so. These days came three times a week, and how Prudence and Sadie groaned when they had to go down to the pool and undress themselves, shivering, in the little wooden cubicles that ran alongside the water.

Carlotta was quite mad in the water, for although she could not swim well or fast, she performed all sorts of antics there, and her diving was lovely to watch. Miss Wilton hardly knew what to make of her.

'You'll never make a swimmer, Carlotta,' she said, 'but I shouldn't be surprised if you take all the prizes for your tricks! That was a lovely swallow-dive you did just now. But please don't come down the chute standing up any more. It's dangerous. And also, do try *not* to jump into the water from the top of the diving platform just when

Prudence is underneath. You scare her terribly.'

'Oh, Miss Wilton, I wouldn't scare Prudence for worlds!' said Carlotta, in her up-and-down voice, and a wicked look in her eyes. And the very next moment she ran along the marble floor, pretended to slip, and landed with an enormous splash in the water, right on top of the unfortunate Prudence! No one ever knew what Carlotta would do next.

The twins hoped against hope that they would be chosen to play against St Christopher's. It would be such fun to play together. 'Won't Mummy be pleased if she hears we've both been chosen?' said Pat. 'I wish Bobby could be our reserve girl and come with us. But I bet Janet or Hilary will be chosen.'

The match was to be the following week, and three girls from each of the three lower forms were to go to St Christopher's School for the matches against girls from similar forms there. Belinda promised to put up the names of the girls on the board the night before.

Before Belinda put up the names, she sent for Bobby. Bobby went to Belinda's study in surprise. The big girl was there, neatly writing out some sports lists.

'Hallo, Bobby,' she said, nodding her head towards a chair. 'Sit down for a minute. I've nearly finished.'

Bobby sat down and studied Belinda's clear-cut profile. She liked Belinda very much, and knew how hard she worked at being sports captain. She wondered what Belinda was going to say to her.

The sports captain looked up and set down her pen.

'Look here, Bobby,' she said, 'I just want to know something. You're pretty good at tennis, and I'd half-thought of making you reserve girl for your form. But I want to know if you've been thinking about it too, and working for it.'

'No, I haven't,' said Bobby, going red. 'I told you that that would be too much like hard work, Belinda! Anyway, reserve girls never play in the matches – they only watch – and I don't want to watch! If I was going to do anything, I'd want to play, not watch!'

'You're very disappointing,' said Belinda. 'You've got such good stuff in you, Bobby – but you won't seem to make the best of it. I believe if you'd practised as hard as the twins, I'd not have known who to choose for the two match players! You put yourself out to let Pat and Isabel practise all they like on you – but yet you won't try to make yourself good too. Don't-Care Bobby is a good name for you – but you won't get far if you don't begin to care about things.'

'I don't want to get far,' said Bobby, her obstinacy rising. 'I've told you, Belinda – I'd like to *play* in the match – but I'm not keen on watching – so choose Janet or Hilary for reserve girl. I don't care!'

'Very well,' said Belinda, coldly. 'I shall choose one of the others. I was hoping you would be able to tell me you really had done a bit of hard practising on your own account – then I would certainly have chosen you for reserve girl – but seeing that you don't seem to care either way, I shall choose somebody else. You can go.'

Bobby went out of the room, red of cheek, and rather

ashamed of herself. She was an odd mixture. She had plenty of brains, plenty of high spirits, plenty of kindliness – but she seemed to have an incurable dislike of working hard at anything, and if anyone tried to make her, she became very obstinate and immovable. Belinda felt really impatient with her.

The sports captain made out the list of three girls chosen for the tennis match next day, and went to pin it on the noticeboard. A crowd came round her immediately.

'Pat! Isabel! You're the two girls!' yelled Doris at the top of her voice. 'Who's reserve girl? Take your fat head out of the way, Prudence!'

The reserve girl was Janet. She was delighted. She turned to Bobby. 'I thought it would be *you,*' she said. 'You're much better than I am, really. I can't think why Belinda chose me instead of you, Bobby!'

Bobby knew quite well, but she said nothing. She was cross because she couldn't help feeling ashamed of herself. 'I'm jolly glad it's you, old girl,' she said to Janet. 'Reserve girls never play – we all know that – but you'll have some fun, anyway!'

13.

Three tennis matches – and an accident

The next day dawned warm and sunny – just right for a tennis match. There was a little breeze, but not enough to worry the players. The match was to start at three o'clock. The nine girls chosen – three from each of the three lower forms – were to go with Belinda and Miss Wilton in a small private bus that the school often used.

Pat and Isabel were in a great state of excitement. They had not played for their school before, and were proud and pleased.

'Isn't it lovely that we're to play *together*?' said Pat joyfully. 'It would have been horrid if one of us had been chosen and not the other.'

Janet was almost as excited as they were, because although she was only reserve girl and hadn't a chance in a hundred of really playing, still it was great fun to go off in the bus to another school. She and the other two reserve girls would be able to sit with Belinda Towers and Miss Wilton and talk with them whilst the game was on.

'Good luck!' said everyone, when the little bus drew up to the school door and the tennis players went to get in. 'Good luck! Mind you win *all* the matches! We'll give you three hearty cheers when you come back, if you do! Good luck!'

Bobby felt a little envious as she saw the happy faces of the twins and Janet smiling in the bus. She knew she herself might have been in that bus if she had really wanted to! But nobody guessed her thoughts, for she shouted 'Good luck!' and waved as wildly as the rest.

It was fun to go driving through the countryside to St Christopher's like that. The girls fingered the strings of their rackets and looked at them anxiously to make sure they were all tight and good. Their tennis shoes shone as white as snow. Their tennis-whites were spotless. They all hoped they would make a good showing in the matches against the opposing school.

They arrived at the school, and were met by the sports captain there, a tall graceful girl in white, and by the girls who were to play against them. They all went to the sports ground, chattering hard.

'Our courts badly want a little rain,' said a St Christopher's girl. 'The service lines are getting very worn. We've hard courts as well as grass ones, but we thought we'd use the grass ones today because they are so much softer to the feet – and also there's more room round our grass courts for the school to watch. We want everyone to see us giving you St Clare girls a beating! You beat us last year, so it's our turn this year!'

Margery Fenworthy was one of the second formers chosen, and she was eager to begin. She was wonderful at all games, and had been practising hard in order to perfect her tennis style. Her friend, Lucy Oriell, had been chosen as her partner, and both girls were delighted. Lucy was inclined to work far too hard, and Margery had made her take as much recreation as possible – and now, here was Lucy, her dark curls dancing round her face, happy at having a whole afternoon away from her scholarship work.

Jane Rickson and Winnie Hill were the third formers chosen. All six St Clare players changed into their tennis shoes and took off their cardigans.

'We thought, as you are nice and early, we would play all three matches separately, instead of at the same time,' said the St Christopher's sports captain. 'The third formers could play first. Are you ready? Will you toss for sides, please? Smooth or rough!'

Jane Rickson and Winnie Hill won the toss and chose the side. The match was to be the best of three sets. The players took their places. Jane was serving. She threw the ball high into the air – and the match began!

It was really exciting to watch. The two sets of partners were very evenly matched, and the games were very close. Practically all of them ran up to deuce. The first set was won by St Clare's, seven-five. The second one was won by St Christopher's, six-four.

'And now for the third set!' said Pat, excitedly. 'Gosh, aren't Jane and Winnie playing well, Belinda? Do you think they'll win?'

'I rather think they will,' said Belinda, smiling at

Pat's eager face. 'The other two seem to me to be getting a little tired.'

Belinda was right. The St Christopher girls were not now so fresh as the St Clare two. All the same the last set was very close and very exciting, and went to five all. Then Jane won her serve straight off. Six-five!

'Play up, Jane and Winnie!' yelled the twins. 'Play up!'

And they played up! They skipped about the court, they hit every ball, they smashed the gentle balls and killed the hard ones – and lo and behold, St Clare's had won the first match, two sets to one!

'Match to St Clare's, two sets to one,' called the umpire. 'Good game, everybody!'

St Christopher's cheered the winners. The girls shook hands across the net, and then went to drink long drinks of sweet lemonade with bits of ice bobbing at the top. How good it tasted!

'Golly, that was a good match,' panted Jane, stretching her long, tired body out over the grass. 'Look – there go the next lot. Play up, Margery. Play up, Lucy! Belinda, I don't think there's any doubt about *this* match, do you? I think Margery and Lucy will just wipe the floor with the St Christopher girls.'

'I shall be very surprised indeed if our two don't win, I must say,' said Belinda. 'I'm jolly pleased *you* two managed to pull it off. There wasn't much in it, you know – but you and Winnie managed to keep a bit fresher. It was fine to see you skipping about like that in the last game. Well done!'

There was never any doubt at all about the result of the second match. Lucy and Margery had it all their own way. The two girls opposing them were very good indeed – but Margery played a marvellous game. She and Lucy made perfect partners, never leaving any part of the court unprotected. Margery won all her serves outright.

'Golly, she's good,' said Belinda. *'Isn't* she good, Miss Wilton?'

'Marvellous,' said the St Clare's sports mistress. 'And how happy she looks too. Quite different from the sulky Margery we had to deal with last term!'

The twins remembered what a sullen, bad-tempered girl Margery Fenworthy had been the term before, and then how her whole outlook had been changed when she had become a heroine in one night, through rescuing another girl in a fire at the sickbay. Now here was that same Margery, winning honours for her school, as proud of St Clare's as St Clare's was proud of her!

The match was over in two sets. 'Match to St Clare's,' called the umpire, 'won outright in two sets, six-one, six-love.'

'Now it's our turn!' said Pat to Isabel, in great excitement, as she watched the second-form girls shaking hands across the net. 'Come on, Isabel. We've just GOT to win!'

'Play a steady game, twins,' said Belinda. 'You *ought* to win. You play almost as well together as Margery and Lucy. My word, how terribly proud St Clare's would be of us if we went back tonight having won all three matches! We simply MUST!'

The twins leapt to their feet, and ran on to the tennis-court, rackets in hand. 'Call for sides!' cried the St Christopher girl, and twisted her racket.

'Rough!' called Pat, and 'rough' it was. Pat chose the side, and the four took up their places. Belinda was pleased to see how steady the twins were. They had practised continually together, and were almost as good partners to one another as Margery and Lucy.

They won the first three games, lost one and won another. And then a dreadful thing happened!

Pat was serving. The ball came back to the left-hand side of Isabel and swerved away unexpectedly. The girl swung herself round to hit it, twisted her ankle and fell over, crashing quite heavily to the ground. She immediately tried to get up but her foot gave way beneath her and she fell again with a surprised cry of pain.

Pat rushed over to her anxiously. 'Isabel! What's happened? Oh, *don't* say you've twisted your ankle!'

'I'll be all right in a minute,' said Isabel, her face rather pale, for her foot hurt her very much. 'Just wait a minute till the pain goes off.'

But the pain didn't go off, and it was not long before the ankle swelled up tremendously. 'You've strained it,' said Miss Wilton. 'Twisted it badly, I'm afraid. Poor old Isabel – what bad luck! I'll have to take you off the court and get Janet to take your place.'

And so it came about that for once the reserve girl *did* play! But alas for poor Janet – the sight of Isabel looking so woe-begone and pale quite upset her, and made her thoroughly nervous. She felt that at any costs she and Pat must win – but somehow she couldn't play as well as she hoped.

For one thing she hadn't practised a great deal with either of the twins, and hadn't learnt how to play a good partnership game. She would keep rushing to Pat's court, leaving her own unguarded, so that her opponent found it easy to place a ball where Janet could not get it. And when Pat went up to the net Janet forgot to run to the back-line, so that balls went over her head and she could not get them.

They lost the first set, four-six – and alas, they lost the second, four-six also. They were very sad and disappointed.

'Cheer up,' said Belinda, as they came off the court. 'You both look like Sour-Milk Prudence! It couldn't be helped.'

'You'd have won if Isabel had been able to play with you,' said Janet to Pat. 'And I believe you'd have won if Bobby had been the reserve girl and not me. Bobby hasn't any nerves at all – she would just have stepped right into Isabel's place, and played magnificently. She always comes up to scratch when she has to. And she's practised with you so often that she knows your game better than I do. She'd have made a much better partner. Belinda, don't you think so?'

'Well,' said Belinda, honestly, 'I agree that Bobby knows Pat's game better than you do – but all the same I'm not sure she'd have won the match.'

But Pat and Isabel, Janet and the others were sure!

They talked about it as they ate a good tea, and discussed it in the bus on the way home.

The St Clare girls were delighted to hear that the third and second forms had won their matches, and were sorry over poor Isabel's fall. Her ankle had now gone down a little, and was feeling very much better.

'It will be all right in a day or two,' said Matron when she examined it. 'Bad luck, Isabel! Just the wrong time to have a fall, in the middle of a most important match!'

Isabel smiled wanly. She had been most bitterly disappointed about the whole thing, especially when she had seen Pat lose the match to the St Christopher girls. She poured out her disappointment to Bobby.

'Bobby, I believe Pat would have won if only Belinda had chosen *you* for reserve girl instead of Janet!' she said. 'Janet did her best – but she isn't as used to Pat's game as you are. Oh, why didn't Belinda choose *you*? I do think that was a great mistake on her part. If you'd played in the match Pat and you would have won it, and then St Clare's would have won all three!'

Bobby listened in silence. She knew quite well why Belinda hadn't chosen her! She had been silly and obstinate. She had let St Clare's down! She felt sure she wouldn't have been so nervous as Janet, and she *did* know Pat's style of game very well indeed.

She was so silent that Isabel was astonished. 'What's up, Bobby?' she said. 'You look awfully glum. You don't mind as much as all that about the match being lost, do you?'

'Yes, I do,' said Bobby. 'It wasn't Belinda's fault that Janet was chosen instead of me. Belinda did give me the chance – and I didn't take it. Don't blame Belinda. Blame me. You heard what Belinda said to me on the courts the other day – well I was sore and angry about it, and I just got all obstinate and thought I jolly well wouldn't do what she said and work hard at my tennis.'

'What a pity, Bobby,' said Isabel. 'You could have been reserve girl – and you weren't!'

'Yes – Belinda sent for me last night,' said poor Bobby. 'I missed my chance – and the match was lost. I don't say I could have won it with Pat any more than Janet could – but I can't get rid of the horrid feeling that I might have – and then think how pleased everyone would have been if we'd won all three matches. I thought I didn't care about anything, so long as I had a good time and did what I wanted to. But I find I do care after all!'

She went off by herself, for once in a way looking unhappy. Poor Bobby! She wasn't really as don't-carish as she pretended to be!

14.

Bobby and the squeaking biscuit

The term went on, passed the half-way mark, and slipped into full summer. It was wonderful weather and the girls thoroughly enjoyed everything – except having to work so hard with Miss Roberts and Mam'zelle!

'Bobby, can't you possibly think of something to stop Mam'zelle making us recite French verbs this morning?' said Pat, with a groan. 'I *have* learnt them – but they all slip out of my head with this lovely summer weather. Just think of a little tiny trick to take Mam'zelle's attention off verbs for even five minutes.'

'You haven't played a trick on anyone for at least a week!' said Isabel.

'Bobby's gone all serious,' laughed Janet.

Bobby smiled. She had certainly turned over a new leaf in some ways, for she had suddenly begun to practise both her tennis and her swimming very hard indeed. She had swum underwater for the whole length of the swimming-pool, and everyone had clapped her. She had even tried diving, which as a rule she avoided because she so often dived in flat on her stomach, and hurt herself.

But although she was working hard at games, she still did as little as she possibly could in class. Miss Roberts looked grim sometimes, when she eyed Bobby. She knew quite well that the girl was not using her good brains to the utmost – but as neither sarcastic remarks nor punishments seemed to move Don't-Care Bobby to work harder, the teacher had almost given her up.

The girls around Bobby went on begging her to play some kind of joke on Mam'zelle to make the French class a little easier that day.

'Mam'zelle's in an awful temper this morning,' said Doris. 'The second form said she almost threw the blackboard chalk at Tessie because she sneezed seven times without stopping.'

The twins grinned. They knew Tessie's famous sneezes. It was quite an accomplishment of Tessie's – she had the ability to sneeze most realistically whenever she wanted to. She often used this gift to relieve the second form from boredom. All the teachers suspected that Tessie's sneezes were not at all necessary, but only Miss Jenks knew how to deal with them properly.

'Tessie! Another cold coming!' she would say. 'Go straight to Matron and ask her to give you a dose out of Bottle Number Three, please.'

Bottle Number Three contained some very nasty-tasting medicine indeed. Tessie could never make up her mind whether it was a concoction specially made up for her, or really was medicine reserved for possible colds. So she used her sneezes rather sparingly in Miss Jenks's presence – but gave Mam'zelle the full benefit of them whenever she could.

This particular morning she had given seven very explosive sneezes, making Mam'zelle nearly jump out of her skin, and reducing the class to a state of helpless giggling. Mam'zelle had been very angry – and all the other classes expecting her to teach them that morning knew they would be in for a bad time.

'If you don't think of some trick or other to play, Mam'zelle will keep our noses to the grindstone every minute of the lesson,' groaned Doris. 'For goodness' sake think of something, Bobby.'

'I can't,' said Bobby, thinking hard. 'At least, I can't think of anything that Mam'zelle wouldn't know was a trick today. Oh – wait a minute though!'

The girls stared at Bobby expectantly. She turned to Janet. 'Where's that squeaking biscuit your brother sent you?' she asked.

Janet had a brother who was every bit as bad as Bobby and Janet where tricks were concerned. He had sent Janet a selection of jokes that week, and among them was a very realistic biscuit which, on being pressed between finger and thumb, squeaked loudly, rather like a cat. The girls had not thought that it was a very good trick.

'Rather babyish,' said Janet. 'Not a very good selection this time!'

But now Bobby had thought of some way to use the biscuit. Janet fished it out of her desk and gave it to her.

'Here you are,' she said. 'What are you going to do with it?'

Bobby pressed the biscuit slowly. It gave a pathetic squeaking sound. 'Doesn't it sound like a kitten?' she said with a grin. 'Now listen, everybody. The school cat has kittens, as you know. Well, when Mam'zelle comes into our classroom, she's going to find us talking about a lost kitten. We'll be very disturbed about it. And then, in the middle of the class, I press this biscuit – and Mam'zelle will think the lost kitten is somewhere in our room.'

Hilary chuckled. 'That's a good idea,' she said. 'And I know how we could improve on it too. I'll be outside in the passage, crawling about on my hands and knees, looking for the lost kitten, when Mam'zelle comes along to our room. I can tell her what I'm looking for.'

'Oooh, yes,' said Pat, looking thrilled. Hilary was very good at acting. 'Golly, we're going to have some fun!'

'Well, what happens in class *after* I've squeaked the biscuit will depend on all of you,' said Bobby. 'Look – there's Prudence coming. Don't tell her a word about it. You know what a sneak she is!'

The first form longed for the French lesson to come. They winked at one another whenever they thought of it. Miss Roberts caught one or two of the winks and pounced on the winkers.

'What is the joke, Hilary?' she asked coldly.

'There isn't a joke, Miss Roberts,' answered Hilary, opening her eyes wide as if astonished.

'Well, there had better *not* be,' said Miss Roberts.

'Go on with your geography map, please.'

Mam'zelle gave her French lesson after break. The girls went to their room quickly when break was over, giggling in delight. Prudence could not think why. Pam was not in the secret either, but she did not notice the chuckles of the girls. Pam was getting very much wrapped up in her own thoughts these days.

Hilary was left outside. The twins popped their heads out of the door and doubled themselves up with laughter when they saw Hilary on hands and knees, looking under a tall cupboard there, calling, 'Kitty, kitty, kitty!'

'Sh! Here comes Mam'zelle!' suddenly cried Pat to the class. She darted back to her seat, leaving Isabel to hold the door for Mam'zelle. Hilary was still outside, of course.

Mam'zelle came hurrying along on her big feet. Everyone always knew when Mam'zelle came, because she wore big, flat-heeled shoes like a man's, and made a loud clip-clap noise down the corridors.

Mam'zelle was most surprised to see Hilary crawling about outside the classroom. She stopped and stared.

'Hilary, *ma petite*! *Que faites-vous*?' she cried. 'What are you doing there? Have you lost something?'

'Kitty, kitty, kitty!' called Hilary. 'Mam'zelle, you haven't seen one of the school cat's kittens by any chance, have you? I'm looking and looking for the poor little lost thing.'

Mam'zelle looked up and down the passage. 'No, I have seen no little cat,' she said. 'Hilary, you must come to your class now. It is good of you to seek for the tiny cat, but it is not to be found.'

'Oh, Mam'zelle, just let me look a little longer,' begged Hilary. 'It might be in this cupboard. I thought I heard a sound.'

She opened the cupboard. The girls in the classroom, hearing the sound of conversation outside, wondered how Hilary was getting on. Isabel peeped out to see.

'Have you found the poor little kitten, Hilary?' she called. 'Oh, Mam'zelle, isn't it a shame? It will be so frightened.'

Mam'zelle marched into the classroom and put her books down on her desk. 'The little cat will be found somewhere,' she said. 'Go to your places. Hilary, for the last time I tell you to stop looking for the tiny cat and come to your French class.'

'Oh, Mam'zelle,' said Bobby, as Hilary came in and shut the door, 'do you think it has climbed up a chimney or something like that? I once knew a cat that got up our chimney at home, and arrived on the top of a chimney-pot!'

'And Mam'zelle, *we* had a kitten once that . . .' began Doris, quick to follow up and waste a few more minutes of the class. But Mam'zelle was not having any more fairytales about cats. She rapped on her desk, and Doris stopped her tale.

'*Assez*!' said Mam'zelle, beginning to frown. 'That is quite enough. Hilary, *will* you sit down? You surely do not imagine that the kitten is anywhere here?'

'Well, Mam'zelle, it *might* be,' said Hilary, looking all round. 'You know, my brother once had a cat that . . .'

'Any more tales about cats and the whole class will write me out two pages in French on the habits of the cat-family,' threatened Mam'zelle. At this threat everyone remained silent. Mam'zelle had a horrid way of carrying out her curious threats.

'Get out your grammar books,' said Mam'zelle. 'Open at page eighty-seven. Today we will devote the whole time to irregular verbs. Doris, you will begin.'

Doris gave a groan. She stood up to recite the verbs she had learnt. Poor Doris! No matter how much time she gave to her French preparation, every bit of it invariably went out of her head when she looked at Mam'zelle's expectant face. She began, in a halting voice.

'Doris, again you have not prepared your work properly,' said Mam'zelle, irritably. 'You will do it again. Pat, stand up. I hope you will give a better performance than Doris. You at least know how to roll your 'r's in the French way. R-r-r-r-r-r!'

The class giggled. Mam'zelle always sounded exactly as if she were growling like a dog when she rolled her r-r-r-r in her throat. Mam'zelle rapped on her desk.

'Silence! Pat, begin.'

But before Pat could begin, Bobby pressed the trick biscuit slowly and carefully between finger and thumb. A piteous squeak sounded somewhere in the room. Everyone looked up.

'The kitten!' said Pat, stopping her recital of verbs. 'The kitten!'

Even Mam'zelle listened. The squeak had been so very

much like a kitten in trouble. Bobby waited until Pat had begun her verbs again, and then she once more pressed the biscuit.

'EEEeeeeeeee!' squeaked the biscuit, exactly like a cat. Pat stopped again and looked all round the room. Mam'zelle was puzzled.

'Where *is* the poor little creature?' said Kathleen. 'Oh, Mam'zelle – where can it be?'

'Mam'zelle, I'm pretty certain it must be up the chimney,' said Hilary, jumping up as if she was going to see.

'*Asseyez-vous*, Hilary!' rapped out Mam'zelle. 'You have looked enough for the little cat. Pat, continue.'

Pat began again, Bobby let her recite her verbs until she made a mistake – and then, before Mam'zelle could pounce on her mistake, Bobby pressed the biscuit once more.

A loud wail interrupted the recital of verbs. A babel of voices arose.

'Mam'zelle, the cat must be in the room!'

'Mam'zelle, do let's look for the poor little thing.'

'Mam'zelle, perhaps it's HURT!'

Bobby made the biscuit wail again. Mam'zelle rapped on her desk in despair.

'Sit still, please. I will see if the little cat is up the chimney.'

She left her desk and went to the fire-place. She bent down and tried to look up the chimney. Bobby pressed the biscuit softly and made a very small mew come. Mam'zelle half thought it came from up the chimney. She got a ruler and felt about there.

A shower of soot came down, and Mam'zelle jumped

back, her hand covered with soot. The class began to giggle.

'Mam'zelle, perhaps the cat's in the cupboard,' suggested Janet. 'Do let me look. I'm sure it's there.'

Mam'zelle was glad to leave the chimney. She gazed in dismay at her sooty hand.

'Hilary, open the cupboard,' she said at last. Hilary leapt to open it. Of course there was no animal there at all, but Hilary rummaged violently over the shelves, sending books and handwork material to the floor.

'Hilary! Is it necessary to do this?' cried Mam'zelle, beginning to lose her temper again. 'I begin to disbelieve in this cat. But I warn you, if it is a trick, I will punish you all with a terrible punishment. I go now to wash my hands. You will all learn the verbs on page eighty-eight while I am gone. You will not talk. You are bad children.'

Mam'zelle disappeared out of the room, holding her sooty hand before her. When the door shut, a gale of laughter burst out. Bobby squeaked the biscuit for all she was worth. Prudence stared in surprise at it. As no one had let her into the secret, she really had believed in the tale of the lost kitten. She looked at Bobby with a sour face. So Bobby had once more got away with a trick. How Prudence wished she could give her away to Mam'zelle!

'Well, wasn't that fine?' said Bobby, putting the biscuit into her pocket. 'Half the lesson gone, and hardly anyone has had to say their verbs. Good old biscuit! You can tell your brother it was a success, Janet!'

When Mam'zelle came back she was in one of her black tempers. She had felt sure, as she washed her hands, that there had been some trick about the lost kitten, but she could not for the life of her imagine what it was. She washed her hands grimly and stalked back to the first form, determined to get her own back somehow.

She chose Prudence to say her verbs next. Prudence stood up. She was bad at French, and she faltered over her verbs, trying in vain to get them right.

'Prrrrrudence! You are even more stupid than Dorrrris!' cried Mam'zelle, rolling her 'r's in her fiercest manner. 'Ah, this first form! You have learnt nothing this term! NOTHING, I say. Ahhhhhh! Tomorrow I will give you a test. A test to see what you have learnt. Prudence, do not stare at me like a duck that is dying! You and Doris are bad girls. You will not work for me. If you do not get more than half-marks tomorrow I shall go and complain to Miss Theobald. Ah, this first form!'

The girls listened in horror. A French test! Of all the things they hated, a French test was the worst. The girls always felt certain that Mam'zelle chose questions that hardly anyone could possibly answer!

Prudence sat down, hating Mam'zelle. She knew she would do badly in the test. She had cribbed most of her written work from Pam – but in a test she would have to rely on her own knowledge – unless she could copy Pam's answers.

The girl sat and brooded. If it hadn't been for Bobby's trick, Mam'zelle wouldn't have lost her temper and suggested a beastly, horrible test! How Prudence wished she could find some way to get out of it. If only she could – or better still, if only she could know what the test questions were to be, so that she might look up the answers first!

15.

Prudence is a cheat

The more Prudence thought about the French test, the angrier she felt with Bobby. I suppose she thinks those silly tricks of hers are clever! thought Prudence to herself. And now look what they've led to – a horrible French test that I know I shall fail hopelessly in. Then I shall get into a frightful row and perhaps be sent down to Miss Theobald!

She went to find Pam to talk to her about it. She felt sure Pam would be in the library, hunting for some learned book or other to read. On the way there she passed the open door of the mistresses' common-room. Prudence glanced in.

Mam'zelle was there alone. She was writing out what looked like a list of questions. Prudence felt certain they were the questions for the test. How she longed to have a look at them!

She stood at the door uncertainly, trying to think of some excuse to go in. Mam'zelle saw her shadow there and glanced up.

'Ah, Prudence!' she said, in rather a fierce voice. 'Ah! Tomorrow you will have this French test, yes? I will show you first formers what hard work really means!'

Prudence made up her mind quickly. She would go

into the common-room, and tell Mam'zelle about the trick – and perhaps she would be able to get a peep at the questions on Mam'zelle's desk! So in she went, looking the picture of wide-eyed innocence and goodness.

'Mam'zelle! I'm awfully sorry we played about so much in your class,' she began. 'It was all that silly trick, you know – the squeaking biscuit.'

Mam'zelle stared at Prudence as if the girl had suddenly gone mad.

'The squeaking biscuit?' said Mam'zelle, in the greatest astonishment. 'What is this nonsense you are saying?'

'Mam'zelle, it isn't nonsense,' said Prudence. 'You see, Bobby had a trick biscuit that squeaked like a cat when it was pressed . . .'

Prudence was doing her best to get a look at the French questions as she spoke. Apparently Mam'zelle had finished making them out. There were about twelve questions. Prudence managed to read the first one.

Mam'zelle listened to what Prudence was saying, and at once knew two things – the true explanation of the lost kitten – and that Prudence was what the English girls called 'sneaking'. Mam'zelle had been in England a long time and had learnt to regard sneaking with dislike, although when she had first arrived she had listened to tale-bearers and thought nothing of it. But through long years of being with English mistresses she had come to the conclusion that they were right about sneaks. On no account must they be encouraged.

So Mam'zelle's face suddenly changed, and became

hard and cold as Prudence went on speaking.

'And Bobby thought it would be a good idea if we wasted some of your lesson by pretending that a kitten was lost . . .' she went on. Then she stopped as she saw Mam'zelle's face.

'Prudence, you are a nasty little girl,' said Mam'zelle. 'Yes – a very nasty little girl. I do not like you. It may seem surprising to you – but I would rather have a silly trick played on me than listen to someone who sneaks about it! Go away at once. I do not like you at all.'

Prudence felt her face flame red. She was angry and hurt – and she hadn't been able to read more than one test question after all! Mam'zelle took up the paper and slipped it inside her desk, taking no more notice of Prudence. The girl went out of the room, ready to burst into angry tears.

'Well, I know *where* the questions are, anyway,' she thought, fiercely. 'I've a good mind to slip out of bed at night and have a look at them. Nobody would know. And I'd have a good chance of being top, then, and giving everyone a surprise! I'd love to see their faces if I got top marks!'

The more she thought about it, the more determined she became. 'I *will* get those questions somehow!' she decided. 'I don't care what happens – I will!'

She wondered if Mam'zelle would punish Bobby for the trick she had played, but to her surprise not a word was said about it that day, though Mam'zelle took prep and even had Bobby up to her desk to explain something to her.

I wonder she doesn't send Bobby to Miss Theobald, thought the girl, spitefully.

Mam'zelle's sense of humour had come to her rescue after Prudence had left the common-room that morning. She had felt angry with Bobby first of all – and then when she thought of herself poking up the chimney to find a kitten that wasn't there, she had begun to laugh. That was one very good thing about Mam'zelle – she really did have a sense of humour, and when she thought something was funny, she could laugh at it whole-heartedly and forget her annoyance. So her anger against the first formers melted away – though she was determined to give them the test, all the same.

She could not, however, resist giving Bobby a little shock. When the girl came up to her desk at prep Mam'zelle made a remark that caused Bobby to feel most uncomfortable.

'Do you like biscuits, Bobby?' she asked, her large brown eyes looking at Bobby through their lenses.

'Er – er – yes, Mam'zelle,' said Bobby, wondering what was coming next.

'I thought so,' said Mam'zelle, and then turned to Bobby's French book. Bobby did not dare to ask her what she meant, but she felt certain that Mam'zelle had found out about her trick. Who could have told her? Prudence, of course! Nasty little sneak! Bobby waited for Mam'zelle to say something more, and it was with great relief that she found Mam'zelle speaking about her French mistakes.

'Now you may go to your place,' said Mam'zelle. She gave Bobby a sharp look. 'You may like to know that I do not like biscuits as much as you do, *ma chère* Bobby!'

'No, Mam'zelle – er, I mean, yes, Mam'zelle,' said poor Bobby, and escaped to her seat as quickly as she could. If Mam'zelle *does* know what I did and isn't going to punish me, it's jolly decent of her, thought the girl. I'll work really hard in her classes if she's as decent as all that!

That night, when all the girls in her dormitory were asleep, Prudence sat up in bed. She listened to the steady breathing of the sleepers around her, and then slipped out of bed. It was very warm, and she did not put on her dressing-gown or slippers. She crept out of the room in her bare feet and went down the stairs to the mistresses' common-room. It was in complete darkness. Prudence had brought a torch with her, and she switched it on to see where Mam'zelle's desk was. Good – there it was, just in front of her.

Now I can just go all through the test questions, and look up the answers! thought Prudence, gleefully. It's lucky nobody woke up and saw me leaving the dormitory.

But somebody *had* seen her leaving the dormitory!

That somebody was Carlotta, who always slept very lightly indeed, waking at the least sound. She had heard the click of the door being opened, and had sat up at once. She dimly saw a figure vanishing through the doorway, and wondered who it was. Perhaps it was someone from the next dormitory. She decided to go and see. Sometimes a girl from another dormitory was dared to slip into someone else's room at night and play some kind of joke.

Carlotta slipped out of bed. She went to the dormitory

where Bobby, Pam, Doris, and others slept. She popped her head inside. All was quiet – but one girl was awake. It was Bobby. She saw the door opening, and the dim light from the passage came into the room, showing up the figure at the door.

'Who's there?' whispered Bobby.

'Me,' said Carlotta. 'I saw somebody slipping out of our dormitory and I thought it might be someone from yours, playing a joke.'

'Well, we're all here,' said Bobby, looking down the line of beds. 'Are you sure it wasn't somebody out of your *own* room?'

'Never thought of that,' whispered back Carlotta. 'I'll go and see.' She went and found that Prudence's bed was empty. She slipped back again to Bobby and went to her bed.

'Prudence is gone,' she whispered. 'What do you think she's doing? I bet she's up to some mischief, don't you?'

'Well, let's go and see,' said Bobby, and slid quietly out of bed. Together the two made their way down the passage, and then down the stairs. They stood and listened at the bottom, wondering where Prudence was.

'There's a light coming from the mistresses' common-room,' whispered Carlotta. 'Perhaps she is in there. What *can* she be doing?'

'I'm not sure I quite like spying like this,' said Bobby, a little uncomfortably. But Carlotta had no doubts of that sort. She went quietly on bare feet to the half open door of the common-room. She looked in – and there she saw

Prudence carefully reading the list of French test questions, a French grammar book beside her. She was looking up the answers one by one.

Both girls knew at once what she was doing. Bobby had very strict ideas of honour and she was really horrified and shocked. Carlotta was not shocked, because she had seen many odd things in her life – also she knew Prudence well and was not at all surprised to find her cheating in such an outrageous way.

Bobby went into the room at once, and Prudence was so startled that she dropped the grammar book on the floor. She stared at Bobby and Carlotta with horror.

'What are you doing?' said Bobby, so angry that she forgot to whisper. 'Cheating?'

'No, I'm not,' said Prudence, making up her mind to brazen it out. 'I just came to look something up in the French grammar book, ready for the test tomorrow. So there!'

Carlotta darted to the desk and picked up the list of questions. 'See, Bobby,' she cried. 'She *is* cheating! Here are the test questions.'

Bobby looked at Prudence with the utmost scorn. 'What a hypocrite you are, Prudence!' she said. 'You go about pretending to be so good and religious and proper – and yet you sneak and cheat whenever you get a chance. You look down on Carlotta because she was a circus girl – but I tell you, *we* look down on *you* because you are all the things people hate worse than any other in school, or in life – you are cunning, deceitful, untruthful – and an out-and-out cheat!'

These were terrible things to hear. Prudence burst out sobbing, and put her head down on the desk. A pile of books upset and fell with thuds to the floor. Nobody noticed the noise they made, for all three girls were too wrapped up in what was happening.

It so happened that Miss Theobald's bedroom was just below the mistresses' common-room. She heard the succession of thuds and wondered what the noise could be. She thought she heard the sound of voices too. She switched on her light and looked at her watch. It was a quarter-past two! Whoever could be up at that time of night?

Miss Theobald put on her dressing-gown, tied the belt firmly round her waist, put on her slippers, and left the room. She went upstairs to the corridor that led to the mistresses' common-room. She arrived at the door just in time to hear the end of Bobby's scornful speech. She paused in the greatest astonishment. Whatever could be happening?

16.

Miss Theobald deals with three girls

'Girls,' said Miss Theobald, in her clear low voice. 'Girls! What are you doing here?'

There was a petrified silence as all three girls saw the head mistress standing at the door. A cold chill came over Prudence's heart, and Bobby had the shock of her life. Only Carlotta seemed undisturbed.

'Well?' said Miss Theobald, going into the room, and shutting the door. 'I really think some explanation of this scene is needed. Roberta, surely you can explain?'

'Yes, I can,' blurted out Bobby. 'Surely you can guess what Carlotta and I discovered Prudence doing, Miss Theobald?'

'She is cheating,' said Carlotta, in her little foreign-sounding voice. 'She is looking at the French test questions and finding the answers, Miss Theobald, so that she will be top tomorrow. But it is nothing surprising. Prudence is like that.'

Prudence broke out into loud sobbing again.

'I wasn't, I wasn't,' she wailed. 'Carlotta only says that because I found out she was nothing but a circus girl. I hate her! I hate Bobby too – but Carlotta is the worst of the lot, always showing off and bragging about her circus life.'

Carlotta laughed. 'I am glad you hate me, Prudence,' she said. 'I would not care to be liked by you! You are worse than anyone I have ever met in circus camps. Much worse!'

'Be quiet, Carlotta,' said Miss Theobald. She was very worried. This was a dreadful thing to happen. 'Go back to bed, all of you. I will deal with this in the morning. Is Prudence in the same dormitory as you two?'

'No, she's in mine, but not in Bobby's,' said Carlotta.

'Well – go back, all of you,' said Miss Theobald. 'If I hear another sound tonight, I shall treat the matter even more seriously tomorrow.'

She watched the three girls go back to their dormitories, and then went to her own room, wondering how to deal with things in the best way. Had she done right in letting Carlotta, the little circus girl, come to St Clare's? She might have known that the secret wouldn't be kept! And now there was Prudence Arnold to deal with – Miss Theobald could not like the girl any more than anyone else did. And Roberta – what should she say to her? She had had bad reports of her work from everyone!

The three girls went back to their beds. Carlotta fell asleep again at once. She rarely worried about anything and she did not feel any cause to be upset. Bobby lay and thought for a long time. She disliked and despised Prudence – but she did not want the girl to get into serious trouble because of her.

Prudence was the most upset of the three. It was a very serious matter to be caught cheating. She had always set herself up to be such a model – so honest and straight and had always condemned underhand, mean, or silly tricks. Now everyone would know she was not what she seemed. And it was all because of that hateful interfering Bobby and Carlotta. She felt a great surge of bitterness against Carlotta, who had so calmly told Miss Theobald what the two girls had found her doing. Prudence did not realize that practically every girl had seen through her silly pretences and had set her down as a smug hypocrite and sneak.

Next day the three girls were called into Miss Theobald's room one by one. First Carlotta, who told Miss Theobald again, quite calmly and straightforwardly, what they had found Prudence doing, and also added a few remarks of her own about Prudence.

'She looks down on me because I was a circus girl,' said Carlotta, 'but Miss Theobald, no circus would keep a person like Prudence for more than a week. I think she is a dangerous girl.'

Miss Theobald said nothing to this but in her heart she agreed with Carlotta. Prudence was dangerous. She would do no good to St Clare's, and privately Miss Theobald doubted if St Clare's would do much good for Prudence. She prided herself on the knowledge that it was very few girls indeed that St Clare's would not benefit – but it seemed to her as if Prudence was one of those few. She was the only child of doting, indulging parents, who believed that Prudence was all she seemed. Poor Prudence! What a pity her father and mother hadn't been sensible with her, and punished her when she did wrong, instead of getting upset and begging her to do better!

Miss Theobald had Bobby in next. Bobby did not want to say much about Prudence, and she was surprised to find that Miss Theobald looked at her coldly, and did not give her even a small smile when she came in.

'It is an unpleasant thing to find anyone in the act of cheating,' said Miss Theobald, looking straight at Bobby. 'I expect you hate the idea of cheating almost worse than anything else, Roberta.'

'Yes, Miss Theobald,' said Bobby, who was an honest and truthful girl, in spite of all the tricks she played. 'I think cheating is horrible. I'd just hate myself if I cheated like Prudence.'

Then Miss Theobald said a surprising thing. 'It is odd to me, Roberta,' she said, 'that you, who seem to have such strict ideas about cheating, should be such a cheat yourself.'

Bobby stared at Miss Theobald as if she couldn't believe her ears. 'What did you say, Miss Theobald?' she asked at last. 'I think I didn't hear it correctly.'

'Yes, you did, Roberta,' said Miss Theobald. 'I said that it was odd that *you* should be a cheat, when you hold such strict ideas about cheating.'

'I'm not a cheat,' said Bobby, her cheeks crimson, and her eyes beginning to sparkle with anger and surprise. 'I've never cheated in my life.'

'I don't know about *all* your life,' said the head mistress, 'but I do know about the last two months of it, Roberta. Why have your parents sent you here? To have a good time and nothing but a good time? Why are they paying high fees for you? In order to let you slack and play tricks the whole time? You *are* cheating, Roberta – yes, cheating badly. You are cheating your parents, who are willing to pay for you to learn what we can teach you here – and you won't learn. You are cheating the school, for you have good brains and could do well for St Clare's – but you won't try. And last of all you are cheating yourself – depriving yourself of all the benefits that hard work, well done, can bring you, and you are weakening your character instead of making it strong and fine, because you will not accept duty and responsibility. You just want to go your own way, do as little work as you can, and make yourself popular by being amusing and thinking out ingenious jokes and tricks to entertain your form. I think, in your own way, you are just as much a cheat as Prudence is.'

Bobby's face went white. No one had ever said anything like this to her before. She had always been popular with girls and teachers alike – but here was the head mistress pointing out cold and horrid truths that Bobby had never even thought of before. It was dreadful.

The girl sat quite still and said nothing at all. 'You had better go now, Roberta,' said Miss Theobald. 'I would like you to think over what I have said and see if your sense of honesty is as high as you think it to be – if it is, you will admit to yourself that I am right, and perhaps I shall then get good reports of you.'

Bobby stood up, still white. She mumbled something to Miss Theobald and went out of the room as if she was in a dream. She had had a real shock. It had never before occurred to Bobby that it was possible to cheat in many more ways than the ordinary one.

Prudence was the last of the three called before the head mistress. She was likely to be the most difficult to deal with. Miss Theobald decided that plain speaking was the best. Prudence must know exactly how she stood – and make her own choice.

The girl came in, looking rather frightened. She tried to look Miss Theobald straight in the eyes but could not. The head told her to sit down, and then looked just as coldly at her as she had looked at Bobby.

'Please, Miss Theobald,' began Prudence, who always believed in getting a word in first, 'please don't think the worst of me.'

'Well, I *do* think the worst of you,' said the head mistress at once. 'The very worst. And unfortunately I know it to be true. Prudence, I know the character of every girl in this school. It is my business to know it. I may not know what type of brain you have, I may not know exactly where you stand in class, or what your gifts and capabilities are, without referring to your form mistress – but at any rate I know your characters – the good and bad in you, the possibilities in your nature, your tendencies, your faults, your virtues. These I know very well. And therefore I know all too clearly, Prudence, what you really are.'

Prudence burst into tears. She often found this useful when people were what she called 'being unkind' to her. The tears had no effect at all on Miss Theobald. She stared at Prudence all the more coldly.

'Cry if you wish,' she said, 'but I would think more of you if you faced up to me and listened with a little courage. I need not tell you what you are, Prudence. I need not show you the dishonesty, deceitfulness and spite in your own nature. You are clever enough to know them yourself – and alas, cunning enough to use them, and to hide them too. St Clare's, Prudence, has nothing to offer a girl like you – unless you have enough courage to face up to yourself, and try to tear out the unpleasant failings that are spoiling and weakening what character you have. I do not want to keep you at St Clare's unless you can do this. Think it over and face things out honestly with yourself. I give you to the end of the term to make up your mind. Otherwise, Prudence, I will not keep you here.'

This was actually the only kind of treatment that Prudence really understood. She stared in horror at Miss Theobald.

'But – but – what would my father and mother say?' she half-whispered.

'That rests with you,' said the head. 'Now go, please. I am busy this morning, and have already wasted too much time on you and the others.'

Prudence went out of the room, as shocked and horrified as poor Bobby had been a few minutes earlier. She had to get her books and go to her form for a lesson, but she heard practically nothing of what Miss Lewis, the history teacher, was saying. Bobby heard very little too. Both girls were busy with their own thoughts.

After school that morning, Bobby disappeared. Pat and Isabel saw her running off in the direction of the tennis-court.

'Doesn't she look white?' said Pat. 'I wonder if anything's up?'

'Let's go and see,' said Isabel. So they went to find Bobby. She was nowhere on the courts – but Pat caught sight of a white blouse and navy skirt in a little copse of trees by the courts. She ran up to see if Bobby was there.

'Bobby, what's up?' she cried, for it was quite plain to see that Bobby was in trouble. Her usually merry face, with its sparkling eyes, was white and drawn.

'Go away, please,' said Bobby, in a tight sort of voice. 'I want to think. I – I – I've been accused of cheating – and – I've got to think about it.'

'*You*! You, accused of cheating!' cried Pat, in angry amazement. 'What rot! Who dared to do that? You tell me, and I'll go and tell them what I think of them.'

'It was Miss Theobald,' said Bobby, lifting her troubled face and looking at the twins.

'Miss *Theobald*!' said the twins, in the greatest astonishment. 'But why? How awful of her! We'll go and tell her she's wrong.'

'Well – she's not wrong,' said Bobby. 'I see she's right. She said I was a cheat because I let my parents pay high fees for me to learn what St Clare's could teach – and I wasted my time and wouldn't work – and that was cheating, because I've got good brains. She said I was cheating my parents – and the school – and myself too. It was – simply awful.'

The twins stared uncomfortably at Bobby. They couldn't think of a word to say. Bobby motioned to them to go away.

'Go away, please,' she said. 'I've got to think this out. I simply must. It's – it's somehow very important. I do play the fool a lot – but I'm not such an idiot as not to see that I've come to a sort of – sort of – cross-roads in my life. I've got to choose which way I'll go. And I've got to choose by myself. So leave me alone for a bit, will you?'

'Of course, Bobby,' said Pat, understanding. She and Isabel ran off, admiring Bobby for her ability to face herself, and make up her own mind what she was going to do.

And there was no doubt as to what Bobby was going to do. Her tremendous sense of honesty and fairness made her see at once that Miss Theobald was perfectly right. She had been given good brains, and she was wasting them. That was cheating. She had good parents who wanted her to go to a fine school and learn from good teachers. She was cheating them too. And perhaps worst of all she was cheating herself, and growing into a weaker and poorer character than she needed to be – and the world wanted fine, strong characters, able to help others on – not poor, weak, don't-care people who themselves needed to be helped all the time.

I badly want to be the sort of person who can lead others, and guide them, thought Bobby, pulling at the grass, as she sat thinking. I want others to lean on me – not me on them. Well – I've had my fun. Now I'll work. I'll just show Miss Roberts what I really can do when I make up my mind. I've already shown Belinda and Miss Wilton what I can do at sports when I try. I'll go straight to Miss Theobald and tell her now. I – I don't feel as if I like her very much now – she had such cold, angry eyes when she looked at me. But I'd better go and tell her – I'll get it off my chest and make a fresh start.

Poor Bobby felt nervous as she ran back to the school. Miss Theobald had given her a real shock, and she dreaded seeing her again, and felt half frightened as she thought of looking into the head mistress's scornful eyes. But Bobby had courage, and she was soon knocking at Miss Theobald's door.

'Come in,' said a calm voice, and Bobby went in. She went straight to the head mistress's desk.

'Miss Theobald,' she said, 'I've come to say I know you were right. I *have* been cheating – and I didn't realize it. But – I'm not going to cheat any more. Please believe me. I really do mean what I say, and you can trust me to – to do my very best from today.'

Bobby said this bravely, looking straight at Miss Theobald as she spoke. Her voice trembled a little, but she said her little speech right to the end.

Miss Theobald smiled her rare, sweet smile, and her eyes became warm and admiring. 'My dear child,' she said, and her voice was warm too, 'my dear child, I knew quite well that you would make this decision, and that you would soon come to tell me. I am proud of you – and I am going to be even more proud of you in the future. You are honest enough by nature to be able to see and judge your own self clearly – and that is a great thing. Never lose that honesty, Bobby – always be honest with yourself, know your own motives for what they are, good or bad, make your own decisions firmly and justly – and you will be a fine, strong character, of some real use in this muddled world of ours!'

'I'll try, Miss Theobald,' said Bobby, happily, so glad to see the warmth and friendliness in the head's face that she felt she could work twelve hours a day if necessary! How could she have thought she didn't like Miss Theobald? How *could* she?

She's one of the finest people I've ever met, thought the girl, as she left the room with a light step. No wonder she's head of a great school like St Clare's! We are jolly lucky to have her.

Miss Theobald was happy too. Bobby had pleased her beyond measure. It was good to feel that she had been successful in handling an obstinate character like Bobby's – now she might hope that the girl would have a splendid influence on the others, instead of the opposite.

If I could only hope that Prudence would have the

same kind of courage as Bobby! thought the head. But Prudence, I'm afraid, is not brave enough to face up to herself. That's her only chance – but I don't believe she will take it!

17.

Sadie gets a letter

Whilst Bobby was thinking out things for herself, and making her big decision, Prudence was also brooding over all that Miss Theobald had said. Mixed up with her brooding was a hatred of Carlotta, who seemed to be at the bottom of Prudence's troubles. Prudence could not see that it was her own jealousy of the girl that caused her troubles, filling her with ideas of spite and revenge. No one can ever see things clearly when jealousy or envy cast a fog over the mind.

Prudence felt that she had to get right with Miss Theobald. The girl could never bear to feel that anyone was despising her. But she had not got Bobby's courage – she dared not face the head again. Also, in her heart of hearts she was afraid that Miss Theobald would see that her repentance was not real – that it was only to make things more comfortable!

So Prudence wrote a note, and slipped it on Miss Theobald's desk, when she knew she was not in her room. The head found it there and opened it. She read it and sighed. She did not believe one word of the letter.

Dear Miss Theobald,

I have thought over what you said to me, and I do assure you I am sorry and ashamed, and I will do my best in future to turn over a new leaf and have a good influence on others.

Little humbug! thought Miss Theobald, sadly. I suppose she really believes she *is* going to turn over a new leaf. Well – we shall see!

Pat and Isabel were glad to see that Bobby looked happier that evening. She smiled at them, and her old merry twinkle came back.

'I'm all right again,' she said. 'But from now on I'm going to play fair – I'm going to use my brains and work. No more squeaking biscuits for *me*!'

The twins and Janet looked sorry. 'Oh,' said Pat in disappointment, 'Bobby – you don't mean to say you're going to go all prim and proper like that awful Prudence – never make another joke or play another trick?'

'Golly!' said Janet. 'I couldn't bear that, Bobby. For pity's sake, tell us you're going to be the same jolly old Bobby – the Don't-Care Bobby we all like so much!'

Bobby laughed and slipped her arm through Janet's. 'Don't worry,' she said. 'I *am* going to play the game now and work hard – but I shan't go all prim and proper. I couldn't. I shall be playing tricks all right – but I don't particularly want to be Don't-Care Bobby any more. I *do* care now, you see!'

Bobby kept her word to Miss Theobald, of course. She worked hard and steadily in class, and was surprised to find how well her mind worked when she really set it to something – and she was even more surprised to find how enjoyable good work was!

'I should never be able to slave at my lessons like you do though, Pam,' she said, looking at the thirteen-year-old girl hunched over a book. 'You're looking awfully pale lately. I'm sure you read too much.'

Pam *was* pale – and not only pale but unhappy-looking too. She was terribly sorry now that she had made firm friends with Prudence, because she was beginning to dislike her heartily, but was not strong enough to tell her so. So she found refuge in her lessons, and was working twice as hard as anyone else. She smiled a pale smile at Bobby, and envied her. Bobby didn't mind saying anything that came into her mind, and was as strong as Pam was weak. How Pam wished she could have made friends with Bobby instead of with Prudence!

Prudence was feeling rather pleased with herself. Miss Theobald had not said anything about her letter and the girl felt sure it had made a good impression on the head. For some reason Mam'zelle had not given the French test after all, so the class had heaved a sigh of relief – especially Prudence, who felt certain that Carlotta would blurt out that she, Prudence, had seen the questions before.

Things are going better, thought Prudence. If only that beastly Carlotta could get into a row! She just flaunts about as if she were a princess and not a common little circus girl! I wonder if she visits any of her low-down friends any more? I saw her going off early yesterday morning before breakfast.

It was true that Carlotta did go off each morning – but not to visit any circus friend. She had discovered that some lovely hunting horses were kept in a field not far off, and the girl was visiting them regularly. Sometimes she rode one or other bareback, if there was nobody about. The girl was quite mad about horses, and never lost a chance of going near them if she could.

Nobody knew this. Prudence knew Carlotta was slipping off, but told no one else, for she had found that none of the girls encouraged her confidences at all. She determined to keep a watch herself.

She and Pam went off one afternoon together, Pam not at all pleased about it, but not daring to say no. Prudence had seen Carlotta going off – but somehow or other she missed following her, and the two girls stopped in a little lane, whilst Prudence tried to think where Carlotta had gone.

A man came riding by on a bicycle. He was not a pleasant-looking fellow and his eyes were set very close together. He got off his bicycle when he came up to the girls, and spoke to them. His voice sounded rather foreign, and had a slow American drawl with it. Prudence felt absolutely certain that he had come to see Carlotta.

'Excuse me,' said the man. 'Am I anywhere near St Clare's school?'

'Well – about a mile away,' said Prudence. 'Why? Do you want to see someone there?'

'I should like to,' said the man. 'It's very important

indeed. I suppose you couldn't take a message for me?'

Prudence's heart beat fast. What trouble she could get Carlotta into now! What would Miss Theobald say if she knew Carlotta was slipping out to see awful people like this?

'Of course I could take a message for you,' she said.

The man took a letter from his pocket and handed it to Prudence. 'Don't you tell a single soul,' he said. 'It's very very important. I'll be here at eleven o'clock tonight without fail.'

'All right,' said Prudence. 'I'll see to it for you.'

'You're a brick,' said the man. 'You're dandy! I'll give you a fine present, see if I don't!'

Someone else came down the lane at that moment, and the man jumped on his bicycle and rode away, saluting the two girls as he went. Pam shivered a little.

'Prudence! I don't like him! I don't think you ought to have spoken to him. You know it's a rule we never speak to strangers. You're not going to get Carlotta into trouble are you?'

'Oh, be quiet!' said Prudence, impatiently. She pushed the letter into her pocket without looking at it. 'Aren't I *doing* something for Carlotta, silly? Aren't I taking a message to her from a friend? What awful friends she has, too!'

Pam was worried. Her head ached, and she felt miserable. She wished she had never, never become friendly with Prudence. Her mind turned once again to her work – she could only forget things if she worked. She hadn't been sleeping well at night, and her work was becoming difficult to do which made her worry all the more.

'Now listen to me, Pam,' said Prudence. 'You and I are going to go out tonight at half-past ten and come here. We are going to hide behind the hedge, and hear what goes on between our dear Carlotta and her circus friend. If she is planning any more escapades, we can report them.'

Pam stared at her friend in distress. 'I can't do that,' she said. 'I can't.'

'You've got to,' said Prudence, and she stared at Pam out of her pale blue eyes. Pam felt too tired and weak to argue. She simply nodded her head miserably and turned back to go home. The girls walked back in silence, Prudence thinking with delight that now she had Carlotta at her mercy!

As soon as they got back to school Hilary hailed Prudence. 'Prudence! You know quite well it's your turn to brush up all the tennis-balls and get them clean this week. You haven't done it once, you lazy creature. You jolly well do it now, or you'll be sorry.'

'I've just got to take a message to somebody,' said Prudence. 'I won't be a minute.'

'You just let somebody else take the message,' said Hilary, annoyed. 'I know your little ways, Prudence – you'll *just* do this and you'll *just* do that – and the little jobs you ought to do aren't done!'

'*I'll* take the letter, Prudence,' said Pam, wearily. She felt that she could not stand arguments a minute more. Prudence handed her the letter with a sulky face. Pam went off to find Carlotta. She was in the common-room with the others. Pam went up to her and gave her the letter.

'This is for you,' she said. Carlotta took the note, and, without looking at the envelope, tore it open. She read the first line or two in evident amazement. Then she looked at the envelope.

'Why, it isn't for me,' she said, looking round for Pam, who, however, had gone. 'It's for Sadie. I suppose Pam didn't see her name on the envelope. How odd! Where's Sadie, Alison?'

'Doing her hair,' said Alison. There was a shout of laughter at this. When Sadie was missed she was always either Doing Her Hair, Doing Her Nails or Doing Her Face. Carlotta grinned and went to find her.

'Hi, Sadie,' she said, 'here's a note for you. Sorry I opened it by mistake, but that little idiot of a Pam gave it to me instead of you. I haven't read it.'

'Who's it from? How did Pam get it?' asked Sadie curiously, taking the note.

'Don't know,' said Carlotta, and went. Sadie opened the envelope and took out the letter inside. She read it and her face changed. She sat down on the bed, and thought hard. She read the letter again.

Dear Miss Sadie,

Do you remember your old nanny, Hannah? Well, I'm over here and I'd like to see you. I don't like to come to the school. Can you come down to the lane by the farm and see me for a few minutes? I'll be there at eleven o'clock tonight.

Hannah

Sadie had been very fond of Hannah, who had been her nanny and her mother's help for some years. She was astonished that Hannah should be in England, for she had thought she was in America. Why did she want to see her? Had anything happened? Sadie wondered whether to tell Alison or not – and then she decided not to. Alison was a nice girl and a pretty one, but she was a feather-head. She might go and bleat it out to somebody!

Sadie tucked the note into her pocket and went down-stairs. 'Hallo!' said Alison. 'I was wondering whenever you were coming down. It's nearly supper-time.'

Sadie was rather silent at supper-time. She felt puzzled and a little worried. She thought she would ask Pam where she had got the note from – but Pam was not at supper.

'She's got a frightful headache and Miss Roberts sent her to Matron,' said Janet. 'She's got a temperature.'

Prudence was quite pleased to think she would not have Pam with her that night after all. She was getting a little tired of pretending to Pam that everything she was doing was for Carlotta's good. She looked at Carlotta to see if the girl showed any signs of receiving the letter. Carlotta saw her glancing her way and made one of her peculiarly rude faces. Prudence looked down her nose in disgust and turned away. Carlotta grinned. She didn't care a ha'-penny for Prudence and delighted in shocking her.

18.

An exciting night

That evening Sadie lay awake until the clock struck a quarter to eleven. It was still fairly light, but everyone in the dormitory was asleep. Sadie got up quietly and dressed. No one heard her. She slipped out of the dormitory and down the stairs. In a few moments she was out of the garden-door and in the school grounds. Behind her slipped a dark little shadow – Prudence! Prudence thought that she was following Carlotta, of course. She had no idea it was Sadie. Prudence had got up at a quarter-past ten, and had slipped out of the dormitory next to Sadie's, afraid that if she waited any later, Carlotta might get away before she had a chance of keeping up with her. She had felt so certain that it was Carlotta the letter had been for – she had never even looked at the envelope to see what name was written there!

Now, at about a quarter-past eleven, Alison awoke suddenly with a sore throat. She cleared it and swallowed. It felt most unpleasant. She knew that Sadie had some lozenges and she decided to wake her and ask for them. So the girl slipped out of bed and went to Sadie's cubicle.

She put out her hand to shake Sadie – and to her great astonishment found that she was not there! Her bed was empty! Her clothes had gone – so she had dressed. Alison sat down on the bed in surprise. She was hurt. Why hadn't Sadie told her she was going somewhere? But where in the world could she have gone? There couldn't be a midnight feast or anything like that – because it was obvious that everyone was in bed – unless the other dormitory was holding a feast and had asked Sadie.

Well, Sadie might at least have told me, even if *I* wasn't asked, thought Alison, aggrieved. I'll go and peep in at the twins' dormitory and see if there's anything going on there.

So she slipped into the next dormitory – but everyone's bed seemed filled – with the exception of one. How odd. Alison stood thinking – and then she heard a whisper. It was Pat.

'Who's that? What are you doing?'

'Oh, Pat – are you awake?' said Alison in a low voice, going to Pat's bed. 'I say – Sadie's gone. She's dressed – and her bed is empty. I don't know why, Pat, but I feel worried about it. Sadie didn't seem herself this evening – she was all quiet and sort of worried. I noticed it.'

Pat sat up. She was puzzled. Sadie didn't usually do anything out of the ordinary at all. 'Wherever can she have gone?' she said.

'There's one bed empty in your dorm, too,' said Alison. 'Whose is it?'

'Golly – it's Prudence's,' said Pat, in astonishment. 'Don't tell me those two are somewhere together! I thought Sadie detested Prudence.'

'She does,' said Alison, more puzzled than ever. A movement in the next bed made them look round. Carlotta's voice came to them, low and guarded.

'What *are* you two doing? You'll wake everyone up! Anything up?'

'Carlotta – it's so funny – both Sadie and Prudence are gone from their beds,' said Pat. Carlotta sat up at once. She remembered the note she had given to Sadie.

'I wonder if it's anything to do with the note that Pam gave to me instead of to Sadie,' she said.

'What note?' asked Alison. Carlotta told her, and Pat and Alison listened in surprise.

'Somehow I think there's something a bit odd about this,' said Carlotta. 'I do really.'

'So do I,' said Alison, uncomfortably. 'I'm awfully fond of Sadie. You don't think – you don't think, do you – that's she being kidnapped – or anything. She said once that she nearly had been, over in America. She's awfully rich, you know. Her mother sent her over here because she was afraid she might be kidnapped again in America. She told me that.'

Carlotta could more readily believe this than the more stolid Pat. She got out of bed.

'I think the first thing we'd better do is to ask Pam where she got that note,' said Carlotta.

'She's in the sickbay,' said Pat.

'Well, we'll go there then,' said Carlotta. 'Let's wake Isabel. Hurry!'

It was not long before the twins, Alison and Carlotta

were creeping across the school grounds to the sickbay. This was where any girl who was ill was kept in bed. The door was locked, but a downstairs window was open. Carlotta got in quietly. She could climb like a cat!

'Stay here,' she whispered to the others. 'We don't want to wake Matron. I'll find Pam and ask her what we want to know.'

She made her way through the dark little room and up the stairs to where a dim light was burning in a bedroom. Here Pam lay, wide awake, trying to cool her burning forehead with a wet handkerchief. She was amazed and frightened when she saw Carlotta creeping into the room.

'Sh!' whispered Carlotta. 'It's only me, Carlotta! Pam – where did you get that note from – the one you gave me?'

'Prudence and I met a funny-looking man down the lane by the farm this afternoon,' said Pam. 'He said he wanted to send a message to someone. So Prudence took the note and meant to give it to you. But I had to give it to you instead. The man wanted you to meet him there at eleven o'clock tonight – or to meet somebody there. Why? What's happened?'

'The note wasn't for me – it was for Sadie,' said Carlotta, feeling puzzled. 'Did the man *say* it was for me?'

'Well, now I come to think of it, no names were mentioned at all,' said Pam, frowning as she tried to remember the conversation. 'But somehow Prudence seemed to think we were talking about you.'

'She would!' said Carlotta, grimly. 'I know where she is too! She thought that the man was one of my low-down circus friends, as she calls them – and she wanted to get me down there – and she would spy on me and report me. I know Prudence! But as it happens, the note *wasn't* for me – and I've a feeling that there's some dirty work going on round poor Sadie. She's gone down to the lane by the farm – and I bet Prudence has gone there too – to spy.'

'Yes, she has,' said Pam, feeling frightened and miserable. Tears ran down her cheeks. 'Oh, Carlotta – I'm supposed to be Prudence's friend – but I do so dislike her. It's making me ill. I'm really afraid of her.'

'Don't you worry,' said Carlotta, comfortingly, and she patted Pam's hot hand. 'We'll deal with Miss Sour-Milk Prudence after this. She'll get herself into serious trouble if she's not careful.'

The girl slipped away and went back to the others, who were waiting impatiently by the open window. She told them in a few words all she had learnt.

'Had we better wake Miss Theobald?' said Pat, troubled.

'No – we'll see what's happening first. It mayn't be anything much,' said Carlotta. 'Come on down to the lane by the farm.'

The four girls took bicycles and cycled away in the dark. The summer twilight was just enough for them to see their way. Half-way to the farm they met a sobbing figure running up towards them. It was Prudence!

'Prudence! What's the matter? What's happening?' cried Pat in alarm.

'Oh, Pat! Is it you? Oh, Pat! Something dreadful has happened!' sobbed Prudence. 'Sadie has been kidnapped!

She has, she has! I thought I was following Carlotta when I went out this evening just before eleven – but it was Sadie after all – and when she got near the farm, two men came up and took hold of her. And they dragged her to a hidden car and put her in. I was hiding behind the hedge.'

'Did you hear them say anything?' demanded Carlotta.

'Yes – they said something about a place called Jalebury,' wept Prudence. 'Where is it?'

'Jalebury!' said Carlotta, in astonishment. 'I know where Jalebury is. Why, that's where the circus camp went to! Are you sure you heard them say they were taking Sadie there, Prudence?'

Prudence was quite sure. Carlotta jumped on her bicycle. 'I'm just going to cycle to the telephone kiosk down the lane,' she called. 'The kidnappers will get a shock when they get to Jalebury!'

She rode to the kiosk, jumped off her bicycle, disappeared into the little telephone box, and looked up a number there. In a minute or two her excited voice filled the kiosk as she poured out her story to someone, and asked for their help.

In about five minutes she was back with the others. 'I telephoned the circus camp,' she said. 'They'll be on the watch for the car. They'll stop it and surround it – and if they don't rescue Sadie, I'll eat my hat!'

'Oh, Carlotta – you really are marvellous!' said Pat. 'But wouldn't it have been better to call the police?'

'I never thought of that,' said Carlotta. 'You see – in circus life we don't somehow call in the police. Now – I'm off to join in the fun! I know my way to Jalebury. But I'm not going by bike!'

'How are you going then?' asked Pat.

'On horseback!' said Carlotta. 'I shall borrow one of the hunters I've ridden on in the early morning. They are quite near here – and any of them will come to me if I call to them. I'm going to be in at the fun!'

The girl disappeared into a field. The twins, Alison, and Prudence stared after her in the starlight. Carlotta was such a surprising person. She went straight for what she wanted, and nothing could stop her. In a few minutes they heard the sound of galloping hoofs – and that was the last they saw of Carlotta that night!

19.

Carlotta to the rescue!

Carlotta knew the countryside around very well. She took the horse across fields and hills, her sense of direction telling her exactly where to go. She thought hard all the time, and smiled grimly when Prudence came into her mind.

'She's gone just too far this time!' she thought, as she galloped on through the night, the horse responding marvellously to the girl's sure hands. 'I do hope I get to Jalebury in time to see the fun.'

She didn't get there in time! But when she reached the little town after some time, she saw lights in the big field where the camp was, and galloped swiftly to it. She put the horse to jump the fence that ran round the field and it rose high in the air.

A voice hailed her. 'Who's that?'

'Oh, Jim – it's me, Carlotta!' she cried. 'Has anything happened? Did you get my message?'

'We did,' said the man, coming up to take the panting horse. 'And we've got the girl for you. Mighty pretty, isn't she?'

'Very,' said Carlotta, with a laugh. 'And if I know anything about Sadie, she wanted to borrow a comb and do her hair, or powder her nose, as soon as you rescued her! Tell me what happened.'

'Well, as soon as we got your message we dragged a caravan out of the field and set it across the road there – see, where it runs down into the town,' said the man, pointing in the starlight to where a road, not much wider than a big lane, ran between high hedges. 'Nobody was about, and not a car came by – till suddenly one appeared, racing along. We guessed it must be the one we wanted.'

'Oh – if only I'd been there!' groaned Carlotta. 'Go on. What happened?'

'Well, when the car saw the caravan by the light of its headlamps, it stopped, of course,' said Jim. 'We pretended that our caravan had got stuck, and we were pulling and heaving at it like anything. One of the men in the car jumped out to see what was up – and he called to the other man to come and help us so that we could shift the caravan out of his way. So I slipped off to the car, and there, in the back, all tied up like a chicken, with a handkerchief round her mouth, was your friend. I got her out in half a tick, of course, and bundled her behind a hedge.'

'Quick work!' said Carlotta, enjoying the tale thoroughly.

'Very quick,' agreed the man. 'Well, then I went back to the others, tipped them the wink, and we moved the caravan away in a jiffy, leaving the road clear. The two men went back to the car, hopped in, never looked behind at all to see if the girl was there – and drove off in the night without her!'

Carlotta began to laugh. It struck her as very funny indeed to think of the two kidnappers being so easily tricked and racing away in the night with an empty car!

'Whatever will they think when they take a look behind and see Sadie is gone?' she said. 'You did awfully well, Jim. Now we don't need to call in the police or have a fuss made or anything. I can just take Sadie back to the school and nobody needs to know anything about it. I'm sure Miss Theobald wouldn't want the papers to splash headlines all about the kidnapping of Miss Sadie Greene!'

'Come along and have a word with her,' said Jim. Carlotta went along with him, leading the horse by a lock of its thick mane. She came to a large caravan and went up the steps. Inside was Sadie, combing out her ruffled hair by the light of an oil-lamp. A woman was sitting watching her. Nobody appeared to think that anything extraordinary had happened. It seemed as if rescuing kidnapped girls was quite an ordinary thing to happen in the middle of the night! Not even Sadie was excited – but then, she seldom was!

'Hallo, Sadie,' said Carlotta. 'Doing Your Hair, as usual!'

'Carlotta!' said Sadie, in surprise. 'How did *you* get here? I was an awful idiot, I got kidnapped again. That note you opened by mistake was supposed to be from an old nanny of ours that I was very fond of – and I went out to see her – and two men caught me. And then somebody bundled me out and rescued me – but I haven't quite got the hang of things yet. And my hair got frightfully untidy, so I'm just putting it right.'

Carlotta grinned. 'If you fell out of an aeroplane you'd wonder if your hair was getting windblown!' she said. She told Sadie all that had happened, and how Prudence had followed her, thinking she was after Carlotta.

'Gracious!' said Sadie. 'What a night. I suppose we'd better go back to St Clare's, hadn't we?'

'Well, I think we had,' said Carlotta. 'You see, Sadie, I guess Miss Theobald won't want this story known all over the country – and I know the circus people won't want the police called in. They never do. So I think we'd better just go quietly back to school, and hush it all up. I've got a horse outside – a hunter I took from a field. Do you think you could manage to ride it with me?'

'I'm sure I couldn't,' said Sadie, promptly.

'Oh, well – you'll have to try, said Carlotta impatiently. 'You can put your arms round my waist and hang on to me. Come on!'

The two girls went to find the horse. Jim had it outside the caravan. Carlotta jumped up and spoke to Jim.

'Thanks for doing all you did,' she said. 'I won't forget it. Hold your tongue about everything, won't you?'

'You bet!' said Jim. 'It's all in a day's work. Come and see us again, Carlotta. I always say and I always shall say you're wasted at school – you ought to be in a circus like you've always been – handling horses. You're a marvel with them.'

'Ah well,' said Carlotta, 'things don't always happen as we want them to. Sadie, what are you doing? Surely you can jump up behind me?'

'I can't,' said Sadie. 'The horse seems so enormous.'

Jim gave her a heave and the surprised girl found herself sitting behind Carlotta. She clung to her with all her might. The horse set off at a gallop. Carlotta put him to jump the fence. Up he went with the two girls on his back and came down lightly the other side. Sadie squealed with fright. She had nearly fallen off.

'Let me off, oh, let me off!' she shouted. 'Carlotta, LET ME OFF!'

But Carlotta didn't. She galloped on through the starlit night, poor Sadie bumping up and down, up and down behind her.

'Oh,' gasped Sadie, 'tell the horse not to bump me so, Carlotta! Carlotta, do you hear?'

'It's you that are bumping the horse!' said Carlotta, with a squeal of laughter. 'Hang on, Sadie! Hang on!'

But it was too much for Sadie. When they had gone about half-way back, she suddenly loosened her hold on Carlotta, and slid right off the horse. She fell to the ground with a bump and gave a yell. Carlotta stopped the horse at once.

'Sadie! Are you hurt? Why did you do that?'

'I'm awfully bruised,' came Sadie's voice from the ground. 'Carlotta, I will NOT ride that bumpy horse another step. I'd rather walk.'

'How tiresome you are!' said Carlotta, springing lightly

to the ground. She pulled Sadie up and soon made sure that the girl was not really hurt. 'It will take us ages to get back. We shall have to walk all the way and I must lead the horse. We shan't get back till daylight!'

'I wonder what the others are thinking,' said Sadie, limping along beside Carlotta. 'I bet they're wondering and wondering what's happened!'

The others had worried and wondered till they were tired! They had all gone back to school, and had awakened the rest of the twins' dormitory. The girls had sat and discussed the night's happenings, wondering whether to go and tell Miss Theobald or not. Hilary at last decided that they really must. Carlotta and Sadie had not come back, and Prudence was almost in hysterics. She really was frightened out of her life to think of the trouble that she had caused through being such a mischief-maker.

'Look – there's the dawn coming,' said Pat, looking to the east, where a pale silvery light was spreading. 'In another half-hour the sun will be up. For goodness' sake – let's tell Miss Theobald now. We can't wait for Carlotta any longer.'

So Pat and Isabel went down to awaken Miss Theobald, and the head listened in growing alarm to their curious tale. She had just reached out to take the telephone receiver in order to get in touch with the police when Pat gave a cry.

'Look! Look, Miss Theobald! There's Carlotta coming back – and she's got Sadie with her! Oh – good old Carlotta!'

Sure enough, there was Carlotta coming up the school grounds, with Sadie limping beside her. They had returned the hunter to its field and had come wearily up the school grounds just as the sun was rising. They had had a long way to walk and were very tired indeed.

Miss Theobald had them in her room in a trice, quite bewildered with the strange tale she had heard. She made the tired girls hot cocoa and gave them biscuits to eat. Then, to Carlotta's immense disgust, she took the sleepy girls across to the sickbay, woke up Matron, and bade her put the girls to bed in peace and quietness and keep them there.

'But Miss Theobald,' began Carlotta. Not a scrap of notice was taken of her, however, and it was not long before both she and Sadie were tucked up in comfortable beds and were sound asleep!

'If I had let them go back to their dormitory they would have talked until the dressing bell,' said Miss Theobald. 'Now go back to your beds too, you others, and we will sort things out in the morning. Really, I feel I must be dreaming all this!'

But it was no dream, and in the morning, as Miss Theobald had said, things had to be 'sorted out'.

It was decided that the matter must certainly be reported to the police, but kept as quiet as possible. Carlotta had the excitement of being interviewed by admiring policemen – and Prudence had the ordeal of being closely questioned too. She was frightened out of her life at it all. She had been able to lie and get away with so many unpleasant things before in her life – but there was no getting away with this.

'I want to go home,' she sobbed to Miss Theobald. 'I feel ill. Let me go home.'

'No,' said Miss Theobald. 'You want to run away from the troubles you have caused, Prudence. You are going to remain here and face them, however unpleasant things may be for you. Unless you want me to tell your parents everything, you will stay here and face things out. I hope this will be a lesson to you. I am not going to keep you at St Clare's after this term, of course. You will never be liked by any of the girls now. But you are going to learn a very bitter lesson for the rest of this term – and I hope, Prudence, you will derive some good from it. You need a punishment to make you learn what you have to learn.'

Sadie's mother had to be told about the attempted kidnapping and she arrived at St Clare's in a great state two weeks before the end of the term. She wanted to take Sadie away at once, but Miss Theobald persuaded her not to.

'You may be sure that such a thing will not be allowed to happen again now,' she said. 'If you wish, of course, you must take her away at the end of the term. Maybe you will want to take her back to America with you. Sadie is too grown up for St Clare's, Mrs Greene. If you *could* leave her for a term or two, so that she might shake down a little and try to become more of a schoolgirl, I should be delighted to have her. But maybe you don't want her to be an ordinary schoolgirl!'

Miss Theobald was right. Mrs Greene was like Alison, a feather-head! She had no brains at all, and her only interests in life were her clothes and entertaining others – and her precious pretty daughter, Sadie! She looked round at the girls of St Clare's, some with pig-tails, some with short hair, some freckled, some plain, some pretty.

'Well,' she said, 'don't you get sore at me for saying it, Miss Theobald – but I don't feel I want Sadie to be like these girls! My Sadie's pretty, and she's cute too. I wouldn't call any of these girls cute. Would you?'

'No, I wouldn't,' said Miss Theobald, smiling. 'We don't teach them to be "cute", Mrs Greene. We teach them to be independent, responsible, kind and intelligent, but we don't teach them to be "cute".'

'Well – I guess I'll leave Sadie here for the rest of the term, anyway,' said Mrs Greene, after a pause. 'I'll stay at the hotel down in the town and keep an eye on her. She seems fond of that pretty little thing called Alison. I'll let her stay on just for the rest of the term. Then I'll take her off to America again – and maybe Alison would like to come along too. She's about the cutest girl here.'

Miss Theobald made a private note in her mind to tell Alison's mother not to let her go with Sadie to America. She was not pleased with Alison that term. The girl had much better stuff in her than she had shown the last two or three months, and Miss Theobald did not want her to be completely spoilt.

So it came about that both Sadie and Prudence stayed on for the rest of the term and did not leave. Sadie was pleased – but Prudence was angry and unhappy. It was terribly difficult to face so many hostile girls every minute of the day. For the first time in her life she was really getting a punishment she deserved.

20.

The end of the term

And now the term drew swiftly to an end. There were tennis matches, swimming matches and other sports. There were, alas, exams too! The days were very full, and everyone had plenty to do from morning to night. The girls were very happy – all but Prudence, and nobody, not even Pam, felt sorry for the little humbug. No one knew she was leaving, and Prudence did not say a word about it.

Pam had been ill for a week or two – and Miss Theobald had come to the conclusion that her illness was due to over-work and unhappiness. Carlotta had told her about Pam's friendship with Prudence and how unhappy she had become about it.

'Now, Carlotta, you can do something for me,' said Miss Theobald. 'You can make friends with Pam, please, and see that Prudence does not try to get her under her thumb again. Pam is a good little thing, too advanced for her age – and it seems to me it will do her good to slack a little, instead of working so hard. Take her under your wing, Carlotta, and make her laugh a bit!'

Carlotta was surprised at this request, but rather proud. She had a great admiration for the sensible and wise head mistress, and the two understood each other very well. So, when Pam came out of the sickbay looking rather white and worn, and afraid that Prudence would attach herself to her once again, Pam had a pleasant surprise. Carlotta always seemed to be there! Carlotta pushed Prudence off, and asked Pam to go for walks with her instead, and got her to help her with her prep. Pam soon felt much happier, and her small face glowed whenever Carlotta came up.

'It's been a funny term, hasn't it?' said Miss Roberts to Mam'zelle. 'First of all I thought the new girls were never going to settle down and work – and I gave up Bobby in despair.'

'Ah, that Bobby!' said Mam'zelle, lifting her hands as she remembered all Bobby's tricks. 'That Bobby! But now she has turned over a new stalk – no, what is it you say – a new leaf – and she works and she works!'

'Yes – something has certainly happened to Bobby,' said Miss Roberts. 'She's using her brains – and she's got good ones too. I'm pleased with her. I'm going easy with little Pam Boardman though – she's inclined to work too hard.'

Mam'zelle smiled. 'Ah yes – but now that she has Carlotta for a friend, she does not work so hard. Always we have to hold Pam back or she would over-work herself – she does not play enough. But Carlotta will help her to do that. It is odd, that friendship.'

'I shouldn't be surprised if the head has something to do with it,' said Miss Roberts. 'She's a very remarkable woman, you know. She knows the girls inside-out.'

'Well – I hear that both Prudence and Sadie are

leaving,' said Mam'zelle. 'That is good. Ah, that Prrrrrrrudence! How I detest her!'

'She has a lot of lessons to learn in life,' said Miss Roberts, seriously. 'She has been taught a very big one here, and has learnt for the first time to see herself as she really is – and for two or three weeks she has to undergo the ordeal of knowing that others see her as she is, too. Ah, well – I don't know how she will turn out. She's a problem – and I'm glad I haven't got to solve it!'

'Sadie will not be missed either,' said Mam'zelle. 'Except by silly little Alison. She has had her head turned properly by that American girl. Ah, how cross they have both made me this term!'

Miss Roberts laughed. 'Yes – you've been in some fine tempers this term, Mam'zelle,' she said. 'But never mind – the term will soon be at an end – then summer holidays – and no tiresome girls to teach!'

'And when September comes, we shall both be saying, "Ah, how nice it will be to see those tiresome girls again!" ' laughed Mam'zelle.

The girls were sorry that the summer term was coming to an end. Margery Fenworthy won the tennis championship for the school, and also the swimming matches. Carlotta won the diving. Bobby put up a record for the first form in swimming under water and was loudly cheered and clapped. Nobody was more surprised than she was!

'You deserve it, Bobby,' said Belinda, clapping her on the back. 'My word, how you've improved in tennis and swimming. I'm proud of you, Don't-Care Bobby!'

Bobby felt happy. Her work had improved as much as her sports, and she had felt a new self-respect and contentment. Janet worked well too, now that Bobby was working, and the twins followed suit.

'You'll be able to go up into the second form next term, and do me credit,' said Miss Roberts, as she gave out the exam marks. 'Bobby, you are top in geography! Simply marvellous! Pam, you have done very well indeed. You O'Sullivan twins have managed to tie for second place in most things – that's very good. Hilary, you are top of the form, as you should be! Prudence, Doris, Alison and Sadie are, I regret to say, settling down near the bottom as usual. The great surprise is Carlotta, who has done far better than I expected! I think, Pam, that your help has done a good deal towards putting Carlotta into a higher place than I expected.'

Pam glowed with pleasure. Carlotta looked surprised and amused. Miss Roberts went on with her remarks, picking out each girl and commenting shrewdly on their term's work and exam results. Most of the first-form girls, with the exception of Pam, who was too young, were to go up into the second form the next term.

'That's good,' said Janet, afterwards. 'We shall all keep together now – and the two we like least, Sadie and Prudence, won't be here. I overheard by accident something Mam'zelle said in her loud voice to Miss Roberts. Well – I must say it's good news that Prudence won't be back.'

'Won't she really?' said Janet. 'Well, I vote if that's so,

we're a bit nicer to her then. She's looking pretty miserable lately.'

So for the last two or three days of term the girls relaxed their hostile attitude towards Prudence and the girl regained some of her confidence and happiness. She had begun to learn her lesson, though, and made no attempt to boast or to lie, as she always used to do. Poor Prudence – she was her own worst enemy, and always would be.

The last day came, and the usual wild rush of packing and saying goodbye. Margery Fenworthy proudly packed the beautiful racket she had won for her tennis prize. Bobby just as proudly packed her swimming-underwater prize – a lovely new swimming-costume. All the girls were happy and excited.

'It's a shame I can't come to America with you,' said Alison to Sadie, half-tearful at the thought of saying goodbye to her friend. 'I can't think why Mother won't let me. Don't forget me, Sadie, will you?'

'Of course not,' said Sadie, quite meaning what she said – but the girl was incapable of remembering anyone for long! Her real interest in life was herself and her looks – her friends would never last with her! But Alison did not know this and squeezed Sadie's arm tightly. She knew she would miss her terribly.

The last minutes came. Goodbyes were shouted as the school-coach came up to the door for the first batch of girls. Mam'zelle screamed as someone dropped a suitcase on her toes.

'Pat! *Que vous êtes . . .*' she began. And a whole chorus of girls finished her sentence for her . . .

'ABOMINABLE!' There was a shriek of laughter as they tried to get away from Mam'zelle's large hands, dealing out friendly slaps all the way round.

'Goodbye, Miss Roberts,' said the twins. 'Goodbye, Miss Roberts,' said Bobby. 'Goodbye, Miss Roberts,' said all the other first formers one by one.

'Goodbye, girls,' said Miss Roberts. 'Well – you won't stand in awe of me any more next term! You'll all be second formers, very important indeed – and I'll be left behind with the first form! Dear me – to think how you all grow up!'

'They'll long to be back with you, Miss Roberts!' laughed Miss Jenks, who was nearby. 'My goodness, they don't know what a dragon they are coming to, next term. How I'll make them work! What terrible punishments I shall have in store for them! How I shall see through all their tricks!'

The girls laughed. They liked Miss Jenks, and were looking forward to going up into her class. It would be fun. A new class and a new teacher – yes, they really would have fun!

The first formers got into the coach that was waiting for them. Alison heaved herself up, and her hat went crooked and then fell off. The girls stared at her hair.

'Alison! You've done your hair all funny again!' cried Pat. 'Piled it all on top as if you were twenty-one or something. You *do* look a freak! Honestly you do.'

Alison went red. She put her hat on again and turned defiantly to the twins.

'Well, Sadie says . . .' she began. And at once, in the greatest delight the whole coachful of girls took up the chorus they knew so well, and chanted it all the way down to the station.

'Sadie says – Sadie says – what does Sadie *say*? Sadie says – oh, Sadie says – what does Sadie *say*?'

And there we will leave them, first formers for the last time, singing on their way home for the holidays. What will happen to them when they are important second formers? Ah – that is another story altogether!

SECOND FORM at ST CLARE'S

'I think we ought to have a midnight
Feast EVERY term, you know!
School doesn't seem really
complete without that!'

The second form have plans
to enjoy themselves. But will
spiteful Elsie spoil the feast?

THERE'S MORE TROUBLE
ST CLARE'S!

The THIRD FORM at ST CLARE'S

Written by Pamela Cox

'Girls!' cried Janet. 'We just have to make sure that the play goes ahead somehow!'

There's lots of drama this term! The third form have written a school play and jealous Fern plots to ruin it. Then there is a terrible accident . . .

THERE'S MORE TROUBLE ST CLARE'S!

The O'Sullivan Twins

Enid Blyton

The O'Sullivan Twins

EGMONT

St Clare's

Enid Blyton

EGMONT

We bring stories to life

First published in Great Britain 1942 by Methuen & Co. Ltd
This edition published 2013
by Egmont UK Limited
The Yellow Building
1 Nicholas Road
London W11 4AN

978 0 6035 6935 7

A CIP catalogue record for this title is available from the British Library
Printed and bound in Great Britain by the CPI Group

56922/1

EGMONT LUCKY COIN

Our story began over a century ago, when seventeen-year-old Egmont Harald Petersen found a coin in the street.

He was on his way to buy a flyswatter, a small hand-operated printing machine that he then set up in his tiny apartment.

The coin brought him such good luck that today Egmont has offices in over 30 countries around the world. And that lucky coin is still kept at the company's head offices in Denmark.

Contents

1.

Easter term at St Clare's

'Mother! Did you know that Cousin Alison, who was at Redroofs School with us, is going to St Clare's next term?' said Pat O'Sullivan, looking up from a letter she was reading. Her twin, Isabel, was reading it too, the two dark heads side by side at the breakfast table.

'Yes, I knew,' said their mother, smiling. 'Your aunt Sarah wrote and told me. When she heard how much you liked St Clare's, she decided to send Alison there too – and you can look after her a little, the first term.'

'Alison is a bit stuck up,' said Pat. 'We saw her these hols, Mummy – full of airs and graces. And she has had her hair permed – think of that!'

'Shocking! At her age!' said Mrs O'Sullivan. 'Quite time she went to St Clare's!'

'I remember two girls who were terribly stuck up last summer holidays,' said Mr O'Sullivan, looking up from his newspaper. His eyes twinkled as he looked at the twins. 'My goodness – *they* didn't want to go to St Clare's! They thought it would be a dreadful school – really horrid.'

Pat and Isabel went very red. 'Don't remind us of that, Daddy,' said Pat. 'We were idiots. We behaved awfully badly at St Clare's at first – everyone called us the Stuck-Up Twins.'

'Or the High-and-Mighties!' said Isabel, with a giggle. 'Gracious – I can't think how anyone put up with us.'

'Well, we had a pretty bad time to start with,' said Pat. 'And serve us right too. I hope Alison won't be as stuck up as we were.'

'She'll be worse,' said Isabel. 'She's so vain! Mummy, couldn't you get Alison to come and stay here for two or three days before we have to go back to St Clare's? Then we could tell her a few things.'

'Well, that would be very kind of you,' said Mrs O'Sullivan.

'It's not *altogether* kindness,' said Isabel, with a smile. 'Neither Pat nor I want to be saddled with a cousin who's going to be silly and vain – and we may be able to prepare her a bit if we have her a few days.'

'Lick her into shape, you mean?' said Mr O'Sullivan, over the top of his paper. 'Well, if you can make that conceited little monkey into somebody nice, I shall be surprised. I never saw anyone so spoilt in all my life.'

'It's a good thing she's going to St Clare's,' said Pat, spreading marmalade on her toast. 'Don't you think Isabel and I are nicer since we went there, Daddy?'

'I'll have to think a little about that,' said their father, teasingly. 'Well – yes – on the whole I'm pleased with you. What do you say, Mother?'

'Oh, I think they settled down very well indeed at St

Clare's,' said Mrs O'Sullivan. 'They did so hate going – and they vowed and declared they wouldn't try a bit – but Miss Theobald, the head mistress, said some very nice things on their report. They will be very happy there this term.'

'I don't want the hols to end, but I can't help feeling quite excited when I think of seeing old Mam'zelle Abominable again,' said Pat, 'and Miss Roberts, and . . .'

'Mam'zelle *Abominable*!' said Mr O'Sullivan, in astonishment. 'Is that really her name?'

'Oh, no, Daddy – we only call her that because she says "*C'est abominable*!" to so many things!' said Pat. 'Isabel and I were awfully bad at French grammar at first and Mam'zelle used to write "Abominable" across our books. But she is a kind old thing, really.'

'It will be fun to see all the girls again too,' said Isabel. 'Mummy, write and tell Aunt Sarah to let Cousin Alison come next week before we go back.'

So Mrs O'Sullivan wrote to her sister-in-law and Cousin Alison arrived two days before the girls were due back at school.

She was a very pretty girl, with curled red-brown hair, a rosebud mouth, and big blue eyes.

'A bit like that doll we used to have, really,' said Pat to Isabel. 'We called her Angela, do you remember? I wish Alison wouldn't smile that silly smile so much.'

'Oh, I expect someone has told her what a sweet smile she has, or something,' said Isabel. 'Really, she seems to think she's a film star, the way she behaves!'

Alison was pleased to be with her cousins so that she might go to St Clare's with them for, like most girls, she felt nervous at going for the first time to a new school. It didn't take long to settle down – but it felt rather strange and new at first.

'Tell me a bit about the school,' she said, as she sat down in the old schoolroom that evening. 'I hope it isn't one of these terribly sensible schools that make you play games if you don't want to, and all that.'

Pat winked at Isabel. 'Alison, St Clare's is just about the most sensible school in the kingdom!' she said, in a solemn voice. 'You have to know how to clean shoes . . .'

'And make tea . . .' said Isabel.

'And toast,' went on Pat. 'And you have to know how to make your own beds . . .'

'And if you tear your clothes you have to mend them yourself,' said Isabel, enjoying Alison's look of horror.

'Wait a minute,' said Alison, sitting up. 'What do you mean – clean shoes, make tea – and toast? Surely you don't do that!'

The twins laughed. 'It's all right,' said Pat. 'You see, Alison, the first form and second form have to wait on the top formers in turn. When they shout for us we have to go and see what they want, and jolly well do it.'

Alison went pink. 'It sounds pretty awful to me,' she said. 'What are the girls like? Are they awful too?'

'Oh, dreadful,' said Pat, solemnly. 'Very like Isabel

and me, in fact. You'll probably hate them!'

'It doesn't sound a bit like Redroofs, the school you went to with me only a term ago,' said Alison, sadly. 'What's our form mistress like? Shall I be in the same form as you?'

'Yes, I should think so,' said Pat. 'We are in the first form – we certainly shan't be moved up into the second yet. Our form mistress is Miss Roberts. She's a good sort – but my word, she's sarcastic! If you get the wrong side of her you'll be sorry.'

'And Mam'zelle is hot stuff too,' said Isabel. 'She's big, with enormous feet – and she's got a fearful temper and she shouts.'

'Isabel, she sounds dreadful,' said Alison, in alarm, thinking of the mouse-like French mistress at Redroofs.

'Oh, she's not a bad sort really,' said Pat, smiling. 'She's got a kind heart. Anyway, you needn't worry, Alison – you'll have Isabel and me to look after you a bit and show you everything.'

'Thanks,' said Alison, gratefully. 'I hope I'm in the same dormitory as you are. What's Matron like?'

'Oh, Matron has been there for years and years and years,' said Pat. 'She dosed our mothers and aunts, and our grandmothers too, for all I know! She knows when we've had midnight feasts – she doesn't stand any nonsense at all. But she's nice when you're ill.'

Alison learnt a great deal about St Clare's during the two days she stayed with the twins. She thought they had changed since they had left Redroofs. She stared at them and tried to think how thcy had changed.

They seem so sensible, she thought. They were . . . always rather up in the air and proud, at Redroofs. Oh well – they were head girls there, and had something to be proud of – now I suppose they're among the youngest in the school – and I shall be too.

The day came for the three to leave for their boarding school. Everything had been packed. Mrs O'Sullivan had got the same cakes and sweets for Alison's tuck-box as she had bought for the twins. Everything was neatly marked and well packed, and now the three big trunks and the three tuck-boxes stood ready in the hall, marked in white paint with the names of the three girls.

Mrs O'Sullivan was to see them off in London. Pat and Isabel were excited at the thought of seeing all their friends again. Alison was rather quiet. She was very glad that she had the twins to go with.

They arrived on the platform from which their train was to go – and then what an excitement there was! 'There's dear old Janet! Hi, Janet, Janet! Did you have good hols? Oh, there's Hilary. Hallo, Hilary – look, this is our Cousin Alison who's coming to St Clare's with us this term. Oh, there's Doris – and Sheila!'

Everyone crowded round the twins, talking and laughing. Alison was made known to them all, and she felt very grateful to the twins for helping her in this difficult first meeting with unknown girls.

A pleasant-faced mistress bustled up with a

notebook in hand. 'Good morning, Pat, good morning, Isabel! Still as like as two peas, I see! Is this your cousin, Alison O'Sullivan? Good – I'll tick her off in my list. How do you do, Alison? I'm Miss Roberts, your form mistress. No doubt the twins have told you exactly how fierce and savage I am!'

She smiled and passed on to the next group. It was her job to see that all the first and second formers were there, and to get them into the train in time.

'Any new girls this term?' wondered Pat, looking round. 'I can't see any – except Alison, of course.'

'Yes – there's one over there – look!' said Isabel, nudging Pat. Pat looked, and saw a tall, rather good-looking girl standing by herself. She had a bad-tempered face, and was not trying to make friends with anyone at all. No one had come to see her off.

'*She's* new,' said Pat. 'I wonder if she'll be in our form. My word, I should think she's got a temper – I wonder what would happen if she and Janet had a row!'

Janet was very quick tempered, and flared up easily. But it was soon over with her; this new girl, however, looked sulky, as well as bad tempered. The twins did not take to her at all.

'There's another new girl, too – look, just walking on to the platform!' said Isabel. 'She looks jolly nice! She'll be in our form, I should think.'

The second new girl was quite different from the one they had just seen. She was small, with dancing black curls, and she had deep blue eyes that sparkled and shone. Her father and mother were both with her.

'Her father must be an artist or a musician or something, his hair's so long!' said Pat.

'*I* know who he is,' said Hilary Wentworth, who was standing just nearby. 'He's Max Oriell – the famous painter. My aunt has just had her portrait painted by him – it's simply marvellous. I saw him once or twice when I went with her to a sitting. That must be his daughter. They're awfully alike.'

'She looks clever,' said Pat. 'I hope she's in our form.'

'Get into your carriages, please!' called Miss Roberts, in her clear voice. 'The train goes in three minutes. Say your goodbyes now.'

So goodbyes were said and the girls scrambled into their carriages, trying to sit by their own special friends. Alison thought that the top formers, walking sedately along the platform, were very grown-up and dignified. She felt small when she saw them.

'There's Winifred James, our head girl,' whispered Pat, as a tall, serious-looking girl went by. 'She's frightfully clever, and most awfully nice.'

'I should be afraid to say a word to her!' said Alison.

'We felt like that at first too,' said Isabel. 'Look – that's Belinda Towers, the sports captain. Pat and I got into a row with her last term – but we soon found she was a good sort. Golly, I hope she puts us down for a few matches this term, don't you, Pat?'

The whistle blew. Handkerchiefs waved from

windows. The train moved out slowly, full to bursting-point with all the girls of St Clare's. They were off to school again!

2.

Settling in

The first day or two of a new term is always an exciting time. There are no proper timetables, rules are not kept strictly, there is a lot of unpacking to be done – and best of all there are tuck-boxes to empty!

The twins missed their home and their mother at first, as did most of the girls – but there was so much to do that there was no time to fret or worry. In any case everyone soon settled down into the school routine. It was fun to greet all the teachers again, fun to sit in the same old classroom, and fun to see if the ink-spot that looked like a cat with two tails was still on Janet's desk.

There were new books to be given out, and new pencils, rubbers, rulers and pens.

'Ah, the nice new books!' said Mam'zelle, her large eyes gleaming with pleasure as she looked round the class. 'The nice new books – to be filled with beautiful French compositions. Did you groan, Doris? Surely you are not going to make my hair grey this term as you did last term? Ah-h-h! See this grey lock, *ma chère* Doris – it was you who caused that last term!'

Mam'zelle pulled out a bit of grey hair from her

thick thatch, and looked comically at Doris.

'I'll do my best, Mam'zelle,' promised Doris. 'But I shall never, never be able to say the French 'r's in the right way. Never!'

'R-r-r-r-!' said Mam'zelle, rolling the 'r' in her throat in a most marvellous manner. The class giggled. Mam'zelle sounded remarkably like a dog growling, but nobody dared to say so.

The other teachers welcomed the girls in their own manner. Miss Roberts had already seen most of her girls in the train. Alison couldn't help liking her very much, though she was a little afraid of Miss Roberts's sharp tongue. Miss Roberts had a way of making an offender feel very small indeed.

The form mistress had a special word for the twins. 'Well, Pat and Isabel, I can see by your faces that you've made up your minds to do well this term. You've got determination written all over you, Pat – and I know that Isabel always follows your example! What about being top in a few things this term?'

'I'd like to be,' said Pat, eagerly. 'We always were at Redroofs – the school we went to before, you know. Now that we've got used to St Clare's we'll be able to work more quickly.'

Matron was in her room, giving out towels, sheets and pillow-cases, and warning everyone that any buttons would have to be sewn on by the girls themselves, and any tears would have to be neatly mended in sewing-class.

'But I can't mend sheets and things,' said Alison, in dismay.

'Maybe that's one of the things your mother sent you here to learn?' suggested Matron with her wide smile. 'You hope to be happily married one day, don't you – and run your own home? Well, you must learn to take care of your own linen and mend it, then. But it doesn't seem to me that you need worry much – your mother has sent you all new things. So unless you *try* to kick holes in your sheets, and tear the buttons off, there won't be much for you to do in the way of mending *this* term!'

All the girls had to go and see Miss Theobald in turn. Alison went with Pat and Isabel. She felt very nervous as she stood outside the sitting-room with them, waiting to go in.

'What do I *say*?' she whispered. 'Is she very solemn?'

The door opened and Janet and Hilary came out. 'You next,' said Hilary, and the waiting three went in. Alison liked Miss Theobald, the head mistress, at once. She had a very serious face that could break into a really lovely smile. She smiled now as she saw the three cousins.

'Well, Pat and Isabel, I am glad to see you back again, looking so happy,' she said. 'I remember last term, when I first saw you, you scowled and said hardly a word! But this term I know you better. You will do your very best for your form, and for the school too.'

'Yes, of course, Miss Theobald,' said the twins, beaming.

Miss Theobald turned to Alison. 'And this is another O'Sullivan, a cousin!' she said. 'Well, with three O'Sullivans all working hard in the same form, Miss Roberts ought to be pleased! You are lucky to have two sensible cousins to help you along in this first term, Alison.'

'Yes, Miss Theobald,' gasped Alison, still very nervous.

'You may go now,' said Miss Theobald. 'And remember, Pat and Isabel, that I am here to help in any difficulty, so don't be afraid to come, will you?'

The three went out, all a little awed, but all liking the head mistress immensely. They rushed to the common-room, which Alison had not yet seen.

'Don't we have studies to ourselves here?' said Alison, in disappointment, looking round the big room that was shared by the first and second formers together. 'What an awful row!'

Certainly there was a noise. Girls were talking and laughing. Someone had put the radio on, and someone else, at the other end of the big room, was tinkering with the record player, which kept making most extraordinary noises.

'You'll soon get used to the noise,' said Pat, happily. 'It's nice and friendly, really. Look – you can have this part of the shelf here for your belongings, Alison – your cake-tins and biscuit-tins – and your sewing or knitting and the library book you're reading. The next part belongs to me and Isabel. Keep your part tidy or you'll take up too much room.'

The twins showed their cousin over the school – the big classrooms with the lovely view from the windows – the enormous gym – the fine art-room, high up under the roof, with a good north light – the laboratory – even the cloakrooms, where each girl had a locker for her shoes, and a peg for her outdoor things and her overall.

'Am I in the same dormitory as you, Pat?' asked Alison, timidly, as she peeped in at the big bedrooms, where eight girls slept in eight little cubicles each night.

'I'll ask Hilary,' said Pat. 'She's head girl of our form, and she'll know. Hi, Hilary – do you know if our cousin Alison is in with us, or not?'

Hilary took out a list of names. 'Dormitory 8,' she read out. 'Hilary Wentworth, Pat and Isabel O'Sullivan, Doris Elward, Kathleen Gregory, Sheila Naylor, Janet Robins and Alison O'Sullivan. There you are – that's our dormitory list – same as last term, except that Vera Johns has gone into number 9 – to make room for Alison, I suppose.'

'Oh, good,' said Pat. 'You're with us, Alison. That's a bit of luck for you.'

The three new girls were in the first form with Miss Roberts. The tall bad-tempered-looking girl was called Margery Fenworthy. She looked old enough to be in the second form, but the girls soon saw that her work was poor – not even up to the standard of the first form, really.

'Isn't she a funny creature?' said Pat to Isabel, after a morning in class with Margery. 'She simply doesn't seem to care a bit what she does or says. I've an idea she can be awfully rude. Goodness – there'll be a row if she gets across Mam'zelle!'

Margery Fenworthy kept herself to herself. She was always reading, and if anyone spoke to her she answered so shortly that nobody said any more. She would have been very good looking if she had smiled – but, as Pat said, she always looked as if she wanted to bite somebody's head off!

Lucy Oriell, the other new girl, was the complete opposite of Margery. She was brilliantly clever, but as she was only fourteen and a half, she was put into the first form for that term at any rate. Nothing was difficult to her. She had a wonderful memory, and was always merry and bright.

'The way she gabbles French with Mam'zelle!' groaned Doris. 'The way she draws in the art class! The way she recites yards and yards of Shakespeare, and it takes me all my time to learn two lines properly.'

Everyone laughed. Doris was a duffer – with one great talent. She could make people laugh! She could dance well and comically, and she could mimic others perfectly, which made it all the more strange that she could not imitate Mam'zelle's French accent. Everyone liked Doris.

'An absolute idiot – but such a nice one!' as Janet said.

'What do you think of the three new girls, Janet?' asked Hilary, biting the end of her pencil as she tried to think out a problem in arithmetic set by Miss Roberts.

Pat and Isabel were nearby, listening. Janet shook back her dark hair, and gave her judgment.

'Lucy Oriell – top-hole! Clever, responsible, kind and bright. Margery Fenworthy – a bad-tempered, don't-care creature with some sort of PAST.'

'Whatever do you mean?' said Pat, astonished.

'Well, mark my words, there's something behind that funny way Margery has of keeping herself to herself, and of not caring tuppence for anything or anybody,' said Janet, who could be very far-seeing when she wanted to. 'And what does a girl of fifteen want to be so bad tempered for? I'd just like to know how she got on at her last school. I bet she didn't make any friends!'

The twins stared across at Margery, who, as usual, had her nose buried in a book. Janet went on to the third new girl, Alison.

'I suppose I mustn't say much about Alison, as she's your cousin – but if you want my real opinion it's this – she's a conceited, stuck-up little monkey without a single idea in her pretty little head!'

'Thanks for your opinions, Janet,' said Hilary, with a laugh. 'You have a wonderful way of putting into words just exactly what everyone else is thinking – and doesn't say!'

3.

Alison learns a lesson

The Easter term opened very cold and dreary. The girls shivered when they got up in the morning. Alison simply hated getting up. Time after time Hilary stripped the clothes from her, and Alison almost wept with anger. Nothing like that had ever happened at her old school!

'Don't do that!' she cried, each time. 'I was *just* going to get up!'

Everyone grinned. They thought Alison was very silly sometimes. She spent ages doing her hair and looking at herself in the mirror – and if she had a spot on her face she moaned about it for days till it went.

'As if anybody would notice if she had twenty spots!' said Janet in disgust. 'She's not worth looking at, the vain little thing!'

In a week or two it seemed to the twins as if they had been back at school for months! Each form was now working steadily to its own timetable. Lacrosse games were played three times a week, and anyone could go to the field and practise in their spare time. Gym was held twice a week, and the twins loved that. The new girl, Margery, was excellent at all the things they did in gym.

'She's strong, isn't she?' said Pat, admiringly, as they watched her climbing up the thick rope that hung down from the ceiling.

'She plays games and does gym as if she was fighting somebody fiercely all the time!' said Janet, hitting the nail on the head, as usual. 'Look at her gritting her teeth as she climbs that rope. My word, I don't like marking her at lacrosse I can tell you. She's given me some bruises across my knuckles even though I wear padded gloves!'

Janet showed the bruises. 'She's a savage creature!' said Doris. 'Belinda ticked her off yesterday for deliberately tripping me up on the field. All the same, she'd be a good one to have in a match! If she wanted to shoot a goal she'd jolly well shoot one, even if she had to knock down every single one of the other side!'

Lucy Oriell was a fine lacrosse player too. She had been captain of the lacrosse team at her old school, and she was as swift as the wind.

'She's good at everything, the lucky creature!' said Hilary. 'Have you seen some of her pictures? They really are lovely. She showed me some water-colours she'd done in the hols with her father. I couldn't believe they were hers. Of course, she gets that from him. He must make a lot of money from his portraits – no wonder all her clothes are so good.'

'It's a pity that silly cousin of yours doesn't try a bit harder at games,' said Janet, watching Alison trying to catch a lacrosse ball in her net. It was a very easy throw sent by Kathleen. But Alison muffed it as usual.

'Alison, haven't you ever played games before?' cried Janet.

'Yes,' said Alison, flushing. 'But I played hockey – much better game than this stupid lacrosse. I'd always rather hit a ball than catch it! I was jolly good at hockey, wasn't I, Pat, at Redroofs?'

Pat did not remember Alison ever being good at any game, so she said nothing. Belinda Towers came up and spoke to the twins.

'I say, can't you do something about that silly little cousin of yours? She just stands and bleats at me when I order her to practise catching and throwing! She wants a bit of pep in her.'

Pat laughed. Alison did bleat – that was just the right word for it.

'I'll try and take her in hand,' she said. 'After all, I was pretty awful myself at first, last term – and I'll try and knock some sense into Alison, in the same way that it was knocked into me and Isabel.'

'She thinks too much about herself,' said Belinda, in her direct way. 'Stupid sickly smile, big blue eyes, bleating little voice – make her skip around a bit, can't you? I really can't stand much more of her.'

So Pat and Isabel made Alison skip around a bit! She was very indignant indeed.

'Why do you always make me go and practise this silly catching just when I want to finish my book!' she grumbled. 'Why do you hustle me out for a walk when it's so cold and windy? If you call this looking after me I'd rather you stopped!'

Soon it was Alison's turn to wait on the two top formers, Rita George and Katie White! They sent a runner for her at tea-time one day. Alison was just finishing her own tea when the message came.

'Alison! Rita wants you. Buck up. It's your turn to do her jobs this week.'

'What jobs?' said Alison crossly, swallowing her last mouthful of cake.

'How do I know? Making her tea, I expect. And I think the fire's gone out in her room. You'll have to rake it out and lay it again for her.'

Alison nearly burst with indignation. 'What, me light a fire! I've never lit one in my life! I don't even know how to lay one.'

'If you don't go, Alison, you'll get into a row,' said Isabel. 'Katie White isn't as patient as Rita. Go on. Don't be a ninny.'

Alison, grumbling under her breath all the while, went slowly off to Rita's study. Rita looked up impatiently as she came in.

'Good Heavens! Are you always as slow as this? What bad luck to have *you* waiting on us this week. We won't get a thing done!'

'Rake out the fire and lay it again quickly,' said Katie White, in her deep voice. 'There's some paper and sticks in that cupboard. Go on, now – we've got some other girls coming in for tea.'

Poor Alison! She raked out the fire as best she could, got the paper and sticks from the cupboard and put them higgledy-piggledy into the grate. The grate was hot and she burnt her hand when she touched it. She let out a loud squeal.

'What's the matter?' said Rita, startled.

'I've burnt my hand on the hot grate,' said Alison, nursing her hand against her chest, though really it hardly hurt at all.

'Well, really – did you imagine the grate would be stone cold after having had a fire in it all day?' asked Rita, impatiently. 'For goodness' sake hurry up and light the fire. There's a box of matches on the mantelpiece.'

Alison took down the matches. She struck one and held it to the paper; it flared up at once. At the same moment three more big girls came in, chattering. One was Belinda Towers. No one took any notice of the first former lighting the fire. Alison felt very small and unimportant.

The paper burnt all away. The sticks of wood did not catch alight at all. Bother! There was no more paper in the cupboard. Alison turned timidly to Rita.

'Please, where is there some more paper?'

'On the desk over there,' said Rita, shortly, scowling at Alison. The top formers went on talking and Alison went to a nearby desk. She looked at the papers there. They were sheets covered with Rita's small neat handwriting.

'I suppose it's old work she doesn't want,' thought

Alison, and picked it up. She arranged the sheets in the fire-place, and then set a match to them. At the same moment she heard a loud exclamation from Rita.

'I say! I say! You surely haven't taken my prep to burn? She has! Oh, the silly donkey, she's taken my French prep!'

There was a rush for the fire. Alison was pushed out of the way. Rita tried to pull some of the blazing sheets out – but the flames had got a good hold of them and she could not save any of her precious prep. It was burnt to black ashes.

'Alison! How dare you do a thing like that?' cried Rita, in a rage. 'You deserve to have your ears boxed.'

'I didn't mean to,' said poor Alison, beginning to cry all over the fire-place near which she was still kneeling. 'You said – take the paper on the desk over there – and . . .'

'Well, can't you tell the difference between yesterday's newspaper and today's French prep?' stormed the angry fifth former. 'Now I shall have to do an hour's extra work and rewrite all that French!'

'*And* she hasn't even lit the fire yet!' said Belinda Towers. 'Just as stupid at doing household jobs as you are in the sports field, Alison.'

'Please let me go,' wept Alison, feeling half dead with shame before the accusing faces of the big girls. 'I can't light a fire. I really can't.'

'Then it's just about time you learnt,' said Rita, grimly. 'Now, where's that paper? Put it like this – and like this. Now get the sticks. Arrange them so that the flames can lick up them and set the coal alight. Now put some coal on the top. Good Heavens, idiot, what's the good of putting an enormous lump like that on top? You've squashed down all the sticks! Take little lumps to start a fire with – like this.'

Alison wept all the time, feeling terribly sorry for herself. She held a match to the paper with a shaking hand. It flared up – the sticks caught – the coal burnt – and there was the fire, burning merrily.

'Now put the kettle on the hob just there, and you can go, baby,' said Katie. 'Where do you get all those tears from? For goodness' sake, come away from the fire or you'll put it out again!'

Alison crept out of the room, tears running down her cheeks. She stopped at a mirror and looked at herself. She thought that she looked a most sad and pathetic sight – rather like a film star she had seen crying in a picture. She went back to the common-room, sniffing, hoping that everyone would sympathize with her.

But to her surprise, nobody did – not even kind-hearted Lucy Oriell. Pat looked up and asked her what was up.

Alison told her tale. When she related how she had burnt Rita's French prep papers the first formers looked horrified.

'Fathead!' said Janet in disgust. 'Letting down our form like that! Golly, the big girls must think we are mutton-heads!'

'It was *awful* being rowed at by so many of the big girls,' wept Alison, thinking that she must look a very pathetic sight. But everyone was disgusted.

'Stop it, Alison. You're not in a kindergarten,' said Hilary. 'If you want to behave like an idiot, you must expect the top formers to treat you like one. For goodness' sake stop sniffing. You look simply awful, I can tell you. Your eyes are red, your nose is swollen, your mouth has gone funny – you look just as ugly as can be!'

That made Alison weep really bitterly. Janet lost her temper. 'Either stop, or go out,' she said roughly to Alison. 'If you don't stop I'll put you out of the room myself. You've no right to disturb us all like this.'

Alison looked up. She saw that sharp-tongued Janet meant what she said. So she stopped crying at once, and the twins grinned at each other.

'Lesson number one!' whispered Pat.

4.

Tessie has a secret

The first real excitement of the term was Tessie's birthday. Tessie was a lively girl in the second form, fond of tricks and jokes. She and Janet were a pair! The girls often laughed when they remembered how the term before Janet had thrown fireworks on the schoolroom fire, and given poor Miss Kennedy such a fright.

'And do you remember how Tessie hid the big black cat in the handwork cupboard, and it jumped out at Miss Kennedy and made her rush out of the room?' giggled Doris. 'Oh, golly – I've never laughed so much in all my life.'

Miss Kennedy had gone, and in her place was Miss Lewis, a first-class history teacher. The girls liked her very much, except for one thing – she would not allow the slightest inattention or cheekiness in her classes. Even free-tongued Janet was a model of good behaviour in Miss Lewis's classes. Only surly Margery seemed to care nothing for anything the history teacher said.

Tessie had great ideas for her birthday. She knew she would have plenty of money sent to her, and plenty of good things to eat. She was a generous girl, and wanted everyone to share.

But there would not be enough for everyone. If Tessie put all her things on the table at tea-time there would only be a tiny bit for each of the forty or fifty first and second formers.

Tessie thought about it. She talked to her great friend, Winnie Thomas.

'Winnie, don't you think it would be better to share my things amongst a few of my *best* friends – and not give everyone only a taste?' said Tessie.

'Yes, I do think that,' said Winnie. 'But when can we give the party? We can't very well just ask a few of the ones we like, and leave the rest to stare jealously!'

'Well, we'll have to have the party when there's no one there except the ones we ask,' said Tessie. 'And that means – at night! On my birthday night!'

'But we can't have it in the dormitory,' said Winnie. 'The others would know then. We must keep it a secret. It won't be any fun if we don't.'

'We won't have it in the dormitory,' said Tessie. 'But where in the world *can* we have it, without being found out?'

'I know! We'll have it in that little music room not far from our dormitory!' said Winnie, her eyes shining. 'It's just the place. No one ever goes there at night. If we pull down the blinds and shut the door no one will ever know we are there. We mustn't make much noise though – it's rather near Mam'zelle's study.'

'It'll be all the more fun if we mustn't make much noise,' giggled Tessie. 'How can we warm that room?

It's awfully cold in there. I know, because I had to practise there last week.'

'Let's borrow an oil-stove out of the cupboard downstairs!' said Winnie. 'Some of them have oil in, I know, because they're not emptied when they are put away in that cupboard.'

'Good idea!' said Tessie, who liked everything to be as perfect as possible when she planned anything. Then a thought struck her – 'Oooh, Winnie – do you think we could fry sausages on the top of the oil-stove if I could buy some? I could get some of those tiny little sausages – I forget what they're called – the kind people often have to put round chickens?'

Winnie stared at Tessie in delight. 'I don't believe ANYONE has ever fried sausages at a birthday party in the middle of the night before!' she said. 'Not anyone. It would be a most marvellous thing to do. Can we get a frying-pan?'

'You bet!' said Tessie. 'I'll ask young Gladys, the kitchen help, to lend me one for the night. She's a good sport and won't tell. And if I can't borrow one, I'll jolly well buy one!'

'Tessie, this is going to be awful fun,' said Winnie, dancing about. 'What do you suppose you'll have for your party – besides your birthday cake and the sausages?'

'Well, Mother always sends me a big fruit cake, a ginger cake, sweets, biscuits and home-made toffee,' said Tessie. 'And I'll have plenty of money to buy anything else we want. I'll get some tins of peaches. We all like those.'

The two girls went into corners and whispered excitedly every day. Mam'zelle noticed their inattention in class and scolded them for it.

'Tessie! Winnie! Do you wish me to send you down into the first form? You sit there staring out of the window and you do not pay one small piece of attention to all I am saying! What mischief are you planning?'

This was so near the mark that both girls went red. 'It's my birthday soon, Mam'zelle,' said Tessie, meekly, knowing that Mam'zelle usually understood an excuse like that.

'Ah, I see – and I suppose it is dear Winnie's birthday also?' said Mam'zelle. 'Well, unless you both wish to write me out a ver-r-r-ry nice composition in your best French all about birthdays you will please pay attention to *me*.'

The two girls decided to ask only six more girls to the party. Tessie didn't see why they should all be from the second form. 'You know, I like those O'Sullivan twins awfully,' she said. 'I'd like to ask them. They're good sports.'

'Yes – but for goodness' sake don't ask that awful cousin of theirs, always strutting about like a peacock,' said Winnie.

'Of course not,' said Tessie. 'I simply couldn't bear her. No – we'll ask Pat and Isabel – and Janet. And out of our own form we'll ask Hetty, Susan and Nora. What do you think of that?'

'Yes – fine,' agreed Winnie.

'We'll have to be careful not to let that sneaky Erica guess about our party,' said Tessie, thoughtfully. 'She's such a Paul-Pry – always sticking her nose into things that don't concern her. She's an awful tell-tale too. I'm sure she sneaked about me to Miss Jenks, when I lost that lacrosse ball.'

'We'll tell everyone to keep it a close secret,' said Winnie. 'I say – won't it be fun?'

Tessie got hold of the twins that day and took them to a corner. 'Listen,' she said. 'I'm having a small birthday party on Thursday – just you and five others. Will you come?'

'Oh, yes, thanks,' said Pat, pleased at being asked by a second former.

'What time?' asked Isabel.

'Twelve o'clock at night,' giggled Tessie. The twins stared in surprise.

'Oh – is it a midnight feast, like we had last term?' asked Pat, eagerly.

'No – not quite,' said Tessie. 'It's not going to be held in the dormitory, like a midnight feast – we are going to have it in that little music room not far from my dormitory. You know the one I mean?'

'Yes,' said Pat. 'I say – what fun! It will be a proper midnight party, all by ourselves. Who else are you asking?'

'Four from my form, not counting myself,' said Tessie, 'and you two and Janet from your form. That's all. Now mind you come at twelve o'clock. And oh – I say!'

'What?' asked the twins.

'Don't say a word to anyone, will you?' begged Tessie. 'You see, I can't ask everyone, and some of the girls might be a bit annoyed they haven't been asked.'

'Of course we won't say a word,' said Pat. The twins went off together, and waited until Tessie had told Janet. Then the three of them whispered together excitedly about the twelve o'clock party! It was fun to have a secret. It was fun to be asked by a second former – chosen out of all the girls in their form!

Alison was very curious, for she knew quite well that her cousins had a secret. She kept badgering them to tell her.

'Oh, shut up, Alison,' said Pat. 'Can't we have a secret without telling the whole form?'

'It wouldn't be telling the whole form, if you only told *me,*' said Alison, opening her blue eyes very wide and looking as beseeching as she could.

'My dear Alison, telling you would be quite the quickest way of telling the whole *school*!' said Pat. 'You can't keep your mouth shut about anything. You just go round and bleat out every single thing.'

This wasn't very kind but it was perfectly true. Alison couldn't keep anything to herself at all, and had so often given away little things that the twins had told her that now they left her out of all their secrets.

Alison went away, pouting. Erica, from the second

form, saw her and went up to her. She was just as curious as Alison about other people's plans and secrets.

'It's a mean trick, to have plans and keep everyone in the dark,' said Erica. 'I know Tessie and Winnie have got some sort of plan too – it's about Tessie's birthday, I think. I wish we could find out about it. That would just serve them right.'

Alison didn't like Erica. Few people did, for she really was a sneak. Not even the mistresses liked her, for they much preferred not to know what was going on rather than have Erica come telling tales.

So Alison would not take Erica's hint and try to find out what was up, though she really longed to do so. Erica asked her again and again if she had discovered anything, but Alison stubbornly shook her head. Silly little vain thing as she was, she was not going to find out things to tell Erica.

Hetty, Susan and Nora kept their mouths shut too, about the party. Winnie, of course, did not say a word to anyone except the four in her form who knew. So it was very difficult for Erica really to find out anything much. She guessed that it was to do with Tessie's birthday – and she guessed it was a party – but how, where and when she had no idea.

The plans went steadily forward. Gladys, the kitchen help, giggled when Tessie asked her for the loan of a frying-pan. She put one under her apron and went to find Tessie. On the way she met Erica.

'Whatever are you hiding under your apron,

Gladys?' said Erica, with the high and mighty air that the staff so much disliked. Gladys tossed her neat little head.

'Nothing to do with you,' she answered pertly. Erica was angry. She pulled Gladys's apron aside and saw the pan.

'Oho! For Tessie's party!' she said. It was only a guess – but Gladys at once thought that Erica knew.

'Well, if you knew, why did you ask me?' she said. 'I'm to take it to the little music room near Tessie's dormitory.'

Erica watched Gladys slip inside the music room and put the pan into a cupboard, under a pile of music. It was Tessie's birthday today. So the party was near – probably at night. The inquisitive girl burnt with curiosity and jealousy.

Tessie was having a marvellous birthday. She was a popular girl, for she was amusing and lively. The girls gave her small presents and wished her many happy returns of the day. Tessie handed round a big box of chocolates to everyone in her form. Her grandmother had sent it for her – and Tessie meant to share something with *all* her friends, even though she could not share her party with everyone.

Erica kept as close as she could to Tessie and Winnie that day, hoping to find out something more about the party. She saw Tessie go to the cupboard where the oil-stoves were kept – and fetch out a big stove!

She did not dare to ask Tessie what she was doing with it, for Tessie had a sharp tongue for Erica. But she hid behind a door and watched Tessie through the crack.

Into the music room went Tessie, carrying the heavy stove. Erica's eyes shone with delight. She felt sure that the party was to be held there. 'It will have to be after eleven,' thought the girl. 'I know pretty well everything now – serves Tessie right for leaving me out! Nasty, sharp-tongued creature! I've a good mind to spoil the party!'

It is quite likely that Erica would have done nothing more, now that she was satisfied she knew the secret, if Winnie and Tessie had not caught her taking a chocolate from the big box that Tessie had handed round. Tessie had left it in her classroom, meaning to ask Miss Lewis, the history teacher, to have one. Erica had seen it there, and had not been able to stop herself from lifting the lid to look at the layers.

She could not resist taking one of the chocolates and popping it into her mouth. After all, there were plenty! But just at that moment Tessie and Winnie came running into the room.

They stopped in amazement when they saw Erica hurriedly shutting the lid of the box. It was quite plain that she had a chocolate in her mouth.

'You are simply disgusting, Erica,' said Tessie, coldly. 'If you'd wanted another and had asked me I'd have willingly given you as many as you wanted. But to sneak in and take one like that – you really are a disgusting creature.'

The two girls went out. Erica had not been able to

say a word. A chocolate was only a chocolate – how dared Tessie speak to her like that? Erica's cheeks burnt and she longed to throw the whole box of sweets out of the window.

But she did not dare to. She went to her desk and slouched down into the seat. 'Calling me disgusting!' said the girl, in a fury. 'I won't have it! I'll pay her out for this! I'll spoil her precious party! I'll keep awake tonight till I see them going out of the dormitory – then I'll find a way to have them all caught!'

5.

What happened at the party

Everything was ready for the party. Tessie had even been into the little music room and lit the oil-stove to get the room warm for her guests!

'No one ever goes in there at night,' she said to Winnie, who was afraid that somebody might see the stove, if they went in. 'The room will be lovely and warm by the time we are ready!'

The two girls were in a great state of excitement. Tessie had had *two* birthday cakes sent to her, which pleased her very much. She had been able to put the bigger one of the two on the tea-table for all her form to share – and had kept the other for the midnight party.

There were biscuits, sweets, chocolates, a big fruit cake, and four tins of peaches, with a tin of Nestlé's milk for cream! There were also the strings of little sausages to fry. It was going to be great fun!

'We haven't anything to drink!' whispered Winnie to Tessie, in arithmetic at the end of that morning.

'Yes, we have. I've got some ginger beer,' whispered back Tessie. Miss Jenks caught the words 'ginger beer'.

'Tessie, how does ginger beer come into our arithmetic lesson?' she enquired, coldly.

'Well – it doesn't,' said Tessie, at a loss what to say. 'Sorry, Miss Jenks.'

Susan, Hetty and Nora winked at one another. They knew quite well where the ginger beer came in! Erica saw the winks and smiled to herself. She was going to spoil that party, ginger beer and all!

Everything was hidden in the music room, ready for that night. The eight girls were in a great state of excitement. They had all been in to peep at the things in the cupboard. The music mistress would have been most surprised if she had taken a peep too – for instead of the usual piles of old music, a metronome or two, old hymn books and so on, she would have seen a big birthday cake with 'Happy returns to Tessie!' on it, and a big tin full of other goodies – to say nothing of eight fat brown ginger beer bottles!

'How are we going to keep awake till twelve o'clock?' said Pat to Isabel and Janet.

'Oh, I'll be awake at twelve,' said Janet, who had lately got the idea that she could wake at any time she liked, merely by repeating the hour to herself half a dozen times before she went to sleep. 'I shall simply say twelve o'clock firmly to myself before I go to sleep. And then I shall wake on the first stroke of midnight! You just see.'

'Well, Janet, I hope you're right,' said Pat, doubtfully. 'I've tried that heaps of times but it never works with me. I just go on sleeping.'

'It's will-power,' said Janet. 'You needn't worry. I shall wake you all right!'

So the twins went peacefully to sleep as usual at half-past nine, trusting to Janet to wake them. Janet went to sleep too, saying 'twelve o'clock, twelve o'clock' steadily to herself, as she dropped off.

But alas for Janet! Midnight came – and she slept on! Her will-power must have been a little weak that night! The three first formers would certainly have missed the party if the second formers hadn't sent to see why they didn't turn up!

Pat was awakened by someone tugging at her arm, and a torch being flashed into her face. She woke with a jump and was just about to give a squeal of fright when she saw that it was Winnie who held the torch. In a flash she remembered the party.

'Pat! For goodness' sake! Aren't you three coming?' whispered Winnie.

'Of course,' said Pat. 'I'll wake the others.' She threw off the bed-clothes, slipped her feet into her slippers and put on her warm dressing-gown. She went to wake Isabel and Janet. Soon the three of them were creeping out of the room, down a few stairs, round a corner past the second form dormitory, and into the music room.

The door opened and shut quietly and the three girls blinked at the bright electric light. The blinds had been drawn and the oil-stove had made the little room as warm as toast. The other five girls were busy opening tins and setting out cake and biscuits.

'Whatever happened to you?' said Tessie, in surprise, 'It's a quarter-past twelve. We waited and waited. Then we sent Winnie.'

'It was my fault,' said Janet, looking ashamed of herself, a most unusual thing for Janet. 'I promised I'd wake them – and I didn't. I say – what a marvellous cake!'

The girls set to work to eat all the good things, giggling at nothing. It was so exciting to be cooped up in the little music room, gobbling all sorts of goodies when everyone else was fast asleep.

'Oh, Susan – you've spilt peach juice all over my toes,' giggled Janet.

'Lick it off then,' said Susan. 'I bet you can't!'

Janet was very supple. She at once tried to reach her foot up to her mouth to lick off the juice from her bare pink toes. She overbalanced and fell off her music-stool.

'Janet! You've sat on the sausages!' hissed Tessie, in dismay. 'Get up, you idiot. Oh, the poor sausages – all squashed as flat as pancakes!'

The girls began to giggle helplessly. Tessie tried to press the little sausages back into their ordinary shape again.

'When are we going to fry them?' asked Isabel, who loved sausages.

'Last thing,' said Tessie. 'That is, if there is anything left of them when Janet has finished with them!'

The ginger beer was opened. Each bottle had a top that had to be taken off with an opener, and each bottle gave a pop as it was opened.

'If anyone hears these pops they'll wonder whatever's happening in this music room,' said Susan.

'Well, nobody *will* hear,' said Tessie. 'Everyone is fast asleep. Not a soul in our own dormitory knows that we slipped out. Not a single person knows our secret!'

But Tessie boasted too soon. Someone was already outside the closed door, with her eye to the keyhole and her sharp ears trying to catch all that was said. Erica knew quite well all that was going on. Soon she caught her own name, and she stiffened outside the door, as she tried to hear what was said.

It was Tessie who was speaking. She was handing round chocolates. 'We caught that nasty little sneak Erica helping herself to the chocolates this afternoon,' she said, in her clear voice. 'Isn't she the limit?'

'Oh, she's always doing things like that,' said Pat. 'You can't trust her an inch.'

Erica felt the tears coming into her eyes. The girls had often told her unpleasant things to her face – but somehow it was horrible hearing them spoken behind her back. But the tears passed into tears of rage.

I'll give them a few frights! thought Erica, furiously. And then I'll go and fetch Miss Jenks. It will serve the wretches right.

Erica knocked softly on the door, and then, quick as lightning, darted into a nearby cupboard. She hoped that her knocking would give the girls a shock.

It gave them a most terrible shock! They all stopped talking at once, and Tessie put down the box of chocolates with a shaking hand. They stared at one another, round-eyed.

'What was that?' whispered Tessie.

'A knock at the d-d-d-door,' stuttered Winnie.

There was dead silence. Everyone waited to see if the door would open. But it didn't.

Erica was still hidden in the cupboard. As nothing happened, she crept out again and knocked once more on the door, this time quite smartly. Then back she hopped to the cupboard again, beginning to enjoy herself.

The eight girls in the music room jumped almost out of their skins when the second knocking came. 'There must be somebody there,' said Tessie, quite pale with fright. 'I'll go and see.'

She went bravely to the door and opened it. There was no one there! Tessie shone her torch into the passage. It was perfectly empty. The girl shut the door and went back to her seat, looking frightened.

'It wasn't anyone,' she said.

'Stuff and nonsense,' said Janet, beginning to recover from her fright. 'Doors don't knock by themselves! It must be someone having a joke.'

'But, Janet, no one knows we are here,' said Isabel.

'Shall we get back to bed – and not fry the sausages?' asked Tessie.

That was too much for Isabel. 'What, not fry the sausages when I've been looking forward to them all the evening!' she said, indignantly.

'Shut up, idiot! Do you want to wake the whole

school?' said Pat, giving her a nudge that nearly sent her off her chair. 'Fry the sausages, Tessie, old girl. I think that knocking must have been the wind!'

So the sausages were fried, and sizzled deliciously in the pan on the top of the oil-stove. Tessie turned them over and over with a fork, trying not to squeal when the hot fat jumped out and burnt her.

Erica had crept out of the cupboard again. She heard the sizzling of the sausages, and the lovely smell made her feel hungry. She wondered what to do next. A noise made her scurry back to her cupboard. What could it be?

Then Erica knew. It was Mam'zelle in her study, having one of her late nights! The French mistress sometimes stayed up very late, reading and studying – and tonight she was still in her study! Erica smiled to herself. She knew what she was going to do now. She wouldn't tell Miss Jenks! She would let hot-tempered Mam'zelle find out – and she herself wouldn't come out into the open at all!

'I'll go and knock at Mam'zelle's door,' said Erica to herself. 'Then I'll skip back to the dormitory. Mam'zelle will open her door in surprise – and when she finds no one there she'll go and prowl around, if I know anything about her! And it won't be long before she smells those sausages!'

So Erica slipped up the passage to the door of the little room that Mam'zelle used as a study. She knocked smartly on it three times – rap-rap-rap!

'*Tiens*!' came Mam'zelle's voice, in the greatest surprise. 'Who is there?'

There was no answer, of course, for Erica had slipped as quietly as a mouse away from the door – not into the cupboard this time, but back into her dormitory. She guessed there would soon be trouble about, and she wasn't going to share in it!

Mam'zelle slid back her chair and went to the door, puzzled. She threw it open, but there was no one there. She stood there for a moment, wondering if she could possibly have been mistaken – and then she heard, from somewhere not very far off, a subdued giggle. And down the passage crept the unmistakable smell of – frying sausages!

6.

Mam'zelle makes a discovery

Mam'zelle could not believe her senses. What – frying sausages at a quarter to one at night! It was not possible. She must be dreaming. Mam'zelle gave herself a hard pinch to see if she *was* dreaming or not. No – she was not. She was wide awake! There would be a bruise tomorrow where she had pinched herself.

'But who should be frying sausages at night?' wondered Mam'zelle in amazement. 'And where did that laugh come from? Surely not from the dormitory nearby?'

She went to see, shuffling along in her old comfortable slippers. She looked into the dormitory where Tessie and the others slept. She switched on the light. Five of the beds were empty!

Mam'zelle had not been at all good-tempered lately. She had not been sleeping well, and she had been difficult in class. She was tired now, with her hours of studying and correcting, and she felt really angry with the five truants.

'It is too much!' she said to herself, as she switched out the light. 'The bad girls! How can they do their lessons well if they are awake to such hours of the night? And they are working for the scholarship exam too – ah, I shall report them to Miss Theobald!'

Mam'zelle stood in the passage, sniffing. She simply could not imagine where the smell of sausages came from. Then she heard a scuffle and a giggle. It came from the music room nearby!

Mam'zelle went to the door. She flung it open and glared into the warm little room.

There was a deep silence. Every girl stared in dismay at the large form of the angry French mistress.

'Oh – Mam'zelle – Mam'zelle,' stammered Tessie, at last.

'Yes, it is I, Mam'zelle!' said the mistress, her eyes flashing. 'And what have you to say for yourselves, acting in this manner at this time of night?'

Tessie couldn't think of a word to say and at last in despair she held out a fried sausage on a fork to Mam'zelle.

'Wouldn't you – wouldn't you have a sausage?' she asked, desperately.

That was too much for Mam'zelle. She didn't see that Tessie was very frightened, she only thought that the girl was being cheeky. And the English 'cheek' was something that always made Mam'zelle see red!

She swept the sausage off the fork, and for half a moment Tessie thought that Mam'zelle was going to box her ears. She ducked – and heard Mam'zelle's booming voice above her head.

'So that is the way you would treat your French mistress? Why did I ever come to England to teach such ungrateful girls? You will come straight to Miss Theobald now, all of you!'

There was a moment's intense astonishment and fright. Go to Miss Theobald now – in the middle of the night – when she was asleep in bed! It couldn't be true!

'Please, Mam'zelle,' said Janet, who was recovering herself more quickly than the others, 'please don't make us do that. Tomorrow morning would do, wouldn't it? We don't want to disturb Miss Theobald now. We're sorry we disturbed you – we thought everyone was asleep.'

'But one of you knocked on my door!' said Mam'zelle in astonishment. 'So – rap-rap-rap.' She rapped on the table as she spoke.

'None of us did that,' said Janet, more and more astonished. 'Somebody came and knocked on our door too. Whoever could it have been?'

But Mam'zelle was not interested in that. Her rage was gradually dying down as she looked at the white, scared faces of the eight girls. She realized that it was impossible to take them all into Miss Theobald's bedroom. It must wait till tomorrow.

'We will not after all disturb Miss Theobald tonight,' she said. 'You will all go back to bed – and in the morning you will expect to be called in front of the head mistress to explain this dreadful behaviour.'

'Could – could we just finish the sausages?' asked Isabel, longingly. But that roused Mam'zelle's anger again. She caught Isabel firmly by the arm and pushed her out of the music room. 'You – a first-form girl – daring to do a thing like this!' she cried. 'Go! You should be well scolded, all of you! Go, before I begin to do it!'

The girls were half afraid that Mam'zelle might be as good as her word. They slipped down the passage and into their dormitories, climbing into bed, shivering with fright. What a dreadful ending to a midnight party!

Mam'zelle turned out the light. Then she saw the glow of the oil-stove and turned out that too. 'These girls!' she said, pursing up her big lips. 'These English girls! How they behave!'

Mam'zelle would never have dared to behave in such a free and easy way at her school in France when she had been a girl. She had worked much harder than any of the girls at St Clare's. She had played no games, had been for hardly any walks, and had never even seen the inside of a gym until she had come to England. She did not really understand the girls at St Clare's, although she had been there for years, and had taught them well. She was quite determined to have every one of the truants well punished.

She reported them to Miss Theobald before breakfast the next morning. She even took the surprised head mistress to the little music room to show her the remains of the feast. Miss Theobald looked at the ginger beer bottles, the frying-pan with its congealed fat and few sausages left in it, and the crumbs on the floor.

'I will see the girls at break,' said the head. 'This kind of thing cannot be allowed, Mam'zelle – but at some time or other most schoolgirls attend a midnight feast! Do not take too serious a view of it!'

'In my school days such a thing was not even thought of!' said Mam'zelle. 'Ah, we knew how to work, we French girls!'

'But did you know how to play, Mam'zelle?' asked Miss Theobald, softly. 'It is just as important to know how to have good fun – as how to do good work, you know!'

Mam'zelle snorted when Miss Theobald left her. She thought that the head was far too lenient with the girls. She went into the big dining-hall to have breakfast. She glanced round the table where the first and second form sat.

It was easy to pick out the eight girls who had been caught the night before. They were pale and looked tired. Isabel and Susan could not eat any breakfast, partly because they had eaten too much the night before, and partly because they were scared at what might be going to happen to them.

Mam'zelle stopped the eight girls when they filed out of the dining-hall. 'You, Janet – and you, Winnie – and you, Susan, and you . . . you will all eight go to Miss Theobald at break.'

'Yes, Mam'zelle,' said the girls, and went to the assembly room for morning prayers and roll-call, feeling rather shaky about the legs!

'Pity we were caught,' said Pat to Isabel, in the middle of the hymn. 'Now Miss Theobald will think we didn't mean to try to do our best this term. Oh blow, Mam'zelle! Mean old thing! I won't try a bit in French this term now.'

The eight girls were bad at their lessons that morning. Erica watched the five in her form, all trying not to yawn, as they did their arithmetic under Miss Jenks's eagle eye.

It was French next, and Tessie put on a sulky face when Mam'zelle entered the room. She felt that she really hated the French mistress that morning. She wasn't going to try a bit!

It wouldn't have mattered if she *had* tried – for poor Tessie was really woolly-headed that day! She had not been able to go to sleep until about five o'clock the night before, and was now so sleepy that her thoughts kept running into one another in a most annoying manner. She was really half asleep.

Mam'zelle chose to think that Tessie was defying her. She scolded the girl roundly, and gave her such a lot of extra prep to do that poor Tessie was almost in tears.

'But I can't possibly get all that done, Mam'zelle, you know I can't,' she protested.

'We shall see!' said Mam'zelle, grimly. And Tessie knew that she would have to do it somehow.

At break the eight girls met together outside the head mistress's door. They were all nervous, even Pat who was usually bold. Tessie knocked.

'Come in!' said Miss Theobald's clear voice. They trooped in and shut the door.

Miss Theobald faced them, and looked at each girl seriously. They all felt upset, and Susan began to cry. Then the head talked to them, and pointed out that it was impossible for good work to be done on half a night's sleep, and that rules must be kept. She said many other things in her low, calm voice, and the listening girls took it all in.

'Now please understand,' said Miss Theobald, 'that although you have broken the rule forbidding any girl to leave her dormitory at night, your escapade is not in the same rank as, for instance, meanness, lying, or disloyalty. Those are serious things – what you have done might be serious if you were allowed to do it often – but I regard it more as silly mischief. But even silly mischief has to be punished – and so you will not be allowed to go down into the town for two weeks. That means no walks together, no shopping, and no visits to the tea-shop or to the cinema.'

There was a silence. This was a horrid punishment. The girls really loved their privilege of going down to the town in twos, spending their pocket-money, and going to the tea-shop for tea. Two weeks seemed a very, very long time.

But nobody dared to protest. They all knew that Miss Theobald was absolutely just. 'You see,' the head went on, 'if you behave like small children instead of senior girls, I shall have to treat you as small children, and take away your senior privileges. Now you may go. Tessie, see that the mess in the music room is cleared up before dinner-time, please.'

'Yes, Miss Theobald,' said Tessie meekly, and all eight girls filed out of the room.

'Well, I'm glad that's over,' said Pat, when they were out of ear-shot of the sitting-room. 'And there's another thing I'm glad about too – that Miss Theobald made that distinction between mischief and mean things. I wouldn't like her to think we'd do anything mean or rotten. A joke's a joke – ours went too far, that's all.'

'Yes,' said Isabel, thoughtfully. 'But there's one very mean thing about this, Pat – and that is – the knocking on Mam'zelle's door, that told her something was up! That's the meanest thing I ever heard of! We'll have to find out who did it – and punish them!'

7.

A bad time for Erica

Erica was pleased when she heard of the punishment meted out to the eight girls. She did not dare to say much because she was so afraid that she might be found out. She knew quite well that the girls must wonder who had made the knocking on the doors.

The girls meant to find out who the tale-teller was. They met that evening, and discussed the matter.

'She shan't get away with it,' declared Tessie, fiercely. 'Golly, wasn't I astonished when Mam'zelle let out that she had been disturbed by someone knocking at her door! It must have been the same horrible person who came knocking at ours to give us a fright and spoil the party. I'm sorry I asked you all now. It was my fault.'

'It was jolly decent of you to think of giving us a treat,' said Pat. 'Don't apologize for that! Nobody would have known a thing about it if it hadn't been for that wretched spoil-sport.'

'Pat,' said Tessie, suddenly, 'you don't think it would have been that silly cousin of yours, do you? You know how she bleats everything all over the place. You didn't tell her anything, did you?'

Pat flushed. 'Not a word,' she said, 'and look here,

Tessie, though you've got a pretty poor opinion of Alison – and so have I – she's not the sort to sneak. Honestly she isn't. She can't keep her tongue still – but she wouldn't do a thing like giving us away to Mam'zelle.'

'All right,' said Tessie. 'Well – I simply don't know who it was – and I don't see how we're to find out! Everyone in our dormitory seemed to be asleep when we got back.'

'And so did everyone in ours,' said Pat. 'It's a puzzle. But I'm going to find out who it was, Tessie. I feel so angry when I think about it. I shan't rest till I know who it was.'

They all felt like that, but it was impossible to find out – or so it seemed! Everyone denied even having known that the party was to take place – though most of the girls said that they guessed something was up.

Alison denied absolutely that she knew anything. 'And if I had, I wouldn't have split for worlds,' she said, an angry flush on her cheek. 'You might know that. You don't seem to have much opinion of me lately, you two – but you might at least know that.'

'We do know that,' Pat hastened to say. 'But it is funny, Alison, that although nobody seems to know anything about the party, somebody knew enough to scare us and to bring Mam'zelle out on the warpath!'

It was quite by accident that the truth came out. Gladys came upstairs to find the frying-pan she had lent to Tessie. It had not been brought back to her, and she was afraid that the cook might miss it.

She couldn't find Tessie, but she met Pat on the stairs. 'Oh, Patricia,' she said, 'could you get me back the frying-pan I lent Tessie for the party? I can't find her. I could have asked Erica, but she disappeared before I could speak to her.'

'Erica wouldn't have known anything about it,' said Pat. 'She didn't go to the party.'

'Oh, but she *did* know about it,' said Gladys. 'I met her when I was bringing it upstairs – and she pulled aside my apron and saw the frying-pan, and she said, in that haughty way of hers – "Oho, for Tessie's party!" '

Pat was astonished. It might have been a guess on Erica's part, of course – but anyway, she had seen the frying-pan – and, if she knew anything about sneaky Erica, she would certainly have kept watch, and have put two and two together – and found out everything without difficulty!

'I said to Erica, I said, "Well, if you knew what the frying-pan was for, why did you ask me?" ' said Gladys, quite enjoying this talk with Pat. 'Oh dear, I heard you'd got into trouble over the party, and I'm so sorry.'

'I'll get you the frying-pan,' said Pat, and she went to the music room, where the pan sat solemnly on top of the piano, cleaned by one of the second formers, but otherwise forgotten.

Gladys took it and scuttled downstairs thankfully. She was just as much in awe of the cook as the girls were in awe of Miss Theobald!

Pat went to find Isabel. She told her what Gladys

had said. 'It was Erica all right,' said Pat, fiercely. 'I'm not a bit surprised either, are you? Everyone says she's a sneak. That's almost one of the worst things you can be. Whatever will Tessie say?'

Tessie said a lot. She was angry and indignant. To think that a girl who had shared her chocolates and her birthday cake could have played such a mean trick!

'We'll jolly well tackle her about it,' said Tessie. 'After tea today. You come into the common-room, Pat – and we'll have it out with her. I'll tell the others.'

'Yes, but everyone else will be there,' said Pat, uneasily. 'Is it quite fair to let everyone hear?'

'Why not?' said Tessie, angrily. 'A sneak deserves to be denounced in public. Anyway, we can't go anywhere else.'

So after tea that day Erica was called by Pat. She was sitting in a corner, writing a letter home.

'Erica, come over here. We want to speak to you,' said Pat, in a cold voice. Erica looked up. She went pale. Could the girls have discovered her mean trick?

'I'm busy,' she said, sulkily. 'I've got to finish this letter.'

She went on writing. Pat lost her temper and snatched away the letter. 'You jolly well come!' she said, fiercely. 'Do you want me and Isabel to lug you over?'

Erica saw that there was nothing for it but to go to the corner of the common-room where the six other girls were waiting for her.

She went, looking pale and sulky. She was determined to deny everything.

'Erica, we know that it was you who knocked on the music-room door the other night,' said Pat. 'And it was you too who gave the game away to Mam'zelle and got us punished. You're a mean pig, a horrid sneak, and you're jolly well going to be punished!'

'I don't know what you are talking about,' said Erica, in a trembling voice, not daring to meet eight pairs of accusing eyes.

'Yes, you do. It's no good pretending,' said Tessie. 'Pat has found out everything. Every single thing. We know that you met Gladys on the stairs when she was bringing up something for us.'

'I don't know anything about the frying-pan,' said Erica.

Pat pounced at once. 'How do you know that it was a frying-pan that Gladys was bringing us? There you are, you see – you do know. You've convicted yourself out of your own mouth!'

The other girls in the common-room, curious to hear what was going on, came round, peeping. Alison came too, her big blue eyes almost popping out of her head.

'Oh, was it Erica who gave you away?' she said. 'Well, I might have guessed! She was always bothering me to find out from you and Isabel, Pat, what the secret was.'

'Well, it's a good thing for you, Alison, that for once you had the common sense not to give anything away,' said Pat, grimly. 'Now, Erica – you're a horrible sneak – but at least you might have the decency to own up!'

'I don't know anything about it,' said Erica, stubbornly. 'It's no good your going on at me like this – I just simply don't know anything about it.'

'Go on, Erica, own up!' cried half a dozen voices from members of the second form, who were now all crowding round in the greatest curiosity.

But Erica wouldn't. She hadn't the sense to see that if she owned up frankly and could even bring herself to say she was sorry, the other girls would at least respect her for confessing.

As it was, she made them all intensely angry. 'Very well,' said Pat. 'Don't own up. But you'll have two punishments instead of one, that's all. You'll be punished for sneaking – and you'll be punished for not owning up too!'

'Yes,' said Tessie. 'And the punishment for sneaking is that you jolly well won't go down into the town for two weeks, like us. See?'

'I shall,' said Erica.

'Well, you won't,' said Tessie. 'I'm head of the second form, and I forbid *anyone* to go with you – and you know you are not allowed to go alone. So there!'

Erica was beaten and she knew it. No girl dared to go to the town alone, for that was strictly forbidden. She flushed and said nothing.

'And the punishment for not owning up decently we leave to the first and second forms,' said Pat, her eyes flashing round. 'I am sure that not one of us, Erica, wants to speak to you, or have anything more to do with you than we can help! That's always the punishment for your sort of behaviour!'

'*I* shan't speak to her,' muttered several girls around. Everyone felt disgusted with the miserable Erica. She would have a bad time! It is hard to see glances of contempt and dislike wherever you look, and to have nobody saying a jolly word.

Erica went off to her corner, but her hand trembled as she tried to finish her letter. She was ashamed – but she was angry too – and with Pat most of all!

'So she found out, did she, and told all the others!' thought Erica. 'All right, Pat – I'll pay you out for that – and your silly twin too!'

8.

Margery gets a chance

The first form did not really see very much of Erica, because she did not have lessons with them. But if ever they met her in a passage or in the art room or gym, they looked the other way. In the common-room at night Erica had a miserable time. Not one of the second-form girls would have anything to do with her.

Loud remarks about sneaks and cowards were made in her hearing. The only person who ever threw her a word at all was the bad-tempered Margery Fenworthy. Erica did not like Margery, any more than the other girls did, but she was so grateful to be spoken to, even by the surly first former, that she almost began to like the girl.

'I'm surprised you speak to Erica, Margery,' said Pat, when she had heard Margery ask to borrow Erica's paints.

'Mind your own business,' said Margery, in her usual rude way. 'You're none of you friendly to me, and I know what it is to have people being beastly to you.'

'But Margery, it's your own fault,' said Pat, in surprise. 'You're so rude and sullen. You never smile and joke.'

'Well, people never smile and joke with *me*,' said

Margery. 'You don't give me a chance.'

'Oh, Margery, what a fib!' cried Pat. 'It's you who never give *us* a chance to be decent to you. You scowl and glower and frown all the time.'

'If you're going to pick me to pieces you can save yourself the trouble,' said Margery, fiercely. 'I don't care tuppence for any of you. And if I want to speak to that wretched Erica, I shall. Who cares for a pack of silly girls, and a crowd of stuck-up teachers? I don't!'

Pat was astonished. What a strange girl Margery was! Did she really want a chance of being friends with the others? Was she terribly shy – what was behind that funny manner of hers?

Pat talked about it with her twin. 'Margery is always making enemies,' she said. 'I spoke to her today about it – and she accused us of never giving her a chance. Do you think we ought to do something about it?'

'Ask Lucy,' said Isabel, seeing Lucy coming up to show them a picture she had just finished. 'Oh, Lucy – what a marvellous drawing! It's Mam'zelle to the life!'

Lucy had a clever pencil with portraits. She could, with a few strokes of her pencil, draw any girl or teacher so that everyone knew at once who it was. The drawing she held out was excellent.

'It's exactly how Mam'zelle looks when she says, "Ah, Dorrrrr-is, you are *insupportable*!"' said Pat. 'Lucy, listen, we've been talking about Margery.'

'I'll draw her,' said Lucy. She sat down and sketched Margery's sullen good-looking face – and then, in a few strokes she sketched another Margery – a smiling one, most delightful to see.

'Before taking a course of St Clare's – and after!' laughed Lucy.

'Golly – that's clever,' said Isabel. 'It's a pity Margery can't always look like that second drawing. Listen now, Lucy. She told Pat this morning that we've never given her a chance to be friendly.'

'All wrong,' said Lucy, beginning to draw again. 'She has never given *us* a chance!'

'Exactly what I said,' said Pat, eagerly. 'Oh, Lucy, is that Erica? Goodness, what a poor creature she looks!'

'And is,' said Lucy. 'I'll be glad when we can speak to her again, in a way. I hate to be beastly to anyone even if they deserve it. It makes me feel horrible myself.'

'Lucy, do you think we'd better give Margery a chance, even though she's so jolly difficult?' asked Pat. 'You know – Isabel and I were simply awful last term – and everyone was decent to us. It seems only fair for us to be decent to somebody else who's new, and who seems awful too.'

'I'm all for it,' said Lucy, shaking back her dark curls from her friendly, pretty face. 'My father says, "Always give the under-dog a chance" – and for some reason or other poor Margery seems to think she's an under-dog – everyone's hand against her – that sort of thing. Goodness knows why she's got that idea, but she has. All right – I'll go out of my way to be friendly, if you will.'

'We'll tell the others, as well,' said Pat. So the first formers were told about the idea, and although most of them thought it was stupid, because they really did dislike Margery, they all agreed to back up Lucy and the twins. Even Alison said she would – and she had suffered very much from Margery's rudeness. Margery thought Alison a silly little feather-head, and had said so, many times.

So, what with avoiding Erica, and trying to be nice to Margery, things were quite exciting. The first time that Margery showed any signs of being pleased was when the first form were in the gym. Margery was excellent at climbing, jumping, and any kind of exercise. When she did an extra good jump in the gym, the girls clapped.

Margery glanced round, surprised. She gave a half-smile, and stepped to her place. The mistress spoke a few words of praise too. Margery tried not to look too pleased, but she couldn't help going red with pleasure.

Afterwards Pat spoke to her. 'Margery, you're jolly good at gym,' she said. 'I wish I could climb and jump like you.'

'I like anything like that,' said Margery, in a civil tone. 'As for games, I simply adore them. I only wish we could play three times as much as we do! I wish we went riding more here too. I used to love that at my old school.'

'What school did you go to before you came here?' asked Isabel, pleased to see that Margery could really talk quite normally!

But for some reason or other Margery would not say any more. She turned away and her old scowling look came over her face. The twins were disappointed.

All the same, Margery felt that everyone was giving her a chance, and she did respond in many ways. She didn't give so many rude answers, and she did occasionally offer to help anyone in difficulties. She even offered to give silly little Alison some practice at catching the ball in lacrosse, because she saw that the twins were really ashamed of their cousin's stupidity at games.

But Alison refused. 'Why does everyone keep badgering me to practise catching?' she grumbled. 'I hate lacrosse. I hate all games. I hate having to run across a dirty field and get hot and out of breath. We all look awful when we've finished playing!'

'Alison! Is there ever a time when you don't think about how you look?' cried Janet. 'You're as vain as a peacock. I hope you get a whole lot of spots tomorrow!'

'Don't be mean!' said Alison, the easy tears coming into her eyes.

'Well, for goodness' sake, act more like a senior girl and not like a baby,' grumbled Janet. 'Your cousins were bad enough when they came last term – but at least they didn't turn on the water tap like you do, at any minute of the day!'

'I should think not!' said Pat, hotly, ready to attack Janet, who was in one of her sharp-tongued moods. But Janet gave her a friendly punch. She never wanted to quarrel with the twins, whom she sincerely liked.

Although Margery seemed to be much more friendly with the girls, she was no better with the mistresses, to whom she was really rude. She did not try at all with her lessons – and the curious thing was that all the mistresses seemed to have endless patience with the sulky girl.

'Golly! If any of us were half as rude to Miss Roberts as Margery is, we'd soon hear about it,' said Pat, half a dozen times a week. 'I can't understand it. Did you see the work that Margery handed in to Miss Lewis too? She only did half a page, and her writing was awful.'

'Well, what about her arithmetic!' said Hilary. 'Honestly, I don't think she got a single sum right this morning – and Miss Roberts never said a word.'

'She won't say how old she is,' said Pat. 'I believe Margery's sixteen! And most of us in the first form are fourteen or just fifteen.'

'Oh well – never mind. She can't help being stupid, I suppose,' said Lucy. 'Anyway, she's jolly good at games – and when we play that match against the Oakdene girls next week, I bet we'll be glad of Margery. She's been put into the match-team, you know.'

'Has she?' said Pat. 'Golly! I wish I'd been put in it too. I haven't seen the list.'

'Well, you're not in it,' said Janet. 'I've looked. No first former except Margery is in it – and only two second formers! The rest are all third formers. It's an honour for Margery to be chosen – but honestly, she's frightfully good at games, and most awfully quick and strong.'

'Well, if she's sixteen, as you say, she *ought* to be quick and strong,' said Alison, cattily.

'Shut up, Alison,' said Pat. 'We don't *know* that she's sixteen. Now don't you go round bleating about *that*!'

'I *don't* bleat,' began Alison, in her pathetic voice, making her blue eyes very wide and hurt. But half a dozen exasperated girls yelled at her and threw cushions – so Alison thought it better to say no more. No one could bear Alison when she went all goofy, as Janet described it.

When the two weeks were nearly up, and the eight girls were looking forward to being allowed to go down into the town again, the Big Row happened. It all centred around Margery, who in ten minutes destroyed the new friendliness that had begun to grow up around her.

It happened in history class, and blew up all in a minute. The girls were horrified – and ever afterwards it was spoken of as the Big Row.

9.

The big row

Miss Lewis was taking the history lesson, and the class were learning about the discovery of America, and its conquest. As usual the class was giving the history teacher close attention, for if there was one thing that Miss Lewis would not put up with, it was inattention.

Even Margery usually attended to Miss Lewis more than to the other teachers – partly because she was interested in history, and partly because she was a little afraid of Miss Lewis and her sharp eyes.

But this morning something seemed to have happened to Margery. The girls had noticed it from the time that she had sat down to breakfast. There had been a letter by her plate which Margery had not opened until she had been by herself. From that time onwards Margery had gone back to her most sullen and don't-care self – though nobody imagined that it was anything to do with the letter, of course.

She had been careless and inattentive in Miss Roberts's arithmetic class, and Miss Roberts had been, as usual, patient with her. In the French class, after a sharp look at her, Mam'zelle had taken no notice of Margery, but had let her sit and sulk by herself.

She had cheered up a little in the history class, but had not taken any part in the discussion that Miss Lewis sometimes allowed at the beginning of the lesson.

Then Hilary had come out with a good idea. 'Miss Lewis! There's a play on in the next town, at the Royal Theatre – and it's called "Drake". Would it be about the same period of history that we're doing?'

'Oh, yes,' said Miss Lewis. 'It's a fine play. Just the right period.'

'Oh, Miss Lewis – do you think you could possibly take us to see it?' cried Hilary, who adored plays of any kind.

'Oh, yes, Miss Lewis!' cried the rest of the form, eagerly. 'An outing to the next town would be marvellous.'

'Hush,' said Miss Lewis, rapping on her desk. 'Do remember there are other classes going on. When is the play being performed, Hilary?'

Hilary had a notice of it in her desk. She rummaged about and found it. 'There's a special performance on Saturday afternoon, this week,' she said. 'Oh, Miss Lewis – do, do take us! I'd so love to see it.'

'That's my weekend off,' said Miss Lewis, regretfully. 'I'd arranged to go for a walking-tour with Miss Walker. We've got it all planned.'

Each mistress had a weekend off during the term, and they looked forward to this very much. The class knew how precious the weekends were to the staff, and they stared in disappointment at Miss Lewis. What a pity! Just the Saturday the play was on. It would have been such fun to go and see it.

'Oh, blow!' said Pat. 'Wouldn't that just be the way! Never mind, Miss Lewis – it can't be helped.'

'Well – I don't know,' said Miss Lewis, slowly. 'Perhaps it *can* be helped! You've been good workers this term, and maybe I could give up the Saturday to take you – and go home on the Sunday morning, for one day instead of two. Miss Walker can find someone else to go walking with, I dare say.'

'Oh, I say – we wouldn't let you do that,' said Janet, at once. 'We're not quite such selfish pigs, Miss Lewis.'

Miss Lewis laughed. She liked the outspoken first formers. 'I'll arrange it,' she said. 'I'll speak to Miss Theobald – and the whole class can go with me in the school bus. We'll book seats at the Royal Theatre, and go and have a lovely time seeing the play – and we'll have a marvellous tea afterwards.'

There were sighs and squeals of delight. Shining eyes looked at Miss Lewis, and everyone beamed with joy. What an unexpected treat! Even Margery Fenworthy looked pleased.

'Miss Lewis, you're a sport!' said Janet. 'You really are! Thanks most awfully. Are you really sure you don't mind taking us on your precious weekend?'

'Oh, I mind awfully,' said Miss Lewis, with a twinkle in her eye. 'Do you suppose it's any pleasure to me to take charge of twenty noisy first formers with no manners at all?'

Everyone laughed. Miss Lewis might be sharp at times – but she really was a good sort!

'Now mind –' said Miss Lewis, warningly. 'You will all work well to show me that you really do appreciate the treat! No slacking this term!'

'Of course not!' said the girls, quite determined to work better for Miss Lewis than they had ever done before.

Ten minutes later came the Big Row. Each girl had her history book open, and was following the map there that Miss Lewis was explaining – all except Margery. She had her book open it was true – but into the open pages she had slipped the letter she had received that morning, and she was re-reading it, a scowl on her face.

Miss Lewis spoke to Margery and got no answer. The girl didn't hear the question at all. She was so engrossed in her own thoughts. Miss Lewis spoke again, sharply.

'Margery! You are not paying the least attention! What is that you have in your book?'

'Nothing,' said Margery, with a jump. She tried to slip the letter out of the pages. Miss Lewis looked angry.

'Bring me that letter,' she said.

'It's mine,' said Margery, with her sullenest look.

'I know that,' said Miss Lewis, irritably. 'You can give it to me till the end of the morning. Then there will not be any temptation for you to read it in another lesson. You certainly will not do a thing like that in my lesson again. Bring me the letter.'

'What! For you to read!' flared up Margery in a rage. 'Nobody's going to read my private letters!'

'Margery! You forget yourself,' said Miss Lewis, coldly. 'Do you suppose I should read the letter? You know better than that. But I shall certainly confiscate it for the rest of the day now. You will bring me the letter, and you will come to me for it this evening, and apologize for your behaviour.'

'I shan't do anything of the sort,' said Margery, rudely. All the girls stared in horror.

'Shut up, Margery,' said Pat, who was sitting next to her. 'Don't you dare to speak like that!'

'*You* shut up!' said Margery, turning a look of rage on Pat. 'I won't be interfered with by anybody – no, not even by Miss Theobald herself! As for Miss Lewis, with her sharp eyes and her sharp nose sticking into my private business, she won't get anything out of *me*!'

'Margery!' cried half a dozen voices in the utmost horror. Nobody could believe their ears. Margery was flushed a bright red, and her eyes flashed angrily. She was in her worst temper, and she didn't care in the least what she said.

Miss Lewis was very angry. She was white, and her nose looked suddenly rather thin, as it always did when she was cross. But this morning she was more than cross. She stood up.

'Leave the room, Margery,' she said, in a cold quiet voice. 'I shall have to consider whether or not I can have you in my history classes again.'

'I'll leave the room all right,' said Margery. 'I'd leave the whole school if I could! I didn't want to come. I knew what would happen! I hate the lot of you!'

The angry girl walked out, her head held high. But once outside she leant her head against the wall and cried bitterly. She was shocked and upset.

Miss Theobald happened to come along just as Margery was wiping her eyes, and wondering where to go. She looked at Margery in silence.

'Come with me, my dear,' she said. 'Something has happened, hasn't it? You must tell me about it.'

'It's no good,' said Margery. 'I'll be sent away from here. And I don't care. I don't care a bit.'

'Yes, you do care,' said Miss Theobald. 'You care a lot. Margery, come with me. Come along, please. We can't stand out here like this. The girls will be pouring out of the classrooms in a little while.'

Margery took a look at Miss Theobald's calm, serious face. The head looked at Margery with a wise and compassionate glance in her deep eyes. The angry girl gave a sob, and then went with the head mistress.

Inside the classroom there was a babel of furious voices.

'The beast! How could she behave like that!'

'Just after Miss Lewis had said she'd give up her Saturday too!'

'It's waste of time to be nice to a creature like that! I'll never speak to her again!'

'She deserves to be expelled! I shouldn't be surprised if she is!'

'Miss Lewis! We all apologize to you for Margery! We do, really.'

'Girls, girls, be quiet, please,' said Miss Lewis, putting on her glasses and looking round the room. 'There is no need to make a noise like this. We have only five minutes of this lesson left. Turn to page fifty-six, please. I don't want to hear another word about Margery.'

So no more was said in class – but plenty was said outside! How they raged against her! The second form heard about it too, and they were amazed and aghast that anyone should dare to behave like that to Miss Lewis.

'I wish I'd been there,' said Tessie, who always enjoyed a row, so long as she wasn't the centre of it. 'Golly! Miss Lewis must have been furious!'

'Where's Margery now?' asked Pat.

Nobody knew. She didn't appear again at all that morning or afternoon – but after tea she came into the common-room, rather white, and looking defiant, for she guessed how the girls felt about her.

'Here comes the meanie!' said Janet. 'I hope you're ashamed of yourself, Margery!'

But Margery refused to say a single word. She sat in a corner, reading – or pretending to read – and would not answer anything said to her. The girls gave her a bad time. Even Erica was forgotten. In fact Erica seemed quite harmless, somehow, after the dreadful way Margery had behaved!

'I wonder if Margery will be allowed to come to the

history lesson tomorrow,' said Janet. 'I bet Miss Lewis won't let her!'

But there was a surprise in store for the class when Miss Lewis came to take history next day. Margery was there too!

'Good morning, girls,' said Miss Lewis, as she came into the room. 'Margery, will you go and speak to Mam'zelle for a minute? She is in her study and wants a word with you. Come back when she has finished.'

Margery went out, looking surprised. Miss Lewis turned to the girls. 'I just want to say that Margery has apologized for her bad behaviour,' said Miss Lewis. 'She had a talk with Miss Theobald who found her, outside the classroom, and she came to me yesterday evening to apologize. I have accepted her apology and am taking her back into my class. I hardly think such a thing will happen again, and I would like you all to forget it as soon as possible, please.'

'But, Miss Lewis – isn't she going to be punished?' asked Janet, indignantly.

'Perhaps she has been,' said Miss Lewis, putting on her glasses. 'I think we can safely leave things to be decided by the head mistress, don't you? Now, not a word more about the subject, please. Turn to page fifty-six.'

The class were turning to page fifty-six when Margery came back. Mam'zelle had wanted her about a very small thing, and the girl could not help feeling that she had been sent out for a few minutes so that Miss Lewis could say something about her. She walked to her desk, red in the face, and found her place. She paid great attention to the lesson, and Miss Lewis hadn't the slightest reason to find fault with her that morning.

But at break the girls had a great deal to say about Margery again! 'Forget it as soon as possible!' snorted Janet. 'How could Miss Lewis say a thing like that? Golly, I think Margery ought to have been expelled from the school! After we'd tried to be so decent to her too. You just simply CAN'T help a girl like that.'

So once more Margery was sent back to her lonely, friendless state. No one spoke to her if they could help it, and nobody even looked at her.

'It's a pity she's playing in the match,' said Pat 'Well – *I* shan't clap if she shoots a goal!'

10.

An exciting match

The days went quickly by. The first form were taken to the play, and enjoyed every minute of it. They had a wonderful tea afterwards, for Miss Lewis really did do things well!

'Buns and jam! Fruit cake! Meringues! Chocolate éclairs!' said Janet, describing it all to the envious second formers when they got back. 'Golly, it *was* a spread! I don't know which I enjoyed most – the play or the tea. They were both marvellous.'

'Did Margery go too?' asked Tessie, curiously. Everyone, of course, had heard of the Big Row. Even the top formers knew about it.

'Yes – she went,' said Pat. 'Though if it had been me I wouldn't have had the cheek to have gone. She didn't say a word the whole time – but she thanked Miss Lewis for taking her. Personally I think it was jolly sporting of Miss Lewis even to *think* of having her!'

'So do I,' said Tessie. 'I heard Belinda say yesterday that if Margery wasn't so awfully good at lacrosse, she would strike her out of the match. She's very fond of Miss Lewis, you know, and she was furious when she heard how Margery had cheeked her.'

'Well, it's about the only good thing you can say of Margery – that's she's good at games,' said Tessie. 'But my word, she's fierce, isn't she? I hope Belinda will give her a word of warning before the match. If she tackles the Oakdene team too savagely she'll be sent off the field. And then we shall be one man short.'

Belinda did warn Margery. The match was to be played on the home field, and the whole school was to watch, if it was fine. Oakdene and St Clare's were well matched. There wasn't much to choose between them. So far the score was eleven matches won by each, so this match would be rather exciting.

'Margery, don't be hauled up on a foul, please,' said Belinda to the girl, as she was changing into her gym things before the match. 'You lose your head sometimes and forget you're so strong. Play fairly, and you'll be jolly useful. Lose your temper and you'll probably be sent off the field!'

Margery scowled and said nothing. She bent over to put on her shoes. Pat and Janet came into the changing-room to look for Isabel and Alison.

'Oh, there you are!' said Pat, seeing the other two. It was dark in the changing-room and she did not see Margery, bending down over her shoes. 'Now don't forget, everybody, if that miserable Margery shoots a goal, we don't clap and we don't cheer. See?'

'Right, Pat,' said the others. 'She doesn't deserve even a whisper – and she won't get it!'

'You horrid beast, Pat!' said Margery, suddenly,

standing up in anger. 'So that's what you've planned to do, have you? Just like you!'

The four girls stared in dismay. None of them had known that Margery was there.

'I don't want your claps or your cheers,' said Margery, stalking out. 'One day, Pat, I'll get even with you! You see if I don't!'

The bell rang for the players to take their places. Margery went on to the field, a tall and scowling figure.

'I'm sorry for the girls she's got to play against!' said Belinda to Rita. 'My word, she's an extraordinary girl!'

The whistle went for the game to begin. It was a fine afternoon, rather cold, but with no wind. The watching girls had on their warm coats and felt hats. They put their hands in their pockets as they sat on the forms, and prepared to shout and cheer and clap when the right times came.

It was always fun to watch a match. It was lovely to be able to yell as loudly as they liked, and to dance about and cheer if anything really exciting happened. The school was always glad when the match was an at-home one, then they could see every goal, and watch all that happened, instead of having to wait until the team came back from an away match.

The game was a bit slow at first. The players hadn't warmed up to it, and everyone was playing rather cautiously. No one above the third form was playing in either school. The Oakdene girls did not look a very big lot, but they were wiry and ran fast. They soon got into the game, and the running, tackling and catching began to get very swift and exciting.

'Go it, Susan! Go it, Tessie!' yelled the second formers, anxious to cheer on their members. Except for the first former, Margery, all the rest but Tessie and Susan were third-form girls. Margery was the tallest, strongest girl of the home team, even bigger than the third formers.

'Well run, Mary! Shoot, shoot!' yelled the school, seeing a swift third former catch the ball from Tessie and tear down the field to the goal. But the Oakdene girl marking her was swift too. She tried to knock the ball from Mary's lacrosse net. Mary swung her net in front of her. The Oakdene girl tried to out-run her but couldn't. She yelled to another girl.

'Tackle her, tackle her!'

Like a hare another Oakdene girl shot out from her place and ran straight at Mary. The two met with a clash. Mary went spinning, and the ball rolled from her net. The Oakdene girl picked it up neatly and tore back in the opposite direction.

'On her, Margery!' yelled Belinda, from the onlookers. 'Go on, go on – run. You can do it!'

Margery Fenworthy shot up like a bullet from a gun! She could run faster than anyone on the field. She raced across to the running girl and did a neat turn round her to get to her lacrosse net. She slashed upwards viciously with her own net – the ball jerked out and Margery caught it deftly. The Oakdene girl slashed back at Margery's net to get the ball, but

Margery had already thrown it hard across the field to where Tessie was waiting for it. Down to the goal sped Tessie. She shot – but alas, the ball rolled wide, and the whistle blew.

'My word, that girl Margery plays well,' said Rita. Nobody, however, had cheered Margery on as she had tackled the girl and got the ball. But how they yelled to Tessie when she had tried to shoot!

The match went on its exciting way. The school yelled itself hoarse as the battle went first this way and then that way. The teams were beautifully matched, there was no doubt about that.

Margery stood out among all the players. She always played well – but today she seemed inspired. Pat knew why, and felt a little uncomfortable.

'She always plays extra well when she's angry,' said Pat to her twin. 'Have you noticed that? She seems to make the game into a fight and goes all out for it. Perhaps it helps her to work off her bad temper.'

Margery soon got the ball again by a swift piece of running. She dodged a girl running at her, and looked for someone to pass to. Susan was ready. Margery threw the ball to her. Susan caught it, was tackled, and threw back to Margery. There was a clear space to goal. Should she run nearer and shoot, risking being tackled – or should she try one of her long hard shots?

A girl shot out to tackle her. Margery raised her net, and shot the ball hard and strong down the field. It went like a bullet! The tackling girl tried to stop it but failed. The goal-keeper saw it coming and put out her net – but the shot was so hard that she couldn't stop it! The ball was in the goal!

'Goal!' yelled the school. And then there was a silence. There was no clapping. No cheering. No shouts of 'Well done, Margery!' It was strange, because after a goal everyone usually yelled their loudest. The watching mistresses looked at one another with pursed lips and raised eyebrows. No girl had ever been so unpopular before as not to be cheered in a match!

Half-time came. Pat ran out with a plate of lemon quarters for the thirsty players. How good they tasted! So sour and clean.

'You've got a good player in your team this term,' said the captain of the other side, to Pat, as she took her piece of lemon. 'But golly, isn't she big? I should have thought she was a top former.'

'Well, she's not,' said Pat. 'She's in the first form!'

'Gracious!' said the girl, staring at Margery in surprise. Margery was not speaking to any of her team, and no one was speaking to her. 'She doesn't seem very popular,' said the Oakdene girl. 'What's up?'

'Oh, nothing,' said Pat, who was not going to talk about Margery's affairs to anyone else. 'Have another piece of lemon?'

'Thanks,' said the girl. 'My word, this is a good match. Anybody's game, really. You're one goal up – but I bet we get even this half!'

The whistle blew. Pat scurried off the field. The

players took their places, at opposite ends to the ones they had had before. The game began again.

It was fast and furious. Everyone was now well-warmed-up and enjoying the game. The Oakdene captain scored an unexpected goal, which Bertha, in goal, should have been able to stop and didn't. The whole school groaned. Poor Bertha went as red as fire.

'One all! Play up, St Clare's!' yelled everyone.

If Margery had played well the first half, she played even better in the second half. She ran like the wind, she tackled fearlessly, she caught accurately and threw well. But she unfortunately lost her temper with an Oakdene girl who neatly dodged her with the ball, and brought down her net with such force on the girl's hand to make her drop the ball that the Oakdene girl squealed in pain. The referee blew her whistle and called Margery to her.

'Gosh! Is she going to send her off the field for a foul?' groaned Belinda, who badly wanted her team to win. 'She deserves it, I know – she's such a savage when she gets excited – but we can't afford to lose her just now!'

But Margery fortunately was not sent off. She was severely reprimanded, and walked back to her place with the usual sullen look on her face. She was much more careful after that, for she hadn't the slightest wish to be sent off in the middle of such an exciting match.

She got the ball again within the next few minutes, and ran for goal. She passed to Mary, who passed back.

Margery shot – and the ball rolled straight into the corner of the goal, though the goal-keeper frantically tried to stop it.

'Goal!' yelled the whole school. But again there was that curious silence afterwards. No cheering, no clapping. Margery noticed it at once, and her eyes flashed with anger. The beasts! She was playing her best for the school – and yet they wouldn't even give her a cheer! All because of that hateful Pat O'Sullivan!

The girl felt a fury of anger rising up in her. Somehow it gave her even more swiftness and strength than before. She was a miracle of swiftness as she darted about the field, tackling and dodging, getting the ball when it seemed almost impossible.

'If only Oakdene don't shoot again!' cried Pat, in the greatest excitement. 'Oh, golly – they're going to. Save it, Bertha, save it!'

But poor Bertha couldn't possibly save the goal that time, though she threw herself flat down on her front to do so. The ball trickled by and came to rest in the goal. Two goals all – and five minutes to play!

And in that five minutes Margery managed to shoot two of the finest goals that any of the school had ever seen. The first one was one of her long shots, straight and true, from halfway down the field. The second was extraordinary. She could not shoot because two girls tackled her just near the goal, and Margery rolled over and over on the ground. The Oakdene girls tried to get the ball from her net but somehow or other Margery managed to hold it safely there – and suddenly, from her position flat on the ground, her nose almost in the mud, Margery jerked her lacrosse net! The ball flew out – and landed in the goal right through the surprised goal-keeper's legs!

At first nobody knew it was a goal – and then the umpire shouted, 'Goal! Four goals to St Clare's, two goals to Oakdene. One more minute to play!'

But before the ball was in play again, time was up. The whistle blew and the players trooped off the field. What a match it had been!

11.

Erica gets her own back

Usually, after a match, the girls who had shot the winning goals were surrounded, patted and cheered. If anyone deserved to be cheered that afternoon it was certainly Margery, for she had done the hardest work, and had stood out as the finest player in the team.

Belinda muttered 'Well done!' as Margery came by. But nobody else said a word. No one went to Margery to clap her on the shoulder. No one shouted, 'Well played, old girl!' No one, in fact, took any notice of her at all.

The Oakdene girls couldn't help noticing this curious behaviour, and were surprised. They stared hard at Margery, who stared back, her head held high.

'I'm glad we won the match – but I wish it hadn't been Margery who did it all,' said Pat. 'I feel a bit uncomfortable now about not cheering her a bit. Do you think we ought to go and say a word to her, Janet?'

'Of course we ought,' said Janet, 'but you know jolly well what would happen if we did! She'd bite our heads off – and I don't wonder! No – we've started this uncomfortable game of sending someone to Coventry – and we've got to stick to it.'

Brave as Margery was, she could not face the school tea with the teams. Usually after a match the two opposing teams had a special tea to themselves, apart from the rest of the school, though in the same dining-hall of course. At the long team-table they chattered and laughed and discussed the match with one another. The home team acted as hostesses to the visiting team, and it was all great fun.

'It's so lovely when you're tired and happy to sit down to buns and butter and fruit cake and chocolate biscuits and big cups of tea!' sighed Tessie. 'And to talk as much as you like about the match. Come on, Susan. I'm ready.'

Everyone noticed that Margery was not at the table. No one liked to say anything about it. The visiting team were quite aware that there was something strange in the air and did not like to discuss it. The St Clare team wondered where Margery was, and looked to see if she was at the table where the first formers were sitting eating their own tea.

But she wasn't. She had gone to the changing-room and changed. Then she had slipped into the deserted classroom and gone to her desk. She was tired, angry and miserable. She wanted a cup of tea to drink, and she was hungry too. But not for anything would she have faced the hostile looks of the other girls that afternoon. She had played so well – and won the match for her team – and if they couldn't even say 'Well played!' she didn't want anything to do with them!

Miss Roberts noticed that Margery was missing. She guessed what had happened. She had heard all about the Big Row, and knew that Margery was being punished by the girls for her misbehaviour. Well – people always *were* punished for that kind of thing, by being disliked. Miss Roberts could not do anything about it.

Erica's meanness had been almost forgotten in the excitement of the Big Row, and the match. But Erica had not forgotten that she meant to pay back Pat for finding out her trick, and punishing her for it. She had spent a good deal of time wondering how to get even with her. It was not so easy as it had seemed at first, because the two girls were in different forms.

But Erica soon found one or two things to do. She saw that Pat was making herself a red jumper, with which she was very pleased. She waited her chance, and then, one evening when she saw that Pat had put the knitting back into her bag on the shelf, she made up her mind to spoil it.

There was a school meeting that evening. 'If I go in late for it, I can sit at the back,' thought Erica. 'Then I can slip out halfway through for a few minutes, and come back without anyone noticing. That will just give me time to get to the common-room and back.'

So that evening, at half-past seven, when the meeting had just begun, Erica slipped in at the back. No one noticed her, for Miss Walker was speaking, and everyone was listening. Margery Fenworthy was at the back too. That was usually her place now – at the back

– for it was horrid to be anywhere where people had the chance of looking disdainfully at you! No one saw you if you sat at the back.

Erica sat for a while, listening. When Miss Walker sat down, and Miss Lewis got up to speak, Erica slipped out. No one saw her at all. She ran at top speed to the empty common-room. She went to Pat's corner of the shelf and took down her knitting bag.

In it was the half-finished jumper, knitted most beautifully, for Pat was very proud of it. Erica took out the knitting and pulled the needles from the wool. She wrenched at the jumper, and half the even knitting came undone. Erica, with a feeling of real spite, tore at the wool again – and it broke in half a dozen places! The girl hurriedly pushed the knitting into the bag, and then ran back to the meeting. Miss Lewis was still speaking, in her clear, sharp tones.

No one saw Erica slip in – no one except Margery, who paid no attention, for she was lost in her own thoughts. Erica hugged herself secretly, pleased with what she had done. In her mean little soul she rejoiced that she had harmed someone who had brought her to justice.

The meeting finished. The girls yawned and stretched. Pat looked at her watch.

'Eight o'clock,' she said. 'Time for a game or something in the common-room. Come on.'

'There's dance music on the radio,' said Doris. 'Let's put that on. I want to dance!'

'I've got some French to finish,' groaned Sheila. 'Blow! I wish I'd done it before. I daren't leave it. Mam'zelle always seems in such a bad temper these days.'

'Yes, doesn't she?' said Isabel, who had noticed the same thing. 'I'm getting quite scared of her!'

They all went back to the common-room. The third formers went to the big room they shared with the fourth form, and the top formers went to their studies. The time before bed was always cosy and friendly and jolly.

'What are you going to do, Isabel?' asked Pat. 'Shall we finish that jigsaw puzzle Tessie lent us?'

'No,' said Isabel. 'I want to mend a stocking. I shall have Matron after me if I don't. She told me to do it three days ago and I forgot.'

'All right. I'll talk to you and knit,' said Pat, reaching up to the shelf for her bag. 'I'm getting on so well with my red jumper. I can't imagine what Mother will say when she sees it! I've never stuck at knitting so long before.'

'Let's see what it looks like,' said Janet, coming up. Pat took out her knitting and undid it. The needles dropped to the floor. The wool hung torn and unravelled.

'Pat!' gasped Isabel, in horror. 'Pat! It's all undone! It's spoilt!'

'Gracious goodness!' said Janet, taking a glance at Pat's horrified face as she saw her ruined work. 'Who's done that?'

'Oh, Pat – I'm so sorry about it,' said Isabel, who

knew what hard and careful work Pat had put into the jumper. 'Oh, Pat – whatever *has* happened to it?'

Pat stared at her spoilt work. It was a shock to her, and she was near tears. She blinked hard and swallowed the lump that suddenly came into her throat.

'Somebody's done this to me,' she said, in a low voice. 'Somebody's done it to pay me out.'

'Margery!' said Isabel, at once. 'She overheard what you said about not clapping or cheering her in the match – and this is her way of paying you out. Oh, the mean, mean thing!'

Janet flushed with anger. She hated meanness of any kind. 'Well, if she's done that, she'll jolly well have to be hauled up about it!' she said. 'Look here, girls – come and look at Pat's knitting.'

The first and second formers crowded round. Erica came too, pretending to be surprised and shocked. She was enjoying herself very much. If only nobody guessed it was she who had done it!

But everyone thought it was Margery. No one imagined it was Erica, for by now they had half forgotten her mean behaviour. They crowded round Pat and sympathized with her.

'It *is* rotten luck,' said Tessie. 'I know what it feels like even to drop a stitch when you're trying to make something really nice. But to have it all spoilt and pulled out like that – and broken in so many places – that's dreadful. What will you do? Can you do anything about it?'

'I shall just have to undo it all and begin again, that's all,' said Pat. It had given the girl a great shock to think that anyone could play such a mean trick on her. Real spite is always horrible – and Pat had never come across it directed at herself before.

'Well, what are we going to do about Margery?' said Janet, fiercely. 'She's got to be dealt with, hasn't she?'

'Where is she?' said Hilary. Just as she spoke Margery came into the room with a book. She had been to the school library to get it. Janet rounded on her at once.

'Margery! Come here! We've all seen your latest display of bad temper!'

Margery looked surprised. 'What do you mean, Janet?' she asked, coldly.

'Oh, don't pretend like that!' said Janet. 'Look here – do you dare to say you didn't do that to Pat's knitting?'

She held up the ruined jumper. Margery stared at it in amazement. 'Of course I didn't,' she said, with dignity. 'I'm bad tempered and sulky, and there's not much that's good about me, according to all of you – but I don't do mean tricks like that. I dislike Pat, and I'd like to get even with her for some of the unkind things she's done to me – but not in that way.'

The girls stared at her. Nobody believed her. Pat went red, and put the knitting back into her bag.

'You *did* do it, Margery, you know you did!' cried Isabel, quite beside herself because her twin had been hurt. 'You must have slipped out whilst we were at the meeting and done it then!'

'No, I didn't,' said Margery. 'It's true I was at the back – but what's the good of being anywhere else when you all send me to Coventry, as you do? But I tell you quite honestly. I didn't play that trick. I could *not* do a trick like that. I might knock Pat or push her, or clash with her at lacrosse – but I wouldn't do a hole-and-corner thing like that.'

'You'd do anything!' said Janet, scornfully. 'I bet you wouldn't stick at anything once you got your knife into somebody!'

'You're just proving the truth of the old saying, "Give a dog a bad name and hang him,"' said Margery. 'Because I'm bad in some things you think I'm capable of doing anything horrid. I'm not.'

Her eyes suddenly filled with tears and she turned away to hide them. Tears were weak. She could not bear anyone to see them. She walked out of the room and left a surprised and furious crowd behind her.

'Well, would you think *any*one would have the nerve to deny it like that?' demanded Kathleen.

'She's absolutely brazen!' declared Tessie.

'Oh, shut up about it,' said Pat. 'Let's not say any more. We can't prove it – and though we're all jolly sure she did it, it's no good going on and on about it. It's hateful, but it's best forgotten.'

'Well, it's decent of you to feel like that,' said Doris, going to the radio. 'I wish I knew exactly how and when she did it. Who'd like a little dance music to cheer us up?'

Soon the radio was blaring out dance tunes and Doris and Janet were dancing round the room, doing all sorts of ridiculous steps to make the others laugh. And the one who laughed the loudest was Erica.

What luck! she thought. No one even thought of me – and they've pinned the blame on to Margery! Now I can think of something else to do to Pat, and nobody will imagine it's anyone but that bad-tempered Margery!

12.

The twins hear a secret

That weekend was half-term. Most of the parents who could do so came by train to see their girls, or drove down to them. Those girls whose parents were not able to visit them either went out with their friends, or were taken into the next town to see a film or play.

Mrs O'Sullivan came by car, and took out Pat and Isabel, and also Alison, whose mother could not come. Janet went joyfully with her parents on a long picnic ride, and took Hilary with her. Margery's parents did not come at all – and no one asked her to go out with them, so she went with Miss Roberts and four other girls to the cinema in the next town.

Isabel was still full of how Pat's jumper had been ruined. She poured it all out to Mrs O'Sullivan, and Alison chattered about it too. Pat said very little. She had been shocked and hurt by it, for she was a friendly girl and had had few enemies in her life.

Mrs O'Sullivan listened. 'You are quite sure that Margery did it?' she asked. 'Don't you think you ought to withhold your judgement until you are quite certain? There is nothing so dreadful as to accuse a person wrongly, you know. It makes them very bitter –

and from what you tell me poor Margery must have already had some unhappiness of some sort in her life.'

Mrs O'Sullivan's remark made the three girls feel a little uncomfortable. They did feel sure that Margery had spoilt the jumper – but it was quite true that they hadn't any real proof.

No one said anything more – but privately Pat and Isabel decided to do as their mother said – and not judge Margery until they actually had some real proof. After all, although she was bad tempered and rude, she had never shown before that she could be either mean or deceitful. Alison looked at the twins and thought she would do as they did – if they told her what that would be! Alison was getting a little better now and hadn't quite such a good opinion of herself.

But their good intentions were quite ruined by a chance meeting with an old friend of theirs that afternoon. They were having lunch in a big town some twenty miles away from the school, and afterwards were going to see a play there. And, having lunch at a nearby table was Pamela Holding, a girl who had been at Redroofs for a year or two whilst the twins had been there.

'Hallo, Pam!' cried Isabel, seeing her first. 'Are you having half-term holiday too?'

'Hallo, Pat, hallo, Isabel – and is that Alison?' cried Pam. 'Yes – I'm at school at St Hilda's, and Mother is taking me to the play here this afternoon for my half-term treat. Don't say you're going too!'

'Well, we are!' said Pat, pleased. 'Let's all go together, and have tea with one another afterwards.'

The two mothers knew and liked each other, so they approved of this idea. The four girls and the two grown-ups set off to the theatre at half-past two, chattering and laughing, exchanging all their news.

Unfortunately their seats were not side by side in the theatre, so they had to part there – but arranged to meet for tea. And it was at tea that the twins heard some strange news about Margery Fenworthy.

Pamela was telling the twins and Alison about someone in her school who had just won the record for long distance running.

'Well, we've a girl at our school who could win any records she liked, I should think,' said Alison. 'She's just a miracle at games and gym. Her name's Margery Fenworthy.'

'Margery Fenworthy!' said Pamela, her eyes opening wide. 'You don't mean to tell me *she's* at St Clare's! Golly! We all wondered where she'd gone.'

'Why – was she at St Hilda's with you last term then?' asked Pat in surprise. 'She never will say anything about the schools she has been to.'

'No wonder,' said Pamela scornfully. 'She's been to about six already!'

'Why so many?' asked Isabel in amazement.

'Can't you guess?' said Pam. 'She's been expelled from the whole lot, as far as I can make out. I know that St Hilda's stuck her for two terms – and then out she went! She was just too unbearable for words. So rude in class that no mistress would have her!'

The twins stared at Pamela. Yes – that was Margery all right! So she had been sent away from one school after another. What a disgrace!

'Good gracious!' said Alison, finding her tongue first. 'Well, I should think she'll be sent away from St Clare's soon too. Do you know what she did to Pat?'

And out came the whole history of the spoilt jumper – and then the story of the Big Row. Pamela listened, her eyes wide with interest.

'Well, I must say the Big Row sounds just exactly like Margery,' she said. 'I could tell you things that are more or less the same about her – but the affair of the jumper doesn't sound quite like Margery. I mean – she might in a temper snatch it out of Pat's hand and pull it to pieces in front of her – but as far as I know Margery never did anything behind anyone's back at St Hilda's. She must be getting worse.'

'What was she expelled from other schools for?' asked Alison, eagerly.

'Oh, bad temper – rudeness – insubordination they called it,' said Pamela. 'She wouldn't work at all at St Hilda's. She's sixteen, you know. I bet she's only in your form, Pat and Isabel.'

'Yes, she is,' said Pat. 'We thought she must be sixteen. Her work isn't even up to our form's, though. She is always bottom – when Alison isn't!'

Alison flushed. 'Don't be mean!' she said. 'I haven't

been bottom for three weeks! I've been trying hard lately.'

'All right, feather-head,' said Pat, good humouredly. 'I think you *have* been trying. Well – it's a race between you and Doris and Margery who'll be bottom the oftenest this term – so you'd better buck up and try a bit harder!'

The three cousins had plenty to talk about as they went back to school in the car. They sat in the back whilst Mrs O'Sullivan drove.

'So Margery is sixteen!' said Isabel. 'Golly, isn't she a dunce? And fancy being expelled so many times! I wonder that St Clare's took her.'

Mrs O'Sullivan chimed in unexpectedly. 'If any school can help that miserable girl you keep talking about it should be St Clare's. Miss Theobald prides herself on getting the best out of the worst – and I'm quite sure she knows all about Margery Fenworthy, and is hoping that St Clare's will be the one school that will keep her.'

The three girls were silent. Secretly they had all been hoping that there might be the excitement of Margery being expelled from St Clare's too. But now the twins' mother had put the matter in rather a different light. It *would* be a score for St Clare's if it could keep Margery.

'Mother – do you think we'd better not tell the other girls about Margery?' asked Pat, at last, voicing what the others had been thinking too.

'I certainly think there's no doubt about it,' said Mrs O'Sullivan. 'Why should you spread tales about the girl when, for all you know, she is simply dreading anyone knowing her secret? You say she will not tell you what schools she has been to. She doesn't boast about being expelled – so she is evidently ashamed of it. She hasn't behaved well, but I think you shouldn't give her away.'

The twins felt the same. Much as they disliked Margery they didn't want to spread round the news they had heard. But Alison was rather disappointed.

'It would have been such a bit of news!' she couldn't help saying.

'Now, Alison, if you start to bleat this all over the place –' began Pat, crossly, but Alison gave her a push.

'Be quiet! I shan't tell a soul. And will you stop saying I bleat? I just hate that word! I've tried not to bleat lately, but you just go on and on saying it.'

Alison's eyes were full of the tears she could call up at a moment's notice. But Pat knew the girl was really upset, so she gave her a friendly pinch.

'Shut up, silly! I know you won't say a word. We can trust you all right, I know.'

But although the three girls did not say a word to anyone, they could not help feeling that such a bad record was terrible – and they felt that Margery might be anything bad – she might be capable of doing the meanest, horridest things. Each of the girls believed she had ruined the jumper, and when anyone said so in their hearing, they all agreed.

Margery took no notice of anyone. She was always

reading, and she did not seem to hear the remarks made by the girls in front of her. Her good-looking face was even more sullen than usual, and she was the despair of all the mistresses!

13.

Erica again

Erica was eagerly on the look-out for another trick to play on Pat or Isabel. If she could make it appear that it was done by Margery, so much the better!

But it was not very easy to play a trick without drawing attention to herself. She waited for a week, and then chance put the opportunity her way.

There was a nature-walk one afternoon. All the first and second formers had to go. They were to take their satchels with them, with their nature notebooks, and their tins for collecting specimens.

Miss Roberts and Miss Jenks were going too. The woods were to be visited, and the ponds. There should be quite a lot of things to observe, draw and collect.

The twins were excited about the outing, which was to take up the whole of one afternoon. It was a brilliantly fine day and the sun was quite warm.

'There might be early tadpoles or frog-spawn in the ponds,' said Pat. 'I think I'll take a little jar in case.'

All the girls prepared their satchels and put into them their nature books, their tins and jars. Pat was proud of her nature notebooks. She had done some beautiful drawings in them, and Miss Roberts had said they were good enough to be exhibited at the end of the term.

'I've just got one more page to fill,' she said to Isabel. 'I'll do it this afternoon. Are you ready? You're walking with me, aren't you?'

'Of course!' said Isabel. It was no good anyone else asking to walk with either of the twins because they always went with each other. They preferred each other to any of the other girls, much as they liked Janet and Hilary and Lucy.

All the girls paired off. No one wanted to go with Erica or Margery, and so it came about that those two found themselves together. They did not like one another and walked in silence. Some of the girls nudged each other and giggled when they saw the silent pair.

'Two bad eggs together!' giggled Winnie. 'I hope they're enjoying each other's conversation! Doesn't Margery's face look black – she's in one of her tempers, I expect.'

Margery *was* feeling rather ill tempered, for she had hoped to walk by herself. She did not like being paired off with the mean little Erica. So she said nothing, hoping that Erica would take the hint and leave her to herself as much as possible.

The afternoon went on happily in the yellow sunshine. The girls wandered over the woods, and made notes and sketches, and collected twigs and moss. Some of them found early primroses and stuck them into their button-holes.

Then they went down to the ponds, and exclaimed in surprise to see frog-spawn already floating at the top of the water.

'I *must* get some!' said Pat at once.

'You can't,' said Isabel. 'It's too far in. You'll get your shoes wet.'

Pat took a quick glance round. 'Where are Miss Roberts and Miss Jenks? Look – they're still at the top of the hill. I've time to take off my shoes and stockings and wade in!'

The girls giggled. 'Pat, you do do some awful things!' said Janet. 'Miss Roberts will *not* be pleased with you – and your feet will be as muddy as anything.'

'Feet can be cleaned,' said Pat. She took off her satchel and hung it on a post not far off. She took out her little jar and put it down on the bank. Then she stripped off her shoes and stockings and waded into the pond.

'Oooooh! The water's jolly cold!' she said. 'And it's mud at the bottom – horrid! Oh – I've trodden on a snail or something!'

Pat made everyone laugh. All the girls crowded round, laughing, watching her as she waded here and there.

She reached the frog-spawn and bent down to get it. It slipped through her fingers back into the pond. Isabel laughed.

'Try again, old girl!' she cried. Pat did her best to catch the slippery spawn, but time after time it slipped down into the water. Soon all the watching girls were in a state of giggles, and did not see Miss Roberts or Miss Jenks coming to the pond!

'Pat!' suddenly cried Miss Roberts's voice, in horror. 'What in the world are you doing? Oh, you naughty girl – you'll get your death of cold, wading into the icy water like that! Come out at once!'

'Oh, Miss Roberts – please, Miss Roberts, let me get some frog-spawn first,' begged Pat, snatching another handful that promptly slithered between her fingers back into the pond again.

'Pat! *Will* you come out!' cried Miss Roberts. 'Really, I can't leave you first formers for a single minute!'

All the girls but two were watching the scene with the greatest interest and amusement. Those two were Erica and Margery. Margery had stayed behind in a field to watch some horses – and Erica had dawdled too.

Erica heard the laughter going on and hastened to see what the excitement was. Before she got to the pond she saw Pat's satchel hanging on the post. On it was Pat's name – P. O'Sullivan.

Erica took a quick look at the pond. Not a single girl was looking her way. Anyway, she was out of sight, behind the hedge. She looked to see where Margery was. But Margery was still up in the field, watching the horses.

Quick as lightning Erica took the satchel off the post and opened it. Down into the mud she flung all Pat's precious nature books, and her tins of nature finds. She ground the books into the mud with her heel and stamped on the tins.

She flung the satchel into the hedge. Then, as silently as she could, she ran behind the hedge and came up to the pond from the opposite direction. No one noticed her. When Tessie saw her there she imagined that Erica had been there all the time.

Pat was wading out of the water. Her feet were terribly cold. She took out her handkerchief and dried them, and Miss Roberts slapped them well to get the circulation back. Then she made Pat put on her shoes and stockings and run up the hill and back to warm herself.

'And after all that I didn't get any frog-spawn!' said Pat, sorrowfully, as she rejoined the others, her feet tingling. 'Where's my satchel? Where did I put it?'

'Over there on the post,' said Isabel, turning to point. But the satchel wasn't there.

'Well, that's funny,' said Isabel. 'I saw you put it there. Look – there's Margery nearby. Margery! Bring Pat's satchel over with you if you can see it.'

'What's that in the hedge?' said Sheila suddenly, pointing. Her sharp eyes had seen the big brown satchel there.

'Golly! It's my satchel!' said Pat, in astonishment. 'How did it get there?'

She ran to get it – and then saw the notebooks stamped down into the mud – and the dented tins with their little collections spilt on the ground. She said nothing, but there was something in her face that made the girls run towards her.

'What's up, Pat?' asked Isabel – and then she too saw

what had happened. There was absolutely no doubt at all but that some spiteful hand had done the mischief. There was the half-imprint of a muddy foot on the exercise book – and someone had stamped on the tins!

'It – it couldn't have been a cow or something, could it?' said Isabel, hating to think that someone had done this to her twin.

Janet shook her head. 'No, of course not. I think we all know who did it – though we didn't see.'

All the girls looked at Margery, who was standing nearby, looking as surprised as the others. 'Who was the only one not at the pond?' said Janet. 'Margery! Why did she stay behind? To play this beastly trick, I suppose!'

'Girls! What is the matter?' asked Miss Roberts, coming up, 'Oh, Pat – are those your books in the mud? How careless! And all your beautiful drawings spoilt too. How did that happen?'

'I don't know, Miss Roberts,' said poor Pat, red with dismay. She could not bring herself to sneak on Margery, even at that moment. Miss Roberts saw that something serious was the matter, and could hear Margery's name being whispered around her.

'Well, pick up your things quickly,' said Miss Roberts, looking at her watch. 'You have made us late with your paddling. Hurry now. This matter can be settled later on.'

The girls walked quickly home. Erica had to walk with Margery. She was pleased that her mean trick had come off so well, and that Margery had once again been blamed for what was not her fault. Margery walked as if she was in a dream. She simply could not understand who had done these things, for she knew quite well that *she* had not! Who could be so amazingly mean as to do them – and let someone else take the blame? Not even Erica, surely!

She took a glance at Erica, walking by her side. There was something in the smug look on the girl's face that made Margery begin to suspect her. She remembered suddenly how she had noticed Erica slipping back into the meeting the night the jumper was spoilt. *Could* it be Erica? She was a mean little sneak – everyone knew it – but could she be so hateful as that?

'Well, it's someone,' thought Margery, bitterly, 'and as usual I get all the blame. What an unlucky creature I am!'

That evening after tea the girls talked about the latest trick on poor Pat. Margery could not bear their scornful glances and went to the school library to pretend to choose a book.

And whilst she was there Alison let the cat out of the bag!

'We didn't mean to tell this,' she began, looking all round, 'but now that we've seen this fresh bit of spite from Margery, I'm going to tell you all a bit of interesting news.'

'Shut up, Alison,' said Pat.

'I'm not going to shut up,' said Alison, with spirit.

'Do you think I'm going to stand by and see these things happen without getting back at Margery if I can? Now just you listen everybody!'

All the girls were silent, listening eagerly. What *could* Alison be going to tell them?

'We met an old friend of ours at half-term,' said Alison. 'She goes to St Hilda's – and Margery went there – and she was expelled from there!'

There was a buzz of horror. Expelled! What a dreadful disgrace! And to think she was at St Clare's! No wonder she would never say what school she had been to!

'Not only that,' went on Alison, her eyes flashing round, 'but she has been to five or six schools altogether – and has been sent away from each one! Do you wonder she's backward? Do you wonder she's still in the first form when she's *sixteen*!'

A loud chatter broke out. The girls were amazed. They couldn't believe it – and yet it was so easy to believe, knowing Margery!

'Well, why should *St Clare's* have to have her?' cried Tessie, in indignation. 'Why have *we* got to put up with her, I'd like to know?'

'Turn her out!' cried Hilary.

'Let's go to Miss Theobald and say we don't want to have a girl like that here!' cried Winnie.

'My mother wouldn't let me stay here if she knew there was a girl like Margery here!' said Erica.

'You be quiet,' said Tessie, giving Erica a push. She

wasn't going to let mean little Erica give herself airs.

'Well, now we know all about dear Margery!' said Doris. 'The girl who has been expelled from six schools – and will soon be expelled from the seventh! And a jolly good thing too. She won't be able to wreak her spite on Pat any more.'

There was a sound at the door. The girls turned. Margery was there, as white as chalk. She had heard what Doris had said, and was fixed to the spot with horror. So her poor secret was out. She didn't know how the girls had learnt it – but evidently someone had found out about her. And now she would have to leave St Clare's.

Margery stared at the girls out of her deep brown eyes. She opened her mouth to say something but no words came. She turned round and left the silent girls there; they heard her footsteps tip-tapping uncertainly along the passage.

'Well, we've done it now!' said Isabel, feeling rather scared. 'The secret's out – and the whole school will know tomorrow!'

14.

Margery makes a discovery

The twins felt most uncomfortable about Margery. Yet they could not blame their cousin for telling the girl's secret. Alison had been very indignant about the trick that had been played on Pat, and it was her way of backing up her cousin, to talk against Margery.

'I say – you don't think Margery will run away or anything like that, do you?' said Pat, to Isabel. 'You know, Isabel – if that sort of thing happened to me, I couldn't stay one moment more at St Clare's. I simply couldn't. I'd have to go home.'

'Maybe Margery hasn't much of a home to go to,' said Isabel. 'You know, she never talks about her home as we all do – she never says anything about her mother and father, or if she has any brothers or sisters. Does she? It seems rather strange to me.'

'I don't think we can leave things like this,' said Lucy Oriell, looking grave. 'I think Miss Theobald must have known all about Margery – and her bad reputation – and I think she must have said she would let her try here, at St Clare's. And I think something else too – I think that all the mistresses were in the secret, and knew about Margery – and that they have been asked to be lenient with her to give her a chance.'

The girls stared at Lucy's serious little face. She was such a sweet-natured girl that everyone listened to her willingly. No one had ever known Lucy say anything horrid about anyone.

'I think you're right, Lucy,' said Pat. 'I've often wondered why Margery seemed to get away with rudeness and carelessness – whilst we got into hot water if we did the same things. I knew of course it wasn't favouritism, for no mistress could possibly like Margery. Now I understand.'

'Yes – Lucy's right,' said Hilary. 'All the mistresses were in the secret, and were trying to help Margery, hoping she'd turn over a new leaf, and be all right at St Clare's. What a hope!'

'It's this meanness I can't stand,' said Pat. 'I can put up with bad manners and rudeness and even sulkiness, but I just hate meanness.'

'Yes, I agree with you there,' said Janet. 'You can't do much with a mean nature. Well – what are we going to do about Margery? Lucy, you said we couldn't leave things as they are now. What do you suggest doing?'

'I suggest that we all sleep on it, and then one or more of us should go to Miss Theobald tomorrow and tell all we know,' said Lucy. 'If Margery can't face us after what has happened, then she ought to be given the chance to go. But if she still wants to stay, and face it out, then she ought to have the chance to do that. But Miss Theobald ought to decide – not us. We don't know enough. Miss Theobald probably knows the reason for Margery's funny behaviour. We don't.'

'All right. Let's sleep on it,' said Janet. 'My mother always says that's a good thing to do. Things often seem different after a night's sleep. Well – we'll do that – and tomorrow we'll go to Miss Theobald and tell her all we know.'

'Lucy must go,' said Hilary. 'She's good at that sort of thing. She's got no spite in her and can tell a story fairly. Pat and Isabel had better go too – because after all, it's against Pat that these hateful tricks have been directed.'

'All right,' said Lucy. 'I'd rather *not* go really, because I hate being mixed up in this sort of thing. But somebody's got to go. Well, that's decided then.'

But although the girls had laid their plans seriously and carefully, they were not to be put into action. For something happened that night that upset them completely, and that changed everything in a few hours.

The girls all went to bed as usual. Erica had complained of a sore throat and had been sent to Matron. Matron had taken her temperature, and found that it was a hundred. So into the sickbay went Erica, where two other girls were, with bad chills.

'You've just got a chill too,' said Matron. 'Now drink this, and settle down quickly into bed. I'll pop in and see you later. You'll probably be normal tomorrow, and can go back to school the next day if you're sensible.'

Erica didn't mind at all. She rather liked missing lessons for a day or two – and she felt that it was lucky to be away when all the fuss was being made about Margery. Erica was a mean soul – but even she had been horrified at the look on Margery's face when she had overheard what the girls were saying about her.

'I wouldn't have played those tricks and made it seem as if they'd been done by Margery if I'd known the girls were going to find out about her being expelled – and blame the tricks on to her as well as despise her for her disgrace,' thought Erica, her conscience beginning to prick her for the first time. 'I wish I hadn't done them now. But I do hate that horrid Pat. It does serve her right to have her jumper spoilt and all her nature books!'

Erica got undressed and into bed. She was alone in a little room at the top of the sickbay, which was a separate building on the west side of the school. Here were put any infectious cases, any girls with measles and so on, or who had perhaps sprained an ankle. Here Matron looked after them and kept them under her eye until they were well enough to go back to their forms.

Erica was put into a room alone because Matron was not quite sure if her cold was going to turn to something infectious. There had been a case of measles among the Oakdene girls who had played the match against St Clare's, and the mistresses had been on the watch in case any of their own girls should have caught it from the Oakdene girl.

So Erica was not put with the two girls who had chills, in case by any chance she was beginning measles, which she hadn't had.

It was a nice little room, tucked away at the top of the sickbay. Erica looked out of the window before she got into bed and saw a sky full of stars. She drew back the curtains so that the sun could come in the next morning and then got into bed.

Matron came along with a hot-water bottle and some hot lemon and honey. Erica enjoyed it. Then Matron tucked her up, switched off the light, and left her to go to sleep.

Erica was soon asleep. Her conscience did not keep her awake, for it was not a very lively one. If Pat or Isabel had done the things that Erica had done lately, neither of them would have been able to sleep at night because of feeling mean and wretched. But Erica went sweetly off to sleep, and slept as soundly as any of the girls in her form.

But one girl did not sleep that night. It was Margery. She lay in her dormitory, wide awake, thinking of what she had heard the girls say about her. Always, always, wherever she went, her secret was found out, and sooner or later she had to go. She didn't want to be at school. She didn't want to stay at home. She wished with all her might that she could go out into the world and find a job and earn her own living. It was dreadful going from school to school like this, getting worse every time!

The other girls slept soundly. Someone snored a little. Margery turned over to her left side and shut her eyes. If only she could go to sleep! If only she could stop thinking and thinking! What was going to happen tomorrow? Now that all the girls knew about her, things would be terrible.

She couldn't go home. She couldn't run away because she didn't have much money. There was simply nothing she could do but stay and be miserable – and when she was miserable she didn't care about anything in the world, and that made her rude and careless and sulky.

'There isn't any way out for me,' thought the girl. 'There's simply nothing I can do. If only there was something – some way of escape from all this. But there isn't.'

She turned over on to her right side, and shut her eyes again. But in a moment they were wide open. It was impossible to go to sleep. She tried lying on her back, staring up into the dark. But that didn't make her sleepy either. She heard the school clock chime out. Eleven o'clock. Twelve o'clock. One o'clock. Two o'clock. Was there ever such a long night as this? At this rate the night would never never be over.

'I'll get myself a drink of water,' said Margery, sitting up. 'Maybe that will help me to go to sleep.'

She put on her dressing-gown and slippers and found her torch. She switched it on. Its light showed her the sleeping forms of the other girls. No one stirred as she went down between the cubicles to the door.

She opened the door and went out into the passage. There was a bathroom not far off, with glasses. She went there and filled a glass with water. She took it to the window to drink it.

And it was whilst she was standing there, drinking the icy-cold water that she saw something that puzzled her. She forgot to finish the water, and set the glass down to peer out of the window.

The bathroom window faced the sickbay, which was a four-storey building, tall and rather narrow. It was in complete darkness except at one place.

A flickering light showed now and again from high up on the third storey. It came from a window there. Margery puzzled over it. She tried to think what it could be.

'It looks like flickering firelight,' she thought. 'But who is sleeping on the third storey, I wonder? Wait a minute – surely that isn't the window of a bedroom? Surely it's the little window that gives light to the stairway that goes up to the top storey?'

She watched for a little while, trying to make certain. But in the darkness she couldn't be sure if it was the staircase window or a bedroom window. The light flickered on and on, exactly as if it were the glow of a bedroom fire, sometimes dancing up into flames and sometimes dying down.

'I'd better go back to bed,' said Margery to herself, shivering. 'It's probably the room where Erica is – and Matron has given her a fire in her bedroom for a treat. It's the flickering glow I can see.'

So back to bed she went – but she kept worrying a

little about that curious light – and in the end she got out of bed once more to see if it was still there.

And this time, looking out of the bathroom window, she knew without any doubt what it was. It was Fire, Fire, Fire!

15.

A wonderful rescue

As soon as Margery saw the light for the second time, she gave a shout. The whole of the staircase window was lit up, and flames were shooting out of it!

'Fire!' yelled Margery, and darted off to Miss Roberts's room. She hammered on her door.

'Miss Roberts! Miss Roberts! Quick, come and look! The sickbay is on fire! Oh, quick!'

Miss Roberts woke with a jump. Her room faced on to the sickbay and she saw at once what Margery had just seen. Dragging on a dressing-gown she ran to the door. Margery clutched hold of her.

'Miss Roberts! Shall I go across and see if Matron knows! I'm sure she doesn't!'

'Yes, run quickly!' said Miss Roberts. 'Don't wake any of the girls in this building, Margery – there's no need for them to know. Hurry now. I'll get Miss Theobald and we'll join you.'

Margery tore down the stairs and undid the side door. She raced across the piece of grass that separated the sickbay from the school. She hammered on the door there and shouted.

'Matron! Matron! Are you there?'

Matron was fast sleep on the second floor. She didn't wake. It was Queenie, one of the girls in bed with a chill who heard Margery shouting. She ran to the window and looked out.

'What is it, what is it?' she cried.

'The sickbay is on fire!' shouted Margery. 'Flames are coming out on the storey above you. Wake Matron!'

The girl darted into the Matron's room. She shook her hard, calling to her in fright. Matron woke up in a hurry and pulled on a coat.

Miss Theobald appeared with some of the other mistresses. Someone had telephoned for the fire-engine. Girls appeared from everywhere, in spite of mistresses' orders to go back to bed.

'Good gracious! Go back to bed when there's a perfectly good fire on!' said Janet who, as usual, was eager to enjoy any experience that came her way. 'Golly, I've never seen a fire before! I'm going to enjoy this one. Nobody's in any danger!'

Girls swarmed all over the place. Matron tried to find the three who had had chills – Queenie, Rita, and Erica. 'They mustn't stand about in this cold night air,' she said, very worried. 'Oh, there you are, Queenie. You are to go at once to the second form dormitory and get into the first bed you see there. Is Rita with you – and where is Erica?'

'Rita's here,' said Queenie, 'and I think I saw Erica somewhere.'

'Well, find her and take her to bed at once,' ordered

Matron. 'Where are the two nurses? Are they safe?'

Yes – they were safe. They were shivering in their coats nearby, watching the flames getting bigger and bigger.

'Matron, is everyone out of the sickbay?' asked Miss Theobald. 'Are you sure? All the girls? The nurses? Anyone else?'

'I've seen Queenie,' said Matron, 'and Rita – and Queenie said she saw Erica. Those are the only girls I had in. And the two nurses are out. They are over there.'

'Well, that's all right then,' said Miss Theobald, in relief. 'Oh, I wish that fire-engine would hurry up. I'm afraid the fourth storey will be completely burnt out.'

Queenie had not seen the right Erica. She *had* seen a girl called Erica, who was in the fourth form, and she had not known that Matron meant Erica of the second form. Erica was still in the sickbay.

No one knew this at all until suddenly Mam'zelle gave a scream and pointed with a trembling hand to the window of the top storey.

'*Oh, que c'est terrible*!' she cried. 'There is someone there!'

Poor Erica was at the window. She had been awakened by the smell of smoke, and had found her bedroom dark with the evil-smelling smoke that crept in under and around her door. Then she had heard the crackling of the flames.

In a terrible fright she had jumped up and tried to switch on her light. But nothing happened. The wires outside had been burnt and there was no light in her room. The girl felt for her torch and switched it on.

She ran to the door – but when she opened it a great roll of smoke unfolded itself and almost choked her. There was no way out down the staircase. It was in flames.

The fire had been started by an electric wire which had smouldered on the staircase, and had kindled the dry wood nearby. The staircase was old and soon burnt fiercely. There was no way out for Erica. She tried to run into the next room, from whose window there was a fire-escape – but the smoke was so thick that it choked her and she had to run back into her own room. She shut the door and rushed to the window.

She threw it open, and thankfully breathed in the pure night air. 'Help!' she shouted, in a weak voice. 'Help!'

No one heard her – but Mam'zelle saw her. Everyone looked up at Mam'zelle's shout, and a deep groan went up as they saw Erica at the window.

Miss Theobald went pale, and her heart beat fast. A girl up there! And the staircase burning!

'The fire-engine isn't here,' she groaned. 'If only we had the fire-engine to run up its ladder to that high window! Oh, when will it come?'

Someone had found the garden-hose and was spraying water on the flames. But the force of water was feeble and made little difference to the fire. Erica shouted again.

'Help! Save me! Oh, save me!' She could see all the crowd of people below and she could not think why someone did not save her. She did not realize that the fire-engine had not yet come, and that there was no ladder long enough to reach her.

'Where is the long garden ladder?' cried Margery, suddenly, seeing a gardener nearby. 'Let's get it. Maybe we can send a rope up or something, even if the ladder isn't long enough!'

The men ran to get the longest ladder. They set it up against the wall and one of them ran up to the top. But it did not nearly reach to Erica's window.

'It's no good,' he said, when he came down. 'It's impossible to reach. Where's that fire-engine? It's a long time coming.'

'It's been called out to another fire,' said one of the mistresses, who had just heard the news. 'It's coming immediately.'

'Immediately!' cried Margery. 'Well, that's not soon enough! Erica will soon be trapped by the flames.'

Before anyone could stop her the girl threw off her dressing-gown and rushed to the ladder. She was up it like a monkey, though Miss Theobald shouted to her to come back.

'You can't do anything, you silly girl!' cried the head mistress. 'Come down!'

Everyone watched Margery as she climbed to the very top of the ladder. The flames lit up the whole scene now, and the dark figure of the climbing girl could be clearly seen.

'What *does* she think she can do?' said Miss Roberts, in despair. 'She'll fall!'

But Margery had seen something that had given her an idea. To the right side of the ladder ran an iron pipe. Maybe she could swarm up that and get to Erica's window. What she was going to do then she didn't know – but she meant to do *some*thing!

She reached the top of the ladder. She put out a hand and caught hold of the strong iron pipe hoping that it was well nailed to the wall. Fortunately it was. Margery swung herself from the ladder to the pipe, clutching hold of it with her knees, and holding for dear life with her hands.

And now all her training in the gym stood her in good stead. All the scores of times she had climbed the ropes there had strengthened her arms and legs, and made them very steady and strong. It was far more difficult to climb an unyielding pipe than to swarm up a pliant rope, but Margery could do it. Up the pipe she went, pulling herself by her arms, and clinging with her knees and feet. Erica saw her coming.

'Oh, save me!' cried the girl, almost mad with fright. Margery came up to the window. Now was the most difficult part. She had to get safely from the pipe to the window-sill.

'Erica! Hold on to something and give me a hand!' yelled Margery, holding out her hand above the window-sill. 'If you can give me a pull I can get there.'

Erica gave her hand to Margery. She held on to a heavy book-case just inside the room, and Margery swung herself strongly across to the sill from the pipe.

She put up a knee, grazing it badly on the sill, but she did not even feel the pain. In half a moment she was inside the room. Erica clung to her, weeping.

'Now don't be silly,' said Margery, shaking herself free and looking round the room, filled with dense black smoke. The flames were already just outside the door and the floor felt hot to her feet. 'There's no time to lose. Where's your bed?'

Erica pointed through the smoke to where her bed was. Margery ran to it, choking, and dragged the sheets and blankets off it. She ran back to the window, and leant her head outside to get some fresh air. Then she quickly tore the sheets in half.

'Oh, what are you doing?' cried Erica, thinking that Margery was quite mad. 'Take me out of the window with you!'

'I will in a moment,' said Margery, as she knotted the sheet-strips firmly together. There were four long strips. Margery looked for something to tie one end to. As she looked, the door fell in with a crash, and flames came into the room.

'Oh, quick, quick!' cried Erica. 'I shall jump!'

'No, you won't,' said Margery. 'You're going to be saved – and very quickly too. Look here – see how I've knotted this sheet – and tied it to the end of your bed. Help me to drag the bed to the window. That's right.'

Margery threw the other end of the sheet-strips out of the window. The end almost reached the top of the ladder! There was no need to climb down the pipe this time!

Margery sat herself on the window-sill and made Erica come beside her. Below, the crowds of girls and mistresses were watching what was happening, hardly daring to breathe. One of the gardeners had gone up the ladder, hoping to help.

'Now do you think you can climb down this sheet-rope I've made?' said Margery to the trembling Erica. 'Look – it should be quite easy.'

'Oh, no, I can't, I can't,' sobbed Erica, terrified. So Margery did a very brave thing. She took Erica on her back, and with the frightened girl clinging tightly to her, her arms holding fast, she began to climb down the sheet-rope herself. Luckily the sheets were new and strong, and they held well.

Down went Margery and down, her arms almost pulled out of their sockets with Erica's weight. She felt with her feet for the ladder, and oh, how thankful she was when at last she felt the top rung, and a loud voice cried, 'Well done, miss! I've got you!'

The gardener at the top of the ladder reached for Erica, and took hold of her. He helped the weeping girl down, and Margery slid down the few remaining feet of the sheet-rope.

What happened next nobody ever knew. It was likely that Margery was tired out with her amazing climb and equally amazing rescue, and that her feet slipped on the ladder – for somehow or other she lost her balance, and half slid, half fell down the ladder. She fell on the gardener, who helped to break her fall a little

– but then she slid right off the ladder to the ground seven or eight feet below.

People rushed over to her – but Margery lay still. She had struck her head against something and was quite unconscious. Careful hands carried her into the big school just as the fire-engine rumbled up with a great clangour of its big bell. In one minute strong jets of water were pouring on to the flames, and in five minutes the fire was under control.

But the top storey, as Miss Theobald had feared, was entirely burnt out. The room where Erica had been sleeping was a mass of black charred timbers.

The girls were ordered back to bed, and this time they went! But there was one name on everyone's lips that night – the name of a real heroine.

'Margery! Wasn't she wonderful! She saved Erica's life. Fancy her climbing that pipe like that. Let's pray she isn't much hurt. Margery! Well, wasn't she *wonderful*!'

16.

A confession

The next morning everyone wanted to know how Margery was. A few remembered to ask about poor Erica, but it was Margery that people worried about.

'She's broken her leg! Poor old Margery! And she's hurt her head too, but not very badly. She's in the dressing-room off Miss Theobald's own bedroom. Miss Theobald is terribly proud of her!'

'I don't wonder!' said Janet, who always intensely admired bravery of any sort. 'I don't care now what Margery has been like in the past few weeks. I've forgotten it all! A girl who can do a big thing like that can be as rude and sulky as she likes, for all I care!'

'And now I find it more difficult than ever to think that Margery can have played any mean tricks!' said Lucy. 'I simply can't help thinking we made a mistake over that. It *must* have been someone else! Courage of the sort that Margery showed last night never goes with a mean nature – never, never, never! It's impossible.'

'I wish we knew for certain,' said Alison, who was now feeling very guilty because she had told Margery's secret, and had let the girls know that she had been expelled from so many schools.

They did know, very soon, who was the guilty one. It was Lucy who found out. She went to see Erica, who was in a little room off one of the dormitories, not much the worse for her adventure except that she was very sorry for herself.

Something had happened to Erica besides the fire. She had lain awake all that night, thinking of it – and thinking of Margery, who had rescued her.

And her conscience had come very much alive! To think that the girl who had so bravely saved her life was the girl who had been taking the blame for Erica's own meanness! Erica's cheeks burnt when she thought of it. She wished it had been any other girl but Margery who had rescued her.

Lucy came to see her at the end of morning school. Nobody had been allowed to see Margery, who was to be kept quite quiet for a few days. No one had wanted very much to see Erica – but kind-hearted Lucy, as usual, thought of the girl lying alone in the little room, and asked Matron if she could see her.

'Yes, of course,' said Matron. 'She's normal this morning and there's nothing wrong with her except a bit of a cold and shock. It will do her good to see you.'

So Lucy went into the little room and sat down beside Erica. They talked for a while, and then Erica asked about Margery. She did not look at Lucy as she asked, for she felt very guilty.

'Haven't they told you about Margery?' said Lucy, in surprise. 'Oh, poor thing, she's broken her right leg.

That means no more gym or games for her for some time – and as they are the only things she cares about, she's going to have a pretty thin time. She hit her head on something too, but not very badly. She was a heroine, Erica!'

Erica was terribly upset. She had thought that Margery was quite all right, and had pictured her receiving the praise of the whole school. And now after all she was in bed with a broken leg and a bad head!

Erica turned her face to the wall, trying to think the matter out. She looked so miserable that Lucy was touched. She didn't like Erica, but misery of any kind must be comforted.

She took Erica's hand. 'Don't worry about it,' she said. 'Her leg will mend – and she will be quite all right again. We are all very proud of her.'

'Do you – do you still think she did those mean things?' asked Erica, not looking at Lucy.

'No, I don't,' said Lucy at once. 'Those kind of tricks don't go with a strong and fearless nature like Margery's. She's got plenty of faults – and bad ones too – but she has no petty, mean faults, as far as I can see.'

Matron popped her head round the door. 'Come along now, Lucy,' she said. 'Your ten minutes is up.'

'Oh, don't go yet, don't go yet!' said Erica, clutching Lucy's hand, and feeling that she did not want to be left alone with her own thoughts. But Lucy had to go.

And then Erica had a very bad time indeed. It is hard enough when anyone thinks contemptuously of us –

but far worse if we have to despise ourselves. And that is what poor Erica found herself doing. She saw herself clearly – a mean, small, spiteful little creature, insincere and dishonest, and she didn't like herself at all.

She turned her face to the wall. She would not eat any dinner at all, and Matron took her temperature, feeling worried. But it was still normal.

'Are you worrying about something?' she asked. Erica's eyes filled with tears at the kind voice.

'Yes,' she said desperately. 'I'm worrying terribly. I can't stop.'

'Tell me all about it,' said Matron, gently.

'No,' said Erica, and turned her face to the wall again. But she knew she could not keep all her thoughts to herself much longer. She had to tell someone, she simply had to. She called to Matron as she was going out of the room.

'Matron! I want Lucy!'

'My dear child, she's in class!' said Matron. 'She can come and see you at tea-time, if you like.'

Erica burst into floods of tears, and sobbed so heart-rendingly that Matron hurried over to her.

'Whatever *is* the matter?' she said.

'Matron, fetch Lucy,' sobbed Erica. 'Oh, do fetch Lucy.'

Matron went out of the room and sent someone for Lucy. There was something strange about Erica's face, and the sooner she told somebody what was worrying her, the better! Lucy came along in surprise.

'Erica has something on her mind, Lucy,' said

Matron. 'Try to get her to tell you, will you? Her temperature will shoot up and she'll be really ill if she goes on like this.'

Lucy went into the little room and sat down on Erica's bed. Erica had stopped crying, and her face was white and pinched. She stared dry-eyed at Lucy.

'What's up, old girl?' asked Lucy, her kind little face glowing with friendliness.

'Lucy! I've got to tell somebody or I'll go quite mad!' said Erica, desperately. '*I* did all those awful things to Pat. It wasn't Margery. It was me.'

'Oh, Erica!' said Lucy, deeply shocked. 'Poor, poor Margery!'

Erica said nothing. She turned her face to the wall again and lay still. She felt ill.

Lucy sat for a moment, taking in what Erica had said. Then, with an effort, she took Erica's cold hand. She knew that she must try to be kind to the girl, though she could hardly bring herself to be, because of her pity for what Margery must have gone through.

'Erica! I'm glad you told me. You know that I must tell the others, don't you? They mustn't for one moment more think that Margery did those things. We have accused her most unjustly, and treated her very unfairly. You see that I must tell the others, don't you?'

'Must you?' said Erica, her eyes filling with tears again. 'But how can I face them all, if you do?'

'I don't know, Erica,' said Lucy. 'That's for you to decide. You have been awfully mean and spiteful. Why don't you tell Miss Theobald, now that you've told me, and see what she says?'

'No. I daren't tell her,' said Erica, trembling as she thought of Miss Theobald's stern face. 'You tell her, Lucy. Oh, Lucy – I want to leave here. I've done so badly. Nobody has ever liked me much – and nobody will ever, ever like me now. And there won't be a chance for me to try properly if nobody feels friendly towards me. I'm a coward, you know. I can't stand up to things.'

'I know,' said Lucy gravely. 'But sooner or later, you'll have to learn to face things that come along, Erica, and you'll have to get that meanness and spite out of your character, or you'll never be happy. I'll see Miss Theobald. Now don't worry too much. I'm very glad you told me all you did.'

Lucy left Erica to her thoughts. She went to Matron. 'Matron,' she said, 'Erica has told me what's worrying her – but it's something I ought to tell Miss Theobald. Can I go now?'

'Of course,' said Matron, thinking that Lucy Oriell was one of the nicest girls who had ever come to St Clare's. 'Hurry along now. I'll send a message to Miss Roberts for you.'

And so it came about that Lucy went to Miss Theobald with Erica's guilty secret, and related it all to the head mistress in her clear, friendly little voice. Miss Theobald listened gravely, not interrupting her at all.

'So Margery was accused wrongly,' she said. 'Poor Margery! She is a most unlucky child! But she did behave amazingly last night. What a plucky girl she is! She has two sides to her character – and the finer side came out very strongly yesterday.'

'Miss Theobald, we know that Margery has been expelled from many schools,' said Lucy, looking the head straight in the eyes. 'And we have guessed that the mistresses have been asked to be lenient with her to give her a chance at St Clare's. And although I'm a new girl too, I do see that any girl with a bad record would have a fine chance here to do better, because there's a wonderful spirit in this school. I've felt it and loved it. I'm so very glad my parents chose this school to send me to.'

Miss Theobald looked at Lucy's honest and sincere face. She smiled one of her rare sweet smiles.

'And I too am glad that your parents sent you here,' she said. 'You are the type of girl that helps to make the spirit of the school a living powerful thing, Lucy.'

Lucy flushed with pleasure, and felt very happy. Miss Theobald went back to the matter they had been discussing.

'Now we have to decide one or two things,' she said, and at that word 'we', Lucy felt proud and delighted. To think that she and Miss Theobald together were going to decide things!

'About Margery. You shall go and see her and tell her what you have told me. She must know as soon as possible that you have all been wrong about her, and that you know it and are sorry. She must know it was

Erica too. How strange that the girl she rescued should be the girl who did her so much wrong! Erica must have felt very upset about it.'

'This will make a great difference to Margery,' said Lucy, her eyes shining. 'Everyone will think of her as a heroine now, instead of as a sulky, rude girl. What a chance for Margery!'

'Yes – I think things may be easier for her now,' said Miss Theobald. 'You may have guessed that Margery's home is not quite a normal one, Lucy, and that has made things hard for her. I can't tell you any more. You must just be content with that! And now – what about Erica?'

They looked at one another gravely, and Lucy felt pride swell up in her as she saw how Miss Theobald trusted her opinion.

'Miss Theobald – things won't be easier for Erica,' said Lucy. 'She's awfully weak, you know. She won't be able to stand up to the girls' unfriendliness after this. If she only could, it would be the making of her. But I'm quite sure she can't. I think it would be better for her to go away and start all over again at another school. I don't mean expel her in disgrace – but couldn't something be arranged?'

'Yes, of course,' said the head mistress. 'I can explain things to her mother – she has no father, you know – and suggest that Erica goes home for the rest of the term, and then is sent to a fresh school in the summer – perhaps with the determination to do a great deal better! Poor Erica! What a good thing she at least had the courage to tell you.'

Lucy left the head mistress feeling contented. It was good to know that someone wise and kindly had the handling of matters such as these. By this time it was teatime and Lucy went to the dining-hall feeling terribly hungry.

'Where *have* you been?' cried a dozen voices, as she came in. 'You missed painting – and you love that!'

'Oh, dear – so I did!' said Lucy, sadly. 'I forgot about that. Well – I couldn't help it.'

'But, Lucy, where have you been and what have you been doing?' asked Pat. 'Do tell us! You look all excited somehow.'

'I've heard some interesting things,' said Lucy, helping herself to bread and butter and jam. 'I'll tell you in the common-room after tea. I'm too hungry to talk now. You must just wait!'

17.

Help for Margery

The first and second formers crowded into their common-room after tea, eager to hear what Lucy had to say. They knew quite well it was something exciting.

Lucy sat on a table and told them everything in her clear, calm voice. There were many interruptions, for the girls were intensely angry when they heard that it was Erica who had spoilt Pat's jumper and books – and had allowed the blame to rest on Margery.

'The beast! The hateful beast!'

'I'd like to pull all her hair out! I do feel a mean pig to think I blamed poor old Margery!'

'Oh, the spiteful creature! I'll never speak to her again as long as I live!'

'Just wait till she comes back into class! I'll give her an awful time. And to think that Margery broke her leg rescuing *that* mean creature!'

'Now listen,' said Lucy, trying to stop the yells and shouts. 'DO LISTEN! I've got something else to say.'

Everyone was quiet. Lucy then told them that Erica was to go home – not to be expelled in disgrace, but simply to go home and start again somewhere else. 'And let's hope she's learnt her lesson and won't be quite so mean in future,' said Lucy.

'She'd learn her lesson all right if only Miss Theobald made her come back into class,' said Janet, grimly.

'Yes, but she'd learn it in the wrong way,' argued Lucy. 'She'd just be scared and frightened out of her life, and terribly miserable. And honestly nobody can ever do much good if they are scared and unhappy.'

'Lucy is always for giving the under-dog a chance!' said Pat, giving Lucy a warm hug. 'You're a good sort, Lucy, old thing. You're quite right, of course.'

And so it came about that Erica was not seen again at St Clare's, except once by Lucy who went to say goodbye to her. That was two days later when Erica was up again, looking pale and unhappy. She was glad to be going away – but dreaded all that her mother would say.

'Now you just tell your mother honestly that you've been a mean and spiteful girl!' said Lucy. 'And tell her you know it and you're going to start all over again and be just the opposite. You can, you know! Write to me next term and tell me how you're getting on.'

So poor, mean little Erica disappeared from St Clare's to start again somewhere else. Nobody missed her, and nobody waved to her as she went down the school drive in a taxi with her trunks. She had made her own punishment, which is always much harder to bear than any other.

'How's Margery getting on?' Matron was asked a dozen times a day, and at last in despair she put up a bulletin on her door, which read:-

'Margery is getting on nicely.'

'Golly! Just like royalty!' said Janet, when she saw the bulletin. 'You know – when kings and queens are ill they put a notice outside the gates about them.'

Lucy and Pat were the first two allowed to see Margery. They brought flowers and grapes and went into the cosy little dressing-room, which was lighted by a dancing fire.

'Hallo, old girl!' said Pat, presenting the flowers. 'How's the heroine?'

'Don't be an idiot!' said Margery. 'Oh, what glorious daffodils! And oh, how did you know that my favourite grapes were those big purple ones?'

'Here's something from Isabel,' said Pat, bringing out a jigsaw puzzle. 'And Janet sent you this. Everybody's got something for you, but Matron won't allow too much at once.'

Margery flushed with pleasure. She looked at the jigsaw from Isabel and the book from Janet. She forgot the pain in her leg in her delight at being spoilt like this.

'How's Erica?' she asked.

'She's gone,' said Lucy. 'She's not coming back again.'

'Gone!' said Margery, startled. 'Why? Is she ill?'

'No,' said Lucy. 'She's gone because she couldn't face the school now that they know it was she who ruined Pat's jumper and spoilt her books.'

Margery stared in the utmost amazement. 'But you said it was I who did those things,' she said. 'How did you find out it was Erica?'

Lucy told her. 'And we all owe you a humble apology for being so unjust,' she said. 'Please accept it, Margery. We will make it up to you when you are out and about again.'

Margery seldom cried, but the tears came shining into her eyes now. She blinked them away in shame. She did not know what to say for a minute.

'Well, I don't wonder you thought I was the one who did those spiteful things,' she said at last. 'I've been so awful. And it's perfectly true I've been expelled from about six schools for rudeness and sulkiness. But you see – nobody cares about me at home – and so I'm miserable, and I'm always badly behaved when I'm miserable.'

'Don't tell us if you don't want to,' said Lucy. 'But if it's going to help – *do* tell us. We'll understand, you may be sure.'

'Well – there's nothing much to tell, really, I suppose,' said Margery, looking into Lucy's friendly eyes. 'It's probably my own silly fault. You see – my mother died when I was little. She was such a darling. And my father married again and my stepmother didn't like me. She said awful things about me to my father and he ticked me off like anything. I – I loved him awfully – I still do, of course. I'd give anything in the world to make him have a good opinion of me. He's so marvellous.'

Margery stopped and bit her lip. The others said nothing.

'My stepmother had three boys, and my father was

terribly pleased. He always wanted boys. So I was pushed into the background and made to feel I wasn't wanted. And of course I got worse and worse and more and more unbearable, I suppose. I gave my stepmother a bad time, I was so rude and hateful. And that made my father angry. So I'm the black sheep of the family, and I just got to feel I didn't care about anything at all.'

'And so you were sent to boarding school and went on being unpleasant there,' said Lucy, taking Margery's big strong hand in her little one. 'Oh, Margery – I'm terribly sorry. You haven't had a chance.'

'But won't your father be awfully bucked when he hears how you rescued Erica?' cried Pat.

'I shan't tell him,' said Margery. 'He won't know. He wouldn't believe it if anyone did tell him! He thinks I'm no use at all. You know, he's wonderful – so brave and courageous. He climbed Mount Everest.'

'Golly!' cried Pat, in astonishment. 'I say, he must be marvellous – and you take after him, don't you? You are so strong, and so good at games and gym – and so frightfully brave too.'

Margery's eyes suddenly lit up. She lay looking up at Pat as if Pat had said something simply miraculous.

'I never, never thought of that before,' she said. 'But I believe I *do* take after him! It's lovely to think that. Yes – I'm awfully strong – and I suppose I *am* brave too, though that's not much to my credit really, because strong people ought always to be brave. Oh, you made me happy by saying that, Pat. I think my father would think a lot more of me if he knew I was like him!'

Matron came in as the conversation reached this interesting point. She was pleased to see Margery's happy face. 'You've done her good,' she said. 'But you must go now. My word, what lovely flowers! Tell Isabel that she and Janet can come tomorrow, Lucy.'

The two of them said goodbye and went out. Pat caught hold of Lucy's arm as soon as they were outside the door. Her eyes were bright.

'Lucy! Oh, Lucy! I've got a most marvellous idea.'

'What?' asked Lucy.

'Listen!' said Pat. 'You know that there's a picture of Margery in the local paper, don't you – and a long bit telling all about how she saved Erica? Well – I'm going to cut that out and send it to Margery's father – with a letter telling all about her and how very proud we are of her at St Clare's!'

'I say – that really *is* a good idea!' said Lucy. 'I wish I'd thought of it. We can get the address from Miss Theobald. My word – that will make Margery's father sit up a bit – to think that St Clare's is so proud of her! That will be a bit different from the opinion of the other schools she's been to. Well – it's time Margery had a bit of luck. I expect it was partly her own fault she didn't get on with her stepmother, because she *is* difficult – but the treatment she had at home only turned her from bad to worse. How silly some parents are! When I think of my own – so kind and understanding – I feel jolly sorry for Margery.'

After this long speech the two girls said nothing till they reached the common-room. Then Pat took the local paper and snipped out the paragraph about 'Brave Schoolgirl Heroine' with Margery's picture.

'What are you doing?' said Isabel, curiously.

'I'll tell *you*, but no one else,' said Pat. So she told Isabel, and she and her twin and Lucy set to work to compose the letter to Margery's father.

Here it is, just as it was written by the three of them.

Dear Mr Fenworthy,

We know that you are a very brave man, because Margery has told us about you. Perhaps you have heard how brave Margery is too, though you may not have been told all the details. Well, here they are.

Margery climbed up an iron pipe to the window-sill of a burning room, and rescued a girl called Erica. She tore sheets into strips and tied them to the bed. She climbed down them with Erica over her shoulder. She fell from the ladder and broke her leg and hurt her head. She saved Erica's life, and is a real heroine.

Margery is awfully strong. You should see her at gym, and she is almost the best in the school already at games. She won the last match for St Clare's. We think that she must take after you, because we are quite sure she is already strong and courageous enough to climb mountains or anything like that. She is getting a bit better now, but we think she is rather lonely, so it would be lovely if you had enough time to spare to come and see her.

We are all as proud of her as we can be, and we hope she will stay at St Clare's till she leaves school altogether. We thought you ought to know all this so that you could be proud of her too.

With kind regards from three of Margery's friends.

Pat and Isabel O'Sullivan, and Lucy Oriell.

The girls were quite pleased with this letter, and they posted it off the same day. It had an immediate effect – for the next day Margery had a message that excited her very much. It was from her father.

'Very, very proud of you. Coming to see you today. Love from Daddy.'

Margery showed the message to Isabel and told her to tell Pat and Lucy. 'I'm so happy,' she kept saying. 'I'm so awfully happy. Fancy my father sparing the time to come and see me. He's proud of me too! It's simply marvellous!'

The girls all watched eagerly for Margery's father to arrive. He was a fine-looking man, tall, broad-shouldered and good looking. He was very like Margery. He was shown into Miss Theobald's room, and then taken to Margery.

What happened between Margery and her father nobody ever knew for certain, for Margery guarded her precious secret jealously. She could not even tell Lucy of those wonderful minutes when her father had taken her into his arms and praised her and loved her. Everything had come right. She had at last what she wanted and had missed so much, and in a few short minutes all that was best in Margery's character came up to the surface – and stayed there.

'Pat – Isabel – Lucy – you wrote to my father!' said Margery, next day, her eyes shining brightly. 'He showed me your letter. You're dears, all of you. It's made all the difference in the world! He didn't know a bit what I was like – and now he does – and he's terribly pleased to know I am so exactly like him! I'm going mountaineering with him next hols! Think of that! And he's going to let me stay on at St Clare's, and then, when I'm eighteen, I'm to go to a training college to train to be a games-mistress. I've always wanted to do that.'

'Margery – you do look different!' said Pat, marvelling at the glow in Margery's good-looking face. All the sullenness was gone.

'I'll be able to work well and happily now,' said Margery. 'I shan't be at the bottom of the form any more!'

'No – you'll be shot up into the top form, I expect, and send for us poor first formers to make your tea and clean your boots!' laughed Lucy. 'Don't you get too swollen-headed, my girl! You'll hear about it from Janet, if you do!'

18.

Bad luck for Lucy

Margery was allowed to hop about on one leg fairly soon, with crutches. Although she had to miss games and gym she didn't fret at all. Nothing seemed to matter to her now, she was so contented and happy. She worked well, and the mistresses began to like this new, cheerful Margery.

Lucy and she made firm friends. Margery could not do enough for the merry, friendly Lucy, who only came up to her friend's shoulder. They were always together, and it was good to hear them joking and laughing.

'Lucy ought always to be happy,' said Pat, as she watched her helping Margery down the passage with her crutches. 'There's something simply lovely about her – she's one of those people you just can't help liking.'

'Well, there's no reason why she shouldn't be happy,' said Isabel. 'She's got a lovely mother – and a famous father – and she's very clever and pretty. She just loves St Clare's too. She told me yesterday that she means to be its head girl some day. I bet she is too.'

But ill fortune came swiftly to poor Lucy the next week. A message came to Miss Theobald and Lucy was sent for out of the history class. She went to the head mistress's study, feeling rather frightened. What was the matter?

Miss Theobald was looking grave. She held out her hand to Lucy as the girl came in, and drew her to her.

'Lucy,' she said, 'I have some rather bad news for you. Can you be brave?'

'Yes,' said Lucy, her lip trembling. 'Tell me quickly.'

'Your father has been in a car accident,' said Miss Theobald. 'He is badly hurt. He wants you to go to him.'

'He won't – die – will he?' said Lucy, her face very white.

'I hope not,' said Miss Theobald. 'Go and ask one of the girls to help you to pack a small bag, and then I will take you to the station. I'm so sorry, my dear – but things may not be so bad as they appear. Be brave.'

Lucy hurried off and asked Margery to help her. The bigger girl was unhappy to see Lucy so upset. She put her arm round her and hugged her. 'Cheer up,' she said. 'You may find things are all right. I'll pack your bag for you. Just you tell me what you want to take.'

Very soon poor white-faced Lucy was driving to the station with Miss Theobald. The first formers were sad and subdued, and Margery missed her friend terribly. It seemed all wrong that anything like this should happen to merry, friendly Lucy.

'I'm going to pray hard for Lucy's father,' said Janet. 'As hard as I can.'

All the girls did the same, and thought a great deal of Lucy and wondered what was happening. Margery had a letter in four or five days. She told the others what it said.

'Lucy's father is out of danger,' she said. 'But an awful thing has happened to him. He'll never be able to use his right hand properly again – and he's a painter!'

The girls listened in dismay. 'It's terribly hard luck on him,' said Margery, 'and hard luck on Lucy too – because if he can't make money by his portrait-painting, there won't be any! So Lucy won't be able to stay on at St Clare's.'

'What a shame!' cried Tessie. 'She's the nicest girl that ever came here!'

'And she had planned to be head girl one day,' said Pat. 'Oh gosh – what bad luck! Poor old Lucy. She must be so terribly upset about her father – and then to see all her future changed in a moment like that – it must be terrible.'

'She'll have to leave school and take a job, I suppose,' said Hilary. 'St Clare's is expensive. What a pity she can't win a scholarship or something.'

'She could if she was in the third form,' said Tessie. 'There's a scholarship set there, sitting for an exam at the end of next term – and the winner has the right to go to one of a dozen special schools, free of fees.'

'But Lucy is only in the first form,' said Pat. 'Oh dear – I wish something could be done. Margery, is she coming back this term at all?'

'Yes, when her father leaves the nursing home in two days' time,' said Margery, looking at the letter. 'We mustn't be all over her when she comes back. That would only upset her. Let's be quite ordinary and friendly. She'll know we are feeling for her all right.'

Lucy got a great welcome when she came back. She was pale and her face had gone thin, but she held her head up and smiled her old sweet smile. She could be as brave in her way as Margery!

The girls did not say too much to her, and Margery took her off to show her what the class had done during the week she had been away. Lucy took her friend's arm and squeezed it.

'You're so nice to me, Margery,' she said. 'Thank you. You sent me a lovely letter. It did help. Poor Daddy – you can't think how brave he is. He knows he will probably never be able to paint again – but he means to try with his left hand. He's so brave. He blames himself terribly now because he never saved any money – so Mummy and I have got hardly any. You see, he always made as much as he wanted to – and spent it all! We none of us bothered about saving. We thought Daddy could always get as much as he wanted.'

'Will you really have to leave St Clare's after this term?' asked Margery.

'Of course,' said Lucy. 'We couldn't possibly afford the fees. If I could only have stayed on I might have won a scholarship to some other school. As it is I'm going to leave and Mummy is looking out for some sort of job for me. I'm quite quick, you know, and I could learn to be a secretary, I'm sure.'

'I shall miss you dreadfully,' said Margery, 'Just as I've got a friend for the first time in my life! Oh, I wish I could do something about it!'

Margery was not a person to sit down lightly under misfortune, and she puzzled and puzzled about how she might do something to help Lucy. And then she suddenly got an idea. If only, only it would work! She told nobody about it at all, not even Lucy, but went straight to Miss Theobald.

The head mistress had someone with her. She called out 'Come in!' when Margery knocked, and the girl went in. Her good-looking face was bright with her idea, and Miss Theobald marvelled to see the difference in her looks.

'Oh, Miss Theobald – I didn't know you had anyone with you,' said Margery, in disappointment. 'I did want to ask you something very badly.'

Miss Walker, the art mistress was there. She had been talking to the head mistress and had not yet finished. Miss Theobald looked at Margery and saw her eagerness.

'What do you want to speak to me about?' she asked. 'Is it anything private?'

'Well – yes, it is rather,' said Margery. 'It's about Lucy.'

'How strange!' said Miss Theobald. 'Miss Walker has also been speaking to me about Lucy. Well – I think you can say what you want to with Miss Walker here. You know that she is very interested in Lucy, because she is so good at art.'

'Miss Theobald – you know Lucy is going to leave after this term, don't you?' said Margery. 'Well, she is awfully unhappy about it, because she does so love St Clare's – and she is exactly the sort of girl you want, isn't she? We all love her. Well, Miss Theobald, I've got an idea.'

'And what is that?' asked the head, trying not to smile as Margery almost fell over her words in her eagerness to get them out.

'Miss Theobald, you do think Lucy is awfully clever, don't you?' said Margery. 'She's always top of our form, and she's got the most wonderful memory. Why she's only just got to *look* at a page and she knows it by heart!'

'That is a gift,' said Miss Theobald. 'I know Lucy has it. She is very lucky. Well – go on, Margery.'

'Don't you think that Lucy is clever enough to sit for the scholarship exam with the third form next term?' said Margery, her eyes shining. 'I'm sure she'd win it, because she'd work so awfully hard! Couldn't you give her a chance to do that, Miss Theobald? She's worth it, honestly she is.'

'You needn't tell me that,' said Miss Theobald. 'We all know that Lucy is worth helping. I would keep her on at St Clare's at reduced fees – but her parents will not hear of that. But, Margery, my dear – Lucy is only fourteen – and all the other girls going in for the exam are sixteen. I know she's clever – but I doubt if she is as clever as that. It would only mean a great deal of very hard work – and probably a bitter disappointment at the end. There are one or two clever girls in the third form, you know.'

Margery looked dismayed. She had set her heart on her idea. She had felt so certain that Lucy was clever enough to win any scholarship, if only she had a few months to prepare for it!

Miss Walker joined in the conversation. 'I don't quite see how going in for the scholarship exam will help Lucy to stay on at St Clare's!' she said.

'Oh, but Miss Walker, it *will*!' cried Margery. 'I've looked at the list of schools that are open to scholarship girls free of fees – and St Clare's is one of them this year! So of course Lucy would choose St Clare's, if she won the scholarship.'

Miss Theobald began to laugh. Margery was so very determined about it all. 'Really, the running of this school is being taken out of my hands!' she said. 'What with Lucy deciding what was to be done about Erica – and writing that letter to your father, Margery – and now you telling me how we can manage to keep Lucy on – I feel a head mistress is not really needed at St Clare's.'

'Oh, Miss Theobald, we all know that it's you that makes the school what it is,' said Margery, going red. 'But you've no idea how popular Lucy is, and how we all want to keep her. She's the first friend I've ever had – and I've been puzzling my brains how to help her. I did think this idea might be some good.'

'Well, Margery, I don't somehow think it will work,'

said Miss Theobald. 'I'm not going to overwork a brilliant brain like Lucy's, two years below the scholarship exam age unless there is a very great hope of her winning it. Miss Walker has also been to me with ideas about Lucy – and we have been talking them over.'

'Oh, how nice of you, Miss Walker!' said Margery, who had never very much liked the art mistress before – entirely her own fault, for she had never tried at all in Miss Walker's excellent classes! Now she felt that she would do anything for Miss Walker because she had taken an interest in Lucy.

'Well, my idea was that we should try to keep Lucy here for a couple of years somehow – and then let her go in for an art scholarship,' said Miss Walker. 'Her art is so brilliant already, that she is bound to be an artist of some sort. She must go to the best art school in the country – but she is too young yet. I didn't somehow feel I wanted her to go in for shorthand and typing and get a job as a junior clerk somewhere, when she could make such good use of her time here – and then win a place at a London art school.'

'I've already offered to let Lucy stay here at reduced fees for two years, so that she might try for an art scholarship then,' said Miss Theobald, 'but her parents will not hear of it – neither will Lucy either, Margery, though I don't suppose she has told you that. She apparently wants to do her bit in helping to keep her family now that her father can't paint.'

'Miss Theobald – couldn't you keep Lucy just one

more term and let her try for the scholarship?' said Margery, eagerly. 'Then she could be here for two or three years if she won it – and then try for an art scholarship. She'd get that easily enough!'

'Well, Margery, we'll see what can be done,' said Miss Theobald. 'It's certainly an idea I hadn't thought of – and I'm still not sure it can possibly be carried out. I shall have to talk to the other mistresses and find out more about Lucy's capabilities. I'll tell you as soon as we have decided something. In the meantime – thank you, my dear, for trying to be so helpful. I am more glad than I can say that you came to St Clare's. We have helped you, I know – and now you are going to help us tremendously.'

19.

And a little good luck too

Margery left the sitting-room on her crutches, her face bright with hope. Surely, surely, something would be arranged for Lucy now! She did not say a word to anyone about what she had suggested, least of all to Lucy, in case nothing came of it.

'I know Miss Theobald will keep her word and look into the idea thoroughly,' thought Margery, as she looked across the classroom at Lucy's rather sad little face. Lucy was brave – but she could not help feeling sad now. Things looked so different. All her bright future was gone.

Miss Theobald kept her word. She called a meeting of the first, second and third form mistresses, and of Mam'zelle and Miss Lewis, the history teacher, too. She told them shortly what Margery had suggested.

They talked the matter out thoroughly. All the teachers liked Lucy Oriell and admired her quick brain and wonderful memory. Miss Lewis said at once that she could coach Lucy for the history section of the exam, and she was certain that Lucy would excel in that, whatever she did in other subjects.

'And her French is already perfect!' said Mam'zelle.

'She has spent many of her holidays in France, and she speaks French almost as well as I do!'

Mathematics were Lucy's weak point. She did not like them and found them difficult, though even here her quick brain helped her over difficulties. But mathematics were Miss Theobald's specialty. She was a wonderful teacher where they were concerned.

'I could give her special coaching there,' she said. 'The child is worth extra trouble. I know I do no coaching now, because the running of the school takes all my time – but I would make an exception for Lucy Oriell.'

The meeting ended after an hour and the mistresses went to their various rooms. Margery, who knew that the mistresses had been summoned to Miss Theobald's room, wondered and wondered if they had been talking about Lucy. She soon knew, for Miss Theobald sent for her.

'Well, Margery,' said the head, coming to the point at once. 'We've been discussing Lucy's future – and we think you are right – we think it *is* possible that she might win the scholarship. So I have written to her parents and put the idea before them. We must see what they say.'

The answer came by telephone the next day. Mrs Oriell had been delighted with the head's suggestion. She knew how very much Lucy had wanted to stay on at St Clare's – and if there really was a chance that the girl could win a scholarship and stay there without the payment of fees, going on to an art school afterwards, then she should certainly be given the chance.

'I'm so glad you think that, Mrs Oriell,' said Miss Theobald, pleased. 'Thank you for letting me know so soon. I will tell Lucy tonight.'

Miss Theobald sent for Lucy and in a few words told her what was suggested. The girl listened with shining eyes. It all seemed too good to be true, after her terrible disappointment and shock.

'Oh, Miss Theobald – thank you very very much!' she said. 'I'll do my best, I promise. I'll work terribly hard – all the holidays too. I'll win that scholarship somehow, and stay on here. It nearly broke my heart to think I'd have to leave just when I was so happy!'

'Well, that's settled then,' said Miss Theobald. 'I have discussed the whole thing with the other mistresses, and they are going to give you special coaching. I shall take you for maths myself, and we must begin this very week, for every day's work will count. I will draw up a special timetable for you, because you will be taking different classes now. You must not be foolish and work *too* hard, though! I think I must tell Margery Fenworthy to keep an eye on you and make you take a rest when you get over-tired!'

'Oh – won't Margery be pleased!' cried Lucy, thinking of her friend with pleasure. 'I shall tell her first of all.'

'Yes – she will be delighted,' said Miss Theobald. 'Go and find her now.'

Lucy rushed off and found Margery in the common-room with one or two others. She pounced on her friend and made her jump.

'Margery! Listen! I've got the most marvellous news!' she cried. 'You won't believe it! I'm staying on at St Clare's!'

'Oh, *Lucy*! Are you going to be allowed to go in for the scholarship exam then?' cried Margery, wishing her leg was better, so that she might dance around.

'Why, Margery – what do *you* know about it?' said Lucy, in astonishment.

'Because it was all my idea!' said Margery, happily. 'I thought of it. I went to Miss Theobald about it. But I couldn't say a word to you till I knew it was decided, in case you might be disappointed. Oh, Lucy – I'm so terribly pleased!'

'What a friend you are!' said Lucy, wonderingly, as she looked into Margery's strong, determined face. 'How lucky I am to have you! Fancy you going to all that trouble for me. Oh, Margery, I'll never never forget this. I'll remember your kindness all my life long.'

'Don't be silly,' said Margery. 'I'm the lucky one, not you! Why, now I shall have you here at St Clare's with me, instead of being all alone. The only thing is – you will have to work so terribly hard. I shall have to keep my eye on you and see that you get some fun sometimes!'

'How funny – that's just what Miss Theobald said!' said Lucy, laughing. 'Well, with the mistresses looking after my work and you looking after my play, I should be all right, shouldn't I?'

'What's the matter?' cried Pat, from her corner of the room. 'What are you two talking about in such excitement? Has one of you got a "Very Good" from Mam'zelle?'

'Not likely, these days!' said Margery. It was quite a joke that Mam'zelle never gave anyone a Very Good now. 'No – the excitement is, that Lucy is staying on here after all – and going in for the third form scholarship exam at the end of next term. What about *that*?'

All the girls came over to say how glad they were. Lucy was happy again. It was lovely to be liked so much. It was lovely to have a friend who would do so much for her. If only her father's poor hand would get right, she would be even happier than she had been before the accident.

'Lucy,' said Margery, that night, just before they went up to bed. 'I've thought of something.'

'Gracious – not another idea so soon!' said Lucy, teasingly.

'Yes – but about me, this time, not you,' said Margery, rather soberly. 'You know, I'm sixteen, and I've no right to be so low down in the school. It's only because I've never been able to settle for long in any school, so my education has been a sort of hotch-potch, all mixed up. But my brains aren't too bad if only I'll use them. Well, I'm going to use them like anything now – so that I can go up in form, and keep with you a bit. I couldn't bear to be in the first form whilst you forged ahead and became one of the top formers, although you are two years younger. It's so difficult to be friends, proper friends, if we are in different forms.'

'Oh, Margery – that would be splendid!' said Lucy at once. 'Yes – I suppose I shall go up next term, and keep up in a higher form, if I *do* win that scholarship – and it would be lovely if you got put up too. Do work hard!'

And so, to every mistress's enormous astonishment, Margery Fenworthy, the dunce of the first form, suddenly produced excellent brains, and worked so much harder that one week she actually tied for top place with Lucy.

'Miracles will never cease!' said Miss Roberts, when she read out the marks to the form. 'Margery, you'll be in the second form before you know where you are! Good gracious, what a surprise this is. Doris, perhaps you will give me a nice surprise next. You have been bottom for three weeks. What about tying for top place with Lucy and Margery *next* week?'

Everyone laughed, Doris too. The first form was a very pleasant place to be in those last few weeks of term.

20.

Janet is up to tricks again

It was Mam'zelle who seemed to spoil things each day. She had always had a very hot temper – but nowadays she seemed to be unusually irritable, and the girls felt the rough edge of her tongue in every lesson.

Janet got tired of it. She was very hot tempered herself, and she found it difficult to control herself when Mam'zelle made some specially biting remark.

'Ah, Janet! Once more you have made the same mistake that you have made at least one hundred times this term!' said Mam'zelle one day, scoring a sentence with a blue pencil, and pressing so hard that it almost tore the page. 'I have no pleasure in teaching a stupid careless girl like you.'

'Well, I've no pleasure in being taught!' muttered Janet, angrily. She said it half under her breath, but Mam'zelle caught enough of it to look up with flashing eyes.

'*Que dites-vous*?' she cried. 'What is that you said? You will please repeat it.'

The class listened breathlessly. Mam'zelle was in one of her rages. That was exciting – providing it was someone else who was getting into trouble!

Janet was bold enough to repeat what she had said, and she said it loudly, so that all the class could hear.

'I said, "I've no pleasure in being taught!" ' she repeated.

'*Méchante fille*!' cried Mam'zelle. 'What has happened to all you girls this term? You are rude and careless and sulky.'

The class knew that it was really Mam'zelle's fault, not theirs. She was so bad tempered. They looked mutinous, and said nothing. Even Lucy would not look at Mam'zelle when her eyes flashed round the class.

'Janet, you will learn the whole of the French poem in this book, and you will write it out for me three times!' said Mam'zelle, her voice trembling with rage. The class gasped. The poem was three pages long!

'Oh, Mam'zelle!' said Janet, startled. 'You know I can't do that. It would take me ages and ages. Besides, I'm not good at learning French poetry. It's as much as I can do to learn eight lines – and there must be about a hundred in that poem.'

'Then it will make you think twice before you are rude to me again,' said Mam'zelle. She took up her spectacle case and put her glasses on her big nose. Her face was flushed an angry red, and her head was aching. Ah, these English girls! They were terrible! How was it she had liked them so much before? She could not bear them now.

After the class Janet talked angrily about her punishment. 'It's not fair,' she said. 'It's all Mam'zelle's own fault, the wretch! Can't she see that we won't stand her sarcastic remarks when we don't deserve them? I'm sure we work just as hard as we did last term – and look at Lucy, how good she is in French, and yet Mam'zelle scolded her like anything yesterday.'

'Wasn't she always as bad tempered as this then?' asked Lucy, in wonder.

'Gracious no,' said Janet. 'This is the fourth term I've been in the first form – and Mam'zelle has always been quite a brick before – well, she always did have a hot temper – but she wasn't *bad* tempered, like she is now.'

'Janet, I'll copy out that poem once for you,' said Kathleen. 'My writing is a bit like yours. Mam'zelle won't know. You can't possibly do it three times yourself today.'

'Oh, thanks, Kath, you're a brick,' said Janet. 'That *will* be a help. I wouldn't let anyone take on a part of my punishments if I could help it. But goodness me, Mam'zelle must be mad if she thinks I've enough time to do all she said!'

Kathleen copied out the poem once in Janet's French book. Sheila did it once too, for her writing was not unlike Janet's. Janet scribbled it out the third time and, with much trouble and pains, learnt it by heart. The whole class was sick of the poem by the time that Janet had it perfect.

She went to Mam'zelle at seven o'clock to take the written work and to say the poem. She said it in a sulky voice and would not look at the French teacher at all. By this time Mam'zelle had recovered a little and was half sorry she had given the girl such a long punishment. But Janet would not smile at Mam'zelle, and would not even say good night to her when she went from the room.

'Ah, these impolite English girls!' said Mam'zelle, with a sigh. 'They should go to school in France – then they would know what good behaviour and hard work are!'

Janet did not forgive Mam'zelle for her hardness. She was a dreadful girl for playing tricks and practical jokes, and had got into great trouble the term before for throwing fireworks into the classroom fire. She had not done anything very bad this term – but now she determined to make Mam'zelle 'sit up', as she called it, the last two or three weeks of term.

She told the others. 'If Mam'zelle thinks she can treat me like that without my getting a bit of my own back, she's jolly well mistaken!' said Janet. 'I'm going to pay her out – so look out for some fun!'

The class was pleasantly excited. They knew Janet's tricks and appreciated them, for Janet was clever and original with her jokes. What would she be up to now?

'You know, it was terribly funny last term when she threw the fireworks into the fire,' said Pat to Margery and Lucy. 'We really meant to play that joke on Miss Kennedy, a timid sort of mistress who took Miss Lewis's place for history last term. Well, Miss Roberts came along just when Janet had thrown about fifty in – and golly, we had fireworks from Miss Roberts then too, I can tell you!'

'I wonder what Janet will do?' said Doris, hugging herself, for she adored a joke, and was pretty good herself at playing them. 'I've got a funny trick my cousin gave me at Christmas – it's a thing that looks exactly like spilt ink!'

'Oh, why haven't you shown it to us?' cried Janet, in delight. 'I know the thing you mean – it's awfully good. Have you got it?'

'Well, I brought it to school meaning to give somebody a shock with it,' said Doris, 'but I couldn't find it. It must be somewhere about.'

'Go and look, Doris. Go and look now,' begged Pat, giggling. 'Look where you haven't looked before. In your tuck-box for instance. You haven't opened that since the beginning of the term, when we ate everything.'

The joke *was* in the neglected tuck-box! Doris pounced on it with glee. It was a thing which, when put down flat on a book looked exactly like a big, irregular, shiny ink-blot – almost as if the ink-pot had been spilt.

Janet took it in delight. 'This is fine!' she said. 'Lend it to me, there's a sport!'

'Rather!' said Doris. 'What will you do with it?'

'Wait and see, tomorrow,' said Janet. So the class waited impatiently till the French lesson came, and Mam'zelle bustled in, out of breath as usual.

It was French dictation that morning. Mam'zelle looked round the class, which was suspiciously good and docile all of a sudden.

'Take down *dictée*,' she said. 'Get out your exercise books, and begin.'

Every girl had to take her book to Mam'zelle to be corrected after *dictée*. Janet took hers up when her turn came and laid it flat on the desk. Mam'zelle took up her fountain pen – and then, before her eyes, there appeared on Janet's perfectly clean book, a very large and shiny ink-blot!

'Oh, Mam'zelle!' cried Janet, in a doleful voice. 'Look what you've done on my book! It must have been your fountain pen! Is it leaking? Oh, and I did try so hard with my *dictée* this morning!'

Mam'zelle stared in horror at the enormous blot. She couldn't believe her eyes.

'Janet! What can have happened?' she cried. She looked at her fountain pen. It seemed all right. And yet there was the tremendous blot, right across Janet's neat book.

'I'll go and blot it, Mam'zelle,' said Janet, and took her book away carefully, as if she were trying not to let the blot run across the page. The class saw it clearly and buried their heads in their hands or under their desks to stiffle their giggles.

Janet slipped the trick blot into her pocket and then pretended to be very busy with blotting-paper. Mam'zelle was shaking her pen with a puzzled air. She simply could not imagine how so much ink had run out of it so suddenly.

Janet took back her book, which was now absolutely clean. Mam'zelle stared at it in the greatest amazement.

'But where is the smudge?' she asked in astonishment. 'You cannot have cleaned it so well!'

'Well, I've got some special blotting-paper, Mam'zelle,' said Janet, in a solemn voice. 'It cleans ink like magic.'

'Ah, but it is indeed magic!' said Mam'zelle, pleased. 'Your *dictée* is now not spoilt at all. Thank you, *ma chère* Janet! I was so sorry to have spoilt your work.'

One or two muffled giggles could be heard from Doris and Kathleen. Mam'zelle looked up sharply. 'There is nothing to laugh at,' she said. '*Taisez-vous*!'

But, of course, there was something to laugh at – and when Janet cleverly managed to slip the ink-blot on to Doris's desk, just as Mam'zelle was leaning over to look at her work, the class nearly had hysterics!

'Oh, Mam'zelle – that wretched pen of yours!' said Doris, in a reproachful voice, looking at the blot. 'It's messed up my desk now.'

Mam'zelle stared at it in surprise and horror. Blots seemed to be following her round this morning. She looked at her fountain pen again and shook it violently. A shower of ink drops flew over the floor. Doris cried out loudly.

'It *is* your pen! Look at all the blots it has made on the floor! Oh, Mam'zelle, please may I borrow Janet's wonderful blotting-paper to wipe up the mess? Miss Roberts will be so angry with me if she sees it there next lesson.'

'I cannot understand it,' murmured poor Mam'zelle, feeling she must be in some sort of a dream, as she looked at the large and shiny blot on Doris's desk. 'I have never made such blots before.'

The class went off into giggles that spread round uncontrollably. Mam'zelle lost her temper.

'Is it so funny that I make blots?' she cried. 'Silence! Another giggle and I will keep the whole class in for break.'

That was enough to keep the class quiet for a while, though there were many handkerchiefs stuffed into mouths when the urge to laugh became too great. Janet was pleased with the success of her joke, and already she was planning another.

'I'm going to put beetles into Mam'zelle's spectacle case,' she giggled to the others, when they were in the common-room after tea, discussing with enjoyment the success of the ink-blot. The second formers had enjoyed the tale immensely and had groaned because they hadn't been able to share in the joke.

'Janet! Not *beetles*!' shuddered Sheila. 'How could you possibly pick them up to put them in?'

'And anyway, how are you going to get them there?' said Pat.

'Easy enough,' said Janet. 'Mam'zelle is always leaving her spectacle case around. The first time she leaves it in our classroom I grab it and put the beetles into the case! What-ho for a squeal from Mam'zelle! That will teach her to make me learn her horrid French poems!'

The very next day Mam'zelle left her glasses in their case on the first form desk. Janet winked at the others. She saw them at once. Immediately Mam'zelle was out of the room on her way to the second form Janet whipped out of her seat and took the case from the desk. She slipped it into her pocket and got back to her seat just as Miss Roberts came in to take arithmetic.

The lesson had hardly been going for more than four minutes when a girl from the second form came in.

'Please, Miss Roberts, Mam'zelle is sorry to interrupt you, but may she have her glasses? She left them in a case on your desk.'

Miss Roberts looked round the big desk and then opened it. No spectacle case was to be seen, which was not surprising considering that it was safely in Janet's pocket.

'It doesn't seem to be here,' said Miss Roberts. 'Mam'zelle will probably find that they are in her pocket.'

The class giggled to itself. They knew quite well that Mam'zelle would find nothing of the sort! Janet looked quite solemn. It made the others giggle to look at her.

'Girls! What is the joke, please?' asked Miss Roberts, impatiently. She did not like giggles. 'Is there anything funny in Mam'zelle losing her glasses?'

As it happened, there was – but Miss Roberts, of

course, didn't know it. The class sobered down.

'Well, Miss Roberts, it's only that Mam'zelle is *always* leaving her glasses about,' said Doris.

'Quite,' said Miss Roberts, drily. 'Turn to page forty-seven, please. KATHLEEN! If you stare round the class any more I'll put you with your back to it! What *is* the matter with you this morning?'

The class had to behave itself. Miss Roberts made it work so hard that most of them thought no more of the next trick Janet was going to play, until break came. Then they all crowded round Janet to see her put the poor surprised beetles into the spectacle case!

21.

Mam'zelle gets another shock

Janet collected various kinds of beetles and grubs from underneath fences at break. Giggling loudly the first and second formers watched her take out Mam'zelle's spectacles and carefully put in the wriggling insects. They were half dazed with their winter sleep. Janet shut the case with a snap.

'I hope the beetles can breathe,' said Kathleen, in a troubled voice. She was passionately fond of animals, and her kindness extended even to spiders, beetles and moths.

'Of course they can breathe,' said Janet. 'This spectacle case is as big as a room to them!'

'What are you going to do with the case?' asked Hilary. 'Are you going to put it back on the desk so that Mam'zelle can open it next day?'

'Of course, silly,' said Janet. 'We all want to see the fun, don't we?'

'I say, Janet – won't Mam'zelle be absolutely furious?' said Lucy. 'She'll tell Miss Theobald, I should think. Better be careful – you don't want to get into a fearful row just before the end of term. You might get a bad report.'

'I don't care,' said Janet. 'I'm going to get even with Mam'zelle, the bad-tempered thing!'

The beetles and grubs passed quite a pleasant time in the spectacle case, and didn't seem to mind at all, though Kathleen kept worrying about them and opening the case to give them a little air. In the morning Janet placed the case on Miss Roberts's desk just before Mam'zelle came to give her daily French lesson. The whole class was in a state of fidget and excitement. They had tried to keep it under whilst Miss Roberts was teaching them, for she was very clever at sensing anything wrong with the class.

She had been rather sharp with them, but had not seemed to suspect anything. She left to go to the second form – and Mam'zelle came in. Mam'zelle had had a bad night. She was not sleeping well these days, and her eyes were circled with big black rings.

'*Bonjour!*' she said, as she came in. She went to the desk, and put down her books. The girls wished her good morning and sat down. Mam'zelle turned to the blackboard and wrote down a few questions which the class had to answer in writing, in French.

Then suddenly Mam'zelle spotted her spectacle case. She pounced on it with delight.

'Ah! Here are my glasses! Now this is a strange thing! I sent to ask for them yesterday and was told they were not here! All day long I looked for them!'

The girls watched in the most intense excitement. The ones at the back craned their necks round the girls in front of them, trying their hardest to see. The girls at the front were thrilled to have such a good view.

Mam'zelle sat down. She did not open the case at once. She looked round the class. '*Dépêchez-vous*!' she cried. 'Why are you so slow at beginning your work today?'

The class took up their pens. Mam'zelle yawned and tapped her big white teeth with her pencil. Why, oh why, didn't she open her spectacle case?

Ah! Now she was going to. She stretched out her hand and picked up the case. She opened it slowly – and out scrambled the quick-legged beetles, and out crawled the grubs, wide awake now because of the warmth of the room!

Mam'zelle stared at them. She took out her handkerchief and rubbed it across her eyes. Then she looked cautiously at the spectacle case again. She simply could not believe her eyes.

It is impossible! thought poor Mam'zelle. My eyes tell me that there are beetles and grubs crawling over my desk, but my sense tells me that my glasses should be there. And no doubt they *are* there. It is because I am tired that I see these insects crawling out of my case!

The girls were trying to smother their giggles. Mam'zelle's face was so funny! It was quite plain that she was immensely astonished and couldn't believe her eyes.

Mam'zelle was trying to think calmly. She hated anything that crawled, and one of her worst nightmares was that beetles were crawling over her. And now here they were walking out of her spectacle case. It was quite impossible. Beetles did not live in spectacle cases. Her eyes must be wrong. She must go to the optician again and get fresh glasses. Perhaps that was why she had such headaches lately! All these thoughts passed through poor Mam'zelle's mind, and the first formers peered over their books and watched eagerly to see what would happen.

'It cannot be that these insects are real,' Mam'zelle was thinking firmly to herself. 'They are in my imagination only! My glasses must be in the case, although it appears to me that there are insects there instead. I must be brave and put my hand into the case to get my glasses. Then, when they are safely on my nose I shall see that the beetles are not really there!'

The girls began to giggle, though they tried their hardest to stop. Mam'zelle was so puzzled and so amazed. It did not seem to enter her mind for one moment that it was a trick. She put out her hand to feel for the glasses she felt sure must really be in her case.

And, of course, all she got hold of were beetles and grubs! When she felt them in her fingers she gave a loud scream. The girls watched in enjoyment. This was simply marvellous!

'What's the matter, Mam'zelle?' asked Doris, demurely, winking round at the others.

'Ah, Doris – Janet – come up here and tell me what there is on my desk,' said poor Mam'zelle, looking down in horror as one beetle ran round and round the ink-pot and finally fell right into it.

Doris and Janet leapt up at once. Janet stared solemnly at Mam'zelle. 'Your glasses are in your case,' said the naughty girl. 'Put them on, Mam'zelle, and maybe you will see properly.'

'My glasses are not there!' cried Mam'zelle. 'But do you not see those insects, girls!'

'What insects?' asked Doris, innocently, and the whole class exploded into stifled giggles. But Mam'zelle hardly noticed them.

'Ah, there is something wrong with me!' she groaned. 'I have feared it all these weeks. I am not the same. My temper is so bad. I am so irritable. And now my eyes are wrong. I see things! I see beetles on this desk! If only I could find my glasses!'

Janet picked up the empty case, quickly slipped Mam'zelle's glasses into it, from her pocket, and then took them out of the case as if they had been there all the time. She handed them to the astonished French mistress.

'Ah, this is worse than ever!' cried Mam'zelle. 'So they were there all the time and I could not even see them! And alas, alas – still the beetles they crawl over my desk! I am ill! I must leave you! You will go on with your French quietly, please, and wait till Miss Roberts comes back. I am ill – *très malade, très malade*!'

Mam'zelle left the room stooping like an old woman. The class were startled and dismayed. This was not the right ending for a joke at all! Mam'zelle had taken it really seriously. She had believed Janet and Doris when they had assured her that the insects were not there. The girls stared at one another in dismay. Janet picked the insects off the desk and put them carefully out of the window.

'Janet, I don't much like this,' said Lucy, in her clear voice. 'We've given Mam'zelle a real shock. It sounded to me as if she hadn't been feeling well for ages and thought that our joke was all part of her illness. I wish we hadn't done it now.'

Everyone wished the same. Nobody giggled. Janet wished that Mam'zelle had seen through the joke and had punished her. This was much worse than any punishment. The girls took up their pens and got on with their work, each feeling decidedly uncomfortable.

In about ten minutes Miss Theobald came in. The girls stood up at once. The head mistress glanced at the board and at the girl's books. She saw that they were working and she was pleased.

'Girls,' she said, in her low, pleasant voice, 'I am sorry to tell you that Mam'zelle is sure she is ill, so she will not come back to you this morning. I have sent for the doctor. Please get on with what work you can, and wait until Miss Roberts returns.'

She went out. The girls sat down. They felt more uncomfortable than ever. Janet was very red. She kicked herself for playing such a trick now. She thought about Mam'zelle and her bad temper. Could it have been because she was feeling ill?

The first form were so subdued that morning that Miss Roberts was quite astonished. She kept looking at the bent heads and wondering what was the matter. But nobody told her.

At the end of the morning there was a regular buzz of talk in the common-room. 'Did you know that Mam'zelle is very ill? Whose form was she in when she was taken ill? Oh, yours, Margery? What happened? Did she faint or something?'

Nobody gave Janet away. They all felt that she was sorry about the trick, and they were ashamed too – so they said nothing about the joke at all. It had gone very wrong and goodness knows how it could be put right.

Mam'zelle was put to bed, and Matron went to see to her. Poor Mam'zelle was more worried about her eyes than about anything else. She kept telling Matron about the insects she had seen, and she declared she was afraid to go to sleep in case her nightmare came back.

Janet went to ask Matron how Mam'zelle was after tea. The doctor had been, so Matron was able to tell the girl all the news.

'It's overwork and strain,' she told Janet. 'Poor Mam'zelle's sister was ill all the Christmas holidays and she went to nurse her. She nursed her day and night, and got very little rest or sleep herself. So she came back tired out, and instead of taking things easy, she worked herself all the harder. I know you girls thought her very bad tempered and irritable this term – but that's the explanation!'

'Did she – did she say anything about her spectacle case?' asked Janet.

Matron stared at Janet in surprise. 'What do you know about her spectacle case?' she said. 'As a matter of fact something seems to be worrying poor Mam'zelle terribly. She keeps saying that her eyes are going wrong because she saw insects coming out of her spectacle case – and she daren't go to sleep and get the rest she needs because she is so afraid she will dream that insects are crawling over her. She is in a very overtired state!'

Janet went away to tell the others. So that was the explanation of Mam'zelle's bad temper that term! She had been nursing her sister day and night – and, knowing Mam'zelle's zeal and thoroughness, Janet could well imagine that she had spared herself nothing in the holidays. Mam'zelle had the kindest heart in the world, in spite of her hot temper.

'I do feel simply awful about that trick,' said Janet to Pat. 'I really do. I've a good mind to go into Mam'zelle's room and tell her about it to set her mind at rest. I simply daren't tell Miss Roberts or Miss Theobald.'

'Well, go and tell Mam'zelle then,' said Pat. 'Take her some flowers from me. And some from Isabel too.'

Every girl in the class put money towards flowers for Mam'zelle. As the next day was Saturday they were able to go down into the town to buy them. They bought daffodils, narcissi, anemones and primroses.

They all felt so guilty that they spent far more money than they could really afford.

Miss Roberts saw the girls coming back with their flowers, and stared in amazement.

'What's this – a flower show?' she asked.

'They're for Mam'zelle,' said Hilary, which astonished Miss Roberts all the more, for she had heard the bitter complaints of her form about the amount of work set by Mam'zelle that term, and her bad temper when it was not done properly.

These first formers have really kind hearts, thought Miss Roberts. She spoke aloud to them. 'This is very nice of you. Mam'zelle will be pleased. She had a very bad night, so I don't expect any of you will be allowed to see her. But you can take the flowers to Matron to give to her.'

But that wasn't Janet's plan at all! She was going to see Mam'zelle somehow, whatever Matron said!

22. Last week of term

Pat and Isabel kept watch for Matron after tea that day. They were to tell Janet when she was not about so that Janet might slip in by herself. Janet was not going to take the flowers in with her. They were outside the room in a cupboard and Janet meant to go and fetch them as a kind of peace-offering when she had confessed everything to Mam'zelle.

Poor Janet was rather white. She didn't at all like the idea of facing Mam'zelle, even when she was ill. But it had to be done. Pat and Isabel saw Matron come out of Mam'zelle's bedroom with her tea-tray and they went to her.

'Matron, please may we have a clean towel?'

'What have you done with yours?' asked Matron, bustling along with the tray. 'Come along and get it then, I haven't much time.'

Pat looked back over her shoulder and winked at Janet to tell her that Matron wouldn't be back for a few minutes. The twins meant to keep her talking and give Janet a clear field.

Janet slipped to Mam'zelle's door. She knocked and a voice said, '*Entrez*!' Janet went in. Mam'zelle was lying in bed, looking up at the ceiling. She looked very unhappy, because she was still worrying about what was suddenly and mysteriously the matter with her eyes. She expected to see insects crawling all over the ceiling. Poor Mam'zelle – she would not have thought these things if she had not been so overworked.

She looked with surprise at Janet. Matron had told her there were to be no visitors that day.

'Mam'zelle,' said Janet, going to the bed. 'Are you better? I had to come and see you. I wanted to tell you something.'

'It is nice to see you, *ma chère* Janet!' said Mam'zelle, who was always touched by any kindness. 'What have you to tell me, *ma petite*?'

'Mam'zelle – Mam'zelle – I don't know how to tell you,' said Janet, 'you'll be so angry. But please believe me when I say I'm terribly sorry – so are we all – and we wouldn't have done it if we'd known you'd been feeling ill – and . . .'

'My dear child, what are you trying to say?' asked Mam'zelle, in the utmost astonishment. 'What is this terrible thing you have done?'

'Mam'zelle – we – I – I put those beetles and things into your spectacle case to pay you out for punishing me the other day,' blurted out Janet, desperately. 'And I put a trick ink-blot on my book too. You see . . .'

Mam'zelle looked at Janet as if she couldn't believe her ears. 'Those – those crawling insects were *real*, then?' she said, at last.

'Yes, Mam'zelle,' said Janet. 'Quite real. I got them from places under the fence. I – I didn't think you'd believe it was your eyes that were wrong. Now you're ill we feel awful.'

Mam'zelle lay quite still. So her eyes and her mind were quite all right. Those insects were not in her imagination, they were real. It was only a joke! If she had been well and quite herself she would have guessed that! But she was tired and could not think properly. How thankful she was that Janet had told her!

She turned to speak to the girl but Janet was not there. She had slipped out to get the flowers. She came back with her arms full of them, and Mam'zelle gasped to see them.

'Mam'zelle, these are from all of us in the first form,' said Janet. 'We are sorry you're ill – and please forgive us, won't you? Honestly we'd have put up with all your rages and everything if we'd known you were so tired!'

'Come here,' said Mam'zelle, and reached out a large hand to Janet. The girl took it shyly. 'I have been *abominable* this term!' said Mam'zelle, a smile coming over her face. '*Insupportable* and *abominable*! You will please tell the O'Sullivan twins that, Janet. I know the nickname they had for me last term – Mam'zelle Abominable, which they gave me because I said so often that their work was abominable! But this term I have really earned that name.'

'You were awfully cross with us lots of times,' said Janet, honestly. 'But we don't mind now. We understand.'

'Ah, you English girls! There is nobody like you when you are nice!' said Mam'zelle, quite forgetting all the dreadful things she had thought and said about them that term. 'You will give my love to the others, Janet – and my best thanks for these beautiful flowers – and you will tell them that if they will forgive me I will forgive them also – and you too, of course! *Méchante fille*! Wicked girl! Ah – but how brave and good of you to come and tell me!'

Janet stared at Mam'zelle and Mam'zelle looked at Janet with her big dark eyes. She began to laugh, for she had a great sense of humour at times.

'To think you put those beetles there – and I did not know it was a trick – and that ink-blot! What bad children you are! But how it makes me laugh now!'

And Mam'zelle went off into a loud burst of laughter. Matron was passing by the door at that moment and heard it in amazement. Thinking that Mam'zelle must have gone mad for a minute, Matron quickly opened the door and went in. She looked in astonishment when she saw the masses of flowers – and Janet!

'Janet! What are you doing in here? You naughty girl! I didn't give you permission to come. Go at once.'

'No, Matron, I will not have Janet sent away,' said Mam'zelle, most surprisingly. 'She stays here to put my flowers in water! She has brought me good news. I feel better already. She makes me laugh, this *méchante fille*!'

Mam'zelle certainly looked better. Matron looked at

her and then nodded to Janet that she might stay and put the flowers in water. Janet swiftly arranged them as well as she could. Mam'zelle watched her.

'The lovely flowers!' she said, contentedly. 'Matron, do you see what beautiful bunches the girls have sent to their bad-tempered, insupportable old Mam'zelle?'

'I see them,' said Matron. 'Now, Janet, you must go. And if you come here again without permission I shall punish you!'

Janet went, with a grin. She ran straight to the common-room to tell the others all that had happened. How glad they were to know that Mam'zelle had been such a brick about it all – and had actually laughed.

'Perhaps things will be better this last week of term,' said Doris, who had suffered very much that term from Mam'zelle's rough tongue. 'If Mam'zelle is well enough to come back for a few days at the end of term she'll be nicer – and if she doesn't I shall be jolly glad to miss French.'

'This term *has* gone quickly!' said Pat. 'It seems no time at all since half-term – and here we are almost at the Easter hols. What a lot has happened this term – almost as much as last term.'

'More,' said Isabel. 'We didn't have a fire last term – or a heroine either!'

Margery blushed. She was getting very clever at using her crutches, and her leg was mending marvellously. Lucy twinkled at her.

'It always makes Margery go red if you say the word

"heroine"!' she said. 'Pat, Margery is coming to stay with me for a week of the hols. We shan't have any home help or anything, because we are poor now, but Margery's going to help all she can – isn't she a brick? I shall be working hard most of the time, but I shall take time off to be with Margery too.'

'And then I'm going on a holiday with my father,' said Margery. 'What are you twins doing for the hols?'

Holidays were certainly in the air. Everyone was making plans for Easter. Some were going shopping to get new clothes. Alison was full of this, of course.

'Vain little creature!' said Pat, pulling Alison's pretty hair teasingly. 'Well, you're coming to stay with us part of the hols and you can bring your new pretties to show us – but we'll only allow you to boast *once* about them. After that – not a word!'

'All right, Pat,' said Alison, who was really learning to be much more sensible. 'I'll have one good glorious boast – and then be the strong silent girl!'

'You couldn't be silent!' said Isabel, who now liked her silly little cousin very much better. 'If your own tongue couldn't talk, the tongues of your shoes would do it for you!'

The last week of term was very happy. Mam'zelle got much better, and the girls went into her room to see her and play a game with her. She was the same old jolly Mam'zelle she used to be, now that she had had a rest, and had changed her ideas about 'these English girls'. She was already making plans for next term's work – but the girls refused to listen!

Lucy had been working hard to prepare for the scholarship exam next term. She had had good news of her father and this made her work with much more zest and happiness. Miss Theobald and the other teachers had worked out her holiday tasks and praised her for the progress she had already made. So Lucy looked much happier, and laughed and joked like her old self.

The twins were happy too. Things had gone well that term. They were top in five subjects. Lucy did not go in for the class exams as she was doing so much extra work, or she would, of course, have been top in everything except maths. Doris and Alison were bottom in most things, but they were both quite cheerful about it.

'Somebody's got to be bottom,' said Doris to Alison, 'and I think it's rather sweet of us to be willing to take such a back seat in everything!'

'Willing! You jolly well can't help it, you duffer!' said Pat. 'But who cares? You can make us laugh more than anybody else in the form – so you go on being bottom, old girl!'

The last day came, and the excitement of packing and saying goodbyes. Mam'zelle was up once more, making jokes and writing down everyone's addresses. There was laughter everywhere, and occasionally Miss Roberts's voice was lifted in complaint.

'Kathleen! Is it necessary to yell like that? Sheila, you don't look at all elegant rolling on the floor to do your packing. PAT! PAT! Stop pummelling Janet. What a zoo! I shall set you all a hundred lines to write out in the train home and send me tomorrow!'

There were giggles and squeals at this. It was fun to be going home – fun to look forward to Easter and Easter eggs, to long walks through the primrose woods, and reunions with dogs and cats and horses at home, to say nothing of mothers and fathers and little sisters and brothers.

'See you next term!' called Pat. 'Don't forget to write, Janet. Be good, Doris! Oh, Isabel, don't drag me like that – I'm coming! We're off in the first coach, everybody! Goodbye! See you all next term!'

Yes – see you all next term. That's what we will hope to do – see them all next term!

The TWINS at St CLARE'S

St Clare's

Enid Blyton

St Clare's
The Twins at St Clare's
The O'Sullivan Twins
Summer Term at St Clare's
The Second Form at St Clare's
The Third Form at St Clare's (written by Pamela Cox)
Claudine at St Clare's
Fifth Formers of St Clare's
The Sixth Form at St Clare's (written by Pamela Cox)

Malory Towers
First Term at Malory Towers
Second Form at Malory Towers
Third Year at Malory Towers
Upper Fourth at Malory Towers
In the Fifth at Malory Towers
Last Term at Malory Towers

The Mysteries
The Mystery of the Burnt Cottage
The Mystery of the Disappearing Cat
The Mystery of the Secret Room
The Mystery of the Spiteful Letters
The Mystery of the Missing Necklace
The Mystery of the Hidden House
The Mystery of the Pantomime Cat
The Mystery of the Invisible Thief
The Mystery of the Vanished Prince
The Mystery of the Strange Bundle
The Mystery of Holly Lane
The Mystery of Tally-Ho Cottage
The Mystery of the Missing Man
The Mystery of the Strange Messages
The Mystery of Banshee Towers

Enid Blyton®

The TWINS at St CLARE'S

EGMONT

St CLARE'S

Enid Blyton

EGMONT

We bring stories to life

First published in Great Britain 1941 by Methuen & Co. Ltd
This edition published 2013
by Egmont UK Limited
The Yellow Building
1 Nicholas Road
London W11 4AN

978 0 6035 6934 0

A CIP catalogue record for this title is available from the British Library
Printed and bound in Great Britain by the CPI Group

56921/1

EGMONT LUCKY COIN

Our story began over a century ago, when seventeen-year-old Egmont Harald Petersen found a coin in the street.

He was on his way to buy a flyswatter, a small hand-operated printing machine that he then set up in his tiny apartment.

The coin brought him such good luck that today Egmont has offices in over 30 countries around the world. And that lucky coin is still kept at the company's head offices in Denmark.

Contents

1. The twins make up their minds

One sunny summer afternoon four girls sat on the grass by a tennis-court, drinking lemonade. Their rackets lay beside them, and the six white balls were scattered over the court.

Two of the girls were twins. Isabel and Patricia O'Sullivan were so alike that only a few people could tell which was Pat and which was Isabel. Both girls had dark brown wavy hair, deep blue eyes and a merry smile, and the Irish lilt in their voices was very pleasant to hear.

The twins were staying for two weeks with friends of theirs, Mary and Frances Waters. The four girls were talking, and Pat was frowning as she spoke. She took up her racket and banged it hard on the grass.

'It's just too bad that Mummy won't let us go to the same school as you, now that we have all left Redroofs School together. We've been friends so long – and now we've got to go to a different school, and we shan't see each other for ages.'

'It's a pity that Redroofs only takes girls up to fourteen,' said Isabel. 'We could have stayed on together and it would have been fun. I loved being head girl with Pat the last year – and it was fun being tennis captain, and Pat being hockey captain. Now we've got to go to another school that doesn't sound a bit nice – and begin at the bottom! We'll be the young ones of the school instead of head girls.'

'I do wish you were coming to Ringmere School with us!' said Frances. 'It's such a nice *exclusive* school, our mother says. *You* know – only girls of rich parents, very well-bred, go there, and you make such nice friends. We have a bedroom to ourselves and our own study, and we have to wear evening dress at night, and they say the food is wonderful!'

'And we are going to St Clare's, where anybody can go, and the dormitories take six or eight girls and aren't nearly as nicely furnished as the maids' bedrooms are at home!' said Pat in a disgusted voice.

'I can't imagine why Mummy made up her mind to send us there instead of to Ringmere,' said Isabel. 'I wonder if she has *quite* decided. We're going home tomorrow and we'll both do our very very best to make her say we can go to Ringmere, Mary and Frances! We'll ring you up in the evening and tell you.'

'We'll jump for joy if you have good news,' said Mary. 'After all, when you've been head girls at a marvellous school like Redroofs, and had your own lovely bedroom and the best study with the best view, and a hundred girls looking up to you, it's awful to have to start again in a school you don't want to go to a bit!'

'Well, do your best to make your parents change their minds,' said Frances. 'Come on – let's have another set before tea!'

They all jumped up and tossed for partners. Isabel was a splendid player, and had won the tennis championship at Redroofs. She was really rather proud of her game. Pat was nearly as good, but much preferred hockey.

'They don't play hockey at St Clare's, they play lacrosse,' said Pat, dismally. 'Silly game, lacrosse – playing with nets on sticks, and catching a ball all the time instead of hitting it! That's another thing I'll tell Mummy – that I don't want to play lacrosse after being hockey captain.'

The twins thought hard of all the reasons they would put before their parents when they got home the next day. They talked about it as they went home in the train.

'I'll say this, and you say that,' said Pat. 'After all, we ought to know the kind of school that would be best for us – and St Clare's does sound too fierce for words!'

So the next evening the girls began to air their thoughts about schools. Pat began and, as was her way, she attacked at once.

'Mummy and Daddy!' she said. 'Isabel and I have been thinking a lot about what school we're to go to next, and, please, we don't want to go to St Clare's. Everyone says it's an awful school.'

Their mother laughed, and their father put down his paper in surprise.

'Don't be silly, Pat,' said Mrs O'Sullivan. 'It's a splendid school.'

'Have you quite decided about it?' asked Isabel.

'Not absolutely,' said her mother. 'But Daddy and I both think it will be the best school for you now. We do think that Redroofs spoilt you a bit, you know – it's a very expensive and luxurious school, and nowadays we have to learn to live much more simply. St Clare's is really a very sensible sort of school, and I know the head and like her.'

Pat groaned. 'A sensible school! How I do hate sensible things – they're always horrid and ugly and stupid and uncomfortable! Oh, Mummy – do let us go to Ringmere School with Mary and Frances.'

'Certainly not!' said Mrs O'Sullivan at once. 'It's a very snobbish school, and I'm not going to have you two girls coming home and turning up your noses at everything and everybody.'

'We wouldn't,' said Isabel, frowning at Pat to make her stop arguing for a while. Pat lost her temper very easily, and that didn't do when their father was there. 'Mummy dear – be a pet – just let's try at Ringmere for a term or two, and then, if you think we're turning into snobs, you can take us away. But you might let us try. They play hockey there, and we do so like that. We'd hate to have to learn a new game, just when we've got so good at hockey.'

Mr O'Sullivan lighted his pipe. 'My dear Isabel, it will be good for you to start at the beginning again, and learn something new! I've thought the last year that both you girls have become very conceited, and thought far too much of yourselves. If you have to learn new things, and find you're not so wonderful as you thought you were, it will be very good for you both!'

The twins went red. They were angry and hurt and

almost ready to cry. Mrs O'Sullivan felt sorry for them.

'Daddy doesn't mean to be unkind,' she said. 'But he is quite right, my dears. You've had a wonderful time at Redroofs, had things all your own way, been head girls and captains, and really lived in luxury. Now you must show us what kind of stuff you are made of when you have to start as youngsters of fourteen and a half in a school where the top classes are eighteen years old!'

Pat looked sulky. Isabel's chin shook as she answered.

'We shan't be happy, and we shan't try to be!' she said.

'Very well. Be *unhappy*!' said their father, sternly. 'If that's the sort of silly attitude you've learnt at Redroofs, I'm sorry we let you stay there so long. I wanted to take you away two years ago, but you begged so hard to stay, that I didn't. Now say no more about it. I shall write to St Clare's myself tonight and enter you for next term. If you want to make me proud of you, you will cheer up and make up your minds to be good and hardworking and happy at your next school.'

Their father relit his pipe and began to read his paper again. Their mother took up her sewing. There was no more to be said. The twins left the room together and went into the garden. They found their own secret place behind the thick old yew hedge and flung themselves down on the ground. The evening sun threw its slanting golden rays around them, and they blinked in its brightness. Tears shone in Isabel's eyes.

'I never thought Mummy and Daddy would be so hard,' she said. 'Never!'

'After all, *we* ought to have some say in the matter,' said Pat, furiously. She took a stick and dug it hard into the ground. 'I wish we could run away!'

'Don't be silly,' said Isabel. 'You know we can't. Anyway, it's cowardly to run away. We'll have to go to St Clare's. But how I shall hate it.'

'We'll both hate it,' said Pat. 'And what's more, I'm jolly well going to turn up my nose at everything there! I'm not going to let them think we're babies of fourteen, just come from some silly prep school. I'll soon let them know that we were head girls, and tennis and hockey captains. How horrid of Daddy to say we are conceited! We're not a bit. We can't help knowing that we're good at nearly everything, besides being pretty and quite amusing.'

'It *does* sound a bit conceited when you talk like that,' said Isabel. 'We'd better not say too much when we get to St Clare's.'

'I'm going to say all I like, and you must back me up,' said Pat. 'People are going to know who we are, and what we can do! All the mistresses are going to sit up and take notice of us too. The O'Sullivan twins are going to be SOMEBODIES! And don't you forget it, Isabel.'

Isabel nodded her dark head with its brown waves of hair. 'I won't forget it,' she said. 'I'll back you up. My word, St Clare's will get a few surprises next term!'

2.

The twins arrive at St Clare's

The time soon came when the twins had to leave for the winter term at St Clare's. Their mother had had a list of things they were to take with them, and the twins examined it carefully.

'It's not nearly such a long list as we had for Redroofs,' said Pat. 'And golly – how few dresses we are allowed! Mary and Frances said that they were allowed to take as many dresses as they liked to Ringmere – and they had both got long evening dresses like their mother! Won't they show off to us when they see us again!'

'And look – lacrosse-sticks instead of hockey-sticks!' said Isabel in disgust. 'They might at least play hockey as *well* as lacrosse! I didn't even bother to *look* at the lacrosse sticks Mummy bought for us, did you? And look – we are even told what to bring in our tuck boxes! We could take what we liked to Redroofs.'

'Just wait till we get to St Clare's. We'll show that we can do as we like,' said Pat. 'What time is the train tomorrow?'

'Ten o'clock from Paddington,' said Isabel. 'Well – we shall get our first glimpse of the St Clare girls there. I bet they'll be an odd-looking crowd!'

Mrs O'Sullivan took the twins to London. They taxied

to Paddington Station, and looked for the St Clare train. There it was, drawn up at the platform, labelled St Clare. On the platform were scores of girls, talking excitedly to one another, saying good-bye to their parents, hailing mistresses, and buying bars of chocolate from the shop.

A simply dressed mistress came up to the twins. She knew that they were St Clare girls because they had on the grey coats that were the uniform of the school. She smiled at Mrs O'Sullivan, and looked at the list in her hand.

'These are new girls,' she said, 'and I am sure they must be Patricia and Isabel O'Sullivan, because they are so exactly alike. I'm your form-mistress, Miss Roberts, and I'm very pleased to see you.'

This was a nice welcome and the twins liked the look of Miss Roberts. She was young and good-looking, tall and smiling – but she had a firm mouth and both Pat and Isabel felt sure that she wouldn't stand much nonsense from her form!

'Your carriage is over here, with the rest of your form,' said Miss Roberts. 'Say good-bye now, and get in. The train will be going in two minutes.'

She went off to talk to someone else and the twins hugged their mother. 'Good-bye,' said Mrs O'Sullivan. 'Do your best this term, and I do hope you'll be happy at your new school. Write to me soon.'

The twins got into a carriage where three or four other girls were already sitting and chattering. They said nothing, but looked with interest at the scores of girls passing by their compartment to their places farther up the train.

At their last school the twins had been the oldest and biggest there – but now they were among the youngest! At Redroofs all the girls had looked at Pat and Isabel with awe and admiration – the two wonderful head girls – but now the twins were looking at others in the same way! Tall, dignified girls from the top form walked by, talking. Merry-voiced girls from other forms ran to get their places, calling out to one another. Younger ones scrambled into the carriages as the guard went along to warn one that the train was about to go.

The journey was quite fun. Everyone had packets of sandwiches to eat at half-past twelve, and the train steward brought bottles of ginger beer and lemonade, and cups of tea. At half-past two the train drew in at a little platform. A big notice said 'Alight here for St Clare's School'.

There were big school-coaches waiting outside and the girls piled themselves in them, chattering and laughing. One of them turned to Pat and Isabel.

'There's the school, look! Up on that hill there!'

The twins looked. They saw a pleasant white building, built of large white stones, with two towers, one at each end. It looked down into the valley, over big playing-fields and gardens.

'Not nearly so nice as Redroofs,' said Pat to Isabel. 'Do you remember how sweet our old school used to look in the evening sun? Its red roof was glowing, and it looked warm and welcoming – not cold and white like St Clare's.'

For a few minutes both girls were homesick for their old school and their old friends. They knew nobody at St

Clare's at all. They couldn't call out 'Hallo, there!' to everyone as they had done each term before. They didn't like the look of any of the girls, who seemed much more noisy and boisterous than the ones at Redroofs. It was all horrid.

'Anyway, we are lucky to have got each other,' said Isabel to Pat. 'I would have hated to come here all alone. Nobody seems to talk to us at all.'

It was the twins' own fault, if they had but known it. They both looked 'stuck-up' as one girl whispered to another. Nobody felt much inclined to talk to them or make friends.

There was the same rush of unpacking and settling in as there is at all boarding schools. The big dormitories were full of girls putting away their things, hanging up their dresses and putting photographs out on their little dressing-tables.

There were a good many dormitories at St Clare's. Pat and Isabel were in number 7, where there were eight white beds, all exactly alike. Each was in its own cubicle surrounded by curtains that could be drawn open or closed, just as the girls pleased. Pat's bed was next to Isabel's, much to their joy.

When the girls had unpacked a tall girl came into the dormitory calling out, 'Any new girls here?'

Pat and Isabel nodded their heads. 'We are new,' said Pat.

'Hallo, twins!' said the tall girl, smiling, as she looked at the two sisters so exactly alike. 'Are you Patricia and

Isabel O'Sullivan? Matron wants to see you.'

Pat and Isabel went with the girl to where the school matron sat in her comfortable room, surrounded by cupboards, chests and shelves. She was a fat, jolly-looking person, but her eyes were very sharp indeed.

'You can't deceive Matron over anything,' whispered their guide. 'Keep in her good books if you can.'

Matron checked over sheets, towels and clothes with them. 'You will be responsible for mending all your own belongings,' she said.

'Good gracious!' said Pat. 'There were sewing-maids at our other school to do that.'

'Shocking!' said Matron, briskly. 'Well, there are no sewing-maids here. So be careful of your things, and remember that they cost your parents money.'

'Our parents don't need to worry about torn clothes,' began Pat. 'Why, once at Redroofs I got caught in some barbed wire, and everything I had on was torn to bits. They were so torn that the sewing-maid said she couldn't mend a thing, and . . .'

'Well, I would have made you mend every hole, every rent, every tear,' said Matron, her eyes beginning to sparkle. 'There's one thing I can't bear, and that's carelessness and waste. Now mind you . . . What is it, Millicent?'

Another girl had come into the room with a pile of towels, and the twins were very glad that Matron's attention was no longer given to them. They slipped out of the room quietly.

'I don't like Matron,' said Pat. 'And I've a jolly good

mind to tear something so badly that it can't be mended, and that would give her something to think about!'

'Let's go and see what the school is like,' said Isabel, slipping her arm into Pat's. 'It seems much barer and colder somehow than dear old Redroofs.'

The twins began to explore. The classrooms seemed much the same as any classrooms, and the view from the windows was magnificent. The twins peeped into the studies. At their old school they had shared a fine study between them, but here there were no studies except for the top form girls and the fifth form. The younger girls shared a big common-room, where there was a radio, a record player and a big library of books. Shelves ran round the common-room and each girl shared part of a shelf, putting her belongings there, and keeping them tidy.

There were small music rooms for practising, a fine art room, an enormous gym, which was also used for assembly and concerts, and a good laboratory. The mistresses had two common-rooms and their own bedrooms, and the head lived in a small wing by herself, having her own bedroom in one of the towers, and a beautiful sitting-room below.

'It's not so bad,' said Pat, after they had explored everywhere. 'And the playing-fields are fine. There are many more tennis-courts here than at Redroofs – but of course it's a much bigger school.'

'I don't like big schools,' said Isabel. 'I like smaller schools, where you are somebody, not just a little nobody tucked away among heaps of others!'

They went into the common-room. The radio was on and a band was playing cheerful music, which was almost drowned by the chatter of the girls. Some of them looked up as Pat and Isabel came in.

'Hallo, twins!' said a cheeky-looking girl with curly golden hair. 'Which is which?'

'I'm Patricia O'Sullivan and my twin sister is Isabel,' said Pat.

'Well, welcome to St Clare's,' said the girl. 'I'm Hilary Wentworth, and you're in the same dormitory as I am. Have you been to boarding school before?'

'Of course,' said Pat. 'We went to Redroofs.'

'The school for snobs!' said a dark haired girl, looking up. 'My cousin went there – and didn't she fancy herself when she came home! Expected to be waited on hand and foot, and couldn't even bear to sew a button on!'

'Shut up,' said Hilary, seeing that Pat went red. 'You always talk too much, Janet. Well, Patricia and Isabel, this isn't the same kind of school as Redroofs – we work hard and play hard here, and we're jolly well taught to be independent and responsible!'

'We didn't want to come here,' said Pat. 'We wanted to go to Ringmere School, where our friends were going. Nobody thought much of St Clare's at Redroofs.'

'Dear, dear, dear, is that so?' said Janet, raising her eyebrows till they were almost lost in the dark hair on her forehead. 'Well, the point is, my dear twins – not what you think of St Clare's – but what St Clare's thinks of *you*! Quite a different thing. Personally, I think it's a pity that you didn't go somewhere else. I've a feeling you won't fit in here.'

'Janet, do be quiet,' said Hilary. 'It's not fair to say things like that to new girls. Let them settle in. Come on, Patricia – come on, Isabel – I'll show you the way to the head's room. You'll have to go and say hallo to her before supper.'

Pat and Isabel were almost boiling over with rage at what dark-haired Janet had said. Hilary pushed the twins out of the room. 'Don't take too much notice of Janet,' she said. 'She always says exactly what she thinks, which is very nice when she thinks complimentary things about people, but not so good when she doesn't. You'll get used to her.'

'I hope we shan't,' said Pat stiffly. 'I like good manners, something that was taught at our school anyway, even if it's not known here!'

'Oh, don't be stuffy,' said Hilary. 'Look, that's the head's room. Knock on the door first – and try some of your good manners on Miss Theobald!'

The twins knocked on the door. A pleasant, rather deep voice called 'Come in!' Pat opened the door and the twins went in.

The head mistress was sitting at her desk, writing. She looked up and smiled at the girls.

'I needn't ask who you are,' she said. 'You are so alike that you must be the O'Sullivan twins!'

'Yes,' said the girls, looking at their new head mistress. She was grey haired, with a dignified, serious face that broke into a lovely smile at times. She shook hands with each twin.

'I am very glad to welcome you to St Clare's,' she said. 'I hope that one day we shall be proud of you. Do your best for us and St Clare's will be able to do its best for you!'

'We'll try,' said Isabel, and then was quite surprised at herself to find that she had said that. She didn't mean to try at all! She looked at Pat. Pat said nothing but stared straight in front of her.

'I know your mother quite well,' said Miss Theobald. 'I was glad when she decided to send you here. You must tell her that when you write to her, and give her my kind regards.'

'Yes, Miss Theobald,' said Pat. The head mistress nodded at them with a smile, and turned to her desk again.

'What funny children!' she thought to herself. 'Anyone might think they hated to be here! Perhaps they are just shy or homesick.'

But they were neither shy nor homesick. They were just two obstinate girls determined to make the worst of things because they hadn't been sent to the school of their choice!

3.
Bad beginning

The twins soon found that St Clare's was quite different from their old school. Even the beds were not nearly so comfortable! And instead of being allowed to have their own pretty bedspreads and quilt to match, every girl had to have the same.

'I hate being the same as everyone else!' said Pat. 'Goodness – if only we were allowed to have what we liked, wouldn't we make everyone stare!'

'What I hate most is being one of the young ones,' said Isabel, dismally. 'I hate being spoken to as if I were about six, when the top form or fifth-form girls say anything to me. It's, "Here, you – get out of my way! Hi, you! Fetch me a book from the library!" It's just too bad.'

The standard of work was higher at St Clare's than at most schools, and although the twins had good brains, they found that they were rather behind their form in many ways, and this, too, annoyed them very much. They had so hoped that they would impress the others in so many ways – and it seemed as if they were even less than nobodies!

They soon got to know the girls in their form. Hilary Wentworth was one and the sharp-tongued Janet Robins. Then there was a quiet, straight-haired girl called Vera

Johns and a rather haughty-looking girl called Sheila Naylor, whose manners were very arrogant. The twins didn't like her at all.

'I don't know what she's got to be so haughty about!' said Pat to Isabel. 'It's true she's got a lovely home because I've seen a photo of it on her dressing-table – but my goodness, she sometimes talks like a rag-and-bone man. Then she seems to remember she mustn't talk like that and goes all haughty and silly.'

Then there was Kathleen Gregory, a frightened-looking girl of fifteen, who was the only one who really tried to make friends with the twins the first week. Most of the other girls left them alone, except for being polite, and telling them the ways of the school. They all thought that Pat and Isabel were very 'stuck-up'.

'Kathleen is funny,' said Isabel. 'She seems so eager to make friends with us, and lend us books and shares her sweets. She's been at St Clare's for a year, and she doesn't seem to have any friends at all. She keeps asking me to walk with her when we go out, and I keep saying I can't because I've got you.'

'I feel rather sorry for her somehow,' said Pat. 'She reminds me of a lost dog trying to find a new master!'

Isabel laughed. 'Yes, that's just it! I think of all the girls that I like Hilary the best in our form. She's so natural and jolly – a real sport.'

The twins were very much in awe of the older girls, who seemed very grown-up to them. The top form especially seemed almost as old and even more dignified than the mistresses! The head girl, Winifred James, spoke a few words to the twins the first week. She was a tall, clever-looking girl with pale blue eyes and pretty soft hair. St Clare's was proud of her, for she had passed many difficult exams with flying colours.

'You are the new girls, aren't you?' she said. 'Settle in and do your best. Come to me if you are in any difficulty. I'm the head girl and I should like to help you if ever I can.'

'Oh, thank you,' said the twins, feeling quite overcome at being addressed by the head girl. Winifred went off with her friends, and the twins stared after her.

'She's rather nice,' said Isabel. 'In fact, I think most of the top form girls are nice, though they're awfully serious and proper.'

They liked their form mistress, Miss Roberts, too, though she would stand no nonsense at all. Sometimes Pat would try to argue about something, and say, 'Well, that's what I was taught at my old school!'

Then Miss Roberts would say, 'Really? Well, do it that way if you like – but you won't get very far up your form! Do remember that what suits one school won't work in another. Still, if you like to be obstinate, that's your own look-out!'

Then Pat would stick out her lower lip, and Isabel would go red, and the rest of the form would smile to itself. Those 'stuck-up' girls were having to learn a lesson!

The art mistress, Miss Walker, was a merry soul, young and jolly, and very good at her work. She was pleased to find that both twins could draw and paint well. Pat and Isabel loved Miss Walker's classes. They were very go-as-you-please, much more like their old school. The girls were allowed to chatter and laugh as they worked, and it was often a very noisy class indeed.

Mam'zelle was not so easy-going. She was very strict, elderly, conscientious and fierce. She wore pince-nez glasses on her nose, and these were always slipping off when she was cross, which was fairly often. She had enormous feet, and a rather harsh voice that the twins hated at first. But Mam'zelle had also a great sense of fun, and if anything tickled her she would go off into enormous roars of laughter that set the whole class laughing too.

Pat and Isabel came up against Mam'zelle very much at first, for although they could speak and understand French quite well, they had never bothered very much about French grammar and rules. And Mam'zelle bothered a great deal about those!

'You girls, Patricia and Isabel!' she cried. 'It is not enough to speak my language! You write it abominably! See this essay – it is abominable, abominable!'

'Abominable' was Mam'zelle's favourite adjective. She used it for everything – the weather, a broken pencil, the girls, and her own glasses when they slipped off her big nose! Pat and Isabel called her 'Mam'zelle Abominable' between themselves, and were secretly more than a little afraid of the loud-voiced, good-hearted big Frenchwoman.

History was taken throughout the school by Miss

Kennedy, and her classes were a riot. Poor Miss Kennedy was a frump, and could not manage any class of girls for more than five minutes. She was nervous and serious, always tremendously polite, listened to every question that was put to her no matter how silly, and explained every difficulty at great length. She never seemed to see that half the time the girls were pulling her leg.

'Before Miss Kennedy came we had her friend Miss Lewis,' said Hilary to the twins. 'She was marvellous. Then she fell ill in the middle of last term, and asked the head to have her friend, Miss Kennedy, until she was well enough to come back. Old Kenny has got umpteen degrees, and is supposed to be even cleverer than the head – but my word, she's a goose!'

Bit by bit the twins sorted out the various girls and mistresses, grew to know the classes and the customs of the school, and settled in. But even when two weeks had gone by they had not got used to being 'nobodies instead of somebodies' as Pat complained.

One thing they found most annoying. It was the custom at St Clare's for the younger girls to wait on the two top forms. The fifth and sixth form girls shared studies, two friends having a study between them.

They were allowed to furnish these studies themselves, very simply and, in cold weather, to have their own fire there, and to have tea by themselves instead of in the hall with the others.

One day a girl came into the common-room where the twins were reading and called to Janet, 'Hi, Janet – Kay

Longden wants you. You're to light her fire and make some toast for her.'

Janet got up without a word and went out. Pat and Isabel stared after her in surprise.

'Golly! What cheek of Kay Longden to send a message to Janet like that! I'm jolly sure I wouldn't go and light anybody's fire!' said Pat.

'And neither would I!' said Isabel. 'Let one of the maids light it – or Kay herself.'

Hilary Wentworth looked up from her embroidery. 'It will be your turn next!' she said. 'Look out next week for sudden messages, twins. If the fifth or sixth want anything doing, they expect us to do it. It's the custom of the school – and anyway, it doesn't hurt us. We can have our turn at sending messages and ordering the lower forms about when we're top formers ourselves!'

'I never heard of such a thing!' cried Pat, furiously. 'I jolly well won't go and do a thing for anyone. Our parents didn't send us here to wait on lazy top formers. Let them light their own fires and make their own toast! Isabel and I won't do a thing! And they can't make us either!'

'Hoity-toity!' said Hilary. 'I never knew such a hot temper. Get further away from me, Pat, you're scorching me!'

Pat slammed down her book and flounced out of the room. Isabel followed her. All the other girls laughed.

'Idiots!' said Hilary. 'Who do they think they are, anyway? Why don't they get some sense? They wouldn't be at all bad if only they would shake down. I vote we knock some of their corners off, else we shall hate them like anything!'

'OK,' said Vera. 'I'm willing. I say, what a shock for them when they find they've got to wait on the top formers too. I hope they get Belinda Towers. I had to wait on her last term, and my word, didn't she make me skip around! She got it into her head that I was lazy, and I'm sure I lost a whole stone rushing round in circles after her one week!'

The girls laughed. Sheila Naylor spoke haughtily. 'The worst of people who think they are somebodies is that so often they are just nobodies. I'm sure I shouldn't even trouble to *know* Patricia and Isabel at home.'

'Oh, come off the high horse, Sheila,' said Hilary. 'The twins aren't as bad as all that. Anyway, there are a few shocks in store for them!'

So there were – and they came the very next week!

4.

A little trouble for the twins

One day, about half-past five when the twins were writing home, one of the fourth formers popped her head in at the door.

'Hi, there!' she said. 'Where are the O'Sullivan twins? Belinda Towers wants one of them.'

Pat and Isabel looked up. Pat went red. 'What does she want us for?' she asked.

'How should I know?' said the messenger. 'She's been out over the fields this afternoon, so maybe she wants her boots cleaned. Anyway, jump to it, or you'll get into a row!'

The messenger disappeared. The twins sat still. Hilary looked at them.

'Go on, idiots,' she said. 'One of you must go and find out what Belinda wants. Don't keep her waiting, for goodness' sake. She's got about as hot a temper as you have, Pat.'

'I'll go,' said Isabel, and got up. But Pat pulled her down.

'No, don't,' she said. 'I'm not going to clean anybody's boots! And you're not, either.'

'Look here, Pat, don't be goofy,' said Janet. 'Belinda may want to tell you something. Golly, she might want to ask you if you'll play in a match. She's captain, you know.'

'Oh,' said Pat. 'Well, I shouldn't think it's that because neither Isabel nor I have ever played lacrosse before, and we were pretty bad at it yesterday.'

'Well, do go!' said Hilary. 'You've got to go in the end, so why not go now?'

Another girl popped her head in at the door. 'I say! Belinda's foaming at the mouth! Where *are* those O'Sullivan twins? They'll get it hot if one of them doesn't go along!'

'Come on,' said Pat to Isabel. 'We'll go and see what she wants. But I'm not doing any boot-cleaning or fire-lighting, that's certain. And neither are you!'

The two got up and went out of the room. Everybody giggled. 'Wish I could go and see what happens!' said Janet. 'I love to see Belinda in a rage!'

Belinda Towers was in her study with Pamela Harrison, the girl who shared it with her. Pat opened the door.

'Knock, can't you!' cried Belinda. 'Barging in like that! And I should jolly well like to know why you've been all this time coming. I sent for you ages ago.'

Pat was rather taken aback, and Isabel did not dare to say anything.

'Well, haven't you a tongue between you?' said Belinda. 'My goodness, Pam, did you ever see such a pair of idiots? Well, as you've *both* come, you can both do a spot of work for me. I want my boots cleaned and Pam's too. And make up my fire for me and put the kettle on to boil. You'll find water just down the passage. Come on, Pam – we'll go and collect our prep and by that time the kettle will be boiling and we'll make tea.'

The two big girls walked to the door. Pat, very red and angry, stopped them.

'I didn't come to St Clare's to wait on the older girls,' she said. 'Neither did my twin. We shan't clean your boots nor put on the kettle, nor make up the fire.'

Belinda stopped as if she had been shot. She stared at Pat as if she was some particularly nasty insect. Then she turned to Pam.

'Did you hear that?' she said. 'Talk about cheek! All right, my girl – no walks down the town for you. Just remember that!'

The twins stared at Belinda in dismay. The St Clare girls were allowed to go down to the town in twos to buy anything they needed, or to look at the shops, or even to go to the cinema if they had permission. Surely Belinda hadn't the power to stop them doing that?

'I don't think you've any right to say that,' said Pat. 'I shall go to Winifred James and tell her what you've said and ask her about it.'

'Well, I'm blessed!' said Belinda, flaring up angrily, her red hair seeming to flame too. 'You *do* want taking down a peg, don't you? Run off to Winifred, by all means. Tell your little tales and see what happens.'

Pat and Isabel went out of the study. Isabel was very much upset, and wanted to stay and do what Belinda had ordered, but Pat was furious. She took hold of her twin's arm and marched her off to Winifred's study. The head girl had her own study, which she shared with no one. Pat dared not go in without knocking. So, she knocked quietly.

'Come in!' said Winifred's voice. The twins went in. Winifred was working at a table, 'What is it?' she said. 'I'm rather busy.'

'Please, Winifred,' said Pat. 'Belinda Towers ordered us to clean her boots, make up her fire and put her kettle on. And when we said we wouldn't she said we weren't to go down into the town. So we've come to ask you about it.'

'I see,' said Winifred. 'Well, it's the custom of this school to get the juniors to wait on the seniors within reason. It doesn't hurt them. When you go to Rome, you must do as Rome does, you know.'

'But we didn't want to come to St Clare's, so we don't want to follow silly customs of that sort,' said Pat. 'Do we, Isabel?'

Isabel shook her head. She couldn't think how Pat could dare to speak to Winifred like that. Her knees were shaking as she stood! She was never so brave as Pat.

'I think I should wait a little while before you call our customs silly,' said Winifred. 'Now listen – can't you clean boots? Don't you know how to make up a fire? Have you never put a kettle on to boil?'

'We never had to at Redroofs,' said Pat, obstinately. 'And we don't at home either.'

'I don't think I'd know how to clean muddy boots!' said Isabel, thinking that perhaps if she said that, Winifred would let them off.

'Good Heavens!' said Winifred in disgust. 'To think you're nearly fifteen and you don't know how to clean boots! How shocking! All the more reason why you should learn at once. Go back to Belinda's study and try to do what she tells you. I know she's hot tempered and will tick you off properly, but honestly I think you both deserve it. Do have a little common sense.'

Winifred turned back to her books. The twins, red in the face, went out of the room and closed the door quietly. They stood outside and looked at each other.

'I shan't clean her beastly boots, even if I have to stay in the school grounds the whole of the term and not go down into the town once,' said Pat, angrily.

'Oh, Pat! I do want to get a new hair brush and some chocolate,' said Isabel, in dismay. 'Come on – we'd better do it. The others will think we're terribly silly if we kick up such a fuss. They laugh at us enough already.'

'Well, you can do it if you like, but *I'm* not going to!' said Pat, and she stalked off, her nose in the air, leaving Isabel by herself.

Isabel stood for a little while, thinking. 'Supposing I go and do the jobs that Belinda wants done,' she thought. 'That means that I can go down into the town if I want to – and as Pat is so exactly like me, she can go down too, if we each go at different times, with somebody else. No one will ever know! That will trick Belinda nicely!'

Isabel went to Belinda's study. It was empty. On the floor lay two pairs of very muddy boots. The owners had evidently been across some very clayey fields. Isabel picked them up. Goodness, however did anyone set about cleaning boots like that?

She heard someone passing and went to the door. She saw Kathleen Gregory and called her.

'Kathleen! Look at these awful boots! How do I clean them?'

Kathleen stopped at once, looking delighted. She was pleased that Isabel should ask her help. 'You want to scrape them first and get all the clay off,' she said. 'Come on, I'll help you.'

Soon the two girls were cleaning the muddy boots thoroughly. They took quite a time. Kathleen talked hard all the time, pouring out all kinds of information about how her mother spoilt her at home, and what a lot of presents she was always getting from her parents, and how much money they sent her for her birthday.

Isabel listened politely, grateful for Kathleen's help, but thinking that she was rather silly. After all, everyone got presents for their birthdays, and everyone had money on their birthdays! When the boots were finished she put them neatly together on the shoe-shelf, and made up the fire. Kathleen showed her where to fill the kettle and set it on to boil. Just then Belinda and Pam came back.

'Oh, so you decided to be sensible, I see,' she said. 'Where's your twin? Did she help you?'

'No,' said Isabel.

'Well, tell her from me that there's to be no going down to the town till she does her bit,' said Belinda, flinging herself down in a chair. 'I won't have new girls behaving as if they owned the place! Is the kettle boiling yet? My goodness, the water's cold! How long has this kettle been on?'

'I've only just this minute put it on, Belinda,' said Isabel.

'I suppose it didn't occur to you that it would be a good idea to make up the fire and put the kettle on *first*, before you did the boots?' said Belinda, sarcastically. 'I suppose you thought it would be a great pity if the kettle boiled whilst you were doing the boots? I don't know what you kids are coming to nowadays. When I was your age I had a lot more common sense. Clear out now. And see that you come running next time I send a message!'

Isabel went out of the room. Just as she was closing the door Belinda yelled to her again. 'And mind you tell that obstinate twin of yours what I said. If she disobeys I'll report her to Miss Theobald.'

Isabel fled. She felt upset and angry and very foolish. Why, why, why hadn't she put the kettle on first? No wonder that Belinda had thought her stupid.

Isabel told Pat what had happened. 'And she says you're not to go down to the town till you do your bit,' she said. 'But you can, Pat – because no one will know if it's you or me going! I don't think anyone can tell the difference between us yet.'

'All right,' said Pat, ungraciously. 'But I don't think much of you for giving in like that, Isabel. Fancy cleaning those dirty boots!'

'Well, I rather enjoyed it,' said Isabel. 'Kathleen helped me. First we . . .'

'Oh, shut up,' said Pat, rudely. 'Go and write an essay

about how to clean boots and boil kettles if you want to, but don't preach to me!'

Isabel was hurt. But Pat could not be angry with her twin for long. Before an hour had gone by she had slipped her arm through Isabel's. 'Sorry, old thing,' she said. 'I wasn't really angry with you. I was furious with Belinda, and took it out on you. Never mind! I'll trick Belinda all right and go down to the town whenever I like, pretending that I am you.'

Pat was as good as her word! She slipped down to the town with one or other of the girls, pretending that she was Isabel, and nobody knew the difference! How the twins giggled about their trick!

And then something happened. Pat had gone down to the town with Kathleen after tea, when a messenger came to the common-room. Isabel was putting on a record, and she jumped when she heard Pat's name called.

'Patricia O'Sullivan! Belinda wants you!'

'Well – I must pretend to be Pat,' thought Isabel. 'But why does Belinda want Pat? I'm the one that does her jobs just now. She knows Pat doesn't.'

She soon knew what Belinda wanted. The sports captain was making out a list and she looked up as Isabel came in.

'Pat O'Sullivan, you played well in the lacrosse practice yesterday,' she said. 'I was watching. You're a silly, obstinate kid, but I'm not counting that against you where lacrosse is concerned. I'm putting you down for the match on Saturday.'

Isabel stared in surprise. How pleased Pat would be! Isabel muttered a thank you and sped, longing for Pat to come back so that she might tell her the good news.

When Pat heard she stood speechless. 'In a match already!' she cried. 'How decent of Belinda! If she'd been spiteful she'd have left me out for months.'

Then she became silent and went away by herself. Isabel knew quite well what she was thinking, because she was worrying about the same thing herself.

Soon Pat came over and put her arm through Isabel's. 'I feel a beast now,' said Pat. 'I've let you do all the jobs – and I've gone down to the town all I wanted to, just to spite Belinda. I thought we were being rather clever to play a trick like that. But now I don't think so.'

'Nor do I,' said Isabel. 'I just feel mean and dishonest. It was decent of Belinda to stick you in the match, although she must have felt furious with you – but we haven't been decent. And, you know, Pat, I don't really mind doing anything for the top formers. They are awfully good sorts, really. After all, why should anyone mind putting a kettle on to boil and making toast? Belinda talks to me quite a lot now, and I like her, though I'm a bit afraid of her hot temper.'

Pat rubbed her nose and frowned. She always did that when she felt uncomfortable. She suddenly got up and went to the door. 'I'm going to tell Belinda I've played her a trick,' she said. 'I'm not playing in the match on Saturday knowing I've been mean.'

She ran out. She went to Belinda's study and knocked

on the door. Belinda yelled, 'Come in!' She looked surprised when she saw Pat.

'Hallo, Isabel!' she said. 'I didn't send for you.'

'I'm not Isabel, I'm Pat,' said Pat. 'I've come about the match on Saturday.'

'Well, there's nothing more to tell you than I told you just now,' said Belinda.

'That's just it. You didn't tell *me* just now – you told my twin, Isabel,' said Pat. 'I was down in the town. I know you said I wasn't to go – but I'm so like my twin that I knew nobody would ever know.'

'Rather a mean trick, Pat,' said Belinda, in a scornful voice.

'I know,' said Pat, in a troubled voice. 'I'm sorry for that. I've come to say thank you for putting me in the match, but of course I don't expect to play now. Anyway, I couldn't have you being decent to me if I was playing a trick just to pay you out. And I'll take my share of the jobs with Isabel now. I was silly before. That's all, Belinda.'

'No – not quite all,' said Belinda, in an unexpectedly gentle voice. 'I've something to say too. You've done something rather mean, but you've been big enough to put it right. We'll say no more about it – but you'll play in the match on Saturday!'

Pat flew off to tell Isabel, her heart leaping for joy. How decent Belinda was! How could she ever have thought her beastly and horrid?

'I'll boil her old kettle and clean her old boots and even scrub the floor now!' thought Pat. 'And my word

I'll shoot a dozen goals on Saturday, see if I don't!'

She didn't – but she shot one very difficult one – and how pleased she was to hear both Isabel *and* Belinda shout, 'Well done, Pat! Oh, good shot, good shot!'

5.

A battle with Mam'zelle

Every week the twins' form had marks for different subjects. Pat and Isabel had been used to being top in most things at Redroofs, and it was with shame and dismay that they found they were nearer the bottom than the top at St Clare's.

Hilary saw them looking unhappy about it and she spoke to them. 'You've got to remember that you are the only new girls in your form,' she said. 'The rest of us have been in the form at least two terms, and we are used to St Clare ways. Cheer up!'

It was 'Mam'zelle Abominable' who really upset the twins. She would not make allowances for them, and when they sent in badly written French essays, she was very angry.

She had the pile of French books on the desk before her, all neatly marked with '*Très bien*' or '*Bien*' or '*Excellent*'. But when she took out Pat's book and Isabel's they were both marked the same. '*Abominable!*'

'This will not do!' cried Mam'zelle, banging her big hand down on the books. '*C'est abominable!* You will write the whole essay again today, and you will bring it to me after supper.'

'We can't write it again today, Mam'zelle,' said Isabel, politely. 'We've got art this afternoon, and after tea we've got permission to go to the cinema together. We shan't have time to rewrite it. Can we do it tomorrow?'

'Oh, *que vous êtes insupportable*!' raged Mam'zelle, stamping her foot on the floor, and making the books on her desk jump and slide. 'How dare you talk to me like this! You present me with a shocking, yes, a shocking essay, and then you talk of going to the cinema. You will not go! You will stay behind and write the essay for me. And if there is more than one mistake you will write it all over again! That is certain!'

'But – but – we've got the tickets,' said Isabel. 'We had to book our seats. We . . .'

'I do not care about seats, I do not care about booking!' shouted Mam'zelle, now quite losing her temper. 'All I care about is that you should learn good French, which is what I am here for. You will bring me the essays tonight.'

Isabel looked ready to cry. Pat looked mutinous, and stuck out her lower lip. Everyone else enjoyed the row and a few of the girls were secretly very pleased to see the twins taken down a peg. Nobody dared to be inattentive after that, and the lesson went very smoothly, though Pat was sulky and joined in the lesson as little as she dared.

When the lesson was over the twins had a few words together. 'I'm going to the cinema!' said Pat.

'Oh, no, Pat!' said Isabel, shocked. 'We can't do that. We'd really get into a terrible row. We'd better stay behind and do the work again. For goodness' sake let's!'

'I'm GOING to the cinema!' said Pat, obstinately. 'I'll fit in the beastly essay somehow, and you must too. Let's do it directly after dinner. I don't care how badly I do it either.'

But after dinner they had to go to a meeting of their form to plan nature rambles, so there was no time then. Art took up the whole of the afternoon. Isabel began to be worried. Suppose Pat insisted on going to the cinema even if they hadn't rewritten their essays? She could not imagine what Mam'zelle would say.

'Let's miss our tea,' said Isabel to Pat as they ran down the stairs after the art lesson. 'We could do our essays then.'

'Miss my tea! No, thank you!' said Pat. 'I'm jolly hungry. I don't know why art makes me hungry, but it always does. And I know Janet has got a big pot of plum jam sent to her that she's opening this tea-time. I'm not going to miss my share!'

Isabel was hungry too, and she weakly gave way. She knew that if they were going to get into the cinema in time they wouldn't have a moment to spare for anything after tea, let alone rewriting essays! 'I really shan't go to the cinema,' she thought. 'I daren't. Honestly, I think Mam'zelle Abominable would go up in smoke if she heard we'd gone.'

But after tea Pat dragged Isabel off to the dormitory to get her hat and coat. 'We're not really going, Pat, surely!' cried Isabel.

'Indeed we are!' said Pat, sticking out her lower lip. 'Come on.'

'But, Pat – we'll really get into a simply enormous

row!' said Isabel. 'It isn't worth it. Perhaps Mam'zelle will give us an hour's extra work every day or something like that. Janet told me that once she had to stop in after tea for a whole week and write out French verbs for cheeking Mam'zelle just a little bit. And she wouldn't count this a little thing.'

'Don't be a coward, Isabel,' said Pat. 'I've got a plan. Mam'zelle said we were to take our essays to her after supper, didn't she? But she didn't say what time after supper! So when we're in bed and think the others are asleep, we'll slip down to the common-room in our dressing-gowns, rewrite our essays then – and give them to Mam'zelle when they're finished!'

'Pat! I'd never dare to!' cried poor Isabel. 'Think of going to find Mam'zelle at that time of night in our dressing-gowns. You must be mad.'

'Well, Mam'zelle has *made* me feel mad,' said obstinate Pat. 'Anyway, I don't care what happens. You know we never wanted to come to St Clare's – and if it's going to treat us like this, I'm jolly sure I won't stay. I'll get expelled!'

'Pat, you're not to say things like that!' said Isabel. 'Think what Mummy and Daddy would say!'

'Well it's their fault for sending us here,' said Pat, who really was in a great rage.

'Yes, but, Pat – think how awful it would be if Redroofs heard that we'd been sent away from St Clare's,' said Isabel, in a low voice.

Pat's eyes filled with tears. She didn't want to think of that. 'Come on,' she said, gruffly. 'I'm not going to change my mind now. If you're coming with me, come. If not, you can jolly well be a coward by yourself!'

But Isabel was not going to be left by herself. She put on her hat and coat. Janet came into the room as the twins were going out.

'Hallo, Hallo!' she said. 'So you *are* going to the cinema after all! Whenever did you find time to rewrite your French?'

'We haven't done it,' said Pat. Janet gave a long whistle and stared at the twins in surprise.

'I wouldn't like to be in your shoes tomorrow when you tell Mam'zelle that!' she said. 'You really are a couple of idiots. I can't think why you should go out of your way to make things difficult for yourselves!'

The twins did not answer. They ran downstairs and were soon in the town. But neither of them really enjoyed the show, although it was a fine film. They had to leave a little before the end to get back to supper in time. There was a debate afterwards that they had to go to, and they both wished they could miss it. But it was taken by Winifred James, the head girl, and neither of the twins dared to ask if they might miss it.

Nine o'clock was the bedtime for their form and the two forms above them. Chattering and laughing, the girls went upstairs and undressed. Usually a mistress came to see that all the girls were in bed, and switched off the lights – but tonight Hilary announced that she was to see to this.

'Miss Roberts is with Miss Theobald,' she said, 'so I'm

on duty tonight. Hurry, all of you, because the light will go off in five minutes' time, and you'll have to finish in the dark if you're not ready.'

Two girls, Joan and Doris, began to have a pillow-fight when they heard that Miss Roberts was not coming. Bang-thud went the two pillows, and the girls shrieked with laughter. But it wasn't quite so funny when one of the pillows split and feathers poured out into the air!

'Golly!' said Joan. 'Look at my pillow. Hilary, for goodness' sake don't turn the lights off yet. I *must* pick up some of these feathers!'

'Sorry,' said Hilary. 'You'll have to do it in the morning. Lights are going out now! Miss Roberts will be along to see we're all right in an hour's time, so let's hope she won't spot the feathers all over the place. She'll think the cat's been chasing hens in our dormitory!'

The lights snapped out. All the girls were in bed except Joan and Doris, who were still groping for feathers. They had to finish undressing and cleaning their teeth in the dark. Joan upset her tooth-mug and Doris banged her ankle on her chest-of-drawers and groaned deeply. Janet giggled, and Kathleen Gregory went off into a spasm of laughter that gave her hiccups.

'Shut up, Kathleen,' ordered Hilary. 'You're hiccupping on purpose. I know you!'

'I'm *not*!' said Kathleen, indignantly, and gave such an enormous hiccup that her bed shook. Janet couldn't stop giggling. Every time she tried to stop, poor Kathleen hiccupped again and Janet went off into more gurgles.

Even the twins, anxious though they were to have everyone going to sleep quickly, could not help laughing. Hilary lost her temper and sat up in bed.

'You're all meanies!' she cried. 'If anyone comes along and hears you making this row I'll be blamed because I'm head of the dormitory. Shut up, Janet – and Kathleen, for goodness' sake get a drink of water. How do you suppose we're going to sleep with you hiccupping like that?'

'Sorry, Hilary,' said Kathleen, with another hiccup. 'I'll get up and get some water.'

'Get into bed, Joan and Doris,' said Hilary, snuggling down again. 'I don't care if you've cleaned your teeth and brushed your hair or not. GET INTO BED!'

In five minutes' time there was peace in the dormitory except for an occasional small and subdued hiccup from Kathleen and a smothered giggle from Janet.

The twins lay awake, listening for the others to go to sleep. They were worried because Miss Roberts was coming in about an hour's time. They could not wait a whole hour before going down to the common-room. For one thing, Mam'zelle would have gone to bed by the time they had finished their essays!

'Isabel!' whispered Pat at last. 'Isabel! I think they're all asleep. Get up and put on your dressing-gown.'

'But Miss Roberts hasn't been in yet,' whispered back Isabel.

'We'll put our bolsters down our beds, so that they'll look like our bodies,' said Pat. 'Come on!'

They got up quietly and slipped on their dressing-gowns. They pushed their bolsters down their beds and hoped that Miss Roberts wouldn't notice anything different when she came. Then out of the door they went, and down the dimly lit stairs to the common-room, which was just below their own dormitory.

Pat shut the door and turned on the light. The two girls sat down and took out their French books. Mam'zelle had marked all the mistakes, and carefully and laboriously the two girls wrote out the essays again.

'Well, mine had fifteen mistakes before, and I hope it hasn't got more than five now!' said Isabel. 'Blow Mam'zelle Abominable! I'm so sleepy. And oh, Pat – *dare* we go and find Mam'zelle now, do you think? My knees are shaking at the very thought!'

'Oh, don't be stupid,' said Pat. 'What can she say to us, anyway? We've done the essays again – and she said give them to her after supper – and we are going to do that, aren't we?'

The essays were finished. Now they had to find Mam'zelle. Where would she be? In one of the mistresses' common-rooms – or in her own bedroom – or where?

'Well, come on,' said Pat, at last. 'We must go and find her. Cheer up, Isabel.'

The twins slipped out of the common-room and went to the first of the mistresses' rooms. The light was out and the room was quite dark. No one was there at all. As they went on their way to the second common-room, they heard Mam'zelle's voice in one of the classrooms! What luck!

'She's in the upper third classroom,' whispered Pat. 'I don't know who's there with her, but it doesn't matter. The art mistress, I expect – Mam'zelle's awfully friendly with Miss Walker.'

They knocked at the upper third door. A surprised voice called, 'Come in! Who's there?'

Pat opened the door and the twins went in. And oh my goodness, who should be with Mam'zelle, studying a big French chart, but the head, Miss Theobald herself!

The twins were so shocked that they stood and stared with wide eyes. Mam'zelle cried '*Tiens*!' in a loud and amazed voice, and Miss Theobald said nothing at all.

Mam'zelle recovered first. 'What is wrong?' she cried. 'Are you ill, *mes petites*?'

'No,' said Pat, in rather a trembling voice. 'We're not ill. We've brought you our rewritten essays. You said we were to bring them after supper, so here they are.'

'But why bring them so late?' asked Miss Theobald, in her deep, serious voice. 'You must have known that Mam'zelle meant you to bring them before you went to bed.'

'We hadn't time to rewrite the essays till just now,' answered Pat, suddenly feeling very foolish indeed. 'We got out of bed and went down to the common-room to do them.'

'Ah! The bad children! They went to the cinema after all, instead of doing my essays!' cried Mam'zelle, guessing everything at once. 'Ah, Miss Theobald, these twins send my hair grey! The work they do! It is impossible that they have gone to a school before they came here! Their work is abominable.'

'We *did* go to a school, and it was a jolly fine one!' cried Pat, indignantly. '*Much* better than St Clares!'

There was a silence after this. Miss Theobald looked thoughtful. Mam'zelle was speechless.

'I think we won't decide anything tonight or talk about this,' said Miss Theobald at last. 'It is too late. Go to bed, twins, and come and see me at ten o'clock tomorrow morning. Ask Miss Roberts to excuse you for fifteen minutes then.'

So back to bed with their French books went the twins, subdued and dismayed. What bad luck to have run into the head herself like that! Now what was going to happen to them? They didn't like to think of ten o'clock in the morning!

6.

Poor Miss Kennedy!

Hilary was awake when they got back into bed and she sat up and demanded to know where they had been.

'Miss Roberts came in and turned on the light and I woke up,' said Hilary. 'I spotted that you'd put bolsters down your beds, but Miss Roberts didn't. Whatever have you been doing?'

Pat told her. Hilary listened in amazement. 'Whatever will you two do next?' she said. 'Honestly, I think you're mad. Nobody would ever think you'd been head girls in your old school. You behave like a couple of babies!'

The twins were annoyed with Hilary, particularly as they each had a kind of feeling that she was right. They got into bed and lay thinking. It was all very well to be defiant and daring – but it wasn't so funny afterwards!

They asked Miss Roberts to excuse them at ten o'clock. Miss Roberts had evidently been told to expect this, for she nodded her head at once, and did not ask any questions. The twins went off together to Miss Theobald's room.

The head was making out timetables and she told them to sit down for a minute. It was rather dreadful waiting for her to finish what she was doing. Both the twins felt much more nervous than they pretended. Pat began to wonder if the head would write home about them to their parents. Much as she had grumbled about going to St Clare's, she didn't want the head to report her for misbehaviour at the school.

At last Miss Theobald was ready. She swung her chair round and faced the twins. She looked very serious, but not angry.

'I have been looking through the reports that your father sent me from your last school,' the head began. 'They are very good, and you seem to have been responsible and conscientious children there. I can't imagine that you can have completely changed your characters in a few weeks, so I am not going to treat you as naughty irresponsible girls. I know there must be a good reason behind all your strange behaviour last night. Really, my dears, you gave Mam'zelle and me quite a shock when you walked into the classroom in your blue dressing-gowns.'

The head smiled. The twins felt most relieved, and Pat began to pour out what had happened in the French class.

'The French isn't the same as at our old school. It isn't much use our trying to do well, because we always get everything wrong. It isn't our fault. And Mam'zelle was simply furious with us yesterday, and . . .'

Miss Theobald heard Pat patiently to the end.

'Well, your French difficulties can easily be put right,' said the head mistress. 'I have spoken to Mam'zelle, and she says that you speak well and understand well, but that you have not been well grounded in the writing of French. She has offered to give you half an hour's extra

French a day until you have caught up the others. This is very kind of her because she is extremely busy. All this bother has come from the fact that you were behind your class in one thing – and if you are willing to help to put it right by working hard with Mam'zelle, there is no need to say any more about your rather silly behaviour last night.'

The twins stared at Miss Theobald with mixed feelings. They were most relieved that nothing more was to be said – but oh dear, oh dear – extra French each day! How tiresome! And yet how decent of Mam'zelle Abominable to be willing to help them.

'Thank you, Miss Theobald,' said Pat at last. 'We'll try. Once we catch up the others, we shan't feel so angry and ashamed when we are scolded in front of the class.'

'Well, you won't be scolded if Mam'zelle really feels you are trying,' said Miss Theobald. 'Now go to her and arrange what time will be best each day for the extra lesson. And don't go marching through the corridors in your dressing-gowns at half-past ten any more!'

'No, Miss Theobald,' said the twins, smiling at the head. Things seemed suddenly brighter. What they had done didn't any longer seem a dreadful piece of misbehaviour likely to be punished in dire ways – but just a silly bit of nonsense that they were both heartily ashamed of. They went out of the room, and skipped down the passage to the common-room. Mam'zelle was there, correcting piles of French essays, and muttering to herself as she ticked the pages.

'*Très bien, ma petite* Hilary! Ah, this dreadful girl. Joan! Ah . . . come in!'

The twins went into the mistresses' common-room. Mam'zelle beamed at them, and patted them on the shoulder. Although she had an extremely quick and hot temper, she was very good hearted and kind.

'Ah, now we will see how clever you can be at catching up the others,' she said. 'Every day you will work with me, and we shall be good friends, *n'est-ce pas*?'

'Thank you, Mam'zelle,' said Pat. 'We were rather idiots yesterday. We won't be again!'

'And thank you for saying you'll help us each day,' said Isabel.

So that was that, and the classes with Mam'zelle went much more smoothly. Mam'zelle was patient with the twins, and they tried hard.

But nobody tried hard with poor Miss Kennedy! Janet was a born tease and leg-puller, and she gave the unfortunate history teacher a terrible time. Janet had a wonderful collection of trick pencils, all of which she tried on Miss Kennedy with enormous success.

One pencil had a point that was made of rubber, so that it wobbled to one side when Miss Kennedy took it to write with. Another pencil had a point that slipped right inside the pencil as soon as anyone wrote with it. The girls all watched with intense eagerness as the unfortunate mistress unwarily used these pencils, and gazed at them in surprise when they behaved so strangely.

Then Janet produced a pencil that wouldn't write at

all, although it appeared to have a most marvellous point. To see poor Miss Kennedy pressing hard with the pencil, trying her best to write 'Very good' with it, sent the whole class into fits of giggles.

'Girls, girls! Please make less noise!' Miss Kennedy said. 'Turn to page eighty-seven of your history books. Today I want to tell you how the people lived in the seventeenth century.'

The class at once began to turn over the pages of their history books in a most feverish manner, making a noise like the whispering of trees in the wind. They went on and on turning over the pages, muttering eighty-seven, eighty-seven to themselves all the time.

'What number did you say, Miss Kennedy?' asked Kathleen, innocently, though she knew very well indeed.

'I said page eighty-seven,' said Miss Kennedy, politely. She was always polite, never rude like Mam'zelle, or sarcastic like Miss Roberts.

'Oh, eighty-seven!' said all the girls at once, and immediately began to turn over their pages the other way, very busy and very serious – until Janet let out a giggle, and then the whole class roared. Miss Kennedy rapped on the desk.

'Please, please,' she said, 'I do beg you to be quiet and let us get on with the lesson.'

'Please, Miss Kennedy, did the people wear clothes in the seventeenth century, or just skins?' asked Janet, in an innocent voice. Miss Kennedy looked surprised.

'Surely you know that they wore clothes,' she said. 'I

have a picture here of the kind of clothes they wore. You should know that they didn't wear skins then, Janet.'

'Not even their *own* skins?' asked Janet. This wasn't really at all funny, but the class was now in a state to giggle at anything, and the twins and everyone else joined in the laughter.

'Perhaps they had jumped *out* of their skins and that's why they didn't wear any,' said Hilary. More giggles followed this, though half the class didn't even catch what Hilary had said.

'Girls, I can't have this, I really can't,' said Miss Kennedy. 'I shall have to report you.'

'Oh, please, please, PLEASE, Miss Kennedy!' chanted the class in a chorus, and one or two girls pretended to sob.

Poor Miss Kennedy! She had to deal with this sort of thing every time, though the upper forms were better behaved. The lower forms did not mean to be cruel or unkind, but they loved a joke and did not stop to think about Miss Kennedy and what she must be feeling. They just thought she was silly and asked for trouble.

One morning, when the class was especially riotous. Janet caught everyone's eye. Kathleen giggled, for she knew what had been planned. When Janet gave the signal every girl was to drop her history text book flat on the floor! Janet nodded, and each girl let go her book.

Crash! Miss Kennedy jumped in fright – and the next minute the door opened and in came Miss Roberts! She had been taking a class in the next room, and when the crash of twenty history books had sounded, like a gunshot, she had decided it was time to investigate.

'Miss Kennedy, I don't know if there are any girls' names you would like to report to me,' said Miss Roberts, in a very cold voice, 'but I shall be glad to have them after morning school. I am sure you find it as difficult as I do to teach with all this noise going on.'

Miss Roberts glared at the form, and they sat silent, half the girls going red. Miss Kennedy went red too.

'I'm so sorry for the noise, Miss Roberts,' she said. 'You see . . .'

But Miss Roberts was gone, shutting the door after her very firmly indeed.

'Kenny won't report anyone,' whispered Janet to Isabel. 'If she did, she'd have to report the whole class, and she would be ashamed to do that.'

Miss Kennedy reported no one – but in the secrecy of her bedroom that night she worried and tossed all night long. She had come to St Clare's because her friend, Miss Lewis, who thought so much of her, was ill – and now Miss Kennedy felt that she was letting her down because the girls were quite out of hand, and she was sure that not one of them had learnt any history worth mentioning that term! And Miss Roberts had come in like that and been so cold and horrid – and had hardly spoken to her in the common-room afterwards. Suppose she complained about her to Miss Theobald? It was dreadful to feel herself a failure, and poor Miss Kennedy did not see how she could possibly turn her failure into anything like success.

'I'm afraid of the girls, that's why!' she said to herself.

'And I do hate reporting them, because if I do they will hate me, and then my classes will be worse than ever.'

And in the dormitory Janet was planning other tricks to play on poor unsuspecting Miss Kennedy! Janet had brothers, monkeys all of them, and they sent her all kinds of tricks which they themselves tried out in their own classes.

'Pat! Isabel! Are you asleep?' whispered Janet. 'I say! My brothers are sending me some fire-cracks! Have you ever heard of them?'

'Never,' said the twins. 'Whatever are they?'

'Well, you throw them on the fire and they crack and spit and hiss,' whispered Janet, in glee. 'My seat is next to the fire – so watch out for some fun next week! I expect the parcel will come tomorrow.'

The twins giggled. Whatever would Kenny say when the fire began to spit and hiss and crack? They hugged themselves and pictured Miss Kennedy's alarmed expression.

'Janet!' whispered Pat. 'Let's . . .'

But Hilary, head of the dormitory, put an end to the whispering. 'Shut up!' she said. 'You know the rules, don't you? For goodness' sake, go to sleep!'

7.

Janet is up to tricks

The parcel of fire-cracks duly arrived for Janet. She giggled when she took it from the post-rack, and winked at the twins.

'I'll undo it in the dormitory after breakfast,' she said. 'Say you've forgotten something and get permission to go up before prayers.'

So Janet and the twins scurried upstairs to the dormitory immediately after breakfast, and for five minutes they gloated over the contents of the parcel. There was a box inside, and this contained about fifty squib-like crackers, small and innocent-looking, coloured red and yellow.

'But will they really make much noise?' asked Pat, taking one up. 'I shouldn't think they'd do much more than make a gentle pop.'

'Don't worry! I'll throw about a dozen on at a time!' said Janet. 'There'll be quite an explosion, I promise you. Golly! We'll have some sport!'

With many giggles the girls hurried downstairs as the bell for prayers went. They could hardly wait for the history lesson to come. It came after the mid-morning break. Janet told some of the other girls what she was going to do, and the whole form was in a great state of expectation. Even Miss Roberts felt there was something up, though the class tried to work well.

At the end of the maths lesson, just before break, Miss Roberts spoke a few dry words to her form.

'After break you will have your history lesson as usual. I expect you to work as well for Miss Kennedy as you do for me. If you don't, I shall have something serious to say to you all. There is to be no disturbance at all this morning. DO YOU HEAR ME, JANET?'

Janet jumped. She couldn't imagine why Miss Roberts had suddenly picked her out. She did not know that she had been looking extremely guilty!

'Yes, Miss Roberts,' said Janet, thinking that, alas, she would not be able to play her fire-crack trick after all.

But the rest of the form crowded round her during break, and insisted that she carried out her promise. They couldn't bear not to have the treat of seeing Miss Kennedy jump and stare with wide eyes at the fire's extraordinary behaviour.

'All right,' said Janet, at last. 'But for goodness' sake don't give me away to Miss Roberts, that's all, if she hears anything. And DO promise not to laugh too loudly. Honestly, we'll get into an awful row if Miss Roberts hears us. And she'll be quite near, you know.'

'No, she won't,' said Kathleen. 'She's taking the sixth for something. I heard her say so. And they're right at the other end of the school! She won't hear a thing.'

'Good,' said Janet, feeling more comfortable. 'Well,

watch out! We'll hear some fine spitting and hissing, I can tell you!'

The whole form were in their places as quiet as mice when Miss Kennedy came in to give them their usual history lesson. She was feeling even more nervous than usual, for she had not forgotten how the form had behaved the last time she had taken them. She was most relieved to see them sitting so quietly in their places.

'Good morning, girls,' said Miss Kennedy, sitting at her desk.

'Good morning, Miss Kennedy,' chorused the form, and the lesson opened. Miss Kennedy had to turn to the blackboard to draw a history chart, and immediately every girl turned her head towards Janet. The time had come!

Janet's seat was just by the fire. The box of fire-cracks was in her desk. Cautiously she lifted the lid, and took out about a dozen. She threw them into the heart of the fire.

Everyone waited tensely. For a moment nothing happened at all except that the fire flamed up a little. Then the excitement began!

Crack! Spit! Hiss! Half the fire-cracks went off at once, and sparks jumped up the chimney and leapt out of the fire on to the floor.

CRACK! Ssssssssss! Everyone watched and listened, their eyes on poor Miss Kennedy, who looked as surprised and as startled as could be!

'Miss Kennedy! Oh, Miss Kennedy! What's happening?' cried Pat, pretending to be frightened.

'It's all right, Pat – it's probably a very gassy piece of

coal,' said Miss Kennedy. 'It's all over now – but it really made me jump.'

'CRACK! CRACK!' Some more fireworks went off, and a shower of sparks flew out of the fire. Janet jumped up, took the blackboard cleaner, and began to beat out the sparks with an enormous amount of quite unnecessary noise.

'Janet! Janet! Stop!' cried Miss Kennedy, afraid that the next class would hear the noise.

By this time the class had begun to giggle, though they had tried hard to keep serious and to smother their laughter. When the fire-cracks went off once more the class nearly went into hysterics, which were not made any better by the sight of Janet again pretending to beat out sparks on the floor by flapping about with the blackboard cleaner, making an enormous dust.

Miss Kennedy went pale. She guessed that some trick had been played, though she couldn't imagine what. She stood up, looking unexpectedly dignified, though bits of straight hair fell rather wildly from the two knots at the sides of her head.

'Girls!' she said. 'There will be no history lesson this morning. I refuse to teach an unruly class like this.'

She went out of the room, her face white and her eyes swimming with tears.

She would have to go to the head and give up her job. She couldn't possibly take fees for teaching girls who simply played the whole of the time. But it was no use going when she felt so upset. She would wait until the end of the morning and go then. She hurriedly scribbled a note to Miss Roberts, and sent it to her by one of the school messengers.

'Am afraid I feel unwell, and have had to leave your form for a while,' said the note.

Miss Roberts was surprised to get the note. She debated with herself whether to let the first form carry on by itself – surely Miss Kennedy would have left them some work to do? Or should she leave the sixth form to get on by themselves, and go back to the first? She decided to give the sixth some questions to answer, and leave them. They would behave themselves, of course – but she wasn't so sure about her own form!

So she began to write out questions on the board, wondering meanwhile what the first form was up to.

They had been rather taken aback when Miss Kennedy walked out. Some of the girls felt guilty and uncomfortable, but when the fire began to hiss and spit again, it all seemed terribly funny once more, and Doris, Joan, Kathleen and the rest began to giggle again.

'*Did* you see old Kenny when the first crack went off?' cried Joan. 'I thought I should die, trying not to laugh. I had an awful stitch in my side, I can tell you.'

'Janet, those fire-cracks are simply marvellous!' cried Hilary. 'Put some more on – Kenny won't be back. All I hope is that she doesn't go and tell Miss Theobald.'

'She didn't go towards the head's room,' said Janet. 'She went the other way. All right – I'll stick some more on. Watch out, everyone!'

Janet shook the box over the fire, meaning to throw

out about a dozen of the little squibs – but the whole lot went in! Janet laughed.

'Golly! They've all gone in. We'll have some fun!'

Doris was at the door of the classroom, keeping guard in case a teacher came along. Suddenly she gave a cry.

'Look out! Miss Roberts is coming! Get to your seats, quick!'

Everyone scurried to their seats at once. They pulled open their history books, and by the time that Miss Roberts came into the room, the class looked fairly peaceful, though it was rather surprising to see so many bent heads. Miss Roberts became suspicious at once – usually the girls all looked up when she came into the room!

'You seem very busy,' she said, drily. 'Did Miss Kennedy leave you history work to do?'

Nobody answered. Janet gave an anxious glance at the fire. Those fire-cracks! How she wished she hadn't put so many on! The fire began to flare up a little. Miss Roberts spoke sharply.

'Can't somebody answer me? Did Miss . . .'

But she did not finish her question, because about twenty fire-cracks went off at once with the most tremendous hissing, spluttering and cracking! Sparks flew out and huge flames shot up the chimney.

'Good Heavens!' said Miss Roberts. 'What in the world is going on there?'

Again nobody said a word. There was no giggling or laughing this time, no smothered gurgles. Everyone looked scared.

Crack! Ssssss! Crack! Some of the fireworks shot themselves up the chimney and exploded there, bringing down showers of soot. It was hot soot, and flew out over the room. Janet and the girls nearest the fire began to cough and choke.

'Come away from the fire, Janet,' ordered Miss Roberts. 'Those sparks will set fire to your tunic.'

The soot flew out again, and black specks began to descend on to books, papers, desks and heads. Miss Roberts's mouth went very straight and thin. She looked round the class.

'Someone has been putting fireworks into the fire,' she said. 'The class will dismiss. I am going to the common-room across the passage. I expect the girl who played this stupid and dangerous joke to come and own up at once.'

She left the room. Everyone stared in dismay. It was all very well to play a joke on stupid old Kenny – but Miss Roberts was a different matter altogether! Miss Roberts knew a great many most annoying punishments.

'Gosh! I'm in for it now!' said Janet, gloomily. 'I'd better go and get it over.'

She went to the door. The twins stared after her. Pat ran to the door too.

'Janet! Wait! I'm coming too. I was as much to blame as you, because I egged you on. I'd have put those fire-cracks on if you hadn't!'

'And I'll come as well,' said Isabel at once.

'Oh, I say! That *is* decent of you!' said Janet, slipping her arm through Pat's, and holding out her other hand to Isabel.

Then Hilary spoke up too. 'Well, I'll come along as well. As a matter of fact, we're all to blame. It's true you got the squibs and put them on – but we all shared the joke, and it's not fair that only you should be punished.'

So it ended in the whole of the class going to the common-room, looking very downcast and ashamed. Miss Roberts looked up, surprised to see so many girls crowding into the room.

'What's all this for?' she asked, sternly.

'Miss Roberts, may I tell you?' said Hilary. 'I'm head of the form.'

'I want the person who played the trick to own up.' said Miss Roberts. 'Who did it?'

'I did,' said poor Janet, going rather white. Her knees shook a little, and she looked on the floor. She could not bear to meet Miss Roberts's sharp hazel eyes.

'But we were all in it,' said Hilary. 'We wanted Janet to do it, and we shared in it.'

'And may I ask if you also treated Miss Kennedy to the same silly trick?' asked Miss Roberts, in her most sarcastic voice.

'Yes,' said Janet, in a low voice.

'So that explains it,' said Miss Roberts, thinking of the note that Miss Kennedy had sent her. 'Well, you will all share the expenses of the chimney being swept and you will all spend two hours each washing down the walls and scrubbing the floor and desks after the sweep has been. That means that you will work in batches of five, each giving up two hours of your free time to do it.'

'Yes, Miss Roberts,' said the class dolefully.

'You will also apologize to Miss Kennedy, of course,' went on Miss Roberts. 'And I should like to say that I am ashamed of you for taking advantage of somebody not able to deal with you as I can!'

The form trooped out. Miss Roberts telephoned for the sweep – and Miss Kennedy was surprised to find relays of girls waylaying her, offering her humble apologies for their behaviour. They did not tell her what had happened, so Miss Kennedy had no idea that Miss Roberts had experienced the same startling explosions from the fire, but had dealt with the whole matter with a firm hand. She really thought that the girls were offering their apologies of their own accord, and she felt almost happy.

'I shan't give in my resignation to Miss Theobald after all,' she thought. 'Anyway, if I did, I would have to say why, and I shouldn't like to give the girls away after they had said they were sorry in such a nice way.'

So the matter rested there for a while – and batches of dismal girls washed and scrubbed that afternoon and evening, instead of playing lacrosse, and going to a concert!

One good thing came out of the row – and that was that the twins' form liked them a great deal better.

'It was decent of Pat and Isabel to go after Janet like that and say they'd share the blame,' said Hilary. 'Good for them!'

8.

The great midnight feast

Miss Roberts kept a very tight hand indeed on her form for the next week or two, and they squirmed under her dry tongue. Pat and Isabel hated being spoken to as if they were nobodies, but they did not dare to grumble.

'It's simply awful being ticked off as if we were in the kindergarten, when we've been used to bossing the whole school at Redroofs,' said Isabel. 'I shall never get used to it!'

'I hate it too,' said Pat. 'But all the same, I can't help liking Miss Roberts, you know. I do respect her awfully, and you can't help liking people you respect.'

'Well, I wish she'd start respecting us, then,' said Isabel gloomily. 'Then maybe she'd like us, and we wouldn't get such a hot time in class. Golly, when I forgot to take my maths book to her this morning you'd have thought she was going to phone up the police station and have me sent to prison!'

Pat laughed. 'Don't be an idiot,' she said. 'By the way, don't forget to give a pound towards buying Miss Theobald something on her birthday. I've given mine in.'

'Oh, my!' groaned Isabel. 'I hope I've got a pound! I had to give something towards the sweep, and I gave a pound to the housemaid for cleaning my tunic for me in case Matron ticked me off about it – and we had to give something to the Babies' Convalescent Home last week. I'm just about broke!'

She went to her part of the shelf in the Common-room and took down her purse. It was empty!

'Golly!' said Isabel in dismay. 'I'm sure I had a pound in my purse. Did you borrow it, Pat?'

'No,' said Pat. 'Or I'd have told you. It must be in your coat pocket, silly.'

But the money was nowhere to be found. Isabel decided she must have lost it, and she had to borrow some money from Pat to give towards buying the head a present.

Then Janet had a birthday, and everyone went down to the town to buy a small present for her – all but Hilary, who discovered, to her dismay, that the money that her granny had sent her had disappeared out of her pocket!

'Oh, my, a whole ten pounds!' wailed Hilary. 'I was going to buy all sorts of things with it. I really must get some new shoelaces, and my lacrosse stick wants mending. Where in the world has it gone?'

Joan lent Hilary some money to buy a present for Janet, and on her birthday Janet was most delighted to find so many gifts. She was very popular, in spite of her bluntness. The finest gift she had was from Kathleen Gregory, who presented her with a gold brooch, with her name inscribed at the back.

'I say! You shouldn't have done that!' said Janet, in amazement. 'Why, it must have cost you a mint of money,

Kathleen! I really can't accept it. It's too generous a gift.'

'But you *must* accept it, because it's got your name inside,' said Kathleen. 'It's no use to anyone else!'

Everyone admired the little gold brooch and read the name inscribed on the back. Kathleen glowed with pleasure at the attention that her gift produced, and when Janet thanked her again, and slipped her arm through hers, she was red with delight.

'It was very generous of Kathleen,' said Janet to the twins, as they went to the classroom. 'But I can't understand why she went such a splash on me! Usually she's awfully mean with her gifts – either gives nothing at all, or something that costs fifty pence! It isn't as if she likes me such a lot, either. I've gone for her heaps of times because she's such a goof!'

Janet had a marvellous hamper sent to her for her birthday, and she and Hilary and the twins unpacked it with glee. 'All the things I love!' said Janet. 'A big chocolate cake! Shortbread biscuits! Sardines in tomato sauce! Nestlé's milk. And look at these peppermint creams! They'll melt in our mouths!'

'Let's have a midnight feast!' said Pat, suddenly. 'We once had one at Redroofs, before we were head girls. I don't know why food tastes so much nicer in the middle of the night than in the daytime, but it does! Oh, Janet – don't you think it would be fun?'

'It might be rather sport,' said Janet. 'But there's not enough food here for us all. The rest of you will have to bring something as well. Each girl had better bring one thing – a cake – or ginger beer – or chocolate. When shall we have the feast?'

'Tomorrow night,' said Isabel, with a giggle. 'Miss Roberts is going to a concert. I heard her say so. She's going to stay the night with a friend and get a train that brings her back in time for prayers.'

'Oh, good! Tomorrow's the night then!' said Janet. 'Let's tell everyone.'

So the whole form was told about the Great feast, and everyone promised to bring something. Pat bought a jam sponge sandwich. Isabel, who again had to borrow from Pat, bought a bar of chocolate. Joan brought candles, because the girls were not allowed to put on the electric light once it was turned out except for urgent reasons, such as illness.

The most lavish contribution was Kathleen's! She brought a really marvellous cake, with almond icing all over it, and pink and yellow sugar roses on the top. Everyone exclaimed over it!

'Golly, Kathleen! Have you come into a fortune or something?' cried Janet. 'That cake must have cost you all your pocket-money for the rest of the term! It's marvellous.'

'The prettiest cake I've ever seen,' said Hilary. 'Jolly decent of you, Kathleen.'

Kathleen was red with pleasure. She beamed round at everyone, and enjoyed the smiles that she and her cake received.

'I wish I could have got something better than my silly

little bar of chocolate,' said Isabel. 'But I even had to borrow from Pat to get that.'

'And I can only bring a few biscuits I had left from a tin that Mother sent me a fortnight ago,' said Hilary. 'I'm quite broke since I lost my money.'

'Anyway, we've got heaps of things,' said Janet, who was busy hiding everything at the bottom of a cupboard just outside the dormitory. 'Golly, I hope Matron doesn't suddenly take it into her head to spring-clean this cupboard! She *would* be surprised to see what's in it. Goodness – who brought this pork pie? How marvellous!'

The whole form was in a state of excitement that day. It was simply gorgeous to have a secret and not to let any of the other forms know. Hilary knew that the upper third had had a midnight feast already that term, and it had been a great success. She meant to make theirs even more of a success!

Miss Roberts couldn't think why the first form girls were so restless. As for Mam'zelle, she sensed the underlying excitement at once, and grew excited too.

'Ah, now, *mes petites*, what is the matter with you today?' she cried, when one girl after another made a mistake in the French translation. 'What is in your thoughts? You are planning something – is it not so? Tell me what it is.'

'Oh, Mam'zelle, whatever makes you think such a thing!' cried Janet. 'What should we be planning?'

'How should I know?' said Mam'zelle. 'All I know is that you are not paying attention. Now, one more mistake and I send you to bed an hour earlier than usual!'

Mam'zelle did not mean this, of course – but it tickled the girls, who were all longing for bedtime that night, and would have been quite pleased to go early. Janet giggled and was nearly sent out of the room.

At last bedtime came, and everyone undressed.

'Who's going to get the stuff out of the cupboard?' said Pat.

'You and I and Hilary and Isabel,' said Janet. 'And for goodness' sake don't drop anything. If you drop the pork pie on the floor there *will* be a mess.'

Everyone laughed. They snuggled down into bed. They all wanted to keep awake, but it was arranged that some of them should take it in turns to sit up and keep awake for half an hour, waking the next girl when it was her turn. Then, at midnight, they should all be awakened and the Feast would begin!

First Janet sat up in bed for half an hour, hugging her knees, and thinking of all the things in the cupboard outside. She was not a bit sleepy. She switched on her torch to look at the time. The half hour was just up. She leant across to the next bed and awoke Hilary.

At midnight everyone was fast asleep except for the girl on watch, who was Pat. As she heard the big clock striking from the west tower of the school, Pat crept out of bed. She went from girl to girl, whispering in her ear and shaking her.

'Hilary! It's time! Wake up! Isabel! It's midnight! Joan! The Feast is about to begin. Kathleen! Kathleen! Do wake up! It's twelve o'clock!'

At last every girl was awake, and with many smothered giggles, they put on their dressing-gowns and slippers.

The whole school was in darkness. Pat lighted two candles, and placed them on a dressing-table in the middle of the dormitory. She had sent Isabel to waken the rest of the form in the next dormitory, and with scuffles and chuckles all the girls crept in. They sat on the beds nearest to the candles, and waited whilst Pat and the others went to get the things out of the cupboard.

Pat took her torch and shone it into the cupboard whilst the others took out the things. A tin of sweetened milk dropped to the floor with a crash. Everyone jumped and stood stock still. They listened, but there was no sound to be heard – no door opened, no one switched on a light.

'Idiot!' whispered Janet to Isabel. 'For goodness' sake don't drop that chocolate cake. Where did that tin roll to? Oh, here it is.'

At last all the eatables were safely in the dormitory, and the door was shut softly. The girls looked at everything, and felt terribly hungry.

'Golly! Pork pie and chocolate cake, sardines and Nestlé's milk, chocolate and peppermint creams, tinned pineapple and ginger beer!' said Janet. 'Talk about a feast! I bet this beats the upper third's feast hollow! Come on – let's begin. I'll cut the cake.'

Soon every girl was munching hard and thinking that food had never tasted quite so nice before. Janet took an opener and opened a ginger beer bottle. The first one was quite all right and Janet filled two tooth-glasses. But the next ginger beer bottle fizzed out tremendously and soaked the bed that Janet was sitting on. Everyone giggled. It went off with a real pop, and sounded quite loud in the silence of the night.

'Don't worry! No one will hear that,' said Janet. 'Here, Pat – open the sardines. I've got some bread and butter somewhere, and we'll make sandwiches.'

The bread and butter was unwrapped from its paper. Janet had brought it up from the tea-table! Every girl had taken a piece from the plate at tea-time, and hidden it to give to Janet.

'Look – take a bite of a sardine sandwich, and then a bite of pork pie, and then a spoonful of Nestlé's milk,' said Pat. 'It tastes gorgeous.'

The chocolate was saved till last. By that time the girls were all unable to eat any more and could only suck the sweets and the chocolate. They sat about and giggled at the silliest jokes.

'Of course, the nicest thing of the whole feast was Kathleen's marvellous cake,' said Hilary. 'The almond icing was gorgeous.'

'Yes – and I had one of the sugar roses,' said Joan. 'Lovely! However much did you pay for that cake, Kath? It was jolly decent of you.'

'Oh, that's nothing,' said Kathleen. 'I'm most awfully glad you liked it.'

She looked very happy. There had not been quite enough cake to go round and Kathleen hadn't even tasted the marvellous cake. But she didn't mind at all. She sat quite happily watching the others feast on it.

Then the girls began to press Doris to do her clown-dance. This was a dance she had learnt during the holidays at some special classes, and it was very funny. Doris was full of humour and could make the others laugh very easily. The clown dance was most ridiculous, because Doris had to keep falling over herself. She accompanied this falling about with many groans and gurgles, which always sent the audience into fits of laughter.

'Well, don't laugh too loudly this time,' said Doris, getting up. 'You made such a row last time I did it in the common-room that Belinda Towers came in and ticked me off for playing the fool.'

She began the dance with a solemn face. She fell over the foot of the bed, on purpose of course, and rubbed herself with a groan. The girls began to chuckle, their hands over their mouths.

Doris loved making people laugh. She swayed about, making comical faces, then pretended to catch one leg in another, and fell, clutching at Pat with a deep groan.

With a giggle Pat fell too, and knocked against the dressing-table. The table shook violently, and everything on it slid to the floor! Brushes, combs, photograph frames, tooth-mugs, a ginger beer bottle – goodness, what a crash!

The girls stared in horror. The noise sounded simply terrific!

'Quick! Clear everything up and get into bed,' cried

Janet, in a loud whisper. 'Golly! We'll have half the mistresses here.'

The girls belonging to the next dormitory fled out of the door at once. The others cleared up quickly, but very soon heard the sound of an electric light being switched on in the passage.

'Into bed!' hissed Hilary, and they all leapt under the sheets. They pulled them up to their chins and lay listening. Hilary remembered that they had left two ginger beer bottles out in the middle of the floor – and they hadn't had time to clear up the remains of the pork pie either. Pork pies were so untidy, and *would* scatter themselves in crumbs every time a bite was taken!

The door opened, and someone was outlined against the light from the passage outside. Pat saw who it was – old Kenny! What bad luck! If she discovered anything she would be sure to report it after the bad behavior of the form. But perhaps she wouldn't switch on the dormitory light.

Miss Kennedy stood listening. One of the girls gave a gentle snore, making believe that she was fast asleep – but that was too much for Kathleen, who was already very strung up. She gave a smothered giggle, and Miss Kennedy heard it. She switched on the light.

The first thing she saw were the two ginger beer bottles standing boldly in the middle of the floor. Then she saw the remains of the pork pie. She saw the paper from the chocolate. She guessed immediately what the girls had been up to.

A little smile came over her face. What monkeys girls were! She remembered the thrill of a midnight feast herself – and how she and the others had been caught and severely punished. She spoke in a low voice to Hilary, the head of the dormitory.

'Hilary! Are you awake?'

Hilary dared not pretend. She answered in a sleepy voice. 'Hallo, Miss Kennedy! Is anything wrong?'

'I thought I heard a noise from this dormitory,' said Miss Kennedy. 'I'm in charge of it tonight as Miss Roberts isn't here. But I may have been mistaken.'

Hilary sat up in bed and saw the ginger beer bottles. She glanced at Miss Kennedy and saw a twinkle in her eye.

'Perhaps you *were* mistaken, Miss Kennedy,' she said. 'Perhaps – perhaps – it was mice or something.'

'Perhaps it *was*,' said Miss Kennedy. 'Er – well, I don't see that there's anything to report to Miss Roberts – but as you're head of the dormitory, Hilary, you might see that it's tidy before Matron does her rounds tomorrow morning. Good night.'

She switched off the light, shut the door and went back to her room. The girls all sat up in bed at once and began to whisper.

'My goodness! Kenny's a sport!'

'Golly! She saw those awful ginger beer bottles all right! And fancy agreeing that that terrific noise we made might have been *mice*!'

'And she as good as said we were to remove all traces

of the feast, and she promised not to report anything to Miss Roberts.'

'Though old Roberts is a sport too, in her way,' said Doris.

'Yes, but we're in her bad books at the moment, don't forget, and anything like this would just about finish things!' said Isabel. 'Good old Kenny!'

9.

A lacrosse match – and a puzzle

The only bad effects of the Great Midnight Feast, as it came to be called, were that Isabel, Doris and Vera didn't feel at all well the next day. Miss Roberts eyed them sharply.

'What have you been eating?' she asked.

'Only what the others have,' answered Doris, quite truthfully.

'Well, go to Matron and she'll dose you,' said Miss Roberts. The three girls went off dolefully. Matron had some most disgusting medicine. She dosed the girls generously and they groaned when she made them lick the spoon round.

Then Joan and Kathleen felt ill and they were sent to Matron too.

'I know these symptoms,' said Matron. 'You are suffering from Midnight Feast Illness! Aha! You needn't pretend to me! If you *will* feast on pork pies and sardines, chocolate and ginger beer in the middle of the night, you can expect a dose of medicine from me the next day.'

The girls stared at her in horror. How did she know?

'Who told you?' asked Joan, thinking that Miss Kennedy had told tales after all.

'Nobody,' said Matron, putting the cork back firmly

into the enormous bottle. 'But I haven't been Matron of a girls' school for twenty-five years without knowing a *few* things! I dosed your mother before you, Joan, and your aunt too. They couldn't stand midnight food any more than you can. Go along now – don't stare at me like that. I shan't tell tales – and I always say there's no need to punish girls for having a midnight feast, because the feelings they get the next day are punishment enough!'

The girls went away. Joan looked at Kathleen. 'You know, I simply loved the pork pie and the sardines last night,' she said, gloomily, 'but the very thought of them makes me feel sick today. I don't believe I'll ever be able to look a sardine in the face again.'

But everyone soon forgot their aches and pains, and the feast passed into a legend that was told throughout the school. Even Belinda Towers heard about it and chuckled when she was told how everything fell off the dressing-table at the last.

It was Kathleen who told Belinda. It was rather strange how Kathleen had altered during the last few weeks. She was no longer nervous and apologetic to everyone, but took her place happily and laughed and joked like the rest. She could even talk to tall Belinda Towers without stammering with nervousness! She was waiting on Belinda that week, and rushed about quite happily, making toast, running errands and not even grumbling when Belinda sent for her in the middle of a concert rehearsal.

Kathleen was to play in an important lacrosse match that week, and so was Isabel. They were the only first form girls chosen – all the others were second formers. At first Pat had been by far the better of the two, but Isabel soon learnt the knack of catching and throwing the ball in the easiest way, and had outstripped her twin. The match was to be against the second form of a nearby day school, and the girls were very keen about it.

'Kathleen's goalkeeper,' said Pat to Isabel. 'Belinda told her today. I say, isn't Kath different? I quite like her now.'

'Yes – and she's so generous!' said Isabel. 'She bought some sweets yesterday and shared the whole lot round without having even one herself. And she bought some chrysanthemums for Vera – they must have cost a lot!'

Vera was in the sickbay, recovering from a bad cold. She had been very surprised and touched when Kathleen had taken her six beautiful yellow chrysanthemums. It was so unlike Kathleen, who had always been rather mean before.

Kathleen got Isabel to practise throwing balls into the goal, so that she might get even better at stopping them. She was very quick. Then she and Isabel practised catching and throwing the ball and running with it and dodging each other.

'If only, only I could shoot two or three goals on Saturday,' Isabel said a dozen times a day. Hilary laughed. Isabel asked her why.

'I'm laughing at *you,*' said Hilary. 'Who turned up her nose at lacrosse a few weeks ago? You did! Who said there wasn't any game worth playing except hockey? You did! Who vowed and declared she would never try to be any good at a silly game like lacrosse? You did. That's why I'm laughing! I have to sit and hear you raving about lacrosse now, talking it all day long. It sounds funny to me.'

Isabel laughed too, but she went rather red. 'I must have seemed rather an idiot,' she said.

'You *were* a bit of a goof,' said Janet, joining in. 'The stuck-up twins! That's what we used to call you.'

'Oh,' said Isabel, ashamed. She made up her mind to play so well on Saturday that her whole form would be proud of her. The stuck-up twins! What a dreadful name! She and Pat must really do something to make the form forget that.

Saturday came, a brilliantly fine winter's day. The first form were excited. The girls from the day school were coming to lunch and they had to entertain them. Dinner was to be sausages and mashed potatoes, with treacle pudding to follow, a very favourite meal.

'Now look here, Isabel and Kathleen, just see you don't eat too much,' ordered Hilary. 'We want you to play your best. You're the only ones from the first form who are playing – all the rest are second formers. We'll stuff the other school all right – give them so much to eat that they won't be able to catch a ball!'

'Oh, I say! Can't I have two sausages?' said Isabel in dismay. 'And I always have two helpings of treacle pudding.'

'Well, you won't today,' said Janet, firmly. 'But if you play well and we win, the whole form will stand you cream buns at tea-time. See?'

So Isabel cheered up and went without a second helping

of treacle pudding quite amiably. It was a pleasant lunch. The guests were all jolly, friendly girls, and how they laughed when they were told the story of the Great Feast!

'We can't have fun like that,' said one of the day girls. 'We always go home at night. What's your lacrosse team like? Any good? We've beaten you each time we've played you so far.'

'And I bet we'll beat them again,' cried the captain, a tall girl with flaming red hair.

'Cream buns for you if you stop their goals, Kathleen!' cried Janet, and everyone laughed.

All the first, second and third forms turned out to watch the match. The fourth form were playing a match of their own away from home, and the sixth rarely bothered to watch the juniors. Some of the fifth turned up, among them Belinda Towers, who arranged all the matches and the players, for she was sports captain, and very keen that St Clare's should win as many matches as possible.

The players took their places. Isabel was tremendously excited. Kathleen was quite cool and calm in goal. The match began.

The day girls made a strong team, and were splendid runners. They got the ball at once, and passed it from one to another whenever they were tackled. But Isabel jumped high into the air and caught the ball as it flew from one day girl to another!

Then she was off like the wind, racing down the field. A girl came out to tackle and tried to knock the ball off Isabel's net – but Isabel jerked it neatly over her head into the waiting net of another St Clare girl – and she was off down the field too. Isabel sped behind – and caught the ball again neatly as the other girl threw it when tackled.

But a very fast girl was after Isabel and took the ball from her. Back the other way raced the day girl, making for the goal. She passed the ball to another girl, who passed it to a third – and the third one shot straight at the goal, where Kathleen stood on guard. Swift as lightning Kathleen put her net down towards the ball, caught it and threw it to Isabel who was waiting not far off.

'Jolly well saved, Kathleen!' roared every one of the St Clare girls, and Kathleen went red with excitement and delight.

So the match went on till half-time, when lemon quarters were taken round on plates to all the hot and panting players. How they loved sucking the cool sour lemon!

'The score is three-one,' said the umpire. 'Three to the day girls of St Christopher's and one to St Clare's.'

'Play up, St Clare's!' cried Belinda. 'Play up. Now, Isabel, score, please!'

The second half of the match began. The players were not quite so fast now, for they were tired. But the excitement ran very high, especially when St Clare's shot two goals in quick succession, one of them thrown by Isabel.

Kathleen hopped about on one leg as the play went on down the other end of the field. She had saved seven goals already. Down the field raced the players, the ball flying from one to another with grace and ease. Kathleen stood tensely, knowing that a goal would be tried.

The ball came down on her, hard and swift. She tried to save the goal, but the ball shot into the corner of the net. Goal! Four-three – and only five minutes to go!

Then St Clare's scored a most unexpected goal in the next two minutes and that made the score equal.

'Only one and a half minutes more!' panted Isabel to a St Clare girl as she passed her the ball. 'For goodness' sake, let's get another goal and win!'

The ball came back to her. A day girl thundered down on Isabel, a big, burly girl. Isabel swung round and dodged, the ball still in her net. She passed it to another girl, who neatly passed it back as soon as she was tackled. And then Isabel took a look at the goal, which, although a good way away, was almost straight in front. It was worth a shot!

She threw the ball hard and straight down the field. The goalkeeper stood ready – but somehow she missed the ball and it rolled into the net, just before the whistle went for time! How the St Clare girls cheered! Pat leapt up and down like a mad thing, Belinda yelled till she was hoarse, and Hilary and Janet thumped one another on the back, though neither of them quite knew why!

'Good old Isabel! She saved the match just in time!' cried Pat. 'Cream buns for her!'

Hot and tired and happy, all the girls trooped off the field to wash and tidy themselves before tea. Janet ran to get her purse to rush off on her bicycle to buy the cream buns.

But her purse only had a few pence inside! How

strange! Janet knew quite well that it had had five pounds in it that very morning – and she certainly hadn't spent any of it.

'I say! My money's gone!' she said in dismay. 'I can't get the cream buns. Dash! Where's it gone?'

'Funny,' said Isabel. 'Mine went a little while ago – and so did Hilary's. Now yours has gone.'

'Well, don't discuss it now,' said Joan. 'We've got to entertain the day girls. But it's a pity about the cream buns.'

'*I'll* buy them!' said Kathleen. 'I'll give you the money, Janet.'

'Oh, no!' said Janet. 'We wanted to buy them for you and Isabel because you did so well in the match. We can't let you buy them for yourselves!'

'Please do,' said Kathleen, and she took some money from her pocket. 'Here you are. Buy buns for everyone!'

'Well – it's jolly decent of you,' said Janet, taking the money. 'Thanks awfully.' She sped off on her bicycle whilst the other girls got ready for tea.

'Well played, kids,' said Belinda Towers, strolling up. 'You stopped some pretty good goals, Kathleen – and you just about saved the match, Isabel, though all the rest did jolly well too.'

Everyone glowed at the sports captain's praise. Then they sat down to tea, and soon the big piles of bread and butter and jam, currant buns and chocolate cake disappeared like magic. Janet was back in a few minutes with a large number of delicious-looking cream buns. The girls greeted them with cheers.

'Thanks, Kathleen! You're a brick, Kathleen!' everyone cried, and Kathleen beamed with delight.

'Well, I *did* enjoy today!' said Isabel to Pat, as they went off to the common-room together, after seeing the day girls off. 'Simply marvellous! Every bit of it.'

'Not quite every bit,' said Pat, rather gravely. 'What about Janet's money? Somebody took that, Isabel. And that's pretty beastly. Who in the world could it be?'

'I simply can't imagine,' said Isabel.

Neither could anyone else. The girls talked about it together, and wondered who had been near Janet's coat. She had hung it on a peg in the sports pavilion, and most of the first and second form had been in and out. But surely, surely no St Clare girl could possibly do such a thing!

'It's stealing, just plain stealing,' said Hilary. 'And it's been going on for some time too, because I know others besides myself and Janet and Isabel have lost money. Belinda lost ten pounds too. She made an awful row about it, but she never found it.'

'Could it be one of the staff?' said Joan.

'Shouldn't think so,' said Hilary. 'They've been here for years. Well – we must all be careful of our money, that's all, and, if we can't *find* the thief, we'll make it difficult for her to *be* one!'

10.

A very muddled girl

One afternoon Rita George, one of the big girls, sent for Kathleen to give her some instructions about a nature ramble she was getting up. Kathleen was head of the nature club in her form. She asked Pat to finish winding the wool that Isabel was holding for her, and ran off.

'Shan't be long,' she said, and disappeared. Pat wound the wool into balls and then threw them into Kathleen's work-basket. She looked at her watch.

'I hope Kath won't be long,' she said. 'We are due for gym in five minutes. I'd better go and remind her. Coming, Isabel?'

The twins went out, and made their way to Rita's study, meaning to see if Kathleen was still there. But when they arrived outside they stood still in dismay.

Someone was sobbing and crying inside! Someone was saying, 'Oh, please forgive me! Oh, please don't tell anyone! Please, please, don't!'

'Gracious! That's not Kathleen, is it?' said Pat, horrified. 'What's happened?'

They did not dare to go in. They waited, hearing more sobs, pitiful, heartbroken sobs, and they heard Rita's rather deep voice, sounding very stern. They could not hear what she said.

Then the door opened and Kathleen came out, her eyes red, and her cheeks tear-stained. She sobbed under her breath, and did not see the twins. She hurried towards the stairs that led to her dormitory.

Pat and Isabel stared after her. 'She's forgotten about gym,' said Pat. 'I don't like to go to her in case she hates anyone seeing her cry.'

'Oh, let's go and comfort her,' said Isabel. 'We'll get into a row for being late for gym – but it's awful to see anyone in trouble like that and not see if we can help.'

So they ran up the stairs to the dormitory. Kathleen was lying on her bed, her face buried in her pillow, sobbing.

'Kathleen! Whatever's happened?' asked Isabel, putting her hand on Kathleen's shoulder. Kathleen shook it off.

'Go away!' she said. 'Go away! Don't come peeping and prying after me.'

'We're not,' said Pat, gently. 'What's the matter? We're your friends, you know.'

'You wouldn't be, if I told you what had happened,' sobbed Kathleen. 'Oh, do go away. I'm going to pack my things and leave St Clare's! I'm going this very night!'

'Kathleen! Do tell us what's happened!' cried Isabel. 'Did Rita tick you off for something? Don't worry about that.'

'It's not the ticking off I'm worrying about – it's the thing I did to *get* the ticking off,' said Kathleen. She sat up, her eyes swollen and red. 'Well, I'll tell you – and you can go and spread it all round the school if you like – and everyone can laugh and jeer at me – but I'll not be here!'

She began to cry again. Pat and Isabel were very much upset. Isabel slipped her arm round the sobbing girl. 'All right – tell us,' she said. 'We won't turn on you, I promise.'

'Yes, you will, yes, you will! What I've done is so dreadful!' sobbed Kathleen. 'You won't believe it! I hardly believe it myself. I'm – I'm – I'm a thief!'

'Kathleen! What do you mean?' asked Pat, shocked. Kathleen stared at her defiantly. She wiped her eyes with a hand that shook.

'*I* took all the money that's been missing!' she said. 'Every bit of it – even yours, Isabel. I couldn't bear never having any money of my own, and saying no when people wanted subscriptions, and not giving any nice birthday presents to anyone, and being thought mean and selfish and ungenerous. I did so want to be generous to everybody, and to make friends. I do so love giving things and making people happy.'

The twins stared at Kathleen in surprise and horror. They could hardly believe what she said. She went on, pouring out her troubles between her sobs.

'I haven't a mother to send me money as you and the other girls have. My father is away abroad and I only have a mean old aunt who gives me about a penny a week! I hated to own up to such a miserable bit of money – and then one day I found a pound belonging to someone and I bought something for somebody with it – and they were so terribly pleased – and I was so happy. I can't tell you how dreadful it is to want to be generous and not to be able to be!'

'Poor Kathleen!' said Isabel, and she patted her on the shoulder. 'Nobody would have minded at all if only you had told them you hadn't any money. We could all have shared with you.'

'But I was too proud to let you do that,' said Kathleen. 'And yet I wasn't too proud to steal. Oh, I can't think how I did it now! I took Janet's money – and Hilary's – and Belinda's. It was all so easy. And this afternoon I – I – I . . .'

She began to cry so bitterly that the twins were quite frightened. 'Don't tell us if you'd rather not,' said Pat.

'Oh, I'll tell you everything now I've begun,' said poor Kathleen. 'It's a relief to tell somebody. Well, this afternoon when I went to Rita's study, she wasn't there – but I saw her coat hanging up and her purse sticking out of it. And I went to it – and oh, Rita came in quietly and caught me! And she's going to Miss Theobald about it, and I shall be known all over the school as a thief, and I'll be expelled and . . .'

She wept again, and the twins looked at one another helplessly. They remembered all Kathleen's sudden generosity – her gifts – the marvellous cake with sugar roses on it – the fine chrysanthemums for Vera – and they remembered too Kathleen's flushed cheeks and shining eyes when she saw her friends enjoying the things she had bought for them.

'Kathleen – go and wash your face and come down to gym,' said Pat at last.

'I'm not going to,' said Kathleen, obstinately. 'I'm going to stay here and pack. I don't want to see anybody again. You two have been decent to me, but I know in your heart of hearts that you simply despise me!'

'We don't, Kath dear,' said Isabel. 'We're terribly, terribly sorry for you – and we do understand why you did it. You so badly wanted to be generous – you did a wrong thing to make a right thing, and that's never any good.'

'Please go, and leave me alone,' said Kathleen. 'Please go.'

The twins went out of the dormitory. Halfway to the gym Isabel stopped and pulled at Pat's arm.

'Pat! Let's go and find Rita if we can. Let's say what we can for poor old Kathleen.'

'All right,' said Pat. The two of them went to Rita's study, but it was empty. 'Blow!' said Pat. 'I wonder if she's gone to Miss Theobald already.'

'Well, come on – let's see,' said Isabel. So to the head's room they went – and coming out of the door, looking very grim indeed, was Rita George!

'What are you two kids doing here?' she said, and went on her way without waiting for an answer. Pat looked at Isabel.

'She's told Miss Theobald,' she said. 'Well – dare we go in and speak to the head about it? I do really think Kathleen isn't an ordinary kind of thief – and if she gets branded as one, and sent away, she may really become one, and be spoilt for always. Come on – let's go in.'

They knocked, and the head called them to come in. She looked surprised to see them.

'Well, twins,' she said. 'What is the matter? You look rather serious.'

Pat didn't quite know how to begin. Then the words came in a rush and the whole story came out about how Kathleen had stolen all the money, and why.

'But oh, Miss Theobald, Kathleen didn't spend a penny on herself,' said Pat. 'It was all for us others. She certainly took our money – but we got it back in gifts and things. She isn't just an ordinary, contemptible sort of thief. She's terribly, terribly upset. Oh, could you possibly do anything about it – not send her away – not let the school know? I'm quite sure Kathleen would try to repay every penny, and Isabel and I would help her all we could never to do such a thing again.'

'You see, it was all because Kathleen got hardly any pocket-money and she was too proud to say so – and she hated to be thought mean and selfish because really she's terribly generous,' said Isabel.

Miss Theobald smiled a very sweet smile at the earnest twins. 'My dears,' she said, 'you tell me such a different story from Rita, and I'm so very glad to hear it. Rita naturally sees poor Kathleen as a plain thief. You see her as she is – a poor muddled child who wants to be generous and chooses an easy but a very wrong way. I am sure I would not have got any explanation from Kathleen, and I might have written to her aunt to take her away. And then I dread what might have happened to her, poor, sensitive child!'

'Oh, Miss Theobald! Do you mean that you will let Kathleen stay?' cried Pat.

'Of course,' said the head. 'I must talk to her first, and get her to tell me all this herself. I shall know how to deal with her, don't worry. Where is she?'

'In her dormitory, packing,' said Pat. Miss Theobald stood up. 'I'll go to her,' she said. 'Now you go off to whatever lesson you are supposed to be at, and tell your teacher please to excuse your being late, but that you have been with me. And I just want to say this – I am proud of you both! You are kind and understanding, two things that matter a great deal.'

Blushing with surprise and pleasure, the twins held open the door for Miss Theobald to go out. They looked at each other in delight.

'Isn't she a sport?' said Pat. 'Oh, how glad I am we dared to come in and tell her. I believe things will be all right for Kath now!'

They sped off to gym, and were excused for being late. They wondered and wondered how Kathleen was getting on with Miss Theobald. They knew after tea when Kathleen, her eyes still red, but looking very much happier, came up to them.

'I'm not going,' she said. 'I'm going to stay here and show Miss Theobald I'm as decent as anyone else. She's going to write to my aunt and ask for a proper amount of pocket-money to be paid to me – and I shall give back all the money I took – and start again. And if I can't be as generous as I'd like for a little while, I'll wait patiently till I can.'

'Yes – and don't be afraid of owning up if you haven't

got money to spare,' said Pat. 'Nobody minds that at all. That's just silly pride, to be afraid of saying when you can't afford something. Oh, Kath – I'm so glad you're not going. Isabel and I had just got to like you very much.'

'You've been good friends to me,' said Kathleen, squeezing their arms as she walked between them. 'If ever I can return your kindness, I will. You *will* trust me again, won't you? It would be so awful not to be trusted. I couldn't bear that.'

'Of course we'll trust you,' said Pat. 'If you go on like that I'll get a hundred pounds out of the bank and ask you to keep it for me! Don't be such a silly-billy!'

11.

Miss Kennedy again

The twins were really beginning to settle down well at St Clare's. They were getting used to being in the lowest form instead of in the top one, and they were no longer called the 'stuck-up twins'. Mam'zelle had helped them a great deal with their French writing, and they had caught up with the rest of the form. Miss Roberts found that they had good brains and occasionally threw them a word of praise, which they treasured very much.

Kathleen was their firm friend. She really was a very generous-hearted girl, and although she now had no longer plenty of money to spend, she gave generously in other ways – mended Pat's stockings for her, stuck together a favourite vase of Mam'zelle's that got broken, and spent what time she could with Doris and Hilary when they had to go to the sickbay with flu. She knew that she would never be dishonest again, and she held her head high and tried to forget the silly things she had done, which were now put right.

Miss Kennedy had a bit better time, for since she had been so nice over their Great Feast, the first formers behaved better. But the second form were not so good. They had discovered that Miss Kennedy was terrified of cats, and it was perfectly astonishing the number of cats that appeared at times in the second form classroom.

The second form found every cat they could lay hands on, and secreted them somewhere in the classroom before their history lesson. They had a big cupboard, and this was a good place to hide a cat.

One morning Miss Roberts was not well. She felt sure that she had flu coming, and she retired to bed, hoping to ward it off quickly. So poor Miss Kennedy had to tackle both first and second forms together. The first formers went into the second form classroom, as it was much bigger than theirs.

They entered in an orderly line. Miss Jenks, the second form mistress, was there, and she gave them their places. 'Now sit quietly till Miss Kennedy comes,' she said, and went off to take needlework with another form.

As soon as she had gone, a perfect babel of noise broke out, and to the enormous astonishment of the first formers, a large black cat was produced from the passage, where Tessie, a girl of the second form, had hidden the cat in a cupboard.

The cat was most amiable. It arched its back and purred, sticking its tail up in the air. The twins stared at it in surprise.

'Why the cat?' asked Pat. 'Is it a member of your class, by any chance?'

'Ha ha! Funny joke, I don't think,' said Pam, stroking the cat. 'No, Pat – it's just going to give old Kenny a fine surprise, that's all! Didn't you know she was terrified of cats? We're going to shut old Sooty up in our handwork cupboard over there – and then, at a good moment Tessie, who sits near, is going to pull the door open – and out will walk dear old Sooty, large as life and twice as natural – and he'll make straight for Kenny, you see if he doesn't!'

The first formers began to giggle. This was marvellous – even better than fire-cracks!

'Sh! She's coming!' came a cry from the door, where someone was keeping guard. 'To your places! Put the cat into the cupboard, quick, Tessie!'

The cat went into the cupboard with a rush, much to its amazement. The door was shut on it. Kathleen, who was passionately fond of animals, began to object.

'I say – can the cat breathe properly in there? Ought we to . . .'

'Shut up!' hissed Tessie, and at that moment in walked Miss Kennedy, her pile of books under her arm. She smiled at the girls and sat down. She felt very nervous, for she did not like handling two forms at once. Also she felt something was in the air, and did not like the one or two chuckles that she heard from the back row. Her book dropped to the floor and she bent to pick it up – and her belt snapped undone, and flew off.

This really wasn't very funny, but it seemed most humorous to the girls in the front row, and they bent over their books, trying not to laugh. Miss Kennedy knew that they were laughing and she determined to be firm for once.

'Any girl who disturbs the class by laughing or playing

will stand the whole of the time,' she announced in as firm a voice as she could. Everyone was astonished to hear the mild Miss Kennedy make such a statement, and for a while the lesson went smoothly.

Tessie was to let the cat out about half-way through the class – but the cat thought otherwise. It had lain down on the handwork, and had got itself mixed up with the coloured raffia that was used by the girls for their basket-making. It tried to lick the raffia off its back legs, but couldn't.

It stood up and shook itself. It turned round and round – but the more it turned, the more entangled it got, and at last it became frightened.

It jumped about on the shelf, and some curious noises came from the cupboard. At first Miss Kennedy could not imagine what the noise was. The girls knew quite well that it was the cat, and they bent their heads over their exercise books, doing their best not to laugh.

The cat got excited. It leapt into the air and knocked its head against the shelf above. Then it scrabbled about and bit savagely at the entangling raffia.

'What *is* in that cupboard?' said Miss Kennedy at last.

'The handwork, Miss Kennedy,' answered Tessie.

'I know that,' answered Miss Kennedy, impatiently. 'But handwork doesn't make a noise. What *can* be causing all that disturbance? It must be mice.'

It certainly wasn't mice. It was just poor old Sooty going completely mad. He tore round and round the big shelf, the raffia catching his legs all the time. The whole class began to giggle helplessly.

'This is too much!' said Miss Kennedy, angrily. She walked quickly to the handwork cupboard and flung open the door. Sooty was thrilled, and leapt out with an enormous yowl. Miss Kennedy gave a shriek when she saw the big black animal springing out, and she rushed to the door. Sooty went with her, thinking she was going to let him out. He rubbed against her ankles and Miss Kennedy went white with fright, for she really was quite terrified of cats.

Sooty and Miss Kennedy went out of the door together, parted, and fled in opposite directions. The girls put down their heads on their desks and almost sobbed with laughter. Tears trickled out of Kathleen's eyes, and as for the twins, they had to hold their sides, for they each got dreadful stitches with laughing so much.

Tessie staggered to the door and shut it, in case any other mistress came by. For at least five minutes the girls let themselves go and laughed till they cried. As soon as they stopped, someone started them off again.

'Oh, I say – *did* you see Sooty when he shot out?' cried Tessie, and everyone giggled again.

'It must be mice!' said Doris, imitating Miss Kennedy's voice. Shrieks of laughter again.

'Sh!' said Tessie, wiping her eyes. 'Someone will hear us. I say – I wonder what's become of old Kenny? She disappeared into the blue. Do you suppose she'll come back and finish the lesson?'

But no Miss Kennedy came back. She was sitting in

one of the empty common-rooms, drinking a glass of water, and looking very pale. She was afraid of cats as some people are afraid of beetles or bats – but that was not all that made her feel worried and ill. It was the thought of the girls playing the trick on her, knowing that she would so easily fall into the trap.

'I'm absolutely no good at taking a class,' thought Miss Kennedy, putting down her glass. 'It was all very well when I coached one or two girls at a time – but this job is too much for me. And yet the money does come in so useful now Mother is ill. Still, it's no use. I must give it up.'

She decided to go down to the town and meet a friend of hers at tea-time. She would talk over the matter with her, then come back and give in her notice to Miss Theobald, confessing that she could neither teach nor keep discipline.

So down to the town she went at four o'clock, after telephoning to her friend, Miss Roper, to meet her at the tea-shop.

And to the same shop went the twins and Kathleen, having tea there by themselves as a great treat! The tea-shop was divided into little cosy partitions with red curtains, and the three girls were already sitting eating buttered buns when Miss Kennedy and Miss Roper came in.

They chose the partition next to the three girls, and sat down. The girls could not see them – but it was possible to hear the voices. And they recognized Miss Kennedy's at once!

'Listen! There's old Kenny! I bet she's going to talk

about the cat!' chuckled Kathleen. The girls had no intention of eavesdropping, but they could not help hearing what was said. And, as they thought, Kenny began to talk about the morning's happenings.

But she talked of something else too – of her old mother, ill and poor; of the money that her teaching had so unexpectedly brought in; of the bills she had to pay. She spoke with sadness of her failure to hold the girls in class.

'I'm a fraud,' she told her friend. 'I take the school's money for teaching the girls, and I don't teach them a thing, because I can't manage them, and they just rag me the whole time. Don't you think I should tell the head this, Clara? It's not honest of me to go on, leaving my classes because they rag me. Miss Lewis, the school's history specialist, can't possibly come back till the end of next term – but I don't see how I can honestly take her place till then.'

'But you do so badly need the money to help your mother whilst she's ill,' said Miss Roper. 'It's bad luck, my dear – those girls must be wretches.'

The three girls listened, stricken dumb. They were horrified. What seemed just teasing and ragging to them, meant losing a job to somebody else, meant being a failure – not being able to help a mother when she was ill.

'Let's go,' muttered Pat, in a low voice. 'We oughtn't to overhear this.'

They crept out, unseen by Miss Kennedy, paid their bill and went back to school. They all felt unhappy. They couldn't let Miss Kennedy give up her post. She was a silly in many ways, but she was kind, and a real sport. And they, the girls, *were* wretches!

'Oh, dash, I do feel mean!' said Kathleen, sitting down in their common-room. 'I just hate myself now. I loved the joke this morning – but a joke's not a joke when it means real unhappiness to somebody else.'

'We can't let Kenny go to Miss Theobald,' said Pat, suddenly. 'It would look awful. Look here – we've got to do something, for goodness' sake. Think hard!'

Isabel looked up. 'There's only one thing to do, really,' she said. 'We ought to get all our form to sign a letter, and the second form too, apologizing for the trick, and swearing we won't rag Kenny again. And we'll have to stick to that.'

'That's not a bad idea at all,' said Pat. 'Kath, you go to the second form – they're having a meeting – and tell them quite shortly what's happened. I'll write out the letter – and each one of us can sign it.'

Kathleen sped off. Pat took a pen and some notepaper, and she and Isabel wrote out the letter. This is what it said:

Dear Miss Kennedy,

We are all ashamed of our behaviour this morning, and we do ask you to accept our very humble apologies. We didn't mean the cat to jump out at you. Please forgive us. If you will, we promise never to rag you again, but to behave much better, and work hard. We thought you were a great sport not to split on us about You Know What.

Yours sincerely,

and then all the names of the girls were to follow, written out by each girl.

The second form came in to sign their names. 'What's "You Know What"?' asked Tessie, curiously.

'It's our Great Midnight Feast,' answered Pat. 'She knew we had one and didn't tell. Now, has everyone signed? You haven't, Lorna. Put your name at the bottom.'

All the girls felt rather ashamed when they heard Kathleen's tale of what they had overheard.

'You shouldn't really have listened,' said Hilary, reprovingly. 'It's mean to overhear things.'

'I know,' said Pat. 'But we really couldn't help it, Hilary. And anyway, I'm glad we did. We can stop Kenny giving up her job, anyway.'

It did prevent Miss Kennedy from going to Miss Theobald when she came in that evening. She saw the letter on her desk, and opened it. When she read it, the tears came into her eyes.

'What a nice letter!' she thought. 'The girls are not little wretches after all! If only they keep their promise! I should be happy teaching them then!'

She thanked each form the next morning, and assured them that she forgave them. And, for the first time that term, her lessons went as smoothly as those of the other teachers, for the girls had no intention of breaking their word.

There would be giggles now and then – sly flippings of paper darts – but no organized ragging, and no unkindness. Kenny was happy. She taught well now that she had no ragging to fight, and the girls became interested and keen.

'I'm glad we did the decent thing,' said Pat, one day, after the history lesson. 'I asked old Kenny how her mother was today, and she said she's much better, and is coming out of the nursing home tomorrow. Wouldn't it have been awful if she had died because we made Kenny lose her job so that her mother couldn't be nursed back to health?'

'*Awful,*' agreed Isabel. And everyone in the form thought the same.

12.

A broken window

One morning Hilary came into the common-room most excited.

'I say! Did you know that the circus was coming to the field just outside the town? Well, it is! I saw the notices up!'

'Golly! I hope we're all allowed to go!' said Pat, who loved a circus.

'It's Galliano's Circus,' said Hilary, and she pulled a handbill out of her pocket. 'Look – clowns, acrobats, dancing horses, everything. If only Miss Theobald gives permission for the school to go!'

Miss Theobald did. She said that each evening two of the forms might go, with their teachers. The first form were thrilled. Pat, Isabel, Kathleen and Janet went down to the town to examine the big coloured posters pasted up everywhere.

They did look exiting. Then the girls went to see the big tents set up in the field. They leant over the gate and watched the sleek satin-skinned horses being galloped round with their trainer. They watched in wonder when a big chimpanzee, dressed up in trousers and jersey, came along hand in hand with a small boy, who had a terrier at his heels.

'Gracious! Look at that big monkey!' cried Isabel.

'Sammy's not a monkey. He's a chimpanzee,' said the boy, smiling. 'Shake hands, Sammy!'

The big chimpanzee solemnly held out his hand to the girls. Isabel and Kathleen were too afraid to take it, but Pat put out her hand at once. Sammy shook it up and down.

'Are you coming to see our show?' asked the boy.

'Rather!' said Pat. 'Are you in the circus? What do you do?'

'I'm Jimmy Brown, and I go into the ring with my famous dog, Lucky. That's Lucky, just by your feet. She knows how to spell and count!'

'Oh, no! Dogs can't do that!' said Isabel.

Jimmy laughed. 'Well, mine can. You'll see when you come! Look – see that girl over there, riding the black horse – that's Lotta. You'll see her in the ring too. She can ride the wildest horse in the world!'

The girls stared at Lotta. She was galloping round the field on a beautiful black horse. As she came near she suddenly stood up on the horse's back and waved to the astonished girls!

'Isn't she awfully clever!' said Pat. 'How I wish I could ride like that! Doesn't she ever fall off?'

'Of course not,' said Jimmy. 'Well, I must go. Come on, Sammy. We'll look out for you four girls when you come to the show!'

He went off with the chimpanzee and the little dog. The girls made their way back to school. They were longing for the night to come when they might go to the circus with the first and second forms.

'There are two shows each night,' said Pat. 'One at six-thirty to eight-thirty, and the second at eight forty-five to ten forty-five. I wish we were going to the later one – it would be sport getting back at eleven o'clock!'

'No such luck,' said Isabel. 'Come on, hurry – we shall be late for tea.'

But a dreadful blow befell the first form the next morning. They came into their classroom, chattering as usual – and saw that one big pane of the middle window was completely broken! Miss Roberts was at her desk, looking stern.

'Gracious! How did the window get broken?' cried Janet in surprise.

'That is exactly what I would like to know,' said Miss Roberts. 'When I was in the common-room I heard a crash, and came to see what caused it. I heard the sound of running feet going round the corner of the corridor – and when I came into the room I saw the broken window!'

'Who did it?' said Pat.

'I don't know,' answered Miss Roberts. 'But this is what broke the window.' She held up a hard rubber lacrosse ball. 'I found it still rolling across the floor when I came in. Somebody must have been playing with it in the classroom – and the window was smashed. It's against the rules to take lacrosse balls out of the locker in the gym, unless you go to games, as you know.'

Everyone listened in silence. They all felt a little guilty

when Miss Roberts mentioned that it was against the rules to take lacrosse balls, because it was a rule nobody bothered to keep. Any girl slipped to the locker to borrow a ball to play with at break.

'Now,' said Miss Roberts, 'I want the girl who broke the window to own up now, or to come to me at break and tell me then. She should, of course, have stayed to own up as soon as the window was broken – but it is quite natural in a moment of fright to run away.'

Nobody spoke. All the girls sat perfectly still in their seats. Nobody looked at anyone else. Miss Roberts looked searchingly along the rows, looking for a guilty face.

But as half the girls were blushing with sheer nervousness, that was no help. Practically all the class looked guilty and ill at ease. They always did when anything went wrong.

'Well,' said Miss Roberts at last, 'it is quite evident that the culprit is not going to own up now. She must come to me at break, without fail. All you girls have a sense of honour, I know, and not one of you is a coward. So I am quite sure that the culprit will be brave enough to come to me. I shall be in the common-room, alone.'

Still nobody said a word. One or two looked round at each other, and everyone wondered who the sinner was. Pat and Isabel smiled nervously at each other. They had been together since breakfast, so they knew that neither of *them* was the sinner!

The first lesson began. It was maths. Miss Roberts was not in a good temper, and nobody dared to utter a word.

Dark and fair heads were bent busily over books, and when the form mistress rapped out an order it was obeyed at once. Everyone knew how dangerous it would be to get into trouble when Miss Roberts was on the warpath.

After maths came French. Mam'zelle came into the room, and exclaimed at the broken window.

'*Tiens*! The window is broken! How did that happen?'

'We don't know, Mam'zelle,' said Hilary. 'Nobody has owned up yet.'

'That is abominable!' cried Mam'zelle, looking round the class with her big dark eyes. 'It is not brave!'

The class said nothing. They all felt uncomfortable, for it was not nice to think that somebody in the class was a coward. Still, maybe the culprit would own up at break. Whoever could it be?

Pat and Isabel thought hard. It couldn't be Janet or Hilary, for both girls were brave spirited and owned to a fault at once. It couldn't be Kathleen, for she had been with them. It might be Vera – or Sheila – or Joan – or Doris. No, surely it couldn't be any of them! They wouldn't be cowards.

At break the first form got together and discussed the matter. 'It wasn't *us*,' said Pat. 'Isabel and I were together all the time after breakfast till we went to the classroom. And Kathleen was with us too.'

'Well, it wasn't *me*,' said Hilary. 'I was doing a job for Rita.'

'And it wasn't *me*,' said Janet. 'I was cleaning the bird-table, and Doris was helping.'

One by one the girls of the first form all said what they had been doing between breakfast-time and the first lesson. Apparently not one of them could have broken the window – though one must be telling an untruth!

After break the girls took their places in their form room. Miss Roberts came in, her mouth in a thin line and her hazel eyes cold. She looked round the class.

'I am sorry to say that no one has owned up,' she said. 'So I have had to report the matter to Miss Theobald. She agrees with me that the window must be paid for by the whole class, as the culprit hasn't owned up. The window is made of special glass, and will cost twenty pounds to mend. Miss Theobald has decided instead of letting you go to the circus, which would cost one pound each, she will use the money for the window.'

There was a gasp of dismay from all the girls. Not go to the circus! That was a terrible blow. They looked round at one another, angry and upset. Why should the whole class suffer because one person had done a wrong thing? It didn't seem fair.

'I am sure that the one who broke the window will not want her whole class to be punished,' went on Miss Roberts. 'So I hope she will still own up, before the night comes when our form is due to go to the show – that is, on Thursday. And I trust that if any of you know who it is you will insist that she does her duty by her form.'

'But Miss Roberts, suppose nobody owns up,' began Hilary, 'couldn't we all put a pound of our own towards the window and still go to the circus?'

'No,' said Miss Roberts. 'There's no argument, Hilary. What I have said stands, and will not be altered. Open your books at page eighty-two, please.'

What a babel there was after morning school was over, in the quarter of an hour before dinner! How angry and indignant the girls were!

'It's a shame!' cried Janet. 'I didn't do it – nor did you, Pat and Isabel – and we jolly well know it. So why should we be punished too?'

'Well, it's the custom in schools to make a whole form suffer for one person in a case like this,' said Hilary. 'They do it at my brother's school too – though it doesn't happen often. I don't see the point of it myself, but there you are. If only I knew who it was! Wouldn't I take them by the scruff of the neck and give them a shaking!'

'Look here – what about one of us owning up to it, so that the rest can go?' said Kathleen, suddenly. 'I don't mind owning up and taking the blame. Then all you others can go.'

'Don't be an idiot,' said Pat, slipping her arm through Kathleen's. 'As if we'd let you do a thing like that!'

'I suppose you *didn't* do it, Kath?' said Sheila, half-laughing.

'Of course she didn't!' cried Isabel. 'She was with Pat and me all the time. It's jolly decent of her to offer to take the blame – but I wouldn't dream of it. If I heard she'd owned up to save our skins I'd go straight to Miss Roberts myself and tell her that Kathleen couldn't possibly have done it!'

'Oh, well,' said Kathleen, 'I shan't say anything, of course, if you feel like that about it. If only we knew which of us had done it!'

The whole of Tuesday slipped by and the whole of Wednesday. Still nobody had owned up. When Thursday came Miss Roberts informed the class that the second form were to go to the circus, but not the first. The class groaned and fidgeted.

'I'm very sorry,' said Miss Roberts. 'It's most unfortunate. I only hope that the culprit is feeling most unhappy and uncomfortable. Now, no more groaning, please. Let's get on with our geography!'

13.

The four truants

That afternoon, after tea, four girls of the first form held a secret meeting in one of the little music rooms. They were the twins, and Kathleen and Janet. They were all furious because they were not allowed to go that night to the show in the town.

'Look here! *Let's* go!' said Janet. 'We can slip off at a quarter past eight on our bikes without anyone noticing, if we go down the path by the lacrosse field. And we can get back in the dark all right.'

'But the school doors are locked at ten,' said Kathleen.

'I know that, idiot!' said Janet. 'But what's the matter with a ladder? There's one alongside the gardener's shed. We can easily get into our dormitory window with that.'

'Yes – but the ladder will be seen the next morning, leading up to our window!' said Isabel.

'Oh, golly, haven't you *any* brains?' sighed Janet. '*One* of us can go up the ladder – and undo the side-door to let the others in – and we can all take the ladder back to the shed before we go in. Is that quite clear, or shall I say it all over again?'

Everyone laughed. Janet was funny when she was

impatient. 'I see,' said Pat. 'But gosh, if we were caught! I don't like to think what would happen to us.'

'Well, don't,' said Janet, 'because we shan't be caught! Miss Roberts never puts the light on at night when she comes to our dormitory now. We shall be all right. We must tell Hilary though. She won't come with us because she's head girl and keeps all the rules – but she won't stop us going.'

Hilary didn't stop them. 'All right,' she said. 'Risk it if you want to. I won't stop you. But for goodness' sake don't get caught!'

The second form went off to the circus with Miss Jenks. The first form stayed behind, sulky and angry. Only the four who were going to slip off by themselves looked at all bright. Most of the first form knew what Janet had planned, but nobody else dared to risk it.

'You'll get expelled if you're caught, I shouldn't wonder,' said Doris.

'We shan't be expelled and we *shan't* be caught,' said Janet, firmly.

When the time came, the four girls put on their hats and coats and slipped down to the side-door. It was dark outside, but the night was clear. Coming home there would be a moon. They went softly to the bicycle shed.

'Golly! What a noise bikes make!' whispered Janet, as the four machines clanked and rattled. 'Now – down the path by the field. Come on.'

Off they all rode, their lamps shining in the darkness. When they arrived at the circus field they saw the people streaming out of the gates. They had been to the six-thirty performance.

'Look out! Hide by the hedge till everyone's gone!' said Janet. 'We don't want to run into Miss Jenks!'

They hid until it was safe. They pushed their bicycles behind the hedge and went to the gate, where people were already going in, under the flare of acetylene lamps. The girls paid and went towards the big circus tent. Soon they had taken their seats, well at the back in case anyone saw them. They took off their school hats.

The circus was marvellous. They saw the girl Lotta, now dressed in a sparkling, shining frock, riding bareback round the ring, standing on her horse, kneeling, jumping, smiling all the time. They saw Jimmy and his dog Lucky, and could not imagine how he could be so clever. They cheered the absurd clowns and the amazing acrobats. They loved big Mr Galliano, with his cracking whip and big moustache. It was a gorgeous show and the four girls enjoyed every minute.

'We'd better slip out a bit before the end,' whispered Janet, watching Sammy the chimpanzee solemnly undress himself and put on a pair of pyjamas. 'I say – isn't he funny? Oh, look – he's getting into bed!'

Just before the show was finished the girls slipped out quietly.

'What a marvellous show!' said Janet, as they made their way to where they had left their bicycles. 'Where's my bike? Oh, here it is.'

They mounted their bicycles and rode off. The moon

was up now and they could see clearly. They were soon back at the school. They put their bicycles into the shed as quietly as they could, and then, with beating hearts, they tiptoed to the shed, outside which the ladder was kept.

They all felt excited and nervous. Just suppose they were caught now! It would be awful. But nobody was about. A dim light showed from a mistress's bedroom in the eastern wing of the school. It was about eleven o'clock, and all the girls and some of the mistresses would be asleep.

They looked for the ladder. There were two, a small one and a much bigger one. Janet tugged at the smaller one.

'I should think this one will just about reach,' she said. So the four of them carried it to where their dormitory windows shone in the moonlight. They kept in the dark shadows and were as quiet as they could be.

They set the ladder up gently against the wall – but to their great dismay it didn't nearly reach to the windowsill!

'Dash!' said Janet. 'Look at that! It's much too dangerous to try and climb to the sill from the top of the ladder – it's so far below the window. Well – come on, let's take it back and get the other ladder. That's long enough to reach to the roof, I should think!'

They took the small ladder back and put it down gently. But then they found they could not possibly carry the big ladder! It was enormously heavy and needed two or three gardeners to handle it. The four girls could hardly move it and certainly would not be able to set it up against the wall.

They stood in the moonlight and stared at one another in dismay. 'Now what are we going to do?' asked Isabel, her voice quivering. 'We can't stay out here all night.'

'Of course not, silly,' said Janet. 'We'll try all the doors. Maybe we'll find one that's unlocked. Cheer up.'

So they tiptoed round the school, trying the doors, but every one of them was safely locked and bolted. The staff did their work well!

Kathleen began to cry. She did not want to be caught breaking the rules, because she had tried very hard to be in Miss Theobald's good books since she had been forgiven for her fault. It suddenly seemed a very dreadful thing to her to be out of doors when all the others were in bed and asleep.

'We shall be discovered in the morning,' she whispered. 'And we shall catch our deaths of cold staying out here.'

'Shut up and don't be such a baby,' said Janet fiercely.

'I know what we can do! We'll throw little pebbles up to our dormitory window!' said Pat. 'They will make a rattling noise and maybe one of the girls will wake. Then she can slip down and open a door for us.'

'Good idea!' said Janet. 'Pick up tiny pebbles, everyone!'

They scooped handfuls up from the gravel, and threw them up. But Kathleen threw very badly and her pebbles rattled against the wrong window – the one above the dormitory, where Mam'zelle slept! And Mam'zelle awoke!

'Quick! Back into the shadows!' whispered Janet, urgently. 'Idiot – you hit Mam'zelle's window!'

The big dark head of Mam'zelle looked out, and they heard her mutter to herself. They squeezed together in a corner, hardly daring to breathe, terrified that Mamzelle would see them. But the shadows were black and she could see nothing. Puzzled, and yawning deeply, she went back to her bed. The girls stayed where they were for a few minutes and then began to whisper.

'This is awful! Really awful. What *are* we going to do?'

'I do wish we hadn't slipped off to the circus!'

'I'm so cold my teeth are chattering.'

Then Pat clutched hold of Isabel's arm and whispered loudly. 'Look – look – isn't that someone looking out of our dormitory window?'

They all looked up – and sure enough a girl's head was peeping from the window. Pat slipped out of the shadows and stood in the moonlight. Hilary's voice came down to her in a whisper.

'Pat! How late you are! Where are the others?'

'Here,' whispered Pat. 'The ladders aren't any good. Open the side-door here and let us in, Hilary, quick! We're so cold.'

Hilary drew in her head and disappeared. A minute later the four girls heard the key turning in the lock of the side-door, and the bolts being slipped back – and the door was open! They crept in quietly and Hilary locked and bolted the door once more.

They all slipped upstairs like mice, and tip-toed in their stockinged feet to their dormitory. Once there they sank on to Janet's bed and began to giggle from sheer excitement and relief.

They told Hilary all that had happened. Doris woke up and joined the little group. The four truants began to feel much better now that they were safe, and boasted of all they had done.

'Did you hear our pebbles rattling on the window?' asked Janet of Hilary. 'Why did you come to the window? Golly, wasn't I glad to hear your voice?'

'Your pebbles came rattling on to the floor!' said Hilary, with a laugh. 'The window was open at the bottom. I left it like that for you to climb in. When I heard the sound of pebbles all over the floor I woke up. At first I couldn't imagine what the noise was – then I switched on my torch and saw the bits of gravel. We'll have to sweep those up in the morning.'

Janet yawned. 'I'm so tired,' she said. 'The circus was marvellous. I wish you could have seen it, Hilary.'

'So do I,' said Hilary. 'Buck up and get undressed now, for goodness' sake. And don't make too much noise or you'll wake Mam'zelle. Her room's just above, remember.'

'We know that all right!' said Pat, giggling as she remembered Mam'zelle's dark head sticking out of the window. 'Where's my nightie? Oh, blow, where's it gone?'

'You won't find it on *my* bed, silly,' said Isabel, who was already undressed and in her nightgown. 'You've got muddled. That's your bed, over there, and there's your nightie on the pillow.'

'Oh, yes,' said Pat, yawning. 'I wish I could go to sleep in my clothes!'

Soon all the dormitory was quiet once more, and every girl was asleep. The four truants slept peacefully – but there was a shock in store for them in the morning!

14.

A great disappointment

The four truants were extremely sleepy the next day. They could hardly wake up. When the dressing-bell went not one of them got out of bed.

'Hi, Janet! Kathleen! Aren't you going to get a move on?' cried Hilary. 'You'll be late. And just look at those lazy twins – they haven't even opened their eyes!'

'Another five minutes!' murmured Pat, sleepily. But the five minutes stretched into ten, and still the four girls hadn't moved. Hilary winked at Doris, and the two of them went swiftly to the four white beds and stripped off all the bedclothes, throwing them on the floor.

'Oooooh!' shivered the girls, for it was a very cold morning. 'You mean things!'

'Come on, get up, or you'll get into a row,' said Hilary. And very slowly and sleepily the four dressed, yawning all the time. They cheered up a bit when the rest of the form clustered round them, asking what happened the night before. They really felt almost heroines as they related their exciting adventures.

'I don't feel in the least like lessons this morning,' said Janet. 'Oh, my goodness – Miss Roberts is taking us for algebra, isn't she? I always am stupid about that anyhow, and I shan't be able to understand a thing today. I hope she's in a good temper.'

The class went into their form room, and took their places. Janet got out her algebra book and hurriedly glanced through the chapter she had been told to learn. It seemed to her as if she had entirely forgotten every word! But that was just because she had had such a short night.

'Here comes Miss Roberts!' hissed Doris, who was at the door. The girls stood. Miss Roberts came in – and goodness, whatever could have happened? She looked very pleased, and her eyes sparkled so that she looked really pretty.

'Sit, girls,' she said, and the girls sat down, wondering why their mistress looked so pleased. Had they done some marvellous prep or something?

'Girls,' said Miss Roberts, 'I feel very happy about something this morning. I have found out that it was not anyone in my form who broke the window!'

The girls looked at her, amazed. Miss Roberts smiled round the class.

'It was one of the second form,' she said. 'Apparently the ball bounced in here, the girl rushed for it, tried to catch it, and it was knocked on to the window, which broke.'

'But why didn't she own up?' cried Hilary, indignantly. 'That was jolly mean of her! We missed going to the circus because of that.'

'Wait,' said Miss Roberts. 'The girl was Queenie Hobart, who, as you know, is now in the sickbay with a bad attack of flu. She was frightened when she broke the window, but meant to own up at the end of the morning. In the middle of the morning she was taken ill and was hurried off to the sickbay where she has been really ill for a few days. Today she is better, and her form mistress, Miss Jenks, went to see her.'

'Did she own up then?' asked Janet.

'Miss Jenks told her that the second form had gone to the circus the night before, but not the first form, and Queenie asked why,' said Miss Roberts. 'When she heard that you had all been punished for something that was her fault, she was very upset and began to cry. She told Miss Jenks, of course, and Miss Jenks came hurrying to tell me.'

'Oh! I *am* glad it wasn't anybody in our form,' said Hilary. 'I did hate to think that somebody was such a mean coward!'

'And I couldn't understand it either,' said Miss Roberts. 'I think I know you all pretty well – and although you are sometimes very stupid, aggravating and, in fact, a set of nuisances – I really couldn't believe that any of you were cowards!'

Miss Roberts smiled as she made these remarks, and the class laughed. They were all most relieved.

'Can we go to the circus after all, then?' asked Hilary. 'There's still tonight or tomorrow.'

'Of course,' said Miss Roberts. 'You are to go tomorrow, Miss Theobald says – and to make up for your disappointment, which was quite undeserved, I am to take you down into the town and give you a real good tea first! What do you think of that?'

The girls thought a lot of it! They said 'Oooh' and 'Ah!' and rubbed their hands together, and looked as cheerful as possible. Tea first – a really scrumptious tea – and then the circus – and it was sure to be good fun on the last night of all! What luck that Queenie had owned up in time!

But there were four girls who were feeling most uncomfortable about the whole thing – and they were the twins, and Kathleen and Janet. They had played truant and seen the show! They looked at one another and felt very guilty. Why hadn't they waited?

They went to Hilary about it afterwards. 'Hilary! We feel awfully mean now somehow – do you think we ought to go tomorrow?' asked Pat.

'Well, if you don't, what excuse will you make?' said Hilary. 'Since you ask me, I say you jolly well oughtn't to go! You've had your pleasure, by breaking the rules – well, everyone breaks rules sometimes, so I'm not blaming you for that. The thing is, it's not fair that you should have a second treat. I should feel like that myself, just as you do. But if you go and tell Miss Roberts why, you certainly will get into a first-class row.'

'Could we say we don't feel well?' said Isabel. 'I really don't feel awfully well today – I had so little sleep.'

'Well, say that tomorrow,' said Hilary. 'But I say, it's bad luck on you, isn't it? You've done yourself out of a gorgeous tea, and everyone knows that a Saturday night is the best night to see a show.'

'I wish we hadn't been so impatient now,' sighed Kathleen. 'I would so love to go with you tomorrow.'

The four were very sad. They talked about it together. 'Let's go anyhow!' said Janet. Then almost immediately she changed her mind. 'No, we can't. I'd feel mean all the time. And the other girls would think us mean too.'

'I only hope Miss Roberts doesn't send us to Matron for some of her disgusting medicine, when we tell her we don't feel well tomorrow,' said Kathleen, who was a perfect coward over taking medicine.

But when the next day came there was no question of telling a story about feeling unwell – for all four girls had bad colds! They had caught a chill standing about waiting to get into the school on Thursday night – and how they sneezed and coughed!

Miss Roberts noticed at once. 'You'd better spend a day in bed,' she said. 'You may be in for flu. Go along to Matron and ask her to take your temperatures. Four of you at once! Wherever could you all have caught such bad colds?'

They didn't tell her. They went to Matron, feeling very sad and sorry. Kathleen had a temperature, and as Matron was not at all sure that the whole lot were not going to have flu she did the sensible thing and popped them all into bed. She gave them each a dose out of one of her enormous bottles, tucked them up, and left them in the sickbay together.

'A-tish-oo!' sneezed Kathleen. 'Golly, weren't we idiots to rush off like that the other night? I do hate having a beastly cold like this.'

'And missing that tea,' sighed Pat. 'Hilary said Miss Roberts had rung up the tea-shop and made sure that they had those special chocolate cakes we like.'

'Well – it's no use grumbling!' said Isabel, sensibly. 'We brought this on ourselves. Now shut up, you others. I want to read.'

The first form went off at five with Miss Roberts and had a gorgeous tea. Miss Roberts bought four of the special chocolate cakes to take back to the girls in the sickbay.

'I think they have been perfect bricks about all this,' she said to Hilary. 'Not a grumble, not one word of complaint!'

Hilary said nothing. Miss Roberts would have been astonished if she had known the real reason why the four truants were not at the circus! But Hilary was certainly not going to tell her.

The circus was at its best that night – and afterwards the girls were allowed to go behind the ring and see the performers at close quarters. Sammy the chimpanzee was delighted to see them and kept taking off his cap to them most politely. Jumbo, the enormous elephant, blew down Hilary's neck and lifted her curls as if they had been blown by the wind! Lotta let them all stroke her magnificent horse, Black Beauty. Altogether, it was a marvellous evening, the girls went back tired, but very happy and talkative.

Miss Roberts slipped into the sickbay to see if the four girls were awake. Matron was just tucking them up for the night.

'There's nothing much wrong with them,' she told Miss Roberts. 'Kathleen's temperature is down to normal. They've just got ordinary bad colds, that's all. As tomorrow is Sunday I'll keep them in bed one more day.'

'I've brought them some of the special chocolate cakes we always have at the tea-shop,' said Miss Roberts. 'I suppose they mustn't have them now.'

'Oh, they can if they feel like it,' said Matron, smiling. 'It won't hurt them!'

All four girls felt like chocolate cakes immediately, and sat up. They thought it was jolly kind of Miss Roberts to think of them. They munched their cakes and listened to their teacher's recital of the evening's happenings.

'Didn't you think Sammy the chimpanzee was funny when he undressed himself and got into bed?' asked Kathleen eagerly, quite forgetting that Miss Roberts had no idea she had seen the circus. Miss Roberts stared in surprise.

'Kathleen saw the posters in the town,' said Pat, hurriedly, glaring at the unfortunate Kathleen with rage.

'I think it's time the girls settled down now, Miss Roberts,' said Matron, coming in, luckily for the four, at that very moment. Miss Roberts said good night at once, and went. The girls lay down, whilst Matron fussed round a bit, then turned out the light, and went.

'Idiot, Kathleen!' said Janet. 'You nearly gave us all away!'

'Sorry,' said Kathleen, sleepily. 'I quite forgot!'

'No more talking!' said Matron, putting her head round the door. 'Another word, and I'll come in and give you all a dose of my very nastiest medicine!'

And after that there wasn't a word!

15.

A terrible quarrel

The weeks went quickly by. Half-term came and went. The twins' mother came to see them at half-term and took them out in the car for the day. She was glad to see them looking so well and happy.

'Well, how are you getting on?' she asked. 'I hope you're not finding St Clare's quite as bad as you feared!'

The twins blushed. 'It's not a bad school,' said Pat.

'It's quite decent,' said Isabel. Their mother smiled to herself. She knew the twins so well – and their few words meant that they liked St Clare's and were happy.

Every week there were lacrosse matches. Sometimes they were played by the lower forms, sometimes by the upper. The twins became very keen indeed, and used to watch all the upper form matches with great enjoyment. They thought Belinda Towers was marvellous. She was as swift as the wind, and her catching was beautiful to watch.

'Do you remember how rude we were to her at the beginning of the term?' said Pat. 'Golly, I wonder how we dared now!'

'We were awful idiots,' said Isabel. 'Honestly, I wonder how everyone put up with us!'

'Well, there's one person I simply *can't* put up with!'

said Pat. 'And that's Sheila Naylor. What is the matter with her? She's so awfully haughty and conceited – always talking about her marvellous home, and her horse, and their three cars. Always pushing herself forward and airing her opinions – which aren't worth twopence, anyway!'

Everyone found Sheila very trying indeed. She was always doing her best to impress people, and to make them think that she was wonderful. Actually she was a plain and ordinary girl, with rather bad manners, who didn't speak very well. All her clothes were good, and she went to no end of trouble to buy the best of everything – and yet she never brushed her hair really well, and if she could forget to wash her neck, she would!

The most impatient girl in the first form was Janet. She could not bear vanity, or conceit, and Sheila's airs and graces irritated her beyond words. She hadn't the patience to put up with Sheila, and usually Sheila knew this and kept out of her way.

One afternoon, just before tea, the first form were enjoying themselves in their common-room. Pat put on the record player, and played the same record four times running. Janet looked up.

'For goodness' sake! Are you trying to learn that record by heart, Pat? Take it off and break it! If I have to hear it again I'll scream!'

'You didn't ought to talk like that,' began Sheila, in a mincing voice – and Janet flung down her book in a rage.

'Hark at Sheila! "Didn't ought to!" Good Heavens, Sheila, where were you brought up? Haven't you learnt by now that people don't say "Didn't ought to!" My goodness, you talk about your house, and your cars, your horse and your lake and goodness knows what – and then you talk like a barrow-boy!'

Sheila went very white. Pat hurriedly put on another record. Janet took up her book again, still angry, but rather ashamed. If Sheila had said nothing more, the whole thing might have blown over. But after a while Sheila raised her voice and addressed Janet.

'I'm sure that if my people knew that I had to put up with girls like *you*, Janet, they would never have sent me to St Clare's,' she began. 'You've no manners at all, you . . .'

'Manners! *You* talk about manners!' raged Janet, flinging down her book again. 'Good Heavens! What about your own manners, I should like to know! You can begin to talk about other people's when you know how to wash your neck and brush your hair, and how to eat decently! And then you pretend you are too grand for us! Huh!'

Janet stamped out of the room. Sheila sat perfectly still, very pale. The twins glanced at her, and Pat put on yet another record, setting it at 'Loud'. What an awful quarrel!

After a while Sheila went out of the room. Pat switched off the record player. 'Didn't she look awful?' she said to Isabel. 'I wish Janet hadn't said all that. It's true it's what we've all thought, and perhaps said to one another in joke – but its rather awful to blurt it all out like that.'

'Well, it's partly Sheila's own silly fault,' said Hilary. 'If she wouldn't swank as she does, and try to make out she's someone marvellous, we wouldn't notice so easily the stupid things she does and says. I mean to say – if people swank about five different bathrooms, one pink, one blue, one green, one yellow and one mauve, and then don't trouble to wash their necks, you do notice it rather!'

'Yes – she's funny about her bathrooms!' said Isabel. 'She's funny altogether. She's the only girl in the form that I really and truly don't know at all. I mean, I don't know if she's generous or mean, kind or unkind, honest or dishonest, truthful or untruthful, jolly or serious – because she's always pretending about herself – putting on airs and graces, swanking, being somebody that she isn't. She might be quite nice, for all we know!'

'I shouldn't think so,' said Hilary, who was heartily tired of Sheila and her nonsense. 'Honestly, I think she's batty.'

Sheila didn't come in for tea, but nobody missed her. When she didn't attend evening preparation in the form room, Miss Roberts sent Pat to find her. Pat hunted all over the place, and at last came across Sheila sitting in a deserted and cold little music room, all by herself.

'Sheila! What in the world are you doing?' asked Pat. 'Have you forgotten it's prep tonight?'

Sheila sat still and said nothing. Pat looked at her closely. She looked ill.

'Don't you feel well?' asked Pat. 'I'll take you to Matron if you like. What's up, Sheila old girl?'

'Nothing,' said Sheila.

'Well, what are you sitting here for, all in the cold?'

asked Pat. 'Don't be an idiot. If you're not ill, come along to prep. Miss Roberts is getting all hot and bothered about you.'

'I'm not coming,' said Sheila. 'I can't face you all again, after what Janet said.'

'Well, really! Fancy taking any notice of Janet!' said Pat, feeling worried. 'You know how she loses her temper with all of us, and says things she doesn't mean. She's forgotten all about it by now. Come along!'

'She didn't say things she didn't mean. That's the whole point,' said Sheila, still in the same quiet, rather strange voice. 'She said things she *did* mean! Oh, I hate her!'

'You can't hate old Janet!' said Pat. 'She's dreadfully quick-tempered and impatient, but she's very kind too. She wouldn't *really* hurt you, Sheila. Look here – I'm sure you're not well. Come with me to Matron. Perhaps you've got a temperature.'

'Leave me alone,' said Sheila, obstinately. So in despair Pat left her, feeling very worried. What a pity Janet had flared out like that, and said those really dreadful things! Pat knew how she would feel if anyone sneered at her in that way in front of everyone. She wondered what to do. What should she tell Miss Roberts?

On her way back to the form room she passed the head girl's study. The door was a little open and Pat could just see Winifred James bent over a book. She hesitated outside, as a thought came into her head.

She couldn't tell Miss Roberts about the awful quarrel. But could she tell Winifred? Something had got to be done about Sheila, and she simply didn't know what! She knocked at Winifred's door.

'Come in!' said the head girl, and raised her serious face as Pat came in.

'Hallo! Is there anything the matter?' asked Winifred. 'Oughtn't you to be at prep?'

'Yes, I ought,' said Pat. 'But Miss Roberts sent me to find somebody. And I'm rather worried about this girl, Winifred, but I can't possibly tell Miss Roberts, so can I tell you?'

'Of course,' said Winifred, 'so long as it isn't just telling tales, Patricia.'

'Of course it's not, Winifred!' said Pat. 'I would never tell tales. But I suddenly remembered that you and this girl come from the same town, so I thought maybe you could help a bit.'

'This is very mysterious,' said Winifred. 'What's it all about?'

Then Pat explained about the quarrel, and told the head girl all that had happened. 'And Sheila looks so funny and so ill,' she said. 'I'm afraid it's something worse than just a silly quarrel.'

Winifred listened in silence. 'I'm glad you came to me,' she said. 'It so happens I'm the only person that can help a little, because I know Sheila's history. You are a sensible person, Pat, so I shall tell you a little. And perhaps between us we can help Sheila.'

'I hope we can,' said Pat. 'I don't like her, Winifred – in fact, I hardly know her at all because she's always hidden behind conceit and swank, if you know what I mean. But she's awfully unhappy and I hate to see that.'

'Sheila's parents were once very poor,' said Winifred. 'Her mother was the daughter of our gardener. Her father kept a kind of village stores. He made a great deal of money, an enormous fortune, in fact, so they rose tremendously in the world. Now they have a wonderful house, almost a mansion, goodness knows how many servants and cars – and they sent Sheila to the best schools possible because they wanted their daughter to be a lady.'

'Oh,' said Pat, suddenly understanding a lot of things. 'So that's why poor Sheila is always swanking and being haughty and arrogant, and showing off – because she's afraid we'll not want to be friends with her. She's afraid we might sneer at her.'

'Yes – her stupid haughtiness is just a sort of smoke-screen to hide the plain, ordinary, rather frightened person she is underneath,' said Winifred. 'And now you see what has happened. Janet has blown away the smoke-screen and pointed out to everyone just those things that Sheila is always trying to hide – the manners and speech she learnt when she was very small.'

'But how awfully silly of Sheila to pretend like that!' said Pat. 'If she'd told us honestly that her people had made a lot of money, and how pleased she was to be able to come to St Clare's, and all that, we'd have understood and liked her for it. But all that silly conceit and pretence! Honestly, Winifred, it was awful.'

'When people feel that they are not so clever, so good

or so well-born as others, they often behave like that, to hide their feelings of inferiority,' said Winifred, sounding rather learned to Pat. 'Be sorry for them and help them.'

'Well – how can I help Sheila?' asked Pat. 'I really don't see how I can.'

'I'll go to her myself,' said Winifred, getting up. 'All I want *you* to do – and Isabel too – is to be extra nice to her for a week or two, and not to laugh at her or point out anything that might hurt her. Now that Janet has dragged away the wall Sheila set up round herself, and shown what a poor thing there is behind it, she will want a little friendship and understanding. If she's got any common sense she'll drop her airs and graces after this, and you'll have a chance of finding out what the real Sheila is like. But do give her a chance, won't you?'

'Of course I will,' said Pat. 'Thanks awfully, Winifred. I'll go back to prep now.'

What Winifred said to Sheila the twins never knew. The head girl was wise beyond her years, and handled the shocked and distressed girl with understanding and gentleness. Sheila appeared in the common-room that night, pale and nervous, and would not meet anyone's eyes. But Pat came to her rescue at once.

'Sheila! You're just the person I wanted! *Please* tell me where I've gone wrong in this jumper I'm knitting. You're so clever at following patterns and I get all muddled. Look – did I go wrong there – or was it here?'

Sheila gladly went to Pat's side, and was soon showing her how to put the wrong stitch right. When that was done, Isabel called to her. 'Hi, Sheila – will you lend me your paints? I can't imagine what's happened to mine.'

'Yes, of course,' said Sheila, and went to fetch her paints. Janet looked up as soon as she was out of the room.

'Why all this sudden friendship for our haughty Sheila?' she asked.

'To make up a bit for the beastly things you said to her,' said Pat. 'Give her a chance, Janet. You've hit her hard on her tenderest places, and taken all the stuffing out of her.'

'Good thing too,' said Janet, gruffly. 'She needed it.'

'Well, she's had it, so now give her a chance,' said Pat. 'Don't be small, Janet.'

'I'm not,' said Janet. 'I'm jolly sorry for what I said now, though you may not think it. All right – I'll do my bit. But I'm not going to say I'm sorry. If I do it'll get her all hot and bothered again. But I don't mind *showing* I'm sorry.'

'Better still,' said Isabel. 'Look out – here she comes!'

Sheila came in with the paints. 'Thanks,' said Isabel. 'Golly, what a lovely box!'

Usually Sheila would have said at once what the box had cost, and would have boasted about it. But she said nothing. Janet glanced at her and saw that she was still pale. Janet was kind-hearted and generous, although her tongue could be sharp and bitter, and her temper was hot. She got down a tin of toffees from her shelf and handed them round. Sheila expected to be missed out and looked away.

'Toffee for you, Sheila, old girl?' said Janet, in her clear, pleasant voice. Sheila looked at Janet and hesitated. She still felt sore and angry with her. But Janet's brown eyes were kind and soft, and Sheila knew that she was trying to make peace. She swallowed her feelings, and put out her hand to take a toffee.

'Thanks, Janet,' she said, in rather a shaky voice. Then all the girls plunged into a discussion of the play they were going to prepare for Christmas, and in the interest of it all Sheila forgot the quarrel, sucked her toffee, and grew happier.

She thought hard when she went to bed that night. She shouldn't have boasted and bragged – but she had only done it because she felt she wasn't as good as the others and she wanted to hide it. And all the time the girls had seen her weak spots, and must have laughed at her boasting. Well – if only they would be friendly towards her and not sneer at her, she would try not to mind. She was not a brave girl, and not a very sensible one – but that night she was brave enough and sensible enough to see that money and cars didn't matter at all. It was the person underneath that mattered.

'And now I'll do what Winifred said I must do – show the girls the person I am underneath,' thought poor Sheila, turning over in bed. 'I don't think I'm much of a person really – but anyway. I'll be better than that awful conceited creature I've pretended to be for a year!'

And that was the end of Sheila's haughty and boastful manner. The other girls followed the example of Janet and the twins, and were friendly to Sheila, and gave her a chance. She took the chance, and although, as she had feared, she wasn't much of a person at first, nevertheless the rather mouse-like gentle Sheila was much nicer than the girl she had been before. As time went on, she would become somebody real, and then as Pat said, she would be worth having for a friend.

'I shall always give people a chance now,' Pat said to Isabel. 'Look at Kathleen – what a brick she is! And Sheila's so different, already.'

'Well,' said Janet, who overheard, 'I should jolly well think you *would* give people a chance! Didn't we all give *you* two a chance? My goodness, you were pretty unbearable when you came, I can tell you. But you're not so bad now. In fact, you're quite passable!'

Pat and Isabel picked up cushions and rushed at the quick-tongued Janet. With squeals and shrieks she tried to get away, but they pummelled her unmercifully.

'We shan't give *you* a chance, you wretch!' giggled Isabel. 'You don't deserve one! Ow, stop pinching, you brute.'

'Well, get off my middle then,' panted Janet. 'Wait till *I* get hold of a cushion!'

But they didn't wait! They tore off to gym with Janet after them, bumping into half a dozen girls on the way.

'Those first form kids!' said Tessie, in disgust. 'Honestly, they ought to be in a kindergarten, the way they behave!'

16.

Sheila does her bit

Only four weeks remained of the winter term. The girls were busy with plays, songs and sketches, ready for the end of the term. The first form were doing a historical play with Miss Kennedy and thoroughly enjoying themselves.

Miss Kennedy had written the play herself with the girls all helping where they could. Miss Ross, the sewing mistress, was helping with the costumes. It was great fun.

'You know, old Kenny is a good sort,' said Pat, who was busily learning her part for the play. 'It's funny – I hardly ever think of playing about in her lesson now. I suppose it's because we're all so interested in the play.'

'Well, I wish I was as interested in our French play!' groaned Doris, whose French accent drove Mam'zelle to despair. 'I simply can NOT roll my '*r*'s in my throat like the rest of you. R-r-r-r-r-r-r!'

Everyone laughed at Doris's funny efforts to say the letter '*r*' in the French way. Doris had no ear for either music or languages, and was the despair of both the music mistress and Mam'zelle. But she was a wonderful dancer, and her sense of humour sent the class into fits of laughter half a dozen times a day.

It was fun preparing for the Christmas concert. All the

different forms were doing something, and there were squabbles over using the gym for rehearsals. Miss Thomas, the gym mistress, complained that the gym was used for everything else but its proper purpose these days!

Lessons went on as usual, of course, and Miss Roberts refused to allow the Christmas preparations to make any difference at all to the work her form did for her. She was very cross with Pat when she found that she was secretly learning her part in the play, when she should have been learning a list of grammar rules.

Pat had copied out her words, and had neatly fitted them into her grammar book. She had a good part in the play and was very anxious to be word-perfect for the rehearsal that afternoon.

'I think, Pat, that you must have got the wrong page in your grammar book,' said Miss Roberts, suddenly. 'Bring it to me.'

Pat went red. She got up with her book. She dropped it purposely on the floor so that it shut, and then picked it up, hoping that Miss Roberts would not notice the words of the play inside. But Miss Roberts did, of course. Her sharp eyes missed nothing!

'I thought so,' she said, dryly, taking out the neatly copied play-words. 'When is the rehearsal?'

'This afternoon, Miss Roberts,' said Pat.

'Well, you will learn your grammar rules instead of going to the rehearsal,' said Miss Roberts. 'That seems quite fair to me, and I hope it does to you. If you learn your part in the play during grammar time, then it seems just that you should learn your grammar rules in rehearsal time.'

Pat looked up in dismay. 'Oh, Miss Roberts! Please don't make me miss rehearsal. I've got an important part in the play, you know.'

'Yes, and next year this form has important exams to take,' said Miss Roberts. 'Well, I'll give you one more chance, Pat. No more of this, please! Learn those rules now and say them to me at the end of the morning. If they are correct, I'll let you off. Go back to your seat!'

Pat went to the rehearsal, of course! It was just no good at all trying to play any tricks in Miss Roberts' class and she had had to learn her grammar in break in order to get it perfect for Miss Roberts by the end of the morning.

But everyone liked the form mistress. She was strict, could be very severe and sarcastic, but she was always perfectly just, and never went back on what she said or promised. Mam'zelle was not always just, but she was so goodhearted that very few of the girls really disliked her.

What with working up for the end-of-term exams, and the concert, the girls had very little time to themselves, but they enjoyed every minute. Doris was to dance a solo dance that she had created herself. Vera was to play the piano, at which she was extremely good. Five of the girls were in the French play, and most of them in the history play. Everybody was in something.

Except one person! Sheila was in nothing! This happened quite by accident. At first Mam'zelle had said she was to be Monsieur Toc-Toc in the play, so Miss Kennedy didn't put her in the history play – and then Mam'zelle changed her mind and put Joan into the French play instead. So Sheila was in neither, and as she didn't play the piano or the violin, could not recite at all, and was no good at dancing, she felt very left out.

She said nothing. At first nobody noticed that she wasn't going to be in anything, because it had all happened accidentally. Then Isabel noticed that Sheila was looking mopey and asked her why.

'What's up? Had bad news from home or something?'

'Oh, no,' said Sheila. 'Nothing's wrong.'

Isabel said no more but watched Sheila for a few days. She soon noticed that she was not in either of the plays and was not doing anything by herself either.

'I say! I believe you're miserable because you're not in the concert!' said Isabel. 'I thought you were going to be in the French play.'

'I was,' said Sheila, uncomfortably. 'But then Mam'zelle chose someone else. I'm not in anything, and everyone will notice it, Isabel. I do so hate being left out.'

'Well, it wasn't done on purpose, silly,' said Isabel, laughing.

'I feel as if it was,' said Sheila. 'I know I'm not much good at anything, but it doesn't make it any better when I'm not even given the *chance* to do anything.'

'Oh, don't be an idiot!' said Isabel. Sheila looked obstinate. Like many weak people she could be really pig-headed.

'Well, I'm fed up!' she said. 'I shan't go to the rehearsal or anything. I'll just go off by myself.'

'Well, anyway, you might at least take an interest in what the form is doing, even if you're not doing anything yourself!' cried Isabel, indignantly. 'That's mean and stupid.'

'I'll be mean and stupid then,' said Sheila, almost in tears, and she went off by herself.

Isabel told Pat. 'Oh blow!' said Pat. 'Just as we were getting Sheila to be sensible too, and giving her a chance. Don't let's bother about her! If she wants to feel she's left out and slighted when she isn't, let her!'

Janet came up and listened to the tale. She had been very good to Sheila the last week or two, for she had really felt very guilty over her loss of temper. She looked thoughtful now. 'No – don't let's undo the good work we've been trying to do!' she said. 'Let's think of something. I know once I was left out of a match when I badly wanted to be in it, and although I'm not such a silly as Sheila, still I did feel pretty awful. I remember thinking that the whole school would be whispering about me, wondering what I had done to be out of the match!'

The twins laughed. Janet was so sensible and jolly that they couldn't imagine her worrying about a thing like that.

'It's all very well to laugh,' said Janet. 'You are twins and have always got each other to back up and laugh over things with – but when you're a naturally lonely person like Sheila, it's different. Little things get awfully big.'

'You *are* sticking up for Sheila all of a sudden,' said Pat, in surprise.

'No, I'm not. All I say is – don't let's spoil what we've been trying to *do*,' said Janet, impatiently.

'Oh, well – you think of something then,' said Isabel. 'I can't!'

The twins went off. Janet sat down and began to think. She was impatient and impulsive, but once she had set her hand to anything she wouldn't give up. Sheila wanted help again, and Janet was going to give it.

'Gosh! I've got it!' said Janet to herself. 'We'll make her prompter, of course! We need someone at rehearsals with the book, ready to prompt any of us who forgets. And my goodness, I forget my words all right! I'll go and ask Sheila if she'll be prompter at rehearsals and on the concert night too.'

She went off to find Sheila. It was some time before she found her, and then at last she ran her to earth in the art room, tidying out the cupboards.

'I say, Sheila! Will you do something for us?' cried Janet. 'Will you be prompter for the play? We get into an awful muddle trying to prompt each other, and it would be an awful help to have someone with the book, who will follow the words and help when we go wrong.'

'I wouldn't be any good at that,' said Sheila, rather sullenly.

'Oh, yes, you would, idiot!' said Janet. 'It *would* be such a help, Sheila. Please do. Some of us are sure to be nervous on the concert night too, and it would be nice to know you were at the side, ready to prompt us with the words.'

'All right,' said Sheila, rather ungraciously. She had felt that if she wasn't in the plays, she jolly well wouldn't help at all. But that was small and mean – and Sheila was doing her best not to be that.

So she became prompter, and attended all the rehearsals with the book of words. She soon began to enjoy it all, and loved the play. She did nothing but stand or sit with the book, prompting those who forgot, whilst the others had the fun of acting. But she didn't grumble or complain, and the twins secretly thought she was behaving rather well.

'Good for Janet to have thought of that,' said Pat.

'Yes – she thought Sheila was going to refuse,' said Isabel. 'I'm not at all sure *I* wouldn't have said no, if it had been me!'

'I shouldn't have let you!' said Pat.

Two weeks before the end of the term an accident happened. Vera, a very quiet girl in the first form, fell during gym and broke her arm. She broke it just by the wrist and had to be taken off to hospital to have it X-rayed. It was set in plaster, and her parents decided that as it was so near the end of the term, she might as well go home, instead of staying the last two weeks.

'It's her right arm, so she won't be able to write at all,' said her mother to Miss Theobald. 'It would be just as well for her to be quiet at home.'

So poor Vera said goodbye and went, promising to be back the next term with her arm mended again! And then there was consternation in the class, because Vera had an important part in the play!

'Golly! What's to be done?' said Pat, in dismay. 'No one

else can possibly learn all the words in time. Vera had such a big part.'

Everyone stared round in despair. Those who were not in the play felt perfectly certain that they could not possibly learn the big part in so short a time. And then Janet spoke.

'There's someone who *does* know all the words!' she cried. 'Sheila, you do! You've been prompting us at every rehearsal, and you know every part! You're the only one who's been following the words page by page in the book. Can't *you* take Vera's part?'

Sheila went bright red. All the girls looked at her expectantly.

'Go on – say you will,' said Pat. 'You can do it just as well as Vera!'

'I should love to,' said Sheila. 'I'm sure I could do it! I know every word! Well – I know every word of every part now, of course – but I'd just love to do Vera's part. I like it best of all.'

'Good!' cried Pat. 'That's settled then. We'll get someone else to be prompter and you must be in the play.'

So at the next rehearsal Sheila was not prompter, but took one of the most important parts. She was quite word-perfect, and because she had so often watched Vera doing the part, she was able to act it very well.

Everyone was pleased. They had all known that Sheila was hurt because she had been left out of everything by accident, and had admired her for taking on the rather dull job of prompter – and now that she had had such an unexpected reward the whole form was delighted.

But nobody was more delighted than Sheila herself. She was really thrilled with her good luck. She went about with a smiling face, and was so unexpectedly jolly that the class could hardly believe it was Sheila.

But Sheila did not forget to write and tell Vera how sorry she was to hear about her accident. She remembered someone else's disappointment in the middle of her own pleasure. Yes – Sheila was well on the way to becoming somebody now!

17.

Kathleen has a secret

One afternoon, when Pat, Isabel and Kathleen were coming back from the town across the fields, they heard a whining noise from the hedge.

'That's a dog!' said Kathleen at once, and she ran to see. The others followed – and there, in the ditch, they saw a half-grown rough-haired terrier, its chest and face bleeding.

'It's been shot!' cried Kathleen indignantly. 'Look at all the pellets in its poor legs! Oh! It's that hateful farmer who lives over the hill. He always swears he'll shoot any dog that goes wandering in his fields.'

'But why?' asked Pat, in surprise. 'Dogs go all over the fields.'

'Yes – but sheep are in these fields, and soon the lambs will be born,' said Kathleen. 'Dogs chase sheep, you know, and frighten them.'

'Well, this poor animal has been shot,' said Pat. 'What are we going to do with it?'

'I'm going to take it back to school with me and look after it,' said Kathleen. She was quite crazy over animals. The twins looked at her in astonishment.

'You won't be able to keep him,' said Pat. 'And anyway, you ought to ring up the police and report him.

Suppose his owner is looking for him?'

'Well, I'll ring up and see if anyone has been asking for him,' said Kathleen. 'But if you think I'm going to leave a dog bleeding all by itself out in the fields, you're jolly well mistaken!'

'All right, all right!' said Isabel. 'But how are you going to take him home? He'll cover you with blood.'

'As if I care about that!' said Kathleen, picking the dog up very gently. He whined again, but snuggled down into the girl's arms, knowing quite well that they were kind and friendly.

They walked back to school with the dog. They debated where to put him. No girl was allowed to keep a dog, and if he were discovered he would certainly be sent off. And Kathleen was quite determined that she was going to nurse him till he was better!

'Could we keep him in the bicycle shed?' asked Pat.

'Oh, no. He would be much too cold,' said Kathleen, standing behind the bushes with the dog in her arms, pondering how to get him into school without being seen. 'Wait a minute – let's think.'

They all thought. Then Pat gave an exclamation. 'I know! What about that little boxroom near the hot tank upstairs in the attics? He'd be warm there, and right away from everyone. Nobody ever goes there.'

'And we're not supposed to either,' said Isabel. 'Dash! We always seem to be doing things we oughtn't to do.'

'Well, this is for the dog's sake,' said Kathleen. 'I'm willing to do anything. Poor darling! Don't whine like that. I promise I'll make you better soon.'

Janet came round the corner and saw the three of them standing by the bushes. 'Hallo!' she said. 'What's up? What have you got there? A dog! Goodness gracious, what's wrong with him?'

'He's been shot,' said Kathleen. 'We're going to keep him in the boxroom upstairs in the attics till he's better. Are you going down to the town, Janet? Well, be a sport and ask at the police station if anyone has reported a lost dog. If they have, ask for their name and address, and I'll tell them I've got him safely.'

'All right,' said Janet. 'But look out that he doesn't make a noise or you'll get into trouble. You're quite batty over animals, Kathleen! Goodbye!'

Janet rushed off to get her bicycle. Kathleen turned to the twins. 'You go and see that the coast is clear,' she said. 'And let's think what to have for a bed for him.'

'There's an old wooden box in the gardener's shed,' said Isabel, eagerly. 'That would do nicely. I'll get it.'

She ran to get it. Pat went indoors to see if it was safe for Kathleen to take the dog in. She whistled a little tune, and Kathleen ran in with the dog. The two of them scurried up the stairs without meeting anyone – but round the corner of the corridor they could hear footsteps coming and the loud voice of Mam'zelle, talking to Miss Jenks.

'Oh, crumbs!' groaned Kathleen, and she turned to go down the stairs again. But someone was now coming up. Pat opened the door of a big broom cupboard and pushed Kathleen and the dog into it. She shut the door, and then dropped on one knee, pretending to do up her shoe. Just as Mam'zelle and Miss Jenks passed her, the dog in the cupboard gave a whine. Mam'zelle looked round in surprise.

'*Tiens*! Why do you whine like a dog?' she asked Pat, and passed on, thinking that girls were indeed funny creatures. Pat giggled, and opened the door when the two mistresses had gone by.

'Did you hear what Mam'zelle said?' she asked. 'Come on – it's all right now. We can get up the attic stairs in no time!'

They went up to the top of the school. The attics were just under the roof, and the boxrooms were a peculiar shape, being small, with slanting roofs, and almost impossible to stand up in. Here were kept the trunks and cases belonging to the girls. The boxrooms were only visited twice a term – once when the trunks were put there, and once when they were brought down to be packed.

After a moment Isabel came up with the box and an old rug she had found in the locker downstairs in the gym. The girls chose the little boxroom next to the hot tanks. It was warm and cosy. They set the wooden box down in a corner and tucked the old rug into it. It made a very cosy bed.

Then Kathleen set to work to bathe the dog's wounds. It took a long time, and the dog lay patiently till it was finished, licking Kathleen's careful hands as she bathed him.

'You're awfully good with animals,' said Pat, watching her. 'And doesn't he love you?'

'I'm going to be a vet when I'm grown up,' said

Kathleen. 'There you are, my beauty. You're all right now. Don't lick off that ointment more than you can help! Lie quietly here now, and you'll soon be all right again! I'll bring you some water and some food.'

The bell went for prep and the three girls hurried downstairs, carefully closing the boxroom door behind them. They met Janet as they went into the classroom.

'I asked at the police station,' whispered Janet. 'But they said nobody had reported a dog. I had to tell them what he was like and they wanted your name and address.'

'Gracious! What an idiot you are!' whispered back Kathleen, as she took her seat. 'Whatever will Miss Theobald say if the police ring up the school and ask for me! Really, Janet!'

'Well, I *had* to give it!' whispered Janet. 'You can't say no to the police, can you? Anyway, I don't expect the dog will be reported, so don't worry!'

But Kathleen did worry. When she heard the telephone bell ringing that evening she was quite sure that it was the police ringing up the head mistress. But it wasn't. The girls breathed with relief when they heard that it was a message for Miss Roberts.

The dog was given water and food. He lay quite quietly in his basket and was as good as gold. 'He ought to have a run before we go to bed,' said Kathleen, anxiously. 'How are we to manage it?'

'Let's bundle him up in a heap of the clothes we are using for the play,' said Pat. 'If anyone meets us they will think we are just taking a pile of clothes for rehearsal. I'll get some!'

So, five minutes before bedtime the girls crept up the attic stairs with a heap of clothes. The surprised dog was carefully tucked up in them, with just his nose showing so that he could breathe.

Then Kathleen carried him downstairs, whispering to him so that he would lie quiet. He did not want to be quiet at all, and struggled violently, but luckily the girls met nobody except Matron. She was in a hurry, and hardly glanced at them.

'You won't be in time for bed if you aren't quick!' she called. The girls giggled, and went out into the garden by a little-used door. They set the dog free in a tiny yard where the gardeners chopped firewood and logs, and he limped about joyfully. Then they packed him up in the pile of clothes again, and scurried indoors.

This time they were not so lucky. They met Belinda Towers! She stopped and glared at them.

'Don't you know that your bed-time bell has gone? What are you doing wandering about here? And what on earth is that in those clothes?'

The dog struggled to get out and its head came out with a jerk. 'Oh, we've been trying so hard not to let anyone see him!' said Kathleen, almost in tears. 'Belinda, he's been shot, he's . . .'

'Don't tell me anything about him and I shan't know,' said Belinda, who was very fond of animals too. 'Go on – take that pile of clothes away – and go to your dormitory quickly.'

'Good old Belinda!' said Pat, as the three of them ran up the stairs to the boxroom. 'Isn't she a sport? Talk about Nelson turning the blind eye – she turned a blind eye on our dog all right! Do hurry, Kath. We really shall get into a row if we're much longer!'

They tucked the dog up again in his basket. He licked their hands and wuffed a very small bark. 'Isn't he clever?' cried Kathleen, in delight. 'He even knows he must whisper a bark.'

'Well, it was a pretty loud whisper,' said Pat. 'Come on. Let's go down and hope that Hilary won't say a word. It's about the first time we've been late, anyway. I hope the dog doesn't bark the place down in the night!'

'Of course he won't!' said Kathleen, shutting the boxroom door carefully. 'He'll sleep all night – and in the morning, very early, I'll take him for a run again.'

They tore down to their dormitory, to find Hilary getting most exasperated with them. 'Where *have* you been?' she demanded. 'You know it's my job to see you're here on time at nine o'clock. It's too bad of you.'

'We've been putting a dog to bed,' whispered Kathleen. Hilary stared in surprise.

'*What* did you say?' she asked. 'Putting *what* to bed?'

'Shall I tell everyone?' said Kathleen to the twins. They nodded. It was lovely to have a secret – but it was great fun to surprise everyone and tell it!

So Kathleen explained about the hurt dog, and everyone listened in amazement. 'Fancy taking a dog to the boxroom!' cried Doris. 'Well, I'd never dare to do that!

Suppose Matron went up there! She'd soon find him!'

'Well, we shall only keep him for a day or two till he's quite better,' said Kathleen. 'Then we'll have found out where he belongs to and can take him back.'

But it wasn't quite as easy as all that!

18.

The secret is out!

The dog made no noise at all in the night. Kathleen managed to wake very early, and creep up to the boxroom to take him for a run in the little wood-yard. He completely refused to be taken down all wrapped up again, so Kathleen had to put a bit of string round his neck and lead him down the stairs. He made rather a noise flopping down, but nobody came to see what was the matter.

It was marvellous the way his legs and chest and face had healed during the night. Kathleen was very pleased. The dog fawned round her legs in the yard, and tried to jump up to lick her hand. The girl thought he was a marvellous dog, and hoped against hope that no one would claim him.

'If only I could keep him until the end of term, and then take him home!' she thought. 'Wouldn't it be lovely!'

She took him back to the boxroom again. This time he didn't want her to leave him, and after she had shut the door and gone back to the dormitory she felt sure she could hear him whining and scraping against the door.

The first form's classroom was just underneath the boxrooms. The room where the dog was was not exactly overhead but more to the right. Kathleen listened anxiously to see if he was making any noise during school time. Her sharp ears heard the patter of feet and small whines, but Miss Roberts apparently heard nothing.

When Mam'zelle came to take a French lesson, however, she heard the dog quite plainly! Her ears were exceedingly keen. The first time that the dog whined, she looked up in surprise.

'What can that noise be?' she said.

'What noise, Mam'zelle?' asked Isabel, with an innocent face.

'The noise of a dog!' said Mam'zelle, impatiently. 'The whine, the bark! Is it possible that you have not heard it, Isabel?'

All the class pretended to listen hard. Then the girls shook their heads.

'You must be mistaken, Mam'zelle,' said Doris, gravely.

'There surely isn't a dog in the school,' said Joan. 'Only the kitchen cats.'

Mam'zelle was really most astonished to think that she was the only one who heard the strange noises.

'Ah, it must be something wrong with my ears, then,' she said, and she shook her big head vigorously. 'I will get the doctor to syringe them for me. I cannot have dogs barking and whining in my head.'

The class, already in a state of giggles, was glad to burst into laughter at this. Mam'zelle rapped on the desk.

'Enough! I made no joke! Take down *dictée*, please.'

The class went on with its work. The dog in the boxroom explored the place thoroughly and, judging by the noise, tried a good deal of scratching at the door and the walls. Mam'zelle looked extremely puzzled once or twice, and glanced at the girls to see if they too had noticed the noises – but one and all went serenely on with their work, and appeared to hear nothing – so Mam'zelle pressed her ears thoughtfully, and made up her mind to see the doctor that very same day.

The twins and Kathleen spent most of their free time in the boxroom with the dog. It was always so pleased to see them, and they all grew very fond of it indeed. The only exasperating thing was that when they left it, it *would* bark and whine after them, and try to scratch the door open. They were always afraid that somebody would hear it then.

But two days went by safely, and it was not discovered. The girls fed it, gave it water, and took it down secretly for runs in the wood-yard. Kathleen really adored the little creature, and indeed it was a very intelligent and affectionate animal.

'As nobody has claimed to be its owner, I really think I might keep it for myself, don't you?' asked Kathleen, anxiously, as she and the twins stroked the dog up in the boxroom one free half-hour. 'I do love him so. He really is a darling. I couldn't bear to take him to the police station now and leave him there. You know, if nobody claimed him at all the police would have him put to sleep.'

'Well, you keep him then,' said Pat. 'There isn't much longer till the end of the term. But you'll have to move him out of here when the cleaners come up to get down our boxes for us. That's very soon. I don't see what you're going to do, really I don't!'

However, the twins and Kathleen did not need to bother about what was going to happen because the dog soon decided things for himself.

One morning, about four days after he had been found, he lay down in a bit of wintry sunshine that came slanting through the attic window. It made him feel restless and he jumped up and prowled round. He came to the door and stood sniffing at it. Then he began to jump at the handle.

After a while he managed, quite by chance, to jerk the catch back – and the door opened! The dog was delighted. He pushed it wide open with his nose and trotted down the attic stairs.

Now all might still have been well if one of the school cats had not been lying fast asleep on a mat underneath one of the corridor radiators. The dog sniffed the cat-smell, and trotted up in delight. What! A cat! And what was more, a cat asleep!

With a loud wuff the dog leapt on the cat in play. It was only a puppy and would not really have hurt it – but the cat was in a most terrible fright. It leapt up, gave an anguished yowl, and fled down the corridor, its tail straight up in the air. The dog gave chase at once, prancing along on all four puppy-legs! And that was how Miss Theobald met the dog.

She was going along to one of the classrooms when first the cat and then the dog shot round her legs. She turned in amazement. Cats there were in the school, because of mice – but where in the world did a dog suddenly appear from?

The cat leapt out of a window. The dog paused, surprised that the cat had disappeared so suddenly. Then he decided to go and find Kathleen. He thought he had smelt her somewhere along the passage. So off he trotted again, and soon came to the first form classroom. He stood up on his hind legs and whined and scratched.

Mam'zelle was once again giving a French lesson, and the whole class was busy correcting its French prep, and writing out various mistakes. When the dog jumped up at the door and whined, Mam'zelle leapt to her feet.

'*Tiens*! This time it is not my ears! It is in truth a dog!' She marched to the door and opened it. In ran the dog, his tail wagging nineteen to the dozen, and went straight to Kathleen. How all the class stared!

And after him came Miss Theobald, determined to unravel the mystery of the dog! She looked into the classroom and saw Mam'zelle stamping up and down, and Kathleen doing her best to quiet the excited dog!

'What is all this disturbance?' asked Miss Theobald, in her quiet, serious voice. Mam'zelle turned to her at once, her hands wagging above her shoulders as she poured out how she had heard a dog some days ago, and how he had come to the door and scratched.

'I think perhaps Kathleen knows more about him than anyone,' said Miss Theobald, noticing how the animal fawned on the girl, and how she stroked and patted him.

'Kathleen, come with me, and perhaps you can give me an explanation.'

Kathleen, rather pale, stood up. She followed the head to her room, the dog trotting amiably at her heels. Miss Theobald made her sit down.

'I didn't mean to do any wrong,' said Kathleen, beginning her tale. 'But he was so hurt, Miss Theobald, and I do so much love dogs, and I've never had any pets of my own, and . . .'

'Begin at the beginning,' said the head. So Kathleen told the whole story, and Miss Theobald listened. At the end she reached for the telephone and took off the receiver. She asked for the police station. Kathleen's heart stood still! Whatever was the head going to say!

Miss Theobald enquired if any dog had been reported missing. Apparently none had. Then she asked what would happen if a dog that had been found hurt was kept. 'It had no collar when it was found,' she explained.

After a while she put down the receiver and turned to Kathleen, who now had the dog on her knee.

'I can't imagine how you have kept the dog hidden all this time,' she said, 'and I am not going to enquire. I know you are fond of animals. Well, apparently there is no reason why you should not keep the dog for yourself, if no one claims it within a certain time. So I propose to let you keep it until you return home for the holidays, and if your aunt will let you have it, you can take it back. But it must be kept in the stables, Kathleen. For once in a way I will relax the rule that says no pet must be kept, and let you have the dog until the holidays.'

If Kathleen had not been in such awe of the head she would certainly have flung her arms round her neck! As it was she could hardly swallow a lump that suddenly appeared in her throat, which made it very difficult for her to say anything. But she managed to stammer out her thanks. The dog was not in awe of Miss Theobald, however – and he went to her and licked her hands solemnly, for all the world as if he knew what had been said!

'Take him to the stables now, and get one of the men to find a good place for him,' said Miss Theobald. 'And next time you want to do anything peculiar, Kathleen, come and ask either me or Miss Roberts first! It really would save quite a lot of trouble!'

Kathleen hurried off, her eyes shining. The dog trotted after her. Before she went to the stables the girl ran back to her classroom and burst in, her cheeks flushed and her eyes sparkling.

'I say!' she cried. 'I'm to keep the dog. I'm to take him home if my aunt . . .'

'Kathleen! I will not have my class interrupted in this scandalous way!' cried Mam'zelle, rising in wrath from her desk. Kathleen took one look at her and disappeared. She went to the stables and found one of the gardeners. He soon gave the dog a place, and Kathleen left him, happy in the thought that now she could come and take him for a walk whenever she wanted to.

On her way back to her form she met Belinda Towers, off for a practice in the lacrosse field. 'Belinda!' she cried.

'The dog escaped and came to me in the classroom! And he chased a cat and Miss Theobald saw him and came after him – and she's letting me keep him!'

'Good for you!' said Belinda. 'Now buzz off back to your form. You first form kids always seem to be doing something extraordinary!'

Kathleen buzzed off. She went very, very quietly back to the French lesson and sat down. Mam'zelle still had a lot to say, but the words rolled off Kathleen's head like water off a duck's back. She sat and dreamt of the dog who was really to be her very own.

'And if you do not pay more attention to me I will give you a three-page essay to write about dogs in French!' she suddenly heard Mam'zelle say, and pulled herself together. The whole class was grinning at her. Mam'zelle was glaring, half-angry, half-amused, for the girl had really not heard a word until then.

Kathleen didn't at all want to write a three-page essay in French. Good gracious! She wouldn't be able to take the dog for a walk. So for the next twenty minutes she worked harder than anyone in the class, and Mam'zelle said no more!

And during the half-hour between morning school and dinner, four girls crowded round an excited dog and quarrelled as to what name he should be given!

'I'm his owner and I'm going to choose!' said Kathleen, firmly. 'His name is Binks. I don't know why – but he looks like a Binks to me.'

So Binks he was, and Binks he remained till the last

day of term came and he went home with Kathleen. What a time he had till then, with dozens of girls clamouring to take him for walks, and bringing him so many things to eat that he grew as fat as a barrel! Even the mistresses loved him and gave him a pat when they met him out with Kathleen.

All but Mam'zelle, who thought that school was no place for dogs! 'He is abominable!' she said, whenever she saw him. 'That dog! How he disturbed my class!' But there was a twinkle in her eye, so nobody took her seriously!

19.

A shock for Isabel

Exams began. The twins were very anxious to do well in them, for they badly wanted to be top in something. They had caught up well with the rest of their form, but as most of the other girls had been there a good deal longer than they had, Miss Roberts told them that they could not expect to come out top that term.

The maths exam came first. It was quite a stiff one, for Miss Roberts had taught her form a good deal that term and expected them to make a good showing. Pat and Isabel groaned over it, but did their best.

'I know I got questions 3, 4 and 5 quite wrong,' said Isabel, when they compared their papers afterwards. 'I think I got the problems right though, but they took me so long to puzzle out that I didn't do them all.'

'I bet I'll be bottom,' said Pat, dismally. She still at times resented being a 'nobody', as she put it, though she was rapidly forgetting all the high-and-mighty ideas she had held at first.

French wasn't so bad. Thanks to 'Mam'zelle Abominable's' coaching the twins were now well up to the average of their class in writing. It was poor Doris who 'fell down' in French. She stammered and stuttered in the oral exam and drove Mam'zelle nearly frantic.

'Have I taught you three terms already and still you speak French like a four-year-old in the kindergarten?' she stormed. 'Now repeat to me again one of the French verses you learnt this term.'

The crosser Mam'zelle got, the worse poor Doris became. She gazed hopelessly round the class, and winked at the twins.

'Ah! You wink! You will soon wink the other side of your face!' cried Mam'zelle, getting all mixed up. 'You will have nought for your oral French.'

As Doris had expected to be bottom anyhow this did not disturb her a great deal. She sat down thankfully. Joan was next, and as she was good at French, Mam'zelle calmed down a little.

The exams went on until only the geography one was left. The twins examined the lists each morning and were sad to see that they were not top in anything at all. They were not even second in anything! Pat managed to get third in nature, and Isabel fifth in history, but that was the highest they reached!

'Golly! Our exam marks won't look too good on our reports,' sighed Pat. 'We were always top in most things at Redroofs, long before we were head of the school. Mother and Daddy won't like us not being top in a single thing here.'

'They'll think we did what we said, and didn't try at all,' said Isabel. 'Oh, blow! And we have been trying. What a pity we said all we did before we came. I don't see how Daddy can help feeling we've slacked all this term. He's so used to getting reports that show us top in nearly everything.'

'Well – there's only the geography exam left,' said Pat. 'We might be top in that – but I doubt it! I don't feel I know an awful lot about Africa, though we've been studying it all term. Which part of it do the Zulus live in? I never can remember.'

'I wish we *could* just be top in it,' said Isabel, getting out her geography textbook, and turning over the pages. 'Pat – let's cram hard all tonight and really see if we can't do well. Come on!'

So the two of them bent their heads over their text-books and solemnly began to read through the whole of the lessons they had had that term on Africa. They looked at the maps they had drawn, and drew them roughly again two or three times. They made lists of towns and ports and said them to one another. They pored over the rivers and learnt those too, and read up about the peoples of Africa, the animals and the products.

'Well, I really feel I know something now,' said Isabel, with a sigh. 'I especially know all the products of Africa, and the rivers.'

'And I especially know all about the climate,' said Pat. 'But I bet we shan't get asked questions about those things! Exam questions always seem to deal with the things you missed because you were ill, or forgot to look up, or for some reason simply can't remember at all!'

'Well, I can't do any more work tonight,' said Isabel. 'I

want to finish the sleeve of the jumper I'm knitting. I've only got a few more rows to do. Where did I put the pattern book?'

'Can't imagine,' said Pat. 'You're always losing it. I think you took it into the form room with you this afternoon.'

'Blow!' said Isabel. 'So I did.'

She got up and went out of the common-room. She quite forgot that she and the others had been told not to go to the first form room that evening, because the exam papers were to be set out there. She sauntered along to the room, opened the door and went in. She walked over to her desk and opened it.

Yes – there was the pattern book. Good! Isabel took it, and then picked up a pencil that belonged to Miss Roberts. She went to the teacher's big desk and put it in the groove that held pencils and pens.

And there, staring up at her from the desk were the exam papers for tomorrow! A list of geography questions was written out very neatly on a sheet of paper. Isabel stared at them with a beating heart.

If only she knew what the questions were she could cram them up and answer them so perfectly that she would be top! Without thinking she hurriedly read down the questions. 'State what you know about the climate of South Africa. What do you know about the race called Pygmies? What do you . . .'

Isabel read the questions from top to bottom, and then went out of the room. Her face was flushed and her heart was beating. 'All those questions are what we've both been looking up this evening,' she said to herself. 'It doesn't matter me seeing the paper at all. I've already crammed up the answers.'

Pat looked up as Isabel came back into the common-room. 'Got the pattern book?' she asked.

Isabel looked down at her empty hands. No – she had left the pattern book behind after all.

'Didn't you find it?' said Pat, surprised.

'Yes – I did,' said Isabel. 'But I've gone and left it behind after all.'

'Well, aren't you going to go and get it?' asked Pat, still more surprised. Isabel hesitated. She could not bear to go back into the form room again.

'What *is* the matter, Isabel?' asked Pat, impatiently. 'Have you gone dumb? What's up?'

'Pat, the geography paper questions were on Miss Roberts' desk,' said Isabel. 'I read them.'

'Isabel! That's cheating!' said Pat.

'I didn't think about whether it was cheating or not,' said Isabel, in a troubled voice. 'But it's all right, Pat – the questions were all about what we've been looking up this evening. So it won't matter.'

Pat stared at Isabel. Isabel would not look at her. 'Isabel, I don't see how in the world you're going to sit for the geography exam tomorrow when you know you've already seen the questions,' she said at last. 'I dare say you could answer them all quite perfectly without any further looking up at all – but if anyone knew about this they'd think you were a cheat. And you're not – you've always been straight and honourable. I just don't understand you.'

'I did it all in a hurry,' said poor Isabel.

'Well, you'd better tell Miss Roberts,' said Pat.

'Oh, I *can't*!' said Isabel, in horror. 'You know how strict she is. I can't.'

'Well, you must answer all the questions so badly that Miss Roberts will be angry with you, and then you can tell her why you've done it,' said Pat. 'If she knows you haven't taken advantage of seeing the questions she can't think you're a cheat. You'll have to own up before or after. Go on now, Isabel, you know you must.'

'Well – I'll own up afterwards,' said Isabel. 'I'll sit for the exam and do the answers so badly that I'll be bottom. Then when Miss Roberts rows me I'll tell her why. Oh, blow! Why was I so silly? I did it all in a hurry. I might even have been top, you know – because all the questions were ones I could answer quite well.'

'Don't tell me what they were,' said Pat. 'I don't want to know, else I'll feel awkward about answering them. Cheer up, Isabel, I know you well enough to know you didn't mean to cheat! Anybody can be silly!'

Isabel was not very happy that night. She tossed and turned, wishing to goodness she hadn't seen the geography questions. She could so easily have answered them correctly and got high marks! What an idiot she had been!

The geography exam was to be held first thing after prayers next day. At nine o'clock all the first form filed into their room, and took their places. Isabel saw that the exam questions were still on the desk. Pat saw them there too, though of course it was impossible for anyone to read them.

Miss Roberts came in. 'Good morning, girls!' she said. 'Good morning, Miss Roberts,' chorused the class, and sat down.

'Geography exam this morning,' said Miss Roberts, briskly. 'Do well, please! Joan, come and give out the questions.'

Isabel watched Joan go up for the slips of paper. She felt miserable. It was not nice to have to do badly on purpose, but there was nothing else to do.

Just as Joan was taking up the papers Miss Roberts gave an exclamation and stopped her. 'Wait! I don't believe these are the right papers! No – they're not! How stupid! They are the exam questions for the second form, who have been doing Africa too. Go to Miss Jenks with these, and ask her to give you the papers I left on her desk. Tell her I've left the first form's exam questions there, and that these are for her form.'

Joan took the papers and disappeared out of the room. Isabel looked at Pat. Pat was smiling in delight. When Miss Roberts turned to write something on the board Pat leant across and whispered to Isabel.

'What luck! Now you can do your best instead of your worst, old girl! You saw the wrong questions! Hurrah!'

Isabel nodded. She was really delighted too. It seemed too good to be true. Miss Roberts turned round. 'No talking! If I catch any girls whispering during exams I shall deduct ten marks from their papers. Do you hear me, Pat?'

'Yes, Miss Roberts,' said Pat, meekly. Joan came back with the right papers and distributed them round the class. Isabel read hers quickly. Yes – they were quite, quite different from the questions she had read last night. How marvellous! Now she could set to work and really do her best to be top. She would never be such an idiot again. She hadn't meant to be a cheat, but it was horrible to feel like one.

But poor Isabel was rather nervous now after her experiences, and did not do nearly such a good paper as Pat. Her hand shook as she drew the maps required, and she made some silly mistakes. So when the papers were gathered up and corrected Isabel was nowhere near the top! She was sixth – but Pat was top! Isabel was as pleased to see Pat's name heading the list as she would have been to see her own. She squeezed her twin's arm hard.

'Good for you, Pat!' she said. 'I'm jolly glad! One of us is top in something anyhow!'

Pat glowed with pleasure. It was marvellous to see her name heading the list. Miss Roberts came up and patted her on the back.

'You did an excellent paper, Patricia,' she said. 'Eighty-three per cent is very good. But I was surprised that Isabel didn't do better? Why was that, Isabel?'

But Isabel did not tell her and Miss Roberts laughed and went on her way. Surprising things happened in exams – probably next term those O'Sullivan twins would be top in nearly everything!

20.
The concert

And now the end of the term was indeed drawing near. Miss Theobald and the other mistresses were busy making out reports, putting up lists, helping the girls with the great concert, and going through exam papers. The girls themselves were restless, looking forward to the holidays, getting ready for the concert, wondering what their reports would be like, and nearly driving Mam'zelle mad with their inattention.

Miss Roberts was more lenient, but even she grew impatient when Isabel told her that there were fourteen ounces in a pound.

'I know you all go *slightly* mad at the end of term,' she said, 'but there really is a limit to my patience. Isabel, if there was a lower form than this I'd send you to it for the rest of the morning!'

The last two weeks were really great fun. For one thing all the cupboards had to be turned out, washed, dried and tidied. The twins had never done this at Redroofs School, and at first were inclined to turn up their noses at such work. But when they saw the others putting on overalls, they couldn't help thinking it would be rather fun, even though the cleaning had to be done in their free time.

'Come on, Pat, come on, Isabel! Don't stand looking stuck up like you used to!' cried Janet, who sensed at once the twins hadn't done work like this before. 'You'll get dirty, but you can always bathe and wash your hair! Come on, high-and-mighties!'

This was not a name that the twins liked at all, so they climbed down at once. They put on overalls, and went to join the others. Hilary was in charge of the first form cleaning.

It really was fun. Everything had to be taken out of the cupboards, and there were squeals and shrieks of delight when things long-lost came to light again.

'Oh! I thought I'd never see that ruler again!' squealed Doris, pouncing on a small ruler in delight. 'Wherever has it been all this time?'

'Golly! Here's Miss Roberts's fountain-pen!' cried Hilary, a little later. 'Look – tangled up in this bundle of raffia. Oooh! I know how it got there. Do you remember, Janet, when you dumped a whole lot of it on to Miss Roberts's desk in handwork one day, and she objected, and you carted it all off to the cupboard again? Well, I bet you took the pen with you! My word, what a hunt we had for it.'

'Well, for pity's sake don't remind her that it might have been *me*,' said Janet. 'She's always going off the deep end about something now. Look – take her the pen, Isabel, and say we found it in the handwork cupboard. You've been in her bad books today, so maybe you'll get an unexpected smile!'

Isabel did! Miss Roberts was delighted to see her pen, and beamed at Isabel with pleasure. Isabel wondered if Miss Roberts was in a good enough temper to be asked something. She tried.

'Miss Roberts! I'm so sorry I made a mess of my maths this morning. If I promise to do better tomorrow, need I do those sums all over again? I've such a lot to do today.'

But Miss Roberts was not to be caught like that! 'My dear Isabel!' she said, 'I am delighted that you have been able to give me back my pen – but I think you'll agree with me that that isn't any real reason why I should forgive you for shockingly bad work! And even if you find me my best hat, which unaccountably flew from my head last Sunday and completely disappeared over the fields, I should still say you must do your sums again!'

The class chuckled. Miss Roberts could be very dry when she liked. Isabel laughed too and went back to the cleaning and tidying.

'I wish I *could* find her hat for her!' she said. 'She's jolly strict, but she's an awful sport!'

There was great excitement when the night of the concert came. For the last few days before the concert the girls had been in a state of great excitement, getting their lines perfect, and rehearsing everything. Each form was to do something, and the concert was to last three hours, with a break in between for refreshments.

Mam'zelle had taught French plays and songs to each form, and pestered the girls continually to make sure that they were word-perfect. The sixth form were doing a short

Greek play. The fifth were doing an absurd sketch that they had written themselves, called 'Mrs Jenkins Pays a Call', and borrowed all kinds of odd hats and clothes from the mistresses, and even from the school cook!

The fourth form had got up a jazz band, which sounded simply marvellous, though Mam'zelle said that she could easily do without the side-drum, which could be heard rat-a-tat-tatting from a music room at all kinds of odd hours. The third form were doing part of a Shakespeare play, and the second and first were doing plays and odd things such as Doris's solo dance, and Tessie's recitations.

Sheila was tremendously excited. She knew that if she had been given a part in the history play at the beginning she would never have had the chance of such a big part. Now, because of Vera's accident, she had a fine part. She practised it continually, thinking about it, putting in actions that Vera had never thought of, and astonishing everyone by her acting.

'She's going to be jolly good!' whispered Janet to Pat. 'I'm quite getting to like old Sheila now. Who would have thought there was a hardworking, interesting little person like that underneath all those old posings and boastings of hers!'

Pat and Isabel worked their hardest for the concert too. All the mistresses and the staff were coming and the whole school would be watching. Nobody must forget their words or do anything silly. Each form had its own honour to uphold!

The great night came. There were gigglings and whisperings all day long. Lessons slacked off that day, except Mam'zelle's French classes. Mam'zelle would surely not allow even an earthquake to spoil her lessons! No wonder that the girls were such excellent French scholars by the time that they reached the top form.

The sewing mistress worked at top speed to alter dresses at the last moment. Matron proved unexpectedly good at providing a real meal in one of the plays, instead of the pretend one that Hilary had arranged for.

'Golly! Isn't that decent of her!' said Hilary, looking at the jug of lemonade and the currant buns that Matron had presented her with. 'I *shall* enjoy my part in the play now!'

'Well, don't stuff your mouth so full that you can't speak,' grinned Janet. 'I say – what about asking Mam'zelle to let us have a meal of some sort in the French play too?'

But nobody dared to mention such a thing to Mam'zelle!

At six o'clock the concert began. Everyone had filed into the gym, where benches and chairs had been set ready. The stage had its curtains and footlights, and looked fine. There were pots of plants borrowed from Miss Theobald's hothouse at the sides.

The mistresses sat in the three front rows, leaving their forms to look after themselves for once. The kitchen staff sat behind the mistresses. The girls were on benches at the back, completely filling the gym.

Everyone had a programme, designed and coloured by the girls themselves. Pat was terribly proud to see that

Miss Theobald had the one that she herself had done. She saw the head looking carefully at the design of the cover, and she wondered if Miss Theobald would see her name in the corner – Pat O'Sullivan.

Every form knew when its turn was coming and knew when it must rise quietly and go to the back of the stage to dress and await its turn. The fifth form were acting their play first, and as soon as the curtains swung aside and showed the girls dressed up most ridiculously in odd hats and coats and shawls, the audience went off into fits of laughter. The school cook squealed out, 'Oh, there's my old hat! I never thought I'd see it on a stage!'

The sketch was really funny and the audience loved it. Then came the Greek play by the sixth which was really a serious and difficult thing to understand. The first formers listened politely and clapped hard at the end, but they secretly thought that the fifth form were very much better!

The fourth form came on with their jazz band, and this was an instant success. The drummer was simply marvellous and Mam'zelle quite forgave the constant irritation that the practising of the drum had given her. Swinging dance tunes were played, and the audience roared the choruses. They kept clapping for encores, but as it was now half-time, the jazz band had to stop at last!

How the girls enjoyed the trifles and jellies, cream buns, sandwiches and lemonade! When they went into the dining-room to have their meal, they gasped at the sight of so much food.

'Golly! We'll never, never eat all that!' cried Pat.

'Patricia O'Sullivan, you don't know what you're talking about!' said Janet, lifting up a plate of asparagus sandwiches. 'Speak for yourself! Have one – or two whilst they're here.'

And sure enough Pat didn't know what she was talking about – for in twenty minutes not a thing was left on the dishes! The girls made a clean sweep of everything – and, hidden under the long cloth of the table, sat someone as hungry as the girls – Binks, the puppy-dog!

Kathleen had let him out secretly and had tied him to a leg of the big table. She gave him bits of sausage roll, which he ate eagerly. He was sensible enough not to poke his nose out in case he was discovered, and nobody guessed he was there except Isabel, who had been filled with astonishment at the amount of sausage rolls that Kathleen was apparently able to eat.

Then she suddenly realized what was happening. 'Oh – you monkey, Kath! You've got Binks there.'

'Sh!' said Kathleen. 'Don't say a word. I didn't see why he should miss the fun. Isn't he good?'

Binks had a marvellous time after that, for there were two people feeding him instead of one!

The concert began again in half an hour. The first form gave their two short plays, and Sheila acted so magnificently that the audience actually roared her name and made her come and give a special bow. The girl was happier than ever she had been in her life, and looked quite pretty as she stood on the stage, flushed and excited.

Winifred, the head girl, smiled across at Pat to let her know how pleased she was, for she guessed that Pat and the others had been giving Sheila the chance she had begged for her.

The French play was a success too, and Mam'zelle beamed round with pleasure when she heard it clapped so heartily. 'Those first form kids aren't half bad,' Isabel heard Belinda Towers say, and she stored it up in her mind to tell the others later on.

Doris did her dance, which was really excellent. She too was encored, and came on again in a clown's dress. She proceeded to do the clown dance which had ended so disastrously on the night of the Great Feast, and this time it ended in plenty of cheers and clapping. Just as she was finishing, a disturbance arrived in the shape of Binks!

He had bitten through his lead and had come to join his mistress. Kathleen was in the wings at the side of the stage, watching Doris dancing. Binks leapt up on to the stage joyfully, to join Kathleen, and tripped Doris up very neatly, for all the world as if he were joining in the dance!

Doris promptly fell over just as the music ended. How the audience laughed and cheered! Binks turned round as he heard them, his pink tongue hanging out, and his tail wagging joyfully. Then he went to Kathleen who, fearful of being scolded, rushed off at once to put him back into the stables.

But nobody scolded her, not even Mam'zelle, who had never ceased to say that she thought it was 'abominable' and 'insupportable' to allow 'that dog' in the school!

The concert ended with the whole school singing the school song, a very swinging, heartening tune that the twins heard for the first time. They were the only ones who did not know it.

'We'll sing it *next* time!' whispered Pat to Isabel. 'Oh, Isabel! What a lovely evening! It beats Redroofs hollow, don't you think?'

Then, yawning hugely, for it was an hour past their usual bedtime, the first formers went up to bed. They chattered and laughed as they undressed, and were just as long as they liked – for this was the last evening of term, and tomorrow they were breaking up and going home!

21. The last day

Next day the trunks were dragged down from the boxroom. Each had its owner's name on in white paint, and soon they were being packed. Matron bustled to and fro, giving out clothes, and seeing that the girls packed at least moderately well. She made Doris take out every single thing and begin again.

'But Matron, I'll never have time!' said Doris, laughing at Matron's annoyed face.

'If you stay here till next week you will pack properly!' said Matron, grimly. 'Doris Elward, your mother and your two aunts came here years ago, and they never learnt to pack – but *you* are going to! It is *not* sensible to put breakable things at the bottom of your trunk, and shoes and boots on the top of your best things. Begin again!'

'Kath! What's your home address?' yelled Pat. 'You said you'd give it to me and you haven't. I want to write to you for Christmas.'

Kathleen went red with pleasure. No one had bothered to ask for her address before. She wrote it down for Pat. Then there was a general exchange of addresses, and promises to telephone, and invitations for parties after Christmas if so-and-so could only manage to come.

The school didn't seem like school any more. Everywhere there was babbling and chattering and giggling, and even when mistresses came into the classrooms and dormitories nobody thought of being quiet. The mistresses were excited too, and talked laughingly among themselves.

'I'm pleased with my lot this term,' said Miss Roberts, watching Sheila throw something across to Pat. 'Two or three of them have altered so much for the better that I hardly know them.'

'What about those O'Sullivan twins?' asked Miss Jenks. 'I thought they were going to be a handful when they came. They were called the "stuck-up twins", you know, and at first I couldn't bear the look of their discontented faces.'

'Oh, they're all right,' said Miss Roberts at once. 'They've settled down well. They've got good stuff in them. One of these days St Clare's will be proud of them, mark my words! They're monkeys, though. Look out when you get them in your form some time next year!'

'Oh, they'll be all right after a term or two in your tender care!' laughed Miss Jenks. 'I never have any trouble with girls that come up into my form from yours. It's only the new girls that come straight into my form that I have bother with.'

Mam'zelle sailed by, beaming. She always entered every girl's address in a little black holiday notebook, and most conscientiously wrote to every one of them in the holidays.

'Good old "Mam'zelle Abominable"!' whispered Pat as she went by. Mam'zelle's sharp ears heard what she said.

'What is that you call me?' she demanded, towering over Pat as she knelt packing her trunk.

'Oh – nothing, Mam'zelle,' said Pat, horror-struck to think that Mam'zelle might have overheard. The other girls looked round, grinning. They all knew the twins' name for Mam'zelle.

'You will tell me, please. I demand it!' insisted Mam'zelle, her eyes beginning to flash.

'Well,' said Pat, reluctantly, 'I only call you "Mam'zelle Abominable" because at first you called me and Isabel and our work abominable so often. Please don't be cross!'

But Mam'zelle was not cross. For some reason the name tickled her sense of humour, and she threw back her head and roared.

'Ha! "Mam'zelle Abominable"! That is a fine name to call your French mistress. And next term your work will be so fine that I shall say you are "*magnifique*" and you will then call me "Mam'zelle Magnifique", *n'est-ce pas*?'

At last all the packing was done. Each girl went to say a polite goodbye to Miss Theobald. When the twins went in together, she looked at them seriously, and then smiled an unusually sweet smile at them.

'I don't think you wanted to come to St Clare's, did you?' she said. 'And now somehow I think you've changed your minds?'

'Yes, we *have* changed our minds!' said Pat honestly. She never minded owning up when she altered her ideas. 'We hated coming here. We were going to be really awful, and we did try to be. But – well – St Clare's is fine.'

'And we shall simply *love* coming back again next term,' said Isabel, eagerly. 'It's hard work here, and things aren't a bit the same as at our old school, and it's odd being one of the young ones after being top of the school – but we've got used to it now.'

'One day maybe you'll be one of the top ones at St Clare's,' said Miss Theobald.

But the thought of being as grand and great as Winifred James was too much for the twins. 'Oh, no!' said Pat. 'We could never, never be that!'

But Miss Theobald smiled a secret smile. She knew far more about the girls than they knew about themselves, and she felt sure that she was right. These troublesome twins had the makings of fine girls, and she and St Clare's would see to it that they fulfilled the promise they showed.

'Here are your reports,' she said, and gave one to each girl. 'Give my love to your mother and tell her that I haven't had to expel you yet!'

'I hope our reports are good,' said Pat. 'We told Daddy we weren't going to try a bit – and if they're bad he'll think we were jolly mean.'

'Well, you'll see when you get home!' said Miss Theobald, smiling. 'But – I wouldn't worry very much, if I were you! Goodbye!'

The twins said goodbye to everyone, and received fat kisses on each cheek from Mam'zelle, who seemed unaccountably fond of every girl that day. Miss Roberts shook hands and warned them not to eat too much plum pudding. Miss Kennedy looked rather sad as she said goodbye, for her friend, Miss Lewis, was now quite well, and was coming back to take up her old post the next term.

'I shan't see you again,' said Kenny, as she said goodbye to the twins. 'I'm going to miss you all very much.'

'Goodbye, Kenny,' said Pat. 'We were pigs to you at first – but you do forgive us for being piggy, don't you? And I do promise to write. I won't forget.'

'Neither will I,' said Isabel, and then Janet and Hilary and the rest came crowding up, and Miss Kennedy grew quite tearful as the girls poured goodbyes and good wishes on her. What a good thing it was that she hadn't been a failure after all!

The most uproarious soul that day was Binks. He was set free and spent his time taking chocolate from his friends, and going round licking people's hands and faces as they knelt to pack. No mistress had the heart to complain about him and he had a marvellous time.

'He *will* hate leaving me when I come back to school again!' said Kathleen, as she patted his wiry head. 'But never mind – we shall have a whole month together. Miss Theobald wrote to my aunt, and Aunt is going to see if he behaves.'

'Of *course* he'll behave!' said Janet. 'But I expect he'll take after you, Kathleen – sometimes he'll behave well – and sometimes he won't!'

Kathleen laughed and gave Janet an affectionate punch. She didn't live a great way from the twins and they had already made plans to cycle over and see one another. She was very happy.

The bell rang to say that the first coach was ready to take the girls to the station. That was for the first form. Shouting goodbyes to their teachers, the girls ran helter-skelter down the stairs and piled into the big coach. What fun to be breaking up! What fun to be going home to Christmas jollities, parties and theatres! There were Christmas presents to buy, Christmas cards to send, all kinds of things to look forward to.

Pat and Isabel got into the train together and sat down with the others to wait for the rest of the school to come down in the coaches. Before very long the engine gave a violent whistle and the carriages jerked. They were off!

The twins craned their heads out of the window to see the last of the big white building they had grown to love.

'Goodbye!' said Pat under her breath. 'We hated you when we first saw you, St Clare's! But now we love you!'

'And we'll be glad to see you again!' whispered Isabel. 'Oh, Pat – it's marvellous that we'll be going back in four weeks' time, isn't it? Good old St Clare's!'

And then the school disappeared from sight, and the train rattled on its noisy way, singing a song that seemed to say over and over again. 'We're-pleased-we're-coming-back-again-to-st-clare's! We're-pleased-we're-coming-back-again-to-st-clare's!'

A funny song, but quite a true one, thought the twins!

The O'Sullivan Twins

'Ah, you English girls!
There is nobody like you
When you are nice!'
said Mam'zelle.

Pat and Isabel are determined to work hard this term. But it's just so tempting to play a few TRICKS on Mam'zelle . . .

There's More Trouble St Clare's!

EGMONT PRESS: ETHICAL PUBLISHING

Egmont Press is about turning writers into successful authors and children into passionate readers – producing books that enrich and entertain. As a responsible children's publisher, we go even further, considering the world in which our consumers are growing up.

Safety First
Naturally, all of our books meet legal safety requirements. But we go further than this; every book with play value is tested to the highest standards – if it fails, it's back to the drawing-board.

Made Fairly
We are working to ensure that the workers involved in our supply chain – the people that make our books – are treated with fairness and respect.

Responsible Forestry
We are committed to ensuring all our papers come from environmentally and socially responsible forest sources.

For more information, please visit our website at www.egmont.co.uk/ethical

FSC MIX Paper FSC® C018306

Egmont is passionate about helping to preserve the world's remaining ancient forests. We only use paper from legal and sustainable forest sources, so we know where every single tree comes from that goes into every paper that makes up every book.

This book is made from paper certified by the Forestry Stewardship Council (FSC®), an organisation dedicated to promoting responsible management of forest resources. For more information on the FSC, please visit **www.fsc.org**. To learn more about Egmont's sustainable paper policy, please visit **www.egmont.co.uk/ethical**.